Bedford Cultural Editions

WILLIAM WELLS BROWN

Clotel;

or,

The President's Daughter: A Narrative of Slave Life in the United States

EDITED BY

Robert S. Levine

University of Maryland

BEDFORD/ST. MARTIN'S   BOSTON • NEW YORK

For Bedford/St. Martin's
Developmental Editor: Katherine A. Retan
Editorial Assistants: Katherine Gilbert and Nicole Simonsen
Senior Production Supervisor: Cheryl Mamaril
Project Management: Stratford Publishing Services, Inc.
Cover Design: Zenobia Rivetna
Cover Art: Detail from *The Death of Clotel,* an original illustration from the 1853 edition of the novel.
Composition: Stratford Publishing Services, Inc.
Printing and Binding: Haddon Craftsmen, an R. R. Donnelley & Sons Company

President: Charles H. Christensen
Editorial Director: Joan E. Feinberg
Director of Marketing: Karen R. Melton
Director of Editing, Design, and Production: Marcia Cohen
Manager, Publishing Services: Emily Berleth

Library of Congress Catalog Card Number: 99-65091

Manufactured in the United States of America.

5   4   3   2   1   0
f   e   d   c   b

For information, write: Bedford/St. Martin's, 75 Arlington Street, Boston, MA 02116   (617-399-4000)

ISBN: 0-312-15265-5 (paperback)
        0-312-22758-2 (hardcover)

Published and distributed outside North America by:
MACMILLAN PRESS, LTD
Houndmills, Basingstoke, Hampshire RG21 2XS and London
Companies and representatives throughout the world
ISBN: 0-333-91437-6
A catalogue record for this book is available from the British Library.

About the Series

The need to "historicize" literary texts — and even more to analyze the historical and cultural issues all texts embody — is now embraced by almost all teachers, scholars, critics, and theoreticians. But the question of how to teach such issues in the undergraduate classroom is still a difficult one. Teachers do not always have the historical information they need for a given text, and contextual documents and sources are not always readily available in the library — even if the teacher has the expertise (and students have the energy) to ferret them out. The Bedford Cultural Editions represent an effort to make available for the classroom the kinds of facts and documents that will enable teachers to use the latest historical approaches to textual analysis and cultural criticism. The best scholarly and theoretical work has for many years gone well beyond the "new critical" practices of formalist analysis and close reading, and we offer here a practical classroom model of the ways that many different kinds of issues can be engaged when texts are not thought of as islands unto themselves.

The impetus for the recent cultural and historical emphasis has come from many directions: the so-called new historicism of the late 1980s, the dominant historical versions of both feminism and Marxism, the cultural studies movement, and a sharply changed focus in older movements such as reader response, structuralism, deconstruction, and psychoanalytic theory. Emphases differ, of course, among schools and individuals, but what these movements and approaches have in common is a commitment to explore — and to have students in the classroom study interactively — texts in their full historical and cultural dimensions. The aim is to discover how older texts (and those from other traditions) differ from our own assumptions and expectations, and thus the focus in teaching falls on cultural and historical difference rather than on similarity or continuity.

The most striking feature of the Bedford Cultural Editions — and the one most likely to promote creative classroom discussion — is the inclusion of a generous selection of historical documents that contextualize the main text in a variety of ways. Each volume contains works (or passages from works) that are contemporary with the main text: legal and social documents, journalistic and autobiographical accounts, histories, sections from conduct books, travel books, poems, novels, and other historical sources. These materials have several uses. Often they provide information beyond what the main text offers. They provide, too, different perspectives on a particular theme, issue, or event central to the text, suggesting the range of opinions contemporary readers would have brought to their reading and allowing students to experience for themselves the details of cultural disagreement and debate. The documents are organized in thematic units — each with an introduction by the volume editor that historicizes a particular issue and suggests the ways in which individual selections work to contextualize the main text.

Each volume also contains a general introduction that provides students with information concerning the political, social, and intellectual context for the work as well as information concerning the material aspects of the text's creation, production, and distribution. There are also relevant illustrations, a chronology of important events, and, when helpful, an account of the reception history of the text. Finally, both the main work and its accompanying documents are carefully annotated in order to enable students to grasp the significance of historical references, literary allusions, and unfamiliar terms. Everywhere we have tried to keep the special needs of the modern student — especially the culturally conscious student of the turn of the millennium — in mind.

For each title, the volume editor has chosen the best teaching text of the main work and explained his or her choice. Old spellings and capitalizations have been preserved (except that the long "s" has been regularized to the modern "s") — the overwhelming preference of the two hundred teacher-scholars we surveyed in preparing the series. Original habits of punctuation have also been kept, except for occasional places where the unusual usage would obscure the syntax for modern readers. Whenever possible, the supplementary texts and documents are reprinted from the first edition or the one most relevant to the issue at hand. We have thus meant to preserve — rather than counter — for modern students the sense of "strangeness" in older texts, expecting that the oddness will help students to see where older texts are *not* like modern ones, and expecting too that today's historically informed teachers will find their own creative ways to make something of such historical and cultural differences.

In developing this series, our goal has been to foreground the kinds of issues that typically engage teachers and students of literature and history now. We have not tried to move readers toward a particular ideological, political, or social position or to be exhaustive in our choice of contextual materials. Rather, our aim has been to be provocative — to enable teachers and students of literature to raise the most pressing political, economic, social, religious, intellectual, and artistic issues on a larger field than any single text can offer.

J. Paul Hunter, University of Chicago
William E. Cain, Wellesley College
Series Editors

About This Volume

Over the last several decades, William Wells Brown's *Clotel; or, The President's Daughter* has come to achieve canonical status as the first published novel by an African American. Although there is little dispute about *Clotel*'s importance to African American and U.S. literary history, the novel remains a difficult, elusive work for many readers. One problem is that Brown assumes an antebellum readership immersed in debates on slavery and race. He does not simply allude to influential texts on these subjects; at times he quotes from them verbatim and at great length. Is Brown a plagiarist? Or are there more complex ways of understanding his authorial strategies and perspectives? This edition is grounded on a set of interrelated assumptions: that *Clotel* is an immensely important literary achievement, and that to appreciate Brown's artistry in the novel it is essential to have some knowledge of the cultural issues and texts that he engages. A principal aim of this edition, then, is to help readers become conversant with a wide range of those issues and texts.

At the same time, this edition aspires to help readers think about *Clotel* not just in relation to its specific antebellum cultural moment but also in relation to the nation's ongoing conversations on race and slavery, and thus in relation to the many texts in the African American and U.S. literary tradition that explore racial issues and the practices and legacies of slavery. One important way this Cultural Edition helps to situate the novel in relation to these larger issues is by providing materials on the "President" and his "daughter." *Clotel* was inspired in part by rumors, in circulation off and on since 1802, that Thomas Jefferson had had sexual relations and children with at least one of his slaves. As elaborated more fully in the Introduction, these rumors may have been based on Jefferson's actual behavior. As Brown well knew, Jefferson the slaveholder was the very embodiment of the contradictory fact that a nation ideologically committed to principles of freedom and equality was also a nation in which slavery was the law of the land. Jefferson's actions as a slaveholder continue to engage the attention of professional historian and layperson alike, for much remains at stake in assessing the legacy of the principal author of the Declaration of Independence. *Clotel*'s bold confrontation with that legacy is one of many aspects of the novel that helps to give it a continued power and relevance in African American and U.S. literary and cultural studies.

The documents and annotations in this edition are intended to help readers situate *Clotel* in its time, the decade of the 1850s, and also to think about the novel's continued pertinence to debates in the United States on race, gender, and slavery's myriad legacies. There are three main groupings of documents. One set provides a number of the principal "source" materials of the novel and allows readers to address knowledgeably the issue of Brown's use of these sources; the second presents a collection of influential writings on race and slavery and allows readers to situate the novel in the midst of cultural conversations on these crucial issues; and the third gathers various African American responses to the problem of white racial dominance in the United States and allows readers to consider Brown's own literary form of resistance in *Clotel*. Brown's novel emerged in response to historically specific cultural problems and literary challenges, but it remains a vital and even prophetic meditation on Jefferson's contradictory legacy of slavery and freedom and on African Americans' heroic efforts to challenge and revise that legacy.

ACKNOWLEDGMENTS

I am grateful for the assistance I have received from a number of individuals and institutions. My thanks to William Cain for entertaining my proposal to do a Cultural Edition of *Clotel* and for remaining a hands-on and committed editor during the several years that I worked on the project. For their continued support and encouragement, I am also pleased to thank Chuck Christensen, Joan Feinberg, and Steve Scipione at Bedford/St. Martin's. I am also grateful to Emily Berleth at Bedford/St. Martin's and Leslie Connor and the staff at Stratford Publishing Services, who guided the book through production, and to Katherine Gilbert and Nicole Simonsen, who assisted with numerous details. I was particularly fortunate in Bedford's choice of project referees. For their cogent readings of the draft of the manuscript, I am indebted to Leonard Cassuto, Russ Castronovo, John Ernest, Dana Nelson, and Karen Sánchez-Eppler. I owe a special debt of thanks to John Ernest for having led me to William C. Nell's 1851 *Services of Colored Americans,* and to Leonard Cassuto for his careful line-by-line editorial suggestions. For their help along the way with various aspects of the edition, I wish also to thank Jonathan Auerbach, Allan Austin, Vincent Carretta, Neil Fraistat, Ivy Goodman, Ezra Greenspan, Patricia Herron, Carla Peterson, Kenneth Price, and Martha Nell Smith.

I did the bulk of my research at the Library of Congress and am pleased to acknowledge the assistance of its expert staff. I am also grateful to librarians at the Boston Athenæum, the Schomburg Center for Research in Black Culture at The New York Public Library, and the University of Maryland's Interlibrary Loan Office.

My greatest debt, however, is to my indefatigable and brilliant editor at Bedford/St. Martin's, Kathy Retan, the sort of editor who supposedly vanished from the publishing landscape long ago. While dealing with personal ups and downs that would have led many an editor to abandon the project, Kathy somehow managed to sustain her enthusiasm for the edition and to prod me almost weekly with sharp editorial interventions. She has my sincere thanks for helping me to make this Cultural Edition of *Clotel* as good and as useful as I could possibly make it.

Robert S. Levine
University of Maryland

Contents

Illustrations

Part One

Clotel;

or,
The President's Daughter
The Complete Text

Introduction:
Cultural and
Historical Background

I know that upon the 4th of July, our 4th of July orators talk of Liberty, Democracy, and Republicanism. They talk of liberty, while three millions of their own countrymen are groaning in abject Slavery. This is called the "land of the free, and home of the brave;" it is called the "Asylum of the oppressed;" and some have been foolish enough to call it the "Cradle of Liberty." If it is the "cradle of liberty," they have rocked the child to death.

— William Wells Brown, *Lecture* (1847)

William Wells Brown's *Clotel; or, The President's Daughter: A Narrative of Slave Life in the United States* is a landmark work, the first novel by an African American. Published in 1853 in London, *Clotel* appeared at a time when Brown, an escaped slave, was still legally regarded as property within the borders of the United States. (His British admirers would purchase his free papers in 1854.) Purporting to tell the stories of Thomas Jefferson's slave mistress, daughters, and granddaughters, *Clotel* "talks back" to U.S. culture, providing a brilliantly ironic challenge to the nation's patriotic narratives, particularly those that celebrate Thomas Jefferson's America as a nation of freedom and equality for all. Brown accomplishes his goals of social critique not only by providing his readers with what he suggests is a secret history of Jefferson's black paramour and descendants but also by appropriating and working transformations on numerous texts

3

published between 1780 and 1853. Those texts include a short story by Lydia Maria Child, factual accounts from abolitionist books and journals, a speech by Andrew Jackson, debates in Congress, slave narratives, earlier writings by Brown, and poems and essays on Jefferson's alleged sexual relationship with his slave Sally Hemings. The critic John Ernest has usefully termed Brown's authorial work in *Clotel* as that of a "cultural editor" (23) — a writer and compiler who presses his readers to rethink their assumptions about race, gender, and slavery by teaching them how they might better read cultural texts and scripts. And yet, as Ernest allows, there are limits to the effectiveness of Brown's narrative strategies, for the fact is that most of his readers, both then and now, "have never seen the sources themselves" (24). This Cultural Edition of *Clotel* seeks to rectify that situation, providing readers with Brown's most important acknowledged sources along with a number of cultural texts that help to put those sources, and the novel itself, into a fuller political, ideological, and literary context.

In the final chapter of *Clotel*, Brown declares that he created his novel by drawing on his personal experiences and wide reading, which he then "combined" into the narrative that "made up my story" (p. 226 in this volume). Brown's comments on his sources suggest the importance of considering his textual appropriations in relation to his career as a former slave who had risen to become a noted abolitionist, reformer, and man of letters. His comments also suggest that he liked to make up stories; in fact, he liked storytelling so much that he told different stories about his own life history in his various autobiographical writings, asserting in some places that he was the grandson of Daniel Boone, describing in others how he unwittingly participated in the power structure of slavery, and detailing in still others his subversive relation to the slave owners. A deadly serious moralist, Brown was also something of a confidence man and trickster whose views on such explosive subjects as race and gender can be difficult to pin down. An artist who challenges the culture's "official" stories, Brown can seem to be suspicious of any kind of coherent or definitive narrative.

But there are certain facts we can state about Brown's life history with relative assurance. The author of over fifteen books and one of the most renowned antislavery lecturers and reformers of the time, Brown was born a slave on a plantation near Lexington, Kentucky, most likely in 1814, the son of a white man and a slave named Elizabeth. As a boy he spent several years in the Missouri territory, and by 1827 he was living in St. Louis with his master, Dr. John Young. After working a variety of jobs, ranging from house servant to assistant to a slave trader, Brown, accompanied by his mother, attempted to escape from slavery in 1833. Captured in Illinois, he was returned to Young and eventually sold to Enoch Price, a St. Louis merchant and steamboat owner. In 1834 Brown made a second escape attempt, this time by himself, and with the help of the Quaker Wells Brown, whose name he subsequently adopted, he successfully made his way to Cleveland, Ohio. Shortly thereafter, he married the free black Elizabeth Schooner, and over the next nine years worked on a steamboat in Lake Erie, regularly helping slaves to escape on the underground railroad. In 1836, after moving to Buffalo, New York, he initiated his career as a reformer, organizing and later serving as president of a black temperance society while continuing his antislavery activities.

Brown began lecturing for the Western New York Anti-Slavery Society in 1843; his reputation as a speaker and reformer grew, and he lectured for several other organizations as well. In 1847 he moved to Boston and commenced working as a paid lecturer for William Lloyd Garrison's Massachusetts Anti-Slavery Society. That same year he published his *Narrative of William W. Brown,* which rivaled Frederick Douglass's 1845 *Narrative* for popularity and consequently made him, as had been true for Douglass, vulnerable to fugitive-slave catchers. Estranged from his wife, Brown traveled to Paris to attend the 1849 International Peace Congress, and after touring Great Britain as an antislavery lecturer, he decided to remain in England when he learned that the U.S. Congress had passed the Fugitive Slave Law in 1850. Thus, when Brown published the first African American novel in 1853, it appeared not in the United States but in England.

Though *Clotel* was Brown's first novel, by 1853 he had published, in addition to his *Narrative, A Lecture Delivered Before the Female Anti-Slavery Society of Salem* (1847), an edition of antislavery songs (1848), a catalogue description of antislavery drawings (1850), and a travel book, *Three Years in Europe* (1852). He would go on to publish three significantly revised versions of *Clotel,* two major histories of blacks in the United States, a play, several memoirs, and some of his most famous speeches. Like Frederick Douglass, who had escaped from slavery in 1838, Brown regarded social reform and writing as significant ways of forwarding the cause of antislavery and antiracism in the United States. He presented himself, as Douglass did (and as Benjamin Banneker did in his famous letter to Thomas Jefferson; see p. 343 in this volume), as living proof, against the claims of proslavery and racist ideology, of an African American's ability to become a learned man of letters.

KIDNAPPING TEXTS

Central to Brown's authorial labors, indeed to his emergence as a man of letters, was his practice of using and reusing textual materials (including his own) that were already circulating in the culture. *Clotel*'s prefatory third-person "Narrative of the Life and Escape of William Wells Brown," for example, draws abundantly from Brown's first-person *Narrative* (1847). But what are we to make of the fact that in *Clotel* itself Brown takes whole passages, sometimes pages and pages of other peoples' writings, and uses those words and paragraphs and pages in his own novel? Some readers (perhaps students asked to write essays on *Clotel*) might well wonder whether Brown was simply a plagiarist. Although it would be anachronistic to accuse Brown of plagiarism in our sense of the term (the nineteenth century had very different notions of copyright and literary ownership, though the modern notion of individual rights to literary property was beginning to emerge), it nonetheless *is* useful to think of Brown as a kind of plagiarist. Stephen Rachman notes that plagiarism can be regarded as a form of literary trickery that "has its roots in *plagiarus,* Latin for 'a kidnapper, a seducer,' as well as a literary thief" (52). According to the *Oxford English Dictionary,* "plagiary" also refers to "one who abducts the child or slave of another." By that definition, the abolitionists who attempted to help the slaves escape from the slave catchers unleashed by the Fugitive Slave Law of 1850 (which legally required all U.S. citizens to return escaped slaves to their masters) could be understood metaphorically as types of plagiarists. And yet if we were to put the interpretive emphasis on theft and kidnapping, we could regard the slave masters themselves as "plagiarists," and Brown's taking of texts as a kind of kidnapping and trickery characteristic of a liberator; he steals the texts of a culture that steals black bodies. Writing *Clotel* in the wake of the Fugitive Slave Law's edict to return escaped blacks to their "proper" place on the southern plantation, Brown attempts to liberate a variety of texts by placing them in "improper" relation within his revisionary narrative. In doing so, Brown presses his readers to raise questions about the arbitrariness and morality of the existing arrangements of the social order.

According to a recent interpreter of nineteenth-century debates on plagiarism, "the plagiarist disrupts the field of significations that the law sets in place, disrupting claims of legitimacy and natural authority" (Weinauer 700). Such disruption can occur when marginalized subjects, who have little access to the power structure, show how easy it is to appropriate, manipulate, and parody the language of the oppressors. Rather than simply using that language to uphold the power structure, the plagiarist in effect inhabits that language, getting inside it, so to speak, in order to explore and ultimately to reveal its cultural uses and abuses. A black author's intelligent mimicry of the proslavery rhetoric that insists upon blacks' lack of intelligence, for example, works quite powerfully to reveal the bankruptcy of such rhetoric, and thus the ways in which that rhetoric serves the ends of racist white enslavers. In *Clotel,* Brown again and again artfully inhabits and arranges various discourses and texts so as to suggest the limits of their truth-telling capacities, thereby undermining the narratives and texts of the dominant culture. At times the various "stolen" cultural texts seem to converse with one another; at other times, such as when we move from descriptions of black victimization to images of violent black rebellion, they seem to challenge or deconstruct one another. Parody, fragmentation, and oddly disruptive juxtapositions of oft-times incompatible cultural discourses characterize Brown's narrative method in *Clotel.*

Ironically inhabiting and mimicking a hodgepodge of discourses (political, sentimental, reformist, and so on), *Clotel* can be read as a stunning example of literary pastiche — a technique of creating a literary work by borrowing from or imitating other works and styles. Unlike the plagiarist, the author of pastiche tends to be fairly open in acknowledging his or her textual sources, for without some acknowledgment, the point of the pastiche, which could range from homage to parody, would be lost. In Brown's case, writing as he does from a marginalized minority position in U.S. culture, there is a powerful socio-critical dimension to his use of pastiche, for he generally wishes to subvert and transform the very discourses that make up his novel. In bringing a variety of cultural discourses and texts into *Clotel,* Brown also makes use of the (post)modernistic technique of bricolage, a close cousin to pastiche, which involves taking bits and pieces of writings (sometimes long pieces) and (re)assembling those "found" cultural materials into something new. The critic Ann duCille nicely describes the new fictive world created by Brown's techniques of pastiche and bricolage in *Clotel* as "an 'unreal estate,' a fictive realm of the fantastic and coincidental . . . an ideologically charged space, created by drawing together a variety of discursive fields — including 'the real' and 'the romantic,' the simple and the sensational, the allegorical and the historical" (18). Within the "unreal estate" of *Clotel,* Brown points to the gaps and blindnesses of much of the materials that he appropriates, with the large aim of helping his readers to see the culture more clearly.

As "cultural editor," Ernest writes, "Brown gathers the documents that reveal the national disunity — not the meaninglessness of the national text but its meaningful incoherence — and he constructs or reshapes his various narrative lines to instruct his readers to read beyond the text" (34). The "meaningful incoherence" that Brown's work reveals is the paradoxical space of an antebellum culture that celebrates democratic freedom while upholding slavery. Brown's narrative method, then, in addressing large questions of slavery and freedom, presses the reader to "read beyond" the nation's founding documents, and thus to rethink the politics and deeds of the nation's Founding Fathers. In fact, among the cultural sources that find their way into *Clotel* are the Declaration of Independence and the histories and counterhistories of Thomas Jefferson's relationship with his slaves at Monticello, his estate in central Virginia, particularly the rumors circulated by abolitionists during the 1830s and 1840s about Jefferson's sexual relationship with his slave Sally Hemings (see Part Two, Chapter 1). Brown took from these abolitionist counterhistories in particular the informing donnée of his novel: that the Father of American Freedom was also the father of slaves. And he asks his readers to wrestle with the large question of what happens to U.S. narratives of progress and freedom when they are disrupted by such a historical contradiction.

AMERICAN GENEALOGIES:
THOMAS JEFFERSON AND SALLY HEMINGS

In a lecture delivered at an August 1854 antislavery meeting in Manchester, England, Brown proclaimed: "No one can read . . . the declaration of the American independence, and compare that document with the history of the legislation of the federal government in the United States, without being struck with the marked inconsistency of the theory of the people and their acts; the one declaring that all men are created equally, endowed by their Creator with certain inalienable rights, among which are life, liberty, and the pursuit of happiness, and the other is the history of the encroachment of slavery upon liberty, or legislation in favour of slavery in that country against the cause of freedom" (Ripley I:399). To a significant extent, that "inconsistency" first manifested itself at the 1787 Constitutional Convention, where the delegates entrusted with establishing the governmental structure of a nation that had rebelled against England, which the patriots had regularly analogized to a slave power, agreed to approve three key provisions on slavery: Article 1, section 2, which allowed the slave states to count slaves as three-fifths of a person when assessing taxation and congressional representation; Article 1, section 9, which stated that Congress could not interfere with the importation of slaves until 1808; and Article 4, section 2, which called for the return of fugitive slaves and thus set the groundwork for Congress's passage of the Fugitive Slave Law of 1793 and the later passage of the Compromise of 1850's infamous Fugitive Slave Law. What remains debatable is whether the delegates of the Constitutional Convention, in search of sectional compromise, had in fact violated the spirit of Jefferson's Declaration of Independence and the American Revolution itself, for Jefferson never seemed all that concerned about the situation of the colonists' blacks. Nevertheless, Northerners opposed to the compromises believed that there had been a violation, and it is no coincidence that nineteenth-century abolitionists would regularly point to that violation and its attendant contradictions by invoking the Revolutionary ideals encapsulated in the Declaration (see, for example, Frederick Douglass's famous speech, "What to the Slave is the Fourth of July?" [pp. 253–58], and the passage from Brown's *Lecture* that serves as the epigraph to this Introduction).

But given the racism of Jefferson and other Revolutionary leaders, an argument can also be made that there had been no violation at all, and that in the emergent United States, slavery and freedom, as Brown and other antislavery writers would lament, went hand in hand. The historian David Brion Davis remarks, for example, that "the American Revolution freed southern slaveholders from various imperial restraints, opening the way for Indian removal and for a westward expansion of slavery that met no serious opposition until the rise of the Republican party in response to the Kansas-Nebraska Act of 1854" (273). And in his magisterial study of the first two centuries of slavery in North America, Ira Berlin comments on the perverse ways in which the Declaration worked to strengthen slaveholders' convictions of the moral soundness of the "peculiar institution," and thus to legitimate their efforts to make slavery the law of the land: "If indeed all men were created equal and some men were slaves — the argument ran — then, perhaps, those who remained in the degraded condition of slaves were not fully men after all. The implications of this twisted reading of the Declaration of Independence . . . would have a powerful influence on

Americans, black and white" (224). But how "twisted" was this reading of the Declaration of Independence? That is one of the large questions that Brown addresses head-on in his novel about the president's daughters and granddaughters.

By deciding to use the most famous propositions of the Declaration of Independence as the epigraph to *Clotel*, Brown immediately calls attention to the disturbing fact that the nation of freedom, equality, and the pursuit of happiness is also the home of slavery. To Jefferson's credit, the epigraph also suggests why blacks and whites opposed to slavery and racial hierarchies in the United States would turn to the Declaration to justify both their quest for equality and their resistance to authoritarian power (see, for example, the selections from David Walker, Frederick Douglass, Henry Highland Garnet, and other abolitionists in Part Two, Chapters 2 and 3). In *Clotel*, the "heroic young slave" (p. 211) George Green proclaims that he participated in Nat Turner's bloody slave conspiracy of 1831 because he was inspired when he heard his "master read in the Declaration of Independence 'that all men are created free and equal' " (p. 212). Like the patriotic abolitionists whom Brown celebrates in his 1847 *Lecture* as occupying "a higher position, than those who put forth their Declaration in 1776, in behalf of American liberty" (96), George is a patriot in the Jeffersonian tradition who outshines even Jefferson. For as Brown reminds his readers in *Clotel*, the Founding Father who helped to give such powerful expression to American ideals of freedom was also a slaveholder who apparently saw no contradiction between his commitment to political equality and his status as a plantation master. Any effort to understand American genealogies of slavery and freedom, Brown suggests, must begin with that basic fact.

As is well known, among the nation's founders Jefferson was not alone in holding slaves. George Washington purchased and traded slaves while running his Mount Vernon estate in Virginia, and during the 1790s owned upwards of three hundred slaves, most of whom he freed at his death. James Madison and other notable Southern political leaders also owned slaves and had important roles in developing the constitutional compromises ensuring that slavery would remain part of the social and legal fabric of the new nation. Jefferson, however, stands as a particularly interesting case, for his views on slavery and on blacks appear to have wavered. In his draft version of the Declaration, Jefferson blamed the British for introducing the practice of slavery to America, and he called for its eventual abolition (pp. 238–44). During the 1780s, he proposed a gradual abolition program that would have ended the slave trade and prohibited slavery in the western territories, and he set a date around the year 1800 after which all children born of slaves would be regarded as free. In 1806, during his second term as president, he signed legislation ending the importation of slaves; and he regularly voiced his hopes that the spread of slavery would lead to its diffusion and demise. But despite views that in their time and place could be regarded as antislavery, Jefferson ran a fairly extensive slave plantation at Monticello, with approximately two hundred slaves, and from the 1790s until his death in 1826 blamed his substantial financial debts for making it impossible for him to end slavery at his own estate. Moreover, in response to the 1819–21 debates on the Missouri Compromise, which ultimately set territorial limits on the spread of slavery (until these limits were repealed by the 1854 Kansas-Nebraska Act), Jefferson's views on slavery hardened. Outraged by Congress's efforts to exclude slavery from Missouri and the unsettled territories to its west and north, Jefferson vociferously defended Southerners' rights to decide when and how to bring about the end of slavery on their own. The Compromise of 1820, which admitted Missouri as a slave state and Maine as a free state, while banning slavery from the remaining unorganized territory north of latitude 36° 30′, did little to assuage his discomfort with what he regarded as a Federalist conspiracy to limit the power of the Southern slave states.

Jefferson's *Notes on the State of Virginia* (1785) can be taken as a key to his contradictory thinking on slavery and race. In *Notes's* chapters on slavery (pp. 335–43), Jefferson expresses an overall abhorrence of the institution, focusing in particular on how slavery corrupts the masters. His implicit argument is that slavery goes against the grain of the Enlightenment political philosophy that encouraged the colonists to challenge England's authoritarianism in the first place. In an eerie and prescient anticipation of Herman Melville's novella of slave revolt, "Benito Cereno" (1855), he imagines the slaves as so angry about their mistreatment, and so hateful toward their white enslavers, that their primary desire is to wage an apocalyptic war of vengeance against the masters. And yet even as Jefferson's imaginings of a bloody race war imply that he understands blacks' all too human resistance to their degradation, he presents the specter of such a war as evidence not for blacks' humanity but rather for the political "fact" that blacks and whites can never live together in the United States. By the 1820s he would come to support the efforts of the American Colonization Society to ship the free blacks to Africa.

Repressing his cross-racial identification with vengeful black rebels, Jefferson in *Notes* presents blacks as physically, morally, and mentally inferior to whites. In this way he anticipated, and even helped to give rise to, the "scientific" racialist writings of the 1840s and 1850s that insisted on the "objective" fact of black inferiority and difference (for examples see Part Two, Chapter 2); those writings served as an intellectual foundation for white supremacist thinking and emerged as a crucial discursive and ideological force in the culture against which Brown and other antebellum black writers had to do battle. Though Jefferson was aware that it was difficult for free blacks to acquire an education, and virtually impossible for slaves to do so, he proclaimed in an 1814 letter to his friend Edward Coles that blacks are "as incapable as children of taking care of themselves, and are extinguished promptly wherever industry is necessary for raising young. In the mean time they are pests in a society by their idleness, and the depredations to which this leads them" (*Writings* 1345). According to Jefferson, blacks' apparent inability to rise in white society revealed not their lack of training or experience (or the barriers erected by white racists) but their essential inferiority. In his letter to Coles he worries over the possibility of "black" blood contaminating "white" blood, asserting that blacks' "amalgamation with the other color produces a degradation to which no lover of his country, no lover of excellence in the human character can innocently consent" (*Writings* 1345). Quite understandably, one historian refers to Jefferson as "the intellectual godfather of the racist pseudo-science of the American school of anthropology" (Finkelman 186).

But even as Jefferson was going on record in *Notes* with his statements on blacks' mental and physical inferiority, he apparently was struck by the beauty (and intelligence) of one of his slaves, Sally Hemings, and may himself have been guilty of the very "crimes" against race and the nation that he later anxiously contemplated in his letter to Coles. Hemings accompanied Jefferson's nine-year-old daughter Mary to Paris in 1787, where Jefferson was serving as U.S. minister to France. Jefferson had assumed that position in 1785, three years after the death of his wife, Martha, and he had summoned Mary and Sally to Paris shortly after his daughter Lucy had died at Monticello. At the time, Jefferson was forty-four and Hemings was fourteen. To a significant extent, the light-skinned Sally was somewhat like family, for in 1773, shortly before he began working on his draft of the Declaration, Jefferson had inherited her mother, Betty Hemings, and ten of Betty's twelve children, from his father-in-law, John Wayles, who was in all likelihood the father of six of those children. Sally Hemings would therefore have been the half sister of Jefferson's wife and may have borne a physical resemblance to her. Hemings remained with Jefferson in Paris for twenty-six months, returning with him to Monticello in 1789. In subsequent years she had at least five children, all of whom were so light-complected that they were often mistaken for white. Most assumed that the father was someone other than Jefferson, perhaps Samuel or Peter Carr, the rakish sons of Jefferson's sister, though the evidence showed that Jefferson, who traveled frequently, was at Monticello nine months before each of the births.

"Amalgamation" thus had an important place in the Jefferson-Wayles family history, and there was ample evidence in the bodies of the light-skinned slaves at Monticello that amalgamation remained part of the family history. Rumors about Jefferson's possible sexual relationship with Sally Hemings were first publicly circulated in 1802 by James Callender, an alcoholic journalist angered by Jefferson's refusal to appoint him postmaster of Richmond, Virginia. Callender attempted to damage Jefferson's reputation in crudely racist fashion, fully aware that perhaps the worst thing he could say about a white leader was that he had had sexual relations with a black slave woman. Callender declared in the 1 September 1802 issue of the Richmond *Recorder:* "It is well known that the man, whom it delighteth the people to honor, keeps and for many years has kept, as his concubine, one of his slaves. Her name is SALLY . . . By this wench Sally, our president has had several children" (2). Following up on his accusations in the 22 September 1802 issue of the *Recorder,* Callender charged Jefferson not only with sexual immorality but also with having committed egregious crimes against the state and the nation: "Put the case that every white man in Virginia had done as much as Thomas Jefferson has done towards the utter destruction of its happiness, that eighty thousand white men had; each of them, been the father of five mulatto children. Thus you have FOUR HUNDRED THOUSAND MULATTOES in addition to the present swarm. The country would be no longer habitable, till after a civil war, and a series of massacres" (2). The controversy over Jefferson's possible relationship with Hemings continued for several months, but abruptly came to an end when Callender drowned in the James River, apparently when attempting to bathe while drunk. Jefferson won his 1804 reelection by a landslide.

Because Callender's charges emerged from a highly partisan perspective, they were not taken very seriously in their own time (and were dismissed, until recently, by most twentieth-century historians).

But rumors persisted about Jefferson's sexual relationships with one or more of his female slaves, and during the 1830s the charges were revived and echoed not by other proslavery and racist writers like Callender, but by antislavery British and American writers (see the several examples in Part Two, Chapter 1). With the upsurge of abolitionist activity and writings during the 1830s, spawned in part by William Lloyd Garrison's founding in 1831 of the abolitionist newspaper *The Liberator*, there was suddenly such a proliferation of texts asserting Jefferson's paternity of slave children that the popular British writer Captain Frederick Marryat could declaim with full authority in his widely read *A Diary in America: With Remarks on Its Institutions* (1839): "It is a well-known fact that a considerable portion of Mr. Jefferson's slaves were his own children. If any of them absconded, he would smile, thereby implying that he should not be very particular in looking after them; and yet this man, this great and GOOD man, . . . who asserted that slavery of the Negro was a violation of the most sacred rights of life and liberty, permitted these his slaves and his children, the issue of his own loins, to be sold at auction after his demise, not even emancipating them, as he might have done, before his death" (281).

Although Jefferson did leave instructions for emancipating the Hemings slaves after his death, William Wells Brown takes as his point of departure in *Clotel* the possibility that two of Jefferson's slave daughters, and his slave mistress, remained enslaved and were sold at auction. By setting *Clotel* after Jefferson's death, Brown chooses to keep Jefferson offstage and to deal with the fate of Currer's children by Jefferson rather than with the president's relationship with Currer (the Hemings character). Thus, rather than presenting a fictionalized version of the Jefferson-Hemings relationship, Brown develops a more metaphorical and clearly fictional account of the travails of Jefferson's black "descendants" — the daughters (and sons) of a failed (or unfinished) American Revolution. That said, Brown, like many abolitionists of the time, probably regarded the rumors about Jefferson and Hemings as literal truth. Near the conclusion of Chapter 1 of *Clotel*, he writes with little irony or ambiguity: "Thus closed a Negro sale, at which two daughters of Thomas Jefferson, the writer of the Declaration of Independence, and one of the presidents of the great republic, were disposed to the highest bidder!" (p. 88). Brown may be telling a fictionalized story but, as with his histories of the 1860s and 1870s, he is also writing an alternative history, one that deauthorizes the heroic founding narrative that has Jefferson at its untroubled center as the "father" of American freedom.

Encouraging its readers to develop a skeptical relationship to glorified stories of the national past, *Clotel* can be regarded as what Lee Quinby terms a "genealogical fiction," a text that "breaks the hold of official truth and the metaphysics of memory, putting in their place the truth of countermemory" (xviii; see also Castronovo 31–66). As a genealogical fiction, *Clotel* shares a good deal with two other novels of the period that also pose challenges to cultural memory by raising questions about the fathers: Nathaniel Hawthorne's *The House of the Seven Gables* (1851) and Herman Melville's *Pierre* (1852). Both novels depict what appears on the surface to be a thriving, prosperous, democratic America, and both ultimately show that beneath that happy surface lies an ambiguous history of violation and deceit. Pierre fears that the woman he is attracted to may be his sister, for he learns that his father may have had a daughter out of wedlock who may well be "black," just as his father before him, a Revolutionary hero, may have had sexual relations with his slaves (see Levine); and in Hawthorne's *House*, the main characters and the reader learn that the esteemed Judge Pyncheon, in the tradition of his esteemed forefather Colonel Pyncheon, is a thief. Both novels develop contrasts between official and unofficial history, locating the truth in the margins and shadows. Like Brown, Hawthorne and Melville encourage the reader to rethink national genealogies and dominant cultural narratives. In contesting those narratives, the genealogical fictionalist takes seriously the "unofficial," marginalized perspectives of cultural outsiders. Access to sites of exclusion and repression, to the truth of conflict and power, Hawthorne remarks in *House*, may best be available from "private, diurnal gossip" (122).

Until very recently, most historians have rejected the "gossip" that Jefferson could have had sexual relations and fathered children with Sally Hemings (but see Fawn Brodie's *Thomas Jefferson: An Intimate History* [1974] and Barbara Chase-Riboud's best-selling historical novel *Sally Hemings* [1979], both of which chronicle Jefferson's sexual relationship with Hemings). In his prize-winning *American Sphinx: The Character of Thomas Jefferson* (1997), for example, the historian Joseph J. Ellis comments only briefly on Jefferson and his slaves at Monticello, exploring other broad intellectual movements before concluding with an appendix, "A Note on the Sally Hemings Scandal," that by its very placement at the end of the volume ensures that the overall study will remain uncontaminated by the "scandal." While conceding that there is suggestive evidence of a relationship between Hemings and Jefferson, and that at "the purely metaphoric level, then, the story of an enduring sexual connection between Jefferson and Sally Hemings conveys an elemental truth about the hidden history of race relations in America" (306), Ellis nonetheless takes the high historiographic road of dismissing the allegations: "Within the scholarly world, especially within the community of Jefferson specialists, there seems to be a clear consensus that the story is almost certainly not true. Within the much murkier world of popular opinion, especially within the black community, the story appears to have achieved the status of a self-evident truth" (305). Unlike Hawthorne, who locates the truth of Judge Pyncheon precisely in the world of popular opinion, Ellis rejects the "murky" world of black popular opinion and places his faith in the "experts."

But as Annette Gordon-Reed argues in her revisionary study, *Thomas Jefferson and Sally Hemings: An American Controversy* (1997), for nearly two hundred years that "murky" black world has based its opinion on less traditional but perhaps more valid sources than rational and "disinterested" scholarly argument — specifically, on an oral and written tradition among the black descendants of Sally Hemings. While the Jefferson family has asserted that one of the Carrs was in all probability the father of Sally's children, some of the Hemings children (and their friends) have talked of their knowledge that Jefferson was the father of some or all of Sally Hemings's children. As Gordon-Reed shows, Madison Hemings, in a memoir published in the 13 March 1873 *Pike County (Ohio) Republican,* made a particularly compelling case for claiming Thomas Jefferson as his father; this account was corroborated by Israel Jefferson, another former slave at Monticello (Gordon-Reed 7–58).

Further corroboration came in 1998 in the form of evidence based on DNA testing. In a study appearing in the highly regarded scientific journal *Nature,* Eugene A. Foster, a pathologist and geneticist, reported that a DNA analysis demonstrated all but conclusively that Thomas Jefferson was the father of Hemings's youngest son, Eston (1808–1852), and thus could have been the father of some of her other children as well. In a series of genetic tests researchers traced the Y chromosome of male descendants of Eston Hemings against the Y chromosome of male descendants of Thomas Jefferson's uncle on his father's side, with whom he shared genetic material, and found a match. This testing also eliminated Peter Carr and Samuel Carr as possible fathers of Eston Hemings, for no match was found among the male descendants of the Carr family (see Foster et al.). Because Jefferson was known to have been at Monticello at the various times of conception, the genetic evidence suggests rather strongly that Jefferson was the father of at least this one slave. Formerly skeptical historians, such as Joseph Ellis, who coauthored an accompanying article in *Nature* with biomedicist Eric S. Lander, quickly concurred with the conclusions of the testing, though questions remain about what the scientific revelations say about Jefferson. Ellis and Lander offer a rather bland conclusion to their essay: "Our heroes — and especially presidents — are not gods or saints, but flesh-and-blood humans, with all of the frailties and imperfections that this entails" (14).

One of the disturbing aspects of Ellis's and other historians' quick capitulation to the scientific "facts" is that the historical evidence that helped to support the findings of the scientists had for a long time been readily available. The difference now is that respected white scientists are finally saying what the Hemings descendants have said all along. What has not changed are the hierarchies of knowledge that dictate social truths. A full consideration of the Jefferson-Hemings relationship should prompt much more than a pious concession of human frailty: It should instead lead to a rethinking of the history of blacks and whites in America, of connections between slavery and freedom, of the dynamics of race in American history, and of the relationship of the politics of gender to the politics of slavery. It should also inspire a rethinking of how those histories traditionally have been told in the U.S. and how they might now be more truthfully revised. Such a reconceptualization would commence approximately one hundred fifty years after William Wells Brown began the process in his phantasmagorical, fragmented, *un*writing of American history in *Clotel*.

RACE, GENDER, AND THE PROBLEM OF THE TRAGIC MULATTA

Brown's assumed knowledge of Jefferson's sexual consortings with at least one of his slave women was certainly taken seriously by the abolitionist press. In the 3 February 1854 *Liberator*, an anonymous reviewer of *Clotel* refers to the "warmest commendations" that the novel has received in England and expresses the hope that the book "might be reprinted in this country, believing it would find many readers." The reviewer then turns to the heart of the matter:

> While the Declaration of Independence is preserved, the memory of Thomas Jefferson, its author, will be cherished, for the clear recognition it makes of the natural equality of mankind, and the inalienable right of every human being to freedom and the pursuit of happiness. But it will

also be to his eternal disgrace that he lived and died a slave-holder, emancipating not one of his slaves at his death, and, it is well understood, leaving some of his own children to be sold to the slave speculators, and thus to drag out a miserable life of servitude. Of the last, 'Clotel' was one — beautiful, intelligent, captivating ("New Work by William W. Brown" 19).

Reviewers in England similarly took for granted that Jefferson had children by at least one of his female slaves, and thus praised Brown for chronicling in the form of a novel what they took to be the historical facts of the lives of those light-complected children (see, for example, the review reprinted from the Hereford *Times* in the 20 January 1854 issue of the *Liberator*).

The Jefferson-Hemings relationship had a particularly resonant connection to Brown's own life history (which has to be taken as an important "source" of the novel) and the life histories of many other black abolitionists. As a "mulatto" (a word used rather loosely in antebellum culture to refer to blacks who showed evidence of having "white" blood in their genealogical lines), Brown could regard himself metaphorically, in James Callender's terms, as part of the "swarm" of Jefferson's "FOUR HUNDRED THOUSAND MULATTOES." Brown's light-complected skin insistently told the story that he owed his very existence to the sexual violation of his mother by a slave owner. In her biography of her father, Josephine Brown proclaimed: "If there is one evil connected with the abominable system of slavery which should be loathed more than another, it is taking from woman the right of self-defence, and making her subject to the control of any licentious villain who may be able to purchase her person" (11). As Brown himself would write in *Three Years in Europe,* the whiteness of the slaves "is attributable, solely to the unlimited power which the slave owner exercises over his victim," and "there seems to be no limits to the system of amalgamation carried on between master and slave" (274). Though Brown is obviously critical of the masters' power, and is concerned in particular about the vulnerability and victimization of slave women, the fact remains that had there been no such violations, neither Brown nor his daughter (nor, for that matter, Frederick Douglass and many other black abolitionists) would have been alive to offer their condemnation of the patriarchal institution. *Clotel* can be read, in part, as a meditation on the history of such violations — one that is informed by a complex mix of Brown's guilt and anger at the violation that brought about his existence. Arguably, it is precisely because of his own personal history that Brown makes an effort to find something redemptive and transformative in the relationship between white men and black women. Although Brown implicitly discounts the possibility that there had been an emotional bond between Jefferson and Currer by focusing on the slave mother's abandonment by her master, the novel, both in the account of the initial attraction between Horatio and Clotel and in the later story of Morton and Althesa, suggests that interracial love is possible and that individuals have the potential to see their way past culturally inscribed racial boundaries and hierarchies. Nevertheless, Brown realistically emphasizes how such individuals are eventually destroyed by these hierarchies.

For his representations of cross-racial sexuality and love, Brown may have been inspired by rumors of the Jefferson-Hemings relationship and by his meditations on his own genealogy, but his specific literary source for the stories of Clotel and Althesa, Jefferson's fictional daughters, was Lydia Maria Child's "The Quadroons," first published in an antislavery journal in 1842 and slightly revised for book publication in 1846. (The story is reprinted on pp. 274–84.) Briefly, the antislavery tale, set in Georgia, tells of Edward's attraction to Rosalie, whom he cannot legally marry because she has black blood. They have a daughter, Xarifa, but after a number of years in which he treats Rosalie as a mistress, the socially ambitious Edward marries Charlotte, the daughter of a wealthy man in the community. Distraught at the marriage, Rosalie eventually dies of grief, and an equally distraught Edward takes up drinking and dies when he falls from a horse. Their daughter Xarifa is sold into slavery, and when her white lover attempts to rescue her, he is shot and killed. In response, Xarifa goes mad and dies of a broken heart.

Despite having nothing much to do with Jefferson, Child's "The Quadroons" spoke to Brown's interest in genealogy and racial politics. Though he changed the names and settings, he used much of Child's language verbatim. In doing so, he risked more than simply being accused of plagiarism; he also risked giving his apparent assent to the notion that stories of whites (or people who look white to the eye) were more important than stories of blacks. It is worth recalling that the reviewer of *Clotel* in the *Liberator* emphasized that Clotel is "beautiful, intelligent, captivating." As Brown makes clear in the opening chapter of the novel, Clotel's conventional attractiveness gives rise to a bidding war among the young white men who compete to possess her. Later in the novel we are told the story of Salome, a free white woman who is mistaken for a mulatto and taken into slavery, and Brown would seem to be suggesting that her tragedy is more worthy of our attention (and even more tragic) than that of a dark-skinned black born into slavery. We are also told how Morton's romantic attraction to Althesa has its origins in his conviction that it is unfair for a woman as white and attractive as Althesa to suffer the life of a slave.

In focusing on the fate of the white-complected daughters and granddaughters of Jefferson, Brown was particularly responsive to Child's use of the figure of the "tragic mulatta" — the woman who looks white to the eye but nonetheless suffers the fate of the black slave. Like Child, Brown in his writings sought to expose the sexual vulnerability and exploitation of black women in Southern slave culture, and in *Clotel* he strategically deploys the trope of the tragic mulatta in an effort to heighten his white readers' concerns about the plight of the slaves by showing how women's vulnerability crosses racial divides; the titles to chapters fourteen and fifteen, "A Free Woman Reduced to Slavery" and "To-day a Mistress, To-morrow a Slave," underscore this important point. In this respect, Brown was influenced not only by Child's story but also by Harriet Beecher Stowe's enormously popular *Uncle Tom's Cabin* (1852). Like Stowe, who presents a number of "tragic mulattas" (Eliza and Cassy being the most prominent), Brown linked himself with literary sentimentalism's project of attempting to make readers feel the plight of the marginalized other by depicting black slaves as not all that different from the whites who were reading about them. This was a literary and political strategy, as duCille argues, which "attempt[ed] to insinuate into the consciousness of white readers the humanity of a people they otherwise constructed as subhuman — beyond the pale of white comprehension" (8). In *Clotel*, the white liberator Georgiana can be taken as an idealized version of such a reader, for as a result of her encounters with Northern antislavery sentiment and her rereading of the Bible, she "had learned to feel deeply for the injured Negro" (p. 109).

And yet even as Child and Brown boldly address the immorality of slavery through the figure of the tragic mulatta, their light-complected black characters can seem perhaps too enamored of the white culture that denies them their rights and humanity. In Child's "The Quadroons," the slave women have no clear relation to the world of the slaves or of blackness; in focusing on the main characters' attraction to white men, the story can appear to uphold racial hierarchies and even to support Jefferson's notion, as expressed in *Notes,* of the physical unattractiveness of blacks. But though Child and Brown can be accused of a certain complicity in the dominant culture's racial valuations, there are important differences between Child's story and

Brown's revision that need to be emphasized. It is crucial to note, for example, that in an effort to put Child's story into conversation with other cultural discourses of the time, Brown breaks it into three sections (see chapters IV, VIII, and XXIII), and at the end of each section moves away from the original narrative to explore other concerns, characters, and generic modes. For example, the sentimental account of Clotel's failed "marriage" to Horatio Green is preceded and immediately followed by more realistic scenes of slave trading. Even more strikingly, in the later account of the deaths of Althesa's daughters, Brown draws on the tragic conclusion of Child's story, yet narrates these deaths in a chapter that begins with descriptions of a yellow fever epidemic and is immediately followed by descriptions of Nat Turner's slave rebellion. Through such juxtapositions, Brown reminds his readers that the daughters' sad story takes place within a larger context of suffering and rebellion.

Presenting his readers with a fractured and somewhat altered version of Child's story, Brown, through his method of literary pastiche and bricolage, suggests the limitations of this "kidnapped" text. Within the larger narrative framework of *Clotel,* much more than in its initial publication, Child's story (as reimagined and recontextualized by Brown) emerges as a much less stable story, one that is overly dependent on conventional notions of race, gender, and sentiment. Unlike Child, Brown points to the possibilities of black rebellion, particularly among the female slaves, presenting most of the black women characters derived from "The Quadroons" as active agents who claim their rights to watch out for themselves and for those they love, and who hold up those rights as markers of their freedom and humanity. Because the Child story is included in this Cultural Edition, it can be left to readers of *Clotel* and "The Quadroons" to make their own determinations about the effectiveness of Brown's appropriation and revisions. But a few additional words should be said about race, genealogy, and sentimentalism in *Clotel* and other writings of the period.

In *Uncle Tom's Cabin,* Augustine St. Clare imagines the possibility of a racial war of extermination (similar to that which haunted Jefferson's *Notes*) and proclaims to his racist brother Alfred: "If ever the San Domingo hour comes, Anglo Saxon blood will lead on the day. Sons of white fathers, with all our haughty feelings burning in their veins, will not always be bought and sold and traded. They will rise, and raise with them their mother's race" (234). Alluding to the massive slave rebellion of the 1790s in San Domingo, which led to the loss of over 60,000 lives, St. Clare's comments are informed by racialist notions of the time that conceived of blacks and whites as essentially different, with the differences penetrating to the very blood. Though most scientists today reject the notion that there are clear, genetically distinct races, and regard "race" as an unworkable biological category dependent upon absurd (and insidious) notions of essential differences between "white" and "black" blood, the fact is that many of the most prestigious biologists and ethnologists of the nineteenth century thought quite differently on this matter, arguing that humankind consisted of a variety of discrete races (for several examples of this racialist writing, see Part Two, Chapter 2).

The historian George M. Fredrickson has coined the term "Romantic Racialism" (97) to describe Harriet Beecher Stowe's and other liberal whites' paternalistic views of blacks' supposed racial differences from whites. Influenced by Alexander Kinmont's *Twelve Lectures on the Natural History of Man* (1839), Stowe celebrates blacks for what she believes are their more naturally Christian ways — domestic, noncompetitive, relatively passive. The aggressive feelings that may lead to a violent rebellion, she suggests, are more characteristic of white males, whose drive toward mastery has important sources in their blood. At times in *Clotel* Brown can seem to share a similar racialist perspective on blood differences. For example, the reader is informed during a discussion of the 1831 Nat Turner rebellion and its aftermath: "The infusion of Anglo-Saxon with African blood has created an insurrectionary feeling among the slaves of America hitherto unknown. Aware of their blood connection with their owners, these mulattoes labour under the sense of their personal and social injuries" (p. 201). Like Stowe, Brown in this passage would appear to be promoting the idea that peoples of different skin colors have different blood that ultimately generates different patterns of behavior. And yet his use of the word "aware" links blacks' anger to their political awareness that intertangled black and white genealogies give the lie to the essentialist claims of racial difference regularly invoked to defend the practice of slavery. Moreover, his positive presentation of the black rebels Nat Turner, Picquilo, and William all argue for Brown's desire to challenge and revise the romantic racialism of the liberal North. In subsequent revisions of *Clotel,* Brown would even make the lightly complected rebel George Green into a full-blooded, prideful black (see the selection from *Clotelle: A Tale of the Southern States* in Part Two, Chapter 1).

With respect to the variously complected blacks of *Clotel,* Brown's approach to the problem of race might more usefully be termed "colorist" than "racialist," which is to say that he ultimately rejects the notion of biological or blood differences and emphasizes instead the inevitable cultural differences among light- and dark-complected slaves (and former slaves) — differences that have almost everything to do with the deleterious influences of white supremacist slave culture. The problem of color, then, emerges as one of the large subjects of *Clotel* (and of at least two important later novels by African American writers who were influenced by *Clotel,* Frances Harper's *Iola Leroy* [1892] and Pauline Hopkins's *Hagar's Daughter* [1901]). The plantation slave Sam, who is described as "one of the blackest of his race" (p. 135), appears virtually pathological in his denial of his blackness. Rather than accept the reality of his physical appearance, he makes pathetic efforts to pass himself off as a mulatto, smearing grease on his hair in an ultimately doomed attempt to straighten it, and pompously asserting his distance from "pure" blacks: "I don't like to see dis malgemation of blacks and mulattoes" (p. 136). Like the typical white in blackface performing on Northeast minstrel stages of the period, Sam initially comports himself in ways that appear contemptible and little short of laughable. But the surprise is that Sam, like all of the slaves of *Clotel,* is presented as possessing a communal political consciousness: soon after his "minstrel" performance as a black who harbors an impossible desire to be white, he learns of the death of his owner, and, along with other slaves of the plantation, sings songs expressing his loathing of slavery and the master. Sam's performance as a loyal black slave who actually hates slavery thus works to undermine the racist ideology that proclaimed blacks were happiest in a subordinate, enslaved position.

As his portrayal of Sam's subversive use of minstrelsy suggests, Brown, unlike Stowe and other racialists of the period, regarded race as anything but a stable biological category. Instead, he portrays race as something that is "performed" within racist culture (see Gilmore). A similar perspective on race and performance informs the novel's accounts of several of the slaves' escape attempts. Inspired by the escape of William and Ellen Craft (see pp. 271–73), Brown presents characters who manage to escape by cleverly performing the roles of lordly white master and subordinate black slave. The cross-dressed and racially "passing" George and Mary, for example, like black Sam who metaphorically puts on blackface, destabilize notions of essential racial difference between whites and blacks that had come to inform the ethnographic racial science and cultural formations of the period. Exposing the limits of such racialism, Brown implicitly calls on his readers to reevaluate the place of African Americans in U.S. culture.

As he would remark in his 1863 *The Black Man:* "There is nothing in race or blood, in color or features, that imparts susceptibility of improvement to one race over another. The mind left to itself from infancy, without culture, remains a blank. Knowledge is not innate. Development makes the man" (35–36).

PARALLEL LINES

Development made William Wells Brown. Having successfully fashioned his own escape from bondage, Brown presents himself in *Clotel*'s prefatory "Narrative of the Life and Escape of William Wells Brown" as "most assiduous in his studies" (p. 78), staying up to the wee hours of the morning "to read when others are asleep" (p. 79). Brown was not alone among antebellum African Americans in presenting himself to his readers as exemplary of blacks' ability to overcome what Frederick Douglass in *My Bondage and My Freedom* (1855) referred to as the "brutification" (152) of slavery. The period between 1845 and 1861 saw a flourishing of African American writing, as authors such as Douglass, Brown, Wilson, and Jacobs depicted blacks' struggles to rise in racist U.S. culture. This "Afro-American Literary Renaissance," as William L. Andrews has termed it, came at a time when blacks were experiencing an increasing despair at their prospects in the United States. The emergence of such powerful texts as Martin R. Delany's *The Condition, Elevation, Emigration, and Destiny of the Colored People of the United States* (1852), Solomon Northup's *Twelve Years a Slave* (1853), James Whitfield's *America and Other Poems* (1853), Frances Harper's *Poems* (1854), Douglass's *My Bondage and My Freedom* (1855), Harriet Wilson's *Our Nig* (1859), and Harriet A. Jacobs's *Incidents in the Life of a Slave Girl* (1861) attest to African Americans' high regard for literature as an expressive and political vehicle for addressing white racism and the dire political developments of the 1850s.

When *Clotel* appeared in England in 1853, the situation in the U.S. looked particularly grim. Following the acquisition of the vast territories gained from the war with Mexico (1846–48), Congress had approved the Compromise of 1850, which allowed California to enter the Union as a free state, left the Utah and New Mexico territories open to the possibility of becoming slave states, abolished the slave trade in the District of Columbia, and, as mentioned, imposed a more stringent Fugitive Slave Law that required all U.S. citizens to return escaped slaves to their masters. Rather than putting an end to antislavery activity, the Fugitive Slave Law outraged black and white abolitionists (and even less politically inclined Northerners with heretofore moderate antislavery sentiments), who regarded the new law as a clear sign that the Southern "slave power" had control of the federal government and that slavery would remain absolutely central to Northern and Southern U.S. culture. As Brown remarked in an 1854 speech to the Pennsylvania Anti-Slavery Society on the pervasive ills of slavery: "We need not go out of the free States to see its cruelties. . . . Look at the coloured people of the free States, thrown out of your schools, your churches and your social circles, deprived of their political rights and debarred from those avenues of employment that are necessary to a proper maintenance of themselves and their families. We find the degrading influences of slavery all about us" (Ripley IV:248).

Those "influences" became only more apparent in the mid to late 1850s. The passage of the 1854 Kansas-Nebraska Act, which repealed the territorial limits on slavery established by the Missouri Compromise, meant that slavery could continue its spread west. A central provision of this bill, which was drafted by the influential senator from Illinois, Stephen A. Douglas, was its support for popular sovereignty — the idea that settlers of future states would have full power to vote on whether to legalize slavery in their state constitutions. Unsurprisingly, the Kansas-Nebraska Act destroyed the sectional "peace" that had supposedly been established by the Compromise of 1850. During the mid-1850s, proslavery and antislavery forces clashed violently in what came to be termed "Bleeding Kansas." For black abolitionists, perhaps the most distressing development of the 1850s was the Supreme Court's 1857 ruling on *Dred Scott* v. *Sanford,* which asserted that African Americans had no legal rights in the U.S. and could never become citizens. The ruling also addressed the territorial issues raised by the Kansas-Nebraska Act, asserting in the broadest and most unambiguous terms that it was unconstitutional for the federal government to exclude slavery from the territories. The Dred Scott decision thus worked to further radicalize antislavery opinion in the North and midwest, and became a point of contention in the increasingly heated (and nationally prominent) political debates between Stephen Douglas and the Republican prairie lawyer Abraham Lincoln, who challenged Douglas for his senate seat in the election of 1858. Following the Dred Scott decision a number of African Americans, including Brown, began to champion black emigration to Haiti or Africa.

The materials in Part Two, Chapter 2, "Race, Slavery, Prejudice," focus on the centrality of slavery and antiblack racism to the dominant culture; the materials in Part Two, Chapter 3, "Resistance and Reform," focus on African Americans' strategies for contesting the dominant culture. The emigration movement of the 1850s was one of many black responses to slavery and racism in the United States; it was an extreme response to extreme circumstances. The majority of African American reformers from the 1770s to the 1860s fought for black citizenship in the U.S., which they hoped could be achieved through abolitionism, black uplift, and concerted challenges to antiblack racist ideologies. To this end, northeast free blacks organized temperance and antislavery societies, developed educational and religious organizations, founded a number of important black newspapers, met in conventions, published a wide variety of antislavery and antiracist documents, lectured in the U.S. and abroad on abolitionism and civil rights, and worked off and on with white political and antislavery organizations to attempt to improve the lot of African Americans. At the forefront of a number of these initiatives was William Wells Brown.

Brown's attraction to Haiti was short lived. Like many black abolitionists, he came to see the Civil War as a war against slavery, and he embraced the Union cause. Committed to a war that he hoped would reform the United States, he wrote three new versions of *Clotel* (1860–61, 1864, 1867), the final version of which, *Clotelle; or, The Colored Heroine,* portrays blacks playing a crucial role in the cultural politics of Reconstruction (for selections from his revisions, see pp. 309–27). Brown himself sought to play a central role in the reconstruction of the nation, as he was initially optimistic about the federal government's post-Civil War efforts to reorder the social and economic structure of the South (and North) by granting African Americans their civil and political rights. He worked as a black temperance leader and antiracist reformer, and authored black histories that he hoped would contribute to black pride and further inform whites about African Americans' crucial contributions to the nation. However, in his last published volume, *My Southern Home* (1880), Brown conveyed his despair at the failure of Reconstruction — which effectively ended in 1877 when President Hayes withdrew federal troops from the South — and urged Southern blacks to consider migrating north. But even with the persistence of antiblack racism and the restoration of segregationist Jim Crow practices in the South, Brown retained a hopeful belief that racial harmony could be achieved in the United States at some future historical moment (see Part Two, Chapter 3).

The bases of Brown's idealistic hopes that the U.S. could one day live up to its (Jeffersonian) ideals as a nation of freedom and opportunity can be found in an especially resonant passage in *Clotel*. At the opening of chapter XXI, the narrator offers a mythic account of the birth of slavery and freedom in the Northern and Southern colonies. On a particular day in 1620, the narrator writes, the Puritans' "Mayflower brought the seed-wheat of states and empire. . . . This ship had the embryo elements of all that is useful, great, and grand in Northern institutions; it was the great type of goodness and wisdom, illustrated in two and a quarter centuries gone by; it was the good genius of America" (p. 180). On that same day in the South "a low rakish ship hastening from the tropics" carried "the first cargo of slaves on their way to Jamestown, Virginia" (pp. 180–81). In the examples of these two ships Brown presents a rather clear allegory (albeit an artful one, as the Puritans did have slaves) of the struggle between slavery and freedom in the nascent republic:

> Behold the May-flower anchored at Plymouth Rock, the slave-ship in James River. Each a parent, one of the prosperous, labour-honouring, law-sustaining institutions of the North; the other the mother of slavery, idleness, lynch-law, ignorance, unpaid labour, poverty, and duelling, despotism, the ceaseless swing of the whip, and the peculiar institutions of the South. These ships are the representation of good and evil in the New World, even to our day. When shall one of those parallel lines come to an end? (p. 181)

By rhetorically asking when the evils spawned by slavery will come to an end, Brown, even in this highly polarized formulation, signals his belief that a reformative social transformation can occur, and that the very spirit needed to bring about that transformation is the same spirit that brought the nation into being. At the same time, with its demythologizing of Jefferson and its ultimate revelation that the idea of "parallel lines" is a fiction, *Clotel* provides no easy solutions and, particularly with its jaded view of Northern racism, no easy choices between "good" and "evil." Instead, Brown challenges his readers to rethink historical narratives and imperatives, and in this way begin the process of reimagining and reconceiving New World possibilities.

Drawn & Engraved   *by R. Woodman*

W. Wells Brown,

William Wells Brown, circa 1855. Frontispiece to Brown's *The American Fugitive in Europe* (1855).

28

Chronology of
Brown's Life and Times

1814
William Wells Brown born on a plantation near Lexington, Kentucky, the son of a slave woman named Elizabeth and a white man, most likely a relative of her owner, Dr. John Young. William is one of Elizabeth's seven children; the evidence suggests that there were several different fathers of her six sons and one daughter.

1816
December: Founding of the American Colonization Society, which sought to transport free blacks to Africa.

Dr. Young moves to the Missouri Territory, taking William and his other slaves with him. Sometime in the next few years, Young adopts into his family a nephew named William Moore and decides to change his slave William's name to Sandford.

1818
Birth of Frederick Douglass in Tuckahoe, Maryland.

1819
Washington Irving (1783–1859), *The Sketch Book*.

1820
Enactment of the Missouri Compromise: Missouri admitted as a slave state, Maine as a free state, and slavery excluded in the Louisiana Territory north of latitude 36°30′.

1821

William Cullen Bryant (1794–1878), *Poems;* James Fenimore Cooper (1789–1851), *The Spy.*

1822

Denmark Vesey's slave conspiracy in Charleston, South Carolina, is betrayed by a house slave; over thirty blacks are executed.

1824

Lydia Maria Child (1802–1880), *Hobomok.*

1826

July 4: Deaths of Thomas Jefferson and John Adams.

Cooper, *The Last of the Mohicans.*

1827

Young moves to St. Louis and buys a farm outside of the city. Pressed by financial circumstances, he sells Brown's mother, sister, and three brothers (two brothers had died), and begins to hire out his remaining slaves. Over the next few years Brown works at a tavern, at a St. Louis hotel, and on a steamboat, the *Missouri.*

New York State abolishes slavery.

First African American newspaper, *Freedom's Journal,* begins publication in New York City.

Catharine Sedgwick (1789–1867), *Hope Leslie.*

1829

David Walker (c.1790–1830) publishes his militant *Appeal* in Boston; Southern whites attempt to prevent its dissemination.

Antiblack riots in Cincinnati; several hundred blacks emigrate to Upper Canada.

William Apess (1798–?), *A Son of the Forest.*

1830

Brown is employed in the printing office of the Reverend Elijah P. Lovejoy, editor of the *Saint Louis Times.* During 1830 and 1831 he is also hired out to the steward's department of the steamboat *Enterprise,* where he first encounters the slave trader James Walker. He also works as an assistant to Dr. Young.

First national black convention convenes in Philadelphia.

1831

January 1: William Lloyd Garrison (1805–1879) publishes the first issue of his abolitionist newspaper, *The Liberator*.

August: Nat Turner leads a slave rebellion in Southampton County, Virginia. Approximately sixty whites and two hundred blacks are killed. Turner is captured in October and executed in November. That same month Thomas Gray publishes *The Confessions of Nat Turner*.

1832

Brown is hired out for a year to the slave trader James Walker.

Founding of the New England Anti-Slavery Society in Boston.

Nullification Crisis: After a special convention in South Carolina nullifies the federal government's new protective tariff and affirms the state's willingness to secede from the Union, President Jackson issues a proclamation of condemnation. The following year Congress lowers tariffs and passes the Force Bill, which authorizes Jackson to use U.S. troops to uphold federal law.

Garrison, *Thoughts on African Colonization*.

1833

Brown returns to Young's plantation and finds his sister has again been sold and is to be taken to Natchez, Mississippi. He attempts to escape from slavery with his mother but is captured in Illinois and returned to Young. Young sells him to Samuel Willi, a St. Louis merchant, for $500. His mother is sold and taken to New Orleans. Later that year Willi sells Brown for approximately $650 to the St. Louis merchant and steamboat owner Enoch Price, who initially employs Brown as a coachman.

Founding of the American Anti-Slavery Society in Philadelphia.

Child, *An Appeal in Favor of That Class of Americans Called Africans*.

1834

January: Brown escapes from slavery, traveling at night from Cincinnati to Cleveland, and receiving much valued help from the Ohio Quakers Wells Brown and his wife. Brown reassumes his name of William and in gratitude also assumes the name of his male benefactor. By the spring Brown has a job on the Lake Erie steamer *Detroit*, and by the end of the summer he has married the free black Elizabeth Schooner. Over the next nine years he works as a steamboatsman on Lake Erie, regularly helping fugitive slaves escape to Canada.

August: Great Britain abolishes slavery in the West Indies; in 1835 African Americans begin annually to celebrate West Indies emancipation on August 1.

Antiblack riots in Philadelphia and New York.

Founding of the *Southern Literary Messenger.*

1835

The Browns' first daughter dies in infancy.

President Jackson calls for the suppression of antislavery writings, thus supporting the bans set in place by most of the Southern states.

William Gilmore Simms (1806–1870), *The Yemassee.*

1836

Birth of Clarissa Brown. Near the end of the year Brown moves his family to Buffalo, New York, where he continues his work as a steamboatsman and conductor on the Underground Railroad, and also organizes and eventually becomes the president of a temperance society.

Abolitionists present to Congress the first of hundreds of petitions to end slavery in the District of Columbia.

Texas proclaims independence from Mexico.

Ralph Waldo Emerson (1803–1882), *Nature;* Richard Hildreth (1807–1865), *The Slave;* Jarena Lee (1783–?), *The Life and Religious Experiences of Jarena Lee, A Coloured Lady.*

1837

Passage of a gag rule prohibiting the reception of antislavery petitions in Congress and restricting congressional debate.

The antislavery newspaper editor Elijah Lovejoy is murdered by a mob in Alton, Illinois.

The Colored American, the second major African American newspaper, begins publication in New York City.

Financial panic: Failures of numerous banks lead to severe unemployment, which persists into the early 1840s.

Catharine Beecher (1800–1878), *An Essay on Slavery and Abolitionism.*

1838

Trail of Tears: Thousands of Native American Cherokees die during a federally mandated march from their native home in Georgia to the Indian Territory in Oklahoma.

Edgar Allan Poe (1809–1849), *The Narrative of Arthur Gordon Pym.*

1839

Birth of Josephine Brown.

Black rebellion on the Spanish slaver *Amistad;* the U.S. Supreme Court grants the rebels their freedom in 1841.

Theodore Dwight Weld (1803–1895), *American Slavery as It Is.*

1840

May: Formation of the antislavery Liberty Party in Albany, New York.

June: Leaders of the World's Antislavery Convention in London vote to ban women from public participation.

According to his later writings, Brown visits Haiti, Cuba, and islands of the West Indies. Upon his return, he resumes his antislavery activities, continuing to help fugitive slaves escape to Canada.

A schism in the American Anti-Slavery Society on key principles and tactics (including whether women, as Garrison argued, should have an important role in antislavery organizations) leads to the formation of the anti-Garrisonian group, the American and Foreign Anti-Slavery Society.

Founding of the Washingtonian Temperance Society, which quickly leads to the emergence of temperance as one of the most popular social reforms of the period.

Richard Henry Dana (1815–1882), *Two Years Before the Mast.*

1841

Slave rebellion on the slaver *Creole* bound from Virginia to New Orleans; the slaves are freed after taking the ship to the British colony of Nassau.

1843

August: Brown meets Frederick Douglass at antislavery meetings in Buffalo. Attending the National Convention of Colored Citizens of the United States in Buffalo, he joins Douglass in voting against the adoption of Henry Highland Garnet's militant "Address to the Slaves of the United States of America," which called on slaves to use violence against their masters.

October: Brown publishes a letter attacking Garnet in the October *National Anti-Slavery Standard;* this is his first known published writing. Around this time Brown becomes a lecturing agent for the Western New York Anti-Slavery Society.

Timothy Shay Arthur (1809–1885), *Temperance Tales;* William Prescott (1796–1859), *History of the Conquest of Mexico.*

1844

May: In New York, Brown attends the tenth anniversary meeting of the American Anti-Slavery Society, which condemns the U.S. Constitution as a proslavery document. He makes his first speech at this convention, which William Lloyd Garrison also attends. When he returns to Buffalo, Brown (according to his account) finds that his wife is involved with another man. This begins a period of public marital discord for him.

1845

July: The *United States Magazine and Democratic Review* proclaims that it is the United States' "manifest destiny to overspread the continent."

December: Texas is admitted to the Union as a slave state.

Brown moves his family to Farmington, New York, where there are integrated schools for his daughters.

Frederick Douglass (1818–1895), *Narrative of the Life of Frederick Douglass, An American Slave;* Margaret Fuller (1810–1850), *Woman in the Nineteenth Century.*

1846

May: The United States declares war on Mexico.

June: Brown attends a meeting of the Liberty Party, where he hears the Reverend Mr. Peck of Rochester scoff at the notion that blacks have natural, inalienable rights.

August: David Wilmot, a congressman from Pennsylvania, proposes that slavery should be banned in any territories acquired from the Mexican war. His proviso is defeated.

December: Attending the annual meeting of the Western New York Anti-Slavery Society in Rochester, Brown gives a speech supporting African Americans' rights to vote.

Herman Melville (1819–1891), *Typee.*

1847

Brown becomes a lecturing agent for the Massachusetts Anti-Slavery Society. After separating from his wife, he takes custody of their two daughters and moves to Boston. During the summer he publishes *Narrative of William W. Brown, A Fugitive Slave,* which is brought out by the Boston Anti-Slavery Office. The *Narrative* goes through four American editions and sells approximately ten thousand copies; it eventually goes through five British editions. Later that year he debates Garnet on moral suasion at the National Convention of Colored

People in Troy, New York, and in November he addresses the Female Anti-Slavery Society of Salem. His speech is published as a pamphlet, *A Lecture Delivered Before the Female Anti-Slavery Society of Salem.*

1848

February: The Mexican War ends with the Treaty of Guadalupe Hidalgo; the U.S. gains one-half-million square miles of new territory in the southwest for $15 million.

July: Brown publishes *The Anti-Slavery Harp: A Collection of Songs for Anti-Slavery Meetings,* which includes "Jefferson's Daughter." That same month Elizabeth Schooner Brown appears in Boston with a baby and demands financial support from Brown. After a mediating committee for the Massachusetts Anti-Slavery Society exonerates Brown, Elizabeth returns to Buffalo. She reportedly dies in 1851.

The first women's rights convention is held in Seneca Falls, New York, led by Lucretia Mott (1793–1880) and Elizabeth Cady Stanton (1815–1902).

1849

January: Brown meets the escaped slaves William and Ellen Craft and lectures with them over the next four months.

July–August: Elected as a delegate to the International Peace Congress in Paris, Brown sails from Boston to Liverpool, arriving on July 28. He attends the Peace Congress in August, and upon his return to London gives the first of hundreds of antislavery lectures delivered in Great Britain over the next five years.

Henry Bibb (1815–1854), *Narrative of the Life and Adventures of Henry Bibb;* Josiah Henson (1789–1883), *The Life of Josiah Henson;* James W. C. Pennington (1807–1870), *The Fugitive Blacksmith;* Henry David Thoreau (1817–1862), *A Week on the Concord and Merrimack Rivers* and "Resistance to Civil Government."

1850

September: Congress approves an omnibus of compromise measures intended to quell sectional discord on slavery. Among the approved bills is the Fugitive Slave Law, which mandates that all U.S. citizens are required to return fugitive slaves to their owners. Brown decides to remain in England after the passage of the Fugitive Slave Law; later that year he once again lectures with the Crafts.

Brown publishes *A Description of William Wells Brown's Original Panoramic Views,* a catalogue accompanying an exhibition of anti-slavery drawings.

Nathaniel Hawthorne (1804–1864), *The Scarlet Letter,* Emerson, *Representative Men;* Olive Gilbert, ed., *The Narrative of Sojourner Truth;* Susan Warner (1819–1885), *The Wide, Wide World.*

1851

July: Brown's daughters arrive in England, and in August he enrolls them in a seminary in Calais, France, where they remain for a year before enrolling in the Home and Colonial School in London, a teacher training school.

The "Maine Law" bans the manufacture and distribution of alcoholic beverages; over the next several years thirteen states adopt versions of this law.

Henry Box Brown (1815–?), *Narrative of the Life of Henry Box Brown;* John C. Calhoun (1782–1850), *A Disquisition on Government;* Hawthorne, *The House of the Seven Gables;* Melville, *Moby-Dick.*

1852

March: Harriet Beecher Stowe (1811–1896), *Uncle Tom's Cabin.* Stowe's tremendously popular antislavery novel sells upwards of one million copies in the U.S. and abroad during the 1850s, and further polarizes the North and South.

Brown writes for pay for London newspapers, and publishes a travel narrative, *Three Years in Europe; or, Places I Have Seen and People I Have Met.* His "A True Story of Slave Life" appears in the December *Anti-Slavery Advocate.*

Martin R. Delany (1812–1885), *The Condition, Elevation, Emigration, and Destiny of the Colored People of the United States;* Melville, *Pierre.*

1853

May: At the anniversary meeting of the British and Foreign Anti-Slavery Society at Exeter Hall, Brown sees Harriet Beecher Stowe for the first time.

November: Brown publishes *Clotel; or, The President's Daughter: A Narrative of Slave Life in the United States* with the London house of Partridge and Oakey.

Formation of the American, or Know-Nothing, Party, which campaigns for repeal of naturalization laws and greater privileges for native-born whites; the Party's activities culminate an upsurge of political nativism.

Douglass, "The Heroic Slave"; Sarah Hale (1788–1879), *Liberia;* Solomon Northup (1808–1863?), *Twelve Years a Slave;* James M. Whitfield (1822–1871), *America and Other Poems.*

1854

May: Sponsored by Senator Stephen A. Douglass (1813–1861) of Illinois, the Kansas-Nebraska Act is approved by Congress; the Act repeals the Missouri Compromise, making it legal for the white voting residents of a territory to determine whether it should be admitted as a slave or free state. The passage of the Act leads to increased violence in the territories

July: Ellen Richardson, who had helped to purchase Frederick Douglass's freedom in 1846, purchases Brown's manumission from Enoch Price for $300.

Formation of the Republican Party, which is opposed to the extension of slavery into the territories.

September–October: Brown returns to the United States, arriving in Philadelphia in late September and in Boston in October. On October 13 a public meeting is held in Boston in Brown's honor.

December: Brown publishes two works, both with 1855 imprints: *The American Fugitive in Europe: Sketches of Places and People Abroad* (an expanded version of *Three Years in Europe*), and *St. Domingo: Its Revolution and Its Patriots.*

After passing their qualifying examinations, Brown's daughters accept teaching positions in England.

Arthur, *Ten Nights in a Bar-room;* Caroline Lee Hentz (1800–1856), *The Planter's Northern Bride;* Thoreau, *Walden;* Frances Ellen Watkins [Harper] (1824–1911), *Poems on Miscellaneous Subjects.*

1855

August: Josephine Brown joins her father in Boston. In December she publishes a life of her father, *Biography of an American Bondman, by His Daughter,* which has an 1856 imprint.

Brown lectures for the American Anti-Slavery Society and the Massachusetts Anti-Slavery Society, and would lecture hundreds of times on the antislavery lecturing circuit the next five years.

Douglass, *My Bondage and My Freedom;* Fanny Fern [Sara Payson Willis] (1812–1889), *Ruth Hall;* Henry Wadsworth Longfellow (1807–1882), *Song of Hiawatha;* Melville, "Benito Cereno" and *Israel Potter;* William C. Nell (1816–1874), *Colored Patriots of the*

American Revolution; Samuel Ringgold Ward (1817–1866), *Autobiography of a Fugitive Negro;* Walt Whitman (1819–1892), *Leaves of Grass.*

1856

May: In the midst of an acrimonious debate on Kansas, South Carolina Congressman Preston Brooks (1819–1857) canes and severely injures Massachusetts Senator Charles Sumner (1811–1874) two days after Sumner delivers an antislavery speech on Kansas.

Brown writes his first play, "Experience, or, How to Give a Northern Man a Backbone," which satirizes the proslavery writings of the Northern minister Nehemiah Adams. Over the next two years, Brown delivers a number of public performances of his unpublished drama.

Josephine Brown returns to England.

Emerson, *English Traits;* Stowe, *Dred: A Tale of the Great Dismal Swamp.*

1857

March: The Supreme Court rules on *Dred Scott v. Sanford,* asserting that African Americans cannot become U.S. citizens and thus have no legal rights.

May: At the annual meeting of the New England Anti-Slavery Convention in Boston, Brown offers a resolution asserting the slaves' right to use revolutionary violence to obtain their freedom.

During the summer, Brown lectures with Frances Ellen Watkins (Harper), and at a fall "disunion convention" he supports the proposition that the Northern states should consider breaking from the Southern states.

Banking failures lead to a severe financial panic in the United States.

Edited by James Russell Lowell (1819–1891), *The Atlantic Magazine* begins publication.

Melville, *The Confidence-Man;* Sedgwick, *Married or Single?*

1858

Brown publishes *The Escape; or, A Leap for Freedom. A Drama in Five Acts,* which he has been publicly performing with "Experience" since the summer of 1857.

Stephen Douglas and Abraham Lincoln engage in widely reported debates during the campaign for the U.S. Senate seat from Illinois; Douglas is reelected.

Henry Highland Garnet founds the African Civilization Society, which promotes black emigration to Africa.

1859

August: At a black convention, Brown attacks black emigration and colonization.

October: Hoping to spark a slave insurrection, John Brown leads a small group of blacks and whites in an unsuccessful raid on the federal arsenal at Harper's Ferry, Virginia. He is hanged for treason on December 2.

Brown publishes *Memoir of William Wells Brown.*

Dion Boucicault (1822?-1890), *The Octoroon;* Dana, *To Cuba and Back;* Delany, *Blake* (1859–62); E. D. E. N. Southworth (1819–1899), *The Hidden Hand;* Stowe, *The Minister's Wooing;* Harriet Wilson (1808?-1870), *Our Nig.*

1860

April 12: Brown marries Anna Elizabeth Gray of Cambridgeport.

November: Abraham Lincoln elected president of the United States.

December: South Carolina secedes from the Union.

Brown begins serialized publication of *Miralda; or, The Beautiful Quadroon,* which appears in sixteen installments in the weekly *Anglo-African,* running from 1 December 1860 to 16 March 1861.

William Craft (1824–1900), *Running a Thousand Miles for Freedom; or, The Escape of William and Ellen Craft from Slavery;* Hawthorne, *The Marble Faun.*

1861

February: Birth of William Wells Brown, Jr., who dies in infancy.

March: Lincoln inaugurated.

April 1: Civil War begins with Confederate troops attacking and seizing Fort Sumter in South Carolina.

April: At a meeting of African American leaders, Brown votes against an approved resolution calling on blacks to fight for the Union cause.

Brown lectures in support of black emigration to Haiti and is listed as one of the "Special Contributors" to the *Pine and Palm,* a newspaper that promotes Haitian emigration. During the late summer and fall, he tours the black communities of Canada; his report on his travels appears over eight issues of *Pine and Palm.*

Rebecca Harding Davis (1831–1910), *Life in the Iron Mills;* Harriet A. Jacobs (1813–1897), *Incidents in the Life of a Slave Girl, Written by Herself;* Frederick Law Olmsted (1822–1903), *The Cotton Kingdom.*

1862

May: Birth of Clotelle Brown.

December: Brown publishes *The Black Man, His Antecedents, His Genius, and His Achievements;* the book has an 1863 imprint and copyright.

Abandoning his support for black emigration to Haiti, Brown chooses to support the Union's effort in the Civil War; on numerous occasions he speaks on the future of blacks in the United States.

Congress abolishes slavery in the District of Columbia.

1863

January: Lincoln's Emancipation Proclamation frees the slaves in the Confederate states.

July: New York City draft riots. Hundreds of blacks are killed or wounded when white workers riot over four days to protest the draft.

A black regiment, the Fifty-Fourth Massachusetts Volunteers, attacks Fort Wagner in Charleston, South Carolina.

Joining Frederick Douglass, Martin Delany, Henry Highland Garnet, and other African American leaders, Brown helps to recruit black soldiers for the Union army.

1864

Brown publishes *Clotelle: A Tale of the Southern States* in James Redpath's "Books for the Camp Fire" series for Union soldiers.

After reading and apprenticing in medicine for two years, Brown, though not formally trained, begins to work as a doctor and sign his name as an "M.D." He practices medicine for the next nineteen years.

Congress authorizes equal pay and treatment for the African American Union troops.

Augusta Jane Evans (1835–1909), *Macaria; or, Altars of Sacrifice.*

1865

April 9: Confederate General Robert E. Lee surrenders to the Union General Ulysses S. Grant at Appomattox Courthouse, Virginia, formally ending the Civil War.

April 15: Lincoln assassinated.

December: Ratification of the Thirteenth Amendment to the Constitution, which abolishes slavery in the United States.

Whitman, *Drum-Taps.*

1866

April: Congress approves the Civil Rights Act, which grants citizenship and legal protections to African Americans.

Brown resumes active work in temperance reform. Over the next seventeen years he participates in the Order of the Sons of Temperance, the John Brown Division of the Sons of Temperance, and the Independent Order of Good Templars.

Melville, *Battle-Pieces*.

1867

January: Congress overrides the veto of President Andrew Johnson and grants voting rights to African American citizens of the District of Columbia.

March: Congress passes the Reconstruction Acts, which are intended to help the former Southern slaves achieve their full rights as citizens. These Acts are enforced by the presence of federal troops in the South.

Brown publishes *The Negro in the American Rebellion* and *Clotelle; or, The Colored Heroine*.

Henry Ward Beecher (1813–1887), *Norwood*; Child, *A Romance of the Republic*; John William De Forest (1826–1906), *Miss Ravenel's Conversion*; Augusta Jane Evans Wilson (1835–1909), *St. Elmo*.

1868

July: Ratification of the Fourteenth Amendment, granting citizenship and equal protection under the law to all individuals born or naturalized in the United States.

Brown helps to found the National Association for the Organization of Night Schools and the Spread of Temperance Among the Freed People of the South.

Louisa May Alcott (1832–1888), *Little Women*; Elizabeth Stuart Phelps (1844–1911), *The Gates Ajar*.

1870

March: Ratification of the Fifteenth Amendment, guaranteeing African Americans the right to vote.

Clotelle Brown dies of typhoid fever.

Thomas Wentworth Higginson (1823–1911), *Army Life in a Black Regiment*.

1871

During a visit to Kentucky, Brown (according to his testimony) is abducted by members of the Ku Klux Klan; he escapes, he says, by using a hypodermic needle to inject a drug into the group's leader while the others lie in a drunken stupor.

1873

Brown publishes *The Rising Son; or, The Antecedents and Advancement of the Colored Race*, with an imprint of 1874.

Widespread financial panic and depression.

Alcott, *Work.*

1874

Founding of the Women's Christian Temperance Union.

1875

Congress approves a Civil Rights act, guaranteeing African Americans equal rights to public facilities and accommodations, and equal rights to serve on juries.

1877

Brown travels to Glasgow to attend a meeting of the Right Worthy Grand Lodge of the World of the Independent Order of Good Templars.

The end of Reconstruction: A compromise decides the close presidential election between the Republican Rutherford B. Hayes and the Democrat Samuel Tilden. Southern democrats grant Hayes the victory in exchange for the withdrawal of federal troops from the South. As a result of the withdrawal, African Americans suffer a precipitous loss of their civil rights and become subject to new Jim Crow laws and a wave of violence.

Henry James (1843–1916), *The American;* Sidney Lanier (1842–1881), *Poems.*

1879

May: Death of William Lloyd Garrison.

Albion Tourgée (1838–1905), *A Fool's Errand.*

1880

After touring several Southern states during the winter of 1879–80, Brown publishes *My Southern Home: Or, The South and Its People.*

Henry Adams (1838–1918), *Democracy;* George Washington Cable (1844–1925), *The Grandissimes.*

1883

The Supreme Court invalidates the 1875 Civil Rights Act.

Frances Willard (1839–1898), *Women and Temperance.*

1884

November 6: Brown dies from a tumor of the bladder. His wife, Anna Brown, who shares her husband's passion for temperance reform, subsequently serves for several years as president of a local branch of the Women's Christian Temperance Union. On 2 September 1902 she dies from burns suffered in a house fire.

Helen Hunt Jackson (1830–1885), *Ramona;* Mark Twain (1835–1910), *The Adventures of Huckleberry Finn.*

A Note on the Text
and Annotations

This volume reprints the 1853 first edition of the text of *Clotel; or, The President's Daughter: A Narrative of Slave Life in the United States,* published in London by Partridge & Oakey. Obvious printer's errors have been silently corrected; otherwise, this edition preserves mid-nineteenth-century usages and spellings, as well as Brown's sometimes peculiar style and syntax. The novel's original four illustrations have also been reprinted.

Wherever possible, the text of the documents in Part Two is that of the original edition or of an edition that would have been available to Brown and his contemporaries. As with the text of *Clotel,* only obvious printer's errors have been corrected.

In *Clotel,* Brown quotes widely from popular poetry, antislavery songbooks, political writings, classic literature, newspapers, the Bible, and many other sources. It was not always possible to track down a particular reference, but the annotations in this edition make a start at identifying his myriad sources. It should be noted that Brown's primary source for Biblical quotations was Noah Webster's idiosyncratic *The Holy Bible, Containing the Old and New Testaments, in the Common Version, with Amendments of the Language* (New Haven: Durrie & Peck, 1833).

C L O T E L ;

OR,

THE PRESIDENT'S DAUGHTER:

A Narrative of Slave Life

IN

THE UNITED STATES.

BY

WILLIAM WELLS BROWN,

A FUGITIVE SLAVE, AUTHOR OF "THREE YEARS IN EUROPE."

With a Sketch of the Author's Life.

———————

"We hold these truths to be self-evident: that all men are created equal; that they are endowed by their Creator with certain inalienable rights, and that among these are LIFE, LIBERTY, and the PURSUIT OF HAPPINESS." — *Declaration of American Independence.*

———————

PREFACE.

More than two hundred years have elapsed since the first cargo of slaves was landed on the banks of the James River, in the colony of Virginia, from the West coast of Africa. From the introduction of slaves in 1620,[1] down to the period of the separation of the Colonies from the British Crown, the number had increased to five hundred thousand; now there are nearly four million. In fifteen of the thirty-one States, Slavery is made lawful by the Constitution, which binds the several Sates into one confederacy.

On every foot of soil, over which *Stars* and *Stripes* wave, the negro is considered common property, on which any white man may lay his hand with perfect impunity. The entire white population of the United States, North and South, are bound by their oath to the constitution, and their adhesion to the Fugitive Slave Law,[2] to hunt down the runaway slave and return him to his claimant, and to suppress any effort that may be made by the slaves to gain their freedom by physical force. Twenty-five millions of whites have banded themselves in solemn conclave to keep four millions of blacks in their chains. In all grades of society are to be found men who either hold, buy, or sell slaves, from the statesmen and doctors of divinity, who can own their hundreds, down to the person who can purchase but one.

Were it not for persons in high places owning slaves, and thereby giving the system a reputation, and especially professed Christians, Slavery would long since have been abolished. The influence of the great "honours the corruption, and chastisement doth therefore hide his head."[3] The great aim of the true friends of the slave should be to lay bare the institution, so that the gaze of the world may be upon it, and cause the wise, the prudent, and the pious to withdraw their support from it, and leave it to its own fate. It does the cause of emancipation but little good to cry out in tones of execration against the traders, the kidnappers, the hireling overseers, and brutal drivers, so long as nothing is said to fasten the guilt on those who move in a higher circle.

The fact that slavery was introduced into the American colonies, while they were under the control of the British Crown, is a sufficient

---

[1] *1620:* Dutch traders brought slaves to the colonial settlement at Jamestown, Virginia, as early as 1619; many of these slaves had already spent time in the New World.

[2] *Fugitive Slave Law:* One of the bills making up the Compromise of 1850, the Fugitive Slave Law imposed fines on anyone who helped a runaway slave, and ordered state and federal authorities to aid in the pursuit of runaways.

[3] *"honours . . . head":* Shakespeare, *Julius Caesar* IV. iii, 13–14.

reason why Englishmen should feel a lively interest in its abolition; and now that the genius of mechanical invention has brought the two countries so near together, and both having one language and one literature, the influence of British public opinion is very great on the people of the New World.

If the incidents set forth in the following pages should add anything new to the information already given to the Public through similar publications, and should thereby aid in bringing British influence to bear upon American slavery, the main object for which this work was written will have been accomplished.

W. Wells Brown.

22, Cecil Street, Strand, London.

CONTENTS.

Narrative of the Life and Escape of William Wells Brown

"Shall tongues be mute when deeds are wrought
Which well might shame extremest Hell?
Shall freemen lack th' indignant thought?
Shall Mercy's bosom cease to swell?
Shall Honour bleed? — shall Truth succumb?
Shall pen, and press, and *soul* be dumb?"[1]

— *Whittier.*

William Wells Brown, the subject of this narrative,[2] was born a slave in Lexington, Kentucky, not far from the residence of the late Hon. Henry Clay.[3] His mother was the slave of Doctor John Young. His father was a slaveholder, and, besides being a near relation of his master, was connected with the Wicklief family, one of the oldest, wealthiest, and most aristocratic of the Kentucky planters. Dr. Young was the owner of forty or fifty slaves, whose chief employment was in cultivating tobacco, hemp, corn, and flax. The Doctor removed from Lexington, when William was five or six years old, to the state of Missouri, and commenced farming in a beautiful and fertile valley, within a mile of the Missouri river.

Here the slaves were put to work under a harsh and cruel overseer named Cook. A finer situation for a farm could not have been selected in the state. With climate favourable to agriculture, and soil rich, the products came in abundance. At an early age William was separated from his mother, she being worked in the field, and he as a servant in his master's medical department. When about ten years of age, the young slave's feelings were much hurt at hearing the cries of his mother, while being flogged by the negro driver for being a few minutes behind the other hands in reaching the field. He heard her cry,

---

[1] *"Shall tongues. . . . be dumb?":* From John Greenleaf Whittier (1807–1892), "Stanzas for the Times" (1835).

[2] *William Wells Brown, the subject of this narrative:* Brown authored this third-person narrative of his life and escape. In doing so, he challenged the convention of the time that had white abolitionists writing such prefaces as a way of "legitimating" the efforts of the black author.

[3] *Henry Clay:* Kentucky Congressman and nationalist, Henry Clay (1777–1852) championed the American Colonization Society's efforts to ship free blacks to Africa and was one of the principal architects of the Compromise of 1850. For a selection from Clay, see pp. 360–65.

"Oh, pray! oh, pray! oh, pray!" These are the words which slaves generally utter when imploring mercy at the hands of their oppressors.
The son heard it, though he was some way off. He heard the crack of
the whip and the groans of his poor mother. The cold chill ran over
him, and he wept aloud; but he was a slave like his mother, and could
render her no assistance. He was taught by the most bitter experience,
that nothing could be more heart-rending than to see a dear and
beloved mother or sister tortured by unfeeling men, and to hear her
cries, and not be able to render the least aid. When William was twelve
years of age, his master left his farm and took up residence near St.
Louis. The Doctor having more hands than he wanted for his own use,
William was let out to a Mr. Freeland, an innkeeper. Here the young
slave found himself in the hands of a most cruel and heartless master.
Freeland was one of the real chivalry of the South; besides being himself a slaveholder, he was a horse-racer, cock-fighter, gambler, and, to
crown the whole, an inveterate drunkard. What else but bad treatment
could be expected from such a character? After enduring the tyrannical and inhuman usage of this man for five or six months, William
resolved to stand it no longer, and therefore ran away, like other slaves
who leave their masters, owing to severe treatment; and not knowing
where to flee, the young fugitive went into the forest, a few miles from
St. Louis. He had been in the woods but a short time, when he heard
the barking and howling of dogs, and was soon satisfied that he was
pursued by the negro dogs; and, aware of their ferocious nature, the
fugitive climbed a tree, to save himself from being torn to pieces. The
hounds were soon at the trunk of the tree, and remained there, howling and barking, until those in whose charge they were came up. The
slave was ordered down, tied, and taken home. Immediately on his
arrival there, he was, as he expected, tied up in the smoke-house, and
whipped till Freeland was satisfied, and then smoked with tobacco
stems. This the slaveholder called *"Virginia play."* After being well
whipped and smoked, he was again set to work. William remained
with this monster a few months longer, and was then let out to Elijah
P. Lovejoy,[4] who years after became the editor of an abolition newspaper, and was murdered at Alton, Illinois, by a mob of slaveholders
from the adjoining state of Missouri. The system of letting out slaves
is one among the worst of the evils of slavery. The man who hires a
slave, looks upon him in the same light as does the man who hires a
horse for a limited period; he feels no interest in him, only to get the

---

[4] *Elijah P. Lovejoy:* The abolitionist editor of the Alton (Illinois) *Observer,* Lovejoy
(1802–1837) was killed by a mob that was attempting to destroy his press.

worth of his money. Not so with the man who owns the slave; he regards him as so much property, of which care should be taken. After being let out to a steamer as an under-steward, William was hired by James Walker, a slave-trader. Here the subject of our memoir was made superintendent of the gangs of slaves that were taken to the New Orleans market. In this capacity, William had opportunities, far greater than most slaves, of acquiring knowledge of the different phases of the *"peculiar institution."* Walker was a negro speculator, who was amassing a fortune by trading in the bones, blood, and nerves, of God's children. The thoughts of such a traffic causes us to exclaim with the poet,

> "——— Is there not some chosen curse,
> Some hidden thunder in the stores of heaven,
> Red with uncommon wrath, to blast the man
> Who gains his fortune from the blood of souls?"[5]

Between fifty and sixty slaves were chained together, put on board a steam-boat bound for New Orleans, and started on the voyage. New and strange scenes began to inspire the young slave with the hope of escaping to a land of freedom. There was in the boat a large room on the lower deck in which the slaves were kept, men and women promiscuously, all chained two and two together, not even leaving the poor slaves the privilege of choosing their partners. A strict watch was kept over them, so that they had no chance of escape. Cases had occurred in which slaves had got off their chains and made their escape at the landing-places, while the boat stopped to take in wood. But with all their care they lost one woman who had been taken from her husband and children, and having no desire to live without them, in the agony of her soul jumped overboard and drowned herself. Her sorrows were greater than she could bear; slavery and its cruel inflictions had broken her heart. She, like William, sighed for freedom, but not the freedom which even British soil confers and inspires, but freedom from torturing pangs, and overwhelming grief.

At the end of the week they arrived at New Orleans, the place of their destination. Here the slaves were placed in a negro pen, where those who wished to purchase could call and examine them. The negro pen is a small yard surrounded by buildings, from fifteen to twenty feet wide, with the exception of a large gate with iron bars. The slaves are

---

[5] " ——— *Is there . . . blood of souls?":* From Joseph Addison (1672–1719), *Cato* (1716) I.1.21–24. Brown significantly revises the final line, which in the original reads, "Who owes his greatness to his country's ruin?"

kept in the buildings during the night, and turned into the pen during the day. After the best of the gang were sold off, the balance was taken to the Exchange coffee-house auction-rooms, and sold at public auction. After the sale of the last slave, William and Mr. Walker left New Orleans for St. Louis.

After they had been at St. Louis a few weeks another cargo of human flesh was made up. There were amongst the lot several old men and women, some of whom had grey locks. On their way down to New Orleans William had to prepare the old slaves for market. He was ordered to shave off the old men's whiskers, and to pluck out the grey hairs where they were not too numerous; where they were, he coloured them with a preparation of blacking with a blacking brush. After having gone through the blacking process, they looked ten or fifteen years younger. William, though not well skilled in the use of scissors and razor, performed the office of the barber tolerably. After the sale of this gang of negroes they returned to St. Louis, and a second cargo was made up. In this lot was a woman who had a child at the breast, yet was compelled to travel through the interior of the country on foot with the other slaves. In a published memoir of his life,[6] William says, "The child cried during the most of the day, which displeased Mr. Walker, and he told the mother that if her child did not stop crying, he would stop its mouth. After a long and weary journey under a burning sun, we put up for the night at a country inn. The following morning, just as they were about to start, the child again commenced crying. Walker stepped up to her and told her to give the child to him. The mother tremblingly obeyed. He took the child by one arm, as any one would a cat by the leg, and walked into the house where they had been staying, and said to the lady, 'Madam, I will make you a present of this little nigger; it keeps making such a noise that I can't bear it.' 'Thank you, sir,' said the lady. The mother, as soon as she saw that her child was to be left, ran up to Mr. Walker, and falling on her knees, begged of him in an agony of despair, to let her have her child. She clung round his legs so closely, that for some time he could not kick her off; and she cried, 'O my child, my child. Master, do let me have my dear, dear child. Oh! do, do. I will stop its crying, and love you for ever if you will only let me have my child again.' But her prayers were not heeded, they passed on, and the mother was separated from her child for ever.

[6] *published memoir of his life:* A reference to William Wells Brown's *Narrative of William W. Brown* (1847), from which he occasionally quotes in this prefatory "Narrative."

"After the woman's child had been given away, Mr. Walker rudely commanded her to retire into the ranks with the other slaves. Women who had children were not chained, but those who had none were. As soon as her child was taken she was chained to the gang."

Some time after this, Walker bought a woman who had a blind child; it being considered worthless, it was given to the trader by the former owner of the woman on the score of humanity, he saying that he wished to keep mother and child together. At first Walker declined taking the child, saying that it would be too much trouble, but the mother wishing to have her boy with her, begged him to take it, promising to carry it the whole distance in her arms. Consequently he took the child, and the gang started on their route to the nearest steamboat landing, which was above one hundred miles. As might have been expected, the woman was unable to carry the boy and keep up with the rest of the gang. They put up at night at a small town, and the next morning, when about to start, Walker took the little boy from its mother and sold it to the innkeeper for the small sum of *one dollar.* The poor woman was so frantic at the idea of being separated from her only child, that it seemed impossible to get her to leave it. Not until the chains were put upon her limbs, and she fastened to the other slaves, could they get her to leave the spot. By main force this slave mother was compelled to go on and leave her child behind. Some days after, a lady from one of the free states was travelling the same road and put up at the same inn: she saw the child the morning after her arrival, and heard its history from one of the slaves, which was confirmed by the innkeeper's wife. A few days after, the following poem appeared in one of the newspapers, from the pen of the lady who had seen the blind child: —

> "Come back to me, mother! why linger away
>   From thy poor little blind boy, the long weary day!
>   I mark every footstep, I list to each tone,
>   And wonder my mother should leave me alone!
>   There are voices of sorrow and voices of glee,
>   But there's no one to joy or to sorrow with me;
>   For each hath of pleasure and trouble his share,
>   And none for the poor little blind boy will care.
>
> "My mother, come back to me! close to thy breast
>   Once more let thy poor little blind one be pressed;
>   Once more let me feel thy warm branch on my cheek,
>   And hear thee in accents of tenderness speak!
>   O mother! I've no one to love me — no heart

Can bear like thy own in my sorrows a part;
No hand is so gentle, no voice is so kind!
Oh! none like a mother can cherish the blind!

"Poor blind one! no mother thy wailing can hear,
No mother can hasten to banish thy fear;
For the slave-owner drives her, o'er mountain and wild,
And for one paltry dollar hath sold thee, poor child!
Ah! who can in language of mortals reveal
The anguish that none but a mother can feel,
When man in his vile lust of mammon hath trod
On her child, who is stricken and smitten of God?

"Blind, helpless, forsaken, with strangers alone,
She hears in her anguish his piteous moan,
As he eagerly listens — but listens in vain,
To catch the loved tones of his mother again!
The curse of the broken in spirit shall fall
On the wretch who hath mingled this wormwood and gall,
And his gain like a mildew shall blight and destroy,
Who hath torn from his mother the little blind boy."[7]

The thought that man can so debase himself as to treat a fellow-creature as here represented, is enough to cause one to blush at the idea that such men are members of a civilised and Christian nation.

Nothing was more grievous to the sensitive feelings of William, than seeing the separation of families by the slave-trader: husbands taken from their wives, and mothers from their children, without the least appearance of feeling on the part of those who separated them. While at New Orleans, on one occasion, William saw a slave murdered. The circumstances were as follows: — In the evening, between seven and eight o'clock, a slave came running down the levee, followed by several men and boys. The whites were crying out, "Stop that nigger! stop that nigger!" while the poor panting slave, in almost breathless accents, was repeating, "I did not steal the meat — I did not steal the meat." The poor man at last took refuge in the river. The whites who were in pursuit of him, ran on board of one of the boats to see if they could discover him. They finally espied him under the bow of the steamboat "Trenton." They got a pike-pole, and tried to drive

---

[7] *"Come back. . . . little blind boy"*: Brown's source for this poem by Margaret Baily (1807–1859) is *The Liberty Minstrel*, ed. George W. Clark (New York, 1845); he reprinted the poem in *The Anti-Slavery Harp*, ed. Brown (Boston, 1848).

him from his hiding-place. When they struck at him he would dive under the water. The water was so cold, that it soon became evident that he must come out or be drowned.

While they were trying to drive him from under the boat or drown him, he in broken and imploring accents said, "I did not steal the meat; I did not steal the meat. My master lives up the river. I want to see my master. I did not steal the meat. Do let me go home to master." After punching and striking him over the head for some time, he at last sunk in the water, to rise no more alive.

On the end of the pike-pole with which they had been striking him was a hook, which caught in his clothing, and they hauled him up on the bow of the boat. Some said he was dead; others said he was "playing 'possum;" while others kicked him to make him get up; but it was of no use — he was dead.

As soon as they became satisfied of this they commenced leaving one after another. One of the hands on the boat informed the captain that they had killed the man, and that the dead body was lying on the deck. The captain, whose name was Hart, came on deck, and said to those who were remaining, "You have killed this nigger; now take him off my boat." The dead body was dragged on shore and left there. William went on board of the boat where the gang of slaves were, and during the whole night his mind was occupied with what he had seen. Early in the morning he went on shore to see if the dead body remained there. He found it in the same position that it was left the night before. He watched to see what they would do with it. It was left there until between eight and nine o'clock, when a cart, which took up the trash from the streets, came along, and the body was thrown in, and in a few minutes more was covered over with dirt, which they were removing from the streets.

At the expiration of the period of his hiring with Walker, William returned to his master, rejoiced to have escaped an employment as much against his own feelings as it was repugnant to human nature. But this joy was of short duration. The Doctor wanted money, and resolved to sell William's sister and two brothers. The mother had been previously sold to a gentleman residing in the city of St. Louis. William's master now informed him that he intended to sell him, and, as he was his own nephew, he gave him the privilege of finding some one to purchase him, who would treat him better than if he was sold on the auction block. William tried to make some arrangement by which he could purchase his own freedom, but the old Doctor would hear nothing of the kind. If there is one thing more revolting in the trade of human flesh than another, it is the selling of one's own blood relations.

He accordingly set out for the city in search of a new master. When he arrived there, he proceeded to the goal with the hope of seeing his sister, but was again disappointed. On the following morning he made another attempt, and was allowed to see her once, for the last time. When he entered the room where she was seated in one corner, alone and disconsolate, there were four other women in the room, belonging to the same man, who were bought, the gaoler[8] said, for the master's own use.

William's sister was seated with her face towards the door when he entered, but her gaze was transfixed on nothingness, and she did not look up when he walked up to her; but as soon as she observed him she sprang up, threw her arms around his neck, leaned her head upon his breast, and without uttering a word, in silent, indescribable sorrow, burst into tears. She remained so for some minutes, but when she recovered herself sufficiently to speak, she urged him to take his mother immediately, and try to get to the land of freedom. She said there was no hope for herself, she must live and die a slave. After giving her some advice, and taking a ring from his finger, he bade her farewell for ever. Reader, did ever a fair sister of thine go down to the grave prematurely, if so, perchance, thou hast drank deeply from the cup of sorrow? But how infinitely better is it for a sister to "go into the silent land"[9] with her honour untarnished, but with bright hopes, than for her to be sold to sensual slave-holders.

William had been in the city now two days, and as he was to be absent for only a week, it was well that he should make the best use of his time if he intended to escape. In conversing with his mother, he found her unwilling to make the attempt to reach the land of liberty, but she advised him by all means to get there himself if he possibly could. She said, as all her children were in slavery, she did not wish to leave them; but he loved his mother so intensely, that he could not think of leaving without her. He consequently used all his simple eloquence to induce her to fly with him, and at last he prevailed. They consequently fixed upon the next night as the time for their departure. The time at length arrived, and they left the city just as the clock struck nine. Having found a boat, they crossed the river in it. Whose boat it was he did not know; neither did he care: when it had served his

---

[8] *gaoler:* Jailer.
[9] *"go into the silent land":* From Henry Wadsworth Longfellow (1807–1882), "Song of the Silent Land" (1839), a translation of a poem by the German poet J. G. Von Salis-Seewis (1762–1834).

purpose, he turned it adrift, and when he saw it last, it was going at a good speed down the river. After walking in the main road as fast as they could all night, when the morning came they made for the woods, and remained there during the day, but when night came again, they proceeded on their journey with nothing but the North Star to guide them. They continued to travel by night, and to bury themselves in the silent solitudes of the forest by day. Hunger and fatigue could not stop them, for the prospect of freedom at the end of the journey nerved them up. The very thought of leaving slavery, with its democratic whips, republican chains, and bloodhounds, caused the hearts of the weary fugitives to leap with joy. After travelling ten nights and hiding in the woods during the day for fear of being arrested and taken back, they thought they might with safety go the rest of their way by day-light. In nearly all the free states there are men who make a business of catching runaway slaves and returning them to their owners for the reward that may be offered; some of these were on the alert for William and his mother, for they had already seen the runaways adver-tised in the St. Louis newspapers.

All at once they heard the click of a horse's hoof, and looking back saw three men on horseback galloping towards them. They soon came up, and demanded them to stop. The three men dismounted, arrested them on a warrant, and showed them a handbill, offering two hundred dollars for their apprehension and delivery to Dr. Young and Isaac Mansfield in St. Louis.

While they were reading the handbill, William's mother looked him in the face, and burst into tears. "A cold chill ran over me," says he, "and such a sensation I never experienced before, and I trust I never shall again." They took out a rope and tied him, and they were taken back to the house of the individual who appeared to be the leader. They then had something given them to eat, and were separated. Each of them was watched over by two men during the night. The religious characteristic of the American slaveholder soon manifested itself, as before the family retired to rest they were all called together to attend prayers; and the very man who, but a few hours before, had arrested poor panting, fugitive slaves, now read a chapter from the Bible and offered a prayer to God; as if that benignant and omnipotent One con-secrated the infernal act he had just committed.

The next morning they were chained and hand-cuffed, and started back to St. Louis. A journey of three days brought the fugitives again to the place they had left twelve days previously with the hope that they would never return. They were put in prison to await the orders of their owners. When a slave attempts to escape and fails, he feels sure of either being severely punished, or sold to the negro traders and taken to the far south, there to be worked up on a cotton, sugar, or rice plantation. This William and his mother dreaded. While they were in suspense as to what would be their fate, news came to them that the mother had been sold to a slave speculator. William was soon sold to a merchant residing in the city, and removed to his new owner's dwelling. In a few days the gang of slaves, of which William's mother was one, were taken on board a steamer to be carried to the New Orleans market. The young slave obtained permission from his new owner to go and take a last farewell of his mother. He went to the boat, and found her there, chained to another woman, and the whole number of slaves, amounting to some fifty or sixty, chained in the same manner. As the son approached his mother she moved not, neither did she weep; her emotions were too deep for tears. William approached her, threw his arms around her neck, kissed her, fell upon his knees begging her forgiveness, for he thought he was to blame for her sad condition, and if he had not persuaded her to accompany him she might not have been in chains then.

She remained for some time apparently unimpressionable, tearless, sighless, but in the innermost depths of her heart moved mighty passions. William says, "She finally raised her head, looked me in the face, and such a look none but an angel can give, and said, 'My dear son, you are not to blame for my being here. You have done nothing more nor less than your duty. Do not, I pray you, weep for me; I cannot last long upon a cotton plantation. I feel that my heavenly Master will soon call me home, and then I shall be out of the hands of the slaveholders.' I could hear no more — my heart struggled to free itself from the human form. In a moment she saw Mr. Mansfield, her master, coming toward that part of the boat, and she whispered in my ear, 'My child, we must soon part to meet no more on this side of the grave. You have ever said that you would not die a slave; that you would be a freeman. Now try to get your liberty! You will soon have no one to look after but yourself!' and just as she whispered the last sentence into my ear, Mansfield came up to me, and with an oath said, 'Leave here this instant; you have been the means of my losing one hundred dollars to get this wench back' — at the same time kicking me with a heavy pair of boots. As I left her she gave one shriek, saying, 'God be with you!' It was the last time that I saw her, and the last word I heard her utter.

"I walked on shore. The bell was tolling. The boat was about to start. I stood with a heavy heart, waiting to see her leave the wharf. As I thought of my mother, I could but feel that I had lost

> 'The glory of my life,
> My blessing and my pride!
> I half forgot the name of slave,
> When she was by my side.'[10]

"The love of liberty that had been burning in my bosom had well-nigh gone out. I felt as though I was ready to die. The boat moved gently from the wharf, and while she glided down the river, I realised that my mother was indeed

> 'Gone — gone — sold and gone,
> To the rice swamp, dark and lone!'[11]

"After the boat was out of sight I returned home; but my thoughts were so absorbed in what I had witnessed, that I knew not what I was about. Night came, but it brought no sleep to my eyes." When once the love of freedom is born in the slave's mind, it always increases and brightens, and William having heard so much about Canada, where a number of his acquaintances had found a refuge and a home, he heartily desired to join them. Building castles in the air in the daytime; incessantly thinking of freedom, he would dream of the land of liberty, but on waking in the morning would weep to find it but a dream.

> "He would dream of Victoria's domain,
> And in a moment he seemed to be there;
> But the fear of being taken again,
> Soon hurried him back to despair."[12]

Having been for some time employed as a servant in an hotel, and being of a very active turn, William's new owner resolved to let him out on board a steamboat. Consequently the young slave was hired out to the steamer St. Louis, and soon after sold to Captain Enoch Price, the owner of that boat. Here he was destined to remain but a short period, as Mrs. Price wanted a carriage-driver, and had set her heart upon William for that purpose.

Scarcely three months had elapsed from the time that William became the property of Captain Price, ere that gentleman's family took

[10] 'The glory . . . side': From Elizabeth Margaret Chandler (1807–1834), "The Bereaved Father," in The Poetical Works of Elizabeth Margaret Chandler; with a Memoir of Her Life and Character, by Benjamin Lundy (Philadelphia, 1836).

[11] 'Gone . . . and lone!': From John Greenleaf Whittier, "The Farewell of a Virginia Slave Mother to Her Daughters Sold into Southern Bondage" (1838).

[12] "He would . . . despair": Brown wrote poetry and he may well have been the author of this and several other of the unattributable quotations; see the Note on the Text and Annotations (p. 44).

a pleasure trip to New Orleans, and William accompanied them. From New Orleans the family proceeded to Louisville. The hope of escape again dawned upon the slave's mind, and the trials of the past were lost in hopes for the future. The love of liberty, which had been burning in his bosom for years, and which at times had been well nigh extinguished, was now resuscitated. Hopes nurtured in childhood, and strengthened as manhood dawned, now spread their sails to the gales of his imagination. At night, when all around was peaceful, and in the mystic presence of the everlasting starlight, he would walk the steamer's decks, meditating on his happy prospects, and summoning up gloomy reminiscences of the dear hearts he was leaving behind him. When not thinking of the future his mind would dwell on the past. The love of a dear mother, a dear and affectionate sister, and three brothers yet living, caused him to shed many tears. If he could only be assured of their being dead, he would have been comparatively happy; but he saw in imagination his mother in the cotton-field, followed by a monster task-master, and no one to speak a consoling word to her. He beheld his sister in the hands of the slave-driver, compelled to submit to his cruelty, or, what was unutterably worse, his lust; but still he was far away from them, and could not do anything for them if he remained in slavery; consequently he resolved, and consecrated the resolve with a prayer, that he would start on the first opportunity.

That opportunity soon presented itself. When the boat got to the wharf[13] where it had to stay for some time, at the first convenient moment Brown made towards the woods, where he remained until night-time. He dared not walk during the day, even in the state of Ohio; he had seen so much of the perfidy of white men, and resolved, if possible, not to get into their hands. After darkness covered the world, he emerged from his hiding-place; but he did not know east from west, or north from south; clouds hid the North Star from his view. In this desolate condition he remained for some hours, when the clouds rolled away, and his friend, with its shining face — the North Star — welcomed his sight. True as the needle to the pole he obeyed its attractive beauty, and walked on till daylight dawned.

It was winter-time; the day on which he started was the 1st of January, and, as it might be expected, it was intensely cold; he had no over-coat, no food, no friend, save the North Star, and the God which made it. How ardently must the love of freedom burn in the poor slave's bosom, when he will pass through so many difficulties, and even look

---

[13] *wharf:* The wharf is in Cincinnati, and Ohio was a free state.

death in the face, in winning his birth-right, freedom. But what crushed the poor slave's heart in his flight most was, not the want of food or clothing, but the thought that every white man was his deadly enemy. Even in the free states the prejudice against color is so strong, that there appears to exist a deadly antagonism between the white and coloured races.

William in his flight carried a tinder-box with him, and when he got very cold he would gather together dry leaves and stubble and make a fire, or certainly he would have perished. He was determined to enter into no house, fearing that he might meet a betrayer.

It must have been a picture which would have inspired an artist, to see the fugitive roasting the ears of corn that he found or took from barns during the night, at solitary fires in the deep solitudes of woods.

The suffering of the fugitive was greatly increased by the cold, from the fact of his having just come from the warm climate of New Orleans. Slaves seldom have more than one name, and William was not an exception to this, and the fugitive began to think of an additional name. A heavy rain of three days, in which it froze as fast as it fell, and by which the poor fugitive was completely drenched, and still more chilled, added to the depression of his spirits already created by his weary journey. Nothing but the fire of hope burning within his breast could have sustained him under such overwhelming trials,

> "Behind he left the whip and chains,
> Before him were sweet Freedom's plains."[14]

Through cold and hunger, William was now ill, and he could go no further. The poor fugitive resolved to seek protection, and accordingly hid himself in the woods near the road, until some one should pass. Soon a traveller came along, but the slave dared not speak. A few moments more and a second passed, the fugitive attempted to speak, but fear deprived him of voice. A third made his appearance. He wore a broad-brimmed hat and a long coat, and was evidently walking only for exercise. William scanned him well, and though not much skilled in physiognomy, he concluded he was the man. William approached him, and asked him if he knew any one who would help him, as he was sick? The gentleman asked whether he was not a slave. The poor slave hesitated; but, on being told that he had nothing to fear, he answered, "Yes." The gentleman told him he was in a pro-slaving

---

[14] *"Behind . . . Freedom's plains"*: From anon., "The Flying Slave," in *The Anti-Slavery Harp*, ed. Brown.

neighbourhood, but, if he would wait a little, he would go and get a covered waggon, and convey him to his house. After he had gone, the fugitive meditated whether he should stay or not, being apprehensive that the broad-brimmed gentleman had gone for some one to assist him: he however concluded to remain.

After waiting about an hour — an hour big with fate to him — he saw the covered waggon making its appearance, and no one on it but the person he before accosted. Trembling with hope and fear, he entered the waggon, and was carried to the person's house. When he got there, he still halted between two opinions, whether he should enter or take to his heels; but he soon decided after seeing the glowing face of the wife. He saw something in her that bid him welcome, something that told him he would not be betrayed.

He soon found that he was under the shed of a Quaker, and a Quaker of the George Fox stamp.[15] He had heard of Quakers and their kindness; but was not prepared to meet with such hospitality as now greeted him. He saw nothing but kind looks, and heard nothing but tender words. He began to feel the pulsations of a new existence. White men always scorned him, but now a white benevolent woman felt glad to wait on him; it was a revolution in his experience. The table was loaded with good things, but he could not eat. If he were allowed the privilege of sitting in the kitchen, he thought he could do justice to the viands. The surprise being over his appetite soon returned.

"I have frequently been asked," says William, "how I felt upon finding myself regarded as a man by a white family; especially having just run away from one. I cannot say that I have ever answered the question yet. The fact that I was, in all probability, a freeman, sounded in my ears like a charm. I am satisfied that none but a slave could place such an appreciation upon liberty as I did at that time. I wanted to see my mother and sister, that I might tell them that 'I was free!' I wanted to see my fellow-slaves in St. Louis, and let them know that the chains were no longer upon my limbs. I wanted to see Captain Price, and let him learn from my own lips that I was no more a chattel, but a MAN. I was anxious, too, thus to inform Mrs. Price that she must get another coachman, and I wanted to see Eliza[16] more than I did Mr. Price or Mrs. Price. The fact that I was a freeman — could walk, talk, eat, and

---

[15] *Quaker of the George Fox stamp:* George Fox (1624–1691) was the founder of the Quakers, or Society of Friends, a Christian sect known for its commitment to nonviolence and abolitionism.

[16] *Eliza:* According to Brown's 1847 *Narrative,* Eliza was a maid belonging to the Price family; Mrs. Price hoped to secure Brown's loyalty by marrying him to Eliza.

sleep as a man, and no one to stand over me with the blood-clotted cow-hide — all this made me feel that I was not myself."

The kind Quaker, who so hospitably entertained William, was called Wells Brown. He remained with him about a fortnight, during which time he was well fed and clothed. Before leaving, the Quaker asked him what was his name besides William? The fugitive told him he had no other. "Well," said he, "thee must have another name. Since thee has got out of slavery, thee has become a man, and men always have two names."

William told him that as he was the first man to extend the hand of friendship to him, he would give him the privilege of naming him.

"If I name thee," said he, "I shall call thee Wells Brown, like myself."

"But," said he, "I am not willing to lose my name of William. It was taken from me once against my will,[17] and I am not willing to part with it on any terms."

"Then," said the benevolent man, "I will call thee William Wells Brown."

"So be it," said William Wells Brown, and he has been known by this name ever since.

After giving the newly-christened freeman "a name," the Quaker gave him something to aid him to get "a local habitation." So, after giving him some money, Brown again started for Canada. In four days he reached a public-house, and went in to warm himself. He soon found that he was not out of the reach of his enemies. While warming himself, he heard some men in an adjoining bar-room talking about some runaway slaves. He thought it was time to be off, and, suiting the action to the thought, he was soon in the woods out of sight. When night came, he returned to the road and walked on; and so, for two days and two nights, till he was faint and ready to perish of hunger.

In this condition he arrived in the town of Cleveland, Ohio, on the banks of Lake Erie, where he determined to remain until the spring of the year, and then to try and reach Canada. Here he was compelled to work merely for his food. "Having lived in that way," said he in a speech at a public meeting in Exeter Hall,[18] "for some weeks, I obtained a job, for which I received a shilling. This was not only the only shilling I had, but it was the first I had received after obtaining my

---

[17] *It was taken . . . against my will:* The name "William" had been taken from Brown during his boyhood when his owner at the time, Dr. John Young, adopted a nephew named William Moore.

[18] *Exeter Hall:* Opened in 1831 in London, Exeter Hall, with a seating capacity of three thousand, was regularly used for antislavery rallies.

freedom, and that shilling made me feel, indeed, as if I had a considerable stock in hand. What to do with my shilling I did not know. I would not put it into the bankers' hands, because, if they would have received it, I would not trust them. I would not lend it out, because I was afraid I should not get it back again. I carried the shilling in my pocket for some time, and finally resolved to lay it out; and after considerable thinking upon the subject, I laid out 6*d*.[19] for a spelling-book, and the other 6*d*. for sugar candy or barley sugar. Well, now, you will all say that the one 6*d*. for the spelling-book was well laid out; and I am of opinion that the other was well laid out too; for the family in which I worked for my bread had two little boys, who attended the school every day, and I wanted to convert them into teachers; so I thought that nothing would act like a charm so much as a little barley sugar. The first day I got my book and stock in trade, I put the book into my bosom, and went to saw wood in the wood-house on a very cold day. One of the boys, a little after four o'clock, passed through the wood-house with a bag of books. I called to him, and I said to him, 'Johnny, do you see this?' taking a stick of barley sugar from my pocket and showing it to him. Says he, 'Yes; give me a taste of it.' Said I, 'I have got a spelling-book too,' and I showed that to him. 'Now,' said I, 'if you come to me in my room, and teach me my A, B, C, I will give you a whole stick.' 'Very well,' said he, 'I will; but let me taste it.' 'No; I can't.' 'Let me have it now.' Well, I thought I had better give him a little taste, until the right time came; and I marked the barley sugar about a quarter of an inch down, and told him to bite that far and no farther. He made a grab, and bit half the stick, and ran off laughing. I put the other piece in my pocket, and after a little while the other boy, little David, came through the wood-house with his books. I said nothing about the barley sugar, or my wish to get education. I knew the other lad would communicate the news to him. In a little while he returned, and said, 'Bill, John says you have got some barley sugar.' 'Well,' I said, 'what of that?' 'He said you gave him some; give me a little taste.' 'Well, if you come to-night and help me to learn my letters, I will give you a whole stick.' 'Yes; but let me taste it.' 'Ah! but you want to bite it.' 'No, I don't, but just let me taste it.' Well, I thought I had better show it to him. 'Now,' said he, 'let me touch my tongue against it.' I thought then that I had better give him a taste, but I would not trust him so far as I trusted John; so I called him to me,

---

[19] 6*d*.: Six pence; *d*. is an abbreviation for the British pence. There were twelve pence in the shilling, which was approximately equivalent to the U.S. dime. Brown uses British terms as a way of clarifying U.S. currency for his British readers.

and got his head under my arm, and took him by the chin, and told him to hold out his tongue; and as he did so, I drew the barley sugar over very lightly. He said, 'That's very nice; just draw it over again. I could stand here and let you draw it across my tongue all day.' The night came on; the two boys came out of their room up into the attic where I was lodging, and there they commenced teaching me the letters of the alphabet. We all laid down upon the floor, covered with the same blanket; and first one would teach me a letter, and then the other, and I would pass the barley sugar from one side to the other. I kept those two boys on my sixpenny worth of barley sugar for about three weeks. Of course I did not let them know how much I had. I first dealt it out to them a quarter of a stick at a time. I worked along in that way, and before I left that place where I was working for my bread, I got so that I could spell. I had a book that had the word *baker* in it, and the boys used to think that when they got so far as that, they were getting on pretty well. I had often passed by the school-house, and stood and listened at the window to hear them spell, and I knew that when they could spell *baker* they thought something of themselves; and I was glad when I got that far. Before I left that place I could read. Finally, from that I went on until I could write. How do you suppose I first commenced writing? for you will understand that up to the present time I never spent a day in school in my life, for I had no money to pay for schooling, so that I had to get my learning first from one and then from another. I carried a piece of chalk in my pocket, and whenever I met a boy I would stop him and take out my chalk and get at a board fence and then commence. First I made some flourishes with no meaning, and called a boy up, and said, 'Do you see that? Can you beat that writing?' Said he, 'That's not writing.' Well, I wanted to get so as to write my own name. I had got out of slavery with only one name. While escaping, I received the hospitality of a very good man, who had spared part of his name to me, and finally my name got pretty long, and I wanted to be able to write it. 'Now, what do you call that?' said the boy, looking at my flourishes. I said, 'Is not that *William Wells Brown?*' 'Give me the chalk,' says he, and he wrote out in large letters *'William Wells Brown,'* and I marked up the fence for nearly a quarter of a mile, trying to copy, till I got so that I could write my name. Then I went on with my chalking, and, in fact, all board fences within half a mile of where I lived were marked over with some kind of figures I had made, in trying to learn how to write. I next obtained an arithmetic, and then a grammar, and I stand here to-night, without having had a day's schooling in my life." Such were some of the efforts made by a fugitive slave to obtain himself an education. Soon after his escape,

Brown was married to a free coloured woman, by whom he has had three daughters, one of whom died in infancy. Having tasted the sweets of freedom himself, his great desire was to extend its blessing to his race, and in the language of the poet he would ask himself,

> "Is true freedom but to break
> Fetters for our own dear sake
> And with leathern hearts forget
> That we owe mankind a debt?

> "No! true freedom is to share
> All the chains our brothers wear,
> And with heart and hand to be
> Earnest to make others free."[20]

While acting as a servant to one of the steamers on Lake Erie, Brown often took fugitives from Cleveland and other ports to Buffalo, or Detroit, from either of which places they could cross to Canada in an hour. During the season of 1842, this fugitive slave conveyed no less than *sixty-nine* runaway slaves across Lake Erie, and placed them safe on the soil of Canada. The following interesting account of Brown's first going into business for himself, which we transcribe from his "Three Years In Europe,"[21] will show the energy of the man. He says, "In the autumn of 1835, having been cheated out of the previous summer's earnings by the captain of the steamer in which I had been employed running away with the money, I was, like the rest of the men, left without any means of support during the winter, and therefore had to seek employment in the neighbouring towns. I went to the town of Monroe in the state of Michigan, and while going through the principal streets looking for work, I passed the door of the only barber in town, whose shop appeared to be filled with persons waiting to be shaved. As there was but one man at work, and as I had, while employed in the steamer, occasionally shaved a gentleman who could not perform that office himself, it occurred to me that I might get employment here as a journeyman[22] barber. I therefore made immediate application for work, but the barber told me he did not need a hand. But I was not to be put off so easily, and after making several offers to work cheap, I frankly told him, that if he would not employ

---

[20] *"Is true. . . . others free"*: From James Russell Lowell (1819–1891), "Stanzas on Freedom" (1844).

[21] *"Three Years in Europe"*: A reference to Brown's *Three Years in Europe; or, Places I Have Seen and People I Have Met* (London, 1852).

[22] *journeyman:* An apprentice or hired help.

me, I would get a room near him, and set up an opposition establishment. This threat, however, made no impression on the barber; and as I was leaving, one of the men, who were waiting to be shaved, said, 'If you want a room in which to commence business, I have one on the opposite side of the street.' This man followed me out; we went over, and I looked at the room. He strongly urged me to set up, at the same time promising to give me his influence. I took the room, purchased an old table, two chairs, got a pole with a red stripe painted around it, and the next day opened, with a sign over the door, 'Fashionable Hairdresser from New York, Emperor of the West.' I need not add that my enterprise was very annoying to the 'shop over the way,' especially my sign, which happened to be the most extensive part of the concern. Of course I had to tell all who came in, that my neighbour on the opposite side did not keep clean towels, that his razors were dull, and, above all, he never had been to New York to see the fashions. Neither had I. In a few weeks I had the entire business of the town, to the great discomfiture of the other barber. At this time, money matters in the Western States were in a sad condition. Any person who could raise a small amount of money was permitted to establish a bank, and allowed to issue notes for four times the sum raised. This being the case, many persons borrowed money merely long enough to exhibit to the bank inspectors, and the borrowed money was returned, and the bank left without a dollar in its vaults, if, indeed, it had a vault about its premises. The result was, that banks were started all over the Western States, and the country flooded with worthless paper. These were known as the 'Wild Cat Banks.'[23] Silver coin being very scarce, and the banks not being allowed to issue notes for a smaller amount than one dollar, several persons put out notes of from 6 to 75 cents in value; these were called 'Shinplasters.'[24] The Shinplaster was in the shape of a promissory note, made payable on demand. I have often seen persons with large rolls of these bills, the whole not amounting to more than five dollars. Some weeks after I had commenced business on my 'own hook,' I was one evening very much crowded with customers; and while they were talking over the events of the day, one of them

[23] *Wild Cat Banks:* Prior to the creation of the national banking system in 1854, wildcat banks (and other institutions and individuals) were known to issue banknotes without adequate financial backing. Their proliferation contributed to the Panic of 1837.

[24] *Shinplasters:* During the antebellum period, the term referred to paper money in denominations of less than one dollar that was issued by institutions or individuals not connected to the Bank of the United States. Reforms of such practices were instituted in the wake of the Panic of 1837.

said to me, 'Emperor, you seem to be doing a thriving business. You should do as other business men, issue your Shinplasters.' This of course, as it was intended, created a laugh; but with me it was no laughing matter, for from that moment I began to think seriously of becoming a banker. I accordingly went a few days after to a printer, and he, wishing to get the job of printing, urged me to put out my notes, and showed me some specimens of engravings that he had just received from Detroit. My head being already filled with the idea of the bank, I needed but little persuasion to set the thing finally afloat. Before I left the printer the notes were partly in type, and I studying how I should keep the public from counterfeiting them. The next day, my Shinplasters were handed to me, the whole amount being twenty dollars; and, after being duly signed, were ready for circulation. The first night I had my money, my head was so turned and dizzy, that I could not sleep. In fact, I slept but little for weeks after the issuing of my bills. This fact satisfied me, that people of wealth pass many sleepless hours. At first my notes did not take well; they were too new, and viewed with a suspicious eye. But through the assistance of my customers, and a good deal of exertion on my part, my bills were soon in circulation; and nearly all the money received in return for my notes was spent in fitting up and decorating my shop. Few bankers get through this world without their difficulties, and I was not to be an exception. A short time after my money had been out, a party of young men, either wishing to pull down my vanity, or to try the soundness of my bank, determined to give it 'a run.'[25] After collecting together a number of my bills, they came one at a time to demand other money for them; and I, not being aware of what was going on, was taken by surprise. One day as I was sitting at my table, stropping some new razors I had just purchased with the avails of my Shinplasters, one of the men entered and said, 'Emperor, you will oblige me if you will give me some other money for these notes of yours.' I immediately cashed the notes with the most worthless of the Wild Cat money that I had on hand, but which was a lawful tender. The young man had scarcely left, when a second appeared with a similar amount, and demanded payment. These were cashed, and soon a third came with his roll of notes. I paid these with an air of triumph, although I had but half a dollar left. I began now to think seriously what I should do, or how to act, provided another demand should be made. While I was thus engaged

---

[25] '*a run*': A banking crisis that occurs when many depositors attempt to withdraw their funds.

in thought, I saw the fourth man crossing the street, with a handful of notes, evidently my Shinplasters. I instantaneously shut the door, and looking out of the window said, 'I have closed business for to-day: come to-morrow and I will see you.' In looking across the street, I saw my rival standing at his shopdoor, grinning and clapping his hands at my apparent downfall. I was completely 'done *Brown*'[26] for the day. However, I was not to be 'used up' in this way; so I escaped by the back door, and went in search of my friend, who had first suggested to me the idea of issuing my notes. I found him, told him of the difficulty I was in, and wished him to point out a way by which I might extricate myself. He laughed heartily at my sad position, and then said, 'You must act as all bankers do in this part of the country.' I inquired how they did; and he said, 'when your notes are brought to you, you must redeem them, and then send them out and get other money for them; and, with the latter, you can keep cashing your own Shinplasters.' This was, indeed, a new idea for me. I immediately commenced putting in circulation the notes which I had just redeemed, and my efforts were crowned with such success, that, together with the aid of my friend, who, like a philanthropist and Western Christian as he was, before I slept that night, my Shinplasters were again in circulation, and my bank once more on a sound basis."

In proportion as his mind expanded under the more favourable circumstances in which Brown was placed, he became anxious, not merely for the redemption of his race from personal slavery, but for the moral and religious elevation of those who were free. Finding that habits of intoxication were too prevalent among his coloured brethren, he, in conjunction with others, commenced a temperance reformation in their body. Such was the success of their efforts that, in three years, in the city of Buffalo alone, a society of upwards of 500 members was raised out of a coloured population of less than 700. Of that society Mr. Brown was thrice elected president. The intellectual powers of our author, coupled with his intimate acquaintance with the workings of the slave system, early recommended him to the Abolitionists, as a man eminently qualified to arouse the attention of the people of the Northern States to the great national sin of America. In 1843, he was engaged by the Western New York Anti-Slavery Society[27] as a lecturing agent. From 1844 to 1847, he laboured in

---

[26] '*done Brown*': Swindled (slang), with a pun on Brown's name (and "race").
[27] *Western New York Anti-Slavery Society:* An affiliate of the American Anti-Slavery Society.

the Anti-Slavery cause in connection with the American Anti-Slavery Society;[28] and from that period up to the time of his departure for Europe, in 1849, he was an agent of the Massachusetts Anti-Slavery Society.[29] The records of these societies furnish abundant evidence of the success of his labours. From the Massachusetts Anti-Slavery Society he early received the following testimonial. "Since Mr. Brown became an agent of this society, he has lectured in very many of the towns of this commonwealth, and gained for himself, the respect and esteem of all whom he met. Himself a fugitive slave, he can experimentally describe the situation of those in bonds as bound with them; and he powerfully illustrates the diabolism of that system which keeps in chains and darkness a host of minds, which, if free and enlightened, would shine among men like stars in the firmament." Another member of that society speaks thus of him: — "I need not attempt any description of the ability and efficiency which characterised the speeches of William Wells Brown throughout the meeting. To you who know him so well, it is enough to say that his lectures were worthy of himself. He has left an impression on the minds of the people, that few could have done. Cold indeed must be the hearts that could resist the appeals of so noble a specimen of humanity, in behalf of a crushed and despised race."

In 1847, Mr. Brown wrote a narrative of his life and escape from slavery, which rapidly ran through several editions. A copy of this he forwarded to his old master, from whom he had escaped, and soon after a friend of Mr. Brown's received the following letter:

"*St. Louis, Jan.* 10*th,* 1848.

"Sir, — I received a pamphlet, or a narrative, so called on the title-page, of the Life of William W. Brown, a fugitive slave, purporting to have been written by himself; and in his book I see a letter from you to the said William W. Brown. This said Brown is named William; he is a slave belonging to me, and ran away from me the first day of January, 1834.

"I purchased him of Mr. S. Willi, the last of September, 1833. I paid six hundred and fifty dollars for him. If I had wanted to speculate on him, I could have sold him for three times as much as I paid for him. I was offered two thousand dollars for him in New Orleans at one time, and fifteen hundred dollars for him at another time, in Louisville, Kentucky. But I would not sell him. I was told that he was going to run away, but I did not believe the man, for I had so much confidence in William. I want you to see him, and see if what I say is not the truth. I do not want him as a slave, but I think that his friends, who sustain him and give him the right hand of fellowship, or he himself, could afford to pay my agent in Boston three hundred and twenty five dollars, and I will give him free papers, so that he may go wherever he wishes to. Then he can visit St. Louis, or any other place he may wish.

"This amount is just half what I paid for him. Now, if this offer suits Mr. Brown, and the Anti-Slavery Society of Boston, or Massachusetts, let me know, and I will give you the name of my agent in Boston, and forward the papers, to be given to William W. Brown as soon as the money is paid.

"Yours respectfully,
"ENOCH PRICE."

"To Edmund Quincy,[30] Esq."

While Mr. Brown would most gladly have accepted manumission papers, relieving him from all future claim of the slaveholder, and thereby making his freedom more secure, he yet felt that he could not conscientiously purchase his liberty, because, by so doing, he would be putting money into the pockets of the manstealer which did not justly belong to him. He therefore refused the offer of Mr. Price. Notwithstanding the celebrity he had acquired in the North, as a man of genius and talent, and the general respect his high character had gained him, the slave spirit of America denied him the rights of a citizen. By the constitution of the United States he was every moment liable to be arrested, and returned to the slavery from which he had fled. His only protection from such a fate was the anomaly of the ascendancy of the public opinion over the law of the country.

It has been for years thought desirable and advantageous to the cause of Negro emancipation in America, to have some talented man of color always in Great Britain, who should be a living refutation of the doctrine of the inferiority of the African race; and it was moreover felt that none could so powerfully advocate the cause of "those in bonds" as one who had actually been "bound with them." Mr. Brown

---

[30] *Edmund Quincy:* The Boston reformer and writer Edmund Quincy (1808–1877) served as the Corresponding Secretary of the Massachusetts Anti-Slavery Society from 1844 to 1853.

having received repeated invitations from distinguished English Abolitionists to visit Great Britain, and being chosen a delegate to the Paris Peace Congress of 1849 by the American Peace Society,[31] and also by a convention of the coloured people of Boston, he resolved to acquiesce in the wishes of his numerous friends, and accordingly sailed from the United States on the 18th of July, 1849.

On leaving America he bore with him the following testimony from the Board of Managers of the Massachusetts Anti-Slavery Society: —

" In consequence of the departure for England of their esteemed friend and faithful co-labourer in the cause of the American slave, William W. Brown, the Board of Management of the Massachusetts Anti-Slavery Society would commend him to the confidence, respect, esteem, and hospitality of the friends of emancipation wherever he may travel: —

"1. Because he is a fugitive slave from the American house of bondage, and on the soil which gave him birth can find no spot on which he can stand in safety from his pursuers, protected by law.

"2. Because he is a man, and not a chattel; and while as the latter, he may at any time be sold at public vendue[32] under the American star-spangled banner, we rejoice to know that he will be recognised and protected as the former under the flag of England.

"3. Because, for several years past, he has nobly consecrated his time and talents, at great personal hazard, and under the most adverse circumstances, to the uncompromising advocacy of the cause of his enslaved countrymen.

"4. Because he visits England for the purpose of increasing, consolidating, and directing British humanity and piety against that horrible system of slavery in America, by which three millions of human beings, by creation the children of God, are ranked with four-footed beasts, and treated as marketable commodities.

"5. Because he has long been in their employment as a lecturing agent in Massachusetts, and has laboured with great acceptance and success; and from the acquaintance thus formed, they are enabled to

[31] *Paris . . . Society:* Convened in August 1849, the Paris Peace Congress drew approximately 800 delegates, including the black abolitionists Brown, Alexander Crummell (1819–1898) and J. W. C. Pennington (1807–1870). The Congress supported developing an international peacekeeping Congress of Nations. A league of nations was also one of the large goals of the American Peace Society, founded in 1828 by William Ladd (1778–1841) and then absorbed by the League of Universal Brotherhood, which was founded in 1846 by Elihu Burritt (1810–1879). Burritt was the guiding spirit of the Paris Peace Congress.

[32] *vendue:* auction.

certify that he has invariably conducted himself with great circumspection, and won for himself the sympathy, respect, and friendship of a very large circle of acquaintance."

The Coloured convention unanimously passed the following resolution:

"*Resolved*, — That we bid our brother, William Wells Brown, God speed in his mission to Europe, and commend him to the hospitality and encouragement of all true friends of humanity."[33]

In a letter to an American journal,[34] announcing his arrival at Liverpool, he speaks as follows: —

"No person of my complexion can visit this country without being struck with the marked difference between the English and the Americans. The prejudice which I have experienced on all and every occasion in the United States, and to some degree on board the *Canada*, vanished as soon as I set foot on the soil of Britain. In America I had been bought and sold as a slave, in the Southern States. In the so-called Free States I had been treated as one born to occupy an inferior position; in steamers, compelled to take my fare on the deck; in hotels, to take my meals in the kitchen; in coaches, to ride on the outside; in railways, to ride in the 'Negro car;' and in churches, to sit in the 'Negro pew.' But no sooner was I on British soil than I was recognised as a man and an equal. The very dogs in the streets appeared conscious of my manhood. Such is the difference, and such is the change that is brought about by a trip of nine days in an Atlantic steamer. * * * For the first time in my life, I can say 'I am truly free.' My old master may make his appearance here, with the constitution of the United States in his pocket, the fugitive slave law in one hand and the chains in the other, and claim me as his property; but all will avail him nothing. I can here stand and look the tyrant in the face, and tell him that I am his equal! England is, indeed, the 'land of the free, and the home of the brave.' "

The reception of Mr. Brown at the Peace Congress in Paris was most flattering. He admirably maintained his reputation as a public speaker. His brief address upon that "war spirit of America which

[33] *. . . humanity"*: For accounts of the 16 July 1849 farewell gathering in Boston, see the *Liberator*, 20 July 1849 and 27 July 1849.

[34] *American journal*: Brown wrote regularly to the *Liberator* about his travels in Great Britain; see, for example, the issue of 2 November 1849 for a letter that bears some resemblance to the letter that follows.

holds in bondage nearly four millions of his brethren," produced a profound sensation. At its conclusion the speaker was warmly greeted by Victor Hugo, the Abbé Duguerry, Emile de Girardin, Richard Cobden,[35] and every man of note in the assembly. At the soirée given by M. de Tocquerelle, the Minister for Foreign Affairs, and the other fêtes given to the members of the Congress, Mr. Brown was received with marked attention.

Having finished his Peace Mission in France, he returned to England, where he was received with a hearty welcome by some of the most influential abolitionists of this country. Most of the fugitive slaves, and in fact nearly all of the coloured men who have visited Great Britain from the United States, have come upon begging missions, either for some society or for themselves. Mr. Brown has been almost the only exception. With that independence of feeling, which those who are acquainted with him know to be one of his chief characteristics, he determined to maintain himself and family by his own exertions — by his literary labours, and the honourable profession of a public lecturer. From nearly all the cities and large provincial towns he received invitations to lecture or address public meetings. The mayors, or other citizens of note, presided over many of these meetings. At Newcastle-upon-Tyne[36] a soirée was given him, and an address presented by the citizens. A large and influential meeting was held at Bolton, Lancashire,[37] which was addressed by Mr. Brown, and at its close the ladies presented to him the following address: —

"An address, presented to Mr. William Wells Brown, the fugitive slave from America, by the ladies of Bolton, March 22nd, 1850: —

"Dear friend and brother, — We cannot permit you to depart from among us without giving expression to the feelings which we entertain towards yourself personally, and to the sympathy which you have awakened in our breasts for the three millions of our sisters and brothers who still suffer and groan in the prison-house of American bondage. You came among us an entire stranger; we received you for the sake of your mission; and having heard the story of your personal

[35] *Victor Hugo . . . Richard Cobden:* Vicomte Victor Marie Hugo (1802–1885), French poet and novelist, who would become best known for *Les Misérables* (1862); Abbé Duguerry (?–1871), curé of the Parish of La Madeleine; Emile de Girardin (1806–1881), prominent journalist and editor of *La Presse;* Richard Cobden (1804–1865), British politician known for his advocacy of free trade.
[36] *Newcastle-upon-Tyne:* A seaport in northern England.
[37] *Bolton, Lancashire:* A city in a northwest county of England which at the time was a cotton-textile center.

wrongs, and gazed with horror on the atrocities of slavery as seen through the medium of your touching descriptions, we are resolved, henceforward, in reliance on divine assistance, to render what aid we can to the cause which you have so eloquently pleaded in our presence.

"We have no words to express our detestation of the crimes which, in the name of liberty, are committed in the country which gave you birth. Language fails to tell our deep abhorrence of the impiety of those who, in the still more sacred name of religion, rob immortal beings not only of an earthly citizenship, but do much to prevent them from obtaining a heavenly one; and, as mothers and daughters, we embrace this opportunity of giving utterance to our utmost indignation at the cruelties perpetrated upon our sex, by a people professedly acknowledging the equality of all mankind. Carry with you, on your return to the land of your nativity, this our solemn protest against the wicked institution which, like a dark and baleful cloud, hangs over it; and ask the unfeeling enslavers, as best you can, to open the prison doors to them that are bound, and let the oppressed go free.

"Allow us to assure you that your brief sojourn in our town has been to ourselves, and to vast multitudes, of a character long to be remembered; and when you are far removed from us, and toiling, as we hope you may be long spared to do, in this righteous enterprise, it may be some solace to your mind to know that your name is cherished with affectionate regard, and that the blessing of the Most High is earnestly supplicated in behalf of yourself, your family, and the cause to which you have consecrated your distinguished talents."

A most respectable and enthusiastic public meeting was held at Sheffield,[38] to welcome Mr. Brown, and the next day he was invited to inspect several of the large establishments there. While going through the manufactory of Messrs. Broadhead and Atkin, silver and electroplaters, &c., in Love-street, and whilst he was being shown through the works, a subscription was hastily set on foot on his behalf, by the workmen and women of the establishment, which was presented to Mr. Brown in the counting-house by a deputation of the subscribers. The spokesman (the designer to Messrs. Broadhead and Atkin) addressing Mr. Brown on behalf of the workpeople, begged his acceptance of the present as a token of esteem, as well as an expression of their sympathy in the cause he advocates, viz. that of the American slave. Mr. Brown briefly thanked the parties for their spontaneous free

[38] *Sheffield:* A factory town and industrial center in northern England.

will offering, accompanied as it was by a generous expression of sympathy for his afflicted brethren and sisters in bondage.

Mr. Brown has been in England nearly four years, and since his arrival he has travelled above twenty thousand miles through Great Britain, addressed one hundred and thirty public meetings, lectured in twenty-three mechanics and literary institutions, and given his services to many of the benevolent and religious societies on the occasion of their anniversary meetings. After a lecture, which he delivered before the Whittington Club, he received from the managers of that institution the following testimonial:

"*Whittington Club and Metropolitan Athenæum,*[39]
"189, *Strand, June* 21, 1850.

"My dear sir,

I have much pleasure in conveying to you the best thanks of the Managing Committee of this institution for the excellent lecture you gave here last evening, and also in presenting you in their names with an honorary membership of the club. It is hoped that you will often avail yourself of its privileges by coming amongst us. You will then see, by the cordial welcome of the members, that they protest against the odious distinctions made between man and man, and the abominable traffic of which you have been the victim.

"For my own part, I shall be happy to be serviceable to you in any way, and at all times be glad to place the advantages of the institution at your disposal.

"I am, my dear sir,
"Yours truly,
"WILLIAM STRUDWICKE,
"Secretary."

"Mr. W. Wells Brown."

On the 1st of August, 1851, a meeting of the most novel character was held at the Hall of Commerce, London, the chief actors being American fugitive slaves. That meeting was most ably presided over by Mr. Brown, and the speeches made on the occasion by fugitive slaves were of the most interesting and creditable description. Although a residence in Canada is infinitely preferable to slavery in America, yet the climate of that country is uncongenial to the constitutions of the

---

[39] *Whittington Club and Metropolitan Athenæum:* At the time a prestigious London club with over two thousand members, including Charles Dickens and several members of Parliament.

Negroes, and their lack of education is an almost insuperable barrier to their social progress. The latter evil Mr. Brown attempted to remedy by the establishment of Manual Labour Schools in Canada for fugitive slaves. A public meeting, attended by between 3,000 and 4,000 persons, was held on the 6th of January 1851, in the City Hall, Glasgow, which was presided over by Alexander Hastie, Esq., M.P., at which resolutions were unanimously passed, approving of Mr. Brown's scheme; which scheme, however, never received that amount of support which would have enabled him to bring it into practice; and the plan at present only remains as an evidence of its author's ingenuity and desire for the elevation of his oppressed and injured race. Mr. Brown subsequently made, through the columns of the *Times,* a proposition for the emigration of American fugitive slaves, under fair and honourable terms, from Canada to the West Indies, where there is a great lack of that labour which they are so capable of undertaking.[40] These efforts all show the willingness of this fugitive slave to aid those of his race. Last year Mr. Brown published his "Three Years in Europe; or, Places I have seen and People I have met." And his literary abilities may be partly judged of from the following commendations of that ably written work: —

"The extraordinary excitement produced by 'Uncle Tom's Cabin'[41] will, we hope, prepare the public of Great Britain and America for this lively book of travels by a real fugitive slave. Though he never had a day's schooling in his life, he has produced a literary work not unworthy of a highly educated gentleman. Our readers will find in these letters much instruction, not a little entertainment, and the beatings of a manly heart, on behalf of a down-trodden race, with which they will not fail to sympathise." — *The Eclectic.*

"When he writes on the wrongs of his race, or the events of his own career, he is always interesting or amusing." — *The Athenæum*

"The appearance of this book is too remarkable a literary event to pass without a notice. At the moment when attention in this country is directed to the state of the coloured people in America, the book appears with additional advantage; if nothing else were attained by its publication, it is well to have another proof of the capability of the

[40] *Mr. Brown . . . undertaking:* Brown's letter on West Indies emigration can be found in the (London) *Times,* 4 July 1851.

[41] *'Uncle Tom's Cabin':* Harriet Beecher Stowe's *Uncle Tom's Cabin* ran serially in the *National Era* from June 1851 to April 1852 and was published in two volumes in the spring of 1852. For a selection from the novel, see pp. 284–95.

Negro intellect. Altogether Mr. Brown has written a pleasing and amusing volume. Contrasted with the caricature and bombast of his white countrymen, Mr. Willis's description of 'People he has met,'[42] a comparison suggested by the similarity of the title, it is both in intellect and in style a superior performance, and we are glad to bear this testimony to the literary merit of a work by a Negro author." — *The Literary Gazette.*

"That a man who was a slave for the first twenty years of his life, and who has never had a day's schooling, should produce such a book as this, cannot but astonish those who speak disparagingly of the African race." — *The Weekly News and Chronicle.*

"This remarkable book of a remarkable man cannot fail to add to the practical protests already entered in Britain against the absolute bondage of 3,000,000 of our fellow creatures. The impression of a self-educated son of slavery here set forth, must hasten the period when the senseless and impious denial of common claims to a common humanity, on the score of color, shall be scouted with scorn in every civilised and Christian country. And when this shall be attained, among the means of destruction of the hideous abomination, his compatriots will remember with respect and gratitude the doings and sayings of William Wells Brown. The volume consists of a sufficient variety of scenes, persons, arguments, inferences, speculations, and opinions, to satisfy and amuse the most *exigeant*[43] of those who read *pour se desennuyer;*[44] while those who look deeper into things, and view with anxious hope the progress of nations and of mankind, will feel that the good cause of humanity and freedom, of Christianity, enlightenment, and brotherhood, cannot fail to be served by such a book as this." — *Morning Advertiser.*

"He writes with ease and ability, and his intelligent observations upon the great question to which he has devoted, and is devoting his life, will be read with interest, and will command influence and respect." — *Daily News.*

Mr. Brown is most assiduous in his studies even at the present time. The following extract from his writings will show how he spends most of his leisure hours: —

[42] *Mr. Willis's . . . 'People he has met'*: Nathaniel Parker Willis (1806–1867) was a popular New York writer, editor, and reviewer who was regarded by some as a dilettante and dandy. His *People I Have Met* was published in 1850.

[43] *exigeant*: Exacting, hard to please.

[44] *pour se desennuyer*: For amusement; to kill time.

"It was eight o'clock before I reached my lodgings. Although fatigued by the day's exertions, I again resumed the reading of Roscoe's 'Leo X.,'[45] and had nearly finished seventy-three pages, when the clock on St. Martin's Church apprised me that it was two. He who escapes from slavery at the age of twenty years without any education, as did the writer of this letter, must read when others are asleep, if he would catch up with the rest of the world. 'To be wise,' says Pope, 'is but to know how little can be known.'[46] The true searcher after truth and knowledge is always like a child; although gaining strength from year to year, he still 'learns to labour and to wait.'[47] The field of labour is ever expanding before him, reminding him that he has yet more to learn; teaching him that he is nothing more than a child in knowledge, and inviting him onward with a thousand varied charms. The son may take possession of the father's goods at his death, but he cannot inherit with the property the father's cultivated mind. He may put on the father's old coat, but that is all; the immortal mind of the first wearer has gone to the tomb. Property may be bequeathed but knowledge cannot. Then let him who would be useful in his generation be up and doing. Like the Chinese student who learned perseverance from the woman whom he saw trying to rub a crowbar into a needle, so should we take the experience of the past to lighten our feet though the paths of the future."

The following testimonial to Mr. Brown's abilities, from an American journal of which Frederick Douglas is editor,[48] shows that his talents are highly appreciated in that country: —

"We have the pleasure to lay before our readers another interesting letter from W. Wells Brown. We rejoice to find our friend still persevering in the pursuit of knowledge, and still more do we rejoice to find such marked evidence of his rapid progress as his several letters afford. But a few years ago he was a despised, degraded, whip-scarred slave, knowing nothing of letters; and now we find him writing accounts of his travels in a distant land, of which a man reared under the most favourable educational advantages might be proud."

[45] *Roscoe's 'Leo X.'*: The British historian William Roscoe (1753–1831) published his four-volume *The Life and Pontificate of Leo the Tenth* in 1805; Leo X (1475–1521) was pope from 1513 to 1521.

[46] *'To be . . . known'*: From Alexander Pope (1688–1744), *An Essay on Man* (1734).

[47] *'learns . . . to wait'*: From Henry Wadsworth Longfellow, "Resignation" (1848).

[48] *"The following . . . editor"*: A testimonial by Frederick Douglass (1818–1895) in the *North Star*, 17 April 1851.

We should have said that it was Mr. Brown's intention to have returned to the United States to his family ere this. But the passage of the infamous "Fugitive Slave Law" prevented his returning.

Mr. Brown's wife[49] died in Buffalo N. Y. in Jan. 1851. He has two daughters[50] who are now in this country, being trained for teachers. Of course we need not add that for their education they are entirely dependent on their father's exertions. During last year, the Rev. Edward Hore, of Ramsgate, through a willingness to assist Mr. Brown in returning to the United States, wrote to his former owner, and offered him £50, if he would relinquish all claim to him, and furnish the fugitive with papers of emancipation, but the following note from the slaveowner speaks for itself: —

"*St. Louis, Feb.* 16*th,* 1852.

"Rev. sir, — I received your note, dated Jan. 6th, concerning a runaway slave of mine now known by the name of William Wells Brown. You state that I offered to take three hundred and twenty five dollars for him, and give him free papers, in 1848. I did so then, but since that time the laws of the United States are materially changed. The Fugitive Slave Bill has passed since then. I can now take him anywhere in the United States, and I have everything arranged for his arrest if he lands at any port in the United States. But I will give him papers of emancipation, properly authenticated by our statutes, for the sum of five hundred dollars (or £100) that will make him as free as any white person. If this suits your views, you can let me know, and I will have the papers made out and forwarded to Boston, to Joseph Gruley, of the firm of Charles Wilkins and Co., 33, Long Wharf. The money must be paid before the papers are handed over to your agent.

"Respectfully your obedient servant,

"To the Rev. Edward Hore."　　　　　　　　"Enoch Price."

---

[49] *Mr. Brown's wife:* Brown married the free black Elizabeth Schooner in 1834; they separated in 1847.

[50] *two daughters:* Brown took custody of Clarissa Brown (1836–?) and Josephine Brown (1839–?) after separating from his wife. For a selection from Josephine Brown, see pp. 302–06.

Clotel;
or,
The President's Daughter

CHAPTER I.
THE NEGRO SALE.

"Why stands she near the auction stand,
    That girl so young and fair?
What brings her to this dismal place,
    Why stands she weeping there?"[1]

With the growing population of slaves in the Southern States of America, there is a fearful increase of half whites, most of whose fathers are slaveowners, and their mothers slaves. Society does not frown upon the man who sits with his mulatto child upon his knee, whilst its mother stands a slave behind his chair. The late Henry Clay, some years since, predicted that the abolition of negro slavery would be brought about by the amalgamation of the races.[2] John Randolph, a distinguished slaveholder of Virginia, and a prominent statesman, said in a speech in the legislature of his native state, that "the blood of the first American statesman coursed through the veins of the slave of the South."[3] In all the cities and towns of the slave states, the real negro, or clear black, does not amount to more than one in every four of the slave population. This fact is, of itself, the best evidence of the

---

[1] *"Why stands she ... there?":* The opening stanza of anon., "The Slave-Auction — A Fact," in *The Anti-Slavery Harp,* ed. Brown (1848).

[2] *The late Henry Clay ... races:* Brown distorts Clay's views by presenting them out of context. Clay saw "amalgamation" as the nightmarish but inevitable outcome of what the abolitionists wanted to impose on the United States. Clay advocated colonizing blacks to Africa precisely because he believed blacks were inferior to whites and that black-white unions were "unnatural." See, for example, his speech to the Senate of 7 February 1839, in which he opposed abolishing slavery in the District of Columbia on the grounds that abolitionists "are in favor or amalgamation" and wish "to contaminate the industrious and laboring classes of society of the North by a revolting admixture of blackness" (*The Papers of Henry Clay,* vol. 9, ed. Robert Seger II and Melba Porter Hay [Lexington: U of Kentucky, 1988], 282).

[3] *John Randolph ... of the South":* The Virginian political leader John Randolph (1773–1833) was a fiery advocate of the doctrine of states' rights and the owner of one of Virginia's largest slave plantations. Nevertheless, he went on record opposing slavery, and in his will he freed his slaves. Consistent with the assertions of this obscure and possibly apocryphal quotation, Randolph regularly boasted of having descended from the Indian princess Pocahontas.

degraded and immoral condition of the relation of master and slave in the United States of America.

In all the slave states, the law says: — "Slaves shall be deemed, sold, taken, reputed, and adjudged in law to be chattels[4] personal in the hands of their owners and possessors, and their executors, administrators and assigns, to all intents, constructions, and purposes whatsoever. A slave is one who is in the power of a master to whom he belongs. The master may sell him, dispose of his person, his industry, and his labour. He can do nothing, possess nothing, nor acquire anything, but what must belong to his master. The slave is entirely subject to the will of his master, who may correct and chastise him, though not with unusual rigour, or so as to maim and mutilate him, or expose him to the danger of loss of life, or to cause his death. The slave, to remain a slave, must be sensible that there is no appeal from his master."[5] Where the slave is placed by law entirely under the control of the man who claims him, body and soul, as property, what else could be expected than the most depraved social condition? The marriage relation, the oldest and most sacred institution given to man by his Creator, is unknown and unrecognised in the slave laws of the United States. Would that we could say, that the moral and religious teaching in the slave states were better than the laws; but, alas! we cannot. A few years since, some slaveholders became a little uneasy in their minds about the rightfulness of permitting slaves to take to themselves husbands and wives, while they still had others living, and applied to their religious teachers for advice; and the following will show how this grave and important subject was treated: —

> "Is a servant, whose husband or wife has been sold by his or her master into a distant country, to be permitted to marry again?"

The query was referred to a committee, who made the following report; which, after discussion, was adopted: —

> "That, in view of the circumstances in which servants in this country are placed, the committee are unanimous in the opinion, that it is better to permit servants thus circumstanced to take another husband or wife."

---

[4] *chattels:* Moveable property; possessions.

[5] *"Slaves shall be deemed ... from his master":* An amalgam of slave law, which particularly echoes the famous ruling by Judge Thomas Ruffin (1787–1870), in the 1829 North Carolina Case of *State v. Mann,* that "The power of the master must be absolute to render the submission of the slave perfect."

Such was the answer from a committee of the "Shiloh Baptist Association;" and instead of receiving light, those who asked the question were plunged into deeper darkness!

A similar question was put to the "Savannah River Association,"[6] and the answer, as the following will show, did not materially differ from the one we have already given: —

> "Whether, in a case of involuntary separation, of such a character as to preclude all prospect of future intercourse, the parties ought to be allowed to marry again."

Answer —

> "That such separation among persons situated as our slaves are, is civilly a separation by death; and they believe that, in the sight of God, it would be so viewed. To forbid second marriages in such cases would be to expose the parties, not only to stronger hardships and strong temptation, but to church-censure for acting in obedience to their masters, who cannot be expected to acquiesce in a regulation at variance with justice to the slaves, and to the spirit of that command which regulates marriage among Christians. The slaves are not free agents; and a dissolution by death is not more entirely without their consent, and beyond their control, than by such separation."

Although marriage, as the above indicates, is a matter which the slaveholders do not think is of any importance, or of any binding force with their slaves; yet it would be doing that degraded class an injustice, not to acknowledge that many of them do regard it as a sacred obligation, and show a willingness to obey the commands of God on this subject. Marriage is, indeed, the first and most important institution of human existence — the foundation of all civilisation and culture — the root of church and state. It is the most intimate covenant of heart formed among mankind; and for many persons the only relation in which they feel the true sentiments of humanity. It gives scope for every human virtue, since each of these is developed from the love and confidence which here predominate. It unites all which ennobles and beautifies life, — sympathy, kindness of will and deed, gratitude, devotion, and every delicate, intimate feeling. As the only asylum for true education, it is the first and last sanctuary of human culture. As husband and wife through each other become conscious of complete

---

[6] *"Savannah River Association"*: Like the aforementioned "Shiloh Baptist Association," a Christian organization based in the South.

humanity, and every human feeling, and every human virtue; so children, at their first awakening in the fond covenant of love between parents, both of whom are tenderly concerned for the same object, find an image of complete humanity leagued in free love. The spirit of love which prevails between them acts with creative power upon the young mind, and awakens every germ of goodness within it. This invisible and incalculable influence of parental life acts more upon the child than all the efforts of education, whether by means of instruction, precept, or exhortation. If this be a true picture of the vast influence for good of the institution of marriage, what must be the moral degradation of that people to whom marriage is denied? Not content with depriving them of all the higher and holier enjoyments of this relation, by degrading and darkening their souls, the slaveholder denies to his victim even that slight alleviation of his misery, which would result from the marriage relation being protected by law and public opinion. Such is the influence of slavery in the United States, that the ministers of religion, even in the so-called free states, are the mere echoes, instead of the correctors, of public sentiment.

We have thought it advisable to show that the present system of chattel slavery in America undermines the entire social condition of man, so as to prepare the reader for the following narrative of slave life, in that otherwise happy and prosperous country.

In all the large towns in the Southern States, there is a class of slaves who are permitted to hire their time of their owners, and for which they pay a high price. These are mulatto women, or quadroons,[7] as they are familiarly known, and are distinguished for their fascinating beauty. The handsomest usually pays the highest price for her time. Many of these women are the favourites of persons who furnish them with the means of paying their owners, and not a few are dressed in the most extravagant manner. Reader, when you take into consideration the fact, that amongst the slave population no safeguard is thrown around virtue, and no inducement held out to slave women to be chaste, you will not be surprised when we tell you that immorality and vice pervade the cities of the Southern States in a manner unknown in the cities and towns of the Northern States. Indeed most of the slave women have no higher aspiration than that of becoming

---

[7] *mulatto . . . or quadroons:* "Quadroon" was a term used in the nineteenth century (and less often in the twentieth century) to refer to people who were thought to be one-fourth "black"; more generally, "quadroon," like "mulatto," was used to refer to light-skinned peoples of mixed racial ancestry.

the finely-dressed mistress of some white man. And at negro balls and parties, this class of women usually cut the greatest figure.

At the close of the year —— the following advertisement appeared in a newspaper published in Richmond, the capital of the state of Virginia: — "Notice: Thirty-eight negroes will be offered for sale on Monday, November 10th, at twelve o'clock, being the entire stock of the late John Graves, Esq. The negroes are in good condition, some of them very prime; among them are several mechanics, able-bodied field hands, plough-boys, and women with children at the breast, and some of them very prolific in their generating qualities, affording a rare opportunity to any one who wishes to raise a strong and healthy lot of servants for their own use. Also several mulatto girls of rare personal qualities: two of them very superior. Any gentleman or lady wishing to purchase, can take any of the above slaves on trial for a week, for which no charge will be made."[8] Amongst the above slaves to be sold were Currer and her two daughters, Clotel and Althesa; the latter were the girls spoken of in the advertisement as "very superior." Currer was a bright mulatto, and of prepossessing appearance, though then nearly forty years of age. She had hired her time for more than twenty years, during which time she had lived in Richmond. In her younger days Currer had been the housekeeper of a young slaveholder; but of later years had been a laundress or washerwoman, and was considered to be a woman of great taste in getting up linen. The gentleman for whom she had kept house was Thomas Jefferson, by whom she had two daughters. Jefferson being called to Washington to fill a government appointment,[9] Currer was left behind, and thus she took herself to the business of washing, by which means she paid her master, Mr. Graves, and supported herself and two children. At the time of the decease of her master, Currer's daughters, Clotel and Althesa, were aged respectively sixteen and fourteen years, and both, like most of their own sex in America, were well grown. Currer early resolved to bring her daughters up as ladies, as she termed it, and therefore imposed little or no work upon them. As her daughters grew older, Currer had to pay a stipulated price for them; yet her notoriety as a

[8] "Notice. . . . made": The advertisement draws on an 1838 advertisement quoted in Theodore Dwight Weld's *Slavery As It Is* (1839); see pp. 265–70.

[9] *government appointment*: Because Jefferson resided in Washington, D.C., for part of his vice presidency and for all of his presidency, overall from the late 1790s to 1809, the information provided here would suggest that the events in *Clotel* begin around 1815. But this dating is inconsistent with the novel's later account of Nat Turner's rebellion of 1831, the election of 1840, and other historical events. As discussed in the Introduction, Brown deliberately skews historical chronology.

laundress of the first class enabled her to put an extra price upon her charges, and thus she and her daughters lived in comparative luxury. To bring up Clotel and Althesa to attract attention, and especially at balls and parties, was the great aim of Currer. Although the term "negro ball" is applied to most of these gatherings, yet a majority of the attendants are often whites. Nearly all the negro parties in the cities and towns of the Southern States are made up of quadroon and mulatto girls, and white men. These are democratic gatherings, where gentlemen, shopkeepers, and their clerks, all appear upon terms of perfect equality. And there is a degree of gentility and decorum in these companies that is not surpassed by similar gatherings of white people in the Slave States. It was at one of these parties that Horatio Green, the son of a wealthy gentleman of Richmond, was first introduced to Clotel. The young man had just returned from college, and was in his twenty-second year. Clotel was sixteen and was admitted by all to be the most beautiful girl, coloured or white, in the city. So attentive was the young man to the quadroon during the evening that it was noticed by all, and became a matter of general conversation; while Currer appeared delighted beyond measure at her daughter's conquest. From that evening, young Green became the favourite visitor at Currer's house. He soon promised to purchase Clotel, as speedily as it could be effected, and make her mistress of her own dwelling; and Currer looked forward with pride to the time when she should see her daughter emancipated and free. It was a beautiful moonlight night in August, when all who reside in tropical climes are eagerly gasping for a breath of fresh air, that Horatio Green was seated in the small garden behind Currer's cottage, with the object of his affections by his side. And it was here that Horatio drew from his pocket the newspaper, wet from the press, and read the advertisement for the sale of the slaves to which we have alluded; Currer and her two daughters being of the number. At the close of the evening's visit, and as the young man was leaving, he said to the girl, "You shall soon be free and your own mistress."

As might have been expected, the day of sale brought an unusual large number together to compete for the property to be sold. Farmers who make a business of raising slaves for the market were there; slave-traders and speculators were also numerously represented; and in the midst of this throng was one who felt a deeper interest in the result of the sale than any other of the bystanders; this was young Green. True to his promise, he was there with a blank bank check in his pocket, awaiting with impatience to enter the list as a bidder for the beautiful slave. The less valuable slaves were first placed upon the auction block, one after another, and sold to the highest bidder. Husbands and wives were separated with a degree of indifference that is unknown in any other relation of life, except that of slavery. Brothers and sisters were torn from each other; and mothers saw their children leave them for the last time on this earth.

It was late in the day, when the greatest number of persons were thought to be present, that Currer and her daughters were brought forward to the place of sale. Currer was first ordered to ascend the auction stand, which she did with a trembling step. The slave mother was sold to a trader. Althesa, the youngest, and who was scarcely less beautiful than her sister, was sold to the same trader for one thousand dollars. Clotel was the last, and, as was expected, commanded a higher price than any that had been offered for sale that day. The appearance of Clotel on the auction block created a deep sensation amongst the crowd. There she stood, with a complexion as white as most of those who were waiting with a wish to become her purchasers; her features as finely defined as any of her sex of pure Anglo-Saxon; her long black wavy hair done up in the neatest manner; her form tall and graceful, and her whole appearance indicating one superior to her position. The auctioneer commenced by saying, that "Miss Clotel had been reserved for the last, because she was the most valuable. How much gentlemen? Real Albino, fit for a fancy girl for any one. She enjoys good health, and has a sweet temper. How much do you say?" "Five hundred dollars." "Only five hundred for such a girl as this? Gentlemen, she is worth a deal more than that sum; you certainly don't know the value of the article you are bidding upon. Here, gentlemen, I hold in my hand a paper certifying that she has a good moral character." "Seven hundred." "Ah, gentlemen, that is some-thing like. This paper also states that she is very intelligent." "Eight hundred." "She is a devoted Christian, and perfectly trustworthy." "Nine hundred." "Nine fifty." "Ten." "Eleven." "Twelve hundred." Here the sale came to a dead stand. The auctioneer stopped, looked around, and began in a rough manner to relate some anecdotes rela-tive to the sale of slaves, which, he said, had come under his own observation. At this juncture the scene was indeed strange. Laughing, joking, swearing, smoking, spitting, and talking kept up a continual hum and noise amongst the crowd; while the slave-girl stood with tears in her eyes, at one time looking towards her mother and sister, and at another towards the young man whom she hoped would become her purchaser. "The chastity of this girl is pure; she has never been from under her mother's care; she is a virtuous creature." "Thirteen." "Fourteen." "Fifteen." "Fifteen hundred dollars," cried the auctioneer, and the maiden was struck for that sum. This was a Southern auction, at which the bones, muscles, sinews, blood, and nerves of a young lady of sixteen were sold for five hundred dollars; her moral character for two hundred; her improved intellect for one hundred; her Christianity for three hundred; and her chastity and virtue for four hundred dollars more. And this, too, in a city thronged with churches, whose tall spires look like so many signals pointing to heaven, and whose ministers preach that slavery is a God-ordained institution![10]

What words can tell the inhumanity, the atrocity, and the immorality of that doctrine which, from exalted office, commends such a crime to the favour of enlightened and Christian people? What indignation from all the world is not due to the government and people who put forth all their strength and power to keep in existence such an institution? Nature abhors it; the age repels it; and Christianity needs all her meekness to forgive it.

Clotel was sold for fifteen hundred dollars, but her purchaser was Horatio Green. Thus closed a negro sale, at which two daughters of Thomas Jefferson, the writer of the Declaration of American Independence, and one of the presidents of the great republic, were disposed of to the highest bidder!

> "O God! my every heart-string cries,
>   Dost thou these scenes behold
>   In this our boasted Christian land,
>   And must the truth be told?
>
> "Blush, Christian, blush! for e'en the dark,
>   Untutored heathen see
>   Thy inconsistency; and, lo!
>   They scorn thy God, and thee!"[11]

---

[10] *God-ordained institution!:* For an early version of a similar auction scene, see William Wells Brown's "A True Story of Slave Life," *Anti-Slavery Advocate,* December 1852.

[11] *"Oh God! . . . and thee!":* From anon., "The Slave-Auction — A Fact," in *The Anti-Slavery Harp,* ed. Brown.

CHAPTER II.
GOING TO THE SOUTH.

"My country, shall thy honoured name,
    Be as a bye-word through the world?
Rouse! for, as if to blast thy fame,
    This keen reproach is at thee hurled;
The banner that above thee waves,
    Is floating o'er three million slaves."[1]

Dick Walker, the slave speculator, who had purchased Currer and Althesa, put them in prison until his gang was made up, and then, with his forty slaves, started for the New Orleans market. As many of the slaves had been brought up in Richmond, and had relations residing there, the slave trader determined to leave the city early in the morning, so as not to witness any of those scenes so common where slaves are separated from their relatives and friends, when about departing for the Southern market. This plan was successful; for not even Clotel, who had been every day at the prison to see her mother and sister, knew of their departure. A march of eight days through the interior of the state, and they arrived on the banks of the Ohio river, where they were all put on board a steamer, and then speedily sailed for the place of their destination.

Walker had already advertised in the New Orleans papers, that he would be there at a stated time with "a prime lot of able-bodied slaves ready for field service; together with a few extra ones, between the ages of fifteen and twenty-five." But, like most who make a business of buying and selling slaves for gain, he often bought some who were far advanced in years, and would always try to sell them for five or ten years younger than they actually were. Few persons can arrive at anything like the age of a negro, by mere observation, unless they are well acquainted with the race. Therefore the slave-trader very frequently carried out this deception with perfect impunity. After the steamer had left the wharf, and was fairly on the bosom of the Father of Waters,[2] Walker called his servant Pompey to him, and instructed him as to "getting the negroes ready for market." Amongst the forty negroes were several whose appearance indicated that they had seen some

---

[1] *"My country . . . slaves":* From R. C. Wateston, "Freedom's Banner," in *The Anti-Slavery Harp,* ed. Brown.
[2] *Father of Waters:* The Mississippi River — a principal U.S. river with numerous tributaries.

years, and had gone through some services. Their grey hair and whiskers at once pronounced them to be above the ages set down in the trader's advertisement. Pompey had long been with the trader, and knew his business; and if he did not take delight in discharging his duty, he did it with a degree of alacrity, so that he might receive the approbation of his master. "Pomp," as Walker usually called him, was of real negro blood, and would often say, when alluding to himself, "Dis nigger is no countefit; he is de genewine artekil." Pompey was of low stature, round face, and, like most of his race, had a set of teeth, which for whiteness and beauty could not be surpassed; his eyes large, lips thick, and hair short and woolly. Pompey had been with Walker so long, and had seen so much of the buying and selling of slaves, that he appeared perfectly indifferent to the heartrending scenes which daily occurred in his presence. It was on the second day of the steamer's voyage that Pompey selected five of the old slaves, took them into a room by themselves, and commenced preparing them for the market. "Well," said Pompey, addressing himself to the company, "I is de gentman dat is to get you ready, so dat you will bring marser a good price in de Orleans market. How old is you?" addressing himself to a man who, from appearance, was not less than forty. "If I live to see next corn-planting time I will either be forty-five or fifty-five, I don't know which." "Dat may be," replied Pompey; "but now you is only thirty years old; dat is what marser says you is to be." "I know I is more den dat," responded the man. "I knows nothing about dat," said Pompey; "but when you get in de market, an anybody axe you how old you is, an you tell 'em forty-five, marser will tie you up an gib you de whip like smoke. But if you tell 'em dat you is only thirty, den he wont." "Well den, I guess I will only be thirty when dey axe me," replied the chattel.

"What your name?" inquired Pompey. "Geemes," answered the man. "Oh, Uncle Jim, is it?" "Yes." "Den you must have off dem dare whiskers of yours, an when you get to Orleans you must grease dat face an make it look shiney." This was all said by Pompey in a manner which clearly showed that he knew what he was about. "How old is you?" asked Pompey of a tall, strong-looking man. "I was twenty-nine last potato-digging time," said the man. "What's your name?" "My name is Tobias, but dey call me 'Toby.' " "Well, Toby, or Mr. Tobias, if dat will suit you better, you is now twenty-three years old, an no more. Dus you hear dat?" "Yes," responded Toby. Pompey gave each to understand how old he was to be when asked by persons who wished to purchase, and then reported to his master that the "old boys" were all right. At eight o'clock on the evening of the third day, the lights of another steamer were seen in the distance, and apparently coming up very fast. This was a signal for a general commotion on the Patriot, and everything indicated that a steamboat race was at hand.[3] Nothing can exceed the excitement attendant upon a steamboat on the Mississippi river. By the time the boats had reached Memphis, they were side by side, and each exerting itself to keep the ascendancy in point of speed. The night was clear, the moon shining brightly, and the boats so near to each other that the passengers were calling out from one boat to the other. On board the Patriot, the firemen were using oil, lard, butter, and even bacon, with the wood, for the purpose of raising the steam to its highest pitch. The blaze, mingled with the black smoke, showed plainly that the other boat was burning more than wood. The two boats soon locked, so that the hands of the boats were passing from vessel to vessel, and the wildest excitement prevailed throughout amongst both passengers and crew. At this moment the engineer of the Patriot was seen to fasten down the safety-valve, so that no steam should escape. This was, indeed, a dangerous resort. A few of the boat hands who saw what had taken place, left that end of the boat for more secure quarters.

The Patriot stopped to take in passengers, and still no steam was permitted to escape. At the starting of the boat cold water was forced into the boilers by the machinery, and, as might have been expected, one of the boilers immediately exploded. One dense fog of steam filled every part of the vessel, while shrieks, groans, and cries were heard on every hand. The saloons and cabins soon had the appearance of a hospital. By this time the boat had landed, and the Columbia, the other boat, had come alongside to render assistance to the disabled steamer. The killed and scalded (nineteen in number) were put on shore, and the Patriot, taken in tow by the Columbia, was soon again on its way.

It was now twelve o'clock at night, and instead of the passengers being asleep the majority were gambling in the saloons. Thousands of dollars change hands during a passage from Louisville or St. Louis to New Orleans on a Mississippi steamer, and many men, and even ladies, are completely ruined. "Go call my boy, steward," said Mr. Smith, as he took his cards one by one from the table. In a few

---

[3] *steamboat race was at hand:* The likely source for the subsequent account of this disastrous steamboat race was the widely reported race of 28 July 1852 between the steamboats *Henry Clay* and *Armenia* on the Hudson, which resulted in an explosion killing over sixty people; for an account of the explosion, see the New York *Daily Tribune*, 31 July 1852.

"BETTING" A NEGRO IN THE SOUTHERN STATES.

moments a fine looking, bright-eyed mulatto boy, apparently about fifteen years of age, was standing by his master's side at the table. "I will see you, and five hundred dollars better," said Smith, as his servant Jerry approached the table. "What price do you set on that boy?" asked Johnson, as he took a roll of bills from his pocket. "He will bring a thousand dollars, any day, in the New Orleans market," replied Smith. "Then you bet the whole of the boy, do you?" "Yes." "I call you, then," said Johnson, at the same time spreading his cards out upon the table. "You have beat me," said Smith, as soon as he saw the cards. Jerry, who was standing on top of the table, with the bank notes and silver dollars round his feet, was now ordered to descend from the table. "You will not forget that you belong to me," said Johnson, as the young slave was stepping from the table to a chair. "No, sir," replied the chattel. "Now go back to your bed, and be up in time tomorrow morning to brush my clothes and clean my boots, do you hear?" "Yes, sir," responded Jerry, as he wiped the tears from his eyes.

Smith took from his pocket the bill of sale and handed it to Johnson; at the same time saying, "I claim the right of redeeming that boy, Mr. Johnson. My father gave him to me when I came of age, and I promised not to part with him." "Most certainly, sir, the boy shall be yours, whenever you hand me over a cool thousand," replied Johnson. The next morning, as the passengers were assembling in the breakfast saloon and upon the guards of the vessel, and the servants were seen running about waiting upon or looking for their masters, poor Jerry was entering his new master's state-room with his boots. "Who do you belong to?" said a gentleman to an old black man, who came along leading a fine dog that he had been feeding. "When I went to sleep last night, I belonged to Governor Lucas; but I understand dat he is bin gambling all night, so I don't know who owns me dis morning." Such is the uncertainty of a slave's position. He goes to bed at night the property of the man with whom he has lived for years, and gets up in the morning the slave of some one whom he has never seen before! To behold five or six tables in a steamboat's cabin, with half-a-dozen men playing at cards, and money, pistols, bowie-knives, &c. all in confusion on the tables, is what may be seen at almost any time on the Mississippi river.

On the fourth day, while at Natchez,[4] taking in freight and passengers, Walker, who had been on shore to see some of his old customers, returned, accompanied by a tall, thin-faced man, dressed in black,

---

[4] *Natchez:* A port town in southwest Mississippi on the Mississippi River.

with a white neckcloth, which immediately proclaimed him to be a clergyman. "I want a good, trusty woman for house service," said the stranger, as they entered the cabin where Walker's slaves were kept. "Here she is, and no mistake," replied the trader. "Stand up, Currer, my gal; here's a gentleman who wishes to see if you will suit him." Althesa clung to her mother's side, as the latter rose from her seat. "She is a rare cook, a good washer, and will suit you to a T, I am sure." "If you buy me, I hope you will buy my daughter too," said the woman, in rather an excited manner. "I only want one for my own use, and would not need another," said the man in black, as he and the trader left the room. Walker and the parson went into the saloon, talked over the matter, the bill of sale was made out, the money paid over, and the clergyman left, with the understanding that the woman should be delivered to him at his house. It seemed as if poor Althesa would have wept herself to death, for the first two days after her mother had been torn from her side by the hand of the ruthless trafficker in human flesh. On the arrival of the boat at Baton Rouge, an additional number of passengers were taken on board; and, amongst them, several persons who had been attending the races. Gambling and drinking were now the order of the day. Just as the ladies and gentlemen were assembling at the supper-table, the report of a pistol was heard in the direction of the Social Hall, which caused great uneasiness to the ladies, and took the gentlemen to that part of the cabin. However, nothing serious had occurred. A man at one of the tables where they were gambling had been seen attempting to conceal a card in his sleeve, and one of the party seized his pistol and fired; but fortunately the barrel of the pistol was knocked up, just as it was about to be discharged, and the ball passed through the upper deck, instead of the man's head, as intended. Order was soon restored; all went on well the remainder of the night, and the next day, at ten o'clock, the boat arrived at New Orleans, and the passengers went to the hotels and the slaves to the market!

> "Our eyes are yet on Afric's shores,
>   Her thousand wrongs we still deplore;
>   We see the grim slave trader there;
>   We hear his fettered victim's prayer;
>   And hasten to the sufferer's aid,
>   Forgetful of *our own 'slave trade.'*
>
> "The Ocean 'Pirate's' fiend-like form
>   Shall sink beneath the vengeance-storm;
>   His heart of steel shall quake before

The battle-din and havoc roar;
The knave shall die, the Law hath said,
While it protects *our own 'slave trade.'*

"What earthly eye presumes to scan
The wily Proteus-heart[5] of man? —
What potent hand will e'er unroll
The mantled treachery of his soul! —
O where is he who hath surveyed
The horrors of *our own 'slave trade?'*

"There is an eye that wakes in light,
There is a hand of peerless might;
Which, soon or late, shall yet assail
And rend dissimulation's veil:
Which *will* unfold the masquerade
Which justifies *our own 'slave trade.' "*

---

[5] *Proteus-heart:* In Greek mythology, Proteus was a prophetic old man of the sea who could change himself into any shape he pleased.

CHAPTER III.
THE NEGRO CHASE.

We shall now return to Natchez, where we left Currer in the hands of the Methodist parson. For many years, Natchez has enjoyed a notoriety for the inhumanity and barbarity of its inhabitants, and the cruel deeds perpetrated there, which have not been equalled in any other city in the Southern States. The following advertisements, which we take from a newspaper published in the vicinity, will show how they catch their negroes who believe in the doctrine that "all men are created free."

"NEGRO DOGS. — The undersigned, having bought the entire pack of negro dogs (of the Hay and Allen stock), *he now proposes to catch runaway negroes.* His charges will be three dollars a day for hunting, and fifteen dollars for catching a runaway. He resides three and one half miles north of Livingston, near the lower Jones' Bluff Road.

"WILLIAM GAMBREL."

"Nov. 6, 1845."

"NOTICE. — The subscriber, living on Carroway Lake, on Hoe's Bayou, in Carroll parish, sixteen miles on the road leading from Bayou Mason to Lake Providence, is ready with a pack of dogs to hunt runaway negroes at any time. These dogs are well trained, and are known throughout the parish. Letters addressed to me at Providence will secure immediate attention. My terms are five dollars per day for hunting the trails, whether the negro is caught or not. Where a twelve hours' trail is shown, and the negro not taken, no charge is made. For taking a negro, twenty-five dollars, and no charge made for hunting.

"JAMES W. HALL"

"Nov. 26, 1847."

These dogs will attack a negro at their master's bidding and cling to him as the bull-dog will cling to a beast. Many are the speculations, as to whether the negro will be secured alive or dead, when these dogs once get on his track. A slave hunt took place near Natchez, a few days after Currer's arrival, which was calculated to give her no favourable opinion of the people. Two slaves had run off owing to severe punishment. The dogs were put upon their trail. The slaves went into the swamps, with the hope that the dogs when put on their scent would be unable to follow them through the water. The dogs soon took to the swamp, which lies between the highlands, which was now covered with water, waist deep: here these faithful animals, *swimming* nearly all the time, followed the zigzag course, the tortuous twistings and windings of these two fugitives, who, it was afterwards discovered, were lost; sometimes scenting the tree wherein they had found a temporary refuge from the mud and water; at other places where the deep mud had pulled off a shoe, and they had not taken time to put it on again. For two hours and a half, for four or five miles, did men and dogs wade through this bushy, dismal swamp, surrounded with grim-visaged alligators, who seemed to look on with jealous eyes at this encroachment of their hereditary domain; now losing the trail — then slowly and dubiously taking it off again, until they triumphantly threaded it out, bringing them back to the river, where it was found that the negroes had crossed their own trail, near the place of starting. In the meantime a heavy shower had taken place, putting out the trail. The negroes were now at least four miles ahead.

It is well known to hunters that it requires the keenest scent and best blood to overcome such obstacles, and yet these persevering and sagacious animals conquered every difficulty. The slaves now made a straight course for the Baton Rouge and Bayou Sara road, about four miles distant.

Feeling hungry now, after their morning walk and perhaps thirsty, too, they went about half a mile off the road, and ate a good, hearty, substantial breakfast. Negroes must eat, as well as other people, but the dogs will tell on them. Here, for a moment, the dogs are at fault, but soon unravel the mystery, and bring them back to the road again; and now what before was wonderful, becomes almost a miracle. Here, in this common highway — the thoroughfare for the whole country around — through mud and through mire, meeting waggons and teams, and different solitary wayfarers, and, what above all is most astonishing, actually running through a gang of negroes, their favourite game, who were working on the road, they pursue the track of the two negroes; they even ran for eight miles to the very edge of the plain — the slaves near them for the last mile. At first they would fain believe it some hunter chasing deer. Nearer and nearer the whimpering pack presses on; the delusion begins to dispel; all at once the truth flashes upon them like a glare of light; their hair stands on end; 'tis Tabor with his dogs. The scent becomes warmer and warmer. What was an irregular cry, now deepens into one ceaseless roar, as the relentless pack rolls on after its human prey. It puts one in mind of Actæon[1] and his dogs.

---

[1] *Actæon:* In Greek mythology, Actæon was transformed by Artemis into a stag in punishment for having viewed her bathing naked, and was subsequently killed by his own dogs.

They grow desperate and leave the road, in the vain hope of shaking them off. Vain hope, indeed! The momentary cessation only adds new zest to the chase. The cry grows louder and louder; the yelp grows short and quick, sure indication that the game is at hand. It is a perfect rush upon the part of the hunters, while the negroes call upon their weary and jaded limbs to do their best, but they falter and stagger beneath them. The breath of the hounds is almost upon their very heels, and yet they have a vain hope of escaping these sagacious animals. They can run no longer; the dogs are upon them; they hastily attempt to climb a tree, and as the last one is nearly out of reach, the catch-dog seizes him by the leg, and brings him to the ground; he sings out lustily and the dogs are called off. After this man was secured, the one in the tree was ordered to come down; this, however, he refused to do, but a gun being pointed at him, soon caused him to change his mind. On reaching the ground, the fugitive made one more bound, and the chase again commenced. But it was of no use to run and he soon yielded. While being tied, he committed an unpardonable offence: he resisted, and for that he must be made an example on their arrival home. A mob was collected together, and a Lynch court[2] was held, to determine what was best to be done with the negro who had had the impudence to raise his hand against a white man. The Lynch court decided that the negro should be burnt at the stake. A Natchez newspaper, the *Free Trader*, giving an account of it says,

"The body was taken and chained to a tree immediately on the banks of the Mississippi, on what is called Union Point. Faggots[3] were then collected and piled around him, to which he appeared quite indifferent. When the work was completed, he was asked what he had to say. He then warned all to take example of him, and asked the prayers of all around; he then called for a drink of water, which was handed to him; he drank it, and said, 'Now set fire — I am ready to go in peace!' The torches were lighted, and placed in the pile, which soon ignited. He watched unmoved the curling flame that grew, until it began to entwine itself around and feed upon his body; then he sent forth cries of agony painful to the ear, begging some one to blow his brains out; at the same time surging with almost superhuman strength, until the staple with which the chain was fastened to the tree (not being well secured) drew out, and he leaped from the burning pile. At that

---

[2] *Lynch court:* Named after Captain William Lynch (1742–1820), the term generally refers to a mob's decision to render summary punishment, usually execution by hanging.

[3] *Faggots:* Bundles of sticks or branches.

moment the sharp ringing of several rifles was heard: the body of the negro fell a corpse on the ground. He was picked up by some two or three, and again thrown into the fire, and consumed, not a vestige remaining to show that such a being ever existed."[4]

Nearly 4,000 slaves were collected from the plantations in the neighbourhood to witness this scene. Numerous speeches were made by the magistrates and ministers of religion to the large concourse of slaves, warning them, and telling them that the same fate awaited them, if they should prove rebellious to their owners. There are hundreds of negroes who run away and live in the woods. Some take refuge in the swamps, because they are less frequented by human beings. A Natchez newspaper gave the following account of the hiding-place of a slave who had been captured: —

"A runaway's den was discovered on Sunday, near the Washington Spring, in a little patch of woods where it had been for several months so artfully concealed under ground, that it was detected only by accident, though in sight of two or three houses, and near the road and fields where there has been constant daily passing. The entrance was concealed by a pile of pine straw, representing a hog-bed, which being removed, discovered a trap-door, and steps that led to a room about six feet square, comfortably ceiled with plank, containing a small fire-place, the flue of which was ingeniously conducted above ground and concealed by straw. The inmates took the alarm, and made their escape; *but Mr. Adams and his excellent dogs being put upon the trail, soon run down and secured one of them,* which proved to be a negro-fellow who had been out about a year. He stated that the other occupant was a woman, who had been a runaway a still longer time. In the den was found a quantity of meal, bacon, corn, potatoes, &c. and various cooking utensils and wearing apparel." — *Vicksburgh Sentinel,* Dec. 6th, 1838.

Currer was one of those who witnessed the execution of the slave at the stake, and it gave her no very exalted opinion of the people of the cotton growing district.

[4] *"The body. . . . ever existed":* From the Natchez, Mississippi, *Free Trader,* 16 June 1842, which Brown also quoted in the 1848 edition of his *Narrative.*

CHAPTER IV.
THE QUADROON'S HOME.

"How sweetly on the hill-side sleeps
     The sunlight with its quickening rays!
The verdant trees that crown the steeps,
     Grow greener in its quivering blaze."

About three miles from Richmond is a pleasant plain, with here and there a beautiful cottage surrounded by trees so as scarcely to be seen.[1] Among them was one far retired from the public roads, and almost hidden among the trees. It was a perfect model of rural beauty. The piazzas that surrounded it were covered with clematis and passion flower. The pride of China mixed its oriental looking foliage with the majestic magnolia, and the air was redolent with the fragrance of flowers, peeping out of every nook and nodding upon you with a most unexpected welcome. The tasteful hand of art had not learned to imitate the lavish beauty and harmonious disorder of nature, but they lived together in loving amity, and spoke in accordant tones. The gateway rose in a gothic arch, with graceful tracery in iron work, surmounted by a cross, round which fluttered and played the mountain fringe, that lightest and most fragile of vines. This cottage was hired by Horatio Green for Clotel, and the quadroon girl soon found herself in her new home.

The tenderness of Clotel's conscience, together with the care her mother had with her and the high value she placed upon virtue, required an outward marriage; though she well knew that a union with her proscribed race was unrecognised by law, and therefore the ceremony would give her no legal hold on Horatio's constancy. But her high poetic nature regarded reality rather than the semblance of things; and when he playfully asked how she could keep him if he wished to run away, she replied, "If the mutual love we have for each other, and the dictates of your own conscience do not cause you to remain my husband, and your affections fall from me, I would not, if I could, hold you by a single fetter." It was indeed a marriage sanctioned by heaven, although unrecognised on earth. There the young couple lived secluded from the world, and passed their time as happily as cir-

---

[1] *About three miles . . . to be seen:* This chapter uses most of the language of the first third of Lydia Maria Child's short story "The Quadroons" (1842). Brown draws on the story for Chapters VIII and XXIII as well. For the text of the complete story, see pp. 274–84.

cumstances would permit. It was Clotel's wish that Horatio should purchase her mother and sister, but the young man pleaded that he was unable, owing to the fact that he had not come into possession of his share of property, yet he promised that when he did, he would seek them out and purchase them. Their first-born was named Mary, and her complexion was still lighter than her mother. Indeed she was not darker than other white children. As the child grew older, it more and more resembled its mother. The iris of her large dark eye had the melting mezzotinto,[2] which remains the last vestige of African ancestry, and gives that plaintive expression, so often observed, and so appropriate to that docile and injured race. Clotel was still happier after the birth of her dear child; for Horatio, as might have been expected, was often absent day and night with his friends in the city, and the edicts of society had built up a wall of separation between the quadroon and them. Happy as Clotel was in Horatio's love, and surrounded by an outward environment of beauty, so well adapted to her poetic spirit, she felt these incidents with inexpressible pain. For herself she cared but little; for she had found a sheltered home in Horatio's heart, which the world might ridicule, but had no power to profane. But when she looked at her beloved Mary, and reflected upon the unavoidable and dangerous position which the tyranny of society had awarded her, her soul filled with anguish. The rare loveliness of the child increased daily, and was evidently ripening into most marvellous beauty. The father seemed to rejoice in it with unmingled pride; but in the deep tenderness of the mother's eye, there was an indwelling sadness that spoke of anxious thoughts and fearful foreboding. Clotel now urged Horatio to remove to France or England, where both her and her child would be free, and where colour was not a crime. This request excited but little opposition, and was so attractive to his imagination, that he might have overcome all intervening obstacles, had not "a change come over the spirit of his dreams."[3] He still loved Clotel; but he was now becoming engaged in political and other affairs which kept him oftener and longer from the young mother; and ambition to become a statesman was slowly gaining the ascendancy over him.

Among those on whom Horatio's political success most depended was a very popular and wealthy man, who had an only daughter. His visits to the house were at first purely of a political nature; but the

---

[2] *mezzotinto:* Literally, a half tint between whiteness and blackness, though the emphasis of the description is on blackness.

[3] *"a change . . . dreams":* From Lord Byron (1788–1824), "The Dream" (1816). Brown changes the phrasing from the first to third person.

young lady was pleasing, and he fancied he discovered in her a sort of timid preference for himself. This excited his vanity, and awakened thoughts of the great worldly advantages connected with a union. Reminiscences of his first love kept these vague ideas in check for several months; for with it was associated the idea of restraint. Moreover, Gertrude, though inferior in beauty, was yet a pretty contrast to her rival. Her light hair fell in silken ringlets down her shoulders, her blue eyes were gentle though inexpressive, and her healthy cheeks were like opening rosebuds. He had already become accustomed to the dangerous experiment of resisting his own inward convictions; and this new impulse to ambition, combined with the strong temptation of variety in love, met the ardent young man weakened in moral principle, and unfettered by laws of the land. The change wrought upon him was soon noticed by Clotel.

CHAPTER V.
THE SLAVE MARKET.

> "What! mothers from their children riven!
> What! God's own image bought and sold!
> Americans to market driven,
> And barter'd as the brute for gold."[1] — *Whittier.*

Not far from Canal-street, in the city of New Orleans, stands a large two story flat building surrounded by a stone wall twelve feet high, the top of which is covered with bits of glass, and so constructed as to prevent even the possibility of any one's passing over it without sustaining great injury. Many of the rooms resemble cells in a prison. In a small room near the "office" are to be seen any number of iron collars, hobbles, handcuffs, thumbscrews, cowhides, whip, chains, gags, and yokes. A back yard inclosed by a high wall looks something like the playground attached to one of our large New England schools, and in which are rows of benches and swings. Attached to the back premises is a good-sized kitchen, where two old negresses are at work, stewing, boiling, and baking, and occasionally wiping the sweat from their furrowed and swarthy brows.

The slave-trader Walker, on his arrival in New Orleans, took up his quarters at this slave pen with his gang of human cattle; and the morning after, at ten o'clock, they were exhibited for sale. There, first of all, was the beautiful Althesa, whose pale countenance and dejected look told how many sad hours she had passed since parting with her mother at Natchez. There was a poor woman who had been separated from her husband and five children. Another woman, whose looks and manner were expressive of deep anguish, sat by her side. There, too, was "Uncle Geemes," with his whiskers off, his face shaved clean, and the grey hair plucked out, and ready to be sold for ten years younger than he was. Toby was also there, with his face shaved and greased, ready for inspection. The examination commenced, and was carried on in a manner calculated to shock the feelings of any one not devoid of the milk of human kindness. "What are you wiping your eyes for?" inquired a fat, red-faced man, with a white hat set on one side of his head, and a cigar in his mouth, of a woman who sat on one of the stools. "I s'pose I have been crying." "Why do you cry?" "Because I have left my man behind." "Oh, if I buy you I will furnish

---

[1] *"What! . . . for gold":* From John Greenleaf Whittier, "Expostulation" (1834).

you with a better man than you left. I have lots of young bucks on my farm." "I don't want, and will never have, any other man," replied the woman. "What's your name?" asked a man in a straw hat of a tall negro man, who stood with his arms folded across his breast, and leaning against the wall. "My name is Aaron, sir." "How old are you?" "Twenty-five." "Where were you raised?" "In old Virginny, sir." "How many men have owned you?" "Four." "Do you enjoy good health?" "Yes, sir." "How long did you live with your first owner?" "Twenty years." "Did you ever run away?" "No, sir." "Did you ever strike your master?" "No, sir." "Were you ever whipped much?" "No, sir, I s'pose I did not deserve it." "How long did you live with your second master?" "Ten years, sir." "Have you a good appetite?" "Yes, sir." "Can you eat your allowance?" "Yes, sir, when I can get it." "What were you employed at in Virginia?" "I worked in de terbacar feel." "In a tobacco field?" "Yes, sir." "How old did you say you were?" "I will be twenty-five if I live to see next sweet potater-digging time." "I am a cotton planter, and if I buy you, you will have to work in the cotton field. My men pick one hundred and fifty pounds a day, and the women one hundred and forty, and those who fail to pick their task receive five stripes from the cat[2] for each pound that is wanting. Now, do you think you could keep up with the rest of the hands?" "I don't know, sir, I 'spec I'd have to." "How long did you live with your third master?" "Three years, sir." "Why, this makes you thirty-three, I thought you told me you was only twenty-five?" Aaron now looked first at the planter, then at the trader, and seemed perfectly bewildered. He had forgotten the lesson given him by Pompey as to his age, and the planter's circuitous talk (doubtless to find out the slave's real age) had the negro off his guard. "I must see your back, so as to know how much you have been whipped, before I think of buying," said the planter. Pompey, who had been standing by during the examination, thought that his services were now required, and stepping forward with a degree of officiousness, said to Aaron, "Don't you hear de gentman tell you he want to zamon your limbs. Come, unharness yeself, old boy, an don't be standing dar." Aaron was soon examined and pronounced "sound;" yet the conflicting statement about the age was not satisfactory.

Fortunate for Althesa she was spared the pain of undergoing such an examination. Mr. Crawford, a teller in one of the banks, had just

[2] *cat:* Short for cat-o'-nine-tails, a whip which had nine cords fastened to a handle and was said to cut and scratch like a cat.

been married, and wanted a maid-servant for his wife; and passing through the market in the early part of the day, was pleased with the young slave's appearance and purchased her, and in his dwelling the quadroon found a much better home than often falls to the lot of a slave sold in the New Orleans market. The heart-rending and cruel traffic in slaves which has been so often described, is not confined to any particular class of persons. No one forfeits his or her character or standing in society, by buying or selling slaves; or even raising slaves for the market. The precise number of slaves carried from the slave-raising to the slave-consuming states, we have no means of knowing. But it must be very great, as more than forty thousand were sold and taken out of the state of Virginia in one year. Known to God only is the amount of human agony and suffering which sends its cry from the slave markets and negro pens, unheard and unheeded by man, up to his ear; mothers weeping for their children, breaking the night-silence with the shrieks of their breaking hearts. From some you will hear the burst of bitter lamentation, while from others the loud hysteric laugh, denoting still deeper agony. Most of them leave the market for cotton or rice plantations,

> "Where the slave-whip ceaseless swings,
> Where the noisome insect stings,
> Where the fever demon strews
> Poison with the falling dews,
> Where the sickly sunbeams glare
> Through the hot and misty air."[3]

---

[3] *"Where . . . misty air":* From John Greenleaf Whittier, "The Farewell of a Virginia Slave Mother to Her Daughter Sold into Southern Bondage" (1838).

CHAPTER VI.
THE RELIGIOUS TEACHER.

"What! preach and enslave men?
Give thanks—and rob thy own afflicted poor?
Talk of thy glorious liberty, and then
Bolt hard the captive's door?"[1] — *Whittier.*

The Rev. John Peck[2] was a native of the state of Connecticut, where he was educated for the ministry, in the Methodist persuasion. His father was a strict follower of John Wesley,[3] and spared no pains in his son's education, with the hope that he would one day be as renowned as the great leader of his sect. John had scarcely finished his education at New Haven, when he was invited by an uncle, then on a visit to his father, to spend a few months at Natchez in the state of Mississippi. Young Peck accepted his uncle's invitation, and accompanied him to the South. Few young men, and especially clergymen, going fresh from a college to the South, but are looked upon as geniuses in a small way, and who are not invited to all the parties in the neighbourhood. Mr. Peck was not an exception to this rule. The society into which he was thrown on his arrival at Natchez was too brilliant for him not to be captivated by it; and, as might have been expected, he succeeded in captivating a plantation with seventy slaves, if not the heart of the lady to whom it belonged. Added to this, he became a popular preacher, had a large congregation with a snug salary. Like other planters, Mr. Peck confided the care of his farm to Ned Huckelby, an overseer of high reputation in his way. The Poplar Farm, as it was called, was situated in a beautiful valley nine miles from Natchez, and near the river Mississippi. The once unshorn face of nature had given way, and now the farm blossomed with a splendid harvest, the neat cottage stood in a grove where Lombardy poplars lift their tufted tops almost to prop the skies; the willow, locust, and horse-chestnut spread their branches, and flowers never cease to blossom. This was the parson's country house, where the family spent only two months during the year.

The town residence was a fine villa, seated upon the brow of a hill at the edge of the city. It was in the kitchen of this house that Currer

---

[1] "What! . . . captive's door?": From Whittier, "Clerical Oppressors" (1838).

[2] *Rev. John Peck:* The character was inspired by the hypocritical Reverend Peck of Rochester, whom Brown described in "The New Liberty Party"; see pp. 270–71.

[3] *John Wesley:* The founder of Methodism, the English Protestant evangelical John Wesley (1703–1791) emphasized a methodical devotion to religious duties and practices; he saw good works rather than divine election as the key to salvation.

found her new home. Mr. Peck was, every inch of him, a democrat, and early resolved that his "people," as he called his slaves, should be well fed and not overworked, and therefore laid down the law and gospel to the overseer as well as the slaves.

"It is my wish," said he to Mr. Carlton, an old school-fellow, who was spending a few days with him, "it is my wish that a new system be adopted on the plantations in this estate. I believe that the sons of Ham[4] should have the gospel, and I intend that my negroes shall. The gospel is calculated to make mankind better, and none should be without it." "What say you," replied Carlton, "about the right of man to his liberty?" "Now, Carlton, you have begun again to harp about man's rights; I really wish you could see this matter as I do. I have searched in vain for any authority for man's natural rights; if he had any, they existed before the fall. That is, Adam and Eve may have had some rights which God gave them, and which modern philosophy, in its pretended reverence for the name of God, prefers to call natural rights. I can imagine they had the right to eat of the fruit of the trees of the garden; they were restricted even in this by the prohibition of one. As far as I know without positive assertion, their liberty of action was confined to the garden. These were not 'inalienable rights,' however, for they forfeited both them and life with the first act of disobedience. Had they, after this, any rights? We cannot imagine them; they were condemned beings; they could have no rights, but by Christ's gift as king. These are the only rights man can have as an independent isolated being, if we choose to consider him in this impossible position, in which so many theorists have placed him. If he had no rights, he could suffer no wrongs. Rights and wrongs are therefore necessarily the creatures of society, such as man would establish himself in his gregarious state. They are, in this state, both artificial and voluntary. Though man has no rights, as thus considered, undoubtedly he has the power, by such arbitrary rules of right and wrong as his necessity enforces." "I regret I cannot see eye to eye with you," said Carlton. "I am a disciple of Rousseau,[5]

---

[4] *sons of Ham:* In Genesis, Noah cursed his son Ham for viewing him when he lay naked in a drunken stupor; see Genesis 9.20–27. Oral traditions collected in the Talmud claimed that the curse resulted in Ham having black descendants; this interpretation was echoed by racists in the eighteenth and nineteenth centuries.

[5] *Rousseau:* The influential French philosopher, writer, and social reformer Jean Jacques Rousseau (1712–1778) was best known in America for his political writings, especially *Origin of Inequality Among Men* (1753) and *Social Contract* (1761). In these works he castigated established governmental and religious institutions as sources of evil and called for social amelioration through a contractual surrendering of individual wills to a General Will.

and have for years made the rights of man my study; and I must confess to you that I can see no difference between white men and black men as it regards liberty." "Now, my dear Carlton, would you really have the negroes enjoy the same rights with ourselves?" "I would, most certainly. Look at our great Declaration of Independence; look even at the constitution of our own Connecticut, and see what is said in these about liberty." "I regard all this talk about rights as mere humbug. The Bible is older than the Declaration of Independence, and there I take my stand. The Bible furnishes to us the armour of proof, weapons of heavenly temper and mould, whereby we can maintain our ground against all attacks. But this is true only when we obey its directions, as well as employ its sanctions. Our rights are there established, but it is always in connection with our duties. If we neglect the one we cannot make good the other. Our domestic institutions can be maintained against the world, if we but allow Christianity to throw its broad shield over them. But if we so act as to array the Bible against our social economy, they must fall. Nothing ever yet stood long against Christianity. Those who say that religious instruction is inconsistent with our peculiar civil polity, are the worst enemies of that polity. They would drive religious men from its defence. Sooner or later, if these views prevail, they will separate the religious portion of our community from the rest, and thus divided we shall become an easy prey. Why, is it not better that Christian men should hold slaves than unbelievers? We know how to value the bread of life, and will not keep it from our slaves."

"Well, every one to his own way of thinking," said Carlton, as he changed his position. "I confess," added he, "that I am no great admirer of either the Bible or slavery. My heart is my guide: my conscience is my Bible. I wish for nothing further to satisfy me of my duty to man. If I act rightly to mankind, I shall fear nothing." Carlton had drunk too deeply of the bitter waters of infidelity, and had spent too many hours over the writings of Rousseau, Voltaire, and Thomas Paine,[6] to place that appreciation upon the Bible and its teachings that it demands. During this conversation there was another person in the room, seated by the window, who, although at work upon a fine piece

---

[6] *Voltaire, and Thomas Paine:* Grouped with Rousseau, the French philosopher Françoise Marie Arouet Voltaire (1694–1778), best known as the author of *Candide* (1759), and the Anglo-American political writer Thomas Paine (1737–1809), best known as the author of *Common Sense* (1776), are presented here as troubling exemplars of Enlightenment rationalism. Although they wrote powerfully in support of political freedom, they ultimately rejected Christianity as authoritarian and unreasonable.

of lace, paid every attention to what was said. This was Georgiana, the only daughter of the parson. She had just returned from Connecticut, where she had finished her education. She had had the opportunity of contrasting the spirit of Christianity and liberty in New England with that of slavery in her native state, and had learned to feel deeply for the injured negro. Georgiana was in her nineteenth year, and had been much benefited by a residence of five years at the North. Her form was tall and graceful; her features regular and well defined; and her complexion was illuminated by the freshness of youth, beauty, and health. The daughter differed from both the father and his visitor upon the subject which they had been discussing, and as soon as an opportunity offered, she gave it as her opinion, that the Bible was both the bulwark of Christianity and of liberty. With a smile she said, "Of course, papa will overlook my differing from him, for although I am a native of the South, I am by education and sympathy a Northerner." Mr. Peck laughed and appeared pleased, rather than otherwise, at the manner in which his daughter had expressed herself.

From this Georgiana took courage and said, "We must try the character of slavery, and our duty in regard to it, as we should try any other question of character and duty. To judge justly of the character of anything, we must know what it does. That which is good does good, and that which is evil does evil. And as to duty, God's designs indicate his claims. That which accomplishes the manifest design of God is right; that which counteracts it, wrong. Whatever, in its proper tendency and general effect, produces, secures, or extends human welfare, is according to the will of God, and is good; and our duty is to favour and promote, according to our power, that which God favours and promotes by the general law of his providence. On the other hand, whatever in its proper tendency and general effect destroys, abridges, or renders insecure, human welfare, is opposed to God's will, and is evil. And as whatever accords with the will of God, in any manifestation of it should be done and persisted in, so whatever opposes that will should not be done, and if done, should be abandoned. Can that then be right, be well doing — can that obey God's behest, which makes a man a slave? which dooms him and all his posterity, in limitless generations, to bondage, to unrequited toil through life? 'Thou shalt love thy neighbour as thyself.'[7] This single passage of Scripture should cause us to have respect to the rights of the slave. True Christian love is of an enlarged, disinterested nature. It loves all who love

---

[7] 'Thou shalt love . . . as thyself.': Leviticus 19.18.

the Lord Jesus Christ in sincerity, without regard to color or condition." "Georgiana, my dear, you are an abolitionist; your talk is fanaticism," said Mr. Peck in rather a sharp tone; but the subdued look of the girl, and the presence of Carlton, caused the father to soften his language. Mr. Peck having lost his wife by consumption, and Georgiana being his only child, he loved her too dearly to say more, even if he felt displeased. A silence followed this exhortation from the young Christian. But her remarks had done a noble work. The father's heart was touched; and the sceptic, for the first time, was viewing Christianity in its true light.

"I think I must go out to your farm," said Carlton, as if to break the silence. "I shall be pleased to have you go," returned Mr. Peck. "I am sorry I can't go myself, but Huckelby will show you every attention; and I feel confident that when you return to Connecticut, you will do me the justice to say, that I am one who looks after my people, in a moral, social, and religious point of view." "Well, what do you say to my spending next Sunday there?" "Why, I think that a good move; you will then meet with Snyder, our missionary." "Oh, you have missionaries in these parts, have you?" "Yes," replied Mr. Peck; "Snyder is from New York, and is our missionary to the poor, and preaches to our 'people' on Sunday; you will no doubt like him; he is a capital fellow." "Then I shall go," said Carlton, "but only wish I had company." This last remark was intended for Miss Peck, for whom he had the highest admiration.

It was on a warm Sunday morning, in the month of May, that Miles Carlton found himself seated beneath a fine old apple tree, whose thick leaves entirely shaded the ground for some distance round. Under similar trees and near by, were gathered together all the "people" belonging to the plantation. Hontz Snyder was a man of about forty years of age, exceedingly low in stature, but of a large frame. He had been brought up in the Mohawk Valley, in the state of New York, and claimed relationship with the oldest Dutch families in that vicinity. He had once been a sailor, and had all the roughness of character that a sea-faring man might expect to possess; together with the half-Yankee, half-German peculiarities of the people of the Mohawk Valley. It was nearly eleven o'clock when a one-horse waggon drove up in haste, and the low squatty preacher got out and took his place at the foot of one of the trees, where a sort of rough board table was placed, and took his books from his pocket and commenced.

"As it is rather late," said he, "we will leave the singing and praying for the last, and take our text, and commence immediately.[8] I shall base my remarks on the following passage of Scripture, and hope to have that attention which is due to the cause of God: — 'All things whatsoever ye would that men should do unto you, do ye even so unto them;'[9] that is, do by all mankind just as you would desire they should do by you, if you were in their place and they in yours.

"Now, to suit this rule to your particular circumstances, suppose you were masters and mistresses, and had servants under you, would you not desire that your servants should do their business faithfully and honestly, as well when your back was turned as while you were looking over them? Would you not expect that they should take notice of what you said to them? that they should behave themselves with respect towards you and yours, and be as careful of every thing belonging to you as you would be yourselves? You are servants: do, therefore, as you would wish to be done by, and you will be both good servants to your masters and good servants to God, who requires this of you, and will reward you well for it, if you do it for the sake of conscience, in obedience to his commands.

"You are not to be eye-servants. Now, eye-servants are such as will work hard, and seem mighty diligent, while they think anybody is taking notice of them; but, when their masters' and mistresses' backs are turned they are idle, and neglect their business. I am afraid there are a great many such eye-servants among you, and that you do not consider how great a sin it is to be so, and how severely God will punish you for it. You may easily deceive your owners, and make them have an opinion of you that you do not deserve, and get the praise of men by it; but remember that you cannot deceive Almighty God, who sees your wickedness and deceit, and will punish you accordingly. For the rule is, that you must obey your masters in all things, and do the work they set you about with fear and trembling, in singleness of heart as unto Christ; not with eye-service, as men-pleasers, but as the servants of Christ, doing the will of God from the heart; with good-will doing service as to the Lord, and not as to men.

"*Take care that you do not fret or murmur, grumble or repine at your condition; for this will not only make your life uneasy, but will*

---

[8] "*. . . . and commence immediately.*": For Snyder's sermon, Brown drew on Thomas Bacon's *Sermons Addressed to Masters and Servants* (1813); see pp. 258–62.
[9] '*All . . . unto them*': Matthew 7.12.

greatly offend Almighty God. Consider that this is not yourselves, it is not the people that you belong to, it is not the men who have brought you to it, but *it is the will of God who hath by providence made you servants, because, no doubt, he knew that condition would be best for you in this world, and help you the better towards heaven, if you would but do your duty in it.* So that any discontent at your not being free, or rich, or great, as you see some others, is quarrelling with your heavenly Master, and finding fault with God himself, who hath made you what you are, and hath promised you as large a share in the kingdom of heaven as the greatest man alive, if you will but behave yourself aright, and do the business he hath set you about in this world honestly and cheerfully. Riches and power have proved the ruin of many an unhappy soul, by drawing away the heart and affections from God, and fixing them on mean and sinful enjoyments; so that, when God, who knows our hearts better than we know them ourselves, sees that they would be hurtful to us, and therefore keeps them from us, it is the greatest mercy and kindness he could show us.

"You may perhaps fancy that, if you had riches and freedom, you could do your duty to God and man with greater pleasure than you can now. But pray consider that, if you can but save your souls through the mercy of God, you will have spent your time to the best of purposes in this world; and he that at last can get to heaven has performed a noble journey, let the road be ever so rugged and difficult. Besides, you really have a great advantage over most white people, who have not only the care of their daily labour upon their hands, but the care of looking forward and providing necessaries for to-morrow and next day, and of clothing and bringing up their children, and of getting food and raiment[10] for as many of you as belong to their families, which often puts them to great difficulties, and distracts their minds so as to break their rest, and take off their thoughts from the affairs of another world. Whereas you are quite eased from all these cares, and have nothing but your daily labour to look after, and, when that is done, take your needful rest. Neither is it necessary for you to think of laying up anything against old age, as white people are obliged to do; for the laws of the country have provided that you shall not be turned off when you are past labour, but shall be maintained, while you live, by those you belong to, whether you are able to work or not.

[10] *raiment:* Clothing

"There is only one circumstance which may appear grievous, that I shall now take notice of, and that is correction.

"Now, when correction is given you, you either deserve it, or you do not deserve it. But whether you really deserve it or not, it is your duty, and Almighty God requires that you bear it patiently. You may perhaps think that this is hard doctrine; but, if you consider it right, you must needs thinks otherwise of it. Suppose, then, that you deserve correction, you cannot but say that it is just and right you should meet with it. Suppose you do not, or at least you do not deserve so much, or so severe a correction, for the fault you have committed, you perhaps have escaped a great many more and are at last paid for all. Or suppose you are quite innocent of what is laid to your charge, and suffer wrongfully in that particular thing, is it not possible you may have done some other bad thing which was never discovered, and that Almighty God who saw you doing it would not let you escape without punishment one time or another? And ought you not, in such a case, to give glory to him, and be thankful that he would rather punish you in this life for your wickedness than destroy your souls for it in the next life? But suppose even this was not the case (a case hardly to be imagined), and that you have by no means, known or unknown, deserved the correction you suffered, there is this great comfort in it, that, if you bear it patiently, and leave your cause in the hands of God, he will reward you for it in heaven, and the punishment you suffer unjustly here shall turn to your exceeding great glory hereafter.

"Lastly, you should serve your masters faithfully, because of their goodness to you. See to what trouble they have been on your account. Your fathers were poor ignorant and barbarous creatures in Africa, and the whites fitted out ships at great trouble and expense and brought you from that benighted land to Christian America, where you can sit under your own vine and fig tree and no one molest or make you afraid. Oh, my dear black brothers and sisters, you are indeed a fortunate and a blessed people. Your masters have many troubles that you know nothing about. If the banks break, your masters are sure to lose something. If the crops turn out poor, they lose by it. If one of you die, your master loses what he paid for you, while you lose nothing. Now let me exhort you once more to be faithful."

Often during the delivery of the sermon did Snyder cast an anxious look in the direction where Carlton was seated; no doubt to see if he had found favour with the stranger. Huckelby, the overseer, was also there, seated near Carlton. With all Snyder's gesticulations, sonorous voice, and occasionally bringing his fist down upon the table with the force of a sledge hammer, he could not succeed in keeping the negroes all interested: four or five were fast asleep, leaning against the trees; as many more were nodding, while not a few were stealthily cracking and eating hazelnuts. "Uncle Simon, you may strike up a hymn," said the preacher as he closed his Bible. A moment more, and the whole company (Carlton excepted) had joined in the well known hymn, commencing with

> "When I can read my title clear
> To mansions in the sky."[11]

After the singing, Sandy closed with prayer, and the following questions and answers read, and the meeting was brought to a close.

"Q. What command has God given to servants concerning obedience to their masters? — A. 'Servants, obey in all things your masters according to the flesh, not with eye-service as men-pleasers, but in singleness of heart, fearing God.'

"Q. What does God mean by masters according to the flesh? — A. 'Masters in this world.'

"Q. What are servants to count their masters worthy of? — A. 'All honour.'

"Q. How are they to do the service of their masters? — A. '*With good will,* doing service as unto the Lord, and not unto men.'

"Q. How are they to try to please their masters? — A. 'Please him well in all things, not answering again.'

"Q. Is a servant who is an eye-servant to his earthly master an eye-servant to his heavenly master? — A. 'Yes.'

"Q. Is it right in a servant, when commanded to do any thing, to be sullen and slow, and answer his master again? — A. 'No.'

"Q. If the servant professes to be a Christian, ought he not to be *as a Christian servant,* an example to all other servants of love and obedience to his master? — A. 'Yes.'

"Q. And, should his master be a Christian also, ought he not on that account specially to love and obey him? — A. 'Yes.'

"Q. But suppose the master is hard to please, and threatens and punishes more than he ought, what is the servant to do? — A. 'Do his best to please him.'

"Q. When the servant suffers *wrongfully* at the hands of his master, and, to please God, takes it patiently, will God reward him for it? — A. 'Yes.'

---

[11] "*When . . . the sky*": From Isaac Watts (1674–1748), *Hymns and Spiritual Songs* (1707).

"Q. Is it right for the servant to *run away*, or is it right to *harbour* a runaway? — A. 'No.'

"Q. If a servant runs away, what should be done with him? — A. 'He should be caught and brought back.'

"Q. When he is brought back, what should be done with him? — A. 'Whip him well.'

"Q. Why may not the whites be slaves as well as the blacks? — A. 'Because the Lord intended the negroes for slaves.'

"Q. Are they better calculated for servants than the whites? — A. 'Yes, their hands are large, the skin thick and tough, and they can stand the sun better than the whites.'

"Q. Why should servants not complain when they are whipped? — A. 'Because the Lord has commanded that they should be whipped.'

"Q. Where has He commanded it? — A. 'He says, He that knoweth his master's will, and doeth it not, shall be beaten with many stripes.'

"Q. Then is the master to blame for whipping his servant? — A. 'Oh, no! he is only doing his duty as a Christian.'"

Snyder left the ground in company with Carlton and Huckelby, and the three dined together in the overseer's dwelling.

"Well," said Joe, after the three white men were out of hearing, "Marser Snyder bin try hesef to-day." "Yes," replied Ned; "he want to show de strange gentman how good he can preach." "Dat's a new sermon he gib us to-day," said Sandy. "Dees white fokes is de very dibble," said Dick; "and all dey whole study is to try to fool de black people." "Didn't you like de sermon?" asked Uncle Simon. "No," answered four or five voices. "He rared and pitched enough," continued Uncle Simon. Now Uncle Simon was himself a preacher, or at least he thought so, and was rather pleased than otherwise, when he heard others spoken of in a disparaging manner. "Uncle Simon can beat dat sermon all to pieces," said Ned, as he was filling his mouth with hazelnuts. "I got no notion of dees white fokes, no how," returned Aunt Dafney. "Dey all de time tellin' dat de Lord made us for to work for dem, and I don't believe a word of it." "Marser Peck give dat sermon to Snyder, I know," said Uncle Simon. "He jest de one for dat," replied Sandy. "I think de people dat made de Bible was great fools," said Ned. "Why?" Uncle Simon. "'Cause dey made such a great big book and put nuttin' in it, but servants obey yer masters." "Oh," replied Uncle Simon, "thars more in de Bible den dat, only Snyder never reads any other part to us; I use to hear it read in Maryland, and thar was more den what Snyder lets us hear." In the overseer's house there was another scene going on, and far indifferent from what we have here described.

CHAPTER VII.
THE POOR WHITES, SOUTH.

"No seeming of logic can ever convince the American people, that thou-sands of our slave-holding brethren are not excellent, humane, and even Christian men, fearing God, and keeping His commandments."
— *Rev. Dr. Joel Parker.*[1]

"You like these parts better than New York," said Carlton to Sny-der, as they were sitting down to dinner in the overseer's dwelling. "I can't say that I do," was the reply; "I came here ten years ago as mis-sionary, and Mr. Peck wanted me to stay, and I have remained. I travel among the poor whites during the week, and preach for the niggers on Sunday." "Are there many poor whites in this district?" "Not here, but about thirty miles from here, in the Sand Hill district; they are as ignorant as horses. Why it was no longer than last week I was up there, and really you would not believe it, that people were so poor off. In New England, and, I may say, in all the free states, they have free schools, and everybody gets educated.[2] Not so here. In Connecti-cut there is only one out of every five hundred above twenty-one years that can neither read nor write. Here there is one out of every eight that can neither read nor write. There is not a single newspaper taken in five of the counties in this state. Last week I was at Sand Hill for the first time, and I called at a farmhouse. The man was out. It was a low log-hut, and yet it was the best house in that locality. The woman and nine children were there, and the geese, ducks, chickens, pigs, and chil-dren were all running about the floor. The woman seemed scared at me when I entered the house. I inquired if I could get a little dinner, and my horse fed. She said, yes, if I would only be good enough to feed him myself, as her 'gal,' as she called her daughter, would be afraid of the horse. When I returned into the house again from the stable, she kept her eyes upon me all the time. At last she said, 'I s'pose you aint never bin in these parts afore?' 'No,' said I. 'Is you gwine to stay here long?' 'Not very long,' I replied. 'On business, I s'pose.' 'Yes,' said I, 'I am hunting up the lost sheep of the house of Israel.' 'Oh,' exclaimed she,

---

[1] *Rev. Dr. Joel Parker:* A Presbyterian clergyman in Philadelphia, Joel Parker (1799–1873) was criticized in Stowe's *Uncle Tom's Cabin* for his equivocating sermons on slavery. His sermons were regularly printed in the New York *Observer.*

[2] *everybody gets educated:* Though public schooling was more readily available in the Northeast than in the South, Snyder exaggerates the extent of that availability: Many poor white children worked by the age of twelve, and most free black children were excluded from public schools or put in separate, poorly funded schools.

'hunting for lost sheep is you? Well, you have a hard time to find 'em here. My husband lost an old ram last week, and he aint found him yet, and he's hunted every day.' 'I am not looking for four-legged sheep,' said I, 'I am hunting for sinners.' 'Ah;' she said, 'then you are a preacher.' 'Yes,' said I. 'You are the first of that sort that's bin in these diggins for many a day.' Turning to her eldest daughter, she said in an excited tone, 'Clar out the pigs and ducks, and sweep up the floor; this is a preacher.' And it was some time before any of the children would come near me; one remained under the bed (which, by the by, was in the same room), all the while I was there. 'Well,' continued the woman, 'I was a tellin' my man only yesterday that I would like once more to go to meetin' before I died, and he said as he should like to do the same. But as you have come, it will save us the trouble of going out of the district.' " "Then you found some of the lost sheep," said Carlton. "Yes," replied Snyder, "I did not find anything else up there. The state makes no provision for educating the poor: they are unable to do it themselves, and they grow up in a state of ignorance and degradation. The men hunt and the women have to go in the fields and labour." "What is the cause of it?" inquired Carlton. "Slavery," answered Snyder, "slavery, — and nothing else. Look at the city of Boston; it pays more taxes for the support of the government than this entire state. The people of Boston do more business than the whole population of Mississippi put together. I was told some very amusing things while at Sand Hill. A farmer there told me a story about an old woman, who was very pious herself. She had a husband and three sons, who were sad characters, and she had often prayed for their conversion but to no effect. At last, one day while working in the cornfield, one of her sons was bitten by a rattlesnake. He had scarce reached home before he felt the poison, and in his agony called loudly on his Maker.

"The pious old woman, when she heard this, forgetful of her son's misery, and everything else but the glorious hope of his repentance, fell on her knees, and prayed as follows, — 'Oh! Lord, I thank thee, that thou hast at last opened Jimmy's eyes to the error of his ways; and I pray that, in thy Divine mercy, thou wilt send a rattlesnake to bite the old man, and another to bite Tom, and another to bite Harry, for I am certain that nothing but a rattle-snake, or something of the kind, will ever turn them from their sinful ways, they are so hard-headed.' When returning home, and before I got out of the Sand Hill district, I saw a funeral, and thought I would fasten my horse to a post and attend. The coffin was carried in a common horse cart, and followed by fifteen or twenty persons very shabbily dressed, and attended by a man whom I took to be the religious man of the place. After the coffin had been placed near the grave, he spoke as follows, —

'Friends and neighbours! you have congregated to see this lump of mortality put into a hole in the ground. You all know the deceased — a worthless, drunken, good-for-nothing vagabond. He lived in disgrace and infamy, and died in wretchedness. You all despised him — you all know his brother Joe, who lives on the hill? He's not a bit better though he has scrap'd together a little property by cheating his neighbours. His end will be like that of this loathsome creature, whom you will please put into the hole as soon as possible. I wont ask you to drop a tear, but brother Bohow will please raise a hymn while we fill up the grave.' "

"I am rather surprised to hear that any portion of the whites in this state are in so low a condition." "Yet it is true," returned Snyder.

"These are very onpleasant facts to be related to ye, Mr. Carlton," said Huckelby; "but I can bear witness to what Mr. Snyder has told ye." Huckelby was from Maryland, where many of the poor whites are in as sad a condition as the Sand Hillers of Mississippi. He was a tall man, of iron constitution, and could neither read nor write, but was considered one of the best overseers in the country. When about to break a slave in, to do a heavy task, he would make him work by his side all day; and if the new hand kept up with him, he was set down as an able bodied man. Huckelby had neither moral, religious, or political principles, and often boasted that conscience was a matter that never "cost" him a thought. "Mr. Snyder aint told ye half about the folks in these parts;" continued he; "we who comes from more enlightened parts don't know how to put up with 'em down here. I find the people here knows mighty little indeed; in fact, I may say they are univarsaly onedicated. I goes out among none on 'em, 'cause they aint such as I have been used to 'sociate with. When I gits a little richer, so that I can stop work, I tend to go back to Maryland, and spend the rest of my days." "I wonder the negroes don't attempt to get their freedom by physical force." "It aint no use for 'em to try that, for if they do, we puts 'em through by daylight," replied Huckelby. "There are some desperate fellows among the slaves," said Snyder. "Indeed," remarked Carlton. "Oh, yes," replied the preacher. "A case has just taken place near here, where a neighbour of ours, Mr. J. Higgerson, attempted to correct a negro man in his employ, who resisted, drew a knife, and stabbed him (Mr. H.) in several places. Mr. J. C. Hobbs (a Tennessean) ran to his assistance. Mr. Hobbs stooped to pick up a

stick to strike the negro, and, while in that position, the negro rushed upon him, and caused his immediate death. The negro then fled to the woods, but was pursued with dogs, and soon overtaken. He had stopped in a swamp to fight the dogs, when the party who were pursuing him came upon him, and commanded him to give up, which he refused to do. He then made several efforts to stab them. Mr. Roberson, one of the party, gave him several blows on the head with a rifle gun; but this, instead of subduing, only increased his desperate revenge. Mr. R. then discharged his gun at the negro, and missing him, the ball struck Mr. Boon in the face, and felled him to the ground. The negro, seeing Mr. Boon prostrated, attempted to rush up and stab him, but was prevented by the timely interference of some one of the party. He was then shot three times with a revolving pistol, and once with a rifle, and after having his throat cut, he still kept the knife firmly grasped in his hand, and tried to cut their legs when they approached to put an end to his life. This chastisement was given because the negro grumbled, and found fault with his master for flogging his wife."
"Well, this is a bad state of affairs indeed, and especially the condition of the poor whites," said Carlton. "You see," replied Snyder, "no white man is respectable in these slave states who works for a living. No community can be prosperous, where honest labour is not honoured. No society can be rightly constituted, where the intellect is not fed. Whatever institution reflects discredit on industry, whatever institution forbids the general culture of the understanding, is palpably hostile to individual rights, and to social well-being. Slavery is the incubus[3] that hangs over the Southern States." "Yes," interrupted Huckelby; "them's just my sentiments now, and no mistake. I think that, for the honour of our country, this slavery business should stop. I don't own any, no how, and I would not be an overseer if I wern't paid for it."

[3] *incubus:* Evil spirit.

CHAPTER VIII.
THE SEPARATION.

"In many ways does the full heart reveal
The presence of the love it would conceal;
But in far more the estranged heart lets know
The absence of the love, which yet it fain would show."[1]

At length the news of the approaching marriage of Horatio met the ear of Clotel. Her head grew dizzy, and her heart fainted within her; but, with a strong effort at composure, she inquired all the particulars, and her pure mind at once took its resolution. Horatio came that evening, and though she would fain have met him as usual, her heart was too full not to throw a deep sadness over her looks and tones. She had never complained of his decreasing tenderness, or of her own lonely hours; but he felt that the mute appeal of her heart-broken looks was more terrible than words. He kissed the hand she offered, and with a countenance almost as sad as her own, led her to a window in the recess shadowed by a luxuriant passion flower. It was the same seat where they had spent the first evening in this beautiful cottage, consecrated to their first loves. The same calm, clear moonlight looked in through the trellis. The vine then planted had now a luxuriant growth; and many a time had Horatio fondly twined its sacred blossoms with the glossy ringlets of her raven hair. The rush of memory almost overpowered poor Clotel; and Horatio felt too much oppressed and ashamed to break the long deep silence. At length, in words scarcely audible, Clotel said: "Tell me, dear Horatio, are you to be married next week?" He dropped her hand as if a rifle ball had struck him; and it was not until after long hesitation, that he began to make some reply about the necessity of circumstances. Mildly but earnestly the poor girl begged him to spare apologies. It was enough that he no longer loved her, and that they must bid farewell. Trusting to the yielding tenderness of her character, he ventured, in the most soothing accents, to suggest that as he still loved her better than all the world, she would ever be his real wife, and they might see each other frequently. He was not prepared for the storm of indignant emotion his words excited. True, she was his slave; her bones, and sinews had been purchased by his gold, yet she had the heart of a true woman, and hers

---

[1] *"In many ways . . . would show"*: The complete text of Samuel T. Coleridge (1772–1834), "Eros aei lalethros etairos" (1828), which can be translated as "Love, always a talkative companion."

was a passion too deep and absorbing to admit of partnership, and her spirit was too pure to form a selfish league with crime.

At length this painful interview came to an end. They stood together by the Gothic gate, where they had so often met and parted in the moonlight. Old remembrances melted their souls. "Farewell, dearest Horatio," said Clotel. "Give me a parting kiss." Her voice was choked for utterance, and the tears flowed freely, as she bent her lips toward him. He folded her convulsively in his arms, and imprinted a long impassioned kiss on that mouth, which had never spoken to him but in love and blessing. With efforts like a death-pang she at length raised her head from his heaving bosom, and turning from him with bitter sobs, "It is our last. To meet thus is henceforth crime. God bless you. I would not have you so miserable as I am. Farewell. A last farewell." "The last?" exclaimed he, with a wild shriek. "Oh God, Clotel, do not say that;" and covering his face with his hands, he wept like a child. Recovering from his emotion, he found himself alone. The moon looked down upon him mild, but very sorrowfully; as the Madonna seems to gaze upon her worshipping children, bowed down with consciousness of sin. At that moment he would have given worlds to have disengaged himself from Gertrude, but he had gone so far, that blame, disgrace, and duels with angry relatives would now attend any effort to obtain his freedom. Oh, how the moonlight oppressed him with its friendly sadness! It was like the plaintive eye of his forsaken one, like the music of sorrow echoed from an unseen world. Long and earnestly he gazed at that cottage, where he had so long known earth's purest foretaste of heavenly bliss. Slowly he walked away; then turned again to look on that charmed spot, the nestling-place of his early affections. He caught a glimpse of Clotel, weeping beside a magnolia, which commanded a long view of the path leading to the public road. He would have sprung toward her but she darted from him, and entered the cottage. That graceful figure, weeping in the moonlight, haunted him for years. It stood before his closing eyes, and greeted him with the morning dawn. Poor Gertrude, had she known all, what a dreary lot would hers have been; but fortunately she could not miss the impassioned tenderness she never experienced; and Horatio was the more careful in his kindness, because he was deficient in love. After Clotel had been separated from her mother and sister, she turned her attention to the subject of Christianity, and received that consolation from her Bible that is never denied to the children of God. Although it was against the laws of Virginia, for a slave to be taught to read, Currer had employed an old free negro, who lived near her, to teach her two daughters to read and write. She felt that the step she had taken in resolving never to meet Horatio again would no doubt expose her to his wrath, and probably cause her to be sold, yet her heart was too guileless for her to commit a crime, and therefore she had ten times rather have been sold as a slave than do wrong. Some months after the marriage of Horatio and Gertrude their barouche[2] rolled along a winding road that skirted the forest near Clotel's cottage, when the attention of Gertrude was suddenly attracted by two figures among the trees by the wayside; and touching Horatio's arm, she exclaimed, "Do look at that beautiful child." He turned and saw Clotel and Mary. His lips quivered, and his face became deadly pale. His young wife looked at him intently, but said nothing. In returning home, he took another road; but his wife seeing this, expressed a wish to go back the way they had come. He objected, and suspicion was awakened in her heart, and she soon after learned that the mother of that lovely child bore the name of Clotel, a name which she had often heard Horatio murmur in uneasy slumbers. From gossiping tongues she soon learned more than she wished to know. She wept, but not as poor Clotel had done; for she never had loved, and been beloved like her, and her nature was more proud: henceforth a change came over her feelings and her manners, and Horatio had no further occasion to assume a tenderness in return for hers. Changed as he was by ambition, he felt the wintry chill of her polite propriety, and sometimes, in agony of heart, compared it with the gushing love of her who was indeed his wife. But these and all his emotions were a sealed book to Clotel, of which she could only guess the contents. With remittances for her and her child's support, there sometimes came earnest pleadings that she would consent to see him again; but these she never answered, though her heart yearned to do so. She pitied his young bride, and would not be tempted to bring sorrow into her household by any fault of hers. Her earnest prayer was, that she might not know of her existence. She had not looked on Horatio since she watched him under the shadow of the magnolia, until his barouche passed her in her rambles some months after. She saw the deadly paleness of his countenance, and had he dared to look back, he would have seen her tottering with faintness. Mary brought water from a rivulet, and sprinkled her face. When she revived, she clasped the beloved child to her heart with a vehemence that made her scream. Soothingly she

---

[2] *barouche:* A four-wheeled carriage, with a seat for a driver and facing seats for two couples.

kissed away her fears, and gazed into her beautiful eyes with a deep, deep sadness of expression, which poor Mary never forgot. Wild were the thoughts that passed round her aching heart, and almost maddened her poor brain; thoughts which had almost driven her to suicide the night of that last farewell. For her child's sake she had conquered the fierce temptation then; and for her sake, she struggled with it now. But the gloomy atmosphere of their once happy home overclouded the morning of Mary's life. Clotel perceived this, and it gave her unutterable pain.

"Tis ever thus with woman's love,
   True till life's storms have passed;
And, like the vine around the tree,
   It braves them to the last."

CHAPTER IX.
THE MAN OF HONOUR.

"My tongue could never learn sweet soothing words,
But now thy beauty is propos'd, my fee,
My proud heart sues, and prompts my tongue to speak."[1]
— *Shakspeare.*

James Crawford, the purchaser of Althesa, was from the green
mountains of Vermont, and his feelings were opposed to the holding
of slaves. But his young wife persuaded him into the idea that it was no
worse to own a slave than to hire one and pay the money to another.
Hence it was that he had been induced to purchase Althesa. Henry
Morton, a young physician from the same state, and who had just
commenced the practice of his profession in New Orleans, was boarding with Crawford when Althesa was brought home.[2] The young
physician had been in New Orleans but a few weeks, and had seen
very little of slavery. In his own mountain home he had been taught
that the slaves of the Southern states were negroes, if not from the
coast of Africa, the descendants of those who had been imported. He
was unprepared to behold with composure a beautiful young white
girl of fifteen in the degraded position of a chattel slave. The blood
chilled in his young heart as he heard Crawford tell how, by bantering
with the trader, he had bought her for two hundred dollars less than he
first asked. His very looks showed that the slave girl had the deepest
sympathy of his heart. Althesa had been brought up by her mother to
look after the domestic concerns of her cottage in Virginia, and knew
well the duties imposed upon her. Mrs. Crawford was much pleased
with her new servant, and often made mention of her in presence of
Morton. The young man's sympathy ripened into love, which was re-
ciprocated by the friendless and injured child of sorrow. There was but
one course left; that was, to purchase the young girl and make her his
wife, which he did six months after her arrival in Crawford's family.
The young physician and his wife immediately took lodgings in
another part of the city; a private teacher was called in, and the young
wife taught some of those accomplishments which are necessary for
one's taking a position in society. Dr. Morton soon obtained a large

[1] *"My Tongue . . . to speak":* Shakespeare, *Richard the Third* I.ii.183–185.
[2] *Henry Morton . . . home:* The story of Althesa and Henry Morton draws on
"View Eighth" of Brown's *A Description of William Wells Brown's Original Panoramic
Views* (1850); see pp. 306–08.

practice in his profession, and with it increased in wealth — but with all his wealth he never would own a slave. Mrs. Morton was now in a position to seek out and redeem her mother, whom she had not heard of since they parted at Natchez. An agent was immediately despatched to hunt out the mother and to see if she could be purchased. The agent had no trouble in finding out Mr. Peck: but all overtures were unavailable; he would not sell Currer. His excuse was, that she was such a good housekeeper that he could not spare her. Poor Althesa felt sad when she found that her mother could not be bought. However, she felt a consciousness of having done her duty in the matter, yet waited with the hope that the day might come when she should have her mother by her side.

CHAPTER X.
THE YOUNG CHRISTIAN.

"Here we see *God dealing in slaves;* giving them to his own favourite
child [Abraham], a man of superlative worth, and as a reward for his
eminent goodness."

— Rev. Theodore Clapp, of New Orleans.[1]

On Carlton's return the next day from the farm, he was overwhelmed with questions from Mr. Peck, as to what he thought of the
plantation, the condition of the negroes, Huckelby and Snyder; and
especially how he liked the sermon of the latter. Mr. Peck was a kind of
a patriarch in his own way. To begin with, he was a man of some talent.
He not only had a good education, but was a man of great eloquence,
and had a wonderful command of language. He too either had, or
thought he had, poetical genius; and was often sending contributions to
the *Natchez Free Trader,* and other periodicals. In the way of raising
contributions for foreign missions, he took the lead of all others in his
neighbourhood. Everything he did, he did for the "glory of God," as he
said: he quoted Scripture for almost everything he did. Being in good
circumstances, he was able to give to almost all benevolent causes to
which he took a fancy. He was a most loving father, and his daughter
exercised considerable influence over him, and, owing to her piety and
judgment, that influence had a beneficial effect. Carlton, though a
schoolfellow of the parson's, was nevertheless nearly ten years his
junior; and though not an avowed infidel, was, however, a free-thinker,
and one who took no note of to-morrow. And for this reason Georgiana took peculiar interest in the young man, for Carlton was but little
above thirty and unmarried. The young Christian felt that she would
not be living up to that faith that she professed and believed in, if she
did not exert herself to the utmost to save the thoughtless man from his
downward career; and in this she succeeded to her most sanguine
expectations. She not only converted him, but in placing the Scriptures
before him in their true light, she redeemed those sacred writings from
the charge of supporting the system of slavery, which her father had
cast upon them in the discussion some days before.

Georgiana's first object, however, was to awaken in Carlton's breast
a love for the Lord Jesus Christ. The young man had often sat under

[1] *Rev. Theodore Clapp, of New Orleans:* A well-known Unitarian clergyman, Theodore Clapp (1792–1866) was born in Easthampton, Massachusetts, and moved to New
Orleans in 1822. In 1834 he founded New Orleans's Unitarian Church of the Messiah.

the sound of the gospel with perfect indifference. He had heard men talk who had grown grey bending over the Scriptures, and their conversation had passed by him unheeded; but when a young girl, much younger than himself, reasoned with him in that innocent and persuasive manner that woman is wont to use when she has entered with her whole soul upon an object, it was too much for his stout heart, and he yielded. Her next aim was to vindicate the Bible from sustaining the monstrous institution of slavery. She said, "'God has created of one blood all the nations of men, to dwell on all the face of the earth.'[2] To claim, hold, and treat a human being as property is felony against God and man. The Christian religion is opposed to slaveholding in its spirit and its principles; it classes men-stealers among murderers; and it is the duty of all who wish to meet God in peace, to discharge that duty in spreading these principles. Let us not deceive ourselves into the idea that slavery is right, because it is profitable to us. Slaveholding is the highest possible violation of the eighth commandment. To take from a man his earnings, is theft; but to take the earner is a compound, life-long theft; and we who profess to follow in the footsteps of our Redeemer, should do our utmost to extirpate slavery from the land. For my own part, I shall do all I can. When the Redeemer was about to ascend to the bosom of the Father, and resume the glory which he had with him before the world was, he promised his disciples that the power of the Holy Ghost should come upon them, and that they should be witnesses for him to the uttermost parts of the earth. What was the effect upon their minds? 'They all continued with one accord in prayer and supplication with the women.'[3] Stimulated by the confident expectation that Jesus would fulfil his gracious promise, they poured out their hearts in fervent supplications, probably for strength to do the work which he had appointed them unto, for they felt that without him they could do nothing, and they consecrated themselves on the altar of God, to the great and glorious enterprise of preaching the unsearchable riches of Christ to a lost and perishing world. Have we less precious promises in the Scriptures of truth? May we not claim of our God the blessing promised unto those who consider the poor: the Lord will preserve them and keep them alive, and they shall be blessed upon the earth? Does not the language, 'Inasmuch as ye did it unto one of the least of these my brethren, ye did it unto me,'[4] belong

[2] 'God has created . . . earth': Act 17.26. Abolitionists regularly cited St. Paul's antiracist preachings.

[3] 'They . . . the women': Acts 1.14.

[4] 'Inasmuch . . . unto me': Matthew 25.40.

to all who are rightly engaged in endeavouring to unloose the bond-man's fetters? Shall we not then do as the apostles did? Shall we not, in view of the two millions of heathen in our very midst, in view of the souls that are going down in an almost unbroken phalanx to utter perdition, continue in prayer and supplication, that God will grant us the supplies of his Spirit to prepare us for that work which he has given us to do? Shall not the wail of the mother as she surrenders her only child to the grasp of the ruthless kidnapper, or the trader in human blood, animate our devotions? Shall not the manifold crimes and horrors of slavery excite more ardent outpourings at the throne of grace to grant repentance to our guilty country, and permit us to aid in preparing the way for the glorious second advent of the Messiah, by preaching deliverance to the captives, and the opening of the prison doors to those who are bound."

Georgiana had succeeded in rivetting the attention of Carlton during her conversation, and as she was finishing her last sentence, she observed the silent tear stealing down the cheek of the newly born child of God. At this juncture her father entered, and Carlton left the room. "Dear papa," said Georgiana, "will you grant me one favour; or, rather, make me a promise?" "I can't tell, my dear, till I know what it is," replied Mr. Peck. "If it is a reasonable request, I will comply with your wish," continued he. "I hope, my dear," answered she, "that papa would not think me capable of making an unreasonable request." "Well, well," returned he; "tell me what it is." "I hope," said she, "that in your future conversation with Mr. Carlton, on the subject of slavery, you will not speak of the Bible as sustaining it." "Why, Georgiana, my dear, you are mad, aint you?" exclaimed he, in an excited tone. The poor girl remained silent; the father saw in a moment that he had spoken too sharply; and taking her hand in his he said, "Now, my child, why do you make that request?" "Because," returned she, "I think he is on the stool of repentance, if he has not already been received among the elect. He, you know, was bordering upon infidelity, and if the Bible sanctions slavery, then he will naturally enough say that it is not from God; for the argument from internal evidence is not only refuted, but actually turned against the Bible. If the Bible sanctions slavery, then it misrepresents the character of God. Nothing would be more dangerous to the soul of a young convert than to satisfy him that the Scriptures favoured such a system of sin." "Don't you suppose that I understand the Scriptures better than you? I have been in the world longer." "Yes," said she, "you have been in the world longer, and amongst slaveholders so long that you do not regard it in the same light that those do who have not become so familiar with its every-day scenes as you. I once heard you say, that you were opposed to the institution, when you first came to the South." "Yes," answered he, "I did not know so much about it then." "With great deference to you, papa," replied Georgiana, "I don't think that the Bible sanctions slavery. The Old Testament contains this explicit condemnation of it, 'He that stealeth a man, and selleth him, or if he be found in his hand, he shall surely be put to death;' and 'Woe unto him that buildeth his house by unrighteousness, and his chambers by wrong; that useth his neighbour's service without wages, and giveth him not for his work;' when also the New Testament exhibits such words to rebuke as these, 'Behold the hire of the labourers who have reaped down your fields, which is of you kept back by fraud, crieth; and the cries of them who have reaped are entered into the ears of the Lord of Sabaoth.' 'The law is not made for a righteous man, but for the lawless and disobedient, for the ungodly and for sinners, for unholy and profane, for murderers of fathers and murderers of mothers, for manslayers, for whoremongers, for them that defile themselves with mankind, for *menstealers,* for liars, for perjured persons.'[5] A more scathing denunciation of the sin in question is surely to be found on record in no other book. I am afraid," continued the daughter, "that the acts of the professed friends of Christianity in the South do more to spread infidelity than the writings of all the atheists which have ever been published. The infidel watches the religious world. He surveys the church, and, lo! thousands and tens of thousands of her accredited members actually hold slaves. Members 'in good and regular standing,' fellowshipped throughout Christendom except by a few anti-slavery churches generally despised as ultra and radical, reduce their fellow men to the condition of chattels, and by force keep them in that state of degradation. Bishops, ministers, elders, and deacons are engaged in this awful business, and do not consider their conduct as at all inconsistent with the precepts of either the Old or New Testaments. Moreover, those ministers and churches who do not themselves hold slaves, very generally defend the conduct of those who do, and accord to them a fair Christian character, and in the way of business frequently take mortgages and levy executions on the bodies of their fellow men, and in some cases of their fellow Christians.

[5] '*He that stealeth.... person':* A compendium of passages intended to demonstrate that the Bible is an antislavery document; the sources are Exodus 21.16, Jeremiah 22.13, James 5.4, and 1 Timothy 1.9.

"Now is it a wonder that infidels, beholding the practice and listening to the theory of professing Christians, should conclude that the Bible inculcates a morality not inconsistent with chattelising human beings? And must not this conclusion be strengthened, when they hear ministers of talent and learning declare that the Bible does sanction slaveholding, and that it ought not to be made a disciplinable offence in churches? And must not all doubt be dissipated, when one of the most learned professors[6] in our theological seminaries asserts that the Bible 'recognises that the relation may still exist, *salva fide et salva ecclesia*' (without injury to the Christian faith or church) and that only 'the *abuse* of it is the essential and fundamental wrong?' Are not infidels bound to believe that these professors, ministers, and churches understand their own Bible, and that, consequently, notwithstanding solitary passages which appear to condemn slaveholding, the Bible sanctions it? When nothing can be further from the truth. And as for Christ, his whole life was a living testimony against slavery and all that it inculcates. When he designed to do us good, he took upon himself the form of a servant. He took his station at the bottom of society. He voluntarily identified himself with the poor and the despised. The warning voices of Jeremiah and Ezekiel were raised in olden time, against sin. Let us not forget what followed. 'Therefore, thus saith the Lord — ye have not hearkened unto me in proclaiming liberty every one to his brother, and every one to his neighbour — behold I proclaim a liberty for you saith the Lord, to the sword, to the pestilence, and to the famine.'[7] Are we not virtually as a nation adopting the same impious language, and are we not exposed to the same tremendous judgments? Shall we not, in view of those things, use every laudable means to awaken our beloved country from the slumbers of death and baptize all our efforts with tears and with prayers, that God may bless them. Then, should our labour fail to accomplish the end for which we pray, we shall stand acquitted at the bar of Jehovah, and although we may share in the national calamities which await unrepented sins, yet that blessed approval will be ours. — 'Well done good and faithful servants, enter ye into the joy of your Lord.' "[8]

"My dear Georgiana," said Mr. Peck, "I must be permitted to entertain my own views on this subject, and to exercise my own judgment."

---

[6] *one of the most learned professors:* In all likelihood a reference to the Reverend Joel Parker; see p. 116.

[7] *'Therefore . . . the famine':* Jeremiah 34.15.

[8] *'Well done . . . Lord':* Matthew 25.23.

"Believe me, dear papa," she replied, "I would not be understood as wishing to teach you, or to dictate to you in the least; but only grant my request, not to allude to the Bible as sanctioning slavery, when speaking with Mr. Carlton."

"Well," returned he, "I will comply with your wish."

The young Christian had indeed accomplished a noble work; and whether it was admitted by the father, or not, she was his superior and his teacher. Georgiana had viewed the right to enjoy perfect liberty as one of those inherent and inalienable rights which pertain to the whole human race, and of which they can never be divested, except by an act of gross injustice. And no one was more able than herself to impress those views upon the hearts of all with whom she came in contact. Modest and self-possessed, with a voice of great sweetness, and a most winning manner, she could, with the greatest ease to herself, engage their attention.

CHAPTER XI.
THE PARSON POET.

"Unbind, unbind my galling chain,
    And set, oh! set me free:
No longer say that I'll disdain
    The gift of liberty."

Through the persuasion of Mr. Peck, and fascinated with the charms of Georgiana, Carlton had prolonged his stay two months with his old school-fellow. During the latter part of the time he had been almost as one of the family. If Miss Peck was invited out, Mr. Carlton was, as a matter of course. She seldom rode out, unless with him. If Mr. Peck was absent, he took the head of the table; and, to the delight of the young lady, he had on several occasions taken part in the family worship. "I am glad," said Mr. Peck, one evening while at the tea table, "I am glad, Mr. Carlton, that my neighbour Jones has invited you to visit him at his farm. He is a good neighbour, but a very ungodly man; I want that you should see his people, and then, when you return to the North, you can tell how much better a Christian's slaves are situated than one who does nothing for the cause of Christ." "I hope, Mr. Carlton," said Georgiana, "that you will spend the Sabbath with him, and have a religious interview with the negroes." "Yes," replied the parson, "that's well thought of, Georgy." "Well, I think I will go up on Thursday next, and stay till Monday," said Carlton; "and I shall act upon your suggestion, Miss Peck," continued he; "and try to get a religious interview with the blacks. By-the-by," remarked Carlton, "I saw an advertisement in the *Free Trader* to-day that rather puzzled me. Ah, here it is now; and," drawing the paper from his pocket, "I will read it, and then you can tell me what it means:

'TO PLANTERS AND OTHERS. — *Wanted fifty negroes.* Any person having *sick negroes,* considered *incurable* by their respective physicians, (their owners of course,) and wishing to dispose of them, Dr. Stillman will pay cash for negroes affected with scrofula or king's evil,[1] confirmed hypochondriacism, apoplexy, or diseases of the brain, kidneys, spleen, stomach and intestines, bladder and its appendages, diarrhœa, dysentery, &c. *The highest cash price will be paid as above.*'

[1] *scrofula or king's evil:* A tuberculous disorder, characterized by lymphatic swelling; legend had it that the disorder could be cured by the touch of the reigning sovereign.

When I read this to-day I thought that the advertiser must be a man of eminent skill as a physician, and that he intended to cure the sick negroes; but on second thought I find that some of the diseases enumerated are certainly incurable. What can he do with these sick negroes?" "You see," replied Mr. Peck, laughing, "that he is a doctor, and has use for them in his lectures. The doctor is connected with a small college. Look at his prospectus, where he invites students to attend, and that will explain the matter to you." Carlton turned to another column, and read the following:

> "Some advantages of a peculiar character are connected with this institution, which it may be proper to point out. No place in the United States offers as great opportunities for the acquisition of anatomical knowledge. Subjects being obtained from among the coloured population in sufficient numbers *for every purpose,* and proper dissections carried on *without offending any individuals in the community!*"[2]

"These are for dissection, then?" inquired Carlton with a trembling voice. "Yes," answered the parson. "Of course they wait till they die before they can use them." "They keep them on hand, and when they need one they bleed him to death," returned Mr. Peck. "Yes, but that's murder." "Oh, the doctors are licensed to commit murder, you know; and what's the difference, whether one dies owing to the loss of blood, or taking too many pills? For my own part, if I had to choose, I would rather submit to the former." "I have often heard what I consider hard stories in abolition meetings in New York about slavery; but now I shall begin to think that many of them are true." "The longer you remain here the more you will be convinced of the iniquity of the institution," remarked Georgiana. "Now, Georgy, my dear, don't give us another abolition lecture, if you please," said Mr. Peck. "Here, Carlton," continued the parson, "I have written a short poem for your sister's album, as you requested me; it is a domestic piece, as you will see." "She will prize it the more for that," remarked Carlton; and taking the sheet of paper, he laughed as his eyes glanced over it. "Read it out, Mr. Carlton," said Georgiana, "and let me hear what it is; I know papa gets off some very droll things at times." Carlton complied with the young lady's request, and read aloud the following rare specimen of poetical genius:

---

[2] *"Some advantages. . . . in the community!":* This passage, and the passage above requesting *"sick negroes,"* were drawn from Theodore Dwight Weld's *Slavery As It Is* (1839); for selections from Weld's book, see pp. 265–70.

"MY LITTLE NIG.

"I have a little nigger, the blackest thing alive,
  He'll be just four years old if he lives till forty-five;
  His smooth cheek hath a glossy hue, like a new polished boot,
  And his hair curls o'er his little head as black as any soot.
  His lips bulge from his countenance — his little ivories shine —
  His nose is what we call a little pug, but fashioned very fine:
  Although not quite a fairy, he is comely to behold,
  And I wouldn't sell him, 'pon my word, for a hundred all in gold.

"He gets up early in the morn, like all the other nigs,
  And runs off to the hog-lot, where he squabbles with the pigs —
  And when the sun gets out of bed, and mounts up in the sky,
  The warmest corner of the yard is where my nig doth lie.
  And there extended lazily, he contemplates and dreams,
  (I cannot qualify to this, but plain enough it seems;)
  Until 'tis time to take in grub, when you can't find him there,
  For, like a politician, he has gone to hunt his share.

"I haven't said a single word concerning my plantation,
  Though a prettier, I guess, cannot be found within the nation;
  When he gets a little bigger, I'll take and to him show it,
  And then I'll say, 'My little nig, now just prepare to go it!'
  I'll put a hoe into his hand — he'll soon know what it means,
  And every day for dinner, he shall have bacon and greens."

CHAPTER XII.
A NIGHT IN THE PARSON'S KITCHEN.

> "And see the servants met,
> Their daily labour's o'er;
> And with the jest and song they set
> The kitchen in a roar."

Mr. Peck kept around him four servants besides Currer, of whom we have made mention: of these, Sam was considered the first. If a dinner-party was in contemplation, or any company to be invited to the parson's, after all the arrangements had been talked over by the minister and his daughter, Sam was sure to be consulted upon the subject by "Miss Georgy," as Miss Peck was called by the servants. If furniture, crockery, or anything else was to be purchased, Sam felt that he had been slighted if his opinion had not been asked. As to the marketing, he did it all. At the servants' table in the kitchen, he sat at the head, and was master of ceremonies. A single look from him was enough to silence any conversation or noise in the kitchen, or any other part of the premises. There is, in the Southern States, a great amount of prejudice against color amongst the negroes themselves. The nearer the negro or mulatto approaches to the white, the more he seems to feel his superiority over those of a darker hue. This is, no doubt, the result of the prejudice that exists on the part of the whites towards both mulattoes and blacks. Sam was originally from Kentucky, and through the instrumentality of one of his young masters whom he had to take to school, he had learned to read so as to be well understood; and, owing to that fact, was considered a prodigy among the slaves, not only of his own master's, but those of the town who knew him. Sam had a great wish to follow in the footsteps of his master, and be a poet; and was, therefore, often heard singing doggrels of his own composition. But there was one great drawback to Sam, and that was his colour. He was one of the blackest of his race. This he evidently regarded as a great misfortune. However, he made up for this in his dress. Mr. Peck kept his house servants well dressed; and as for Sam, he was seldom seen except in a ruffled shirt. Indeed, the washerwoman feared him more than all others about the house.

Currer, as we have already stated, was chief of the kitchen department, and had a general supervision of the household affairs. Alfred the coachman, Peter, and Hetty made up the remainder of the house servants. Besides these, Mr. Peck owned eight slaves who were

masons. These worked in the city. Being mechanics, they were let out
to greater advantage than to keep them on the farm. However, every
Sunday night, Peck's servants, including the bricklayers, usually
assembled in the kitchen, when the events of the week were freely discussed and commented on. It was on a Sunday evening, in the month
of June, that there was a party at Mr. Peck's, and, according to custom
in the Southern States, the ladies had their maid-servants with them.
Tea had been served in "the house," and the servants, including the
strangers, had taken their seats at the tea table in the kitchen. Sam,
being a "single gentleman," was unusually attentive to the "ladies" on
this occasion. He seldom or ever let the day pass without spending at
least an hour in combing and brushing up his "hair." Sam had an idea
that fresh butter was better for his hair than any other kind of grease;
and therefore, on churning days, half a pound of butter had always to
be taken out before it was salted. When he wished to appear to great
advantage, he would grease his face, to make it "shiny." On the
evening of the party therefore, when all the servants were at the table,
Sam cut a big figure. There he sat with his wool well combed and but-
tered, face nicely greased, and his ruffles extending five or six inches
from his breast. The parson in his own drawing-room did not make a
more imposing appearance than did his servant on this occasion. "I jist
bin had my fortune told last Sunday night," said Sam, as he helped one
of the girls to some sweet hash. "Indeed," cried half-a-dozen voices.
"Yes," continued he; "Aunt Winny told me I is to hab de prettiest
yaller gall in town, and dat I is to be free." All eyes were immediately
turned toward Sally Johnson, who was seated near Sam. "I speck I see
somebody blush at dat remark," said Alfred. "Pass dem pancakes and
molasses up dis way, Mr. Alf, and none of your insinawaysion here,"
rejoined Sam. "Dat reminds me," said Currer, "dat Dorcas Simpson is
gwine to git married." "Who to, I want to know?" inquired Peter. "To
one of Mr. Darby's field-hands," answered Currer. "I should tink dat
dat gal would not trow herself away in dat manner," said Sally. "She
good enough looking to get a house servant, and not to put up wid a
fiel' nigger," continued she. "Yes," said Sam, "dat's a wery insensible
remark of yours, Miss Sally. I admire your judgment wery much, I
assure you. Dah's plenty of suspectible and well-dressed house servants dat a gal of her looks can get, wid out taken up wid dem common darkies." "Is de man black or a mulatto?" inquired one of the
company. "He's nearly white," replied Currer. "Well den, dat's some
exchuse for her," remarked Sam; "for I don't like to see dis malgemation of blacks and mulattoes, no how," continued Sam. "If I had my
rights I would be a mulatto too, for my mother was almost as light-

coloured as Miss Sally," said he. Although Sam was one of the black-est men living, he nevertheless contended that his mother was a mulatto, and no one was more prejudiced against the blacks than he. A good deal of work, and the free use of fresh butter, had no doubt done wonders for his "hare" in causing it to grow long, and to this he would always appeal when he wished to convince others that he was part of an Anglo-Saxon. "I always thought you was not clear black, Mr. Sam," said Agnes. "You are right dahr, Miss Agnes. My hare tells what company I belong to," answered Sam. Here the whole company joined in the conversation about colour, which lasted for some time, giving unmistakeable evidence that caste is owing to ignorance. The evening's entertainment concluded by Sam's relating a little of his own experience while with his first master in old Kentucky.

Sam's former master was a doctor, and had a large practice among his neighbours, doctoring both masters and slaves. When Sam was about fifteen years of age, his old master set him to grinding up the ointment, then to making pills. As the young student grew older and became more practised in his profession, his services were of more importance to the doctor. The physician having a good business, and a large number of his patients being slaves, the most of whom had to call on the doctor when ill, he put Sam to bleeding, pulling teeth, and administering medicine to the slaves. Sam soon acquired the name amongst the slaves of the "Black Doctor." With this appellation he was delighted, and no regular physician could possibly have put on more airs than did the black doctor when his services were required. In bleeding, he must have more bandages, and rub and smack the arm more than the doctor would have thought of. We once saw Sam taking out a tooth for one of his patients, and nothing appeared more amus-ing. He got the poor fellow down on his back, and he got a straddle of the man's chest, and getting the turnkeys on the wrong tooth, he shut both eyes and pulled for his life. The poor man screamed as loud as he could, but to no purpose. Sam had him fast. After a great effort, out came the sound grinder, and the young doctor saw his mistake; but consoled himself with the idea that as the wrong tooth was out of the way, there was more room to get at the right one. Bleeding and a dose of calomel[1] was always considered indispensable by the "Old Boss;" and, as a matter of course, Sam followed in his footsteps.

---

[1] *Bleeding and a dose of calomel:* Central to allopathic medicine, the practice of bleeding patients, usually through the use of bloodsucking leeches, was believed to restore a healthy balance to the body's blood. Calomel pills consisted of organic mer-cury compounds and were used as purgatives.

NEGRO DENTISTRY.

On one occasion the old doctor was ill himself, so as to be unable to attend to his patients. A slave, with pass in hand, called to receive medical advice, and the master told Sam to examine him and see what he wanted. This delighted him beyond measure, for although he had been acting his part in the way of giving out medicine as the master ordered it, he had never been called upon by the latter to examine a patient, and this seemed to convince him that, after all, he was no sham doctor. As might have been expected, he cut a rare figure in his first examination, placing himself directly opposite his patient, and folding his arms across his breast, and looking very knowingly, he began, "What's de matter wid you?" "I is sick." "Where is you sick?" "Here," replied the man, putting his hand upon his stomach. "Put out your tongue," continued the doctor. The man run out his tongue at full length. "Let me feel your pulse," at the same time taking his patient's hand in his, placing his fingers on his pulse, he said, "Ah, your case is a bad one; if I don't do something for you, and dat pretty quick, you i'll be a gone coon, and dat's sartin." At this the man appeared frightened and inquired what was the matter with him: in answer, Sam said, "I done told you dat your case is a bad one, and dat's enough." On Sam's returning to his master's bedside, the latter said, "Well, Sam, what do you think is the matter with him?" "His stomach is out of order, sir," he replied. "What do you think had best be done for him?" "I think I better bleed him and give him a dose of calomel," returned Sam. So to the latter's gratification the master let him have his own way. We need not further say, that the recital of Sam's experience as a physician gave him a high position amongst the servants that evening, and made him a decided favourite with the ladies, one of whom feigned illness, when the black doctor, to the delight of all, and certainly to himself, gave medical advice. Thus ended the evening amongst the servants in the parson's kitchen.

CHAPTER XIII.
A SLAVE HUNTING PARSON.

" 'Tis too much prov'd — that with devotion's visage,
And pious action, we do sugar o'er the devil himself." [1]
— *Shakspeare*

"You will, no doubt, be well pleased with neighbour Jones," said Mr. Peck, as Carlton stepped into the chaise [2] to pay his promised visit to the "ungodly man." "Don't forget to have a religious interview with the negroes," remarked Georgiana, as she gave the last nod to her young convert. "I will do my best," returned Carlton, as the vehicle left the door. As might have been expected, Carlton met with a cordial reception at the hands of the proprietor of the Grove Farm. The servants in the "Great House" were well dressed, and appeared as if they did not want for food. Jones knew that Carlton was from the North, and a non-slaveholder, and therefore did everything in his power to make a favourable impression on his mind. "My negroes are well clothed, well fed, and not over worked," said the slaveholder to his visitor, after the latter had been with him nearly a week. "As far as I can see, your slaves appear to good advantage," replied Carlton. "But," continued he, "if it is a fair question, do you have preaching among your slaves on Sunday, Mr. Jones?" "No, no," returned he, "I think that's all nonsense; my negroes do their own preaching." "So you do permit them to have meetings." [3] "Yes, when they wish. There's some very intelligent and clever chaps among them." "As to-morrow is the Sabbath," said Carlton, "if you have no objection, I will attend meeting with them." "Most certainly you shall, if you will do the preaching," returned the planter. Here the young man was about to decline, but he remembered the parting words of Georgiana, and he took courage and said, "Oh, I have no objection to give the negroes a short talk." It was then understood that Carlton was to have a religious interview with the blacks the next day, and the young man waited with a degree of impatience for the time.

In no part of the South are slaves in a more ignorant and degraded state than in the cotton, sugar, and rice districts.

If they are permitted to cease labour on the Sabbath, the time is spent in hunting, fishing, or lying beneath the shade of a tree, resting for

---

[1] " *'Tis . . . the devil himself*": Shakespeare, *Hamlet* III.i.51–53.
[2] *chaise:* A horse-drawn carriage.
[3] *meetings:* Religious gatherings.

the morrow. Religious instruction is unknown in the far South, except among such men as the Rev. C. C. Jones, John Peck, and some others who regard religious instruction, such as they impart to their slaves, as calculated to make them more trustworthy and valuable as property. Jones, aware that his slaves would make rather a bad show of intelligence if questioned by Carlton, resolved to have them ready for him, and therefore gave his driver orders with regard to their preparation. Consequently, after the day's labour was over, Dogget, the driver, assembled the negroes together and said, "Now, boys and gals, your master is coming down to the quarters to-morrow with his visitor, who is going to give you a preach, and I want you should understand what he says to you. Now many of you who came of Old Virginia and Kentuck, know what preaching is, and others who have been raised in these parts do not. Preaching is to tell you that you are mighty wicked and bad at heart. This, I suppose, you all know. But if the gentleman should ask you who made you, tell him the Lord; if he ask if you wish to go to heaven, tell him yes. Remember that you are all Christians, all love the Lord, all want to go to heaven, all love your masters, and all love me. Now, boys and gals, I want you to show yourselves smart to-morrow: be on your p's and q's, and, Monday morning, I will give you all a glass of whiskey bright and early." Agreeable to arrangement the slaves were assembled together on Sunday morning under the large tree near the great house, and after going through another drilling from the driver, Jones and Carlton made their appearance. "You see," said Jones to the negroes, as he approached them, "you see here's a gentleman that's come to talk to you about your souls, and I hope you 'ill all pay that attention that you ought." Jones then seated himself in one of the two chairs placed there for him and the stranger.

Carlton had already selected a chapter in the Bible to read to them, which he did, after first prefacing it with some remarks of his own. Not being accustomed to speak in public, he determined, after reading the Bible, to make it more of a conversational meeting than otherwise. He therefore began asking them questions. "Do you feel that you are a Christian?" asked he of a full-blooded negro that sat near him. "Yes, sir," was the response. "You feel, then, that you shall go to heaven." "Yes, sir." "Of course you know who made you?" The man put his hand on his head and began to scratch his wool; and, after a little hesitation, answered, "De overseer told us last night who made us, but indeed I forgot the gentmun's name." This reply was almost too much for Carlton, and his gravity was not a little moved. However, he bit his tongue, and turned to another man, who appeared, from his looks, to be more intelligent. "Do you serve the Lord?" asked he. "No, sir, I don't serve anybody but Mr. Jones; I neber belong to anybody else." To hide his feelings at this juncture, Carlton turned and walked to another part of the grounds, to where the women were seated, and said to a mulatto woman who had rather an anxious countenance, "Did you ever hear of John the Baptist?"[4] "Oh yes, marser, John de Baptist; I know dat nigger bery well indeed; he libs in Old Kentuck, where I come from." Carlton's gravity here gave way, and he looked at the planter and laughed right out. The old woman knew a slave near her old master's farm in Kentucky, and was ignorant enough to suppose that he was the John the Baptist inquired about. Carlton occupied the remainder of the time in reading Scripture and talking to them. "My niggers aint shown off very well to-day," said Jones, as he and his visitor left the grounds. "No" replied Carlton. "You did not get hold of the bright ones," continued the planter. "So it seems," remarked Carlton. The planter evidently felt that his neighbour, Parson Peck, would have a nut to crack over the account that Carlton would give of the ignorance of the slaves, and said and did all in his power to remove the bad impression already made; but to no purpose. The report made by Carlton, on his return, amused the parson very much. It appeared to him the best reason why professed Christians like himself should be slave-holders. Not so with Georgiana. She did not even smile when Carlton was telling his story, but seemed sore at heart that such ignorance should prevail in their midst. The question turned upon the heathen of other lands, and the parson began to expatiate upon his own efforts in foreign missions, when his daughter, with a child-like simplicity, said,

> "Send Bibles to the heathen;
> On every distant shore,
> From light that's beaming o'er us,
> Let streams increasing pour
> But keep it from the millions
> Down-trodden at our door.

> "Send Bibles to the heathen,
> Their famished spirits feed;
> Oh! haste, and join your efforts,
> The priceless gift to speed;
> Then flog the trembling negro
> If he should learn to read."

---

[4] *John the Baptist?*": Jewish prophet and forerunner of Jesus, John baptized Jesus, whom he recognized as the Son of God. He was beheaded at the request of Salome, daughter of the aristocrats Herod and Herodias.

"I saw a curiosity while at Mr. Jones's that I shall not forget soon," said Carlton. "What was it?" inquired the parson. "A kennel of blood-hounds; and such dogs I never saw before. They were of a species between the bloodhound and the foxhound, and were ferocious, gaunt, and savage-looking animals. They were part of a stock imported from Cuba, he informed me. They were kept in an iron cage, and fed on Indian corn bread. This kind of food, he said, made them eager for their business. Sometimes they would give the dogs meat, but it was always after they had been chasing a negro." "Were those the dogs you had, papa, to hunt Harry?" asked Georgiana. "No, my dear," was the short reply: and the parson seemed anxious to change the conversation to something else. When Mr. Peck had left the room, Carlton spoke more freely of what he had seen, and spoke more pointedly against slavery; for he well knew that Miss Peck sympathised with him in all he felt and said.

"You mentioned about your father hunting a slave," said Carlton, in an under tone. "Yes," replied she; "papa went with some slave-catchers and a parcel of those nasty negro-dogs, to hunt poor Harry. He belonged to papa and lived on the farm. His wife lies in town, and Harry had been to see her, and did not return quite as early as he should; and Huckelby was flogging him, and he got away and came here. I wanted papa to keep him in town, so that he could see his wife more frequently; but he said they could not spare him from the farm, and flogged him again, and sent him back. The poor fellow knew that the overseer would punish him over again, and instead of going back he went into the woods." "Did they catch him?" asked Carlton. "Yes," replied she. "In chasing him through the woods, he attempted to escape by swimming across a river, and the dogs were sent in after him, and soon caught him. But Harry had great courage and fought the dogs with a big club; and papa seeing the negro would escape from the dogs, shot at him, as he says, only to wound him, that he might be caught; but the poor fellow was killed." Overcome by relating this incident, Georgiana burst into tears.

Although Mr. Peck fed and clothed his house servants well, and treated them with a degree of kindness, he was, nevertheless, a most cruel master. He encouraged his driver to work the field-hands from early dawn till late at night; and the good appearance of the house-servants, and the preaching of Snyder to the field negroes, was to cause himself to be regarded as a Christian master. Being on a visit one day at the farm, and having with him several persons from the Free States, and wishing to make them believe that his slaves were happy, satisfied, and contented, the parson got out the whiskey and gave each one a

A NEGRO HUNT IN THE SOUTHERN STATES.

dram, who in return had to drink the master's health, or give a toast of some kind. The company were not a little amused at some of the sentiments given, and Peck was delighted at every indication of contentment on the part of the blacks. At last it came to Jack's turn to drink, and the master expected something good from him, because he was considered the cleverest and most witty slave on the farm.

"Now," said the master, as he handed Jack the cup of whiskey; "now, Jack, give us something rich. You know," continued he, "we have raised the finest crop of cotton that's been seen in these parts for many a day. Now give us a toast on cotton; come, Jack give us something to laugh at." The negro felt not a little elated at being made the hero of the occasion, and taking the whiskey in his right hand, put his left to his head and began to scratch his wool, and said,

> "The big bee flies high,
> The little bee make the honey;
> The black folks makes the cotton,
> And the white folks gets the money."

CHAPTER XIV.
A FREE WOMAN REDUCED TO SLAVERY.

Althesa found in Henry Morton a kind and affectionate husband; and his efforts to purchase her mother, although unsuccessful, had doubly endeared him to her. Having from the commencement resolved not to hold slaves, or rather not to own any, they were compelled to hire servants[1] for their own use. Five years had passed away, and their happiness was increased by two lovely daughters. Mrs. Morton was seated, one bright afternoon, busily engaged with her needle, and near her sat Salome, a servant that she had just taken into her employ. The woman was perfectly white; so much so, that Mrs. Morton had expressed her apprehensions to her husband, when the woman first came, that she was not born a slave. The mistress watched the servant, as the latter sat sewing upon some coarse work, and saw the large silent tear in her eye. This caused an uneasiness to the mistress, and she said, "Salome, don't you like your situation here?" "Oh yes, madam," answered the woman in a quick tone, and then tried to force a smile. "Why is it that you often look sad, and with tears in your eyes?" The mistress saw that she had touched a tender chord, and continued, "I am your friend; tell me your sorrow, and, if I can, I will help you." As the last sentence was escaping the lips of the mistress, the slave woman put her check apron to her face and wept. Mrs. Morton saw plainly that there was cause for this expression of grief, and pressed the woman more closely. "Hear me, then," said the woman calming herself: "I will tell you why I sometimes weep. I was born in Germany, on the banks of the Rhine. Ten years ago my father came to this country, bringing with him my mother and myself. He was poor, and I, wishing to assist all I could, obtained a situation as nurse to a lady in this city. My father got employment as a labourer on the wharf, among the steamboats; but he was soon taken ill with the yellow fever, and died. My mother then got a situation for herself, while I remained with my first employer. When the hot season came on, my master, with his wife, left New Orleans until the hot season was over, and took me with them. They stopped at a town on the banks of the Mississippi river, and said they should remain there some weeks. One day they went out for a ride, and they had not been gone more than half an hour, when two men came into the room and told me that they had bought me, and that I was their slave. I was bound and taken to prison, and that

---

[1] *hire servants:* The practice of paying slave masters for the use of their slaves.

night put on a steamboat and taken up the Yazoo river,[2] and set to work on a farm. I was forced to take up with a negro, and by him had three children. A year since my master's daughter was married, and I was given to her. She came with her husband to this city, and I have ever since been hired out."

"Unhappy woman," whispered Althesa, "why did you not tell me this before?" "I was afraid," replied Salome, "for I was once severely flogged for telling a stranger that I was not born a slave." On Mr. Morton's return home, his wife communicated to him the story which the slave woman had told her an hour before, and begged that something might be done to rescue her from the situation she was then in. In Louisiana as well as many others of the slave states, great obstacles are thrown in the way of persons who have been wrongfully reduced to slavery regaining their freedom. A person claiming to be free must prove his right to his liberty. This, it will be seen, throws the burden of proof upon the slave, who, in all probability, finds it out of his power to procure such evidence. And if any free person shall attempt to aid a freeman in regaining his freedom, he is compelled to enter into security in the sum of one thousand dollars, and if the person claiming to be free shall fail to establish such fact, the thousand dollars are forfeited to the state. This cruel and oppressive law has kept many a freeman from espousing the cause of persons unjustly held as slaves. Mr. Morton inquired and found that the woman's story was true, as regarded the time she had lived with her present owner; but the latter not only denied that she was free, but immediately removed her from Morton's. Three months after Salome had been removed from Morton's and let out to another family, she was one morning cleaning the door steps, when a lady passing by, looked at the slave and thought she recognised some one that she had seen before. The lady stopped and asked the woman if she was a slave. "I am," said she. "Were you born a slave?" "No, I was born in Germany." "What's the name of the ship in which you came to this country?" inquired the lady. "I don't know," was the answer. "Was it the *Amazon*?" At the sound of this name, the slave woman was silent for a moment, and then the tears began to flow freely down her care-worn cheeks. "Would you know Mrs. Marshall, who was a passenger in the *Amazon*, if you should see her?" inquired the lady. At this the woman gazed at the lady with a degree of intensity that can be imagined better than described, and then fell at the lady's

[2] *Yazoo river:* A river flowing from northern Mississippi into the Mississippi River at Vicksburg.

feet. The lady was Mrs. Marshall. She had crossed the Atlantic in the same ship with this poor woman. Salome, like many of her countrymen, was a beautiful singer, and had often entertained Mrs. Marshall and the other lady passengers on board the *Amazon*. The poor woman was raised from the ground by Mrs. Marshall, and placed upon the door step that she had a moment before been cleaning. "I will do my utmost to rescue you from the horrid life of a slave," exclaimed the lady, as she took from her pocket her pencil, and wrote down the number of the house, and the street in which the German woman was working as a slave.

After a long and tedious trial of many days, it was decided that Salome Miller was by birth a free woman, and she was set at liberty. The good and generous Althesa had contributed some of the money toward bringing about the trial, and had done much to cheer on Mrs. Marshall in her benevolent object. Salome Miller is free, but where are her three children? They are still slaves, and in all human probability will die as such.

This, reader, is no fiction; if you think so, look over the files of the New Orleans newspaper of the years 1845–6, and you will there see reports of the trial.[3]

[3] *the trial:* Brown draws on the Louisiana trial of Salome Müller, who in 1844 lost her suit to regain her freedom but triumphed in the state's supreme court in 1845. An article about the trial appeared in the *National Anti-Slavery Standard*, 1 January 1846. The case is also discussed in William Craft's *Running a Thousand Miles for Freedom* (1860).

CHAPTER XV.
TO-DAY A MISTRESS, TO-MORROW A SLAVE.

"I promised thee a sister tale
Of man's perfidious cruelty;
Come, then, and hear what cruel wrong
Befel the dark ladie."[1]
— *Coleridge.*

Let us return for a moment to the home of Clotel. While she was passing lonely and dreary hours with none but her darling child, Horatio Green was trying to find relief in that insidious enemy of man, the intoxicating cup. Defeated in politics, forsaken in love by his wife, he seemed to have lost all principle of honour, and was ready to nerve himself up to any deed, no matter how unprincipled. Clotel's existence was now well known to Horatio's wife, and both her and her father demanded that the beautiful quadroon and her child should be sold and sent out of the state. To this proposition he at first turned a deaf ear; but when he saw that his wife was about to return to her father's roof, he consented to leave the matter in the hands of his father-in-law. The result was, that Clotel was immediately sold to the slave-trader, Walker, who, a few years previous, had taken her mother and sister to the far South. But, as if to make her husband drink of the cup of humiliation to its very dregs, Mrs. Green resolved to take his child under her own roof for a servant. Mary was, therefore, put to the meanest work that could be found, and although only ten years of age, she was often compelled to perform labour, which, under ordinary circumstances, would have been thought too hard for one much older. One condition of the sale of Clotel to Walker was, that she should be taken out of the state, which was accordingly done. Most quadroon women who are taken to the lower countries to be sold are either purchased by gentlemen for their own use, or sold for waiting-maids; and Clotel, like her sister, was fortunate enough to be bought for the latter purpose. The town of Vicksburgh stands on the left bank of the Mississippi, and is noted for the severity with which slaves are treated. It was here that Clotel was sold to Mr. James French, a merchant.

Mrs. French was severe in the extreme to her servants. Well dressed, but scantily fed, and overworked were all who found a home with her.

---

[1] *"I promised . . . dark ladie":* From Samuel T. Coleridge, "Introduction to the Tale of the Dark Ladie" (1799).

The quadroon had been in her new home but a short time ere she found that her situation was far different from what it was in Virginia. What social virtues are possible in a society of which injustice is the primary characteristic? in a society which is divided into two classes, masters and slaves? Every married woman in the far South looks upon her husband as unfaithful, and regards every quadroon servant as a rival. Clotel had been with her new mistress but a few days, when she was ordered to cut off her long hair. The negro, constitutionally, is fond of dress and outward appearance. He that has short, woolly hair, combs it and oils it to death. He that has long hair, would sooner have his teeth drawn than lose it. However painful it was to the quadroon, she was soon seen with her hair cut as short as any of the full-blooded negroes in the dwelling.

Even with her short hair, Clotel was handsome. Her life had been a secluded one, and though now nearly thirty years of age, she was still beautiful. At her short hair, the other servants laughed, "Miss Clo needn't strut round so big, she got short nappy har well as I," said Nell, with a broad grin that showed her teeth. "She tinks she white, when she come here wid dat long har of hers," replied Mill. "Yes," continued Nell; "missus make her take down her wool so she no put it up to-day."

The fairness of Clotel's complexion was regarded with envy as well by the other servants as by the mistress herself. This is one of the hard features of slavery. To-day the woman is mistress of her own cottage; to-morrow she is sold to one who aims to make her life as intolerable as possible. And be it remembered, that the house servant has the best situation which a slave can occupy. Some American writers have tried to make the world believe that the condition of the labouring classes of England is as bad as the slaves of the United States.[2]

The English labourer may be oppressed, he may be cheated, de-frauded, swindled, and even starved; but it is not slavery under which he groans. He cannot be sold; in point of law he is equal to the prime minister. "It is easy to captivate the unthinking and the prejudiced, by eloquent declamation about the oppression of English operatives being worse than that of American slaves, and by exaggerating the wrongs on one side and hiding them on the other. But all informed and reflecting minds, knowing that bad as are the social evils of England,

---

[2] *Some American writers . . . United States:* Proslavery writers regularly argued that "wage slavery" in the North and in European industrial centers was far worse than slav-ery on the plantation. See, for example, the selection from George Fitzhugh on pp. 397–403.

those of Slavery are immeasurably worse."[3] But the degradation and harsh treatment that Clotel experienced in her new home was nothing compared with the grief she underwent at being separated from her dear child. Taken from her without scarcely a moment's warning, she knew not what had become of her. The deep and heartfelt grief of Clotel was soon perceived by her owners, and fearing that her refusal to take food would cause her death, they resolved to sell her. Mr. French found no difficulty in getting a purchaser for the quadroon woman, for such are usually the most marketable kind of property. Clotel was sold at private sale to a young man for a housekeeper; but even he had missed his aim.

---

[3] *"It is. . . . worse":* Probably an example of self-quotation, as Brown delivered a number of lectures with similar arguments; see, for example, the transcription of a speech he gave in the Lecture Hall at Croyden, Surrey, on 5 September 1849, in the *Liberator,* 28 September 1849.

CHAPTER XVI.
DEATH OF THE PARSON.

Carlton was about thirty years of age, standing on the last legs of a young man, and entering on the first of a bachelor. He had never dabbed in matters of love, and looked upon all women alike. Although he respected woman for her virtues, and often spoke of the goodness of heart of the sex, he had never dreamed of marriage. At first he looked upon Miss Peck as a pretty young woman, but after she became his religious teacher, he regarded her in that light, that every one will those whom they know to be their superiors. It was soon seen, however, that the young man not only respected and reverenced Georgiana for the incalculable service she had done him, in awakening him to a sense of duty to his soul, but he had learned to bow to the shrine of Cupid. He found, weeks after he had been in her company, that when he met her at table, or alone in the drawingroom, or on the piazza, he felt a shortness of breath, a palpitating of the heart, a kind of dizziness of the head; but he knew not its cause.

This was love in its first stage. Mr. Peck saw, or thought he saw, what would be the result of Carlton's visit, and held out every inducement in his power to prolong his stay. The hot season was just commencing, and the young Northerner was talking of his return home, when the parson was very suddenly taken ill. The disease was the cholera, and the physicians pronounced the case incurable. In less than five hours John Peck was a corpse. His love for Georgiana, and respect for her father, had induced Carlton to remain by the bedside of the dying man, although against the express orders of the physician. The act of kindness caused the young orphan henceforth to regard Carlton as her best friend. He now felt it his duty to remain with the young woman until some of her relations should be summoned from Connecticut. After the funeral, the family physician advised that Miss Peck should go to the farm, and spend the time at the country seat; and also advised Carlton to remain with her, which he did.

At the parson's death his negroes showed little or no signs of grief. This was noticed by both Carlton and Miss Peck, and caused no little pain to the latter. "They are ungrateful," said Carlton, as he and Georgiana were seated on the piazza. "What," asked she, "have they to be grateful for?" "Your father was kind, was he not?" "Yes, as kind as most men who own slaves; but the kindness meted out to blacks would be unkindness if given to whites. We would think so, should we not?" "Yes," replied he. "If we would not consider the best treatment which a slave receives good enough for us, we should not think he ought to be grateful for it. Everybody knows that slavery in its best and mildest form is wrong. Whoever denies this, his lips libel his heart. Try him! Clank the chains in his ears, and tell him they are for him; give him an hour to prepare his wife and children for a life of slavery; bid him make haste, and get ready their necks for the yoke, and their wrists for the coffle chains,[1] then look at his pale lips and trembling knees, and you have nature's testimony against slavery."

"Let's take a walk," said Carlton, as if to turn the conversation. The moon was just appearing through the tops of the trees, and the animals and insects in an adjoining weed kept up a continued din of music. The croaking of bull-frogs, buzzing of insects, cooing of turtle-doves, and the sound from a thousand musical instruments, pitched on as many different keys, made the welkin[2] ring. But even all this noise did not drown the singing of a party of the slaves, who were seated near a spring that was sending up its cooling waters. "How prettily the negroes sing," remarked Carlton, as they were wending their way towards the place from whence the sound of the voices came. "Yes," replied Georgiana; "master Sam is there, I'll warrant you: he's always on hand when there's any singing or dancing. We must not let them see us, or they will stop singing." "Who makes their songs for them?" inquired the young man. "Oh, they make them up as they sing them; they are all impromptu songs." By this time they were near enough to hear distinctly every word; and, true enough, Sam's voice was heard above all others. At the conclusion of each song they all joined in a hearty laugh, with an expression of "Dats de song for me;" "Dems dems."

"Stop," said Carlton, as Georgiana was rising from the log upon which she was seated; "stop, and let's hear this one." The piece was sung by Sam, the others joining in the chorus, and was as follows:

Sam.
"Come, all my brethren, let us take a rest,
    While the moon shines so brightly and clear;
Old master is dead, and left us at last,
    And had gone at the Bar to appear.
Old master has died, and lying in his grave,
    And our blood will awhile cease to flow;
He will no more trample on the neck of the slave;
    For he's gone where the slaveholders go.

---

[1] *coffle chains:* Used to chain slaves together to form a train.
[2] *welkin:* Sky or heavens.

Chorus.

"Hang up the shovel and the hoe —
    Take down the fiddle and the bow —
    Old master has gone to the slaveholder's rest;
    He has gone where they all ought to go.

Sam.

"I heard the old doctor say the other night,
    As he passed by the dining-room door —
'Perhaps the old man may live through the night,
    But I think he will die about four.'
Young mistress sent me, at the peril of my life,
    For the parson to come down and pray,
For she says, 'Your old master is now about to die,'
    And says I, 'God speed him on his way.'

    "Hang up the shovel, &c.

"At four o'clock at morn the family was called
    Around the old man's dying bed;
And oh! but I laughed to myself when I heard
    That the old man's spirit had fled.
Mr. Carlton cried, and so did I pretend;
    Young mistress very nearly went mad;
And the old parson's groans did the heavens fairly rend;
    But I tell you I felt mighty glad.

    "Hang up the shovel, &c.

"We'll no more be roused by the blowing of his horn,
    Our backs no longer he will score;
He no more will feed us on cotton-seeds and corn;
    For his reign of oppression now is o'er.
He no more will hang our children on the tree,
    To be ate by the carrion crow;
He no more will send our wives to Tennessee;
    For he's gone where the slaveholders go.

"Hang up the shovel and the hoe,
    Take down the fiddle and the bow,
    We'll dance and sing,
    And make the forest ring,
    With the fiddle and the old banjo."

The song was not half finished before Carlton regretted that he had caused the young lady to remain and hear what to her must be anything but pleasant reflections upon her deceased parent. "I think we will walk," said he, at the same time extending his arm to Georgiana. "No," said she; "let's hear them out. It is from these unguarded expressions of the feelings of the negroes, that we should learn a lesson." At its conclusion they walked towards the house in silence: as they were ascending the steps, the young man said, "They are happy, after all. The negro, situated as yours are, is not aware that he is deprived of any just rights." "Yes, yes," answered Georgiana: "you may place the slave where you please; you may dry up to your utmost the fountains of his feelings, the springs of his thought; you may yoke him to your labour, as an ox which liveth only to work, and worketh only to live; you may put him under any process which, without destroying his value as a slave, will debase and crush him as a rational being; you may do this, and *the idea that he was born to be free will survive it all.* It is allied to his hope of immortality; it is the ethereal part of his nature, which oppression cannot reach; it is a torch lit up in his soul by the hand of Deity, and never meant to be extinguished by the hand of man."

On reaching the drawing-room, they found Sam snuffing the candles, and looking as solemn and as dignified as if he had never sung a song or laughed in his life. "Will Miss Georgy have de supper got up now?" asked the negro. "Yes," she replied. "Well," remarked Carlton, "that beats anything I ever met with. Do you think that was Sam we heard singing?" "I am sure of it," was the answer. "I could not have believed that that fellow was capable of so much deception," continued he. "Our system of slavery is one of deception; and Sam, you see, has only been a good scholar. However, he is as honest a fellow as you will find among the slave population here. If we would have them more honest, we should give them their liberty, and then the inducement to be dishonest would be gone. I have resolved that these creatures shall all be free." "Indeed!" exclaimed Carlton. "Yes, I shall let them all go free, and set an example to those about me." "I honour your judgment," said he. "But will the state permit them to remain?"[3] "If not, they can go where they can live in freedom. I will not be unjust because the state is."

---

[3] "*. . . will the state permit them to remain?*": In order to discourage mass emancipations, most slave states had legal or de facto requirements that slaves liberated under such circumstances must emigrate to nonslave states.

CHAPTER XVII.
RETALIATION.

"I had a dream, a happy dream;
I thought that I was free:
That in my own bright land again
A home there was for me."

With the deepest humiliation Horatio Green saw the daughter of
Clotel, his own child, brought into his dwelling as a servant. His wife
felt that she had been deceived, and determined to punish her deceiver.
At first Mary was put to work in the kitchen, where she met with little
or no sympathy from the other slaves, owing to the fairness of her
complexion. The child was white, what should be done to make her
look like other negroes, was the question Mrs. Green asked herself. At
last she hit upon a plan: there was a garden at the back of the house
over which Mrs. Green could look from her parlour window. Here the
white slave-girl was put to work, without either bonnet or handkerchief upon her head. A hot sun poured its broiling rays on the naked
face and neck of the girl, until she sank down in the corner of the garden, and was actually broiled to sleep. "Dat little nigger ain't working
a bit, missus," said Dinah to Mrs. Green, as she entered the kitchen.
"She's lying in the sun, seasoning; she will work better by and by,"
replied the mistress. "Dees white niggers always tink dey sef good as
white folks," continued the cook. "Yes, but we will teach them better;
won't we, Dinah?" "Yes, missus, I don't like dees mularter niggers, no
how; dey always want to set dey sef up for something big." The cook
was black, and was not without that prejudice which is to be found
among the negroes, as well as among the whites of the Southern States.
The sun had the desired effect, for in less than a fortnight Mary's fair
complexion had disappeared, and she was but little whiter than any
other mulatto children running about the yard. But the close resemblance between the father and child annoyed the mistress more than
the mere whiteness of the child's complexion. Horatio made proposition after proposition to have the girl sent away, for every time he
beheld her countenance it reminded him of the happy days he had
spent with Clotel. But his wife had commenced, and determined to
carry out her unfeeling and fiendish designs. This child was not only
white, but she was the granddaughter of Thomas Jefferson, the man
who, when speaking against slavery in the legislature of Virginia, said,

"The whole commerce between master and slave is a perpetual exercise of the most boisterous passions; *the most unremitting despotism on the one part, and degrading submission on the other.* With what execration should the statesman be loaded who, permitting one half the citizens thus to trample on the rights of the other, transforms those into despots and these into enemies, destroys the morals of the one part, and the *amor patriæ*[1] of the other! For if the slave can have a country in this world, it must be any other in preference to that in which he is born to live and labour for another; in which he must lock up the faculties of his nature, contribute as far as depends on his individual endeavours to the evanishment of the human race, or entail his own miserable condition on the endless generations proceeding from him. And can the liberties of a nation be thought secure when we have removed their only firm basis, a conviction in the minds of the people that these liberties are a gift of God? that they are not to be violated but with his wrath? Indeed, I tremble for my country when I reflect that God is just; that his justice cannot sleep for ever; that, considering numbers, nature, and natural means only, a revolution of the wheel of fortune, an exchange of situation, is among possible events; that it may become probable by supernatural interference! The Almighty has no attribute which can take side with us in such a contest.

. . . .

"What an incomprehensible machine is man! Who can endure toil, famine, stripes, imprisonment, and death itself, in vindication of his own liberty, and the next moment be deaf to all those motives, whose power supported him through his trial, and inflict on his fellow-men a bondage, *one hour of which is fraught with more misery than ages of that which he rose in rebellion to oppose!* But we must wait with patience the workings of an overruling Providence, and hope that that is preparing the deliverance of these our suffering brethren. When the measure of their tears shall be full — when their tears shall have involved heaven itself in darkness — doubtless a God of justice will awaken to their distress, and by diffusing light and liberality among their oppressors, or at length by his exterminating thunder, manifest his attention to things of this world, and that they are not left to the guidance of blind fatality."[2]

The same man, speaking of the probability that the slaves might some day attempt to gain their liberties by a revolution, said,

---

[1] *amor patriæ:* Love of native land.
[2] *"The whole commerce. . . . blind fatality":* The first passage is from Thomas Jefferson's *Notes on the State of Virginia* (1785); the second is from his "Observations" (1786). For selections from *Notes,* see pp. 335–43.

"I tremble for my country, when I recollect that God is just, and that His justice cannot sleep for ever. The Almighty has no attribute that can take sides with us in such a struggle."[3]

But, sad to say, Jefferson is not the only American statesman who has spoken high-sounding words in favour of freedom, and then left his own children to die slaves.

---

[3] *"I tremble. . . . struggle":* From Jefferson's *Notes on the State of Virginia.*

CHAPTER XVIII.
THE LIBERATOR.

"We hold these truths to be self-evident, that all men are created free and equal; that they are endowed by their Creator with certain inalienable rights; among these are life, *liberty*, and the pursuit of happiness."
— *Declaration of American Independence.*

The death of the parson was the commencement of a new era in the history of his slaves. Only a little more than eighteen years of age, Georgiana could not expect to carry out her own wishes in regard to the slaves, although she was sole heir to her father's estate. There were distant relations whose opinions she had at least to respect. And both laws and public opinion in the state were against any measure of emancipation that she might think of adopting; unless, perhaps, she might be permitted to send them to Liberia.[1] Her uncle in Connecticut had already been written to, to come down and aid in settling up the estate. He was a Northern man, but she knew him to be a tight-fisted yankee, whose whole counsel would go against liberating the negroes. Yet there was one way in which the thing could be done. She loved Carlton, and she well knew that he loved her; she read it in his countenance every time they met, yet the young man did not mention his wishes to her. There were many reasons why he should not. In the first place, her father was just deceased, and it seemed only right that he should wait a reasonable time. Again, Carlton was poor, and Georgiana was possessed of a large fortune; and his high spirit would not, for a moment, allow him to place himself in a position to be regarded as a fortune-hunter. The young girl hinted, as best she could, at the probable future; but all to no purpose. He took nothing to himself. True, she had read much of "woman's rights;" and had even attended a meeting, while at the North, which had been called to discuss the wrongs of woman;[2] but she could not nerve herself up to the point of putting the question to Carlton, although she felt sure that she should not be rejected. She waited, but in vain. At last, one evening, she came out of her room rather late, and was walking on the piazza for fresh air. She passed near Carlton's room, and heard the voice of Sam. The negro had just come in to get the young man's boots, and had stopped,

---

[1] *Liberia:* The American Colonization Society founded this east African colony in the early 1820s as the appropriate "home" for the colonized free blacks.

[2] *the wrongs of woman:* The first women's rights convention was held at Seneca Falls, New York, in 1848.

as he usually did, to have some talk. "I wish," said Sam, "dat Marser Carlton an Miss Georgy would get married; den, I 'spec, we'd have good times." "I don't think your mistress would have me," replied the young man. "What make tink dat, Marser Carlton?" "Your mistress would marry no one, Sam, unless she loved him." "Den I wish she would lub you, cause I tink we have good times den. All our folks is de same 'pinion like me," returned the negro, and then left the room with the boots in his hands. During the conversation between the Anglo-Saxon and the African, one word had been dropped by the former that haunted the young lady the remainder of the night — "Your mistress would marry no one unless she loved them." That word awoke her in the morning, and caused her to decide upon this important subject. Love and duty triumphed over the woman's timid nature, and that day Georgiana informed Carlton that she was ready to become his wife. The young man, with grateful tears, accepted and kissed the hand that was offered to him. The marriage of Carlton and Miss Peck was hailed with delight by both the servants in the house and the negroes on the farm. New rules were immediately announced for the working and general treatment of the slaves on the plantation. With this, Huckleby, the overseer, saw his reign coming to an end; and Snyder, the Dutch preacher, felt that his services would soon be dispensed with, for nothing was more repugnant to the feelings of Mrs. Carlton than the sermons preached by Snyder to the slaves. She regarded them as something intended to make them better satisfied with their condition, and more valuable as pieces of property, without preparing them for the world to come. Mrs. Carlton found in her husband a congenial spirit, who entered into all her wishes and plans for bettering the condition of their slaves. Mrs. Carlton's views and sympathies were all in favour of immediate emancipation; but then she saw, or thought she saw, a difficulty in that. If the slaves were liberated, they must be sent out of the state. This, of course, would incur additional expense; and if they left the state, where had they better go? "Let's send them to Liberia," said Carlton. "Why should they go to Africa, any more than the Free States or to Canada?" asked the wife. "They would be in their native land," he answered. "Is not this their native land? What right have we, more than the negro, to the soil here, or to style ourselves native Americans? Indeed it is as much their homes as ours, and I have sometimes thought it was more theirs. The negro has cleared up the lands, built towns, and enriched the soil with his blood and tears; and in return, he is to be sent to a country of which he knows nothing. Who fought more bravely for American independence than the blacks? A negro, by the name of Attucks,[3] was the first that fell in Boston at the commencement of the revolutionary war; and, throughout the whole of the struggles for liberty in this country, the negroes have contributed their share. In the last war with Great Britain,[4] the country was mainly indebted to the blacks in New Orleans for the achievement of the victory at that place; and even General Jackson, the commander in chief, called the negroes together at the close of the war, and addressed them in the following terms: —

"Soldiers! — When on the banks of the Mobile I called you to take up arms, inviting you to partake the perils and glory of your *white fellow citizens, I expected much from you;* for I was not ignorant that you possessed qualities most formidable to an invading enemy. I knew with what fortitude you could endure hunger and thirst, and all the fatigues of a campaign. *I knew well how you loved your native country,* and that you, as well as ourselves, had to defend what *man* holds most dear — his parents, wife, children, and property. *You have done more than I expected.* In addition to the previous qualities I before knew you to possess, I found among you a noble enthusiasm, which leads to the performance of great things.

" 'Soldiers! The President of the United States shall hear how praiseworthy was your conduct in the hour of danger, and the representatives of the American people will give you the praise your exploits entitle you to. Your general anticipates them in applauding your noble ardour.' "[5]

"And what did these noble men receive in return for their courage, their heroism? Chains and slavery. Their good deeds have been consecrated only in their own memories. Who rallied with more alacrity in response to the summons of danger? If in that hazardous hour, when our homes were menaced with the horrors of war, we did not disdain to call upon the negro to assist in repelling invasion, why should we, now that the danger is past, deny him a home in his native land?" "I see," said Carlton, "you are right, but I fear you will have difficulty in persuading others to adopt your views." "We will set the example," replied she, "and then hope for the best; for I feel that the people of the Southern States will one day see their error. Liberty has always been

[3] *Attucks:* On 5 March 1770, Crispus Attucks (1723–1770), a mulatto who had escaped from slavery in Framingham, Massachusetts, led a group protesting the British army's presence in Boston. British soldiers fired into the crowd, killing Attucks and four others. Attucks's bravery and patriotism were regularly celebrated by nineteenth-century African Americans.

[4] *the last war with Great Britain:* The War of 1812.

[5] *"Soldiers! . . . noble ardour' ":* For Andrew Jackson's complete speech to the black troops on this famous battle of 1815, see "Two Proclamations" on pp. 262–65.

our watchword, as far as profession is concerned. Nothing has been held so cheap as our common humanity, on a national average. If every man had his aliquot proportion[6] of the injustice done in this land, by law and violence, the present freemen of the northern section would many of them commit suicide in self-defence, and would court the liberties awarded by Ali Pasha of Egypt[7] to his subjects. Long ere this we should have tested, in behalf of our bleeding and crushed American brothers of every hue and complexion, every new constitution, custom, or practice, by which inhumanity was supposed to be upheld, the injustice and cruelty they contained, emblazoned before the great tribunal of mankind for condemnation; and the good and available power they possessed, for the relief, deliverance and elevation of oppressed men, permitted to shine forth from under the cloud, for the refreshment of the human race."

Although Mr. and Mrs. Carlton felt that immediate emancipation was the right of the slave and the duty of the master, they resolved on a system of gradual emancipation, so as to give them time to accomplish their wish, and to prepare the negro for freedom. Huckelby was one morning told that his services would no longer be required. The negroes, ninety-eight in number, were called together and told that the whip would no longer be used, and that they would be allowed a certain sum for every bale of cotton produced. Sam, whose long experience in the cotton-field before he had been taken into the house, and whose general intelligence justly gave him the first place amongst the negroes on the Poplar Farm, was placed at their head. They were also given to understand that the money earned by them would be placed to their credit; and when it amounted to be a certain sum, they should all be free.

The joy with which the news was received by the slaves, showed their grateful appreciation of the boon their benefactors were bestowing upon them. The house servants were called and told that wages would be allowed them, and what they earned set to their credit, and they too should be free. The next were the bricklayers. There were eight of these, who had paid their master two dollars per day, and boarded and clothed themselves. An arrangement was entered into with them, by which the money they earned should be placed to their

---

[6] *aliquot proportion:* Comprising a definite, fixed part of a whole.

[7] *Ali Pasha of Egypt:* Known as a despotic military governor of a province of the Ottoman Empire, Ali Pasha (1744?–1822) battled the French, made an alliance with England in 1814, and was eventually assassinated by a Turkish agent.

credit; and they too should be free, when a certain amount should be accumulated; and great was the change amongst all these people. The bricklayers had been to work but a short time, before their industry was noticed by many. They were no longer apparently the same people. A sedateness, a care, an economy, an industry, took possession of them, to which there seemed to be no bounds but in their physical strength. They were never tired of labouring, and seemed as though they could never effect enough. They became temperate, moral, religious, setting an example of innocent, unoffending lives to the world around them, which was seen and admired by all. Mr. Parker, a man who worked nearly forty slaves at the same business, was attracted by the manner in which these negroes laboured. He called on Mr. Carlton, some weeks after they had been acting on the new system, and offered 2,000 dollars for the head workman, Jim. The offer was, of course, refused. A few days after the same gentleman called again, and made an offer of double the sum that he had on the former occasion. Mr. Parker, finding that no money would purchase either of the negroes, said, "Now, Mr. Carlton, pray tell me what it is that makes your negroes work so? What kind of people are they?" "I suppose," observed Carlton, "that they are like other people, flesh and blood." "Why, sir," continued Parker, "I have never seen such people; building as they are next door to my residence, I see and have my eye on them from morning till night. You are never there, for I have never met you, or seen you once at the building. Why, sir, I am an early riser, getting up before day; and do you think that I am not awoke every morning in my life by the noise of their trowels at work, and their singing and noise before day; and do you suppose, sir, that they stop or leave off work at sundown? No, sir, but they work as long as they can see to lay a brick, and then they carry up brick and mortar for an hour or two afterward, to be ahead of their work the next morning. And again, sir, do you think that they walk at their work? No, sir, they run all day. You see, sir, those immensely long ladders, five stories in height; do you suppose they walk up them? No, sir, they run up and down them like so many monkeys all day long. I never saw such people as these in my life. I don't know what to make of them. Were a white man with them and over them with a whip, then I should see and understand the cause of the running and incessant labour; but I cannot comprehend it; there is something in it, sir. Great man, sir, that Jim; great man; I should like to own him." Carlton here informed Parker that their liberties depended upon their work; when the latter replied, "If niggers can work so for the promise of freedom, they ought to be made to work without it." This last remark was in the true spirit of the slave-holder, and reminds us of the fact that, some years since, the overseer of General Wade Hampton[8] offered the niggers under him a suit of clothes to the one that picked the most cotton in one day; and after that time that day's work was given as a task to the slaves on that plantation; and, after a while, was adopted by other planters.

The negroes on the farm, under "Marser Sam," were also working in a manner that attracted the attention of the planters round about. They no longer feared Huckelby's whip, and no longer slept under the preaching of Snyder. On the Sabbath, Mr. and Mrs. Carlton read and explained the Scriptures to them; and the very great attention paid by the slaves showed plainly that they appreciated the gospel when given to them in its purity. The death of Currer, from yellow fever, was a great trial to Mrs. Carlton; for she had not only become much attached to her, but had heard with painful interest the story of her wrongs, and would, in all probability, have restored her to her daughter in New Orleans.

[8] *Wade Hampton:* A prominent South Carolina slave owner, Wade Hampton (1818–1902) owned over nine hundred slaves on six plantations.

CHAPTER XIX.
ESCAPE OF CLOTEL.

"The fetters galled my weary soul —
A soul that seemed but thrown away:
I spurned the tyrant's base control,
Resolved at last the man to play."[1]

No country has produced so much heroism in so short a time, connected with escapes from peril and oppression, as has occurred in the United States among fugitive slaves, many of whom show great shrewdness in their endeavours to escape from this land of bondage. A slave was one day seen passing on the high road from a border town in the interior of the state of Virginia to the Ohio river. The man had neither hat upon his head or coat upon his back. He was driving before him a very nice fat pig, and appeared to all who saw him to be a labourer employed on an adjoining farm. "No negro is permitted to go at large in the Slave States without a written pass from his or her master, except on business in the neighbourhood." "Where do you live, my boy?" asked a white man of the slave, as he passed a white house with green blinds. "Jist up de road, sir," was the answer. "That's a fine pig." "Yes, sir, marser like dis choat[2] berry much." And the negro drove on as if he was in great haste. In this way he and the pig travelled more than fifty miles before they reached the Ohio river. Once at the river they crossed over; the pig was sold; and nine days after the runaway slave passed over the Niagara river,[3] and, for the first time in his life, breathed the air of freedom. A few weeks later, and, on the same road, two slaves were seen passing; one was on horseback, the other was walking before him with his arms tightly bound, and a long rope leading from the man on foot to the one on horseback. "Oh, ho, that's a runaway rascal, I suppose," said a farmer, who met them on the road. "Yes, sir, he bin runaway, and I got him fast. Marser will tan his jacket for him nicely when he gets him." "You are a trustworthy fellow, I imagine," continued the farmer. "Oh yes, sir; marser puts a heap of confidence in dis nigger." And the slaves travelled on. When the one on foot was fatigued they would change positions, the other being tied

---

[1] *"The fetters . . . play"*: From Elizur Wright, Jr. (1814–1885), "The Fugitive Slave to the Christian," in *The Anti-Slavery Harp*, ed. Brown.

[2] *choat:* Shoat, a weaned pig.

[3] *the Niagara river:* A river along the New York-Canada border flowing from Lake Erie to Lake Ontario.

and driven on foot. This they called "ride and tie." After a journey of more than two hundred miles they reached the Ohio river,[4] turned the horse loose, told him to go home, and proceeded on their way to Canada. However they were not to have it all their own way. There are men in the Free States, and especially in the states adjacent to the Slave States, who make their living by catching the runaway slave, and returning him for the reward that may be offered. As the two slaves above mentioned were travelling on towards the land of freedom, led by the North Star, they were set upon by four of these slave-catchers, and one of them unfortunately captured. The other escaped. The captured fugitive was put under the torture, and compelled to reveal the name of his owner and his place of residence. Filled with delight, the kidnappers started back with their victim. Overjoyed with the prospect of receiving a large reward, they gave themselves up on the third night to pleasure. They put up at an inn. The negro was chained to the bed-post, in the same room with his captors. At dead of night, when all was still, the slave arose from the floor upon which he had been lying, looked around, and saw that the white men were fast asleep. The brandy punch had done its work. With palpitating heart and trembling limbs he viewed his position. The door was fast, but the warm weather had compelled them to leave the window open. If he could but get his chains off, he might escape through the window to the piazza, and reach the ground by one of the posts that supported the piazza. The sleeper's clothes hung upon chairs by the bedside; the slave thought of the padlock key, examined the pockets and found it. The chains were soon off, and the negro stealthily making his way to the window: he stopped and said to himself, "These men are villains, they are enemies to all who like me are trying to be free. Then why not I teach them a lesson?" He then undressed himself, took the clothes of one of the men, dressed himself in them, and escaped through the window, and, a moment more, he was on the high road to Canada. Fifteen days later, and the writer of this gave him a passage across Lake Erie, and saw him safe in her Britannic Majesty's[5] dominions.

We have seen Clotel sold to Mr. French in Vicksburgh, her hair cut short, and everything done to make her realise her position as a servant. Then we have seen her re-sold, because her owners feared she would die through grief. As yet her new purchaser treated her with

---

[4] *the Ohio river:* The Ohio river marked an important boundary between free (Ohio and Pennsylvania) and slave (Kentucky and Virginia) states.

[5] *Britannic Majesty's:* Great Britain's.

respectful gentleness, and sought to win her favour by flattery and presents, knowing that whatever he gave her he could take back again. But she dreaded every moment lest the scene should change, and trembled at the sound of every footfall. At every interview with her new master Clotel stoutly maintained that she had left a husband in Virginia, and would never think of taking another. The gold watch and chain, and other glittering presents which he purchased for her, were all laid aside by the quadroon, as if they were of no value to her. In the same house with her was another servant, a man, who had from time to time hired himself from his master. William was his name. He could feel for Clotel, for he, like her, had been separated from near and dear relatives, and often tried to console the poor woman. One day the quadroon observed to him that her hair was growing out again. "Yes," replied William, "you look a good deal like a man with your short hair." "Oh," rejoined she, "I have often been told that I would make a better looking man than a woman. If I had the money," continued she, "I would bid farewell to this place." In a moment more she feared that she had said too much, and smilingly remarked, "I am always talking nonsense." William was a tall, full-bodied negro, whose very countenance beamed with intelligence. Being a mechanic, he had, by his own industry, made more than what he paid his owner; this he laid aside, with the hope that some day he might get enough to purchase his freedom. He had in his chest one hundred and fifty dollars. His was a heart that felt for others, and he had again and again wiped the tears from his eyes as he heard the story of Clotel as related by herself. "If she can get free with a little money, why not give her what I have?" thought he, and then he resolved to do it. An hour after, he came into the quadroon's room, and laid the money in her lap, and said, "There, Miss Clotel, you said if you had the means you would leave this place; there is money enough to take you to England, where you will be free. You are much fairer than many of the white women of the South, and can easily pass for a free white lady." At first Clotel feared that it was a plan by which the negro wished to try her fidelity to her owner; but she was soon convinced by his earnest manner, and the deep feeling with which he spoke, that he was honest. "I will take the money only on one condition," said she; "and that is, that I effect your escape as well as my own." "How can that be done?" he inquired. "I will assume the disguise of a gentleman and you that of a servant, and we will take passage on a steamboat and go to Cincinnati, and thence to Canada." Here William put in several objections to the plan. He feared detection, and he well knew that, when a slave is once caught when attempting to escape, if returned is sure to be worse treated than before. However, Clotel satisfied him that the plan could be carried out if he would only play his part.[6]

The resolution was taken, the clothes for her disguise procured, and before night everything was in readiness for their departure. That night Mr. Cooper, their master, was to attend a party, and this was their opportunity. William went to the wharf to look out for a boat, and had scarcely reached the landing ere he heard the puffing of a steamer. He returned and reported the fact. Clotel had already packed her trunk, and had only to dress and all was ready. In less than an hour they were on board the boat. Under the assumed name of "Mr. Johnson," Clotel went to the clerk's office and took a private state room for herself, and paid her own and servant's fare. Besides being attired in a neat suit of black, she had a white silk handkerchief tied round her chin, as if she was an invalid. A pair of green glasses covered her eyes; and fearing that she would be talked to too much and thus render her liable to be detected, she assumed to be very ill. On the other hand, William was playing his part well in the servants' hall; he was talking loudly of his master's wealth. Nothing appeared as good on the boat as in his master's fine mansion. "I don't like dees steamboats no how," said William; "I hope when marser goes on a journey agin he will take de carriage and de hosses." Mr. Johnson (for such was the name by which Clotel now went) remained in his room, to avoid, as far as possible, conversation with others. After a passage of seven days they arrived at Louisville, and put up at Gough's Hotel.[7] Here they had to await the departure of another boat for the North. They were now in their most critical position. They were still in a slave state, and John C. Calhoun,[8] a distinguished slave-owner, was a guest at this hotel. They feared, also, that trouble would attend their attempt to leave this place for the North, as all persons taking negroes with them have to give bail that such negroes are not runaway slaves. The law upon this point is very stringent: all steamboat and other public conveyances are liable to a fine for every slave that escapes by them, besides paying the full

---

[6] *the plan . . . part:* Clotel and William's plan is modeled on the 1848 escape of Ellen and William Craft. In a letter printed in the *Liberator,* Brown was the first to report on their amazing escape; see "Singular Escape," pp. 271–73.

[7] *Gough's Hotel:* One of many hotels named in honor of the popular British temperance reformer John Bartholomew Gough (1817–1886).

[8] *John C. Calhoun:* The South Carolina politician and political theorist John C. Calhoun (1782–1850) was the South's most prominent advocate of the doctrine of states' rights. For a selection from Calhoun, see pp. 371–74.

value for the slave. After a delay of four hours, Mr. Johnson and servant took passage on the steamer Rodolph, for Pittsburgh. It is usual, before the departure of the boats, for an officer to examine every part of the vessel to see that no slave secretes himself on board. "Where are you going?" asked the officer of William, as he was doing his duty on this occasion. "I am going with marser," was the quick reply. "Who is your master?" "Mr. Johnson, sir, a gentleman in the cabin." "You must take him to the office and satisfy that captain that all is right, or you can't go on this boat." William informed his master what the officer had said. The boat was on the eve of going, and no time could be lost, yet they knew not what to do. At last they went to the office, and Mr. Johnson, addressing the captain, said, "I am informed that my boy can't go with me unless I give security that he belongs to me." "Yes," replied the captain, "that is the law." "A very strange law indeed," rejoined Mr. Johnson, "that one can't take his property with him." After a conversation of some minutes, and a plea on the part of Johnson that he did not wish to be delayed owing to his illness, they were permitted to take their passage without farther trouble, and the boat was soon on its way up the river. The fugitives had now passed the Rubicon,[9] and the next place at which they would land would be in a Free State. Clotel called William to her room, and said to him, "We are now free, you can go on your way to Canada, and I shall go to Virginia in search of my daughter." The announcement that she was going to risk her liberty in a Slave State was unwelcome news to William. With all the eloquence he could command, he tried to persuade Clotel that she could not escape detection, and was only throwing her freedom away. But she had counted the cost, and made up her mind for the worst. In return for the money he had furnished, she had secured for him his liberty, and their engagement was at an end.

After a quick passage the fugitives arrived at Cincinnati, and there separated. William proceeded on his way to Canada, and Clotel again resumed her own apparel, and prepared to start in search of her child. As might have been expected, the escape of these two valuable slaves created no little sensation in Vicksburgh. Advertisements and messages were sent in every direction in which the fugitives were thought to have gone. It was soon, however, known that they had left the town as master and servant; and many were the communications which

---

[9] *Rubicon:* In 49 B.C., in defiance of the Roman senate, Julius Caesar crossed the Rubicon, a stream flowing into the Adriatic Sea, to invade Pompey. Crossing or passing the Rubicon has come to signify taking a bold and irrevocable action.

appeared in the newspapers, in which the writers thought, or pretended, that they had seen the slaves in their disguise. One was to the effect that they had gone off on a chaise; one as master, and the other as servant. But the most probable was an account given by a correspondent of one of the Southern newspapers, who happened to be a passenger in the same steamer in which the slaves escaped, and which we here give: —

"One bright starlight night, in the month of December last, I found myself in the cabin of the steamer Rodolph, then lying in the port of Vicksburgh, and bound to Louisville. I had gone early on board, in order to select a good berth, and having got tired of reading the papers, amused myself by watching the appearance of the passengers as they dropped in, one after another, and I being a believer in physiognomy, formed my own opinion of their characters.

"The second bell rang, and as I yawningly returned my watch to my pocket, my attention was attracted by the appearance of a young man who entered the cabin supported by his servant, a strapping negro.

"The man was bundled up in a capacious overcoat; his face was bandaged with a white handkerchief, and its expression entirely hid by a pair of enormous spectacles.

"There was something so mysterious and unusual about the young man as he sat restless in the corner, that curiosity led me to observe him more closely.

"He appeared anxious to avoid notice, and before the steamer had fairly left the wharf, requested, in a low, womanly voice, to be shown his berth, as he was an invalid, and must retire early: his name he gave as Mr. Johnson. His servant was called, and he was put quietly to bed. I paced the deck until Tybee light[10] grew dim in the distance, and then went to my berth.

"I awoke in the morning with the sun shining in my face; we were then just passing St. Helena.[11] It was a mild beautiful morning, and most of the passengers were on deck, enjoying the freshness of the air, and stimulating their appetites for breakfast. Mr. Johnson soon made his appearance, arrayed as on the night before, and took his seat quietly upon the guard of the boat.

"From the better opportunity afforded by daylight, I found that he was a slight built, apparently handsome young man, with black hair and eyes, and of a darkness of complexion that betokened Spanish extraction. Any notice from others seemed painful to him; so to satisfy

[10] *Tybee light:* Light from the Tybee Lighthouse, one of the tallest lighthouses in the nineteenth-century U.S. The lighthouse was located on the Georgia coast.
[11] *St. Helena:* One of the sea islands off the coast of South Carolina.

my curiosity, I questioned his servant, who was standing near, and gained the following information.

"His master was an invalid — he had suffered for a long time under a complication of diseases, that had baffled the skill of the best physicians in Mississippi; he was now suffering principally with the 'rheumatism,' and he was scarcely able to walk or help himself in any way. He came from Vicksburgh and was now on his way to Philadelphia, at which place resided his uncle, a celebrated physician, and through whose means he hoped to be restored to perfect health.

"This information, communicated in a bold, off-hand manner, enlisted my sympathies for the sufferer, although it occurred to me that he walked rather too gingerly for a person afflicted with so many ailments."

After thanking Clotel for the great service she had done him in bringing him out of slavery, William bade her farewell. The prejudice that exists in the Free States against coloured persons, on account of their color, is attributable solely to the influence of slavery, and is but another form of slavery itself. And even the slave who escapes from the Southern plantations, is surprised when he reaches the North, at the amount and withering influence of this prejudice. William applied at a railway station for a ticket for the train going to Sandusky,[12] and was told that if he went by that train he would have to ride in the luggage-van. "Why?" asked the astonished negro. "We don't send a Jim Crow[13] carriage but once a day, and that went this morning." The "Jim Crow" carriage is the one in which the blacks have to ride. Slavery is a school in which its victims learn much shrewdness, and William had been an apt scholar. Without asking any more questions, the negro took his seat in one of the first-class carriages. He was soon seen and ordered out. Afraid to remain in the town longer, he resolved to go by that train; and consequently seated himself on a goods' box in the luggage-van. The train started at its proper time, and all went on well. Just before arriving at the end of the journey, the conductor called on William for his ticket. "I have none," was the reply. "Well, then, you can pay your fare with me," said the officer. "How much is it?" asked the black man. "Two dollars." "What do you charge those in the passenger-carriage?" "Two dollars." "And do you charge me the same as you do those who ride in the best carriage?" asked the

---

[12] *Sandusky:* A port town in northern Ohio, on Lake Erie.
[13] *Jim Crow:* A term first used in the 1830s to describe a song and dance routine by blackface minstrel performers, "Jim Crow" came to be understood as an adjective indicating discrimination based on race.

Clotel; or, The President's Daughter

negro. "Yes," was the answer. "I shan't pay it," returned the man. "You black scamp, do you think you can ride on this road without paying your fare?" "No, I don't want to ride for nothing; I only want to pay what's right." "Well, launch out two dollars, and that's right." "No, I shan't; I will pay what I ought, and won't pay any more." "Come, come, nigger, your fare and be done with it," said the conductor, in a manner that is never used except by Americans to blacks. "I won't pay you two dollars, and that enough," said William. "Well, as you have come all the way in the luggage-van, pay me a dollar and a half and you may go." "I shan't do any such thing." "Don't you mean to pay for riding?" "Yes, but I won't pay a dollar and a half for riding up here in the freight-van. If you had let me come in the carriage where others ride, I would have paid you two dollars." "Where were you raised? You seem to think yourself as good as white folks." "I want nothing more than my rights." "Well, give me a dollar, and I will let you off." "No, sir, I shan't do it." "What do you mean to do then — don't you wish to pay anything?" "Yes, sir, I want to pay you the full price." "What do you mean by full price?" "What do you charge per hundred-weight for goods?" inquired the negro with a degree of gravity that would have astonished Diogenes[14] himself. "A quarter of a dollar per hundred," answered the conductor. "I weigh just one hundred and fifty pounds," returned William, "and will pay you three-eighths of a dollar." "Do you expect that you will pay only thirty-seven cents for your ride?" "This, sir, is your own price. I came in a luggage-van, and I'll pay for luggage." After a vain effort to get the negro to pay for more, the conductor took the thirty-seven cents, and noted in his cash-book, "Received for one hundred and fifty pounds of luggage, thirty-seven cents." This, reader, is no fiction;[15] it actually occurred in the railway above described.

Thomas Corwin,[16] a member of the American Congress, is one of the blackest white men in the United States. He was once on his way to Congress, and took passage in one of the Ohio river steamers. As he came just at the dinner hour, he immediately went into the dining saloon, and took his seat at the table. A gentleman with his whole

[14] *Diogenes:* A Greek Cynic philosopher, Diogenes (412?–323 B.C.) expounded on the virtues of self-control.
[15] *This, reader, is no fiction:* For a description of Brown's own encounter with such discriminatory practices, see the selection from Josephine Brown, pp. 302–06.
[16] *Thomas Corwin:* Thomas Corwin (1794–1865) held a number of political offices in Ohio, including the governorship and a senate seat. He was best known for an 1847 speech in Congress that attacked the Mexican War and predicted increasing sectional conflict.

party of five ladies at once left the table. "Where is the captain," cried the man in an angry tone. The captain soon appeared, and it was sometime before he could satisfy the old gent. that Governor Corwin was not a nigger. The newspapers often have notices of mistakes made by innkeepers and others who undertake to accommodate the public, one of which we give below.

On the 6th inst.,[17] the Hon. Daniel Webster[18] and family entered Edgartown,[19] on a visit for health and recreation. Arriving at the hotel, without alighting from the coach, the landlord was sent for to see if suitable accommodation could be had. That dignitary appearing, and surveying Mr. Webster, while the hon. senator addressed him, seemed woefully to mistake the dark features of the traveller as he sat back in the corner of the carriage, and to suppose him a *coloured man,* particularly as there were two coloured servants of Mr. W. outside. So he promptly declared that there was no room for him and his family, and he could not be accommodated there — at the same time suggesting that he might perhaps find accommodation at some of the huts "up back," to which he pointed. So deeply did the prejudice of looks possess him, that he appeared not to notice that the stranger introduced himself to him as Daniel Webster, or to be so ignorant as not to have heard of such a personage; and turning away, he expressed to the driver his astonishment that he should bring *black* people there for *him* to take in. It was not till he had been repeatedly assured and made to understand that the said Daniel Webster was a real live senator of the United States, that he perceived his awkward mistake and the distinguished honour which he and his house were so near missing.

In most of the Free States, the coloured people are disfranchised on account of their color. The following scene, which we take from a newspaper in the state of Ohio, will give some idea of the extent to which this prejudice is carried.

"The whole of Thursday last was occupied by the Court of Common Pleas for this county in trying to find out whether one Thomas West was of the VOTING COLOUR, as some had very *constitutional doubts* as to whether his colour was orthodox, and whether his hair was of the official crisp! Was it not a dignified business? Four profound judges, four acute lawyers, twelve grave jurors, and I don't know how many venerable

---

[17] *inst.:* Of the present month; from the Latin "instans."
[18] *Hon. Daniel Webster:* A much admired senator from Massachusetts, Daniel Webster (1782–1852) alienated many abolitionists when he supported the Compromise of 1850. For a selection from Webster, see pp. 394–97.
[19] *Edgartown:* A town in Martha's Vineyard, an island off southeast Massachusetts.

witnesses, making in all about thirty men, perhaps, all engaged in the profound, laborious, and illustrious business, of finding out whether a man who pays tax, works on the road, and is an industrious farmer, has been born according to the republican, Christian constitution of Ohio — so that he can vote! And they wisely, gravely and 'JUDGMAT-ICALLY' decided that he should not vote! What wisdom — what research it must have required to evolve this truth! It was left for the Court of Common Pleas for Columbian county, Ohio, in the United States of North America, to find out what Solomon never dreamed of — the courts of all civilised, heathen, or Jewish countries, never contemplated. Lest the wisdom of our courts should be circumvented by some such men as might be named, who are so near being born constitutionally that they might be taken for white by sight, I would suggest that our court be invested with SMELLING powers, and that if a man don't exhale the constitutional smell, he shall not vote! This would be an additional security to our liberties."

William found, after all, that liberty in the so-called Free States was more a name than a reality; that prejudice followed the coloured man into every place that he might enter. The temples erected for the worship of the living God are no exception. The finest Baptist church in the city of Boston has the following paragraph in the deed that conveys its seats to pewholders:[20]

> "And it is a further condition of these presents, that if the owner or owners of said pew shall determine hereafter to sell the same, it shall first be offered, in writing, to the standing committee of said society for the time being, at such price as might otherwise be obtained for it; and the said committee shall have the right, for ten days after such offer, to purchase said pew for said society, at that price, first deducting therefrom all taxes and assessments on said pew then remaining unpaid. And if the said committee shall not so complete such purchase within said ten days, then the pew may be sold by the owner or owners thereof (after payment of all such arrears) to any one respectable *white person,* but upon the same conditions as are contained in this instrument; and immediate notice of such sale shall be given in writing, by the vendor, to the treasurer of said society."

Such are the conditions upon which the Rowe Street Baptist Church, Boston, disposes of its seats. The writer of this is able to put that whole congregation, minister and all, to flight, by merely putting his coloured

---

[20] *pewholders:* Those who rent or own a pew, an enclosed area of seats or benches in a church. The system of pewholding was widespread in nineteenth-century churches.

face in that church. We once visited a church in New York that had a place set apart for the sons of Ham. It was a dark, dismal looking place in one corner of the gallery, grated in front like a hen-coop, with a black border around it. It had two doors; over one was B. M. — black men; over the other B. W. — black women.

CHAPTER XX.
A TRUE DEMOCRAT.

"Who can, with patience, for a moment see
The medley mass of pride and misery,
Of whips and charters, manacles and rights,
Of slaving blacks and democratic whites,
And all the piebald policy that reigns
In free confusion o'er Columbia's plains?
To think that man, thou just and gentle God!
Should stand before thee with a tyrant's rod,
O'er creatures like himself, with souls from thee,
Yet dare to boast of perfect liberty!"[1]
— *Thomas Moore.*

Educated in a free state, and marrying a wife who had been a victim to the institution of slavery, Henry Morton became strongly opposed to the system. His two daughters, at the age of twelve years, were sent to the North to finish their education, and to receive that refinement that young ladies cannot obtain in the Slave States. Although he did not publicly advocate the abolition of slavery, he often made himself obnoxious to private circles, owing to the denunciatory manner in which he condemned the "peculiar institution." Being one evening at a party, and hearing one of the company talking loudly of the glory and freedom of American institutions, he gave it as his opinion that, unless slavery was speedily abolished, it would be the ruin of the Union. "It is not our boast of freedom," said he, "that will cause us to be respected abroad. It is not our loud talk in favour of liberty that will cause us to be regarded as friends of human freedom; but our acts will be scrutinised by the people of other countries. We say much against European despotism; let us look to ourselves. That government is despotic where the rulers govern subjects by their own mere will — by decrees and laws emanating from their uncontrolled will, in the enactment and execution of which the ruled have no voice, and under which they have no right except at the will of the rulers. Despotism does not depend upon the numbers of the rulers, or the number of the subjects. It may have one ruler or many. Rome was a despotism under Nero; so

---

[1] *"Who can.... perfect liberty!":* From Thomas Moore (1779–1852), "To the Lord Viscount Forbes. From the City of Washington," in *The Poetical Works* (1840–41).

she was under the triumvirate. Athens was a despotism under Thirty Tyrants; under her Four Hundred Tyrants; under her Three Thousand Tyrants.[2] It has been generally observed that despotism increases in severity with the number of despots; the responsibility is more divided, and the claims more numerous. The triumvirs each demanded his victims. The smaller the number of subjects in proportion to the tyrants, the more cruel the oppression, because the less danger from rebellion. In this government, the free white citizens are the rulers — the sovereigns, as we delight to be called. All others are subjects. There are, perhaps, some sixteen or seventeen millions of sovereigns, and four millions of subjects.

"The rulers and the ruled are of all colours, from the clear white of the Caucasian[3] tribes to the swarthy Ethiopian. The former, by courtesy, are all called white, the latter black. In this government the subject has no rights, social, political, or personal. He has no voice in the laws which govern him. He can hold no property. His very wife and children are not his. His labour is another's. He, and all that appertain to him, are the absolute property of his rulers. He is governed, bought, sold, punished, executed, by laws to which he never gave his assent, and by rulers whom he never chose. He is not a serf merely, with half the rights of men like the subjects of despotic Russia; but a native slave, stripped of every right which God and nature gave him, and which the high spirit of our revolution declared inalienable — which he himself could not surrender, and which man could not take from him. Is he not then the subject of despotic sway?

"The slaves of Athens and Rome were free in comparison.[4] They had some rights — could acquire some property; could choose their own masters, and purchase their own freedom; and, when free, could rise in social and political life. The slaves of America, then, lie under

[2] *Rome . . . Tyrants:* Nero was emperor of Rome, A.D. 54–A.D. 68; a triumvirate, a ruling body of three men, governed in ancient Rome circa B.C. 60–B.C. 31. Athens's oligarchical Thirty Tyrants were overthrown in 403 B.C. Morton's reference to the Four Hundred and Three Thousand Tyrants are more likely jabs at what Brown regards as Southerners' false forms of democracy.

[3] *Caucasian:* A term coined by the German naturalist and anthropologist Johann Friedrich Blumenbach (1752–1840) to designate what he classified to be the white race. Based on a comparative study of human skulls, his widely disseminated *On the Natural Varieties of Mankind* (1775) divided mankind into five racial classifications and helped give rise to racial "science."

[4] *The slaves . . . comparison:* In his *Appeal* (1829), the black nationalist David Walker similarly argued that the Roman slaves were better off than U.S. slaves; for selections from the *Appeal,* see pp. 348–60.

the most absolute and grinding despotism that the world ever saw. But who are the despots? The rulers of the country — the sovereign people! Not merely the slaveholder who cracks the lash. He is but the instrument in the hands of despotism. That despotism is the government of the Slave States, and the United States, consisting of all its rulers — all the free citizens. Do not look upon this as a paradox, because you and I and the sixteen millions of rulers are free. The rulers of every despotism are free. Nicholas of Russia is free. The grand Sultan of Turkey is free. The butcher of Austria is free. Augustus, Anthony, and Lepidus were free, while they drenched Rome in blood.[5] The Thirty Tyrants — the Four Hundred — the Three Thousand, were free while they bound their countrymen in chains. You, and I, and the sixteen millions are free, while we fasten iron chains, and rivet manacles on four millions of our fellow-men — tear their wives and children from them — separate them — sell them, and doom them to perpetual, eternal bondage. Are we not then despots — despots such as history will brand and God abhor?

"We, as individuals, are fast losing our reputation for honest dealing. Our nation is losing its character. The loss of a firm national character, or the degradation of a nation's honour, is the inevitable prelude to her destruction. Behold the once proud fabric of a Roman empire — an empire carrying its arts and arms into every part of the Eastern continent; the monarchs of mighty kingdoms dragged at the wheels of her triumphal chariots; her eagle waving over the ruins of desolated countries; — where is her splendour, her wealth, her power, her glory? Extinguished for ever. Her mouldering temples, the mournful vestiges of her former grandeur, afford a shelter to her muttering monks. Where are her statesmen, her sages, her philosophers, her orators, generals? Go to their solitary tombs and inquire? She lost her national character, and her destruction followed. The ramparts of her national pride were broken down, and Vandalism[6] desolated her classic fields. Then let the people of our country take warning ere it is too late. But most of us say to ourselves,

---

[5] *Nicholas. . . . blood:* A listing of representative despots: Nicholas I (1796–1855) was czar of Russia from 1825 to 1855; Abd al-Majid (1823–1861) reigned as the Ottoman sultan from 1839 to 1861; Franz Joseph (1830–1916) was emperor of Austria from 1848 to 1916; Augustus (63 B.C.–A.D. 14) was the first Roman emperor; Marc Anthony (c. 83 B.C.–30 B.C.) and Marcus Aemilius Lepidus (?–13 B.C.) formed Rome's Second Triumvirate circa 43 B.C.

[6] *Vandalism:* Derives from the Vandals, the Germanic people who sacked Rome in A.D. 455.

"'Who questions the right of mankind to be free?
Yet, what are the rights of the *negro* to me?
I'm well fed and clothed, I have plenty of pelf[7] —
I'll care for the blacks when I turn black myself.'

"New Orleans is doubtless the most immoral place in the United States. The theatres are open on the Sabbath. Bull-fights, horse-racing, and other cruel amusements are carried on in this city to an extent unknown in any other part of the Union. The most stringent laws have been passed in that city against negroes, yet a few years since the State Legislature passed a special act to enable a white man to marry a coloured woman, on account of her being possessed of a large fortune. And, very recently, the following paragraph appeared in the city papers: —

"'There has been quite a stir recently in this city, in consequence of a marriage of a white man, named Buddington, a teller in the Canal Bank, to the negro daughter of one of the wealthiest merchants. Buddington, before he could be married, was obliged to swear that he had negro blood in his veins, and to do this he made an incision in his arm, and put some of her blood in the cut. The ceremony was performed by a Catholic clergyman, and the bridegroom has received with his wife a fortune of fifty or sixty thousand dollars.'

"It seems that the fifty or sixty thousand dollars entirely covered the negro woman's black skin, and the law prohibiting marriage between blacks and whites was laid aside for the occasion."

Althesa felt proud, as well she might, at her husband's taking such high ground in a slaveholding city like New Orleans.

[7] *pelf:* Money (generally a disparaging term).

CHAPTER XXI.
THE CHRISTIAN'S DEATH.

"O weep, ye friends of freedom weep!
Your harps to mournful measure sweep."[1]

On the last day of November, 1620, on the confines of the Grand Bank of Newfoundland, lo! we behold one little solitary tempest-tost and weather-beaten ship; it is all that can be seen on the length and breadth of the vast intervening solitudes, from the melancholy wilds of Labrador[2] and New England's iron-bound shores, to the western coasts of Ireland and the rock-defended Hebrides,[3] but one lonely ship greets the eyes of angels or of men, on this great thoroughfare of nations in our age. Next in moral grandeur, was this ship, to the great discoverer's: Columbus found a continent; the May-flower[4] brought the seed-wheat of states and empire. That is the May-flower, with its servants of the living God, their wives and little ones, hastening to lay the foundations of nations in the occidental lands of the setting-sun. Hear the voice of prayer to God for his protection, and the glorious music of praise, as it breaks into the wild tempest of the mighty deep, upon the ear of God. Here in this ship are great and good men. Justice, mercy, humanity, respect for the rights of all; each man honoured, as he was useful to himself and others; labour respected, law-abiding men, constitution-making and respecting men; men, whom no tyrant could conquer, or hardship overcome, with the high commission sealed by a Spirit divine, to establish religious and political liberty for all. This ship had the embryo elements of all that is useful, great, and grand in Northern institutions; it was the great type of goodness and wisdom, illustrated in two and a quarter centuries gone by; it was the good genius of America.

But look far in the South-east, and you behold on the same day, in 1620, a low rakish ship hastening from the tropics, solitary and alone, to the New World. What is she? She is freighted with the elements of unmixed evil. Hark! hear those rattling chains, hear that cry of despair and wail of anguish, as they die away in the unpitying distance. Listen

---

[1] "*O Weep. . . . measures sweep*": From D. H. Jacques, "Your Brother Is a Slave," in *The Anti-Slavery Harp*, ed. Brown.

[2] *Labrador:* Peninsula containing the Canadian provinces of Newfoundland and Quebec.

[3] *Hebrides:* Scottish islands West of Scotland.

[4] *May-flower:* The *Mayflower* brought William Bradford (1590–1657) and other English Puritans to Cape Cod on 9 November 1620.

to those shocking oaths, the crack of that flesh-cutting whip. Ah! it is the first cargo of slaves on their way to Jamestown, Virginia.[5] Behold the May-flower anchored at Plymouth Rock, the slave-ship in James River. Each a parent, one of the prosperous, labour-honouring, law-sustaining institutions of the North; the other the mother of slavery, idleness, lynch-law, ignorance, unpaid labour, poverty, and duelling, despotism, the ceaseless swing of the whip, and the peculiar institutions of the South. These ships are the representation of good and evil in the New World, even to our day. When shall one of those parallel lines come to an end?

The origin of American slavery is not lost in the obscurity of by-gone ages. It is a plain historical fact, that it owes its birth to the African slave trade, now pronounced by every civilised community the greatest crime ever perpetrated against humanity. Of all causes intended to benefit mankind, the abolition of chattel slavery must necessarily be placed amongst the first, and the negro hails with joy every new advocate that appears in his cause. Commiseration for human suffering and human sacrifices awakened the capacious mind, and brought into action the enlarged benevolence, of Georgiana Carlton. With respect to her philosophy — it was of a noble cast. It was, that all men are by nature equal; that they are wisely and justly endowed by the Creator with certain rights, which are irrefragable; and that, however human pride and human avarice may depress and debase, still God is the author of good to man — and of evil, man is the artificer to himself and to his species. Unlike Plato and Socrates,[6] her mind was free from the gloom that surrounded theirs; her philosophy was founded in the school of Christianity; though a devoted member of her father's church, she was not a sectarian.

We learn from Scripture, and it is a little remarkable that it is the only exact definition of religion found in the sacred volume, that "pure religion and undefiled before God, even the Father, is this, to visit the fatherless and widows in their affliction, and to keep oneself unspotted from the world." "Look not every man on his own things, but every man also on the things of others." "Remember them that are in bonds

---

[5] *the first cargo of slaves on their way to Jamestown, Virginia:* In fact, twenty slaves purchased from a Dutch man-of-war were brought to the early English settlement of Jamestown in August 1619.

[6] *Plato and Socrates:* Committed to a philosophical idealism that conceived of the Good as the divine, ordering principal of the cosmos, the ancient Greek philosophers Plato (427?–347 B.C.) and Socrates (469–399 B.C.) are presented as gloomy for lacking a sense of the Christian God.

as bound with them." "Whatsoever ye would that others should do to you, do ye even so to them."[7]

This was her view of Christianity, and to this end she laboured with all her energies to convince her slaveholding neighbours that the negro could not only take care of himself, but that he also appreciated liberty, and was willing to work and redeem himself. Her most sanguine wishes were being realized when she suddenly fell into a decline. Her mother had died of consumption, and her physician pronounced this to be her disease. She was prepared for this sad intelligence, and received it with the utmost composure. Although she had confidence in her husband that he would carry out her wishes in freeing the negroes after her death, Mrs. Carlton resolved upon their immediate liberation. Consequently the slaves were all summoned before the noble woman, and informed that they were no longer bondsmen. "From this hour," said she, "you are free, and all eyes will be fixed upon you. I dare not predict how far your example may affect the welfare of your brethren yet in bondage. If you are temperate, industrious, peaceable, and pious, you will show to the world that slaves can be emancipated without danger. Remember what a singular relation you sustain to society. The necessities of the case require not only that you should behave as well as the whites, but better than the whites; and for this reason: if you behave no better than they, your example will lose a great portion of its influence. Make the Lord Jesus Christ your refuge and exemplar. His is the only standard around which you can successfully rally. If ever there was a people who needed the consolations of religion to sustain them in their grievous afflictions, you are that people. You had better trust in the Lord than to put confidence in man. Happy is that people whose God is the Lord. Get as much education as possible for yourselves and your children. An ignorant people can never occupy any other than a degraded station in society; they can never be truly free until they are intelligent. In a few days you will start for the state of Ohio, where land will be purchased for some of you who have families, and where I hope you will all prosper. We have been urged to send you to Liberia, but we think it wrong to send you from your native land. We did not wish to encourage the Colonization Society,[8] for it originated in hatred of the free coloured people. Its pretences are false, its doctrines odious, its means contemptible. Now,

---

[7] *"pure religion. . . . to them"*: James 1.27, Philippians 2.4, Hebrews 13.3, Matthew 7.12.

[8] *Colonization Society*: Founded in 1816 in Washington, D.C., the American Colonization Society sought to ship the free blacks to Africa.

whatever may be your situation in life, 'Remember those in bonds as bound with them.'[9] You must get ready as soon as you can for your journey to the North."

Seldom was there ever witnessed a more touching scene than this. There sat the liberator, — pale, feeble, emaciated, with death stamped upon her countenance, surrounded by the sons and daughters of Africa; some of whom had in former years been separated from all that they had held near and dear, and the most of whose backs had been torn and gashed by the negro whip. Some were upon their knees at the feet of their benefactress; others were standing round her weeping. Many begged that they might be permitted to remain on the farm and work for wages, for some had wives and some husbands on other plantations in the neighbourhood, and would rather remain with them.

But the laws of the state forbade any emancipated negroes remaining, under penalty of again being sold into slavery. Hence the necessity of sending them out of the state. Mrs. Carlton was urged by her friends to send the emancipated negroes to Africa. Extracts from the speeches of Henry Clay, and other distinguished Colonization Society men, were read to her to induce her to adopt this course. Some thought they should be sent away because the blacks are vicious; others because they would be missionaries to their brethren in Africa. "But," said she, "if we send away the negroes because they are profligate and vicious, what sort of missionaries will they make? Why not send away the vicious among the whites for the same reason, and the same purpose?"

Death is a leveller, and neither age, sex, wealth, nor usefulness can avert when he is permitted to strike. The most beautiful flowers soon fade, and droop, and die; this is also the case with man; his days are uncertain as the passing breeze. This hour he glows in the blush of health and vigour, but the next he may be counted with the number no more known on earth.

Although in a low state of health, Mrs. Carlton had the pleasure of seeing all her slaves, except Sam and three others, start for a land of freedom. The morning they were to go on board the steamer, bound for Louisville, they all assembled on the large grass plot, in front of the drawing-room window, and wept while they bid their mistress farewell. When they were on the boat, about leaving the wharf, they were heard giving the charge to those on shore — "Sam, take care of

[9] 'Remember . . . with them': Hebrews 13.3.

Misus, take care of Marser, as you love us, and hope to meet us in de Hio (Ohio), and in heben; be sure and take good care of Misus and Marser."

In less than a week after her emancipated people had started for Ohio, Mrs. Carlton was cold in death. Mr. Carlton felt deeply, as all husbands must who love their wives, the loss of her who had been a lamp to his feet, and a light to his path. She had converted him from infidelity to Christianity; from the mere theory of liberty to practical freedom. He had looked upon the negro as an ill-treated distant link of the human family; he now regarded them as a part of God's children. Oh, what a silence pervaded the house when the Christian had been removed. His indeed was a lonesome position.

> " 'Twas midnight, and he sat alone —
>   The husband of the dead,
> That day the dark dust had been thrown
>   Upon the buried head."

In the midst of the buoyancy of youth, this cherished one had drooped and died. Deep were the sounds of grief and mourning heard in that stately dwelling, when the stricken friends, whose office it had been to nurse and soothe the weary sufferer, beheld her pale and motionless in the sleep of death.

Oh what a chill creeps through the breaking heart when we look upon the insensible form, and feel that it no longer contains the spirit we so dearly loved! How difficult to realise that the eye which always glowed with affection and intelligence — that the ear which had so often listened to the sounds of sorrow and gladness — that the voice whose accents had been to us like sweet music, and the heart, the habitation of benevolence and truth, are now powerless and insensate as the bier[10] upon which the form rests. Though faith is strong enough to penetrate the cloud of gloom which hovers near, and to behold the freed spirit safe, *for ever,* safe in its home in heaven, yet the thoughts *will* linger sadly and cheerlessly upon the grave.

Peace to her ashes! she fought the fight, obtained the Christian's victory, and wears the crown. But if it were that departed spirits are permitted to note the occurrences of this world, with what a frown of disapprobation would hers view the effort being made in the United States to retard the work of emancipation for which she laboured and so wished to see brought about.

[10] *bier:* A stand holding a corpse or coffin.

In what light would she consider that hypocritical priesthood who gave their aid and sanction to the infamous "Fugitive Slave Law." If true greatness consists in doing good to mankind, then was Georgiana Carlton an ornament to human nature. Who can think of the broken hearts made whole, of sad and dejected countenances now beaming with contentment and joy, of the mother offering her free-born babe to heaven, and of the father whose cup of joy seems overflowing in the presence of his family, where none can molest or make him afraid. Oh, that God may give more such persons to take the whip-scarred negro by the hand, and raise him to a level with our common humanity! May the professed lovers of freedom in the new world see that true liberty is freedom for all! and may every American continually hear it sounding in his ear: —

> "Shall every flap of England's flag
>   Proclaim that all around are free,
> From 'farthest Ind' to each blue crag
>   That beetles o'er the Western Sea?
> And shall we scoff at Europe's kings,
>   When Freedom's fire is dim with us,
> And round our country's altar clings
>   The damning shade of Slavery's curse?"[11]

---

[11] *"Shall. . . . Slavery's curse?":* From John Greenleaf Whittier, "Expostulation" (1834).

CHAPTER XXII.
A RIDE IN A STAGE-COACH.

We shall now return to Cincinnati, where we left Clotel preparing to go to Richmond in search of her daughter. Tired of the disguise in which she had escaped, she threw it off on her arrival at Cincinnati. But being assured that not a shadow of safety would attend her visit to a city in which she was well known, unless in some disguise, she again resumed men's apparel on leaving Cincinnati. This time she had more the appearance of an Italian or Spanish gentleman. In addition to the fine suit of black cloth, a splendid pair of dark false whiskers covered the sides of her face, while the curling moustache found its place upon the upper lip. From practice she had become accustomed to high-heeled boots, and could walk without creating any suspicion as regarded her sex. It was on a cold evening that Clotel arrived at Wheeling,[1] and took a seat in the coach going to Richmond. She was already in the state of Virginia, yet a long distance from the place of her destination.

A ride in a stage-coach, over an American road, is unpleasant under the most favourable circumstances. But now that it was winter, and the roads unusually bad, the journey was still more dreary. However, there were eight passengers in the coach, and I need scarcely say that such a number of genuine Americans could not be together without whiling away the time somewhat pleasantly. Besides Clotel, there was an elderly gentleman with his two daughters — one apparently under twenty years, the other a shade above. The pale, spectacled face of another slim, tall man, with a white neckerchief, pointed him out as a minister. The rough featured, dark countenance of a stout looking man, with a white hat on one side of his head, told that he was from the sunny South. There was nothing remarkable about the other two, who might pass for ordinary American gentlemen. It was on the eve of a presidential election, when every man is thought to be a politician. Clay, Van Buren, and Harrison were the men who expected the endorsement of the Baltimore Convention.[2] "Who does this town go

---

[1] *Wheeling:* A city in the northwest section of Virginia (now West Virginia) on the Ohio River.

[2] *Clay . . . Convention:* In 1839, Henry Clay and William Henry Harrison (1773–1841) competed as presidential candidates at the Whig nominating convention in Harrisburg, Pennsylvania; the incumbent president Martin Van Buren (1782–1862) was renominated at the Democratic convention in Baltimore in 1840. The Whigs' nominee, Harrison, defeated Van Buren to become the nation's ninth president, and died shortly after his inauguration.

for?" asked the old gent. with the ladies, as the coach drove up to an inn, where groups of persons were waiting for the latest papers. "We are divided," cried the rough voice of one of the outsiders. "Well, who do you think will get the majority here?" continued the old gent. "Can't tell very well; I go for 'Old Tip,' "[3] was the answer from without. This brought up the subject fairly before the passengers, and when the coach again started a general discussion commenced, in which all took a part except Clotel and the young ladies. Some were for Clay, some for Van Buren, and others for "Old Tip." The coach stopped to take in a real farmer-looking man, who no sooner entered than he was saluted with "Do you go for Clay?" "No," was the answer. "Do you go for Van Buren?" "No." "Well, then, of course you will go for Harrison." "No." "Why, don't you mean to work for any of them at the election?" "No." "Well, who will you work for?" asked one of the company. "I work for Betsy and the children, and I have a hard job of it at that," replied the farmer, without a smile. This answer, as a matter of course, set the new comer down as one upon whom the rest of the passengers could crack their jokes with the utmost impunity. "Are you an Odd Fellow?"[4] asked one. "No, sir, I've been married more than a month." "I mean, do you belong to the order of Odd Fellows?" "No, no; I belong to the order of married men." "Are you a mason?"[5] "No, I am a carpenter by trade." "Are you a Son of Temperance?"[6] "Bother you, no; I am a son of Mr. John Gosling." After a hearty laugh in which all joined, the subject of Temperance became the theme for discussion. In this the spectacled gent. was at home. He soon showed that he was a New Englander, and went the whole length of the "Maine Law."[7] The minister was about having it all his own way, when the Southerner, in the white hat, took the opposite side of the question. "I don't bet a red cent on these teetotlars,"[8]

---

[3] *"Old Tip"*: Nickname of William Henry Harrison, which he acquired for having led U.S. forces against the Shawnee Indians in the 1811 Battle of Tippecanoe at what was later named Battle Ground, Indiana.

[4] *Odd Fellow?"*: A secretive, benevolent organization founded in England in the eighteenth century.

[5] *mason?"*: Like the Odd Fellows, the Free and Accepted Masons are a secretive, fraternal organization. Modern Masonry had its origins in early-eighteenth-century England.

[6] *Son of Temperance?"*: Founded in 1843, the Sons of Temperance was a secretive, fraternal organization committed to the cause of total abstinence from alcoholic beverages. By 1850, the organization boasted of having 250,000 dues-paying members.

[7] *"Maine Law"*: Passed by Maine's state legislature in 1851, the law banned the sale and manufacture of alcoholic beverages within the state.

[8] *teetotalers"*: People who abstain from intoxicating beverages.

said he, and at the same time looking round to see if he had the approbation of the rest of the company. "Why?" asked the minister. "Because they are a set who are afraid to spend a cent. They are a bad lot,
the whole on 'em." It was evident that the white hat gent. was an uneducated man. The minister commenced in full earnest, and gave an
interesting account of the progress of temperance in Connecticut, the
state from which he came, proving, that a great portion of the prosperity of the state was attributable to the disuse of intoxicating drinks.
Every one thought the white hat had got the worst of the argument,
and that he was settled for the remainder of the night. But not he; he
took fresh courage and began again. "Now," said he, "I have just been
on a visit to my uncle's in Vermont, and I guess I knows a little about
these here teetotlars. You see, I went up there to make a little stay of a
fortnight. I got there at night, and they seemed glad to see me, but they
didn't give me a bit of anything to drink. Well, thinks I to myself, the
jig's up: I sha'n't get any more liquor till I get out of the state. We all
sat up till twelve o'clock that night, and I heard nothing but talk about
the 'Juvinal Temperance Army,' the 'Band of Hope,' the 'Rising Generation,' the 'Female Dorcas Temperance Society,' 'The None Such,'[9]
and I don't know how many other names they didn't have. As I had
taken several pretty large 'Cock Tails' before I entered the state, I
thought upon the whole that I would not spile for the want of liquor.
The next morning, I commenced writing back to my friends, and
telling them what's what. Aunt Polly said, 'Well, Johnny, I s'pose you
are given 'em a pretty account of us all here.' 'Yes,' said I; 'I am tellin'
'em if they want anything to drink when they come up here, they had
better bring it with 'em.' 'Oh,' said aunty, 'they would search their
boxes; can't bring any spirits in the state.' Well, as I was saying, jist as
I got my letters finished, and was going to the post office (for uncle's
house was two miles from the town), aunty says, 'Johnny, I s'pose
you'll try to get a little somethin' to drink in town won't you?' Says I,
'I s'pse it's no use.' 'No,' said she, 'you can't; it aint to be had no how,
for love nor money.' So jist as I was puttin' on my hat, 'Johnny,' cries
out aunty, 'What,' says I. 'Now I'll tell you, I don't want you to say
nothin' about it, but I keeps a little rum to rub my head with, for I am
troubled with a headache; now I don't want you to mention it for the
world, but I'll give you a little taste, the old man is such a teetotaller,
that I should never hear the last of it, and I would not like for the boys
to know it, they are members of the "Cold Water Army." '[10]

[9] *'Juvinal . . . None Such'*: Various temperance organizations.
[10] *"Cold Water Army" '*: Founded in 1834, an organization of Sunday-school youth
that campaigned against alcohol as a destroyer of families.

"Aunty now brought out a black bottle and gave me a cup, and told me to help myself, which I assure you I did. I now felt ready to face the cold. As I was passing the barn I heard uncle thrashing oats, so I went to the door and spoke to him. 'Come in, John,' says he. 'No,' said I; 'I am goin' to post some letters,' for I was afraid that he would smell my breath if I went too near to him. 'Yes, yes, come in.' So I went in, and says he, 'It's now eleven o'clock; that's about the time you take your grog,[11] I s'pose, when you are at home.' 'Yes,' said I. 'I am sorry for you, my lad; you can't get anything up here; you can't even get it at the chemist's, except as medicine, and then you must let them mix it and you take it in their presence.' 'This is indeed hard,' replied I; 'Well, it can't be helped,' continued he: 'and it ought not to be if it could. It's best for society; people's better off without drink. I recollect when your father and I, thirty years ago, used to go out on a spree and spend more than half a dollar in a night. Then here's the rising generation; there's nothing like settin' a good example. Look how healthy your cousins are — there's Benjamin, he never tasted spirits in his life. Oh, John, I would you were a teetotaller.' 'I suppose,' said I, 'I'll have to be one till I leave the state.' 'Now,' said he, 'John, I don't want you to mention it, for your aunt would go into hysterics if she thought there was a drop of intoxicating liquor about the place, and I would not have the boys to know it for anything, but I keep a little brandy to rub my joints for the rheumatics, and being it's you, I'll give you a little dust.' So the old man went to one corner of the barn, took out a brown jug and handed it to me, and I must say it was a little the best cogniac that I had tasted for many a day. Says I, 'Uncle, you are a good judge of brandy.' 'Yes,' said he, 'I learned when I was young.' So off I started for the post office. In returnin' I thought I'd jist go through the woods where the boys were chopping wood, and wait and go to the house with them when they went to dinner. I found them hard at work, but as merry as crickets. 'Well, cousin John, are you done writing?' 'Yes,' answered I. 'Have you posted them?' 'Yes.' 'Hope you didn't go to any place inquiring about grog.' 'No, I knowed it was no good to do that.' 'I suppose a cock-tail would taste good now.' 'Well, I guess it would,' said I. The three boys then joined in a hearty laugh. 'I suppose you have told 'em that we are a dry set up here?' 'Well, I aint told 'em anything else.' 'Now, cousin John,' said Edward, 'if you wont say anything, we will give you a small taste. For mercy's sake don't let father or mother know it; they are such rabid teetotallers, that they would not sleep a wink to-night if they thought there was any spirits

---

[11] *grog:* Generally refers to a mixture of water and hard liquor.

about the place.' 'I am mum,' says I. And the boys took a jug out of a hollow stump, and gave me some first-rate peach brandy. And during the fortnight that I was in Vermont, with my teetotal relations, I was kept about as well corned[12] as if I had been among my hot water friends in Tennessee."

This narrative, given by the white hat man, was received with unbounded applause by all except the pale gent. in spectacles, who showed, by the way in which he was running his fingers between his cravat and throat, that he did not intend to "give it up so." The white hat gent. was now the lion of the company.

"Oh, you did not get hold of the right kind of teetotallers." said the minister. "I can give you a tale worth a dozen of yours," continued he. "Look at society in the states where temperance views prevail, and you will there see real happiness. The people are taxed less, the poor houses are shut up for want of occupants, and extreme destitution is unknown. Every one who drinks at all is liable to become an habitual drunkard. Yes, I say boldly, that no man living who uses intoxicating drinks, is free from the danger of at least occasional, and if of occasional, ultimately of habitual excess. There seems to be no character, position, or circumstances that free men from the danger. *I have known* many young men of the finest promise, led by the drinking habit into vice, ruin, and early death. *I have known* many tradesmen whom it has made bankrupt. *I have known* Sunday scholars whom it has led to prison — teachers, and even superintendents, whom it has dragged down to profligacy. *I have known* ministers of high academic honours, of splendid eloquence, nay, of vast usefulness, whom it has fascinated, and hurried over the precipice of public infamy with their eyes open, and gazing with horror on their fate. *I have known* men of the strongest and clearest intellect and of vigorous resolution, whom it has made weaker than children and fools — gentlemen of refinement and taste whom it has debased into brutes — poets of high genius whom it has bound in a bondage worse than the galleys, and ultimately cut short their days. *I have known* statesmen, lawyers, and judges whom it has killed — kind husbands and fathers whom it has turned into monsters. *I have known* honest men whom it has made villains — elegant and Christian *ladies* whom it has *converted into bloated sots.*"[13]

<hr/>

[12] *well corned:* Well supplied with hard drink; the expression derived from the popularity of corn whiskey.

[13] *"Look at society. . . . bloated sots":* The likely source of the minister's remarks on temperance is "Important Testimony to the Maine Law from a Minster at Large," in *Frederick Douglass' Paper,* 1 April 1852.

"But you talk too fast," replied the white hat man. "You don't give a feller a chance to say nothin'." "I heard you," continued the minister, "and now you hear me out. It is indeed wonderful how people become lovers of strong drink. Some years since, before I became a teetotaller I kept spirits about the house, and I had a servant who was much addicted to strong drink. He used to say that he could not make my boots shine, without mixing the blacking with whiskey. So to satisfy myself that the whisky was put in the blacking, one morning I made him bring the dish in which he kept the blacking, and poured in the whiskey myself. And now, sir, what do you think?" "Why, I s'pose your boots shined better than before," replied the white hat. "No," continued the minister. "He took the blacking out, and I watched him, and he drank down the whiskey, blacking, and all."

This turned the joke upon the advocate of strong drink, and he began to put his wits to work for arguments. "You are from Connecticut, are you?" asked the Southerner. "Yes, and we are an orderly, pious, peaceable people. Our holy religion is respected, and we do more for the cause of Christ than the whole Southern States put together." "I don't doubt it," said the white hat gent. "You sell wooden nutmegs and other spurious articles enough to do some good. You talk of your 'holy religion;' but your robes' righteousness are woven at Lowell and Manchester;[14] your paradise is high per centum on factory stocks; your palms of victory and crowns of rejoicing are triumphs over a rival party in politics, on the questions of banks and tariffs. If you could, you would turn heaven into Birmingham,[15] make every angel a weaver, and with the eternal din of looms and spindles drown all the anthems of the morning star. Ah! I know you Connecticut people like a book. No, no, all hoss;[16] you can't come it on me." This last speech of the rough featured man again put him in the ascendant, and the spectacled gent. once more ran his fingers between his cravat and throat. "You live in Tennessee, I think," said the minister. "Yes," replied the Southerner, "I used to live in Orleans, but now I claim to be a Tennessean." "Your people of New Orleans are the most ungodly set in the United States," said the minister. Taking a New Orleans newspaper from his pocket he continued, "Just look here, there are not less than three advertisements of bull fights to take place on the Sabbath. You people of the Slave States have no regard for the Sabbath, religion, morality or anything else intended to make mankind better."

[14] *Lowell and Manchester:* In the mid-nineteenth century, Lowell, Massachusetts, and Manchester, England, were major manufacturing centers.
[15] *Birmingham:* A factory town in central England.
[16] *hoss:* Horse (slang), suggestive of feistiness (or horse manure).

Here Clotel could have borne ample testimony, had she dared to have taken sides with the Connecticut man. Her residence in Vicksburgh had given her an opportunity of knowing something of the character of the inhabitants of the far South. "Here is an account of a grand bull fight that took place in New Orleans a week ago last Sunday. I will read it to you." And the minister read aloud the following:

"Yesterday, pursuant to public notice, came off at Gretna,[17] opposite the Fourth District, the long heralded fight between the famous grizzly bear, General Jackson[18] (victor in fifty battles), and the Attakapas[19] bull, Santa Anna.[20]

"The fame of the coming conflict had gone forth to the four winds, and women and children, old men and boys, from all parts of the city, and from the breezy banks of Lake Pontchartrain and Borgne,[21] brushed up their Sunday suit, and prepared to see the fun. Long before the published hour, the quiet streets of the rural Gretna were filled with crowds of anxious denizens, flocking to the arena, and before the fight commenced, such a crowd had collected as Gretna had not seen, nor will be likely to see again.

"The arena for the sports was a cage, twenty feet square, built upon the ground, and constructed of heavy timbers and iron bars. Around it were seats, circularly placed, and intended to accommodate many thousands. About four or five thousand persons assembled, covering the seats as with a cloud, and crowding down around the cage, were within reach of the bars.

"The bull selected to sustain the honour and verify the pluck of Attakapas on this trying occasion was a black animal from the Opelousas,[22] lithe and sinewy as a four year old courser,[23] and with eyes like burning coals. His horns bore the appearance of having been filed at the tips, and wanted that keen and slashing appearance so common with others of his kith and kin; otherwise it would have been 'all day' with Bruin at the first pass, and no mistake.

[17] *Gretna:* City in southeastern Louisiana, along the west bank of the Mississippi River.

[18] *General Jackson:* The bear is named for Andrew Jackson (1767–1845), who, during his career as general and president, achieved a reputation as a pugnacious fighter for having battled the British, the Spanish, and the Indians; Jackson also fought several duels.

[19] *Attakapas:* City in southern Louisiana.

[20] *Santa Anna:* Mexican politician and general, Antonio López de Santa Anna (1794–1876) was regarded by many in the U.S. as particularly brutal for having led the 1836 attack on the Alamo, which resulted in the deaths of approximately 150 Texas revolutionaries.

[21] *Lake Pontchartrain and Borgne:* Connected lakes north of New Orleans.

[22] *Opelousas:* A town in southeast Louisiana.

[23] *courser:* A swift horse.

"The bear was an animal of note, and called General Jackson, from the fact of his licking up everything that came in his way, and taking 'the responsibility' on all occasions. He was a wicked looking beast, very lean and unamiable in aspect, with hair all standing the wrong way. He had fought some fifty bulls (so they said), always coming out victorious, but that either one of the fifty had been an Attakapas bull, the bills of the performances did not say. Had he tackled Attakapas first it is likely his fifty battles would have remained unfought.

"About half past four o'clock the performances commenced.

"The bull was first seen, standing in the cage alone, with head erect, and looking a very monarch in his capacity. At an appointed signal, a cage containing the bear was placed alongside the arena, and an opening being made, bruin stalked into the battle ground — not, however, without sundry stirrings up with a ten foot pole, he being experienced in such matters, and backwards in raising a row.

"Once on the battle-field, both animals stood, like wary champions, eyeing each other, the bear cowering low, with head upturned and fangs exposed, while Attakapas stood wondering, with his eyes dilated, lashing his sides with his long and bushy tail, and pawing up the earth in very wrath.

"The bear seemed little inclined to begin the attack, and the bull, standing a moment, made steps first backward and then forward, as if measuring his antagonist, and meditating where to plant a blow. Bruin wouldn't come to the scratch no way, till one of the keepers, with an iron rod, tickled his ribs and made him move. Seeing this, Attakapas took it as a hostile demonstration, and, gathering his strength, dashed savagely at the enemy, catching him on the points of his horns, and doubling him up like a sack of bran against the bars. Bruin 'sung out' at this, and made a dash for his opponent's nose.

"Missing this, the bull turned to the 'about face,' and the bear caught him by the ham, inflicting a ghastly wound. But Attakapas with a kick shook him off, and renewing the attack, went at him again, head on and with a rush. This time he was not so fortunate, for the bear caught him above the eye, burying his fangs in the tough hide, and holding him as in a vice. It was now the bull's turn to 'sing out,' and he did it, bellowing forth with a voice more hideous than that of all the bulls of Bashan.[24] Some minutes stood matters thus, and the cries of the bull, mingled with the hoarse growls of the bear, made hideous music, fit only for a dance of devils. Then came a pause (the bear having relinquished his hold), and for a few minutes it was doubtful whether the fun was not up. But the magic wand of the keeper (the ten foot pole) again stirred up bruin, and at it they went, and with a rush.

[24] *Bashan:* Region in ancient Palestine.

"Bruin now tried to fasten on the bull's back, and drove his tusks in him in several places, making the red blood flow like wine from the vats of Luna.[25] But Attakapas was pluck to the back bone, and, catching bruin on the tips of his horns, shuffled him up right merrily, making the fur fly like feather in a gale of wind. Bruin cried 'Nuff' (in bear language), but the bull followed up his advantage, and, making one furious plunge full at the figure head of the enemy, struck a horn into his eye, burying it there, and dashing the tender organ into darkness and atoms. Blood followed the blow, and poor bruin, blinded, bleeding, and in mortal agony, turned with a howl to leave, but Attakapas caught him in the retreat, and rolled him over like a ball. Over and over again this rolling over was enacted, and finally, after more than an hour, bruin curled himself up on his back, bruised, bloody, and dead beat. The thing was up with California,[26] and Attakapas was declared the victor amidst the applause of the multitude that made the heavens ring."

"There," said he, "can you find anything against Connecticut equal to that?" The Southerner had to admit that he was beat by the Yankee. During all this time, it must not be supposed that the old gent. with the two daughters, and even the young ladies themselves, had been silent. Clotel and they had not only given their opinions as regarded the merits of the discussion, but that sly glance of the eye, which is ever given where the young of both sexes meet, had been freely at work. The American ladies are rather partial to foreigners, and Clotel had the appearance of a fine Italian. The old gentleman was now near his home, and a whisper from the eldest daughter, who was unmarried but marriageable, induced him to extend to "Mr. Johnson" an invitation to stop and spend a week with the young ladies at their family residence. Clotel excused herself upon various grounds, and at last, to cut short the matter, promised that she would pay them a visit on her return. The arrival of the coach at Lynchburgh[27] separated the young ladies from the Italian gent., and the coach again resumed its journey.

[25] *Luna:* Roman goddess of the moon.

[26] *The thing was up with California:* An allusion to the end of the California gold rush of 1849, or perhaps an allusion to the bruins of California. Because the United States acquired California following the war with Mexico, Brown may have used this newspaper story to comment ironically on U.S. expansionism as incarnated by Andrew Jackson.

[27] *Lynchburgh:* A city in central Virginia.

CHAPTER XXIII.
TRUTH STRANGER THAN FICTION.

"Is the poor privilege to turn the key
Upon the captive, freedom? He's as far
From the enjoyment of the earth and air
Who watches o'er the chains, as they who wear."[1]
— *Byron.*

During certain seasons of the year, all tropical climates are subject to epidemics of a most destructive nature. The inhabitants of New Orleans look with as much certainty for the appearance of the yellow-fever, small-pox, or cholera, in the hot-season, as the Londoner does for fog in the month of November. In the summer of 1831, the people of New Orleans were visited with one of these epidemics.[2] It appeared in a form unusually repulsive and deadly. It seized persons who were in health, without any premonition. Sometimes death was the immediate consequence. The disorder began in the brain, by an oppressive pain accompanied or followed by fever. The patient was devoured with burning thirst. The stomach, distracted by pains, in vain sought relief in efforts to disburden itself. Fiery veins streaked the eye; the face was inflamed, and dyed of a dark dull red color; the ears from time to time rang painfully. Now mucous secretions surcharged the tongue, and took away the power of speech; now the sick one spoke, but in speaking had a foresight of death. When the violence of the disease approached the heart, the gums were blackened. The sleep, broken, troubled by convulsions, or by frightful visions, was worse than the waking hours; and when the reason sank under a delirium which had its seat in the brain, repose utterly forsook the patient's couch. The progress of the heat within was marked by yellowish spots, which spread over the surface of the body. If, then, a happy crisis came not, all hope was gone. Soon the breath infected the air with a fetid odour, the lips were glazed, despair painted itself in the eyes, and sobs, with long intervals of silence, formed the only language. From each side of the mouth spread foam, tinged with black and burnt blood. Blue streaks mingled with the yellow all over the frame. All remedies were useless. This was the Yellow Fever. The disorder spread alarm and confusion throughout the city. On an average, more than 400 died

[1] "*Is the poor. . . . who wear*": From Lord Byron, *Don Juan* (1819–24), Canto X.
[2] *epidemics:* In fact a cholera outbreak hit New Orleans in the summer of 1832. For his descriptions of yellow fever, Brown borrowed from John R. Beard, *The Life of Toussaint L'Ouverture, the Negro Patriot of Hayti* (London, 1853).

daily. In the midst of disorder and confusion, death heaped victims on victims. Friend followed friend in quick succession. The sick were avoided from the fear of contagion, and for the same reason the dead were left unburied. Nearly 2000 dead bodies lay uncovered in the burial-ground, with only here and there a little lime[3] thrown over them, to prevent the air becoming infected.

The negro, whose home is in a hot climate, was not proof against the disease. Many plantations had to suspend their work for want of slaves to take the places of those carried off by the fever. Henry Morton and wife were among the thirteen thousand swept away by the raging disorder that year.[4] Like too many, Morton had been dealing extensively in lands and stocks; and though apparently in good circumstances was, in reality, deeply involved in debt. Althesa, although as white as most white women in a southern clime, was, as we already know, born a slave. By the laws of all the Southern States the children follow the condition of the mother. If the mother is free the children are free; if a slave, they are slaves. Morton was unacquainted with the laws of the land; and although he had married Althesa, it was a marriage which the law did not recognise; and therefore she whom he thought to be his wife was, in fact, nothing more than his slave. What would have been his feelings had he known this, and also known that his two daughters, Ellen and Jane, were his slaves? Yet such was the fact. After the disappearance of the disease with which Henry Morton had so suddenly been removed, his brother went to New Orleans to give what aid he could in settling up the affairs. James Morton, on his arrival in New Orleans, felt proud of his nieces, and promised them a home with his own family in Vermont; little dreaming that his brother had married a slave woman, and that his nieces were slaves. The girls themselves had never heard that their mother had been a slave, and therefore knew nothing of the danger hanging over their heads. An inventory of the property was made out by James Morton and placed in the hands of the creditors; and the young ladies, with their uncle, were about leaving the city to reside for a few days on the banks of Lake Pontchartrain, where they could enjoy a fresh air that the city could not afford. But just as they were about taking the train, an officer arrested the whole party; the young ladies as slaves, and the uncle upon the charge of attempting to conceal the property of his deceased

---

[3] *lime:* An odorless calcium compound.

[4] *Henry Morton . . . that year:* Brown skews chronology and historical facts, for if the Mortons died in 1831 they would have been unable to help Salome Miller in the mid-1840s.

brother. Morton was overwhelmed with horror at the idea of his nieces being claimed as slaves, and asked for time, that he might save them from such a fate. He even offered to mortgage his little farm in Vermont for the amount which young slave women of their ages would fetch. But the creditors pleaded that they were "an extra article," and would sell for more than common slaves; and must, therefore, be sold at auction. They were given up, but neither ate nor slept, nor separated from each other, till they were taken into the New Orleans slave market, where they were offered to the highest bidder. There they stood, trembling, blushing, and weeping; compelled to listen to the grossest language, and shrinking from the rude hands that examined the graceful proportions of their beautiful frames.

After a fierce contest between the bidders, the young ladies were sold, one for 2,300 dollars, and the other for 3,000 dollars. We need not add that had those young girls been sold for mere house servants or field hands, they would not have brought one half the sums they did. The fact that they were the grand-daughters of Thomas Jefferson, no doubt, increased their value in the market. Here were two of the softer sex, accustomed to the fondest indulgence, surrounded by all the refinements of life, and with all the timidity that such a life could produce, bartered away like cattle in Smithfield market.[5] Ellen, the eldest, was sold to an old gentleman, who purchased her, as he said, for a housekeeper. The girl was taken to his residence, nine miles from the city. She soon, however, knew for what purpose she had been bought; and an educated and cultivated mind and taste, which made her see and understand how great was her degradation, now armed her hand with the ready means of death. The morning after her arrival, she was found in her chamber, a corpse. She had taken poison. Jane was purchased by a dashing young man, who had just come into the possession of a large fortune. The very appearance of the young Southerner pointed him out as an unprincipled profligate; and the young girl needed no one to tell her of her impending doom. The young maid of fifteen was immediately removed to his country seat, near the junction of the Mississippi river with the sea. This was a most singular spot, remote, in a dense forest spreading over the summit of a cliff that rose abruptly to a great height above the sea; but so grand in its situation, in the desolate sublimity which reigned around, in the reverential murmur of the waves that washed its base, that, though picturesque, it was a forest prison. Here the young lady saw no one, except an old negress

---

[5] *Smithfield market:* London's main meat market is in the Smithfield district.

who acted as her servant. The smiles with which the young man met her were indignantly spurned. But she was the property of another, and could hope for justice and mercy only through him.

Jane, though only in her fifteenth year, had become strongly attached to Volney Lapuc, a young Frenchman, a student in her father's office. The poverty of the young man, and the youthful age of the girl, had caused their feelings to be kept from the young lady's parents. At the death of his master, Volney had returned to his widowed mother at Mobile, and knew nothing of the misfortune that had befallen his mistress, until he received a letter from her. But how could he ever obtain a sight of her, even if he wished, locked up as she was in her master's mansion? After several days of what her master termed "obstinacy" on her part, the young girl was placed in an upper chamber, and told that that would be her home, until she should yield to her master's wishes. There she remained more than a fortnight, and with the exception of a daily visit from her master, she saw no one but the old negress who waited upon her. One bright moonlight evening as she was seated at the window, she perceived the figure of a man beneath her window. At first, she thought it was her master; but the tall figure of the stranger soon convinced her that it was another. Yes, it was Volney! He had no sooner received her letter, than he set out for New Orleans; and finding on his arrival there, that his mistress had been taken away, resolved to follow her. There he was; but how could she communicate with him? She dared not trust the old negress with her secret, for fear that it might reach her master. Jane wrote a hasty note and threw it out the window, which was eagerly picked up by the young man, and he soon disappeared in the woods. Night passed away in dreariness to her, and the next morning she viewed the spot beneath her window with the hope of seeing the footsteps of him who had stood there the previous night. Evening returned, and with it the hope of again seeing the man she loved. In this she was not disappointed; for daylight had scarcely disappeared, and the moon once more rising through the tops of the tall trees, when the young man was seen in the same place as on the previous night. He had in his hand a rope ladder. As soon as Jane saw this, she took the sheets from her bed, tore them into strings, tied them together, and let one end down the side of the house. A moment more, and one end of the rope ladder was in her hand, and she fastened it inside the room. Soon the young maiden was seen descending, and the enthusiastic lover, with his arms extended, waiting to receive his mistress. The planter had been out on an hunting excursion, and returning home, saw his victim as her lover was receiving her in his arms. At this moment the sharp sound of a rifle was heard and the young man fell weltering in his blood, at the feet of his mistress. Jane fell senseless by his side. For many days she had a confused consciousness of some great agony, but knew not where she was, or by whom surrounded. The slow recovery of her reason settled into the most intense melancholy, which gained at length the compassion even of her cruel master. The beautiful bright eyes, always pleading in expression, were now so heart-piercing in their sadness, that he could not endure their gaze. In a few days the poor girl died of a broken heart, and was buried at night at the back of the garden by the negroes; and no one wept at the grave of her who had been so carefully cherished, and so tenderly beloved.

This, reader, is an unvarnished narrative of one doomed by the laws of the Southern States to be a slave. It tells not only its own story of grief, but speaks of a thousand wrongs and woes beside, which never see the light; all the more bitter and dreadful, because no help can relieve, no sympathy can mitigate, and no hope can cheer.

CHAPTER XXIV.
THE ARREST.

"The fearful storm — it threatens lowering,
   Which God in mercy long delays;
Slaves yet may see their masters cowering,
   While whole plantations smoke and blaze!"[1]
                                    — *Carter.*

It was late in the evening when the coach arrived at Richmond, and Clotel once more alighted in her native city. She had intended to seek lodgings somewhere in the outskirts of the town, but the lateness of the hour compelled her to stop at one of the principal hotels for the night. She had scercely entered the inn, when she recognised among the numerous black servants one to whom she was well known; and her only hope was, that her disguise would keep her from being discovered. The imperturbable calm and entire forgetfulness of self which induced Clotel to visit a place from which she could scarcely hope to escape, to attempt the rescue of a beloved child, demonstrate that over-willingness of woman to carry out the promptings of the finer feelings of her heart. True to woman's nature, she had risked her own liberty for another.

She remained in the hotel during the night, and the next morning, under the plea of illness, she took her breakfast alone. That day the fugitive slave paid a visit to the suburbs of the town, and once more beheld the cottage in which she had spent so many happy hours. It was winter, and the clematis and passion flowers were not there; but there were the same walks she had so often pressed with her feet, and the same trees which had so often shaded her as she passed through the garden at the back of the house. Old remembrances rushed upon her memory, and caused her to shed tears freely. Clotel was now in her native town, and near her daughter; but how could she communicate with her? How could she see her? To have made herself known, would have been a suicidal act; betrayal would have followed, and she arrested. Three days had passed away, and Clotel still remained in the hotel at which she had first put up; and yet she had got no tidings of her child. Unfortunately for Clotel, a disturbance had just broken out amongst the slave population in the state of Virginia, and all strangers were eyed with suspicion.

[1] *"The fearful . . . blaze!":* From Mrs. J. G. Carter, "Ye Sons of Freedom," in *The Anti-Slavery Harp*, ed. Brown.

The evils consequent on slavery are not lessened by the incoming of one or two rays of light. If the slave only becomes aware of his condition, and conscious of the injustice under which he suffers, if he obtains but a faint idea of these things, he will seize the first opportunity to possess himself of what he conceives to belong him. The infusion of Anglo-Saxon with African blood has created an insurrectionary feeling among the slaves of America hitherto unknown. Aware of their blood connection with their owners, these mulattoes labour under the sense of their personal and social injuries; and tolerate, if they do not encourage in themselves, low and vindictive passions. On the other hand, the slave owners are aware of their critical position, and are ever watchful, always fearing an outbreak among the slaves.[2]

True, the Free States are equally bound with the Slave States to suppress any insurrectionary movement that may take place among the slaves. The Northern freemen are bound by their constitutional obligations to aid the slaveholder in keeping his slaves in their chains. Yet there are, at the time we write, four millions of bond slaves in the United States. The insurrection to which we now refer was headed by a full-blooded negro, who had been born and brought up a slave. He had heard the twang of the driver's whip, and saw the warm blood streaming from the negro's body; he had witnessed the separation of parents and children, and was made aware, by too many proofs, that the slave could expect no justice at the hand of the slave owner. He went by the name of "Nat Turner."[3] He was a preacher among the negroes, and distinguished for his eloquence, respected by the whites, and loved and venerated by the negroes. On the discovery of the plan for the outbreak, Turner fled to the swamps, followed by those who had joined in the insurrection. Here the revolted negroes numbered some hundreds, and for a time bade defiance to their oppressors. The Dismal Swamps cover many thousands of acres of wild land, and a dense forest, with wild animals and insects, such as are unknown in any other part of Virginia. Here runaway negroes usually seek a hiding-place, and some have been known to reside here for years. The revolters were joined by one of these. He was a large, tall, full-blooded negro, with a stern and savage countenance; the marks on his face showed that he was from one of the barbarous tribes in Africa, and

[2] *The evils ... slaves:* For this paragraph, Brown borrowed from John R. Beard's *The Life of Toussaint L'Ouverture* (1853).

[3] *"Nat Turner":* Nat Turner's bloody slave rebellion occurred in Southampton County, Virginia, in 1831; see pp. 427–43 for the complete text of *The Confessions of Nat Turner.*

claimed that country as his native land; his only covering was a girdle around his loins, made of skins of wild beasts which he had killed; his only token of authority among those that he led, was a pair of epaulettes made from the tail of a fox, and tied to his shoulder by a cord. Brought from the coast of Africa when only fifteen years of age to the island of Cuba, he was smuggled from thence into Virginia. He had been two years in the swamps, and considered it his future home. He had met a negro woman who was also a runaway; and, after the fashion of his native land, had gone through the process of oiling her as the marriage ceremony. They had built a cave on a rising mound in the swamp; this was their home. His name was Picquilo. His only weapon was a sword, made from the blade of a scythe, which he had stolen from a neighbouring plantation. His dress, his character, his manners, his mode of fighting, were all in keeping with the early training he had received in the land of his birth. He moved about with the activity of a cat, and neither the thickness of the trees, nor the depth of the water could stop him. He was a bold, turbulent spirit; and from revenge imbrued his hands in the blood of all the whites he could meet. Hunger, thirst, fatigue, and loss of sleep he seemed made to endure as if by peculiarity of constitution. His air was fierce, his step oblique, his look sanguinary. Such was the character of one of the leaders in the Southampton insurrection.[4] All negroes were arrested who were found beyond their master's threshold, and all strange whites watched with a great degree of alacrity.

Such was the position in which Clotel found affairs when she returned to Virginia in search of her Mary. Had not the slave-owners been watchful of strangers, owing to the outbreak, the fugitive could not have escaped the vigilance of the police; for advertisements, announcing her escape and offering a large reward for her arrest, had been received in the city previous to her arrival, and the officers were therefore on the look-out for the runaway slave. It was on the third day, as the quadroon was seated in her room at the inn, still in the disguise of a gentleman, that two of the city officers entered the room, and informed her that they were authorised to examine all strangers, to assure the authorities that they were not in league with the revolted negroes. With trembling heart the fugitive handed the key of her trunk

---

[4] *He was a large. . . . insurrection:* For his description of the fictional Picquilo, Brown borrowed from Beard's description of the Haitian revolutionary Lamour de Rance in *The Life of Toussaint L'Ouverture.* Again, Brown skews chronology, for Clotel returns to Virginia in the wake of the 1831 Nat Turner rebellion after taking a stagecoach ride set during the 1839 election campaign.

to the officers. To their surprise, they found nothing but a woman's apparel in the box, which raised their curiosity, and caused a further investigation that resulted in the arrest of Clotel as a fugitive slave. She was immediately conveyed to prison, there to await the orders of her master. For many days, uncheered by the voice of kindness, alone, hopeless, desolate, she waited for the time to arrive when the chains were to be placed on her limbs, and she returned to her inhuman and unfeeling owner.

The arrest of the fugitive was announced in all the newspapers, but created little or no sensation. The inhabitants were too much engaged in putting down the revolt among the slaves; and although all the odds were against the insurgents, the whites found it no easy matter, with all their caution. Every day brought news of fresh outbreaks. Without scruple and without pity, the whites massacred all blacks found beyond their owners' plantations: the negroes, in return, set fire to houses, and put those to death who attempted to escape from the flames. Thus carnage was added to carnage, and the blood of the whites flowed to avenge the blood of the blacks. These were the ravages of slavery. No graves were dug for the negroes; their dead bodies became food for dogs and vultures, and their bones, partly calcined by the sun, remained scattered about, as if to mark the mournful fury of servitude and lust of power. When the slaves were subdued, except a few in the swamps, bloodhounds were put in this dismal place to hunt out the remaining revolters. Among the captured negroes was one of whom we shall hereafter make mention.

CHAPTER XXV.
DEATH IS FREEDOM.

"I asked but freedom, and ye gave
Chains, and the freedom of the grave."[1]
— *Snelling.*

There are, in the District of Columbia, several slave prisons, or "negro pens," as they are termed. These prisons are mostly occupied by persons to keep their slaves in, when collecting their gangs together for the New Orleans market. Some of them belong to the government, and one, in particular, is noted for having been the place where a number of free coloured persons have been incarcerated from time to time. In this district is situated the capital of the United States. Any free coloured persons visiting Washington, if not provided with papers asserting and proving their rights to be free, may be arrested and placed in one of these dens. If they succeed in showing that they are free, they are set at liberty, provided they are able to pay the expenses of their arrest and imprisonment; if they cannot pay these expenses, they are sold out. Through this unjust and oppressive law, many persons born in the Free States have been consigned to a life of slavery on the cotton, sugar, or rice plantations of the Southern States. By order of her master, Clotel was removed from Richmond and placed in one of these prisons, to await the sailing of a vessel for New Orleans. The prison in which she was put stands midway between the capitol at Washington and the president's house. Here the fugitive saw nothing but slaves brought in and taken out, to be placed in ships and sent away to the same part of the country to which she herself would soon be compelled to go. She had seen or heard nothing of her daughter while in Richmond, and all hope of seeing her now had fled. If she was carried back to New Orleans, she could expect no mercy from her master.

At the dusk of the evening previous to the day when she was to be sent off, as the old prison was being closed for the night, she suddenly darted past her keeper, and ran for her life. It is not a great distance from the prison to the Long Bridge,[2] which passes from the lower part

---

[1] *"I asked . . . grave":* From a poem by William J. Snelling (1804–1848), whose antislavery poems regularly appeared in the *Liberator.*

[2] *Long Bridge:* Crossing the Potomac River and linking Washington, D.C. to Virginia, the Long Bridge was built in 1835 and remained in use until 1903. For a photograph of the Long Bridge circa 1863, see p. 296.

of the city across the Potomac, to the extensive forests and woodlands of the celebrated Arlington Place, occupied by that distinguished relative and descendant of the immortal Washington, Mr. George W. Custis.[3] Thither the poor fugitive directed her flight. So unexpected was her escape, that she had quite a number of rods[4] the start before the keeper had secured the other prisoners, and rallied his assistants in pursuit. It was at an hour when, and in a part of the city where, horses could not be readily obtained for the chase; no bloodhounds were at hand to run down the flying woman; and for once it seemed as though there was to be a fair trial of speed and endurance between the slave and slave-catchers. The keeper and the forces raised the hue and cry on her pathway close behind; but so rapid was the flight along the wild avenue, that the astonished citizens, as they poured forth from their dwellings to learn the cause of alarm, were only able to comprehend the nature of the case in time to fall in with the motley mass in pursuit, (as many a one did that night,) to raise an anxious prayer to heaven, as they refused to join in the pursuit, that the panting fugitive might escape, and the merciless soul dealer for once be disappointed of his prey. And now with the speed of an arrow — having passed the avenue — with the distance between her and her pursuers constantly increasing, this poor hunted female gained the "Long Bridge," as it is called, where interruption seemed improbable, and already did her heart begin to beat high with the hope of success. She had only to pass three-fourths of a mile across the bridge, and she could bury herself in a vast forest, just in time when the curtain of night would close around her, and protect her from the pursuit of her enemies.

But God by his Providence had otherwise determined. He had determined that an appalling tragedy should be enacted that night, within plain sight of the President's house and the capital of the Union, which should be an evidence wherever it should be known, of the unconquerable love of liberty the heart may inherit; as well as a fresh admonition to the slave dealer, of the cruelty and enormity of his crimes. Just as the pursuers crossed the high draw for the passage of sloops,[5] soon after entering upon the bridge, they beheld three men slowly approaching from the Virginia side. They immediately called to them to arrest the fugitive, whom they proclaimed a runaway slave.

---

[3] *George W. Custis:* Grandson of Martha Washington and heir to part of Washington's Mt. Vernon estate, George W. Custis (1781–1857) gained repute as a playwright and in 1860 published *Recollections and Private Memoirs of Washington.*

[4] *rods:* A unit of linear measurement, a rod equals five-and-a-half yards.

[5] *sloops:* Sailing vessels.

THE DEATH OF CLOTEL.

True to their Virginian instincts as she came near, they formed in line across the narrow bridge, and prepared to seize her. Seeing escape impossible in that quarter, she stopped suddenly, and turned upon her pursuers. On came the profane and ribald crew, faster than ever, already exulting in her capture, and threatening punishment for her flight. For a moment she looked wildly and anxiously around to see if there was no hope of escape. On either hand, far down below, rolled the deep foamy water of the Potomac, and before and behind the rapidly approaching step and noisy voices of pursuers, showing how vain would be any further effort for freedom. Her resolution was taken. She clasped her *hands* convulsively, and raised *them*, as she at the same time raised her *eyes* towards heaven, and begged for that mercy and compassion *there*, which had been denied her on earth; and then, with a single bound, she vaulted over the railings of the bridge, and sunk for ever beneath the waves of the river!

Thus died Clotel, the daughter of Thomas Jefferson, a president of the United States; a man distinguished as the author of the Declaration of American Independence, and one of the first statesmen of that country.

Had Clotel escaped from oppression in any other land, in the disguise in which she fled from Mississippi to Richmond, and reached the United States, no honour within the gift of the American people would have been too good to have been heaped upon the heroic woman. But she was a slave, and therefore out of the pale of their sympathy. They have tears to shed over Greece and Poland; they have an abundance of sympathy for "poor Ireland;" they can furnish a ship of war to convey the Hungarian refugees from a Turkish prison to the "land of the free and home of the brave." They boast that America is the "cradle of liberty;" if it is, I fear they have rocked the child to death.[6] The body of Clotel was picked up from the bank of the river, where it had been washed by the strong current, a hole dug in the sand, and there deposited, without either inquest being held over it, or religious service being performed. Such was the life and such the death of a woman whose virtues and goodness of heart would have done honour to one in a higher station of life, and who, if she had been born in any other

---

[6] *They have tears. . . . to death:* In this passage, Brown joins with many abolitionists in decrying nineteenth-century Americans' tendencies to rally behind various European revolutionary movements while ignoring the plight of U.S. slaves. Brown and William Lloyd Garrison were particularly disturbed by the hero's welcome accorded the Hungarian revolutionary Louis Kossuth (1802–1894) during his 1851–52 tour of the United States, for Kossuth insisted on remaining neutral on abolitionism.

land but that of slavery, would have been honoured and loved. A few days after the death of Clotel, the following poem appeared in one of the newspapers:

"Now, rest for the wretched! the long day is past,
  And night on yon prison descendeth at last.
  Now lock up and bolt! Ha, jailor, look there!
  Who flies like a wild bird escaped from the snare?
      A woman, a slave — up, out in pursuit,
        While linger some gleams of day!
      Let thy call ring out! — now a rabble rout
        Is at thy heels — speed away!

"A bold race for freedom! — On, fugitive, on!
  Heaven help but the right, and thy freedom is won.
  How eager she drinks the free air of the plains;
  Every limb, every nerve, every fibre she strains;
      From Columbia's glorious capitol,
        Columbia's daughter flees
      To the sanctuary God has given —
        The sheltering forest trees.

"Now she treads the Long Bridge — joy lighteth her eye —
  Beyond her the dense wood and darkening sky —
  Wild hopes thrill her heart as she neareth the shore:
  O, despair! there are *men* fast advancing before!
      Shame, shame on their manhood! they hear, they heed
        The cry, her flight to stay,
      And like demon forms with their outstretched arms,
        They wait to seize their prey!

"She pauses, she turns! Ah, will she flee back?
  Like wolves, her pursuers howl loud on their track;
  She lifteth to Heaven one look of despair —
  Her anguish breaks forth in one hurried prayer —
      Hark! her jailor's yell! like a bloodhound's bay
        On the low night wind it sweeps!
      Now, death or the chain! to the stream she turns,
        And she leaps! O God, she leaps!

"The dark and the cold, yet merciful wave,
  Received to its bosom the form of the slave:
  She rises — earth's scenes on her dim vision gleam,
  Yet she struggleth not with the strong rushing stream:
      And low are the death-cries her woman's heart gives,
        As she floats adown the river,

Faint and more faint grows the drowning voice,
And her cries have ceased for ever!

"Now back, jailor, back to thy dungeons, again,
To swing the red lash and rivet the chain!
The form thou would'st fetter — returned to its God;
The universe holdeth no realm of night
More drear than her slavery —
More merciless fiends than here stayed her flight —
Joy! the hunted slave is free!

"That bond woman's corse[7] — let Potomac's proud wave
Go bear it along *by our Washington's grave,*
And heave it high up on that hallowed strand,
To tell of the freedom he won for our land.
A weak woman's corse, by freemen chased down;
Hurrah for our country! hurrah!
To freedom she leaped, through drowning and death —
Hurrah for our country! hurrah!"[8]

---

[7] *corse:* Corpse.
[8] *"Now, rest. . . . hurrah!":* The poem, titled "The Leap from the Long Bridge," is by Grace Greenwood (1823–1904), and is included in her *Poems* (1851). Brown changed some of the wording and added the final stanza; for the text of the original, which Greenwood claimed was based on an actual incident, see pp. 297–98.

CHAPTER XXVI.
THE ESCAPE.

"No refuge is found on our unhallowed ground,
For the wretched in Slavery's manacles bound;
While our star spangled banner in vain boasts to wave
O'er the land of the free and the home of the brave!"[1]

We left Mary,[2] the daughter of Clotel, in the capacity of a servant in her own father's house, where she had been taken by her mistress for the ostensible purpose of plunging her husband into the depths of humiliation. At first the young girl was treated with great severity; but after finding that Horatio Green had lost all feeling for his child, Mrs. Green's own heart became touched for the offspring of her husband, and she became its friend. Mary had grown still more beautiful, and, like most of her sex in that country, was fast coming to maturity.

The arrest of Clotel, while trying to rescue her daughter, did not reach the ears of the latter till her mother had been removed from Richmond to Washington. The mother had passed from time to eternity before the daughter knew that she had been in the neighbourhood. Horatio Green was not in Richmond at the time of Clotel's arrest; had he been there, it is not probable but he would have made an effort to save her. She was not his slave, and therefore was beyond his power, even had he been there and inclined to aid her. The revolt amongst the slaves had been brought to an end, and most of the insurgents either were put to death or sent out of the state. One, however, remained in prison. He was the slave of Horatio Green, and had been a servant in his master's dwelling. He, too, could boast that his father was an American statesman. His name was George. His mother had been employed as a servant in one of the principal hotels in Washington, where members of Congress usually put up. After George's birth his mother was sold to a slave trader, and he to an agent of Mr. Green, the father of Horatio. George was as white as most white persons. No one would suppose that any African blood coursed through his veins. His hair was straight, soft, fine, and light; his eyes blue, nose prominent, lips thin, his head well formed, forehead high and prominent; and he was often taken for a free white person by those who did know

---

[1] *"No refuge . . . brave!"*: From A. E. Atlee, "The Star Spangled Banner," in the *Liberator*, 13 September 1844.
[2] *Mary*: For the story of Mary in this and the next two chapters, Brown reworked the story he initially told in Letter XXII of his *Three Years in Europe* (London, 1852).

him. This made his condition still more intolerable; for one so white seldom ever receives fair treatment at the hands of his fellow slaves; and the whites usually regard such slaves as persons who, if not often flogged, and otherwise ill treated, to remind them of their condition, would soon "forget" that they were slaves, and "think themselves as good as white folks." George's opportunities were far greater than most slaves. Being in his master's house, and waiting on educated white people, he had become very familiar with the English language. He had heard his master and visitors speak of the down-trodden and oppressed Poles; he heard them talk of going to Greece to fight for Grecian liberty, and against the oppressors of that ill-fated people. George, fired with the love of freedom, and zeal for the cause of his enslaved countrymen, joined the insurgents, and with them had been defeated and captured. He was the only one remaining of these unfortunate people, and he would have been put to death with them but for a circumstance that occurred some weeks before the breakout. The court house had, by accident, taken fire, and was fast consuming. The engines could not be made to work, and all hope of saving the building seemed at an end. In one of the upper chambers there was a small box containing some valuable deeds belonging to the city; a ladder was placed against the house, leading from the street to the window of the room in which the box stood. The wind blew strong, and swept the flames in that direction. Broad sheets of fire were blown again and again over that part of the building, and then the wind would lift the pall of smoke, which showed that the work of destruction was not yet accomplished. While the doomed building was thus exposed, and before the destroying element had made its final visit, as it did soon after, George was standing by, and hearing that much depended on the contents of the box, and seeing no one disposed to venture through the fiery element to save the treasure, mounted the ladder and made his way to the window, entered the room, and was soon seen descending with the much valued box. Three cheers rent the air as the young slave fell from the ladder near the ground; the white men took him up in their arms, to see if he had sustained any injury. His hair was burnt, eyebrows closely singed, and his clothes smelt strongly of smoke; but the heroic young slave was unhurt. The city authorities, at their next meeting, passed a vote of thanks to George's master for the lasting benefit that the slave had rendered the public, and commended the poor boy to the special favour of his owner. When George was on trial for participating in the revolt, this "meritorious act," as they were pleased to term it, was brought up in his favour. His trial was put off from session to session, till he had been in prison more than a year. At last, however, he was convicted of high treason, and sentenced to be hanged within ten days of that time. The judge asked the slave if he had anything to say why sentence of death should not be passed on him. George stood for a moment in silence, and then said, "As I cannot speak as I should wish, I will say nothing." "You may say what you please," said the judge. "You had a good master," continued he, "and still you were dissatisfied; you left your master and joined the negroes who were burning our houses and killing our wives." "As you have given me permission to speak," remarked George, "I will tell you why I joined the revolted negroes.[3] I have heard my master read in the Declaration of Independence 'that all men are created free and equal,' and this caused me to inquire of myself why I was a slave. I also heard him talking with some of his visitors about the war with England, and he said, all wars and fightings for freedom were just and right. If so, in what am I wrong? The grievances of which your fathers complained, and which caused the Revolutionary War, were trifling in comparison with the wrongs and sufferings of those who were engaged in the late revolt. Your fathers were never slaves, ours are; your fathers were never bought and sold like cattle, never shut out from the light of knowledge and religion, never subjected to the lash of brutal task-masters. For the crime of having a dark skin, my people suffer the pangs of hunger, the infliction of stripes, and the ignominy of brutal servitude. We are kept in heathenish darkness by laws expressly enacted to make our instruction a criminal offence. What right has one man to the bones, sinews, blood, and nerves of another? Did not one God make us all? You say your fathers fought for freedom — so did we. You tell me that I am to be put to death for violating the laws of the land. Did not the American revolutionists violate the laws when they struck for liberty? They were revolters, but their success made them patriots — we were revolters, and our failure makes us rebels. Had we succeeded, we would have been patriots too. Success makes all the difference. You make merry on the 4th of July; the thunder of cannon and ringing of bells announce it as the birthday of American independence. Yet while these cannons are roaring and bells ringing, one-sixth of the people of this land are in chains and slavery. You boast that this is the 'Land of the Free;' but a traditionary freedom will not save you. It will not do to praise your fathers and build their sepulchres.[4]

---

[3] *"I will tell you . . . negroes:* George's speech echoes Frederick Douglass's "What to the Slave is the Fourth of July?" (1852); see pp. 253–58.
[4] *sepulchres:* Tombs or burial places.

Worse for you that you have such an inheritance, if you spend it foolishly and are unable to appreciate its worth. Sad if the genius of a true humanity, beholding you with tearful eyes from the mount of vision, shall fold his wings in sorrowing pity, and repeat the strain, 'O land of Washington, how often would I have gathered thy children together, as a hen doth gather her brood under her wings, and ye would not; behold your house is left unto you desolate.'[5] This is all I have to say; I have done." Nearly every one present was melted to tears; even the judge seemed taken by surprise at the intelligence of the young slave. But George was still a slave, and an example must be made of him, and therefore he was sentenced. Being employed in the same house with Mary, the daughter of Clotel, George had become attached to her, and the young lovers fondly looked forward to the time when they should be husband and wife.

After George had been sentenced to death, Mary was still more attentive to him, and begged and obtained leave of her mistress to visit him in his cell. The poor girl paid a daily visit to him to whom she had pledged her heart and hand. At one of these meetings, and only four days from the time fixed for the execution, while Mary was seated in George's cell, it occurred to her that she might yet save him from a felon's doom. She revealed to him the secret that was then occupying her thoughts, viz. that George should exchange clothes with her, and thus attempt his escape in disguise. But he would not for a single moment listen to the proposition. Not that he feared detection; but he would not consent to place an innocent and affectionate girl in a position where she might have to suffer for him. Mary pleaded, but in vain — George was inflexible. The poor girl left her lover with a heavy heart, regretting that her scheme had proved unsuccessful.

Towards the close of the next day, Mary again appeared at the prison door for admission, and was soon by the side of him whom she so ardently loved. While there the clouds which had overhung the city for some hours broke, and the rain fell in torrents amid the most terrific thunder and lightning. In the most persuasive manner possible, Mary again importuned George to avail himself of her assistance to escape from an ignominious death. After assuring him that she, not being the person condemned, would not receive any injury, he at last consented, and they began to exchange apparel. As George was of small stature, and both were white, there was no difficulty in his passing out without detection; and as she usually left the cell weeping, with

---

[5] *'O land . . . desolate'*: A paraphrase of Jesus's admonition in Matthew 23.37–38. In his speech, George substitutes "Washington" for "Jerusalem."

handkerchief in hand, and sometimes at her face, he had only to adopt this mode and his escape was safe. They had kissed each other, and Mary had told George where he would find a small parcel of provisions which she had placed in a secluded spot, when the prison-keeper opened the door and said, "Come, girl, it is time for you to go." George again embraced Mary, and passed out of the jail. It was already dark, and the street lamps were lighted, so that our hero in his new dress had no dread of detection. The provisions were sought out and found, and poor George was soon on the road to Canada. But neither of them had once thought of a change of dress for George when he should have escaped, and he had walked but a short distance before he felt that a change of his apparel would facilitate his progress. But he dared not go amongst even his coloured associates for fear of being betrayed. However, he made the best of his way on towards Canada, hiding in the woods during the day, and travelling by the guidance of the North Star at night.

With the poet he could truly say,

> "Star of the North! while blazing day
> Pours round me its full tide of light,
> And hides thy pale but faithful ray,
> I, too, lie hid, and long for night."[6]

One morning, George arrived on the banks of the Ohio river, and found his journey had terminated, unless he could get some one to take him across the river in a secret manner, for he would not be permitted to cross in any of the ferry boats, it being a penalty for crossing a slave, besides the value of the slave. He concealed himself in the tall grass and weeds near the river, to see if he could embrace an opportunity to cross. He had been in his hiding place but a short time, when he observed a man in a small boat, floating near the shore, evidently fishing. His first impulse was to call out to the man and ask him to take him over to the Ohio side, but the fear that the man was a slaveholder, or one who might possibly arrest him, deterred him from it. The man after rowing and floating about for some time fastened the boat to the root of a tree, and started to a neighbouring farmhouse.

This was George's moment, and he seized it. Running down the bank, he unfastened the boat, jumped in, and with all the expertness of

---

[6] *"Star. . . . for night"*: From John Pierpont (1785–1866), "The Fugitive Slave's Apostrophe to the North Star," in *Airs of Palestine and Other Poems* (1840).

one accustomed to a boat, rowed across the river and landed on the Ohio side.

Being now in a Free State, he thought he might with perfect safety travel toward Canada. He had, however, gone but a very few miles when he discovered two men on horseback coming behind him. He felt sure that they could not be in pursuit of him, yet he did not wish to be seen by them, so he turned into another road leading to a house near by. The men followed, and were but a short distance from George, when he ran up to a farmhouse, before which was standing a farmer-looking man, in a broad-brimmed hat and straight-collared coat, whom he implored to save him from the "slave-catchers." The farmer told him to go into the barn near by; he entered by the front door, the farmer following, and closing the door behind George, but remaining outside, and gave directions to his hired man as to what should be done with George. The slaveholders by this time had dismounted, and were in front of the barn demanding admittance, and charging the farmer with secreting their slave woman, for George was still in the dress of a woman. The Friend, for the farmer proved to be a member of the Society of Friends,[7] told the slave-owners that if they wished to search his barn, they must first get an officer and a search warrant. While the parties were disputing, the farmer began nailing up the front door, and the hired man served the back door the same way. The slaveholders, finding that they could not prevail on the Friend to allow them to get the slave, determined to go in search of an officer. One was left to see that the slave did not escape from the barn, while the other went off at full speed to Mount Pleasant, the nearest town. George was not the slave of either of these men, nor were they in pursuit of him, but they had lost a woman who had been seen in that vicinity, and when they saw poor George in the disguise of a female, and attempting to elude pursuit, they felt sure they were close upon their victim. However, if they had caught him, although he was not their slave, they would have taken him back and placed him in jail, and there he would have remained until his owner arrived.

After an absence of nearly two hours, the slave-owner returned with an officer and found the Friend still driving large nails into the door. In a triumphant tone and with a corresponding gesture, he handed the search-warrant to the Friend, and said, "There, sir, now I will see if I can't get my nigger." "Well," said the Friend, "thou hast gone to work according to law, and thou canst now go into my barn."

---

[7] *Society of Friends:* Quakers.

"Lend me your hammer that I may get the door open," said the slave-holder. "Let me see the warrant again." And after reading it over once more, he said, "I see nothing in this paper which says I must supply thee with tools to open my door; if thou wishest to go in, thou must get a hammer elsewhere." The sheriff said, "I will go to a neighbour-ing farm and borrow something which will introduce us to Miss Dinah;" and he immediately went in search of tools. In a short time the officer returned, and they commenced an assault and battery upon the barn door, which soon yielded; and in went the slaveholder and officer, and began turning up the hay and using all other means to find the lost property; but, to their astonishment, the slave was not there. After all hope of getting Dinah was gone, the slave-owner in a rage said to the Friend, "My nigger is not here." "I did not tell thee there was any one here." "Yes, but I saw her go in, and you shut the door behind her, and if she was not in the barn, what did you nail the door for?" "Can't I do what I please with my own barn door? Now I will tell thee; thou need trouble thyself no more, for the person thou art after entered the front door and went out at the back door, and is a long way from here by this time. Thou and thy friend must be some-what fatigued by this time; wont thou go in and take a little dinner with me?" We need not say that this cool invitation of the good Quaker was not accepted by the slaveholders. George in the meantime had been taken to a friend's dwelling some miles away, where, after laying aside his female attire, and being snugly dressed up in a straight collared coat, and pantaloons to match, was again put on the right road towards Canada.

The fugitive now travelled by day, and laid by during night. After a fatiguing and dreary journey of two weeks, the fugitive arrived in Canada, and took up his abode in the little town of St. Catherine's,[8] and obtained work on the farm of Colonel Street. Here he attended a night-school, and laboured for his employer during the day. The cli-mate was cold, and wages small, yet he was in a land where he was free, and this the young slave prized more than all the gold that could be given him. Besides doing his best to obtain education for himself, he imparted what he could to those of his fellow-fugitives about him, of whom there were many.

[8] *St. Catherine's:* A town in southern Ontario.

CHAPTER XXVII.
THE MYSTERY.

George, however, did not forget his promise to use all the means in his power to get Mary out of slavery. He, therefore, laboured with all his might to obtain money with which to employ some one to go back to Virginia for Mary. After nearly six months' labour at St. Catherine's, he employed an English missionary to go and see if the girl could be purchased, and at what price. The missionary went accordingly, but returned with the sad intelligence that, on account of Mary's aiding George to escape the court had compelled Mr. Green to sell her out of the state, and she had been sold to a negro trader, and taken to the New Orleans market. As all hope of getting the girl was now gone, George resolved to quit the American continent for ever. He immediately took passage in a vessel laden with timber, bound for Liverpool, and in five weeks from that time he was standing on the quay of the great English seaport. With little or no education, he found many difficulties in the way of getting a respectable living. However he obtained a situation as porter in a large house in Manchester, where he worked during the day, and took private lessons at night. In this way he laboured for three years, and was then raised to the situation of clerk. George was so white as easily to pass for a white man, and being somewhat ashamed of his African descent, he never once mentioned the fact of having been a slave. He soon became a partner in the firm that employed him, and was now on the road to wealth.

In the year 1842, just ten years after George Green (for he adopted his master's name) arrived in England, he visited France, and spent some time at Dunkirk.[1] It was towards sunset, on a warm day in the month of October, that Mr. Green, after strolling some distance from the Hotel de Leon, entered a burial ground, and wandered long alone among the silent dead, gazing upon the many green graves and marble tombstones of those who once moved on the theatre of busy life, and whose sounds of gaiety once fell upon the ear of man. All nature around was hushed in silence, and seemed to partake of the general melancholy which hung over the quiet resting-place of departed mortals. After tracing the varied inscriptions which told the characters or conditions of the departed, and viewing the mounds beneath which the dust of mortality slumbered, he had now reached a secluded spot, near to where an aged weeping willow bowed its thick foliage to the

---

[1] *Dunkirk:* A seaport in northern France.

ground, as though anxious to hide from the scrutinising gaze of curiosity the grave beneath it. Mr. Green seated himself upon a marble tomb, and began to read Roscoe's *Leo X.*,[2] a copy of which he had under his arm. It was then about twilight, and he had scarcely gone through half a page, when he observed a lady in black, leading a boy, some five years old, up one of the paths; and as the lady's black veil was over her face, he felt somewhat at liberty to eye her more closely. While looking at her, the lady gave a scream, and appeared to be in a fainting position, when Mr. Green sprang from his seat in time to save her from falling to the ground. At this moment, an elderly gentleman was seen approaching with a rapid step, who, from his appearance, was evidently the lady's father, or one intimately connected with her. He came up, and, in a confused manner, asked what was the matter. Mr. Green explained as well as he could. After taking up the smelling bottle which had fallen from her hand, and holding it a short time to her face, she soon began to revive. During all this time the lady's veil had so covered her face, that Mr. Green had not seen it. When she had so far recovered as to be able to raise her head, she again screamed, and fell back into the arms of the old man. It now appeared quite certain, that either the countenance of George Green, or some other object, was the cause of these fits of fainting; and the old gentleman, thinking it was the former, in rather a petulant tone said, "I will thank you, sir, if you will leave us alone." The child whom the lady was leading, had now set up a squall; and amid the death-like appearance of the lady, the harsh look of the old man, and the cries of the boy, Mr. Green left the grounds, and returned to his hotel.

Whilst seated by the window, and looking out upon the crowded street, with every now and then the strange scene in the grave-yard vividly before him, Mr. Green thought of the book he had been reading, and, remembering that he had left it on the tomb, where he had suddenly dropped it when called to the assistance of the lady, he immediately determined to return in search of it. After a walk of some twenty minutes, he was again over the spot where he had been an hour before, and from which he had been so unceremoniously expelled by the old man. He looked in vain for the book; it was nowhere to be found: nothing save the bouquet which the lady had dropped, and which lay half-buried in the grass from having been trodden upon, indicated that any one had been there that evening. Mr. Green took up the bunch of flowers, and again returned to the hotel.

[2] *Roscoe's Leo X.*: See note 45, p. 78.

After passing a sleepless night, and hearing the clock strike six, he dropped into a sweet sleep, from which he did not awake until roused by the rap of a servant, who, entering his room, handed him a note which ran as follows: — "Sir, — I owe you an apology for the inconvenience to which you were subjected last evening, and if you will honour us with your presence to dinner to-day at four o'clock, I shall be most happy to give you due satisfaction. My servant will be in waiting for you at half-past three. I am, sir, your obedient servant, J. Devenant. October 23. To George Green, Esq."

The servant who handed this note to Mr. Green, informed him that the bearer was waiting for a reply. He immediately resolved to accept the invitation, and replied accordingly. Who this person was, and how his name and the hotel where he was stopping had been found out, was indeed a mystery. However, he waited impatiently for the hour when he was to see this new acquaintance, and get the mysterious meeting in the grave-yard solved.

CHAPTER XXVIII.
THE HAPPY MEETING.

"Man's love is of man's life, a thing apart;
'Tis woman's whole existence."[1]
— *Byron.*

The clock on a neighbouring church had scarcely ceased striking three, when the servant announced that a carriage had called for Mr. Green. In less than half an hour he was seated in a most sumptuous barouche, drawn by two beautiful iron greys, and rolling along over a splendid gravel road completely shaded by large trees, which appeared to have been the accumulating growth of many centuries. The carriage soon stopped in front of a low villa, and this too was embedded in magnificent trees covered with moss. Mr. Green alighted and was shown into a superb drawing room, the walls of which were hung with fine specimens from the hands of the great Italian painters, and one by a German artist representing a beautiful monkish legend connected with "The Holy Catherine," an illustrious lady of Alexandria.[2] The furniture had an antique and dignified appearance. High backed chairs stood around the room; a venerable mirror stood on the mantle shelf; rich curtains of crimson damask hung in folds at either side of the large windows; and a rich Turkey carpet covered the floor. In the centre stood a table covered with books, in the midst of which was an old-fashioned vase filled with fresh flowers, whose fragrance was exceedingly pleasant. A faint light, together with the quietness of the hour, gave beauty beyond description to the whole scene.

Mr. Green had scarcely seated himself upon the sofa, when the elderly gentleman whom he had met the previous evening made his appearance, followed by the little boy, and introduced himself as Mr. Devenant. A moment more, and a lady — a beautiful brunette — dressed in black, with long curls of a chestnut color hanging down on her cheeks, entered the room. Her eyes were of a dark hazel, and her whole appearance indicated that she was a native of a southern clime. The door at which she entered was opposite to where the two gentlemen were seated. They immediately rose; and Mr. Devenant was in the act of introducing her to Mr. Green, when he observed that the latter had sunk back upon the sofa, and the last word that he remembered to

[1] *"Man's love . . . existence":* From Lord Byron, *Don Juan* (1819–24), Canto I.
[2] *illustrious lady of Alexandria:* Virgin martyr of the fourth century, St. Catherine was popularly represented in Renaissance art as married to Christ.

have heard was, "It is her." After this, all was dark and dreamy: how long he remained in this condition it was for another to tell. When he awoke, he found himself stretched upon the sofa, with his boots off, his neckerchief removed, shirt collar unbuttoned, and his head resting upon a pillow. By his side sat the old man, with the smelling bottle in the one hand, and a glass of water in the other, and the little boy standing at the foot of the sofa. As soon as Mr. Green had so far recovered as to be able to speak, he said, "Where am I, and what does this mean?" "Wait a while," replied the old man, "and I will tell you all." After a lapse of some ten minutes he rose from the sofa, adjusted his apparel, and said, "I am now ready to hear anything you have to say." "You were born in America?" said the old man. "Yes," he replied. "And you were acquainted with a girl named Mary?" continued the old man. "Yes, and I loved her as I can love none other." "The lady whom you met so mysteriously last evening is Mary," replied Mr. Devenant. George Green was silent, but the fountains of mingled grief and joy stole out from beneath his eye-lashes, and glistened like pearls upon his pale and marble-like cheeks. At this juncture that lady again entered the room. Mr. Green sprang from the sofa, and they fell into each other's arms, to the surprise of the old man and little George, and to the amusement of the servants who had crept up one by one, and were hid behind the doors, or loitering in the hall. When they had given vent to their feelings, they resumed their seats, and each in turn related the adventures through which they had passed. "How did you find out my name and address?" asked Mr. Green. "After you had left us in the grave-yard, our little George said, 'O, mamma, if there aint a book!' and picked it up and brought it to us. Papa opened it, and said, 'The gentleman's name is written in it, and here is a card of the Hotel de Leon, where I suppose he is stopping.' Papa wished to leave the book, and said it was all a fancy of mine that I had ever seen you before, but I was perfectly convinced that you were my own George Green. Are you married?" "No, I am not." "Then, thank God!" exclaimed Mrs. Devenant. "And are you single now?" inquired Mr. Green. "Yes," she replied. "This is indeed the Lord's doings," said Mr. Green, at the same time bursting into a flood of tears. Mr. Devenant was past the age when men should think upon matrimonial subjects, yet the scene brought vividly before his eyes the days when he was a young man, and had a wife living. After a short interview, the old man called their attention to the dinner, which was then waiting. We need scarcely add, that Mr. Green and Mrs. Devenant did very little towards diminishing the dinner that day.

After dinner the lovers (for such we have to call them) gave their experience from the time that George left the jail dressed in Mary's clothes. Up to that time Mr. Green's was substantially as we have related it. Mrs. Devenant's was as follows: — "The night after you left the prison," said she, "I did not shut my eyes in sleep. The next morning, about eight o'clock, Peter the gardener came to the jail to see if I had been there the night before, and was informed that I had, and that I had left a little after dark. About an hour after, Mr. Green came himself, and I need not say that he was much surprised on finding me there, dressed in your clothes. This was the first tidings they had of your escape." "What did Mr. Green say when he found that I had fled?" "Oh!" continued Mrs. Devenant, "he said to me when no one was near, I hope George will get off, but I fear you will have to suffer in his stead. I told him that if it must be so I was willing to die if you could live." At this moment George Green burst into tears, threw his arms around her neck, and exclaimed, "I am glad I have waited so long, with the hope of meeting you again."

Mrs. Devenant again resumed her story: — "I was kept in jail three days, during which time I was visited by the magistrates, and two of the judges. On the third day I was taken out, and master told me that I was liberated, upon condition that I should be immediately sent out of the state. There happened to be just at the time in the neighbourhood a negro-trader, and he purchased me, and I was taken to New Orleans. On the steam-boat we were kept in a close room, where slaves are usually confined, so that I saw nothing of the passengers on board, or the towns we passed. We arrived in New Orleans, and were all put into the slave-market for sale. I was examined by many person, but none seemed willing to purchase me, as all thought me too white, and said I would run away and pass as a free white woman. On the second day, while in the slave-market, and while planters and others were examining slaves and making their purchases, I observed a tall young man, with long black hair, eyeing me very closely, and then talking to the trader. I felt sure that my time had now come, but the day closed without my being sold. I did not regret this, for I had heard that foreigners made the worst of masters, and I felt confident that the man who eyed me so closely was not an American.

"The next day was the Sabbath. The bells called the people to the different places of worship. Methodists sang, and Baptists immersed, and Presbyterians sprinkled, and Episcopalians read their prayers, while the ministers of the various sects preached that Christ died for all; yet there were some twenty-five or thirty of us poor creatures confined in the 'Negro Pen,' awaiting the close of the holy Sabbath, and the dawn of another day, to be again taken into the market, there to be examined like so many beasts of burden. I need not tell you with what anxiety we waited for the advent of another day. On Monday we were again brought out and placed in rows to be inspected; and, fortunately for me, I was sold before we had been on the stand an hour. I was purchased by a gentleman residing in the city, for a waiting-maid for his wife, who was just on the eve of starting for Mobile, to pay a visit to a near relation. I was then dressed to suit the situation of a maid-servant; and upon the whole, I thought that, in my new dress, I looked as much the lady as my mistress.

"On the passage to Mobile, who should I see among the passengers but the tall, long-haired man that had eyed me so closely in the slave-market a few days before. His eyes were again on me, and he appeared anxious to speak to me, and I was reluctant to be spoken to. The first evening after leaving New Orleans, soon after twilight had let her curtain down, and pinned it with a star, and while I was seated on the deck of the boat near the ladies' cabin, looking upon the rippled waves, and the reflection of the moon upon the sea, all at once I saw the tall young man standing by my side. I immediately rose from my seat, and was in the act of returning to my cabin, when he in a broken accent said, 'Stop a moment; I wish to have a word with you. I am your friend.' I stopped and looked him full in the face, and he said, 'I saw you some days since in the slave-market, and I intended to have purchased you to save you from the condition of a slave. I called on Monday, but you had been sold and had left the market. I inquired and learned who the purchaser was, and that you had to go to Mobile, so I resolved to follow you. If you are willing I will try and buy you from your present owner, and you shall be free.' Although this was said in an honest and off-hand manner, I could not believe the man to be sincere in what he said. 'Why should you wish to set *me* free?' I asked. 'I had an only sister,' he replied. 'who died three years ago in France, and you are so much like her that had I not known of her death, I would most certainly have taken you for her.' 'However much I may resemble your sister, you are aware that I am not her, and why take so much interest in one whom you never saw before?' 'The love,' said he, 'which I had for my sister is transferred to you.' I had all along suspected that the man was a knave, and this profession of love confirmed me in my former belief, and I turned away and left him.

"The next day, while standing in the cabin and looking through the window, the French gentleman (for such he was) came to the window while walking on the guards, and again commenced as on the previous evening. He took from his pocket a bit of paper and put it into my hand, at the same time saying, 'Take this, it may some day be of service to you; remember it is from a friend,' and left me instantly. I unfolded the paper, and found it to be a 100 dollars bank note, on the United States Branch Bank, at Philadelphia. My first impulse was to give it to my mistress, but, upon a second thought, I resolved to seek an opportunity, and to return the hundred dollars to the stranger.

"Therefore I looked for him, but in vain; and had almost given up the idea of seeing him again, when he passed me on the guards of the boat and walked towards the stem of the vessel. It being now dark, I approached him and offered the money to him. He declined, saying at the same time, 'I gave it to you — keep it.' 'I do not want it,' I said. 'Now,' said he, 'you had better give your consent for me to purchase you, and you shall go with me to France.' 'But you cannot buy me now,' I replied, 'for my master is in New Orleans, and he purchased me not to sell, but to retain in his own family.' 'Would you rather remain with your present mistress than be free?' 'No,' said I. 'Then fly with me to-night; we shall be in Mobile in two hours from this, and when the passengers are going on shore, you can take my arm, and you can escape unobserved. The trader who brought you to New Orleans exhibited to me a certificate of your good character, and one from the minister of the church to which you were attached in Virginia; and upon the faith of these assurances, and the love I bear you, I promise before high heaven that I will marry you as soon as it can be done.' This solemn promise, coupled with what had already transpired, gave me confidence in the man; and rash as the act may seem, I determined in an instant to go with him. My mistress had been put under the charge of the captain; and as it would be past ten o'clock when the steamer would land, she accepted an invitation of the captain to remain on board with several other ladies till morning. I dressed myself in my best clothes, and put a veil over my face, and was ready on the landing of the boat. Surrounded by a number of passengers, we descended the stage leading to the wharf, and were soon lost in the crowd that thronged the quay. As we went on shore we encountered several persons announcing the names of hotels, the starting of boats for the interior, and vessels bound for Europe. Among these was the ship Utica, Captain Pell, bound for Havre.[3] 'Now,' said Mr. Devenant, 'this is our chance.' The ship was to sail at twelve o'clock

---

[3] *Havre:* Le Havre is a seaport in northern France.

that night, at high tide; and following the men who were seeking passengers, we went immediately on board. Devenant told the captain of the ship that I was his sister, and for such we passed during the voyage. At the hour of twelve the Utica set sail, and we were soon out at sea.

"The morning after we left Mobile, Devenant met me as I came from my state-room, and embraced me for the first time. I loved him, but it was only that affection which we have for one who has done us a lasting favour: it was the love of gratitude rather than that of the heart. We were five weeks on the sea, and yet the passage did not seem long, for Devenant was so kind. On our arrival at Havre we were married and came to Dunkirk, and I have resided here ever since."

At the close of this narrative, the clock struck ten, when the old man, who was accustomed to retire at an early hour, rose to take leave, saying at the same time, "I hope you will remain with us to-night." Mr. Green would fain have excused himself, on the ground that they would expect him and wait at the hotel, but a look from the lady told him to accept the invitation. The old man was the father of Mrs. Devenant's deceased husband, as you will no doubt long since have supposed. A fortnight from the day on which they met in the graveyard, Mr. Green and Mrs. Devenant were joined in holy wedlock; so that George and Mary, who had loved each other so ardently in their younger days, were now husband and wife.

A celebrated writer has justly said of woman, "A woman's whole life is a history of the affections. The heart is her world; it is there her ambition strives for empire; it is there her avarice seeks for hidden treasures. She sends forth her sympathies on adventure; she embarks her whole soul in the traffic of affection; and, if shipwrecked, her case is hopeless, for it is a bankruptcy of the heart."[4]

Mary had every reason to believe that she would never see George again; and although she confesses that the love she bore him was never transferred to her first husband, we can scarcely find fault with her for marrying Mr. Devenant. But the adherence of George Green to the resolution never to marry, unless to Mary, is, indeed, a rare instance of the fidelity of man in the matter of love. We can but blush for our country's shame when we recall to mind the fact, that while George and Mary Green, and numbers of other fugitives from American slavery, can receive protection from any of the governments of Europe, they cannot return to their native land without becoming slaves.

[4] *"A woman's. . . . heart"*: From Washington Irving (1783–1859), "The Broken Heart," in *The Sketch Book* (1819–20).

CHAPTER XXIX.
CONCLUSION.

My narrative has now come to a close. I may be asked, and no doubt shall, Are the various incidents and scenes related founded in truth? I answer, Yes. I have personally participated in many of those scenes. Some of the narratives I have derived from other sources; many from the lips of those who, like myself, have run away from the land of bondage. Having been for nearly nine years employed on Lake Erie, I had many opportunities for helping the escape of fugitives, who, in return for the assistance they received, made me the depositary of their sufferings and wrongs. Of their relations I have made free use. To Mrs. Child, of New York, I am indebted for part of a short story.[1] American Abolitionist journals are another source from whence some of the characters appearing in my narrative are taken. All these combined have made up my story. Having thus acknowledged my resources, I invite the attention of my readers to the following statement, from which I leave them to draw their own conclusions: — "It is estimated that in the United States, members of the Methodist church own 219,363 slaves; members of the Baptist church own 226,000 slaves; members of the Episcopalian church own 88,000 slaves; members of the Presbyterian church own 77,000 slaves; members of all other churches own 50,000 slaves; in all, 660,563 slaves owned by members of the Christian church in this pious democratic republic!"[2]

May these facts be pondered over by British Christians, and at the next anniversaries of the various religious denominations in London may their influence be seen and felt! The religious bodies of American Christians will send their delegates to these meetings. Let British feeling be publicly manifested. Let British sympathy express itself in tender sorrow for the condition of my unhappy race. Let it be understood, unequivocally understood, that no fellowship can be held with slaveholders professing the same common Christianity as yourselves. And until this stain from America's otherwise fair escutcheon[3] be wiped away, let no Christian association be maintained with those

---

[1] *To Mrs. Child . . . story:* Brown's acknowledgment of Lydia Maria Child's "The Quadroons" (1842), of which he used more than a "part."

[2] *"It is estimated . . . republic":* From Reverend Edward S. Mathews (1812–?), "Statistical Account of the Connection of the Religious Bodies in America with Slavery" (1851). A Welsh-born clergyman, Mathews worked as a lecturing agent for the American Baptist Free Mission Society.

[3] *escutcheon:* Shield bearing a coat of arms; reputation.

who traffic in the blood and bones of those whom God has made of one flesh as yourselves. Finally, let the voice of the whole British nation be heard across the Atlantic, and throughout the length and breadth of the land of the Pilgrim Fathers, beseeching their descendants, as they value *the* common salvation, which knows no distinction between the bond and the free, to proclaim the Year of Jubilee.[4] Then shall the "earth indeed yield her increase, and God, even our own God, shall bless us; and all the ends of the earth shall fear Him."[5]

---

[4] *Year of Jubilee:* A yearlong period during which all the slaves would be freed; see Leviticus 25.

[5] *"earth indeed . . . fear him":* Psalms 67.6–7.

Part Two

Clotel;
or,
The President's Daughter
Cultural Contexts

1

Sources and Revisions

What is a "source" of a literary text? The answer can initially seem fairly straightforward. To take the example of a novel published two years before *Clotel:* one might initially respond that the source of Herman Melville's *Moby-Dick* (1851), an account of the pursuit of a mythically powerful white whale, is J. N. Reynolds's "Mocha Dick," an account of the pursuit of a mythically powerful white whale that Melville read in the May 1839 issue of the *Knickerbocker* magazine. But not only are there numerous other accounts of whale pursuits that Melville may have read and borrowed from, there are also numerous aspects of Melville's complex text that owe nothing to whaling stories. The portrayal of Captain Ahab raging in the stormy seas, finding solace only in the company of the black cabin boy Pip, owes much to Shakespeare's portrayal of King Lear raging in a storm, finding solace only in the company of the Fool. Melville's conception of the blasphemous Ahab also clearly draws on Milton's conception of the blasphemous Satan in *Paradise Lost;* the numerous comic descriptions of human and whale bodies owe much to the bawdy writings of François Rabelais and Jonathan Swift; and one could go on and on tracing Melville's indebtedness to such key literary sources as Dante's *Inferno,* Hawthorne's short fiction, Dickens's novels, and the Bible. Critics have also identified a different set of sources for Melville's great novel: contemporaneous discourses that have traditionally been viewed as non- or extraliterary, such as debates on race, gender, religion, economics, politics, and sexuality printed in books, magazines, and newspapers. The presentation of the developing friendship between Ishmael and the tattooed South Sea islander Queequeg, for example, draws heavily on debates of the 1840s and early 1850s on colonialism, sexuality, race, and religion. Moreover, the white whale itself would appear to be conceived not only in relation to folk accounts of mighty whales but also in relation to images of a white United States championed in very different ways by John C. Calhoun and Daniel Webster. And literary and "nonliterary" printed materials do not completely cover the range of Melville's sources, for Melville himself went to sea and spent some time on a whaler; surely his life experiences, and those of the sailors he talked to, are also important sources for *Moby-Dick*. Ultimately, when the question of textual origins and sources is pushed to its limits, one might quickly come to the semiparanoiac conclusion of Edgar Allan Poe, who became convinced of the impossibility, or near impossibility, of writing an "original" text, and consequently became obsessed with the problem of plagiarism, accusing Henry Wadsworth Longfellow, Nathaniel Hawthorne, and many others of lifting from his own and other works.

But with the exception of those unhappy instances when a writer attempts to pass off another's work as his or her own, authors do not simply "lift" texts; they work revisionary transformations, making something new from their sources. Appropriation and revision are part of an author's ongoing dialogue with the present and the past; arguably, these practices can be understood as central aspects of what could be termed authorial power. For instance, Melville does not simply draw on Shakespeare's *King Lear;* he aggressively revises this canonical text by encouraging his readers to see royalty and grandeur both in the strivings of an American sea captain and in the existential despair of a black cabin boy. From a somewhat different perspective, Melville's sympathetic portrayals of the black Pip, the Native American Tashtego, and the South Sea islander Queequeg, which drew on his reading of contemporaneous writings on race, ultimately pose a subtle though aggressive challenge to the white supremacist ideologies that inform much of the racial writing of the period.

Though William Wells Brown similarly poses an aggressive challenge to racist ideologies, when he discusses his use of sources in the "Conclusion" to *Clotel,* he presents himself as simply a collector of texts and testimonials. Like Harriet Beecher Stowe in her 1853 *Key to Uncle Tom's Cabin,* his main purpose in acknowledging his sources appears to be to underscore the fact that his antislavery novel is based on truth: the terrible dehumanizing practices of slavery that he hopes his novel will help to abolish. Because of the urgent political purposes of his novel, and because he feels a strong sense of community with other antislavery writers, he chooses to celebrate, rather than to be embarrassed by, his indebtedness to a range of sources, particularly those that attack slavery. He acknowledges autobiographical sources ("I have personally participated in many of those scenes" [p. 226]), sources in the oral testimonies of "those who, like myself, have run away from the land of bondage" (p. 226), and sources in printed texts that, in some cases, he lifted verbatim from "American Abolitionist journals" (p. 226). He expresses his particular indebtedness to Lydia Maria Child "for part of a short story" (p. 226), "The Quadroons," which by twentieth-century standards he could be accused of having plagiarized. Referring to the wide range of antislavery source materials that helped him to create *Clotel*, Brown states: "All these combined have made my story" (p. 226).

On the basis of Brown's own discussion of his relation to his source materials, we might initially think of him as a kind of documentary historian who combines fact and fiction to reveal the evils of slavery. In this sense there would seem to be a crucial difference in the ways in which Melville and Brown use their sources. Melville revises his source materials by reconceiving them; Brown presents his source materials pretty much as he found them.

Or does he? For Brown "found" his materials in a white supremacist culture in which slavery was the law of the land; he "combined" those materials in a black-authored novel whose primary purpose is simultaneously to contest and provide a fuller historical understanding of that racist culture. Central to Brown's revisionary relation to his sources, then, is a massive, complex, often brilliant effort to recontextualize his source materials, using techniques of pastiche (a typically ironic rearticulation of cultural discourses) and bricolage (a reassembling of "found" documents) to raise questions about the ways in which meanings are produced in a white racist culture, and ultimately to suggest new ways of reading that culture.

In his "Conclusion," it should be emphasized, Brown mentions only a few of the sources that he "combined" in *Clotel*. In addition to drawing on antislavery writings, he also made considerable use of proslavery texts and other contemporaneous materials — speeches on slavery by Northern and Southern politicians, sermons by proslavery ministers, reports about slavery from Southern newspapers, writings on race by "scientific" racialists, tracts by temperance advocates and other reformers, proslavery and antislavery fictions, slave narratives, and numerous other writings ranging from the Declaration of Independence to Andrew Jackson's proclamations to the free people of color. Brown's use of all these sources prompts one to ask a key interpretive question: What is the difference, say, between reading a proslavery sermon as it initially appeared in a book of sermons for masters to read to their slaves, and then reading it again, with only minor variations, as spoken by a fictional character in an antislavery novel? Nothing much has changed in the sermon, but then again, everything has changed. Or what happens to the iconic image of Thomas Jefferson when rumors of his consortings with at least one of his slave women, allegations that were pretty much dismissed in white culture, are transported into a black-authored novel where the truth of these assertions is presented as a given? What happens to the author of the Declaration of Independence when he is viewed, however obliquely, in the light of a legacy of slavery and miscegenation? And perhaps most important, what happens to the Declaration of Independence when it is regularly alluded to in a novel that traces the careers of Jefferson's enslaved "black" children?

Clearly, Brown's every act of textual appropriation becomes an act of cultural revisioning. He does not simply "combine" sources; he creates something new, and in the process of unsettling established truths and hierarchies he encourages his readers, then and now, to participate in a complex process of ideological critique. In this respect it is worth emphasizing another important difference between Melville's and Brown's conception of their relationship to their sources. In revising the works of such authors as Shakespeare and Milton, for example, Melville revises a literary and cultural tradition that he regards relatively unproblematically as his own. Brown, as an African American author, necessarily has a very different relation to the sources he draws on, as most of those sources come from a culture and tradition that regards him as an outsider. Working with the texts that constitute the culture that had enslaved him, Brown, particularly in his allusions to Jefferson, produces what was referred to in the general Introduction as a genealogical fiction (p. 15), an historical novel that investigates and ultimately attempts to desacralize the political, cultural, and ideological origins of the United States.

In his own way, then, Brown, like Melville, assumes a highly aggressive relation to his sources, wresting them from their place in white supremacist culture and repositioning them in a genealogical fiction that works to demonumentalize the Founding Fathers and ultimately to raise large questions about the nation's putative commitment to liberty and freedom for all. As will become apparent by looking at some of Brown's acknowledged source materials in relation to his actual use of them, when Brown appropriates textual sources, he really does appropriate them, at times making use of much of the language of the original text. Rather than portraying himself as the creator of a discrete, transcendent work, however, Brown makes it clear in *Clotel*'s final chapter that he regards himself as being engaged in dialogue with a range of texts and sources. Unlike Poe, who strives for authorial originality, he conceives of revision (and in a sense plagiary) as fundamental to authorship itself.

Breaking down the perceived dichotomy between literary text and source, *Clotel* suggests the slipperiness of the very concepts of "sources" and "revisions." Notwithstanding the title of this section, virtually every text in this Cultural Edition of *Clotel* can be regarded as a source, particularly given Brown's genealogical understanding of the ways in which texts permeate other texts and undergird a history of social practices and beliefs. Moreover, given Brown's broad sense of what constitutes a source (cultural practices, discourses, oral traditions, literary texts, personal experiences and testimony, and so on), the texts in this edition cover only a fraction of the sources that inform Brown's novel. Writing from a minority position as a black and a former slave, Brown assumes that there are intimate connections between his novel's sources and the sources of the nation, which is hardly surprising in a novel that repeatedly invokes the Declaration. By revising his textual and cultural sources, through appropriation (theft) and recontextualization, Brown hoped to inspire larger efforts to revise the nation.

This chapter prints nineteen selections that can best be thought of in relation to the category of "Sources and Revisions." Though the selections could be read at random in accordance with different readers' particular interests, the chapter is roughly divided into three distinct areas of emphasis. The first six selections, beginning with Jefferson's "Declaration" and ending with Douglass's "What to the Slave is the Fourth of July?," focus attention on Brown's recontextualization of Jefferson, and thus of the nation's political and ideological sources; they help us to take stock of Brown's efforts to explore the interconnections between slavery and freedom at the time of the nation's founding. A striking aspect of Jefferson's draft of the Declaration, as he presents it in his "Autobiography," is that it both expresses

and expunges his antislavery views. That erasure can be read as analogous to the suppression of rumors during Jefferson's lifetime about his
involvement with Hemings. After Jefferson's death, the rumors were
recirculated by abolitionists who were outraged by the nation's failure
to live up to its Revolutionary ideals. Douglass's Fourth of July speech,
delivered a year before the publication of *Clotel,* similarly calls into
question the hypocrisies of a nation that tells a progressive, democratic
story about its commitment to the principles of the Declaration even
as it enslaves millions of African descent. Douglass's lecture, which
influenced Brown's ironic perspective on the Declaration (and Jefferson), may well have been inspired by Brown's earlier writings, particularly his 1847 *Lecture.*

The next eight selections, beginning with the excerpts from Thomas
Bacon's *Sermons* and ending with Grace Greenwood's "The Leap
from the Long Bridge," represent some of the texts that Brown "kidnapped" into his text, and thus allow us better to understand how his
recontextualizing techniques of bricolage and pastiche transformed
these source materials. Included among these selections are the
proslavery remarks of Bacon and Peck, proslavery documents collected in Weld's antislavery *American Slavery As It Is* (1839), the story
of William and Ellen Craft's incredible escape from slavery (as told by
Brown), and three literary texts. Two of the literary texts, Lydia Maria
Child's "The Quadroons" and Grace Greenwood's "The Leap from
the Long Bridge," are reproduced nearly word for word in Brown's
novel, and yet many readers will find the experience of reading them
outside of this context to be quite different from reading them as
part of *Clotel.* In *Clotel,* the story and poem lose their identity as
autonomous works with a clear beginning, middle, and end, and necessarily exist in conversation with other appropriated texts and
Brown's own writing. This is particularly true of the Child story,
which Brown divides into three sections that are strategically placed at
key points in the novel. The chapter from Stowe's *Uncle Tom's Cabin,*
which is a more suggestive, lightly borrowed source, helps us to consider ongoing processes of revision in the culture, for the story of
Cassy, who ultimately escapes from slavery and is reunited with her
daughter, can itself be read as a revisionary account of the story of
Rosalie in "The Quadroons." Brown's own revisions of Child may
well have been inspired by Stowe's. Both the Child and Stowe selections, moreover, point to the centrality of the figure of the tragic
mulatta in antislavery writing. Concerned about the vulnerability of

slave women, Brown, like Child and Stowe, sought to engage white readers' sympathies by focusing on the situation of slave women who looked white to the eye. As mentioned in the general Introduction, there are risks to such a rhetorical strategy, specifically, that white readers will continue to be concerned only about the fate of the nation's "whites." Stowe took different sorts of risks in idealizing the Christlike character of the black Uncle Tom. Brown's depiction of the rebellious black militant Picquilo suggests that he is working with and against not just Stowe's characterization of the tragic mulatta but also her celebration of the heroic black martyr.

Throughout his career as a writer, Brown continually reworked his books, publishing numerous revised versions not only of his histories of others but also of his accounts of himself. The selections from Brown's *Narrative* and Josephine Brown's biography of her father indicate that Brown's own experiences were important sources for *Clotel.* Brown emphasized the close connection between his life and fiction by prefacing *Clotel* with a third-person account of his life history. But the selections from *Narrative* and *Biography* can also be read in relation to the final three selections of the chapter — beginning with Brown's *Original Panoramic Views* and ending with his 1867 version of *Clotelle* — which provide examples of how Brown revised his own texts, including *Clotel,* to create new versions and new texts. Just as Brown's use of cultural materials challenged the notion of the finished, discrete text, so his acts of authorial revision challenged the notion of regarding his own works as completed artifacts bounded by the act of publication.

Brown reworked a section from his 1850 *Original Panoramic Views* for his 1853 *Clotel,* and then over the next fourteen years published three major revisions of the novel that responded to the Civil War and its aftermath and reflected his own changing cultural politics, particularly his attitude toward race and reform. In the revisions, he celebrates blackness and more optimistically locates possibilities for black uplift in the United States. As these new versions of the novel make clear, once Brown published *Clotel,* a compendium of sources, he came to see the novel itself as an "incomplete" and historically limited source that remained a prime target for revision. Sharing Melville's suspicion of totalized systems of meaning, Brown would no doubt have offered his assent to Ishmael's paean to the revisionary process: "God keep me from ever completing anything" (Melville 145).

THOMAS JEFFERSON

A Declaration by the Representatives of the United States of America, in General Congress Assembled

Thomas Jefferson (1743–1826), the great Virginian polymath and politician, was the nation's first secretary of state, second vice president, and third president (1801–09). As the principal author of the Declaration of Independence, he continues to occupy a sacred place in American culture for having expressed the nation's ideals of democracy and equality in their most powerful written form. Yet because he was a slave owner, his reputation has fluctuated and the genuineness of his commitment to freedom has come under repeated scrutiny. In his defense, Jefferson seemed uncomfortable with slavery and was reluctant to present the institution as a "positive good." But the fact remains that he owned slaves throughout his career and at his death manumitted only the slaves of the Hemings family. Some therefore view Jefferson as a hypocrite who extolled human liberty while simultaneously defending his — and his fellow Southerners' — rights to enslave black people; others regard him as a visionary Founding Father who, despite being influenced by the sectional and racist ideologies of his day, championed humankind's inalienable rights to freedom and equality. The tensions and contradictions informing Jefferson's (and the new nation's) founding ideals are displayed with no greater clarity than in the draft of the Declaration of Independence printed in his "Autobiography." The draft, "Declaration by the Representatives of the United States of America," includes his original attack on the slave trade, along with the revisions made by the General Congress that cut those antislavery sentiments from the final document. Jefferson wrote the "Autobiography" in 1821 but it was left unpublished until after his death. The text is from *The Works of Thomas Jefferson*, vol. 1, ed. Paul Leicester Ford (New York: G. P. Putnam's Sons, 1904), 32–43.

Congress proceeded the same day to consider the declaration of Independance which had been reported & lain on the table the Friday preceding, and on Monday referred to a commee[1] of the whole. The pusillanimous idea that we had friends in England worth keeping

---

[1] *commee:* Committee.

terms with, still haunted the minds of many. For this reason those passages which conveyed censures on the people of England were struck out, lest they should give them offence. The clause too, reprobating the enslaving the inhabitants of Africa, was struck out in complaisance to South Carolina and Georgia, who had never attempted to restrain the importation of slaves, and who on the contrary still wished to continue it. Our northern brethren also I believe felt a little tender under those censures; for tho' their people have very few slaves themselves yet they had been pretty considerable carriers of them to others. The debates having taken up the greater parts of the 2d 3d & 4th days of July were, in the evening of the last, closed the declaration was reported by the commee, agreed to by the house and signed by every member present except Mr. Dickinson.[2] As the sentiments of men are known not only by what they receive, but what they reject also, I will state the form of the declaration as originally reported. The parts struck out by Congress shall be distinguished by a black line drawn under them; & those inserted by them shall be placed in the margin or in a concurrent column.[3]

A Declaration

When in the course of human events it becomes necessary for one people to dissolve the political bands which have connected them with another, and to assume among the powers of the earth the separate & equal station to which the laws of nature and of nature's God entitle them, a decent respect to the opinions of mankind requires that they should declare the causes which impel them to the separation.

We hold these truths to be self-evident: that all men are created equal; that they are endowed by their creator with <u>inherent and</u>* inalienable rights; that among these are life, liberty, & the pursuit of happiness:[4] that to secure these rights, governments are instituted

---

Note: In this edition, Jefferson's marginal notations, which contain Congress's inserted text, have been replaced by footnotes with symbols (*, †, ‡, §, ||, #).

   * certain

---

[2] *Mr. Dickinson:* The Pennsylvanian John Dickinson (1732–1808) was a leader of the conservative patriots who hoped for reconciliation with England.

[3] *The parts . . . column:* Jefferson fails to note that he uses brackets to indicate where Congress added words to the body of the text.

[4] *life, liberty, & the pursuit of happiness:* Principles derived from John Locke (1632–1704), *Treatises of Civil Government* (1690); Locke also emphasized the right to own property.

among men, deriving their just powers from the consent of the governed; that whenever any form of government becomes destructive of these ends, it is the right of the people to alter or abolish it, & to institute new government, laying it's foundation on such principles, & organizing it's powers in such form, as to them shall seem most likely to effect their safety & happiness. Prudence indeed will dictate that governments long established should not be changed for light & transient causes; and accordingly all experience hath shown that mankind are more disposed to suffer while evils are sufferable, than to right themselves by abolishing the forms to which they are accustomed. But when a long train of abuses & usurpations <u>begun at a distinguished period and</u> pursuing invariably the same object, evinces a design to reduce them under absolute despotism, it is their right, it is their duty to throw off such government, & to provide new guards for their future security. Such has been the patient sufferance of these colonies; & such is now the necessity which constrains them to <u>expunge</u>* their former systems of government. The history of the present king of Great Britain[5] is a history of <u>unremitting</u>† injuries & usurpations, <u>among which appears no solitary fact to contradict the uniform tenor of the rest but all have</u>‡ in direct object the establishment of an absolute tyranny over these states. To prove this let facts be submitted to a candid world <u>for the truth of which we pledge a faith yet unsullied by falsehood.</u>

He has refused his assent to laws the most wholesome & necessary for the public good.

He has forbidden his governors to pass laws of immediate & pressing importance, unless suspended in their operation till his assent should be obtained; & when so suspended, he has utterly neglected to attend to them.

He has refused to pass other laws for the accommodation of large districts of people, unless those people would relinquish the right of representation in the legislature, a right inestimable to them, & formidable to tyrants only.

He has called together legislative bodies at places unusual, uncomfortable, and distant from the depository of their public records, for the sole purpose of fatiguing them into compliance with his measures.

---

* alter
† repeated
‡ all having

[5] *the present king of Great Britain:* George III (1738–1820), who reigned from 1760 to 1820.

He has dissolved representative houses repeatedly & continually for opposing with manly firmness his invasions on the rights of the people.

He has refused for a long time after such dissolutions to cause others to be elected, whereby the legislative powers, incapable of annihilation, have returned to the people at large for their exercise, the state remaining in the meantime exposed to all the dangers of invasion from without & convulsions within.

He has endeavored to prevent the population of these states; for that purpose obstructing the laws for naturalization of foreigners, refusing to pass others to encourage their migrations hither, & raising the conditions of new appropriations of lands.

He has suffered* the administration of justice totally to cease in some of these states† refusing his assent to laws for establishing judiciary powers.

He has made our judges dependant on his will alone, for the tenure of their offices, & the amount & paiment of their salaries.

He has erected a multitude of new offices by a self assumed power and sent hither swarms of new officers to harass our people and eat out their substance.

He has kept among us in times of peace standing armies and ships of war without the consent of our legislatures.

He has affected to render the military independant of, & superior to the civil power.

He has combined with others[6] to subject us to a jurisdiction foreign to our constitutions & unacknowledged by our laws, giving his assent to their acts of pretended legislation for quartering large bodies of armed troops among us; for protecting them by a mock-trial from punishment for any murders which they should commit on the inhabitants of these states; for cutting off our trade with all parts of the world; for imposing taxes on us without our consent; for depriving us [   ]‡ of the benefits of trial by jury; for transporting us beyond seas to be tried for pretended offences; for abolishing the free system of English laws in a neighboring province,[7] establishing therein an arbitrary government, and enlarging it's boundaries, so as to render it at once an

* obstructed
† by
‡ in many cases

[6] *others:* The British Parliament.
[7] *abolishing . . . province:* A reference to the Quebec Act of 1774, which recognized Roman Catholicism in Quebec and allowed the province to extend its boundaries to the Ohio River. The colonists' Protestant majority regarded this Act as but one of the "Intolerable Acts" of 1774.

example and fit instrument for introducing the same absolute rule into these states;* for taking away our charters, abolishing our most valuable laws, and altering fundamentally the forms of our governments; for suspending our own legislatures, & declaring themselves invested with power to legislate for us in all cases whatsoever.

He has abdicated government here withdrawing his governors, and declaring us out of his allegiance & protection.†

He has plundered our seas, ravaged our coasts, burnt our towns, & destroyed the lives of our people.

He is at this time transporting large armies of foreign mercenaries[8] to compleat the works of death, desolation & tyranny already begun with circumstances of cruelty and perfidy [ ]‡ unworthy the head of a civilized nation.

He has constrained our fellow citizens taken captive on the high seas to bear arms against their country, to become the executioners of their friends & brethren, or to fall themselves by their hands.

He has [ ]§ endeavored to bring on the inhabitants of our frontiers the merciless Indian savages, whose known rule of warfare is an undistinguished destruction of all ages, sexes, & conditions of existence.

He has incited treasonable insurrections of our fellow-citizens, with the allurements of forfeiture & confiscation of our property.

He has waged cruel war against human nature itself, violating it's most sacred rights of life and liberty in the persons of a distant people who never offended him, captivating & carrying them into slavery in another hemisphere, or to incur miserable death in their transportation thither. This piratical warfare, the opprobium of INFIDEL powers, is the warfare of the CHRISTIAN king of Great Britain. Determined to keep open a market where MEN should be bought & sold, he has prostituted his negative for suppressing every legislative attempt to prohibit or to restrain this execrable commerce. And that this assemblage of horrors might want no fact of distinguished die, he is now exciting those very people to rise in arms among us, and to purchase that liberty of which he has deprived them, by murdering the people on whom he also obtruded them: thus paying off former crimes committed against the LIBERTIES of one people, with crimes which he urges them to commit against the LIVES of another.

---

* colonies
† by declaring us out of his protection, and waging war against us.
‡ scarcely paralleled in the most barbarous ages, & totally
§ excited domestic insurrection among us, & has

---

[8] *foreign mercenaries:* German soldiers, financed by the British.

In every stage of these oppressions we have petitioned for redress in the most humble terms: our repeated petitions have been answered only by repeated injuries.

A prince whose character is thus marked by every act which may define a tyrant is unfit to be the ruler of a [ ]* people who mean to be free. Future ages will scarcely believe that the hardiness of one man adventured, within the short compass of twelve years only, to lay a foundation so broad & so undisguised for tyranny over a people fostered & fixed in principles of freedom.

Nor have we been wanting in attention to our British brethren. We have warned them from time to time of attempts by their legislature to extend a† jurisdiction over these our states.‡ We have reminded them of the circumstances of our emigration & settlement here, no one of which could warrant so strange a pretension: that these were effected at the expense of our own blood & treasure, unassisted by the wealth or the strength of Great Britain: that in constituting indeed our several forms of government, we had adopted one common king, thereby laying a foundation for perpetual league & amity with them: but that submission to their parliament was no part of our constitution, nor ever in idea, if history may be credited: and, we [ ]§ appealed to their native justice and magnanimity as well as to‖ the ties of our common kindred to disavow these usurpations which were likely to# interrupt our connection and correspondence. They too have been deaf to the voice of justice & of consanguinity, and when occasions have been given them, by the regular course of their laws, of removing from their councils the disturbers of our harmony, they have, by their free election, re-established them in power. At this very time too they are permitting their chief magistrate to send over not only soldiers of our common blood, but Scotch & foreign mercenaries to invade & destroy us. These facts have given the last stab to agonizing affection, and manly spirit bids us to renounce forever these unfeeling brethren. We must endeavor to forget our former love for them, and hold them as we hold the rest of mankind, enemies in war, in peace friends. We might have been a free and a great people together; but a communication of grandeur & of freedom it seems is below their dignity. Be it so,

---

* free
† an unwarrantable
‡ us
§ have
‖ and we have conjured them by
would inevitably

since they will have it. The road to happiness & to glory is open to us too. We will tread it apart from them, and* acquiesce in the necessity which denounces[9] our eternal separation [   ]!†

We[10] therefore the representatives of the United States of America in General Congress assembled do in the same & by authority of the good people of these states reject & renounce all allegiance & subjection to the kings of Great Britain & all others who may hereafter claim by, through or under them: we utterly dissolve all political connection which may heretofore have subsisted between us & the people or parliament of Great Britain: & finally we do assert & declare these colonies to be free & independent states, & that as free & independent states, they have full power to levy war, conclude peace, contract alliances, establish commerce, & to do all other acts & things which independent states may of right do.

And for the support of this declaration we mutually pledge to each other our lives, our fortunes, & our sacred honor.

We therefore the representatives of the United States of America in General Congress assembled, appealing to the supreme judge of the world for the rectitude of our intentions, do in the name, & by the authority of the good people of these colonies, solemnly publish & declare that these united colonies are & of right ought to be free & independent states; that they are absolved from all allegiance to the British crown, and that all political connection between them & the state of Great Britain is, & ought to be, totally dissolved; & that as free & independent states they have full power to levy war, conclude peace, contract alliances, establish commerce & to do all other acts & things which independant states may of right do.

And for the support of this declaration, with a firm reliance on the protection of divine providence we mutually pledge to each other our lives, our fortunes, & our sacred honor.

The Declaration thus signed on the 4th, on paper was engrossed on parchment, & signed again on the 2d of August.

---

* We must therefore
† and hold them as we hold the rest of mankind, enemies in war, in peace friends.

---

[9] *denounces:* Announces.
[10] *We . . .:* In this closing section Jefferson prints his version in the left column and the final adopted version in the right column.

FRANCES TROLLOPE

From *Domestic Manners of the Americans*

In 1827 the British writer Frances Trollope (1780–1863) traveled from England to America with the intention of setting up a department store in Cincinnati. She also wanted to participate in the racially integrated social-ist community founded at Nashoba, Tennessee, by her Scottish-born friend Frances Wright. Unsuccessful in her commercial ventures, though impressed by Wright's radical antislavery efforts, Trollope returned to England three years later and soon afterwards published her acerbic, widely read *Domestic Manners of the Americans* (London: Whittaker, Treacher, & Co., 1832), from which this selection is taken. (Some twenty years later, her son Anthony Trollope would emerge as an internationally celebrated novelist.) Frances Trollope's biting remarks on Jefferson's hyp-ocritical sexual relationship with one of his slave women infuriated Amer-ica's literary nationalists. In his 1839 *A Diary in America, with Remarks on Its Institutions,* a book William Wells Brown probably read, Cap-tain Frederick Marryat echoed Trollope's (and others') charges against Jefferson.

Few names are held in higher estimation in America than that of Jefferson; it is the touchstone of the democratic party, and all seem to agree that he was one of the greatest of men; yet I have heard his name coupled with deeds which would make the sons of Europe shudder. The facts I allude to are spoken openly by all, not whispered privately by a few; and in a country where religion is the tea-table talk, and its strict observance a fashionable distinction, these facts are recorded and listened to without horror, nay, without emotion.

Mr. Jefferson is said to have been the father of children by almost all his numerous gang of female slaves. These wretched offspring were also the lawful slaves of their father, and worked in his house and plantations as such; in particular, it is recorded that it was his especial pleasure to be waited upon by them at table, and the hospitable orgies for which his Monticello[1] was so celebrated, were incomplete, unless

---

[1] *Monticello:* Located near Charlottesville, Virginia, the 640-acre estate of Monti-cello was Jefferson's home for over fifty years. He designed the mansion, which was built by his artisan slaves.

the goblet he quaffed were tendered by the trembling hand of his own slavish offspring.

I once heard it stated by a democratical adorer of this great man, that when, as it sometimes happened, his children by Quadroon slaves were white enough to escape suspicion of their origin, he did not pursue them if they attempted to escape, saying laughingly, "Let the rogues get off, if they can; I will not hinder them." This was stated in a large party, as a proof of his kind and noble nature, and was received by all with approving smiles.

If I know any thing of right or wrong, if virtue and vice be indeed something more than words, then was this great American an unprincipled tyrant and most heartless libertine.

WILLIAM GOODELL

Sale of a Daughter of Tho's Jefferson

Though this selection consists almost entirely of a letter from the obscure New York abolitionist Dr. Gaylord on his conversation with the equally obscure Missouri slavery apologist Otis Reynolds, the piece is ultimately the work of the well-known New York abolitionist William Goodell (1792–1878). Goodell helped to found the American Anti-Slavery Society in 1833, and went on to edit a number of antislavery newspapers, including the *Emancipator,* the *Friend of Man,* and the *Radical Abolitionist.* During the 1840s he championed "Come-Outerism," a movement encouraging abolitionists to withdraw from churches that supported or even remained neutral on slavery. Among his most important books are *Views on American Constitutional Law in Its Bearing on American Slavery* (1844) and *Slavery and Anti-Slavery* (1852). Goodell saw the rumors about Jefferson's sexual involvement with his slaves as performing useful ideological critique; he published Gaylord's account of his putative conversation about Jefferson in the 22 August 1838 issue of his Utica newspaper, *Friend of Man.* The letter, with Goodell's commentary, was reprinted in the 21 September 1838 *Liberator,* which is the source of the text below.

"A Slave Auction in Virginia." Wood engraving in *The Illustrated London News*, 16 February 1861. Courtesy of the Photographs and Prints Division, Schomburg Center for Research in Black Culture, The New York Public Library, Astor, Lennox and Tilden Foundations.

[A SCENE AT NEW ORLEANS]
Sale of a Daughter of Tho's Jefferson.
'Going for a Thousand Dollars! Who Bids?
'Going? going! gone! Who's the buyer?'

The following fact was related in our hearing, by the writer, Dr. GAYLORD, of Sodus,[1] at the Wayne County Anti-Slavery Society's meeting, at Palmyra,[2] last June. At our request, he has now furnished it for publication. Read it, fellow citizens, and ponder. If a daughter of THOMAS JEFFERSON may be sold at auction, what security can you, or any of us, have, that *our* daughters may not, one day, be sold in the same manner? COLOR IS NO PROTECTION. *'Bleached or unbleached!'* says Gov. M'Duffie![3] 'CLEAR WHITE *complexion'* — say the slave advertisements!

From the *Friend of Man.*

MR. GOODELL, — My apology for not furnishing you with an earlier communication, in regard to the following fact, must be found in my having been absent to the 'far West,' for several weeks, whence I have just returned.

Gladly, Mr. Editor, would I draw the mantle of oblivion over a transaction disclosing so dark a spot on the moral escutcheon of the man, whose name stands enrolled so high on the archives of our proud republic, did I not believe, that like the faithful delineations on our sacred pages, of the sin of David,[4] and other eminently great men, it should descend on record, as a solemn beacon, not only to excite disgust and warning against the crime, but also to awaken the lovers of our country, of morality, humanity, and religion, to see the *natural results* connected with the *'practical operations'* of slavery — and hoping, also, that it may assist in prostrating the power of lawless passion, and legalized cruelty; and in preventing similar scenes of disgrace from being either enacted or tolerated, by high or low, as they frequently are, to the burning shame of our beloved country.

---

[1] *Sodus:* A city in northern New York.

[2] *Palmyra:* A town in northern New York.

[3] *Gov. M'Duffie!:* The South Carolina proslavery politician George McDuffie (1790–1851) served as congressman (1821–1834), governor (1834–1835), and senator (1842–1846).

[4] *the sin of David:* A reference to David's sexual relationship with Bathsheba; see 2 Samuel 11.1–12.

In a recent conversation with Mr. OTIS REYNOLDS, a gentleman from *St. Louis, Missouri,* himself a practical, as well as theoretical supporter of slavery, in our discussion of the subject, Mr. Reynolds endeavored to find an apology for the 'domestic institution' of the South, by assuming, as a fact, the alleged inferiority of the colored race.

I replied, that it was currently reported here, that 'the best blood of Virginia, flowed in the veins of the slaves;' and the argument therefore could have no force, in regard to the amalgamated portion of the slaves. Said he, with much emphasis,

'That's true; I saw myself, the DAUGHTER of THOMAS JEFFERSON SOLD in New Orleans, for ONE THOUSAND DOLLARS.'

What a fact for the contemplation of this free republic!! and what a comment on our *professions* of love of liberty, and practice of slavery!!!

The Daughter of the President of the United States, the boasted land of Freedom, sold into interminable bondage!!! Look at it, citizens of our free republic! Here is no violation of law — you have the natural, legalized, common working of the system.

I do not wonder that Jefferson said, 'I tremble for my country when I remember that God is just, and that his justice cannot sleep forever.'[5] If slavery has so far annihilated parental and kindred ties, that the natural offspring of our highest officers of government, are sold under the hammer of the auctioneer, and driven under the lash of unfeeling tyrants,

> 'With stripes that mercy, with a bleeding heart,
> Weeps when she sees inflicted on a beast,'[6]

or turned over to mercenary lust of involuntary prostitution — let it be sounded longer and louder, through the length and breadth of the land, until a virtuous indignation shall kindle in every American bosom, and the guilty apologists and participators of such deeds of infamy, shall hide their heads in merited shame and contempt.

The authenticity of the above fact, rests on the sober testimony of a southern man, whose credibility is unquestioned, in the presence of some respectable merchants of our village, whose names can be given,

---

[5] *I tremble ... forever:* From Jefferson's *Notes on the State of Virginia;* see pp. 335–43.

[6] *With stripes ... inflicted on a beast:* From William Cowper (1731–1800), *The Task* (1784).

if necessary; and as it may be highly important to the full development of a system, in which amalgamation, and an utter disregard to the claims of consanguinity and domestic ties, are perfectly commonplace, it is my deliberate opinion, that such astounding facts should be spread before the community, to awaken them to the repulsive workings of that system of wrongs and wretchedness, which has so long been the foulest blot on the fair fame of our republic.

Very respectfully, yours,
LEVI GAYLORD.

Sodus, August 13, 1838.

Jefferson's Daughter

"Jefferson's Daughter," along with the epigraph from the *London Morning Chronicle* on Jefferson's alleged trafficking of his alleged slave daughter, first appeared in the July 1839 issue of *Tait's Edinburgh Magazine*. The "American Newspaper" mentioned in the epigraph was in all probability the *Liberator,* which would suggest that Levi Gaylord's 1838 letter to William Goodell, printed above, may well have inspired the poem. A slightly different version of "Jefferson's Daughter" appeared in the 26 May 1848 issue of the *Liberator,* and a virtually identical version of that poem appeared in William Wells Brown's antislavery songbook, *The Anti-Slavery Harp: A Collection of Songs for Anti-Slavery Meetings. Compiled by William W. Brown, A Fugitive Slave* (Boston: Bela Marsh, 1848), which is the source of the selection below. Convinced that the communal singing of songs at antislavery meetings would help to advance the cause, Brown compiled a songbook that included Garrison's "I Am an Abolitionist," John Greenleaf Whittier's "The Yankee Girl," James Russell Lowell's "Stanzas on Freedom," and the anonymous "The Blind Slave Boy." "Jefferson's Daughter" anticipates the concerns about genealogy and ideology that would come to inform Brown's novel of "The President's Daughter."

> "It is asserted, on the authority of an American Newspaper, that the daughter of Thomas Jefferson, late President of the United States, was sold at New Orleans for $1,000."

— Morning Chronicle

Can the blood that, at Lexington,[1] poured o'er the plain,
   When the sons warred with tyrants their rights to uphold,
Can the tide of Niagara wipe out the stain?
   No! Jefferson's child has been bartered for gold!

Do you boast of your freedom? Peace, babblers — be still;
   Prate[2] not of the goddess who scarce deigns to hear;
Have ye power to unbind?   Are ye wanting in will?
   Must the groans of your bondman still torture the ear?

The daughter of Jefferson sold for a slave!
   The child of a freeman for dollars and francs!
The roar of applause, when your orators rave,
   Is lost in the sound of her chain, as it clanks.

Peace, then, ye blasphemers of Liberty's name!
   Though red was the blood by your forefathers spilt,
Still redder your cheeks should be mantled with shame,
   Till the spirit of freedom shall cancel the guilt.

But the brand of the slave is the tint of his skin,
   Though his heart may beat loyal and true underneath;
While the soul of the tyrant is rotten within,
   And his white the mere cloak to the blackness of death.

Are ye deaf to the plaints that each moment arise?
   Is it thus ye forget the mild precepts of Penn,[3] —
Unheeding the clamor that "maddens the skies,"
   As ye trample the rights of your dark fellow-men?

When the incense that glows before Liberty's shrine,
   Is unmixed with the blood of the galled and oppressed, —
O, then, and then only, the boast may be thine,
   That the stripes and stars wave o'er a land of the blest.

---

[1] *Lexington:* On 19 April 1775, Lexington, Massachusetts, was the site of the first battle of the American Revolution.
[2] *Prate:* To babble or talk pointlessly.
[3] *Penn:* William Penn (1644–1718) was an English Quaker and the founder of Pennsylvania. The Quakers were strongly opposed to the institution of slavery.

JAMES McCUNE SMITH

From Letter to *Frederick Douglass' Paper*

A regular contributor to *Frederick Douglass' Paper* during the 1850s, James McCune Smith (1813–1865) was one of the most prominent black intellectuals and abolitionists of the period. The son of former slaves, Smith, who was born and educated in New York City, enrolled in Glasgow University in 1832 after he was denied entry to American colleges. By 1837 he had received three degrees, including a doctorate of medicine, whereupon he returned to New York City and established a successful medical and pharmacy practice. Committed to political abolitionism, he edited and contributed to a number of black newspapers and magazines, published several important pamphlets, including *The Destiny of the People of Color* (1843), wrote the introduction to Douglass's *My Bondage and My Freedom* (1855), and participated in black conventions and a number of other abolitionist and antiracist initiatives. Like Douglass in the 1850s, Smith regarded the Constitution as an antislavery document, and thus he was particularly troubled by the contradictions he perceived at the heart of Jefferson's writings and social practices. Published under the pseudonym "Communipaw," Smith's Letter, from which these passages on Jefferson and slavery are drawn, appeared in the 25 March 1852 issue of *Frederick Douglass' Paper*.

. . . [I]t is well known that Jefferson contradicted his philosophy of negro hate, by seeking the dalliance of black women as often as he could, and by leaving so many descendants of mixed blood, that they are to be found as widely scattered as his own writings throughout the world. One at least, a grand daughter, is a shouting Methodist, in Liberia.[1] I have heard, from an eye witness, that on more than one occasion, when the sage of Monticello left that retreat, for the Presidential abode, at Washington, there would be on the top of the same coach, a yellow boy of his own begetting, "running away." And when told that one of his slaves was going off without leave, Jefferson said,

---

[1] *Liberia:* At the time a colony in West Africa governed in large part by agents and representatives of the American Colonization Society, whose goal was to ship free African Americans to Africa.

well! let him go, his right is as good as his father's! And, somehow, *that* boy would get a doceur[2] before the "parting of the ways."

Ah me! The pride of old Virginia! I might exclaim of it as Black Dan[3] did of our Republic, *Epese, Epese.* "Thou hast fallen, thou hast fallen!" These crocus colored products of unphilosophical lust, are now reared, and penned up, and branded, and sold, by slaveholding fathers in Old Dominion,[4] who go to Presbyterian and Methodist churches, and to the altars of Episcopacy, and drink the "blood which Christ shed for all;" and thank God that they are not heathen Circassians[5] who sell their daughters as prostitutes to *Mahommedan*[6] [*sic*], not *Christian,* lust!

[2] *doceur:* A gratuity or small amount of money.

[3] *Black Dan:* A reference to Daniel Webster; see *Clotel*, note 18, p. 173.

[4] *Old Dominion:* Virginia.

[5] *Circassians:* Natives of Circassia, a region in Europe bordering the Black Sea.

[6] *Mahommedan:* Usually *Mahammadan;* a reference to the Islamic followers of Muhammed (570–632).

FREDERICK DOUGLASS

What to the Slave Is the Fourth of July?

In a searing indictment of the nation's contradictory Revolutionary origins in slavery and freedom, Frederick Douglass called attention to the limits (and promise) of Jefferson's Declaration in a Fourth of July speech delivered on 5 July 1852 in Rochester, New York, before a racially mixed audience of approximately six hundred people. The best-known and most influential African American leader of the nineteenth century, Douglass (1818–1895) escaped from slavery in Maryland in 1838, and in 1841 was appointed a lecturing agent for William Lloyd Garrison's Anti-Slavery Society. His widely read *The Narrative of the Life of Frederick Douglass,* an important influence on Brown's own *Narrative,* appeared in 1845. Following a British tour, during which his freedom was purchased, Douglass returned to the United States in 1847 and commenced a career in journalism and abolitionism. For the most part Brown and Douglass greatly respected one another. They met in Buffalo in 1843 at the National Convention of Colored Citizens, and as Garrisonians committed to a nonviolent use of moral persuasion joined hands in voting against endorsing

Henry Highland Garnet's insurrectionary "Address to the Slaves" (see pp. 471–80). During the early 1850s, Brown contributed a number of letters to *Frederick Douglass' Paper*. In the mid-1850s, however, Brown and Douglass quarreled in print after Douglass publicly repudiated Garrison, whom Brown continued to admire. At an 1855 meeting of the Anti-Slavery Society, Douglass attacked Brown for urging the free states to break from, rather than reform, the slave states. That same year Douglass published a much revised and expanded narrative of his life, *My Bondage and My Freedom* (New York and Auburn: Miller, Orton, and Mulligan, 1855). In the appendix to that volume Douglass included an abridgment of his Fourth of July speech, which is printed below.

FELLOW-CITIZENS — Pardon me, and allow me to ask, why am I called upon to speak here to-day? What have I, or those I represent, to do with your national independence? Are the great principles of political freedom and of natural justice, embodied in that Declaration of Independence, extended to us? and am I, therefore, called upon to bring our humble offering to the national altar, and to confess the benefits, and express devout gratitude for the blessings, resulting from your independence to us?

Would to God, both for your sakes and ours, that an affirmative answer could be truthfully returned to these questions? Then would my task be light, and my burden easy and delightful. For who is there so cold that a nation's sympathy could not warm him? Who so obdurate and dead to the claims of gratitude, that would not thankfully acknowledge such priceless benefits? Who so stolid and selfish, that would not give his voice to swell the hallelujahs of a nation's jubilee, when the chains of servitude had been torn from his limbs? I am not that man. In a case like that, the dumb might eloquently speak, and the "lame man leap as an hart."[1]

But, such is not the state of the case. I say it with a sad sense of the disparity between us. I am not included within the pale of this glorious anniversary! Your high independence only reveals the immeasurable distance between us. The blessings in which you this day rejoice, are not enjoyed in common. The rich inheritance of justice, liberty, prosperity, and independence, bequeathed by your fathers, is shared by you, not by me. The sunlight that brought life and healing to you, has

---

[1] *"lame . . . hart":* Isaiah 35.6; a "hart" is a male red deer.

brought stripes and death to me. This Fourth of July is *yours,* not *mine. You* may rejoice, *I* must mourn. To drag a man in fetters into the grand illuminated temple of liberty, and call upon him to join you in joyous anthems, were inhuman mockery and sacrilegious irony. Do you mean, citizens, to mock me, by asking me to speak to-day? If so, there is a parallel to your conduct. And let me warn you that it is dangerous to copy the example of a nation whose crimes, towering up to heaven, were thrown down by the breath of the Almighty, burying that nation in irrecoverable ruin![2] I can to-day take up the plaintive lament of a peeled and woe-smitten people.

"By the rivers of Babylon, there we sat down. Yea! we wept when we remembered Zion. We hanged our harps upon the willows in the midst thereof. For there, they that carried us away captive, required of us a song; and they who wasted us required of us mirth, saying, Sing us one of the songs of Zion. How can we sing the Lord's song in a strange land? If I forget thee, O Jerusalem, let my right hand forget her cunning. If I do not remember thee, let my tongue cleave to the roof of my mouth."[3]

Fellow-citizens, above your national, tumultuous joy, I hear the mournful wail of millions, whose chains, heavy and grievous yesterday, are to-day rendered more intolerable by the jubilant shouts that reach them. If I do forget, if I do not faithfully remember those bleeding children of sorrow this day, "may my right hand forget her cunning, and may my tongue cleave to the roof of my mouth!" To forget them, to pass lightly over their wrongs, and to chime in with the popular theme, would be treason most scandalous and shocking, and would make me a reproach before God and the world. My subject then, fellow-citizens, is AMERICAN SLAVERY. I shall see this day and its popular characteristics from the slave's point of view. Standing there, identified with the American bondman, making his wrongs mine, I do not hesitate to declare, with all my soul, that the character and conduct of this nation never looked blacker to me than on this Fourth of July. Whether we turn to the declarations of the past, or to the professions of the present, the conduct of the nation seems equally hideous and revolting. America is false to the past, false to the present, and solemnly binds herself to be false to the future. Standing with God and the crushed and bleeding slave on this occasion, I will, in the name of

---

[2] *a nation whose crimes . . . ruin!:* The Israelites of the Old Testament. Douglass here is addressing (and critiquing) nineteenth-century Americans' tendency to regard the U.S. as a New Israel.

[3] *"By the rivers . . . mouth":* Psalms 137.1–6.

humanity which is outraged, in the name of liberty which is fettered, in the name of the constitution and the bible, which are disregarded and trampled upon, dare to call in question and to denounce, with all the emphasis I can command, everything that serves to perpetuate slavery — the great sin and shame of America! "I will not equivocate; I will not excuse;"[4] I will use the severest language I can command; and yet not one word shall escape me that any man, whose judgment is not blinded by prejudice, or who is not at heart a slaveholder, shall not confess to be right and just.

But I fancy I hear some one of my audience say, it is just in this circumstance that you and your brother abolitionists fail to make a favorable impression on the public mind. Would you argue more, and denounce less, would you persuade more and rebuke less, your cause would be much more likely to succeed. But, I submit, where all is plain there is nothing to be argued. What point in the anti-slavery creed would you have me argue? On what branch of the subject do the people of this country need light? Must I undertake to prove that the slave is a man? That point is conceded already. Nobody doubts it. The slaveholders themselves acknowledge it in the enactment of laws for their government. They acknowledge it when they punish disobedience on the part of the slave. There are seventy-two crimes in the state of Virginia, which, if committed by a black man, (no matter how ignorant he be,) subject him to the punishment of death; while only two of these same crimes will subject a white man to the like punishment. What is this but the acknowledgment that the slave is a moral, intellectual, and responsible being. The manhood of the slave is conceded. It is admitted in the fact that southern statute books are covered with enactments forbidding, under severe fines and penalties, the teaching of the slave to read or write. When you can point to any such laws, in reference to the beasts of the field, then I may consent to argue the manhood of the slave. When the dogs in your streets, when the fowls of the air, when the cattle on your hills, when the fish of the sea, and the reptiles that crawl, shall be unable to distinguish the slave from a brute, then will I argue with you that the slave is a man!

For the present, it is enough to affirm the equal manhood of the negro race. Is it not astonishing that, while we are plowing, planting, and reaping, using all kinds of mechanical tools, erecting houses, constructing bridges, building ships, working in metals of brass, iron,

---

[4] "*I will . . . not excuse;*": From "To the Public," an editorial by William Lloyd Garrison in the inaugural issue of the *Liberator*, reprinted on pp. 444–46.

copper, silver, and gold; that, while we are reading, writing, and cypher-
ing, acting as clerks, merchants, and secretaries, having among us
lawyers, doctors, ministers, poets, authors, editors, orators, and teachers; that, while we are engaged in all manner of enterprises common to
other men — digging gold in California, capturing the whale in the
Pacific, feeding sheep and cattle on the hillside, living, moving, acting,
thinking, planning, living in families as husbands, wives, and children,
and, above all, confessing and worshiping the christian's God, and
looking hopefully for life and immortality beyond the grave, — we are
called upon to prove that we are men!

Would you have me argue that man is entitled to liberty? that he is
the rightful owner of his own body? You have already declared it.
Must I argue the wrongfulness of slavery? Is that a question for repub-
licans? Is it to be settled by the rules of logic and argumentation, as a
matter beset with great difficulty, involving a doubtful application of
the principle of justice, hard to be understood? How should I look to-
day in the presence of Americans, dividing and subdividing a discourse, to show that men have a natural right to freedom, speaking of
it relatively and positively, negatively and affirmatively? To do so,
would be to make myself ridiculous, and to offer an insult to your
understanding. There is not a man beneath the canopy of heaven that
does not know that slavery is wrong *for him.*

What! am I to argue that it is wrong to make men brutes, to rob
them of their liberty, to work them without wages, to keep them ignorant of their relations to their fellow-men, to beat them with sticks, to
flay their flesh with the lash, to load their limbs with irons, to hunt
them with dogs, to sell them at auction, to sunder their families, to
knock out their teeth, to burn their flesh, to starve them into obedience
and submission to their masters? Must I argue that a system, thus
marked with blood and stained with pollution, is wrong? No; I will
not. I have better employment for my time and strength than such
arguments would imply.

What, then, remains to be argued? Is it that slavery is not divine;
that God did not establish it; that our doctors of divinity are mistaken?
There is blasphemy in the thought. That which is inhuman cannot be
divine. Who can reason on such a proposition! They that can, may; I
cannot. The time for such argument is past.

At a time like this, scorching irony, not convincing argument, is
needed. Oh! had I the ability, and could I reach the nation's ear, I
would to-day pour out a fiery stream of biting ridicule, blasting
reproach, withering sarcasm, and stern rebuke. For it is not light that

is needed, but fire; it is not the gentle shower, but thunder. We need the storm, the whirlwind, and the earthquake. The feeling of the nation must be quickened; the conscience of the nation must be roused; the propriety of the nation must be startled; the hypocrisy of the nation must be exposed; and its crimes against God and man must be proclaimed and denounced.

What to the American slave is your Fourth of July? I answer, a day that reveals to him, more than all other days in the year, the gross injustice and cruelty to which he is the constant victim. To him, your celebration is a sham; your boasted liberty, an unholy license; your national greatness, swelling vanity; your sounds of rejoicing are empty and heartless; your denunciations of tyrants, brass-fronted impudence; your shouts of liberty and equality, hollow mockery; your prayers and hymns, your sermons and thanksgivings, with all your religious parade and solemnity, are to him mere bombast, fraud, deception, impiety, and hypocrisy — a thin veil to cover up crimes which would disgrace a nation of savages. There is not a nation on the earth guilty of practices more shocking and bloody, than are the people of these United States, at this very hour.

Go where you may, search where you will, roam through all the monarchies and despotisms of the old world, travel through South America, search out every abuse, and when you have found the last, lay your facts by the side of the every-day practices of this nation, and you will say with me, that, for revolting barbarity and shameless hypocrisy, America reigns without a rival.

THOMAS BACON

From *Sermons Addressed to Masters and Servants*

Proslavery religious writers regularly turned to the Bible to defend the master-slave relationship as a "natural," divinely ordained relationship that placed a spiritual burden on the master and slave alike. According to these writers, masters were responsible for caring for their slaves' bodies and souls, while the slaves were responsible for pursuing their salvation by remaining true to their worldly "duty" of serving their masters. In his influential *Christian Directory* (1673), the Anglican Richard Baxter (1615–1691) argued that slavery offered masters and slaves myriad opportunities for spiritual growth and redemption. Maryland's Reverend

Thomas Bacon (1700–1768) took up Baxter's arguments and published a number of sermons on the mutual obligations of masters and slaves. Several of those sermons were reprinted by Bishop William Meade (1789–1862) of the Episcopal Diocese of Virginia in an edited collection, *Sermons Addressed to Masters and Servants, and Published in the Year 1743, by the Rev. Thomas Bacon, Minister of the Protestant Episcopal Church in Maryland. Now Republished with other Tracts and Dialogues on the Same Subject, and Recommended to all Masters and Mistresses to be Used in Their Families. By the Rev. William Meade* (Winchester, Virginia: John Heiskell, 1813), from which the selection below is drawn. The arguments of Baxter, Bacon, Meade, and other divines were adduced by antebellum proslavery writers to defend the social and racial hierarchies central to slavery. Antislavery writers countered that slaveholders blasphemously usurped God's place as the "master" of humankind. In *Clotel,* Brown lifts liberally from Bacon's sermons to the slaves, putting his words into the mouth of the cynical Northern proslavery "missionary" Hontz Snyder.

And now, *my dear* BLACK *brethren and sisters,* I beg that you will listen seriously to what I shall say — You all know what love and affection I have for you, and I do believe that most of you have the like love for me, as you have always found me ready to serve you, when you wanted my help. — I doubt not therefore, that you will readily hearken to the good advice I shall now give you, (as you know me to be your friend and wellwisher) and hope you will remember it hereafter, and think upon it at home, and talk of it to your fellow-servants that are not here, that they may receive advantage by it, as well as you, that hear it from my own mouth. [*Here masters may begin to read to their servants.*] . . .

That you may easier understand, and better carry away in your memory what you shall hear, I shall endeavour, by GOD's help, to lay before you, in the plainest words,

I. Why you ought to serve GOD.

II. What service, or what good things GOD expects from you.

III. What kind of reward you may expect to receive from him.

I. And the first reason why you ought to serve GOD, is, — BECAUSE THAT GOD MADE YOU; — and he *made* you, and all men, to *serve* him. — You know that when you were born, you did not come into the world by any power or help of your own: — Nay, you were so far from

knowing any thing about it, or how you came here; — whether you
were found in the woods, or grew out of the ground, — that it was
some years before you could help yourselves, or had so much sense as
to know your right hand from your left. — It was Almighty GOD,
therefore, who made you, and all the world, that sent you here, as he
had sent your fathers and mothers, your masters and mistresses before
you, to take care of you, and provide for you, while you could take no
care of, or help, or provide for yourselves. — And can you think that
Almighty GOD, who is so wise and good himself, would send you into
the world for any bad purposes? — Can you be so silly as to fancy, that
he, who made every thing so good and useful in its kind, sent you here
to be idle, to be wicked, or to make a bad use of any thing he hath
made? — No, my brethren, the most ignorant among you has more
sense than to think any such thing: — And there is none of you but
knows that you ought to be good; — and whosoever is good, let him be
ever so poor and mean, is serving GOD. — For this whole world is but
one large family, of which Almighty GOD is the head and master: — . . .

II. Having thus shown you the chief duties you owe to your great
master in heaven, I now come to lay before you the duties you owe to
your *masters* and *mistresses* here upon earth.

And for this, you have one general rule that you ought always to
carry in your minds; — and that is, — *to do all service for them, as if
you did it for GOD himself.* — Poor creatures! you little consider,
when you are idle and neglectful of your master's business, — when
you *steal* and *waste,* and *hurt* any of their substance, — when you are
saucy and *impudent,* — when you are telling them *lies,* and deceiving
them, — or when you prove *stubborn* or *sullen,* and will not do the
work you are set about without stripes and vexation; — you do not
consider, I say, that what faults you are guilty of towards your masters
and mistresses are faults done against GOD himself, who hath set your
masters and mistresses over you, in his own stead, and expects that
you will do for them, just as you would do for him. — And pray, do
not think that I want to deceive you, when I tell you, that your *masters*
and *mistresses* are GOD's *overseers,* — and that if you are faulty
towards them, GOD himself will punish you severely for it in the next
world, unless you repent of it, and strive to make amends, by your
faithfulness and *diligence,* for the time to come; — for GOD himself
hath declared the same. And you have at the same time this comfort,
that if any of your *owners* should prove *wicked overseers,* and use
you, who are his under servants here, as they ought not to do; —
though you must submit to it, and can have no remedy in this world,

yet, when GOD calls you and them together face to face before him in the next world, and examines into these matters, he will do you strict justice, and punish those that have been bad stewards and overseers over you with the greater severity, as they had more of this world entrusted to their care: — and that whatever you have suffered *unjustly* here, GOD will make you amends for it in heaven. . . .

You are *not* to be *eye-servants*. — Now *eye-servants* are such as will *work hard*, and seem mighty diligent, while they think that any body is taking notice of them, but when their masters and mistresses backs are turned, they are idle, and neglect their business.

— I am afraid that there are a great many such *eye servants* among you, — and that you do not consider how great a sin it is to be so, and how severely GOD will punish you for it. — You may easily deceive your owners, and make them have an opinion of you that you do not deserve, and get the praise of men by it. But remember, that you cannot deceive Almighty GOD, who sees your wickedness and deceit, and will punish you accordingly. For the rule is, that you must *obey your masters in all things*, & do the work they set you about *with fear and trembling, in singleness of heart, as unto Christ, not with eye-service, as men pleasers, but as the servants of Christ, doing the will of God from the heart: With good will doing service, as to the Lord, and not as to men.* — If then, you would but think, and say within yourselves, — "My master hath set me about this work, and his back is turned, so that I may loiter and idle if I please, for he does not see me. — But there is my great *master* in heaven, whose overseer my other master is—and his eyes are always upon me, and taking notice of me, and I cannot get any where out of his sight, not be idle without his knowing it, and what will become of me if I loose his good will, and make him angry with me." — If, I say, you would once get the way of thinking and saying thus, upon all occasions, you then would do what GOD commands you, and serve your masters with singleness of heart, — that is, with honesty and sincerity; you would do the work you are set about *with fear and trembling,* not for fear of your masters and mistresses upon earth (for you may easily cheat them, and make them believe you are doing their business when you do not) — but with *fear and trembling,* lest GOD, your heavenly master, whom you cannot deceive, should call you to account, and punish you in the next world, for your *deceitfulnes,* and *eye-service* in this.

3. You are to be *faithful and honest to your masters and mistresses—not purloining* (or wasting their goods or substance) *but showing all good fidelity in all things.* . . .

Thus I have endeavoured to show you, why you ought to serve GOD, and what duty in particular you owe to him: — I have also shown you, that while you are serving your masters and mistresses, or doing any thing that GOD hath commanded, you are at the same time *serving* him; and have endeavoured to show you what duty or service you owe to your owners, in obedience to GOD, and that in so plain a manner, as I hope the greatest part of you did well understand. — The other parts of your duty and the rewards which GOD hath promised to you (if you will honestly set about doing it) I shall endeavour to lay before you at our next meeting here for that purpose. — In the mean time, consider well what hath been said. — Think upon it, and talk about it one with another, and strive to fix it on your memories. — And may GOD of his infinite mercy grant, that it may sink deep into your hearts, and, taking root there, may bring forth in you the fruit of good living, to the honour and praise of his holy name, the spreading abroad of his gospel, and the eternal salvation of your precious souls, through our Lord and Saviour JESUS CHRIST, to whom, with the father, and the holy spirit, be all honor and glory, world without end. — *Amen.*

ANDREW JACKSON

Two Proclamations

Andrew Jackson (1767–1845), the seventh president of the United States, was celebrated as the champion of the common man. During the 1830s he led a popular fight against what he portrayed as the elitist, oligarchical Bank of the United States, and in 1833 he faced down a Southern bloc led by John C. Calhoun (see pp. 371–74) that was attempting to nullify a federal tariff. Informing Jackson's egalitarianism and unionism, however, was an even larger commitment to white supremacy, for he was a slaveholder who also supported, indeed spearheaded, the Indian removal policies of the 1820s and 1830s. Nevertheless, Jackson was celebrated by many free blacks for having issued two proclamations during the War of 1812: a proclamation calling on blacks to join the white troops in defending New Orleans against the British army, and a proclamation praising the black troops for their heroic conduct under fire. Issued in 1814 when Jackson was serving as major general, the proclamations asserted African Americans' rights to citizenship, and came to assume a sort of sacred status within the free black community. In 1851, two years before the publication of *Clotel*, the proclamations were reprinted in W. C. Nell's influential *Services of Colored Americans*.

Born in Boston, William Cooper Nell (1816–1874) devoted his life to the causes of antislavery and black civil rights. He founded one of the first African American antislavery societies, the Massachusetts Colored Association; he campaigned to integrate Boston's public schools; and he worked closely with both William Lloyd Garrison and Frederick Douglass, contributing essays and letters to Garrison's *Liberator* and helping Douglass to publish *The North Star*. Though he remained committed to Garrison's principles of nonviolence and moral suasion, he actively opposed the Fugitive Slave Law during the 1850s. He also wrote two books celebrating black military service to the United States, *Services of Colored Americans in the Wars of 1776 and 1812* (Boston: Prentiss & Sawyer, 1851), from which this selection is taken, and an expanded volume, *Colored Patriots of the American Revolution* (1855). Nell's main argument in both volumes is that blacks' participation in the American Revolution and the War of 1812, along with their overall contributions to the development of the nation, should have earned them rights to citizenship. Drawing on Nell's account in *Services*, Brown makes a similar point in *Clotel* when Georgiana Peck, in the course of freeing her slaves, quotes from General Andrew Jackson's proclamation on the black soldiers' heroic defense of New Orleans.

In 1814, when New Orleans was in danger, and the proud and criminal distinctions of caste were again demolished by one of those emergencies in which nature puts to silence for the moment the base partialities of art, the free Colored people were called into the field in common with the whites; and the importance of their services was thus acknowledged by General Jackson: —

"HEAD QUARTERS, SEVENTH MILITARY DISTRICT, MOBILE, SEPTEMBER 21, 1814.

"*To the Free Colored Inhabitants of Louisiana*:

"Through a mistaken policy, you have heretofore been deprived of a participation in the glorious struggle for national rights, in which *our* country is engaged. This no longer shall exist.

"As Sons of Freedom, you are now called upon to defend our most inestimable blessings. *As Americans,* your country looks with confidence to her adopted children, for a valorous support, as a faithful return for the advantages enjoyed under her mild and equitable government. As fathers, husbands, and brothers, you are summoned to rally round the standard of the Eagle, to defend all which is dear in existence.

"*Your country,* although calling for your exertions, does not wish you to engage in her cause, without remunerating you for the services rendered. Your intelligent minds are not to be led away by false representations — your love of honor would cause you to despise the man who should attempt to deceive you. In the sincerity of a soldier, and the language of truth, I address you.

"To every noble hearted free man of Color, volunteering to serve during the present contest with Great Britain, and no longer, there will be paid the same bounty in money and lands, now received by the white soldiers of the United States, namely, one hundred and twenty-four dollars in money, and one hundred and sixty acres of land. The non-commissioned officers and privates will also be entitled to the same monthly pay and daily rations, and clothes furnished to any American soldier.

"On enrolling yourselves in companies, the Major General commanding will select officers for your government, from your white fellow citizens. Your non-commissioned officers will be appointed from among yourselves.

"Due regard will be paid to the feelings of freemen and soldiers. You will not, by being associated with white men in the same corps be exposed to improper comparisons, or unjust sarcasm. As a distinct, independent battalion or regiment, pursuing the path of glory, you will, undivided, receive the applause and gratitude of your countrymen.

"To assure you of the sincerity of my intentions, and my anxiety to engage your invaluable services to our country, I have communicated my wishes to the Governor of Louisiana, who is fully informed as to the manner of enrolments, and will give you every necessary information on the subject of this address.

ANDREW JACKSON,
Major General Commanding."

The second proclamation is one of the highest compliments ever paid by a military chief to his soldiers.

On December 18, 1814, General Jackson issued, in the French language, the following address to the free people of Color: —

"SOLDIERS! When on the banks of the Mobile I called you to take up arms, inviting you to partake the perils and glory of your *white fellow citizens, I expected much from you*: for I was not ignorant that you possessed qualities most formidable to an invading enemy. I knew with what fortitude you could endure hunger and thirst, and all the fatigues of a campaign. *I knew well how you loved your native country*, and that you, as well as ourselves, had to defend what *man* holds most dear — his parents, wife, children, and property. *You have done more than I expected*. In addition to the previous qualities I before knew you to possess, I found among you a noble enthusiasm, which leads to the performance of great things.

"Soldiers! The President of the United States shall hear how praiseworthy was your conduct in the hour of danger, and the representatives of the American people will give you the praise your exploits entitle you to. Your General anticipates them in applauding your noble ardor."

"The enemy approaches; his vessels cover our lakes; our brave citizens are united, and all contention has ceased among them. Their only dispute is who shall win the prize of valor, or who the most glory, its noblest reward.

By Order,
THOMAS BUTLER,[1] Aid-de Camp."

[1] *THOMAS BUTLER*: A lawyer from Louisiana, Thomas Butler (1787–1847) fought in the Mississippi territory in the early 1800s and eventually served as a judge and congressman.

THEODORE DWIGHT WELD

From *American Slavery As It Is*

A massive compendium of testimony about the horrors of slavery, Weld's *American Slavery As It Is*, published in 1839, was one of the most influential antislavery books of the time, serving as a kind of source book for Brown, Stowe, and many other antislavery writers. Born in Connecticut, Theodore Dwight Weld (1803–1895) converted to Presbyterianism in

1825, and in 1832 enrolled at the Lane Theological Seminary in Cincinnati, Ohio. Convinced that slavery was a crime against God, he emerged as the leader of the "Lane Rebels," a group of students who decided to leave the Seminary after the faculty, trustees, and president Lyman Beecher (Harriet Beecher Stowe's father) attempted to suppress students' antislavery activities. Thereafter, Weld became an important lecturer and organizer in the American Anti-Slavery Society, taking on the major responsibility of training its traveling agents. In 1838 he married the notorious South Carolina abolitionist Angelina E. Grimké (see pp. 451–56 for a selection from Grimké). He continued his antislavery efforts into the 1840s, and in 1854 established a racially integrated school in Eagelswood, New Jersey. The selections below, taken from *American Slavery As It Is: Testimony of a Thousand Witnesses* (New York: American Anti-Slavery Society, 1839), provided Brown with sources for the important advertisements in Chapters I and XI of *Clotel*.

As slaveholders and their apologists are volunteer witnesses in their own cause, and are flooding the world with testimony that their slaves are kindly treated; that they are well fed, well clothed, well housed, well lodged, moderately worked, and bountifully provided with all things needful for their comfort, we propose — first, to disprove their assertions by the testimony of a multitude of impartial witnesses, and then to put slaveholders themselves through a course of cross-questioning which shall draw their condemnation out of their own mouths. We will prove that the slaves in the United States are treated with barbarous inhumanity; that they are overworked, underfed, wretchedly clad and lodged, and have insufficient sleep; that they are often made to wear round their necks iron collars armed with prongs, to drag heavy chains and weights at their feet while working in the field, and to wear yokes, and bells, and iron horns; that they are often kept confined in the stocks day and night for weeks together, made to wear gags in their mouths for hours or days, have some of their front teeth torn out or broken off, that they may be easily detected when they run away; that they are frequently flogged with terrible severity, have red pepper rubbed into their lacerated flesh, and hot brine, spirits of turpentine, &c., poured over the gashes to increase the torture; that they are often stripped naked, their backs and limbs cut with knives, bruised and mangled by scores and hundreds of blows with the paddle, and terribly torn by the claws of cats, drawn over them by their tormentors; that they are often hunted with blood hounds and shot down like beasts, or torn in pieces by dogs; that they are often suspended by the arms and whipped and beaten till they faint, and when revived by restoratives, beaten again till they faint, and sometimes till they die; that their ears are often cut off, their eyes knocked out, their bones broken, their flesh branded with red hot irons; that they are maimed, mutilated and burned to death over slow fires. All these things, and more, and worse, we shall *prove*. Reader, we know whereof we affirm, we have weighed it well; *more and worse* WE WILL PROVE. Mark these words, and read on; we will establish all these facts by the testimony of scores and hundreds of eye witnesses, by the testimony of *slaveholders* in all parts of the slave states, by slaveholding members of Congress and of state legislatures, by ambassadors to foreign courts, by judges, by doctors of divinity, and clergy men of all denominations, by merchants, mechanics, lawyers and physicians, by presidents and professors in colleges and *professional* seminaries, by planters, overseers and drivers. We shall show, not merely that such deeds are committed, but that they are frequent; not done in corners, but before the sun; not in one of the slave states, but in all of them; not perpetrated by brutal overseers and drivers merely, but by magistrates, by legislators, by professors of religion, by preachers of the gospel, by governors of states, by "gentlemen of property and standing," and by delicate females moving in the "highest circles of society." . . .

A late PROSPECTUS of the South Carolina Medical College, located in Charleston, contains the following passage: —

"Some advantages of a *peculiar* character are connected with this Institution, which it may be proper to point out. No place in the United States offers as great opportunities for the acquisition of anatomical knowledge, SUBJECTS BEING OBTAINED FROM AMONG THE COLORED POPULATION IN SUFFICIENT NUMBER FOR EVERY PURPOSE, AND PROPER DISSECTIONS CARRIED ON WITHOUT OFFENDING ANY INDIVIDUALS IN THE COMMUNITY!!"

Without offending any individuals in the community! More than half the population of Charleston, we believe, is 'colored;' *their* graves may be ravaged, their dead may be dug up, dragged into the dissecting room, exposed to the gaze, heartless gibes, and experimenting knives, of a crowd of inexperienced operators, who are given to understand in the prospectus, that, if they do not acquire manual dexterity in dissection, it will be wholly their own fault, in neglecting to improve the unrivalled advantages afforded by the institution — since each can have as many human bodies as he pleases to experiment upon — and as to the fathers, mothers, husbands, wives, brothers, and sisters, of those whom they cut to pieces from day to day, why, they are not 'individuals in the community,' but 'property,' and however *their* feelings may be tortured, the 'public opinion' of slaveholders is entirely too 'chivalrous' to degrade itself by caring for them! . . .

In the "Charleston (South Carolina) Mercury" of October 12, 1838, we find an advertisement of half a column, by a Dr. T. Stillman, setting forth the merits of another 'Medical Infirmary,' under his own special supervision, at No. 110 Church street, Charleston. The doctor, after inveighing loudly against 'men totally ignorant of medical science,' who flood the country with quack nostrums backed up by 'fabricated proofs of miraculous cures,' proceeds to enumerate the diseases to which his 'Infirmary' is open, and to which his practice will be mainly confined. Appreciating the importance of 'interesting cases,' as a stock in trade, on which to commence his experiments, he copies the example of the medical professors, and advertises for them. But, either from a keener sense of justice, or more generosity, or greater confidence in his skill, or for some other reason, he proposes to *buy up* an assortment of *damaged* negroes, given over, as incurable, by others, and to make such his 'interesting cases,' instead of experimenting on those who are the 'property' of others.

Dr. Stillman closes his advertisement with the following notice: —

"To PLANTERS AND OTHERS. — Wanted *fifty negroes*. Any person having sick negroes, considered incurable by their respective physicians, and wishing to dispose of them, Dr. S. will pay cash for negroes affected with scrofula or king's evil, confirmed hypocondriasm, apoplexy, diseases of the liver, kidneys, spleen, stomach and intestines, bladder and its appendages, diarrhea, dysentery, &c. The highest cash price will be paid on application as above."

The absolute barbarism of a 'public opinion' which not only tolerates, but *produces* such advertisements as this, was outdone by nothing in the dark ages. If the reader has a heart of flesh, he can feel it without help, and if he has not, comment will not create it. The total indifference of slaveholders to such a cold blooded proposition, their utter unconsciousness of the paralysis of heart, and death of sympathy, and every feeling of common humanity for the slave, which it reveals, is enough, of itself, to show that the tendency of the spirit of slaveholding is, to kill in the soul whatever it touches. It has no eyes to see, nor ears to hear, nor mind to understand, nor heart to feel for its victims as *human beings*. To show that the above indication of the savage state is not an index of individual feeling, but of 'public opinion,' it is sufficient to say, that it appears to be a standing advertisement in the Charleston Mercury, the leading political paper of South Carolina, the organ of the Honorables John C. Calhoun, Robert Barnwell Rhett,[1] Hugh S. Legare,[2] and others regarded as the elite of her statesmen and literati. Besides, candidates for popular favor, like the doctor who advertises for the fifty 'incurables,' take special care to conciliate, rather than outrage, 'public opinion.' Is the doctor so ignorant of 'public opinion' in his own city, that he has unwittingly committed violence upon it in his advertisement? We trow not. The same 'public opinion' which gave birth to the advertisement of doctor Stillman, and to those of the professors in both the medical institutions, founded the Charleston 'Work House' — a soft name for a Moloch temple[3] dedicated to torture, and reeking with blood, in the midst of the city; to which masters and mistresses send their slaves of both sexes to be stripped, tied up, and cut with the lash till the blood and mangled flesh flow to their feet, or to be beaten and bruised with the terrible paddle, or forced to climb the tread-mill till nature sinks, or to experience other nameless torments. . . .

That the 'public opinion' of *the highest class of society* in South Carolina, regards slaves as mere *cattle,* is shown by the following advertisement, which we copy from the "Charleston (S.C.) Mercury" of May 16:

"NEGROES FOR SALE. — A GIRL about twenty years of age, (raised in Virginia,) and her two female children, one four and the other two years old — is remarkably strong and healthy — never having had a day's sickness, with the exception of the small pox, in her life. The children are fine and healthy. She is VERY PROLIFIC IN HER GENERATING QUALITIES, *and affords a rare opportunity to any person who wishes to raise a family of strong and healthy servants for their own use.*

"Any person wishing to purchase, will please leave their address at the Mercury office."

The Charleston Mercury, in which this advertisement appears, is the *leading political paper in South Carolina,* and is well known to be

---

[1] *Robert Barnwell Rhett:* An ardent supporter of Southern states' rights, the South Carolina politician Robert B. Rhett (1800–1876) emerged as a leading secessionist by the 1850s.

[2] *Hugh S. Legare:* A prominent South Carolina politician, Hugh Swinton Legare (1797–1843) rejected nullification in favor of unionism.

[3] *Moloch temple:* A temple dedicated to the Canaanite god of fire, Moloch. In the Bible, the Jewish prophets strongly objected to such worship.

the political organ of Messrs. Calhoun, Rhett, Pickens,[4] and others of the most prominent politicians in the state. Its editor, John Stewart, Esq., is a lawyer of Charleston, and of a highly respectable family. He is a brother-in-law of Hon. Robert Barnwell Rhett, the late Attorney-General, now a Member of Congress, and Hon. James Rhett, a leading member of the Senate of South Carolina; his wife is a niece of the late Governor Smith, of North Carolina, and of the late Hon. Peter Smith, Intendant (Mayor) of the city of Charleston; and a cousin of the late Hon. Thomas S. Grimké.[5]

The circulation of the 'Mercury' among the wealthy, the literary, and the fashionable, is probably much larger than that of any other paper in the state.

These facts in connection with the preceding advertisement, are a sufficient exposition of the 'public opinion' towards slaves, prevalent in these classes of society.

[4] *Pickens*: Francis Wilkinson Pickens (1805–1869) supported Southern states' rights and was governor of South Carolina when the state seceded from the Union.
[5] *Thomas S. Grimké*: A peace reformer from South Carolina, Thomas Grimké (1786–1834) was the brother of Angelina E. Grimké (see the selection from Angelina Grimké on pp. 451–56).

WILLIAM WELLS BROWN

From *The New Liberty Party*

Founded in 1840 under the leadership of the abolitionists Gerrit Smith (1797–1874) and James Birney (1792–1857), the Liberty Party was committed to fighting a broadly conceived "Slave Power" but was somewhat vague about its specific programs for eradicating slavery. A number of abolitionists, including William Wells Brown and Frederick Douglass, were suspicious of the Liberty Party's constituency and political goals, and thus continued to support the moral suasion abolitionism of William Lloyd Garrison. In a letter to Sydney Howard Gay (1814–1888), editor of the *National Anti-Slavery Standard,* Brown reported skeptically on the New York State Liberty Party's 1846 convention in Farmington, New York. The letter appeared under the title "The New Liberty Party, or Reorganization" in the 25 June 1846 issue of the *Standard,* the source of this selection. Of particular interest in the letter is Brown's account of a remark on Jefferson by one Reverend Peck of Rochester, clearly a source for *Clotel*'s Reverend John Peck of Connecticut.

The Liberty party of this State, or at least, the wire-pullers of that party, have just closed the last session of a two days' Convention, called for the purpose of finding out where the Liberty party is. The Convention was well attended. . . . I saw among the speakers five clergymen, with whom I was acquainted; how many more there were present, I cannot say. One of them, (Mr. Peck, of Rochester,) said, "Mr. President, it has been said in this Convention, 'that all men had inalienable rights;' now I deny that. I know that Jefferson wrote that sentiment, but it is false! It is utterly untrue. The doctrine that all men are created equal, and with inalienable rights, is a humbug. Let that doctrine be carried out, and in a short time every gallows will be cut down, every prison will be empty, and over their doors will be written in red, — for it should be in blood, — 'All men are born free and equal, and have inalienable rights.'" This clergyman was a Liberty party man.

WILLIAM WELLS BROWN

Singular Escape

In a letter of 4 January 1849 to William Lloyd Garrison, printed in the 12 January 1849 *Liberator* under the title "Singular Escape," William Wells Brown became the first person to report on the amazing escape from slavery of William Craft (1824–1900) and Ellen Craft (1826–1900). Slaves on a Georgia plantation, the Crafts, whose marriage had no legal basis in Southern culture, escaped in December 1848 by having the light-complected Ellen masquerade as a Southern gentleman accompanied by "his" servant William. Brown's letter on the Crafts in the *Liberator,* the source of the selection below, described some of the other creative tactics contributing to their escape. During 1849, the Crafts regularly spoke with Brown at antislavery meetings. In 1850, under threat from fugitive slave hunters, the Crafts sailed to England, and in 1851 they joined Brown for a tour on the British antislavery lecture circuit. The Crafts' story of their escape through gender and racial cross-dressing was an important source for Brown's representations of some of the slaves' stratagems in *Clotel.* In 1860 William Craft published his own account of the couple's ingenious escape, *Running a Thousand Miles for Freedom; or, The Escape of William and Ellen Craft from Slavery.*

"Ellen Craft, A Fugitive Slave." Wood engraving in *The Illustrated London News*, 19 April 1851. Courtesy of the Photographs and Prints Division, Schomburg Center for Research in Black Culture, The New York Public Library, Astor, Lennox and Tilden Foundations.

PINEVILLE, (Pa.) Jan. 4, 1849.

DEAR FRIEND GARRISON:

One of the most interesting cases of the escape of fugitives from American slavery that have ever come before the American people, has just occurred, under the following circumstances: — William and Ellen Craft, man and wife, lived with different masters in the State of Georgia. Ellen is so near white, that she can pass without suspicion for a white woman. Her husband is much darker. He is a mechanic, and by working nights and Sundays, he laid up money enough to bring himself and his wife out of slavery. Their plan was without precedent; and though novel, was the means of getting them their freedom. Ellen dressed in man's clothing, and passed as the *master*, while her husband passed as the *servant*. In this way they travelled from Georgia to Philadelphia. They are now out of the reach of the blood-hounds of the South. On their journey, they put up at the best hotels where they stopped. Neither of them can read or write. And Ellen, knowing that she would be called upon to write her name at the hotels, &c., tied her right hand up as though it was lame, which proved of some service to her, as she was called upon several times at hotels to 'register' her name. In Charleston, S.C., they put up at the hotel which Gov. M'Duffie and John C. Calhoun generally make their home, yet these distinguished advocates of the 'peculiar institution' say that the slaves cannot take care of themselves. They arrived in Philadelphia, in four days from the time they started. Their history, especially that of their escape, is replete with interest. They will be at the meeting of the Massachusetts Anti-Slavery Society, in Boston, in the latter part of this month, where I know the history of their escape will be listened to with great interest. They are very intelligent. They are young, Ellen 22, and Wm. 24 years of age. Ellen is truly a heroine.

Yours, truly,

WM. W. BROWN.

P.S. They are now hid away within 25 miles of Philadelphia, where they will remain until the 6th, when they will leave with me for New England. Will you please say in the Liberator that I will lecture, in connexion with them, as follows: —

At Norwich, Ct., Thursday evening, Jan. 18
" Worcester,   Mass., Friday evening, 19.
" Pawtucket,   "   Saturday evening, 20.
" New Bedford,   "   Sunday afternoon and evening, 28.

LYDIA MARIA CHILD

The Quadroons

The Massachusetts-born fiction writer, abolitionist, educator, editor, domestic theorist, feminist, and Indian rights advocate Lydia Maria Child (1802–1880), née Lydia Francis, was one of the greatest literary activists of nineteenth-century America. Her well-received first book, the novel *Hobomok, A Tale of Early Times,* which favorably represented an interracial marriage between a white woman and an Indian man, appeared in 1824, when she was twenty-two years old. Soon after, she published another highly regarded novel, *The Rebels* (1825), and founded the children's magazine *Juvenile Miscellany.* In 1828 she married David Child and began writing advice manuals for women. *The Frugal Housewife* (1829) went through over thirty editions and established her as one of America's most popular domestic writers. However, she became ostracized from genteel Boston culture in 1833 when she published *An Appeal in Favor of that Class of Americans Called Africans,* which advocated immediate emancipation. (For a selection from *An Appeal,* see pp. 447–51). Child remained passionately committed to antiracist reforms for the rest of her long, prolific career. Among her important books are *Letters from New York* (1843), *Correspondence between Lydia Maria Child and Gov. Wise and Mrs. Mason* (1860), *A Romance of the Republic* (1867), and *An Appeal for the Indians* (1868). In 1860 she edited Harriet Jacobs's *Incidents of the Life of a Slave Girl* (1861).

One of the major literary sources of *Clotel,* "The Quadroons" first appeared in the 1842 *The Liberty Bell* and was reprinted, with minor revisions, in Child's *Fact and Fiction: A Collection of Stories* (New York: C. S. Francis, 1846), the source of the text below. Though Brown changed the names and the settings of Child's story, he lifted large swatches of text verbatim for his novel. Surely an important motivation for his appropriation of Child's story was his admiration for her brave antislavery writings. But it is important to note that, in his reworking of "The Quadroons," Brown strategically broke the story into three different sections and, through his use of pastiche and bricolage, put Child's sentimental discourse, plotting, and motifs into dialogue with discourses, plottings, and motifs that granted greater agency to rebellious blacks. Unlike Child's Rosalie and Xarifa, Brown's Clotel and Mary do not die of despair or dementia. With his portrayal of Mary and George at the end of *Clotel* (and, later, Clotelle and Jerome at the end of the two versions of *Clotelle*), Brown moved beyond the somewhat truncated, melodramatic ending of Child's story.

> "I promised thee a sister tale,
> Of man's perfidious cruelty:
> Come then and hear what cruel wrong
> Befell the dark Ladie."[1]
>
> — COLERIDGE.

Not far from Augusta, Georgia, there is a pleasant place called Sand-Hills, appropriated almost exclusively to summer residences for the wealthy inhabitants of the neighbouring city. Among the beautiful cottages that adorn it was one far retired from the public roads, and almost hidden among the trees. It was a perfect model of rural beauty. The piazzas that surrounded it were wreathed with Clematis and Passion Flower. Magnificent Magnolias, and the superb Pride of India, threw shadows around it, and filled the air with fragrance. Flowers peeped out from every nook, and nodded to you in bye-places, with a most unexpected welcome. The tasteful hand of Art had not learned to *imitate* the lavish beauty and harmonious disorder of Nature, but they lived together in loving unity, and spoke in according tones. The gateway rose in a Gothic arch, with graceful tracery in iron-work, surmounted by a Cross, around which fluttered and played the Mountain Fringe, that lightest and most fragile of vines.

The inhabitants of this cottage remained in it all the year round, and peculiarly enjoyed the season that left them without neighbours. To one of the parties, indeed, the fashionable summer residents, that came and went with the butterflies, were merely neighbours-in-law. The edicts of society had built up a wall of separation between her and them; for she was a quadroon. Conventional laws could not be reversed in her favour, though she was the daughter of a wealthy merchant, was highly cultivated in mind and manners, graceful as an antelope, and beautiful as the evening star. She had early attracted the attention of a handsome and wealthy young Georgian; and as their acquaintance increased, the purity and bright intelligence of her mind, inspired him with far deeper interest than is ever excited by mere passion. It was genuine love; that mysterious union of soul and sense, in which the lowliest dew-drop reflects the image of the highest star.

The tenderness of Rosalie's conscience required an outward form of marriage; though she well knew that a union with her proscribed race was unrecognised by law, and therefore the ceremony gave her no legal hold on Edward's constancy. But her high poetic nature regarded

---

[1] *"I promised . . . dark Ladie"*: See *Clotel*, note 1, p. 149.

the reality, rather than the semblance of things; and when he playfully asked how she could keep him if he wished to run away, she replied, "Let the church that my mother loved sanction our union, and my own soul will be satisfied, without the protection of the state. If your affections fall from me, I would not, if I could, hold you by a legal fetter."

It was a marriage sanctioned by Heaven, though unrecognised on earth. The picturesque cottage at Sand-Hills was built for the young bride under her own direction; and there they passed ten as happy years as ever blessed the heart of mortals. It was Edward's fancy to name their eldest child Xarifa; in commemoration of a quaint old Spanish ballad, which had first conveyed to his ears the sweet tones of her mother's voice. Her flexile form and nimble motions were in harmony with the breezy sound of the name; and its Moorish[2] origin was most appropriate to one so emphatically "a child of the sun." Her complexion, of a still lighter brown than Rosalie's, was rich and glowing as an autumnal leaf. The iris of her large, dark eye had the melting, mezzotinto outline, which remains the last vestige of African ancestry, and gives that plaintive expression, so often observed, and so appropriate to that docile and injured race.

Xarifa learned no lessons of humility or shame, within her own happy home; for she grew up in the warm atmosphere of father's and mother's love, like a flower open to the sunshine, and sheltered from the winds. But in summer walks with her beautiful mother, her young cheek often mantled at the rude gaze of the young men, and her dark eye flashed fire, when some contemptuous epithet met her ear, as white ladies passed them by, in scornful pride and ill-concealed envy.

Happy as Rosalie was in Edward's love, and surrounded by an outward environment of beauty, so well adapted to her poetic spirit, she felt these incidents with inexpressible pain. For herself, she cared but little; for she had found a sheltered home in Edward's heart, which the world might ridicule, but had no power to profane. But when she looked at her beloved Xarifa, and reflected upon the unavoidable and dangerous position which the tyranny of society had awarded her, her soul was filled with anguish. The rare loveliness of the child increased daily, and was evidently ripening into most marvellous beauty. The father rejoiced in it with unmingled pride; but in the deep tenderness

---

[2] *Moorish:* In the style of the Moors—Arab-African Muslims of Northwest Africa celebrated for their art and architecture.

of the mother's eye there was an in-dwelling sadness, that spoke of anxious thoughts and fearful forebodings.

When Xarifa entered her ninth year, these uneasy feelings found utterance in earnest solicitations that Edward would remove to France, or England. This request excited but little opposition, and was so attractive to his imagination, that he might have overcome all intervening obstacles, had not "a change come o'er the spirit of his dream."[3] He still loved Rosalie, but he was now twenty-eight years old, and, unconsciously to himself, ambition had for some time been slowly gaining an ascendency over his other feelings. The contagion of example had led him into the arena where so much American strength is wasted; he had thrown himself into political excitement, with all the honest fervour of youthful feeling. His motives had been unmixed with selfishness, nor could he ever define to himself when or how sincere patriotism took the form of personal ambition. But so it was, that at twenty-eight years old, he found himself an ambitious man, involved in movements which his frank nature would have once abhorred, and watching the doubtful game of mutual cunning with all the fierce excitement of a gambler.

Among those on whom his political success most depended, was a very popular and wealthy man, who had an only daughter. His visits to the house were at first of a purely political nature; but the young lady was pleasing, and he fancied he discovered in her a sort of timid preference for himself. This excited his vanity, and awakened thoughts of the great worldly advantages connected with a union. Reminiscences of his first love kept these vague ideas in check for several months; but Rosalie's image at last became an unwelcome intruder; for with it was associated the idea of restraint. Moreover Charlotte, though inferior in beauty, was yet a pretty contrast to her rival. Her light hair fell in silken profusion, her blue eyes were gentle, though inexpressive, and her delicate cheeks were like blush-rose-buds.

He had already become accustomed to the dangerous experiment of resisting his own inward convictions; and this new impulse to ambition, combined with the strong temptation of variety in love, met the ardent young man weakened in moral principle, and unfettered by laws of the land. The change wrought upon him was soon noticed by Rosalie.

---

[3] *"a change . . . dream"*: See *Clotel*, note 3, p. 101.

"In many ways does the full heart reveal
The presence of the love it would conceal;
But in far more the estranged heart lets know
The absence of the love, which yet it fain would show."[4]

At length the news of his approaching marriage met her ear. Her head grew dizzy, and her heart fainted within her; but, with a strong effort at composure, she inquired all the particulars; and her pure mind at once took its resolution. Edward came that evening, and though she would have fain met him as usual, her heart was too full not to throw a deep sadness over her looks and tones. She had never complained of his decreasing tenderness, or of her own lonely hours; but he felt that the mute appeal of her heart-broken looks was more terrible than words. He kissed the hand she offered, and with a countenance almost as sad as her own, led her to a window in the recess, shadowed by a luxuriant Passion Flower. It was the same seat where they had spent the first evening in this beautiful cottage, consecrated to their youthful loves. The same calm, clear moonlight looked in through the trellis. The vine then planted had now a luxuriant growth; and many a time had Edward fondly twined its sacred blossoms with the glossy ringlets of her raven hair. The rush of memory almost overpowered poor Rosalie; and Edward felt too much oppressed and ashamed to break the long, deep silence. At length, in words scarcely audible, Rosalie said, "Tell me, dear Edward, are you to be married next week?" He dropped her hand, as if a rifle-ball had struck him; and it was not until after long hesitation, that he began to make some reply about the necessity of circumstances. Mildly, but earnestly, the poor girl begged him to spare apologies. It was enough that he no longer loved her, and that they must bid farewell. Trusting to the yielding tenderness of her character, he ventured, in the most soothing accents, to suggest that as he still loved her better than all the world, she would ever be his real wife, and they might see each other frequently. He was not prepared for the storm of indignant emotion his words excited. Hers was a passion too absorbing to admit of partnership; and her spirit was too pure and kind to enter into a selfish league against the happiness of the innocent young bride.

At length this painful interview came to an end. They stood together by the Gothic gate, where they had so often met and parted in the moonlight. Old remembrances melted their souls. "Farewell, dearest Edward," said Rosalie. "Give me a parting kiss." Her voice was

---

[4] *"In many . . . would show"*: See *Clotel*, note 1, p. 120.

choked for utterance, and the tears flowed freely, as she bent her lips toward him. He folded her convulsively in his arms, and imprinted a long, impassioned kiss on that mouth, which had never spoken to him but in love and blessing.

With effort like a death-pang, she at length raised her head from his heaving bosom, and turning from him with bitter sobs, she said, "It is our *last*. God bless you. I would not have you so miserable as I am. Farewell. A *last* farewell." "The *last!*" exclaimed he, with a wild shriek. "Oh, Rosalie, do not say that!" and covering his face with his hands, he wept like a child.

Recovering from his emotion, he found himself alone. The moon looked down upon him mild, but very sorrowful; as the Madonna seems to gaze on her worshipping children, bowed down with consciousness of sin. At that moment he would have given worlds to have disengaged himself from Charlotte; but he had gone so far, that blame, disgrace, and duels with angry relatives, would now attend any effort to obtain his freedom. Oh, how the moonlight oppressed him with its friendly sadness! It was like the plaintive eye of his forsaken one; like the music of sorrow echoed from an unseen world.

Long and earnestly he gazed at that dwelling, where he had so long known earth's purest foretaste of heavenly bliss. Slowly he walked away; then turned again to look on that charmed spot, the nestling-place of his young affections. He caught a glimpse of Rosalie, weeping beside a magnolia, which commanded a long view of the path leading to the public road. He would have sprung toward her, but she darted from him, and entered the cottage. That graceful figure, weeping in the moonlight, haunted him for years. It stood before his closing eyes, and greeted him with the morning dawn.

Poor Charlotte! had she known all, what a dreary lot would hers have been; but fortunately, she could not miss the impassioned tenderness she had never experienced; and Edward was the more careful in his kindness, because he was deficient in love. Once or twice she heard him murmur, "dear Rosalie," in his sleep; but the playful charge she brought was playfully answered, and the incident gave her no real uneasiness. The summer after their marriage, she proposed a residence at Sand-Hills; little aware what a whirlwind of emotion she excited in her husband's heart. The reasons he gave for rejecting the proposition appeared satisfactory; but she could not quite understand why he was never willing that their afternoon drives should be in the direction of those pleasant rural residences, which she had heard him praise so much. One day, as their barouche rolled along a winding road that skirted Sand-Hills, her attention was suddenly attracted by two figures among the trees by the way-side; and touching Edward's arm, she exclaimed, "Do look at that beautiful child!" He turned, and saw Rosalie and Xarifa. His lips quivered, and his face became deadly pale. His young wife looked at him intently, but said nothing. There were points of resemblance in the child, that seemed to account for his sudden emotion. Suspicion was awakened, and she soon learned that the mother of that lovely girl bore the name of Rosalie; with this information came recollections of the "dear Rosalie," murmured in uneasy slumbers. From gossiping tongues she soon learned more than she wished to know. She wept, but not as poor Rosalie had done; for she never had loved, and been beloved, like her, and her nature was more proud. Henceforth a change came over her feelings and her manners; and Edward had no further occasion to assume a tenderness in return for hers. Changed as he was by ambition, he felt the wintry chill of her polite propriety, and sometimes in agony of heart, compared it with the gushing love of her who was indeed his wife.

But these, and all his emotions, were a sealed book to Rosalie, of which she could only guess the contents. With remittances for her and her child's support, there sometimes came earnest pleadings that she would consent to see him again; but these she never answered, though her heart yearned to do so. She pitied his fair young bride, and would not be tempted to bring sorrow into their household by any fault of hers. Her earnest prayer was that she might never know of her existence. She had not looked on Edward since she watched him under the shadow of the magnolia, until his barouche passed her in her rambles some months after. She saw the deadly paleness of his countenance, and had he dared to look back, he would have seen her tottering with faintness. Xarifa brought water from a little rivulet, and sprinkled her face. When she revived, she clasped the beloved child to her heart with a vehemence that made her scream. Soothingly she kissed away her fears, and gazed into her beautiful eyes with a deep, deep sadness of expression, which Xarifa never forgot. Wild were the thoughts that pressed around her aching heart, and almost maddened her poor brain; thoughts which had almost driven her to suicide the night of that last farewell. For her child's sake she conquered the fierce temptation then; and for her sake, she struggled with it now. But the gloomy atmosphere of their once happy home overclouded the morning of Xarifa's life.

"She from her mother learnt the trick of grief,
And sighed among her playthings."[5]

Rosalie perceived this; and it gave her gentle heart unutterable pain. At last, the conflicts of her spirit proved too strong for the beautiful frame in which it dwelt. About a year after Edward's marriage, she was found dead in her bed, one bright autumnal morning. She had often expressed to her daughter a wish to be buried under a spreading oak, that shaded a rustic garden-chair, in which she and Edward had spent many happy evenings. And there she was buried; with a small white cross at her head, twined with the cypress vine. Edward came to the funeral, and wept long, very long, at the grave. Hours after midnight, he sat in the recess-window, with Xarifa folded to his heart. The poor child sobbed herself to sleep on his bosom; and the convicted murderer had small reason to envy that wretched man, as he gazed on the lovely countenance, which so strongly reminded him of his early and his only love.

From that time, Xarifa was the central point of all his warmest affections. He hired an excellent old negress to take charge of the cottage, from which he promised his darling child that she should never be removed. He employed a music master, and dancing master, to attend upon her; and a week never passed without a visit from him, and a present of books, pictures, or flowers. To hear her play upon the harp, or repeat some favourite poem in her mother's earnest accents and melodious tones, or to see her pliant figure float in the garland-dance, seemed to be the highest enjoyment of his life. Yet was the pleasure mixed with bitter thoughts. What would be the destiny of this fascinating young creature, so radiant with life and beauty? She belonged to a proscribed race; and though the brown colour on her soft cheek was scarcely deeper than the sunny side of a golden pear, yet was it sufficient to exclude her from virtuous society. He thought of Rosalie's wish to carry her to France: and he would have fulfilled it, had he been unmarried. As it was, he inwardly resolved to make some arrangement to effect it in a few years, even if it involved separation from his darling child.

But alas for the calculations of man! From the time of Rosalie's death, Edward had sought relief for his wretched feelings in the free use of wine. Xarifa was scarcely fifteen, when her father was found

---

[5] "*She . . . sighed among her playthings*": From William Wordsworth, *The Excursion* (1814), Book First.

dead by the road-side; having fallen from his horse, on his way to visit her. He left no will; but his wife, with kindness of heart worthy of a happier domestic fate, expressed a decided reluctance to change any of the plans he had made for the beautiful child at Sand-Hills.

Xarifa mourned her indulgent father; but not as one utterly desolate. True, she had lived "like a flower deep hid in rocky cleft;" but the sunshine of love had already peeped in upon her. Her teacher on the harp was a handsome and agreeable young man of twenty, the only son of an English widow. Perhaps Edward had not been altogether unmindful of the result, when he first invited him to the flowery cottage. Certain it is, he had more than once thought what a pleasant thing it would be, if English freedom from prejudice should lead him to offer legal protection to his graceful and winning child. Being thus encouraged, rather than checked, in his admiration, George Elliot could not be otherwise than strongly attracted toward his beautiful pupil. The lonely and unprotected state in which her father's death left her, deepened this feeling into tenderness. And lucky was it for her enthusiastic and affectionate nature; for she could not live without an atmosphere of love. In her innocence, she knew nothing of the dangers in her path; and she trusted George with an undoubting simplicity, that rendered her sacred to his noble and generous soul. It seemed as if that flower-embosomed nest was consecrated by the Fates to Love. The French have well named it *La Belle Passion;* for without it life were "a year without spring, or a spring without roses." Except the loveliness of infancy, what does earth offer so much like Heaven, as the happiness of two young, pure, and beautiful beings, living in each other's hearts?

Xarifa inherited her mother's poetic and impassioned temperament; and to her, above others, the first consciousness of these sweet emotions was like a golden sunrise on the sleeping flowers.

> "Thus stood she at the threshold of the scene
> Of busy life.   *   *   *   *
> How fair it lay in solemn shade and sheen!
> And he beside her, like some angel, posted
> To lead her out of childhood's fairy land,
> On to life's glancing summit, hand in hand."

Alas, the tempest was brooding over their young heads. Rosalie, though she knew it not, had been the daughter of a slave, whose wealthy master, though he remained attached to her to the end of her days, yet carelessly omitted to have papers of manumission recorded.

His heirs had lately failed, under circumstances which greatly exasperated their creditors; and in an unlucky hour, they discovered their claim on Angelique's grand-child.

The gentle girl, happy as the birds in spring-time accustomed to the fondest indulgence, surrounded by all the refinements of life, timid as a fawn, and with a soul full of romance, was ruthlessly seized by a sheriff, and placed on the public auction-stand in Savannah. There she stood, trembling, blushing, and weeping; compelled to listen to the grossest language, and shrinking from the rude hands that examined the graceful proportions of her beautiful frame. "Stop that!" exclaimed a stern voice. "I bid two thousand dollars for her, without asking any of their d — d questions." The speaker was probably about forty years of age, with handsome features, but a fierce and proud expression. An older man, who stood behind him, bid two thousand five hundred. The first bid higher; then a third, a dashing young man, bid three thousand; and thus they went on, with the keen excitement of gamblers, until the first speaker obtained the prize, for the moderate sum of five thousand dollars.

And where was George, during this dreadful scene? He was absent on a visit to his mother, at Mobile. But, had he been at Sand-Hills, he could not have saved his beloved from the wealthy profligate, who was determined to obtain her at any price. A letter of agonized entreaty from her brought him home on the wings of the wind. But what could he do? How could he ever obtain a sight of her, locked up as she was in the princely mansion of her master? At last, by bribing one of the slaves, he conveyed a letter to her, and received one in return. As yet, her purchaser treated her with respectful gentleness, and sought to win her favour, by flattery and presents; but she dreaded every moment, lest the scene should change, and trembled at the sound of every footfall. A plan was laid for escape. The slave agreed to drug his master's wine; a ladder of ropes was prepared, and a swift boat was in readiness. But the slave, to obtain a double reward, was treacherous. Xarifa had scarcely given an answering signal to the low cautious whistle of her lover, when the sharp sound of a rifle was followed by a deep groan, and a heavy fall on the pavement of the court-yard. With frenzied eagerness she swung herself down by the ladder of ropes, and, by the glancing light of lanthorns, saw George, bleeding and lifeless at her feet. One wild shriek, that pierced the brains of those who heard it, and she fell senseless by his side.

For many days she had a confused consciousness of some great agony, but knew not where she was, or by whom she was surrounded.

The slow recovery of her reason settled into the most intense melancholy, which moved the compassion even of her cruel purchaser. The beautiful eyes, always pensive in expression, were now so heart-piercing in their sadness, that he could not endure to look upon them. For some months, he sought to win her smiles by lavish presents, and delicate attentions. He bought glittering chains of gold, and costly bands of pearl. His victim scarcely glanced at them, and her attendant slave laid them away, unheeded and forgotten. He purchased the furniture of the Cottage at Sand-Hills, and one morning Xarifa found her harp at the bedside, and the room filled with her own books, pictures, and flowers. She gazed upon them with a pang unutterable, and burst into an agony of tears; but she gave her master no thanks, and her gloom deepened.

At last his patience was exhausted. He grew weary of her obstinacy, as he was pleased to term it; and threats took the place of persuasion.

* * * * * * *

In a few months more, poor Xarifa was a raving maniac. That pure temple was desecrated; that loving heart was broken; and that beautiful head fractured against the wall in the frenzy of despair. Her master cursed the useless expense she had cost him; the slaves buried her; and no one wept at the grave of her who had been so carefully cherished, and so tenderly beloved.

HARRIET BEECHER STOWE

The Quadroon's Story

With the publication of *Uncle Tom's Cabin* in 1852, the heretofore little-known New England regionalist writer Harriet Beecher Stowe (1811–1896), author of *The Mayflower; or, Sketches of Scenes and Characters Among the Descendants of the Puritans* (1843), became famous. But fame had always gone hand in hand with the Beecher family. Her father, Lyman Beecher, was a prominent Congregationalist clergyman who in 1832 became president of the soon-to-be embattled Lane Theological Seminary; her sister Catharine Beecher was a pioneer in women's education and the best-known domestic writer of the time; and her brother Henry Ward Beecher was a celebrated New York preacher. (Her husband, Calvin Ellis Stowe, a professor of biblical literature at Lane when she married him in 1836, was rather more retiring.) Harriet Beecher Stowe became interested in the debate on slavery in the mid-1830s, when Theodore Dwight Weld and the other "Lane Rebels" challenged her father's authority, and in 1845 Stowe wrote her first antislavery sketch, "Immediate Emancipation." *Uncle Tom's Cabin,* serialized in the *National Era* between 1851 and 1852, was inspired in large part by her angry response to the Fugitive Slave Law, though her haunting depictions of slave mothers separated from their children may have been inspired by her grief at the death of her young son Samuel in 1849. The novel was widely read in the United States and abroad, selling approximately 350,000 copies during its first year in print, and around one million copies by the end of the decade. African Americans had a mixed but mostly positive response to the novel. Frederick Douglass, for example, thought the book a godsend that would help to inspire worldwide sympathy for the plight of the American slave; Martin Delany, however, found the novel to be racist and overly sympathetic to the colonizationists' agenda of shipping African Americans to Africa. In a letter to William Lloyd Garrison printed in the 3 June 1853 issue of the *Liberator,* Brown praised Stowe, declaring that her novel "has come down upon the dark abodes of slavery like a morning's sunlight, unfolding to view its enormities in a manner which has fastened all eyes upon the 'peculiar institution,' and awakening sympathy in hearts that never before felt for the slave." Whatever their views on Stowe, it was difficult for African Americans writing in the wake of *Uncle Tom's Cabin* to ignore its images, rhetorical strategies, and ideas. In 1856 Stowe published a second antislavery novel, *Dred; A Tale of the Great Dismal Swamp.*

Like Lydia Maria Child's "The Quadroons," Stowe's chapter "The Quadroon's Story," which comes late in *Uncle Tom's Cabin,* works with the figure of the "tragic mulatta." Tom has been purchased by the satanic slave master Simon Legree, who has also purchased and brought to his Louisiana plantation the young slave woman Emmeline, whom he intends to make into his concubine. At the plantation is the older slave woman Cassy, Legree's former forced concubine, who regards the slaves' situation with an apparently hopeless despair. The prideful and embittered Cassy, who wields a certain power over Legree, tells Tom her life history after he has been viciously flogged by Legree's overseers. Though by reputation a passive, Christ-like hero, Tom has been flogged for actively refusing Legree's command to flog an infirm slave woman. The selection is from *Uncle Tom's Cabin; Or, Life Among the Lowly* (Boston: John P. Jewett and Company, 1852), 198–212.

And behold the tears of such as are oppressed; and on the side of their
oppressors there was power. Wherefore I praised the dead that are already dead more than the living that are yet alive.

— Eccl. 4 : 1.

It was late at night, and Tom lay groaning and bleeding alone, in an
old forsaken room of the gin-house, among pieces of broken machinery, piles of damaged cotton, and other rubbish which had there accumulated.

The night was damp and close, and the thick air swarmed with
myriads of mosquitos, which increased the restless torture of his
wounds; whilst a burning thirst — a torture beyond all others — filled
up the uttermost measure of physical anguish.

"O, good Lord! *Do* look down, — give me the victory! — give me
the victory over all!" prayed poor Tom, in his anguish.

A footstep entered the room, behind him, and the light of a lantern
flashed on his eyes.

"Who 's there? O, for the Lord's massy, please give me some water!"

The woman Cassy — for it was she — set down her lantern, and,
pouring water from a bottle, raised his head, and gave him drink.
Another and another cup were drained, with feverish eagerness.

"Drink all ye want," she said; "I knew how it would be. It is n't the
first time I 've been out in the night, carrying water to such as you."

"Thank you, Missis," said Tom, when he had done drinking.

"Don't call me Missis! I 'm a miserable slave, like yourself, — a
lower one than you can ever be!" said she, bitterly; "but now," said
she, going to the door, and dragging in a small pallaise,[1] over which
she had spread linen cloths wet with cold water, "try, my poor fellow,
to roll yourself on to this."

Stiff with wounds and bruises, Tom was a long time in accomplish-
ing this movement; but, when done, he felt a sensible relief from the
cooling application to his wounds.

The woman, whom long practice with the victims of brutality had
made familiar with many healing arts, went on to make many applica-
tions to Tom's wounds, by means of which he was soon somewhat
relieved.

"Now," said the woman, when she had raised his head on a roll of
damaged cotton, which served for a pillow, "there 's the best I can do
for you."

[1] *pallaise:* A mattress filled with sawdust or straw; from the French *paillasse*, and in
English usually *palliasse*.

Tom thanked her; and the woman, sitting down on the floor, drew up her knees, and embracing them with her arms, looked fixedly before her, with a bitter and painful expression of countenance. Her bonnet fell back, and long wavy streams of black hair fell around her singular and melancholy face.

"It 's no use, my poor fellow!" she broke out, at last, "it 's of no use, this you 've been trying to do. You were a brave fellow, — you had the right on your side; but it 's all in vain, and out of the question, for you to struggle. You are in the devil's hands; — he is the strongest, and you must give up!"

Give up! and, had not human weakness and physical agony whispered that, before? Tom started; for the bitter woman, with her wild eyes and melancholy voice, seemed to him an embodiment of the temptation with which he had been wrestling.

"O Lord! O Lord!" he groaned, "how can I give up?"

"There 's no use calling on the Lord, — he never hears," said the woman, steadily; "there is n't any God, I believe; or, if there is, he 's taken sides against us. All goes against us, heaven and earth. Everything is pushing us into hell. Why should n't we go?"

Tom closed his eyes, and shuddered at the dark, atheistic words.

"You see," said the woman, "*you* don't know anything about it; — I do. I 've been on this place five years, body and soul, under this man's foot; and I hate him as I do the devil! Here you are, on a lone plantation, ten miles from any other, in the swamps; not a white person here, who could testify, if you were burned alive, — if you were scalded, cut into inch-pieces, set up for the dogs to tear, or hung up and whipped to death. There 's no law here, of God or man, that can do you, or any one of us, the least good; and, this man! there 's no earthly thing that he 's too good to do. I could make any one's hair rise, and their teeth chatter, if I should only tell what I 've seen and been knowing to, here, — and it 's no use resisting! Did I *want* to live with him? Was n't I a woman delicately bred; and he — God in heaven! what was he, and is he? And yet, I 've lived with him, these five years, and cursed every moment of my life, — night and day! And now, he 's got a new one, — a young thing, only fifteen, and she brought up, she says, piously. Her good mistress taught her to read the Bible; and she 's brought her Bible here — to hell with her!" — and the woman laughed a wild and doleful laugh, that rung, with a strange, supernatural sound, through the old ruined shed.

Tom folded his hands; all was darkness and horror.

"O Jesus! Lord Jesus! have you quite forgot us poor critturs?" burst forth, at last; — "help, Lord, I perish!"

The woman sternly continued:

"And what are these miserable low dogs you work with, that you should suffer on their account? Every one of them would turn against you, the first time they got a chance. They are all of 'em as low and cruel to each other as they can be; there 's no use in your suffering to keep from hurting them."

"Poor critturs!" said Tom, — "what made 'em cruel? — and, if I give out, I shall get used to 't, and grow, little by little, just like 'em! No, no, Missis! I 've lost everything, — wife, and children, and home, and a kind Mas'r, — and he would have set me free, if he 'd only lived a week longer; I 've lost everything in *this* world, and it 's clean gone, forever, — and now I *can't* lose Heaven, too; no, I can't get to be wicked, besides all!"

"But it can't be that the Lord will lay sin to our account," said the woman; "he won't charge it to us, when we 're forced to it; he 'll charge it to them that drove us to it."

"Yes," said Tom; "but that won't keep us from growing wicked. If I get to be as hard-hearted as that ar' Sambo,[2] and as wicked, it won't make much odds to me how I come so; it 's the *bein' so,* — that ar 's what I 'm a dreadin'."

The woman fixed a wild and startled look on Tom, as if a new thought had struck her; and then, heavily groaning, said,

"O God a' mercy! you speak the truth! O — O — O!" — and, with groans, she fell on the floor, like one crushed and writhing under the extremity of mental anguish.

There was a silence, a while, in which the breathing of both parties could be heard, when Tom faintly said, "O, please, Missis!"

The woman suddenly rose up, with her face composed to its usual stern, melancholy expression.

"Please, Missis, I saw 'em throw my coat in that ar' corner, and in my coat-pocket is my Bible; — if Missis would please get it for me."

Cassy went and got it. Tom opened, at once, to a heavily marked passage, much worn, of the last scenes in the life of Him by whose stripes we are healed.

"If Missis would only be so good as read that ar', — it 's better than water."

Cassy took the book, with a dry, proud air, and looked over the passage. She then read aloud, in a soft voice, and with a beauty of intona-

---

[2] *Sambo:* The name given to this particular slave overseer on Simon Legree's planta-tion; usually a derogatory term for the supposedly loyal and happy black slave.

tion that was peculiar, that touching account of anguish and of glory. Often, as she read, her voice faltered, and sometimes failed her altogether, when she would stop, with an air of frigid composure, till she had mastered herself. When she came to the touching words, "Father forgive them, for they know not what they do,"[3] she threw down the book, and, burying her face in the heavy masses of her hair, she sobbed aloud, with a convulsive violence.

Tom was weeping, also, and occasionally uttering a smothered ejaculation.

"If we only could keep up to that ar'!" said Tom; —"it seemed to come so natural to him, and we have to fight so hard for 't! O Lord, help us! O blessed Lord Jesus, do help us!"

"Missis," said Tom, after a while, "I can see that, some how, you 're quite 'bove me in everything; but there 's one thing Missis might learn even from poor Tom. Ye said the Lord took sides against us, because he lets us be 'bused and knocked round; but ye see what come on his own Son, — the blessed Lord of Glory, — wan't he allays poor? and have we, any on us, yet come so low as he come? The Lord han't forgot us, — I 'm sartin' o' that ar'. If we suffer with him, we shall also reign, Scripture says; but, if we deny Him, he also will deny us. Did n't they all suffer? — the Lord and all his? It tells how they was stoned and sawn asunder, and wandered about in sheep-skins and goat-skins, and was destitute, afflicted, tormented. Sufferin' an't no reason to make us think the Lord 's turned again us; but jest the contrary, if only we hold on to him, and does n't give up to sin."

"But why does he put us where we can't help but sin?" said the woman.

"I think we *can* help it," said Tom.

"You 'll see," said Cassy; "what 'll you do? To-morrow they 'll be at you again. I know 'em; I 've seen all their doings; I can't bear to think of all they 'll bring you to; — and they 'll make you give out, at last!"

"Lord Jesus!" said Tom, "you *will* take care of my soul? O Lord, do! — don't let me give out!"

"O dear!" said Cassy; "I 've heard all this crying and praying before; and yet, they 've been broken down, and brought under. There 's Emmeline, she 's trying to hold on, and you 're trying, — but what use? You must give up, or be killed by inches."

"Well, then, I *will* die!" said Tom. "Spin it out as long as they can, they can't help my dying, some time! — and, after that, they can't do

[3] *"Father forgive . . . do":* Christ's words on the Cross; see Luke 23.34.

no more. I 'm clar, I 'm set! I *know* the Lord 'll help me, and bring me through."

The woman did not answer; she sat with her black eyes intently fixed on the floor.

"May be it 's the way," she murmured to herself; "but those that *have* given up, there 's no hope for them! — none! We live in filth, and grow loathsome, till we loathe ourselves! And we long to die, and we don't dare to kill ourselves! — No hope! no hope! no hope! — this girl now, — just as old as I was!

"You see me now," she said, speaking to Tom very rapidly; "see what I am! Well, I was brought up in luxury; the first I remember is, playing about, when I was a child, in splendid parlors; — when I was kept dressed up like a doll, and company and visitors used to praise me. There was a garden opening from the saloon windows; and there I used to play hide-and-go-seek, under the orange-trees, with my brothers and sisters. I went to a convent, and there I learned music, French and embroidery, and what not; and when I was fourteen, I came out to my father's funeral. He died very suddenly, and when the property came to be settled, they found that there was scarcely enough to cover the debts; and when the creditors took an inventory of the property, I was set down on it. My mother was a slave woman, and my father had always meant to set me free; but he had not done it, and so I was set down in the list. I 'd always known who I was, but never thought much about it. Nobody ever expects that a strong, healthy man is a going to die. My father was a well man only four hours before he died; — it was one of the first cholera cases in New Orleans. The day after the funeral, my father's wife took her children, and went up to her father's plantation. I thought they treated me strangely, but did n't know. There was a young lawyer who they left to settle the business; and he came every day, and was about the house, and spoke very politely to me. He brought with him, one day, a young man, whom I thought the handsomest I had ever seen. I shall never forget that evening. I walked with him in the garden. I was lonesome and full of sorrow, and he was so kind and gentle to me; and he told me that he had seen me before I went to the convent, and that he had loved me a great while, and that he would be my friend and protector; — in short, though he did n't tell me, he had paid two thousand dollars for me, and I was his property, — I became his willingly, for I loved him. Loved!" said the woman, stopping. "O, how I *did* love that man! How I love him now, — and always shall, while I breathe! He was so beautiful, so high, so noble! He put me into a beautiful house, with servants, horses, and carriages, and furniture, and dresses. Everything that money could buy, he gave me; but I did n't set any value on all that, — I only cared for him. I loved him better than my God and my own soul; and, if I tried, I could n't do any other way from what he wanted me to.

"I wanted only one thing — I did want him to *marry* me. I thought, if he loved me as he said he did, and if I was what he seemed to think I was, he would be willing to marry me and set me free. But he convinced me that it would be impossible; and he told me that, if we were only faithful to each other, it was marriage before God. If that is true, was n't I that man's wife? Was n't I faithful? For seven years, did n't I study every look and motion, and only live and breathe to please him? He had the yellow fever, and for twenty days and nights I watched with him. I alone, — and gave him all his medicine, and did everything for him; and then he called me his good angel, and said I 'd saved his life. We had two beautiful children. The first was a boy, and we called him Henry. He was the image of his father, — he had such beautiful eyes, such a forehead, and his hair hung all in curls around it; and he had all his father's spirit, and his talent, too. Little Elise, he said, looked like me. He used to tell me that I was the most beautiful woman in Louisiana, he was so proud of me and the children. He used to love to have me dress them up, and take them and me about in an open carriage, and hear the remarks that people would make on us; and he used to fill my ears constantly with the fine things that were said in praise of me and the children. O, those were happy days! I thought I was as happy as any one could be; but then there came evil times. He had a cousin come to New Orleans, who was his particular friend, — he thought all the world of him; — but, from the first time I saw him, I could n't tell why, I dreaded him; for I felt sure he was going to bring misery on us. He got Henry to going out with him, and often he would not come home nights till two or three o'clock. I did not dare say a word; for Henry was so high-spirited, I was afraid to. He got him to the gaming-houses; and he was one of the sort that, when he once got a going there, there was no holding back. And then he introduced him to another lady, and I saw soon that his heart was gone from me. He never told me, but I saw it, — I knew it, day after day, — I felt my heart breaking, but I could not say a word! At this, the wretch offered to buy me and the children of Henry, to clear off his gambling debts, which stood in the way of his marrying as he wished; — and *he sold us*. He told me, one day, that he had business in the country, and should be gone two or three weeks. He spoke kinder than usual, and said he should come back; but it did n't deceive me. I knew that the time had come; I was just like one turned into stone; I could n't speak, nor shed a tear. He kissed me and kissed the children, a good many times, and went out. I saw him get on his horse, and I watched him till he was quite out of sight; and then I fell down, and fainted.

"Then *he* came, the cursed wretch! he came to take possession. He told me that he had bought me and my children; and showed me the papers. I cursed him before God, and told him I 'd die sooner than live with him.

"'Just as you please,' he said; 'but, if you don't behave reasonably, I'll sell both the children, where you shall never see them again.' He told me that he always had meant to have me, from the first time he saw me; and that he had drawn Henry on, and got him in debt, on purpose to make him willing to sell me. That he got him in love with another woman; and that I might know, after all that, that he should not give up for a few airs and tears, and things of that sort.

"I gave up, for my hands were tied. He had my children; — whenever I resisted his will anywhere, he would talk about selling them, and he made me as submissive as he desired. O, what a life it was! to live with my heart breaking, every day, — to keep on, on, on, loving, when it was only misery; and to be bound, body and soul, to one I hated. I used to love to read to Henry, to play to him, to waltz with him, and sing to him; but everything I did for this one was a perfect drag, — yet I was afraid to refuse anything. He was very imperious, and harsh to the children. Elise was a timid little thing; but Henry was bold and high-spirited, like his father, and he had never been brought under, in the least, by any one. He was always finding fault, and quarrelling with him; and I used to live in daily fear and dread. I tried to make the child respectful; — I tried to keep them apart, for I held on to those children like death; but it did no good. *He sold both those children.* He took me to ride, one day, and when I came home, they were no-where to be found! He told me he had sold them; he showed me the money, the price of their blood. Then it seemed as if all good forsook me. I raved and cursed, — cursed God and man; and, for a while, I believe, he really was afraid of me. But he did n't give up so. He told me that my children were sold, but whether I ever saw their faces again, depended on him; and that, if I was n't quiet, they should smart for it. Well, you can do anything with a woman, when you 've got her children. He made me submit; he made me be peaceable; he flattered me with hopes that, perhaps, he would buy them back; and so things went on,

a week or two. One day, I was out walking, and passed by the calaboose;[4] I saw a crowd about the gate, and heard a child's voice, — and
suddenly my Henry broke away from two or three men who were
holding him, and ran, screaming, and caught my dress. They came up
to him, swearing dreadfully; and one man, whose face I shall never
forget, told him that he would n't get away so; that he was going with
him into the calaboose, and he 'd get a lesson there he 'd never forget. I
tried to beg and plead, — they only laughed; the poor boy screamed
and looked into my face, and held on to me, until, in tearing him off,
they tore the skirt of my dress half away; and they carried him in,
screaming 'Mother! mother! mother!' There was one man stood there
seemed to pity me. I offered him all the money I had, if he 'd only interfere. He shook his head, and said that the boy had been impudent and
disobedient, ever since he bought him; that he was going to break him
in, once for all. I turned and ran; and every step of the way, I thought
that I heard him scream. I got into the house; ran, all out of breath, to
the parlor, where I found Butler. I told him, and begged him to go and
interfere. He only laughed, and told me the boy had got his deserts.
He 'd got to be broken in, — the sooner the better; 'what did I expect?'
he asked.

"It seemed to me something in my head snapped, at that moment. I
felt dizzy and furious. I remember seeing a great sharp bowie-knife on
the table; I remember something about catching it, and flying upon
him; and then all grew dark, and I did n't know any more — not for
days and days.

"When I came to myself, I was in a nice room, — but not mine. An
old black woman tended me; and a doctor came to see me, and there
was a great deal of care taken of me. After a while, I found that he had
gone away, and left me at this house to be sold; and that 's why they
took such pains with me.

"I did n't mean to get well, and hoped I should n't; but, in spite of
me, the fever went off, and I grew healthy, and finally got up. Then,
they made me dress up, every day; and gentlemen used to come in and
stand and smoke their cigars, and look at me, and ask questions, and
debate my price. I was so gloomy and silent, that none of them wanted
me. They threatened to whip me, if I was n't gayer, and did n't take
some pains to make myself agreeable. At length, one day, came a
gentleman named Stuart. He seemed to have some feeling for me; he
saw that something dreadful was on my heart, and he came to see me

---

[4] *calaboose:* Building used as a jail, prison, or, in this instance, slave pen.

alone, a great many times, and finally persuaded me to tell him. He bought me, at last, and promised to do all he could to find and buy back my children. He went to the hotel where my Henry was; they told him he had been sold to a planter up on Pearl river;[5] that was the last that I ever heard. Then he found where my daughter was; an old woman was keeping her. He offered an immense sum for her, but they would not sell her. Butler found out that it was for me he wanted her; and he sent me word that I should never have her. Captain Stuart was very kind to me; he had a splendid plantation, and took me to it. In the course of a year, I had a son born. O, that child! — how I loved it! How just like my poor Henry the little thing looked! But I had made up my mind, — yes, I had. I would never again let a child live to grow up! I took the little fellow in my arms, when he was two weeks old, and kissed him, and cried over him; and then I gave him laudanum,[6] and held him close to my bosom, while he slept to death. How I mourned and cried over it! and who ever dreamed that it was anything but a mistake, that had made me give it the laudanum? but it 's one of the few things that I 'm glad of, now. I am not sorry, to this day; he, at least, is out of pain. What better than death could I give him, poor child! After a while, the cholera came, and Captain Stuart died; everybody died that wanted to live, — and I, — I, though I went down to death's door, — *I lived!* Then I was sold, and passed from hand to hand, till I grew faded and wrinkled, and I had a fever; and then this wretch bought me, and brought me here, — and here I am!"

The woman stopped. She had hurried on through her story, with a wild, passionate utterance; sometimes seeming to address it to Tom, and sometimes speaking as in a soliloquy. So vehement and overpowering was the force with which she spoke, that, for a season, Tom was beguiled even from the pain of his wounds, and, raising himself on one elbow, watched her as she paced restlessly up and down, her long black hair swaying heavily about her, as she moved.

"You tell me," she said, after a pause, "that there is a God, — a God that looks down and sees all these things. May be it 's so. The sisters in the convent used to tell me of a day of judgment, when everything is coming to light; — won't there be vengeance, then!

"They think it 's nothing, what we suffer, — nothing, what our children suffer! It 's all a small matter; yet I 've walked the streets when it

---

[5] *Pearl river:* River in central Mississippi.
[6] *laudanum:* A solution of alcohol and opium.

seemed as if I had misery enough in my one heart to sink the city. I 've wished the houses would fall on me, or the stones sink under me. Yes! and, in the judgment day, I will stand up before God, a witness against those that have ruined me and my children, body and soul!

"When I was a girl, I thought I was religious; I used to love God and prayer. Now, I 'm a lost soul, pursued by devils that torment me day and night; they keep pushing me on and on — and I 'll do it, too, some of these days!" she said, clenching her hand, while an insane light glanced in her heavy black eyes. "I 'll send him where he belongs, — a short way, too, — one of these nights, if they burn me alive for it!" A wild, long laugh, rang through the deserted room, and ended in a hysteric sob; she threw herself on the floor, in convulsive sobbings and struggles.

In a few moments, the frenzy fit seemed to pass off; she rose slowly, and seemed to collect herself.

"Can I do anything more for you, my poor fellow?" she said, approaching where Tom lay; "shall I give you some more water?"

There was a graceful and compassionate sweetness in her voice and manner, as she said this, that formed a strange contrast with the former wildness.

Tom drank the water, and looked earnestly and pitifully into her face.

"O, Missis, I wish you 'd go to him that can give you living waters!"

"Go to him! Where is he? Who is he?" said Cassy.

"Him that you read of to me, — the Lord."

"I used to see the picture of him; over the altar, when I was a girl," said Cassy, her dark eyes fixing themselves in an expression of mournful reverie; "but, *he is n't here!* there 's nothing here, but sin and long, long, long despair! O!" She laid her hand on her breast and drew in her breath, as if to lift a heavy weight.

Tom looked as if he would speak again; but she cut him short, with a decided gesture.

"Don't talk, my poor fellow. Try to sleep, if you can." And, placing water in his reach, and making whatever little arrangements for his comfort she could, Cassy left the shed.

The Long Bridge, circa 1862. Courtesy of the Library of Congress.

GRACE GREENWOOD

The Leap from the Long Bridge.
An Incident at Washington.

Born Sara Jane Clarke, Grace Greenwood (1823–1904), the popular
journalist, children's writer, and poet, adopted her pen name at the age
of nineteen after moving from New York to Pennsylvania and beginning
her career as a journalist. She wrote for *Godey's Lady's Book,* the antislavery *National Era,* and other magazines and journals. Among her best-
known books are *Greenwood Leaves* (1850), a collection of her
periodical sketches, and *Haps and Mishaps of a Tour in Europe* (1854).
She regularly lectured on social reform, and during the Civil War earned
President Lincoln's praise as "Grace Greenwood, the Patriot" for her
many visits to Union hospitals and camps. An important source for a key
scene in *Clotel,* "The Leap from the Long Bridge" appeared in Grace
Greenwood, *Poems* (Boston: Ticknor, Reed, and Fields, 1851), 73–75,
from which this text is taken. In *Clotel,* Brown also "takes" the text,
reprinting it with several minor changes and one major change — a new
final stanza.

A woman once made her escape from the slave-prison, which stands mid-
way between the Capitol and the President's house, and ran for the Long
Bridge, crossing the Potomac to the extensive grounds and woodlands of
Arlington Place.

> Now rest for the wretched. The long day is past,
> And night on yon prison descendeth at last.
> Now lock up and bolt. — Ha, jailer! look there!
> Who flies like a wild bird escaped from the snare?
>> A woman, — a slave! Up! out in pursuit,
>> While linger some gleams of the day!
> Ho! rally thy hunters, with halloo and shout,
>> To chase down the game, — and away!
>
> A bold race for freedom! — On, fugitive, on!
> Heaven help but the right, and thy freedom is won.
> How eager she drinks the free air of the plains!
> Every limb, every nerve, every fibre, she strains;

From Columbia's glorious Capitol
   Columbia's daughter flees
To the sanctuary God hath given,
   The sheltering forest-trees.

Now she treads the Long Bridge, — joy lighteth her eye, —
Beyond her the dense wood and darkening sky;
Wild hopes thrill her breast as she neareth the shore, —
O despair! — there are *men* fast advancing before!
   Shame, shame on their manhood! — they hear, they heed,
     The cry her flight to stay,
   And, like demon-forms, with their outstretched arms
     They wait to seize their prey!

She pauses, she turns, — ah! will she flee back?
Like wolves her pursuers howl loud on her track;
She lifteth to Heaven one look of despair,
Her anguish breaks forth in one hurried prayer.
   Hark, her jailer's yell! — like a bloodhound's bay
     On the low night-wind it sweeps!
   Now death, or the chain! — to the stream she turns,
     And she leaps, O God, she leaps!

The dark and the cold, yet merciful wave
Receives to its bosom the form of the slave.
She rises, — earth's scenes on her dim vision gleam,
But she struggleth not with the strong, rushing stream,
   And low are the death-cries her woman's heart gives
     As she floats adown the river;
   Faint and more faint grows her drowning voice,
     And her cries have ceased for ever!

Now back, jailer, back to thy dungeons again,
To swing the red lash and rivet the chain!
The form thou wouldst fetter a valueless clod,
The soul thou wouldst barter returned to her God!
   She lifts in His light her unmanacled hands;
     She flees through the darkness no more;
   To freedom she leaped through drowning and death,
     And her sorrow and bondage are o'er.

WILLIAM WELLS BROWN

From *Narrative of William W. Brown*

Brown's experiences as a slave formed a major source for *Clotel*. Inspired by the success of Frederick Douglass's *Narrative,* Brown wrote a narrative of his bondage and eventual escape from slavery, which was published in 1847 by the Anti-Slavery Society of Boston. Brown's *Narrative* proved to be highly popular, selling approximately ten thousand copies and helping to make him one of the most prominent black abolitionists of the time. After publishing the *Narrative,* Brown would retell his life history as a slave in a number of other writings, including the third-person "Narrative of the Life and Escape of William Wells Brown" prefacing *Clotel*. In the selection that follows from *Narrative of William W. Brown, A Fugitive Slave. Written By Himself* (Boston: Anti-Slavery Society, 1847), 52–58, Brown, in a complex and troubling moment, shows how he used his wits to save himself from a flogging ordered by his master, Mr. Walker, but only at the expense of a fellow slave. When he described the scene again in his 1880 *My Southern Home*, Brown, perhaps out of a sense of guilt, displaced the same action onto a slave named "Pompey." The depiction of Pompey (and Sam) in *Clotel* may have similarly complicated autobiographical sources in Brown's firsthand knowledge of the ways in which slavery, as he puts it, "makes its victims lying and mean."

Mr. Walker, though not a good master, had not flogged a slave since I had been with him, though he had threatened me. The slaves were kept in the pen, and he always put up at the best hotel, and kept his wines in his room, for the accommodation of those who called to negotiate with him for the purchase of slaves. One day while we were at Vicksburg,[1] several gentlemen came to see him for this purpose, and as usual the wine was called for. I took the tray and started around with it, and having accidentally filled some of the glasses too full, the gentlemen spilled the wine on their clothes as they went to drink. Mr. Walker apologized to them for my carelessness, but looked at me as though he would see me again on this subject.

---

[1] *Vicksburg:* A city in western Mississippi, on the Mississippi River.

After the gentlemen had left the room, he asked me what I meant by my carelessness, and said that he would attend to me. The next morning, he gave me a note to carry to the jailer, and a dollar in money to give him. I suspected that all was not right, so I went down near the landing where I met with a sailor, and walking up to him, asked him if he would be so kind as to read the note for me. He read it over, and then looked at me. I asked him to tell me what was in it. Said he,

"They are going to give you hell."

"Why?" said I.

He said, "This is a note to have you whipped, and says that you have a dollar to pay for it."

He handed me back the note, and off I started. I knew not what to do, but was determined not to be whipped. I went up to the jail — took a look at it, and walked off again. As Mr. Walker was acquainted with the jailer, I feared that I should be found out if I did not go, and be treated in consequence of it still worse.

While I was meditating on the subject, I saw a colored man about my size walk up, and the thought struck me in a moment to send him with my note. I walked up to him, and asked him who he belonged to. He said he was a free man, and had been in the city but a short time. I told him I had a note to go into the jail, and get a trunk to carry to one of the steamboats; but was so busily engaged that I could not do it, although I had a dollar to pay for it. He asked me if I would not give him the job. I handed him the note and the dollar, and off he started for the jail.

I watched to see that he went in, and as soon as I saw the door close behind him, I walked around the corner, and took my station, intending to see how my friend looked when he came out. I had been there but a short time, when a colored man came around the corner, and said to another colored man with whom he was acquainted —

"They are giving a nigger scissors in the jail."

"What for?" said the other. The man continued,

"A nigger came into the jail, and asked for the jailer. The jailer came out, and he handed him a note, and said he wanted to get a trunk. The jailer told him to go with him, and he would give him the trunk. So he took him into the room, and told the nigger to give up the dollar. He said a man had given him the dollar to pay for getting the trunk. But that lie would not answer. So they made him strip himself, and then they tied him down, and are now whipping him."

I stood by all the while listening to their talk, and soon found out that the person alluded to was my customer. I went into the street opposite the jail, and concealed myself in such a manner that I could not be seen by any one coming out. I had been there but a short time, when the young man made his appearance, and looked around for me. I, unobserved, came forth from my hiding-place, behind a pile of brick, and he pretty soon saw me and came up to me complaining bitterly, saying that I had played a trick upon him. I denied any knowledge of what the note contained, and asked him what they had done to him. He told me in substance what I heard the man tell who had come out of the jail.

"Yes," said he, "they whipped me and took my dollar, and gave me this note."

He showed me the note which the jailer had given him, telling him to give it to his master. I told him I would give him fifty cents for it, — that being all the money I had. He gave it to me, and took his money. He had received twenty lashes on his bare back, with the negro-whip.

I took the note and started for the hotel where I had left Mr. Walker. Upon reaching the hotel, I handed it to a stranger whom I had not seen before, and requested him to read it to me. As near as I can recollect, it was as follows: —

"DEAR SIR: — By your direction, I have given your boy twenty lashes. He is a very saucy boy, and tried to make me believe that he did not belong to you, and I put it on to him well for lying to me.

I remain,
Your obedient servant."

It is true that in most of the slave-holding cities, when a gentleman wishes his servants whipped, he can send him to the jail and have it done. Before I went in where Mr. Walker was, I wet my cheeks a little, as though I had been crying. He looked at me, and inquired what was the matter. I told him that I had never had such a whipping in my life, and handed him the note. He looked at it and laughed; — "and so you told him that you did not belong to me." "Yes, sir," said I. "I did not know that there was any harm in that." He told me I must behave myself, if I did not want to be whipped again.

This incident shows how it is that slavery makes its victims lying and mean; for which vices it afterwards reproaches them, and uses them as arguments to prove that they deserve no better fate. I have often, since my escape, deeply regretted the deception I practised upon this poor fellow; and I heartily desire that it may be, at some time or other, in my power to make him amends for his vicarious sufferings in my behalf.

JOSEPHINE BROWN

From *Biography of an American Bondman*

Not much is known about Josephine Brown, the second daughter of William Wells Brown and Elizabeth Schooner Brown. Born in Buffalo in 1839, she was educated at a school in New Bedford following the separation of her parents in 1847. In 1851 Brown summoned to London both Josephine and her older sister, Clarissa (b. 1836), and subsequently placed them in a seminary in Calais, France. They completed their education at the Home and Colonial School in London, where they received their teaching certificates in 1854. Soon after, they both found teaching jobs in England — the fifteen-year-old Josephine at the East Plumstead School in Woolwich. Returning to the United States in 1855, Josephine accompanied her father on his antislavery speaking engagements, and in 1856 published a biography of him. That same year she returned to England to take up a teaching position, and vanished from the historical record.

In Chapter XIX of *Clotel*, the fictional character William challenges Jim Crow practices on Northern railways. The account in Josephine Brown's biography of her father's own challenge to Jim Crow practices suggests that his life history was a source of the railway scene in *Clotel*. Yet the possibility remains that Josephine Brown's account was shaped by her reading of *Clotel*. The text of the selection is taken from *Biography of An American Bondman, by His Daughter* (Boston: R. F. Wallcut, 1856).

If there is one thing at the North which seems more cruel and hateful than another, connected with American slavery, it is the way in which colored persons are treated by the whites. The withering influence which this hatred exerts against the elevation of the free colored people, can scarcely be imagined. Wherever the black man makes his appearance in the United States, he meets this hatred. In some sections of the country it is worse than in others. As you advance nearer to the slave States, you feel this prejudice the more. Twenty years ago, if colored persons travelled by steamboat, they were put on the deck; if by coach, on the outside; if by railway, in the *Jim Crow car*. Even the respectable eating saloons have been closed against colored persons. In New York and Philadelphia, the despised race are still excluded from most places of refreshment. To the everlasting shame of the Church, she still holds on to this unchristian practice of separating persons on

"Negro Expulsion from Railway Car, Philadelphia." Wood engraving in *The Illustrated London News*, 27 September 1856. Courtesy of the Photographs and Prints Division, Schomburg Center for Research in Black Culture, The New York Public Library, Astor, Lennox and Tilden Foundations.

account of their complexion. In the refined city of Boston, there was a church, as late as 1847, deeded its pews upon condition that no colored person should ever be permitted to enter them! Most of these churches have a place set off in the gallery, where the negro may go if he pleases. A New York D.D.,[1] while on a visit to England, some years since, was charged by a London divine with putting his colored members in the furthest part of the gallery. The American clergyman, with a long face and upturned eyes, exclaimed, "Ah! my dear brother, I think more of my colored members than I do of the whites, and therefore I place them in the top of the house, so as to get them nearer to heaven." CHARLES LENOX REMOND,[2] during the many years that he has labored in the Anti-Slavery cause, has, in all probability, experienced greater insults and more hardships than any other person of color. To hear him relate what he has undergone, while travelling to and from the places of his meetings, makes one's blood chill.

This pretended fastidiousness on the part of the whites has produced some of the most ridiculous scenes. WILLIAM WELLS BROWN, while travelling through Ohio in 1844, went from Sandusky to Republic, on the Mad River and Lake Erie Railroad. On arriving at Sandusky, he learned that colored people were not allowed to take seats in the cars with whites, and that, as there was no *Jim Crow car* on that road, blacks were generally made to ride in the baggage-car. Mr. Brown, however, went into one of the best passenger cars, seated himself, crossed his legs, and looked as unconcerned as if the car had been made for his sole use. At length, one of the railway officials entered the car, and asked him what he was doing there. "I am going to Republic," said Mr. Brown. "You can 't ride here," said the conductor. "Yes I can," returned the colored man. "No you can 't," rejoined the railway man. "Why?" inquired Mr. Brown. "Because we don 't allow *niggers* to ride with white people," replied the conductor. "Well, I shall remain here," said Mr. Brown. "You will see, pretty soon, whether you will or not," retorted the railway man, as he turned to leave the car. By this time, the passengers were filling up the seats, and every thing being made ready to start. After an absence of a few minutes, the conductor again entered the car, accompanied by two stout men, and took Mr. Brown by the collar and pulled him out. Pressing business demanded that Mr. Brown should go, and by that train; he

[1] *D.D.:* Doctor of Divinity.
[2] *CHARLES LENOX REMOND:* A pioneering African American abolitionist, Charles Remond (1810–1873) of Salem, Massachusetts, was best known for his work as a lecturing agent for William Lloyd Garrison's Massachusetts Anti-Slavery Society.

therefore got into the freight car, just as the train was moving off. Seating himself on a flour barrel, he took from his pocket the last number of the *Liberator,* and began reading it. On went the train, making its usual stops, until within four or five miles of Republic, when the conductor, (who, by-the-by, was the same man who had moved Mr. Brown from the passenger car) demanded his ticket. "I have no ticket," returned he. "Then I will take your fare," said the conductor. "How much is it?" inquired Mr. Brown. "One dollar and a quarter," was the answer. "How much do you charge those who ride in the passenger cars?" inquired the colored man. "The same," said the conductor. "Do you suppose that I will pay the same price for riding up here in the freight car, that those do who are in the passenger car?" asked Mr. Brown. "Certainly," replied the conductor. "Well, you are very much mistaken, if you think any such thing," said the passenger. "Come, black man, out with your money, and none of your nonsense with me," said the conductor. "I won't pay you the price you demand, and that's the end of it," said Mr. Brown. "Don't you intend paying your fare?" inquired the conductor. "Yes," replied the colored man; "but I won't pay you a dollar and a quarter." "What do you intend to pay, then?" demanded the official. "I will pay what's right, but I don't intend to give you all that sum." "Well, then," said the conductor, "as you have had to ride in the freight car, give me one dollar and you may go." "I won't do any such thing," returned Mr. Brown. "Why won't you?" inquired the railway man. "If I had come in the passenger car, I would have paid as much as others do; but I won't ride up here on a flour barrel, and pay you a dollar." "You think yourself as good as white people, I suppose?" said the conductor; and his eyes flashed as if he meant what he said. "Well, being you seem to feel so bad because you had to ride in the freight car, give me seventy-five cents, and I'll say no more about it," continued he. "No, I won't. If I had been permitted to ride with the other passengers, I would pay what you first demanded; but I won't pay seventy-five cents for riding up here, astride a flour barrel, in the hot sun." "Don't you intend paying any thing at all?" asked the conductor. "Yes, I will pay what is right." "Give me half a dollar, and I will say no more about it." "No, I won't," returned the other; "I shall not pay fifty cents for riding in a freight car." "What will you pay, then?" demanded the conductor. "What do you charge per hundred on this road?" asked Mr. Brown. "Twenty-five cents," answered the conductor. "Then I will pay you thirty-seven and a half cents," said the passenger, "for I weigh just one hundred and fifty pounds." "Do you expect to get off by paying that trifling sum?"

"I have come as freight, and I will pay for freight, and nothing more," said Mr. Brown. The conductor took the thirty-seven and a half cents, declaring, as he left the car, that that was the most impudent negro that ever travelled on that road.

WILLIAM WELLS BROWN

From *Original Panoramic Views*

During his 1850 tour of Great Britain, Brown commissioned several artists to paint a twenty-four-scene canvas depicting slavery in the United States. He used the canvas to dramatic effect during some of his antislavery lectures. To accompany the canvas, which he first displayed in October of 1850, he authored a pamphlet offering short descriptions of each scene, titled *A Description of William Wells Brown's Original Panoramic Views of the Scenes in the Life of An American Slave, from His Birth in Slavery to His Death or His Escape to His First Home of Freedom on British Soil* (London: Charles Gilpin, 1850), the source of this selection. "View Eighth" contains the germ of *Clotel*'s story of Henry and Althesa Morton.

VIEW EIGHTH.

The New Orleans Calaboose — Sale of Slaves — Mode of Punishment.

One of the oldest and most celebrated public buildings in New Orleans, is the Calaboose. This building is built mainly of stone and iron, and is very large and strong. Some parts of the building are let out to Slave-traders, who use it as a depository for their slaves; although the building is the public property of the city.

You here see the mode of punishing slaves. If an owner wishes his slaves whipped, he can have it done to "order," by sending them to the Calaboose, and paying a fee of one dollar. I was once sent to be whipped in this way (see "Narrative of W. W. BROWN"), but escaped the infliction.

The sale before us is a sale of Slaves, although that woman on the auction-stand who is now being sold, together with the other who is standing among the bystanders, is perfectly white. Unfortunately for these poor girls, their mother was a Slave; and therefore they are also Slaves by the Slave-laws of all the American Slave States.

These are the facts as regards the two white girls now before us. A young physician from one of the Free States went to New Orleans, to commence the practice of his profession. On arriving in the city, he took lodgings at a house, where he observed occasionally waiting on the mistress, a young woman apparently white; and knowing that white persons seldom or never acted as servants in the Slave States, he was induced to make some inquiries respecting her. He was much astonished to learn that she was a Slave. Not being accustomed to see persons in a state of Slavery, he felt very much interested in her behalf. This feeling eventually warmed into love; and he determined to purchase the Slave and to make her his wife. He saw the owner, and ascertained that he was actually the father of the girl, and on this account professed some feelings of paternal affection. When he found the purpose for which the young physician wanted her, he sold her, as an especial favour (!) under the circumstances, for 800 dollars, which he gladly paid, and they were united in marriage. They resided in the city of New Orleans, and spent many years in the happy enjoyment of each other's company, in wealth and affluence. At length they both died, and the physician's brother came down to see to his estate, on behalf of two beautiful and handsome daughters whom they had left behind them. He found that his brother's estate was heavily involved in debt; and the case coming before the Courts, the barristers discovered, amongst his papers, the document of the purchase of his wife for 800 dollars. He had failed to manumit his wife from slavery, to save the fact of her having been a slave from becoming known to his friends, and thus causing them probably to look upon her with less kindly and friendly feelings than they otherwise did. The laws of the United States provide, that, if a Slave should be sold out of Slavery, and live for many years a life of freedom, notwithstanding the fact of her becoming married and living in perfect freedom, yet, if the documents of manumission are not taken out, she is still a Slave in the eye of the law, and all the children are Slaves also. Well, the consequence was, that the schedule of the property was handed back to the brother, with an information that he had not given a correct return of his brother's property, and requiring him to amend it, under the penalties of the law. On inquiring where the incorrectness of the return lay, he was told he had not entered his brother's Slaves; and on his replying that he had none, he was coolly referred to these two girls. "Why," said he, "they are my brother's daughters." Nevertheless, they were, he was told, his brother's Slaves. The document was handed to him; and for the first time the painful fact of their mother having been a Slave was made known to her beautiful daughters, accompanied with the still more painful reality that they were, in the eye of the law, Slaves also. The brother was compelled to enter the girls in the schedule as property, with a heavy amount to each as their value; and there not being assets sufficient to cover the debts, the brother tried hard to raise the purchase-money to release them from their unhappy position. But the sale was hurried on before he could do so; and these handsome but unfortunate girls were placed on the auction-stand, and sold; one for 1,500 dollars and the other for 2,000 dollars. For what purpose such high sums were given all those who were acquainted with the iniquities of American Slavery will readily suspect.

The following advertisements, taken from the *New Orleans Picayune*, will give some idea of the American internal Slave-trade, now in active operation: —

[From the *New Orleans Picayune*.]
Slaves for Sale. — HOPE H. SLATTER, who has retired from the trade, has sold to me his establishment in Baltimore, and leased for a number of years his old stand at the corner of Esplanade and Moreau streets, at which place I shall keep up a large and general assortment of *Slaves* for sale, imported direct from Maryland and Virginia.
WALTER L. CAMPBELL,
Successor to Hope H. Slater.

Negroes — Negroes. — Just received, and for sale at No. 7, Moreau-street, Third Municipality, a large and likely lot of *Negroes*, consisting of field hands, house servants, and mechanics. Will be receiving new lots regularly from Virginia during the season.
WM. F. TALBOTT.

Negroes for Sale on Time. — Nine valuable and well trained Negroes, consisting of men, women, and boys, for sale on a credit of four to six months.
PEGRAM & BRYAN.

WILLIAM WELLS BROWN

From *Clotelle: A Tale of the Southern States*

In late 1860, during a time when he was considering the possibility of emigrating to Haiti, Brown dramatically reconceived *Clotel* for serial publication in the *Weekly Anglo-African,* a New York newspaper whose principal audience was the city's free black population. The new narrative, titled *Miralda; or, The Beautiful Quadroon. A Romance of American Slavery, Founded on Fact,* appeared in the issues of 1 December 1860 to 16 March 1861. To highlight just some of the significant changes from *Clotel* to *Miralda:* Brown renamed most of the characters, jettisoned his collage narrative technique for a more traditional narrative storytelling, extended the tale past the European reunion and marriage that concludes *Clotel,* and included just one passing reference to Jefferson. In late 1863, at a time when Brown had come to embrace the Civil War as a war of emancipation, he revised *Miralda* for James Redpath's "Books for the Camp Fires" series — cheaply produced books for Union soldiers and sympathizers. It was published as *Clotelle: A Tale of the Southern States* (Boston: James Redpath Publishers, 1864), the source of the selection below. Indicative of Brown's commitment to what he came to regard as the antislavery politics of the Declaration of Independence and the Constitution, he cuts *all* references to Jefferson in this revised version.

This selection presents in full the final two chapters of the 1864 *Clotelle.* Jerome and Clotelle (George and Mary in *Clotel*) are on their wedding journey in a small town outside of Geneva. They are surprised to meet Clotelle's father, Henry Linwood, who tells the story of one Mrs. Miller, the mother of his wife, Gertrude. While Mrs. Miller in both versions of *Clotelle* goes out of her way to inflict suffering on the slaves, Gertrude is presented as considerably kinder than Horatio Green's wife, also named Gertrude, in *Clotel.* Significantly, Jerome, unlike his white-skinned predecessor George in *Clotel,* is presented as black to the eye. Racial reconciliation, black pride, and hopes for emancipation are addressed at the end of *Clotelle* in ways very different from the more pessimistic *Clotel.*

CHAPTER XXXIV.
CLOTELLE MEETS HER FATHER.

The clouds that had skirted the sky during the day broke at last, and the rain fell in torrents, as Jerome and Clotelle retired for the night, in the little town of Ferney, on the borders of Lake Leman.[1] The peals of thunder, and flashes of vivid lightening, which seemed to leap from mountain to mountain and from crag to crag, reverberating among the surrounding hills, foretold a heavy storm.

"I would we were back at Geneva," said Clotelle, as she heard groans issuing from an adjoining room. The sounds, at first faint, grew louder and louder, plainly indicating that some person was suffering extreme pain.

"I did not like this hotel, much, when we came in," said Jerome, relighting the lamp, which had been accidentally extinguished.

"Nor I," returned Clotelle.

The shrieks increased, and an occasional "She's dead!" "I killed her!" "No, she is not dead!" and such-like expressions, would be heard from the person, who seemed to be deranged.

The thunder grew louder, and the flashes of lightening more vivid, while the noise from the sick-room seemed to increase.

As Jerome opened the door, to learn, if possible, the cause of the cries and groans, he could distinguish the words, "She's dead! yes, she's dead! but I did not kill her. She was my child! my own daughter. I loved her, and yet I did not protect her."

"Whoever he is," said Jerome, "he's crack-brained; some robber, probably, from the mountains."

The storm continued to rage, and the loud peals of thunder and sharp flashes of lightening, together with the shrieks and moans of the maniac in the adjoining room, made the night a fearful one. The long hours wore slowly away, but neither Jerome nor his wife could sleep, and they arose at an early hour in the morning, ordered breakfast, and resolved to return to Geneva.

"I am sorry, sir, that you were so much disturbed by the sick man last night," said the landlord, as he handed Jerome his bill. "I should be glad if he would get able to go away, or die, for he's a deal of trouble to me. Several persons have left my house on his account."

"Where is he from?" inquired Jerome.

"He's from the United States, and has been here a week to-day, and has been crazy ever since."

"Has he no friends with him?" asked the guest.

"No, he is alone," was the reply.

Jerome related to his wife what he had learned from the landlord, respecting the sick man, and the intelligence impressed her so strongly,

---

[1] *Ferney, on the borders of Lake Leman:* On the French-Swiss frontier, near Geneva.

that she requested him to make further inquiries concerning the stranger.

He therefore consulted the book in which guests usually register their names, and, to his great surprise, found that the American's name was Henry Linwood, and that he was from Richmond, Va.

It was with feelings of trepidation that Clotelle heard these particulars from the lips of her husband.

"We must see this poor man, whoever he is," said she, as Jerome finished the sentence.

The landlord was glad to hear that his guests felt some interest in the sick man, and promised that the invalid's room should be got ready for their reception.

The clock in the hall was just striking ten, as Jerome passed through and entered the sick man's chamber. Stretched upon a mattress, with both hands tightly bound to the bedstead, the friendless stranger was indeed a pitiful sight. His dark, dishevelled hair prematurely gray, his long, unshaven beard, and the wildness of the eyes which glanced upon them as they opened the door and entered, caused the faint hope which had so suddenly risen in Clotelle's heart, to sink, and she felt that this man could claim no kindred with her. Certainly, he bore no resemblance to the man whom she had called her father, and who had fondly dandled her on his knee in those happy days of childhood.

"Help!" cried the poor man, as Jerome and his wife walked into the room. His eyes glared, and shriek after shriek broke forth from his parched and fevered lips.

"No, I did not kill my daughter! — I did not! she is not dead! Yes, she is dead! but I did not kill her — poor girl! Look! that is she! No, it cannot be! she cannot come here! it cannot be my poor Clotelle."

At the sound of her own name, coming from the maniac's lips, Clotelle gasped for breath, and her husband saw that she had grown deadly pale. It seemed evident to him that the man was either guilty of some terrible act, or imagined himself to be. His eyeballs rolled in their sockets, and his features showed that he was undergoing "the tortures of that inward hell,"[2] which seemed to set his whole brain on fire.

After recovering her self-possession and strength, Clotelle approached the bedside, and laid her soft hand upon the stranger's hot and fevered brow.

One long, loud shriek rang out on the air, and a piercing cry, "It is

---

[2] *"tortures . . . hell"*: From Lord Byron, *The Giaour: A Fragment of a Turkish Tale* (1813).

she! — Yes, it is she! I see, I see! Ah! no, it is not my daughter! She would not come to me if she could!" broke forth from him.

"I am your daughter," said Clotelle, as she pressed her handkerchief to her face, and sobbed aloud.

Like balls of fire, the poor man's eyes rolled and glared upon the company, while large drops of perspiration ran down his pale and emaciated face. Strange as the scene appeared, all present saw that it was indeed a meeting between a father and his long-lost daughter. Jerome now ordered all present to leave the room, except the nurse, and every effort was at once made to quiet the sufferer. When calm, a joyous smile would illuminate the sick man's face, and a strange light beam in his eyes, as he seemed to realize that she who stood before him was indeed his child.

For two long days and nights did Clotelle watch at the bedside of her father before he could speak to her intelligently. Sometimes, in his insane fits, he would rave in the most frightful manner, and then, in a few moments, would be as easily governed as a child. At last, however, after a long and apparently refreshing sleep, he awoke suddenly to a full consciousness that it was indeed his daughter who was watching so patiently by his side.

The presence of his long absent child had a soothing effect upon Mr. Linwood, and he now recovered rapidly from the sad and almost hopeless condition in which she had found him. When able to converse, without danger of a relapse, he told Clotelle of his fruitless efforts to obtain a clew to her whereabouts after old Mrs. Miller had sold her to the slave-trader. In answer to his daughter's inquiries about his family affairs up to the time that he left America, he said, —

"I blamed my wife for your being sold and sent away, for I thought she and her mother were acting in collusion; but I afterwards found that I had blamed her wrongfully. Poor woman! she knew that I loved your mother, and feeling herself forsaken, she grew melancholy and died in a decline three years ago."

Here both father and daughter wept at the thought of other days. When they had recovered their composure, Mr. Linwood went on again:

"Old Mrs. Miller," said he, "after the death of Gertrude, aware that she had contributed much toward her unhappiness, took to the free use of intoxicating drinks, and became the most brutal creature that ever lived. She whipped her slaves without the slightest provocation, and seemed to take delight in inventing new tortures with which to punish them. One night last winter, after having flogged one of her slaves nearly to death, she returned to her room, and by some means the bedding took fire, and the house was in flames before any one was awakened. There was no one in the building at the time but the old woman and the slaves, and although the latter might have saved their mistress, they made no attempt to do so. Thus, after a frightful career of many years, this hard-hearted woman died a most miserable death, unlamented by a single person."

Clotelle wiped the tears from her eyes, as her father finished this story, for, although Mrs. Miller had been her greatest enemy, she regretted to learn that her end had been such a sad one.

"My peace of mind destroyed," resumed the father, "and broke down in health, my physician advised me to travel, with the hope of recruiting myself, and I sailed from New York two months ago."

Being brought up in America, and having all the prejudice against color which characterizes his white fellow-countrymen, Mr. Linwood very much regretted that his daughter, although herself tinctured with African blood, should have married a black man, and he did not fail to express to her his dislike of her husband's complexion.

"I married him," said Clotelle, "because I loved him. Why should the white man be esteemed as better than the black? I find no difference in men on account of their complexion. One of the cardinal principles of Christianity and freedom is the equality and brotherhood of man."

Every day Mr. Linwood became more and more familiar with Jerome, and eventually they were on the most intimate terms.

Fifteen days from the time that Clotelle was introduced into her father's room, they left Ferney for Geneva. Many were the excursions Clotelle made under the shadows of Mont Blanc,[3] and with her husband and father for companions; she was now in the enjoyment of pleasures hitherto unknown.

CHAPTER XXXV.
THE FATHER'S RESOLVE.

Aware that her father was still a slave-owner, Clotelle determined to use all her persuasive power to induce him to set them free, and in this effort she found a substantial supporter in her husband.

---

[3] *Mont Blanc:* Alpine mountain range southeast of Geneva; one of its highest peaks is also called Mont Blanc.

"I have always treated my slaves well," said Mr. Linwood to Jerome, as the latter expressed his abhorrence of the system; "and my neighbors, too, are generally good men; for slavery in Virginia is not like slavery in the other States," continued the proud son of the Old Dominion.

"Their right to be free, Mr. Linwood," said Jerome, "is taken from them, and they have no security for their comfort, but the humanity and generosity of men, who have been trained to regard them not as brethren, but as mere property. Humanity and generosity are, at best, but poor guaranties for the protection of those who cannot assert their rights, and over whom law throws no protection."

It was with pleasure that Clotelle obtained from her father a promise that he would liberate all his slaves on his return to Richmond. In a beautiful little villa, situated in a pleasant spot, fringed with hoary rocks and thick dark woods, within sight of the deep blue waters of Lake Leman, Mr. Linwood, his daughter, and her husband, took up their residence for a short time. For more than three weeks, this little party spent their time in visiting the birth-place of Rousseau, and the former abodes of Byron, Gibbon, Voltaire, De Stael, Shelley,[4] and other literary characters.

We can scarcely contemplate a visit to a more historic and interesting place than Geneva and its vicinity. Here, Calvin,[5] that great luminary in the Church, lived and ruled for years; here, Voltaire, the mighty genius, who laid the foundation of the French Revolution, and who boasted, "When I shake my wig, I powder the whole republic," governed in the higher walks of life.

Fame is generally the recompense, not of the living, but of the dead, — not always do they reap and gather in the harvest who sow the seed; the flame of its altar is too often kindled from the ashes of the great. A distinguished critic has beautifully said, "The sound which the stream of high thought, carried down to future ages, makes, as it flows — deep, distant, murmuring ever more, like the waters of the mighty ocean." No reputation can be called great that will not endure this test. The distinguished men who had lived in Geneva transfused

---

[4] *Byron . . . De Stael, Shelley:* References to the British Romantic poets Lord Bryon (1788–1824) and Percy Shelley (1792–1822), or to Byron and the novelist Mary Shelley (1797–1851), and to the English historian Edward Gibbon (1737–1794), the French philosopher François Voltaire (1694–1778), and the French-Swiss woman of letters Germaine de Staël (1766–1817).

[5] *Calvin:* The French Protestant theologian John Calvin (1509–1564) was one of the leaders of the Protestant Reformation.

their spirit, by their writings, into the spirit of other lovers of literature and everything that treated of great authors. Jerome and Clotelle lingered long in and about the haunts of Geneva and Lake Leman.

An autumn sun sent down her bright rays, and bathed every object in her glorious light, as Clotelle, accompanied by her husband and father set out one fine morning on her return home to France. Throughout the whole route, Mr. Linwood saw by the deference paid to Jerome, whose black complexion excited astonishment in those who met him, that there was no hatred to the man in Europe, on account of his color; that what is called prejudice against color is the offspring of the institution of slavery; and he felt ashamed of his own countrymen, when he thought of the complexion as distinctions, made in the United States, and resolved to dedicate the remainder of his life to the eradication of this unrepublican and unchristian feeling from the land of his birth, on his return home.

After a stay of four weeks at Dunkirk, the home of the Fletchers,[6] Mr. Linwood set out for America, with the full determination of freeing his slaves, and settling them in one of the Northern States, and then to return to France to end his days in the society of his beloved daughter.

THE END.

NOTE. — The author of the foregoing tale was formerly a Kentucky slave. If it serves to relieve the monotony of camp-life to the soldiers of the Union, and therefore of Liberty, and at the same time kindles their zeal in the cause of universal emancipation, the object both of its author and publisher will be gained.   J.R.[7]

---

[6] *Fletchers:* Jerome and Clotelle.

[7] *J.R.:* James Redpath (1833–1891). A Scottish-born American journalist, publisher, and abolitionist, Redpath ran the Haytian Emigration Bureau in Boston during the early 1860s before embracing the cause of the Civil War.

WILLIAM WELLS BROWN

From *Clotelle; or, The Colored Heroine*

Following the Civil War, Brown published a revised and expanded version of *Clotelle: A Tale of the Southern States*. He made several small changes in the prefatory matter, added four chapters on the Civil War and its aftermath, and supplied a new title, *Clotelle; or, The Colored Heroine*.

A Tale of the Southern States (Boston: Lee & Shepard, 1867). The selection below presents in full the final four chapters of the 1867 edition. Like Frances Harper in *Iola Leroy* (1892), a book very much influenced by *Clotel* and the two *Clotelles*, Brown portrays black patriotism and sacrifice during the Civil War in order to develop black pride, assert claims for black citizenship, and mobilize white support for Reconstruction. Harper and other African American women writers of the Reconstruction period were also influenced, indeed inspired, by Brown's implicit critique of patriarchal marriage and, perhaps more important, by his portrayal of "the colored heroine" as an "Angel of Mercy" for her selfless community-building work. Brown's concluding vignette of Jim and Dinah, however, raises questions about the depth of his commitment to an antipatriarchal politics.

CHAPTER XXXVI.
THE RETURN HOME

The first gun fired at the American Flag, on the 12th of April, 1861, at Fort Sumter,[1] reverberated all over Europe, and was hailed with joy by the crowned heads of the Old World, who hated republican institutions, and who thought they saw, in this act of treason, the downfall of the great American experiment. Most citizens, however, of the United States, who were then sojourning abroad, hastened home to take part in the struggle, — some to side with the rebels, others to take their stand with the friends of liberty. Among the latter, none came with swifter steps or more zeal than Jerome and Clotelle Fletcher. They arrived in New Orleans a week after the capture of that city by the expedition under the command of Major-Gen. B. F. Butler.[2] But how changed was society since Clotelle had last set feet in the Crescent City! Twenty-two years had passed; her own chequered life had been through many shifting scenes, her old acquaintances in New Orleans had all disappeared; and with the exception of the black faces which she beheld at every turn, and which in her younger days were her associates, she felt herself in the midst of strangers; and these were arrayed

---

[1] *Fort Sumter:* The Confederate troops' attack on the Federally controlled Fort Sumter, in the harbor of Charleston, South Carolina, helped to inaugurate the Civil War.
[2] *Major-Gen. B. F. Butler:* The Union military leader Benjamin Franklin Butler (1818–1893) acted as the military governor of New Orleans from May 1862 to December 1862.

against each other in mortal combat. Possessed with ample means, Mr. and Mrs. Fletcher set about the work of assisting those whom the rebellion had placed in a state of starvation and sickness.

With a heart overflowing with the milk of human kindness, and a tear for every sufferer, no matter of what color or sect, Clotelle was soon known as the "Angel of Mercy."

The "General Order No. 63," issued on the 22d of August, 1862, by Gen. Butler, recognizing, and calling into the service of the Federal Government, the battalion of colored men known as the "Native Guard," at once gave full scope to Jerome's military enthusiasm; and he made haste to enlist in the organization.

The "Native Guard" did good service in New Orleans and vicinity, till ordered to take part in the seige of Port Hudson,[3] where they appeared under the name of the "First Louisiana," and under the immediate command of Lieut.-Col. Bassett. The heroic attack of this regiment, made on the 27th of May, 1863, its unsurpassed "charge," its great loss, and its severe endurance on the field of battle, are incidents which have passed into history. The noble daring of the First Louisiana gained for the black soldiers in our army the praise of all Americans who value Republican institutions.

There was, however, one scene, the closing one in the first day's attack on Port Hudson, which, while it reflects undying credit upon the bravery of the negro, pays but a sorry tribute to the humanity of the white general who brought the scene into existence. The field was strewn with the dead, the dying, and the wounded; and as the jaded regiments were leaving the ground, after their unsuccessful attack, it was found that Capt. Payne, of the Third Louisiana, had been killed; and his body, which was easily distinguished by the uniform, was still on the battle-field. The colonel of the regiment, pointing to where the body lay, asked "Are there four men here who will fetch the body of Capt. Payne from the field?" Four men stepped out, and at once started. But, as the body lay directly under the range of the rebel batteries, they were all swept down by the grape, canister, and shell which were let loose by the enemy. The question was again repeated, "Are there four men who will go for the body?" The required number came forth, and started upon a run; but, ere they could reach the spot, they were cut down. "Are there four more men who will try?" The third

[3] *the seige of Port Hudson:* After taking Vicksburg, Mississippi, in July 1863, Union troops stormed the Confederate garrision of Port Hudson, approximately 250 miles south of Vicksburg. Two Union regiments of Louisiana blacks played a heroic role in this successful assault.

call was answered in the affirmative, and the men started upon the double-quick. They, however, fell before getting as far as the preceding four. Twelve men had been killed in the effort to obtain the body of the brave Payne, but to no purpose. Humanity forbade another trial, and yet it was made. "Are there four more men in the regiment who will volunteer to go for Capt. Payne's body?" shouted the officer. Four men sprang forward, as if fearful that they would miss the opportunity of these last: one was Jerome Fletcher, the hero of our story. They started upon the run; and, strange to tell, all of them reached the body, and had nearly borne it from the field, when two of the number were cut down. Of these, one was Jerome. His head was entirely torn off by a shell. The body of the deceased officer having been rescued, an end was put to the human sacrifice.

CHAPTER XXXVII.
THE ANGEL OF MERCY.

The sad intelligence of Jerome's death was brought to Clotelle while she was giving her personal attention to the sick and wounded that filled the hospitals of New Orleans. For a time she withdrew from the gaze of mankind, and gave herself up to grief. Few unions had been productive of more harmonious feelings than hers. And this blow, so unexpected and at a time when she was experiencing such a degree of excitement caused by the rebellion, made her, indeed, feel the affliction severely.

But the newspaper accounts of the intense suffering of Union prisoners in the rebel States aroused her, and caused her to leave her retirement. In the month of October, 1863, Clotelle resolved to visit Andersonville, Ga., for the purpose of alleviating the hardships of our sick and imprisoned soldiers,[4] and at once put her resolution into effect by going immediately to that place. After crossing the lines, she passed as a rebel lady, to enable her the more successfully to carry out her object. On her arrival at Andersonville, Clotelle took up her abode with a private family, of Union proclivities, and commenced her work

---

[4] *Andersonville . . . soldiers:* Located in southwest Georgia, the Confederates' prison in the villlage of Andersonville confined tens of thousands of Union soldiers under brutal conditions.

of mercy. She first visited the hospitals, the buildings of which were merest excuses for hospitals.

It was the beginning of November; and, even in that southern latitude, the cold made these miserable abodes uncomfortable nights and mornings. The dirty, unventilated rooms, with nothing but straw upon the cold, damp floor, for beds, upon which lay the ragged, emaciated Union prisoners, worn down to skin and bone with disease and starvation, with their sunken eyes and wild looks, made them appear hideous in the extreme. The repulsive scenes, that showed the suffering, neglect, and cruelty which these poor creatures had experienced, made her heart sink within her.

Having paid considerable attention to hospital life in Europe, and so recently from amongst the sick at New Orleans, Clotelle's experience, suggestions, and liberal expenditure of money, would have added greatly to the comfort of these helpless men, if the rebel authorities had been so disposed. But their hatred to Union prisoners was so apparent, that the interest which this angel of humanity took in the condition of the rebel sick could not shield her from the indignation of the secession officials for her good feeling for Union men. However, with a determination to do all in her power for the needy, she labored in season and out.

The brutal treatment and daily murders committed upon our soldiers in the Andersonville prisons caused Clotelle to secretly aid prisoners in their escape. In the latter work, she brought to her assistance the services of a negro man named Pete. This individual was employed about the prison, and, having the entire confidence of the commandant, was in a position to do much good without being suspected. Pete was an original character, of a jovial nature, and, when intending some serious adventure, would appear very solemn, and usually singing a doleful ditty, often the following, which was a favorite with him: —

"Come listen, all you darkies, come listen to my song:
It am about ole Massa, who use me bery wrong.
In de cole, frosty mornin', it an't so bery nice,
Wid de water to de middle, to hoe among de rice;

When I neber hab forgotten
How I used to hoe de cotton,
How I used to hoe de cotton,
On de ole Virginny shore;

> But I'll neber hoe de cotton,
> Oh! neber hoe de cotton,
>> Any more.

"If I feel de drefful hunger, he tink it am a vice,
And he gib me for my dinner a little broken rice, —
A little broken rice and a bery little fat,
And he grumble like de debbil if I eat too much of dat;

> When I neber hab forgotten, etc.

"He tore me from my Dinah; I tought my heart would burst:
He made me lub anoder when my lub was wid de first;
He sole my picanninnies becase he got dar price,
And shut me in de marsh-field to hoe among de rice;

> When I neber hab forgotten, etc.

"And all de day I hoe dar, in all de heat and rain;
And, as I hoe away dar, my heart go back again, —
Back to de little cabin dat stood among de corn,
And to de ole plantation where she and I war born!

> Oh! I wish I had forgotten, etc.

"Den Dinah am beside me, de chil'ren on my knee,
And dough I am a slave dar, it 'pears to me I'm free,
Till I wake up from my dreaming, and wife and chil'ren gone,
I hoe away and weep dar, and weep dar all alone!

> Oh! I wish I had forgotten, etc.

"But soon a day am comin', a day I long to see,
When dis darky in de cole ground, foreber will be free,
When wife and chil'ren wid me, I'll sing in Paradise,
How He, de blessed Jesus, hab bought me wid a price;

> How de Lord hab not forgotten
> How well I hoed de cotton,
>> On de ole Virginny shore;
> Dar I'll neber hoe de cotton,
> Oh! I'll neber hoe de cotton
>> Any more."

When away from the whites, and among his own class, Pete could often be heard in the following strains: —

> "A storm am brewin' in de Souf,
> A storm am brewin' now.

Oh! hearken den, and shut your mouf,
    And I will tell you how:
And I will tell you how, ole boy,
    De storm of fire will pour,
And make de darkies dance for joy,
    As dey neber danced afore;
So shut your mouf as close as deafh,
And all you niggas hole your breafh,
    And I will tell you how.

"De darkies at de Norf am ris,
    And dey am comin' down —
Am comin'down, I know dey is,
    To do de white folks brown!
Dey'll turn ole Massa out to grass,
    And set de niggas free,
And when dat day am come to pass
    We'll all be dar to see!
So shut your mouf as close as deafh,
And all you niggas hole your breafh,
    And do de white folks brown!

"Den all de week will be as gay
    As am de Chris'mas time;
We'll dance all night and all de day,
    And make de banjo chime —
And made de banjo chime, I tink,
    And pass de time away,
Wid 'nuf to eat and nuf to drink,
    And not a bit to pay!
So shut your mouf as close as deafh,
And all you niggas hole your breafh,
    And make de banjo chime."

How to escape from prison was ever the thoughts by day and dreams by night of the incarcerated. Plans were concocted, partly put into execution, and then proved failures. Some of these caused increased suffering to the prisoners after their discovery; for, where the real parties could not be found, the whole were ill-treated as a punishment to the guilty. Tunnelling was generally the mode for escape;. and tunnelling became the order of the day, or, rather, the work for the night. In the latter part of November, 1863, the unusual gaiety of the prisoners showed that some plan of exit from the prison was soon to be exhibited.

CHAPTER XXXVIII.
THE GREAT TUNNEL AND THE MISTAKE.

For several weeks, some ten or fifteen of the most able-bodied of the prisoners had been nightly at work; and the great tunnel, the *largest* ever projected by men for their escape from prison, was thought to be finished, with the exception of the tapping outside of the prison wall. The digging of a tunnel is not an easy job, and, consequently, is of slow progress. The Andersonville prisoners had to dig ten feet down into the earth, after cutting through the floor, and then went a distance of fifty feet to get beyond the wall. The digging was done in the following way: As soon as the operator was below the surface, and had a place large enough to admit the body, he laid down upon his face, at full length, and with his knife, spoon, piece of earthenware, or old iron, dug away with all his energies, throwing the dirt behind him, which was gathered up by a confederate, carried off, and hid. This mode of operating was carried on night after night, and the flooring replaced during the day, to prevent suspicion. The want of fresh air in the tunnel, as it progressed to completion, often drove the men from their work, and caused a delay, which proved fatal to their successful escape.

The long-looked for day arrived. More than three hundred had prepared to leave this hated abode, by the tunnel. All they waited for was the tapping and the signal. The time came, the place of egress was tapped, and the leader had scarcely put his head out of the hole, ere he was fired upon by the sentinels, which soon alarmed and drew the entire guard to the spot. Great was the commotion throughout the prison, and all who were caught in the tunnel were severely punished.

This failure seemed to depress the spirits of the men more than any previous attempt. Heavy irons were placed upon the limbs of many of the prisoners, and their lot was made otherwise harder by the keepers. Clotelle, though often permitted to see the prisoners and contribute to their wants, and, though knowing much of their designs, knew nothing of the intended escape, and therefore was more bold in her intercessions in their behalf when failure came upon them.

The cruelty which followed this mishap, induced Clotelle to interest herself in another mode of escape for the men thus so heavily ironed.

Pete, the man of all work, whose sympathies were with the Union prisoners, was easily gained over to a promise of securing the keys of the prison and letting the men escape, especially when Clotelle offered him money to enable him to make good his own way to the North.

The night of the exodus came. It was favored with darkness; and it so happened that the officials were on a spree, owing to the arrival of Confederate officers with news of a rebel victory.

Before getting the keys, Pete supplied the sentinels on duty with enough whiskey, which he had stolen from the keepers' store-room, to make them all drunk. At the chosen moment, the keys were obtained by Pete, the doors and gates were opened, and ninety-three prisoners, including the tunnel workers, whose irons were taken off, made their escape, allowing the faithful negro to accompany them. Nothing was known of the exit of the men till breakfast hour on the next morning. On examination of the store-room, it was found, that, in addition to the whiskey Pete had taken a large supply of stores for the accommodation of the party. Added to this, a good number of arms with ammunition had been furnished the men by the African.

The rebels were not prepared to successfully pursue the fleeing prisoners, although armed men were sent in different directions. Nothing, however, was heard of them till they reached the Union lines. Long suspected of too freely aiding Union prisoners, Clotelle was now openly charged with a knowledge of the escape of these men, and was compelled to leave Andersonville.

CHAPTER XXXIX.
CONCLUSION.

The fiendish and heartless conduct of a large number of the people of the South towards Union men during the war, and especially the unlady-like demeanor of rebel women at New Orleans and other points, is a matter that has passed into history. In few places were the women more abusive to those of Union proclivities than the female portion of the inhabitants of Greenville, Alabama. While passing through this town, on her return from Andersonville to New Orleans, Clotelle had to encounter the fierce ill-treatment of these chivalrous daughters of the South. There were, during the rebellion, many brave and generous women, who, in the mountains and lowlands of Alabama, gave aid to Federals, — soldiers and civilians, — in their wanderings and escape from the cruelties of the traitors. One of these patriotic women was arrested while on a visit to Greenville for the purpose of procuring medicine and other necessaries for sick Union men then hid away in the woods. This large-hearted woman — Eunice Hastings — had her horse taken from her, robbed of the goods she had purchased, and, after experiencing almost death at the hands of the rebel women, was released and turned out penniless, and without the means of reaching her home in the country; when Clotelle, who had just arrived at the dilapidated and poorly kept hotel, met her, and, learning the particulars of her case, offered assistance to the injured woman, which brought down upon her own head the condemnation of the secesh[5] population of the place. However, Clotelle purchased a fine horse from the landlord, gave it to Miss Hastings, who, after securing some articles for which she had come to Greenville, left town under cover of night, and escaped further molestation. This act of kindness to a helpless sister at once stirred up the vilest feelings of the people.

"The worst of slaves is he whom passion rules."[6]

As has already been said, there was nothing in the appearance of Clotelle to indicate that a drop of African blood coursed through her veins, except, perhaps, the slight wave in the hair, and the scarcely perceptible brunettish tinge upon the countenance. She passed as a rebel lady; yet the inhabitants of Greenville could not permit sympathy with, and aid to, a Union woman to pass unnoticed, and therefore resolved on revenge.

"Revenge, at first though sweet,
Bitter ere long, back on itself recoils."[7]

Clotelle's person, trunks, and letters were all searched with the hope and expectation of finding evidences of a spy. Nothing of the kind being found, she was then rigorously interrogated as to her sympathies with the two contending armies. With no wish whatever to conceal her opinions, she openly avowed that she was a Union woman. This was enough. After being persecuted during the day, she was put in charge of a committee of rebel women for the night, with a promise of more violent treatment on the morrow. The loyalty of the negroes of the South, during the severest hours of the rebellion, reflects the greatest possible credit on the race. Through their assistance, hundreds of Union men were enabled to make their escape from prisons, and thousands kept from starvation when on their way to the Federal

---

[5] *secesh:* Secessionist.
[6] *"The worst . . . rules":* From Thomas Francklin (1721–1784), *The Earl of Warwick* (1766), I.iii.109.
[7] *"Revenge . . . recoils":* From John Milton (1608–1674), *Paradise Lost* (1667), book IX.

lines, or while keeping out of the way of rebel recruiting gangs. They seldom, if ever, hesitated to do the white Unionists a service, at the risk even of life, and, under the most trying circumstances, revealed a devotion and a spirit of self-sacrifice that were heroic. No one ever made an appeal to them they did not answer. They were degraded and ignorant, which was attributable to the cruel laws and equally unchristian practices of the people of the South; but their hearts were always open, and the slightest demand upon their sympathies brought forth their tears. They never shunned a man or woman who sought food or shelter on their way to freedom. The goodness of heart and the guileless spirit of the blacks was not better understood by any one than Clotelle; and she felt a secret joy at seeing all the servants in the Greenville hotel negroes. She saw from their very looks that she had their undivided sympathies. One of the servants overheard the rebels in a conversation, in which it was determined to send Clotelle to the county town, for safe keeping in the jail, the following day; and this fact was communicated to the unfortunate woman. The slave woman who gave the information told her that she could escape if she desired.

Having already been robbed of every thing except the apparel upon her person and some money she had concealed about her, she at once signified to the black woman her wish to get out of the reach of her persecutors. The old worn-out clock in the narrow dining hall had struck one; a cold rain was patting upon the roof, and the women watchers, one after another, had fallen asleep; and even the snuff-dippers, whose dirty practice creates a nervousness that keeps them awake longer than any other class, had yielded to the demands of Morpheus,[8] when Aggy, the colored servant, stealthily entered the room, beckoned to Clotelle, and both left in silence.

Cautiously and softly the black woman led the way, followed by the "Angel of Mercy," till, after passing down through the cellar with the water covering the floor, they emerged into the back yard. Two horses had been provided. Clotelle mounted one, and a black man the other; the latter leading the way. Both dashed off at a rapid pace, through a drenching storm, with such a pall-like darkness that they could not see each other. After an hour's ride the negro halted, and informed Clotelle that he must leave her, and return with the horses, but that she was with friends. He then gave a whistle, and for a moment held his breath. Just as the faithful black was about to repeat the signal, he heard the response; and in a moment the lady alighted, and with

[8] *Morpheus:* Greek and Roman god of dreams.

dripping garments, limbs chilled to numbness, followed her new guide to a place of concealment, near the village of Taitsville.

"You is jes as wet as a drownded rat," said the mulatto woman, who met Clotelle as she entered the negro's cabin.

"Yes," replied the latter, "this is a stormy night for one to be out."

"Yes mam, dese is hard times for eberybody dat 'bleves in de Union. I 'spose deys cotched your husband, an' put him in de army, ain't dey?"

"No: my husband died at Port Hudson, fighting for the Union," said Clotelle.

"Oh, mam, dats de place whar de black people fight de rebels so, wasn't it?" remarked Dinah, for such was her name.

"Yes, that was the place," replied the former. "I see that your husband has lost one of his hands: did he lose it in the war?"

"Oh no, missus," said Dinah. "When dey was taken all de men, black an white, to put in de army, dey cotched my ole man too, and took him long wid 'em. So you see, he said he'd die afore he'd shoot at de Yanks. So you see, missus, Jimmy jes took and lay his left han' on a log, and chop it off wid de hatchet. Den, you see, dey let him go, an' he come home. You see, missus, my Jimmy is a free man: he was born free, an' he bought me, an' pay fifteen hundred dollars for me."

It was true that Jim had purchased his wife; nor had he forgotten the fact, as was shown a day or two after, while in conversation with her. The woman, like many of her sex, was an inveterate scold, and Jim had but one way to govern her tongue. "Shet your mouf, madam, an' hole your tongue," said Jim, after his wife had scolded and sputtered away for some minutes. "Shet your mouf dis minit, I say: you shan't stan' dar, an' talk ter me in dat way. I bought you, an' paid my money fer you, an' I ain't a gwine ter let you sase me in dat way. Shet your mouf dis minit: ef you don't I'll sell you; 'fore God I will. Shet up, I say, or I'll sell you." This had the desired effect, and settled Dinah for the day.

After a week spent in this place of concealment, Jim conveyed Clotelle to Leaksville, Mississippi, through the Federal lines, and from thence she proceeded to New Orleans.

The Rebellion was now drawing to a close. The valley of the Mississippi was in full possession of the Federal government. Sherman was on his raid, and Grant was hemming in Lee.[9] Everywhere the condi-

---

[9] *Sherman . . . Lee:* The Union general William T. Sherman (1820–1891) led the Atlanta Campaign (May–September 1864), and presided over the burning of Atlanta on 15 November 1864 and the subsequent devastation of Savannah, Georgia. Ulysses S. Grant (1822–1885), commander in chief of the Union Army, led Union forces against Robert E. Lee (1807–1870), general in chief of the Confederate Army, whose surrender at Virginia's Appomattox Courthouse on 9 April 1865 ended the Civil War.

tion of the freedmen attracted the attention of the friends of humanity, and no one felt more keenly their wants than Clotelle; and to their education and welfare she resolved to devote the remainder of her life, and for this purpose went to the State of Mississippi, and opened a school for the freedmen; hired teachers, paying them out of her own purse. In the summer of 1866, the Poplar Farm, on which she had once lived as a slave, was confiscated and sold by Government authority, and was purchased by Clotelle, upon which she established a Freedmen's School, and where at this writing, — now June, 1867, — resides the "Angel of Mercy."

2

Race, Slavery, Prejudice

William Wells Brown's *Clotel* was published in 1853. Although African Americans had contributed in crucial ways to the economic and cultural life of the nation, and continued to do so, most U.S. whites of the time remained convinced that blacks were essentially inferior to whites, and thus should be denied the political and social privileges that the Declaration of Independence had proclaimed were among the "inalienable" rights of humankind. In fact, in an effort to quell increasing sectional tensions on the slavery issue, Congress had passed the Compromise of 1850, which, among its provisions, made it the law of the land that all U.S. citizens were required to return fugitive slaves to their masters, just as one would be expected to return stolen property to its legal owner. Following the passage of the Compromise, the fugitive slaves William and Ellen Craft barely escaped slave catchers in Boston and subsequently fled to Liverpool, where they met up with William Wells Brown. In a letter to Frederick Douglass printed in the 16 January 1851 issue of the *North Star,* Brown assailed the new Fugitive Slave Law: "You will have seen that the press of this country [England] has been unsparing in its denunciation of the 'Fugitive Slave Bill.' Of the many acts of cruelty and injustice committed by the American Legislature against the colored people of the United States, none has done so much to crown them with infamy, and to cause the people of this country to detest and abhor the American character, as the enactment of this new law" (3). For Brown, the Compromise of 1850 revealed not only that Southern proslavery forces controlled the federal government but also that Northerners were equally complicitous in perpetuating the nation's slave culture.

This chapter and the next provide a range of texts that figured in the debates on slavery and race in the U.S. from the Constitutional period to the outbreak of the Civil War. Most of the documents in Chapter 2 display the racist beliefs and politics that contributed to the making of the Compromise of 1850, and to the equally noxious Kansas-Nebraska Act (1854) and Dred Scott decision (1857), while most of the documents in Chapter 3 show how those beliefs and practices were challenged by black abolitionists. It should be emphasized, however, as *Clotel*'s multiple perspectives and voices suggest, that debate on slavery and race in the U.S. did not proceed by a simple process of white racist proposition and black antiracist rebuttal. As Brown well knew, white racists were often responding to blacks' assertions of their humanity and political rights; and African Americans' resistance to white domination was often couched in the very terms of the culture that was being contested. In this light, the ordering of Chapters 2 and 3 is somewhat arbitrary, for one could easily reverse the order of the chapters and conceive of the documents in Chapter 3 as the proposition and the documents in Chapter 2 as the rebuttal.

Whether conceived of as proposition or rebuttal (or a complex rhetorical mix), Chapter 2 presents materials that will help readers of *Clotel* to better understand the racist ideology of the dominant white culture. The chapter also includes some oppositional voices. Indeed, the chapter begins with three documents that could be considered as a unit of proposition and rebuttal: Thomas Jefferson's highly influential remarks on slavery and race in his one published book, *Notes on the State of Virginia* (1785); a letter exchange between Jefferson and the black scientist Benjamin Banneker; and an excerpt from the black militant David Walker's *Appeal* (1829), which responds to Jefferson's *Notes*. According to the historian Winthrop D. Jordan, Jefferson's reflections on slavery and race in *Notes* "were more widely read, in all probability, than any others until the mid-nineteenth century," and "became a fixed and central point of reference and influence" (429). Influenced by the racist theories of David Hume and other Enlightenment philosophers who regarded blacks as less "civilized" than whites, Jefferson became convinced of blacks' inferiority, and wondered if they might not belong to a different species. At the same time, he was attracted to the views of late-eighteenth-century naturalists, such as the German physical anthropologist Friedrich Blumenbach and the influential French geographer George Leclerc Buffon, who argued that despite apparent racial differences, all humans belonged to a common species. This led Jefferson to a moral and intellectual conundrum. On the one hand he believed that blacks had the same moral sense and natural rights as whites; on the other, he was a slave owner who found it useful to regard blacks as less human than whites. In *Notes*, he attempts to make the "scientific" case for black inferiority and difference, commenting on blacks' supposed failings as artists and purveyors of culture, and almost obsessively sharing his impressions of blacks' physical unattractiveness and sensuality. Ultimately, despite efforts to rationalize the practice of slavery by invoking notions of racial hierarchy, he presents a very bleak picture of the institution, portraying anything but the kind masters and loyal slaves who would populate the fabled plantation of antebellum proslavery writers. Contemplating the future, Jefferson worries over the possibility of a bloody war of extermination between the races. Given this fear, and his inability to imagine blacks and whites living together in free society, it is not surprising that several decades later he would support the American Colonization Society's program of shipping free blacks to Africa.

A number of Northern antislavery writers responded to Jefferson's remarks on slavery and race, most prominently the Princeton theologian Samuel Stanhope Smith (1751–1819), who insisted on the intellectual and moral equality of blacks and whites, and the Philadelphia physician Benjamin Rush (1745–1813), who theorized that blacks' dark skin was a biologically transmitted response to leprosy but that otherwise blacks were intellectually, physically, and morally equal to whites. Some of the most compelling responses to Jefferson, however, came from African Americans. In his letter to Jefferson, Banneker posed a compelling challenge to Jefferson's racialism; and one can detect some bending in Jefferson's position on black inferiority when he concedes to Banneker that his "empirical" observations on the plantation may not have done justice to African Americans' capabilities. In addition to responding warmly to Banneker, Jefferson wrote a follow-up letter to the French scientist the Marquis de Condorcet, in which he proclaimed: "I am happy to be able to inform you that we have now in the United States a negro, the son of a black man born in

Africa, and of a black woman born in the United States, who is a very respectable mathematician. . . . I have seen very elegant solutions of Geometrical problems by him. Add to this that he is a very worthy & respectable member of society. He is a free man. I shall be delighted to see instances of moral eminence so multiplied as to prove that the wants of talents observed in them is merely the effect of their degraded condition, and not proceeding from any difference in the structure of the parts on which intellect depends" (*Works* VI: 311). Similarly, nearly twenty years later, Jefferson remarked in a letter of 25 February 1809 to the Abbé Henri Gregoire, who had sent him a volume on blacks' accomplishments in literature: "Be assured that no person living wishes more sincerely than I do, to see a complete refutation of the doubts I have myself entertained and expressed on the grade of understanding allotted to them [blacks] by nature, and to find that in this respect they are on a par with ourselves. My doubts were the result of personal observation on the limited sphere of my own State, where the opportunities for the development of their genius were not favorable, and those of exercising it still less so" (*Writings* 1202). Of course the possibility exists that Jefferson was being disingenuous in his letters to Condorcet and Gregoire, and that like many Southerners he was incapable of regarding blacks as fully human. Such is the unattractive image of Jefferson that emerges in David Walker's *Appeal* (1829), published just three years after Jefferson's death on 4 July 1826. According to Walker, Jefferson was a hypocrite who bequeathed to the nation a loathsome racist ideology of white supremacy. In Walker's view, Jefferson also bequeathed to the nation a host of unresolved political and cultural conflicts that made the apocalyptic racial war he envisioned in *Notes* little more than a self-fulfilling prophecy.

In the late eighteenth century, then, Jefferson somewhat provisionally made claims for black inferiority and difference — claims that perhaps covered both his attraction to Sally Hemings and his recognition of the arbitrariness of racial categories in a household characterized by miscegenation. In the nineteenth century the "scientific" racism exemplified by Jefferson hardened, as white Americans became more intent on asserting the "fact" of black inferiority — and thus the rightness of relegating peoples of African descent to the slave plantation, the social margins, or Africa. As slavery became increasingly central to Southern culture, proslavery writers proclaimed that the plantation served the needs of allegedly inferior blacks, giving them a home and duties under the paternalistic guidance of the master. The master's supposedly beneficent supervisory rule was celebrated by these writers as sanctified by the teachings of the Bible, and the plantation itself was extolled as blacks' haven from the ruthless capitalist world of Northern market culture. Though many white Northerners resented Southerners' negative characterizations of market culture, and were equally distrustful of celebrations of the slave plantation, they remained as convinced as white Southerners of whites' superiority to blacks. As a result, most "free" Northern blacks remained disenfranchised noncitizens and the victims of discriminatory laws that kept them from having access to schools and workplaces. To be sure, slavery was abolished in Northern states in the late eighteenth and early nineteenth centuries, but most Northern political leaders were content to develop compromises with Southern politicians. Antislavery voices remained in the minority, even as sectional conflict became increasingly tense during the late 1840s and 1850s.

The remaining documents in this chapter provide a glimpse of the ways in which debates on slavery and race developed into the mid–nineteenth century. Significantly, these debates had their sources in the unfinished, racist work of Thomas Jefferson. The selections from Henry Clay, Thomas R. Dew, and John C. Calhoun can all be read in relation to Jefferson's *Notes*. Jefferson's imagining of a happy future for the nation in which blacks have vanished from the social landscape was the fantasy that informed the founding in 1816 of the American Colonization Society, which sought to transport the free blacks to Africa. Henry Clay, who would eventually become one of the principal architects of the Compromise of 1850, assumed an important leadership role in the American Colonization Society, for he was convinced that "returning" blacks to Africa would help to unite the North and South and bring about progress and prosperity in the United States. Jefferson's fears of black-white racial conflict had a fulfillment of sorts in the Nat Turner rebellion of 1831, and the selection from Dew shows how Southerners responded to this realization of their fears by revising Jefferson's notion of the immorality of slavery. Unlike Jefferson, who argued that slavery was bad for the morals of the masters, Dew argued that granting even greater power to the masters would help to stave off black rebellion and further develop Southern civilization. Similarly, in response to abolitionists' efforts to end the slave trade in the District of Columbia, John C. Calhoun attempted to make the case that, in the wake of the Nat Turner rebellion, slavery could be regarded as a "positive good" for keeping blacks under whites' control and contributing to the progress of U.S. civilization.

The subsequent three selections, from Albert Barnes, Martin R. Delany, and Frederick Douglass, provide examples of abolitionists' resistance to proslavery arguments that were based on the Bible or on "scientific" notions of black inferiority. Barnes raises questions about the morality of reading the Bible as a proslavery document, and Delany and Douglass suggest the ludicrousness of attempting to argue for the superiority of "white" over "black" blood. As Brown would in *Clotel*, Delany and Douglass also foreground connections between racism and sexuality, exploring the ways in which whites' racism was informed by an anxious obsession with black bodies.

Douglass and Delany attacked whites' racism at a time not only when Southerners were citing the Bible to support white supremacy but also when scientists and physical anthropologists in the North and South were disseminating the arguments of what has been dubbed the "American School" of ethnography. According to writers of this school, which included such eminent Northern scientists as Samuel Morton of the Philadelphia Academy and Louis Agassiz of Harvard University, blacks and other peoples of color were not of the same species as whites, and were ultimately intellectually, physically, and morally inferior. These views went hand in hand with the emerging Anglo-Saxonism of the time, a nationalistic and racist ideology which maintained that the white Protestant majority was of superior racial stock because it descended from the supposedly pure-blooded and freedom-loving English tribes who attempted to resist the Norman conquest of 1066. Anglo-Saxon ideology was invoked by U.S. political leaders to justify the 1846–48 war with Mexico as a battle between a civilized superior race and an uncivilized inferior race; Anglo-Saxonism and the American School's scientific racialism, which was based on the comparative study of the skulls and bones of peoples from around the world, also led many highly regarded thinkers to argue for polygenesis (separate origins for peoples of different races) as opposed to monogenesis (a single origin) and was used to justify discriminatory practices against blacks in the North and slavery in the South. The selection from Josiah C. Nott and George R. Gliddon's *Types of Mankind* (1854) gives a sense of how scientific racialism was codified during the 1850s; and the selection from Samuel A. Cartwright shows how the rhetoric of racial "science" was employed by the slave masters to deny blacks their humanity.

The final six selections in this chapter address the Compromise of 1850 and its aftermath. The support for the Compromise from the influential Northern senator Daniel Webster helped to ensure its passage. Yet instead of quelling tensions, as was hoped, the Compromise only further exacerbated sectional conflict, particularly following the publication of Harriet Beecher Stowe's *Uncle Tom's Cabin* (1852), which became many Northerners' guidebook to the Southern slave plantation. The selections from George Fitzhugh, Nehemiah Adams, and Caroline Lee Hentz all have a defensiveness to them, signaling the writers' awareness that Stowe's portrayal of the South had contributed to a growing resistance to slavery. In response to Stowe and other Northern antislavery writers, Fitzhugh developed a two-pronged defense of Southern slave culture: he celebrated slavery as an orderly and harmonious institution that provided all concerned, masters and slaves, with a sense of purpose and place; and he attacked Northern market culture as a heartless competitive world in which individuals struggled to best their neighbors and the poor simply fell by the wayside. Adams, a Northerner sympathetic to Southern enslavers, made a case similar to Fitzhugh's for the harmonious social relations of slavery by attempting to refute Stowe's claims of the havoc slavery wreaks on the black family. Also responding to *Uncle Tom's Cabin*, Hentz, in an anti-*Uncle Tom* novel, portrayed the slaves' dissatisfactions with their condition as the deleterious consequences of abolitionist meddling. But the very fact that she could imagine the possibility of a slave rebellion suggests that she shared the fears informing Jefferson's *Notes* and Dew's *Review*.

Whereas Hentz blamed slave unrest on meddling Northerners, Harriet Jacobs showed that efforts to smear abolitionists and to deride blacks' potential to thrive as free citizens were all part of a concerted Southern effort to deceive the slaves. Her autobiography ends, however, with a bleak portrayal of the pervasiveness of antiblack racism in the North. Walt Whitman's 1858 newspaper editorial on the elections in Oregon to create a new state constitution provides chilling support for Jacobs's pessimistic assessment. Whitman detested slavery, and in "Song of Myself" (1855) even made the creative leap to imagine himself as a fugitive slave. Nevertheless, his journalism of the late 1850s suggests that he also regarded blacks as not "naturally" part of the United States. Thus, in the spirit of Stowe's *Uncle Tom's Cabin*, which concludes by advocating African colonization for the free blacks, he endorses the proposed Oregon constitution, which would abolish slavery *and* prohibit blacks from the new state. Whitman's vision in 1858 of an all-white America suggests just how compelling Jefferson's similar future vision of a nation that no longer had slavery — and no longer had any blacks — remained for many whites of successive generations.

THOMAS JEFFERSON

From *Notes on the State of Virginia*

Jefferson wrote *Notes on the State of Virginia* (1785) in response to a series of queries about the state from the Marquis de Barbé-Marbois, secretary to the French legation in Philadelphia. The main purpose of the text was to refute Europe's leading naturalists, Abbé Reynal and the Count de Buffon, who had argued that the New World showed signs of physical and natural degeneration. Jefferson, then governor of Virginia, devoted a number of his chapters to careful, naturalistic descriptions of landscapes, animals, and even the Native Americans, with an aim toward demonstrating the nation's bounty, vigor, and future potential. His discussion of slavery constituted a small but important part of the book. At the time Jefferson disapproved of slavery, but his antislavery views were grounded in a racialist belief in black inferiority and a conviction that blacks could never become citizens of the United States. As he became more economically dependent on his slaves, Jefferson became more of a defender of the South's right to own slaves for the time being, particularly after slavery was banned from the Northwest territories by the Missouri Compromise of 1820. But he continued to look forward to a national future in which slavery had come to an end and blacks had gone to other countries. The selection is taken from *The Works of Thomas Jefferson*, ed. Paul Leicester Ford, vol. 4 (New York: G. P. Putnam's Sons, 1904), 47, 48–54, 55–59, 82–84.

QUERY XIV
*The administration of justice
and the description of the laws?*

Many of the laws which were in force during the monarchy being relative merely to that form of government, or inculcating principles inconsistent with republicanism, the first assembly which met after the establishment of the commonwealth, appointed a committee to revise the whole code, to reduce it into proper form and volume, and report it to the assembly. This work has been executed by three gentlemen, and reported; but probably will not be taken up till a restoration of peace shall leave to the legislature leisure to go through such a work.[1] . . .

The following are the most remarkable alterations proposed:

To change the rules of descent, so as that the lands of any person dying intestate shall be divisible equally among all his children, or other representatives, in equal degree.

To make slaves distributable among the next of kin, as other movables.

To have all public expences, whether of the general treasury, or of a parish or county, (as for the maintenance of the poor, building bridges, courthouses, &c.,) supplied by assessments on the citizens, in proportion to their property.

To hire undertakers for keeping the public roads in repair, and indemnify individuals through whose lands new roads shall be opened.

To define with precision the rules whereby aliens should become citizens, and citizens make themselves aliens.

To establish religious freedom on the broadest bottom.

To emancipate all slaves born after passing the act. The bill reported by the revisers does not itself contain this proposition; but an amendment containing it was prepared, to be offered to the legislature whenever the bill should be taken up, and further directing, that they should continue with their parents to a certain age, then be brought up, at the public expence, to tillage, arts, or sciences, according to their geniusses, till the females should be eighteen, and the males twenty-one years of age, when they should be colonized to such place as the circumstances of the time should render most proper, sending them out with arms, implements of household and of the handicraft arts, seeds, pairs of the useful domestic animals, &c. to declare them a free and independant people, and extend to them our alliance and protection, till they shall have acquired strength; and to send vessels at the same time to other parts of the world for an equal number of white inhabitants; to induce whom to migrate hither, proper encouragements were to be proposed. It will probably be asked, Why not retain and incorporate the blacks into the state, and thus save the expence of supplying by importation of white settlers, the vacancies they will

---

[1] *such a work:* A reference to the *Report of the Revisors,* a revision of Virginia's state laws, which was prepared by Thomas Jefferson, George Wythe (1726–1806), and Edmund Pendleton (1721–1803), and submitted to the state legislature on 18 June 1779.

leave? Deep rooted prejudices entertained by the whites; ten thousand recollections, by the blacks, of the injuries they have sustained; new provocations; the real distinctions which nature has made; and many other circumstances will divide us into parties, and produce convulsions, which will probably never end but in the extermination of the one or the other race. — To these objections, which are political, may be added others, which are physical and moral. The first difference which strikes us is that of colour. Whether the black of the negro resides in the reticular membrane between the skin and scarfskin,[2] or in the scarfskin itself; whether it proceeds from the colour of the blood, the colour of the bile, or from that of some other secretion, the difference is fixed in nature, and is as real as if its seat and cause were better known to us. And is this difference of no importance? Is it not the foundation of a greater or less share of beauty in the two races? Are not the fine mixtures of red and white, the expressions of every passion by greater or less suffusions of colour in the one, preferable to that eternal monotony, which reigns in the countenances, that immovable veil of black which covers all the emotions of the other race? Add to these, flowing hair, a more elegant symmetry of form, their own judgment in favour of the whites, declared by their preference of them as uniformly as in the preference of the Oran ootan[3] for the black woman over those of his own species. The circumstance of superior beauty, is thought worthy attention in the propagation of our horses, dogs, and other domestic animals; why not in that of man? Besides those of colour, figure and hair, there are other physical distinctions proving a difference of race. They have less hair on the face and body. They secrete less by the kidnies, and more by the glands of the skin, which gives them a very strong and disagreeable odour. This greater degree of transpiration, renders them more tolerant of heat, and less so of cold than the whites. Perhaps too a difference of structure in the pulmonary apparatus, which a late ingenious experimentalist[4] has discovered to be the principal regulator of animal heat, may have disabled them from extricating, in the act of inspiration, so much of that fluid from the outer air, or obliged them in expiration, to part with more of it. They seem to require less sleep. A black after hard labour through the day, will be induced by the slightest amusements to sit up

[2] *scarfskin:* The outermost layer of skin.
[3] *Oran ootan:* Orangutan.
[4] *a late ingenious experimentalist:* A reference to Adair Crawford (1748–1795), a British physician and chemist best known for his *Experiments and Observations on Animal Heat* (1779).

till midnight or later, though knowing he must be out with the first
dawn of the morning. They are at least as brave, and more adventure-
some. But this may perhaps proceed from a want of forethought,
which prevents their seeing a danger till it be present. When present,
they do not go through it with more coolness or steadiness than the
whites. They are more ardent after their female; but love seems with
them to be an eager desire, than a tender delicate mixture of sentiment
and sensation. Their griefs are transient. Those numberless afflictions,
which render it doubtful whether heaven has given life to us in mercy
or in wrath, are less felt, and sooner forgotten with them. In general,
their existence appears to participate more of sensation than reflection. To this must be ascribed their disposition to sleep when ab-
stracted from their diversions, and unemployed in labour. An animal
whose body is at rest, and who does not reflect, must be disposed to
sleep of course. Comparing them by their faculties of memory, reason,
and imagination, it appears to me that in memory they are equal to the
whites; in reason much inferior, as I think one could scarcely be found
capable of tracing and comprehending the investigations of Euclid:[5]
and that in imagination they are dull, tasteless, and anomalous. It
would be unfair to follow them to Africa for this investigation. We will
consider them here, on the same stage with the whites, and where the
facts are not apochryphal on which a judgment is to be formed. It will
be right to make great allowances for the difference of condition, of
education, of conversation, of the sphere in which they move. Many
millions of them have been brought to, and born in America. Most of
them, indeed, have been confined to tillage, to their own homes, and
their own society: yet many have been so situated, that they might
have availed themselves of the conversation of their masters; many
have been brought up to the handicraft arts, and from that circumstance have always been associated with the whites. Some have been
liberally educated, and all have lived in countries where the arts and
sciences are cultivated to a considerable degree, and have had before
their eyes samples of the best works from abroad. The Indians, with
no advantages of this kind, will often carve figures on their pipes not
destitute of design and merit. They will crayon out an animal, a plant,
or a country, so as to prove the existence of a germ in their minds
which only wants cultivation. They astonish you with strokes of the
most sublime oratory; such as prove their reason and sentiment
strong, their imagination glowing and elevated. But never yet could I

[5] *Euclid:* Greek mathematician circa 300 B.C.

find that a black had uttered a thought above the level of plain narration; never seen even an elementary trait of painting or sculpture. In music they are more generally gifted than the whites, with accurate ears for tune and time, and they have been found capable of imagining a small catch.[6] Whether they will be equal to the composition of a more extensive run of melody, or of complicated harmony, is yet to be proved. Misery is often the parent of the most affecting touches in poetry. — Among the blacks is misery enough, God knows, but no poetry. Love is the peculiar œstrum[7] of the poet. Their love is ardent, but it kindles the senses only, not the imagination. Religion, indeed, has produced a Phyllis Whately[8]; but it could not produce a poet. The compositions published under her name are below the dignity of criticism. The heroes of the Dunciad[9] are to her, as Hercules to the author of that poem. Ignatius Sancoh[10] has approached nearer to merit in composition; yet his letters do more honour to the heart than the head. They breathe the purest effusions of friendship and general philanthropy, and show how great a degree of the latter may be compounded with strong religious zeal. He is often happy in the turn of his compliments, and his style is easy and familiar, except when he affects a Shandean[11] fabrication of words. But his imagination is wild and extravagant, escapes incessantly from every restraint of reason and taste, and, in the course of its vagaries, leaves a tract of thought as incoherent and eccentric, as is the course of a meteor through the sky. His subjects should often have led him to a process of sober reasoning; yet we find him always substituting sentiment for demonstration. Upon the whole, though we admit him to the first place among those of his own color who have presented themselves to the public judgment, yet when we compare him with the writers of the race among whom he lived and particularly with the

[6] "The instrument proper to them is the Banjar, which they brought hither from Africa, and which is the original of the guitar, its chords being precisely the four lower chords of the guitar." [Jefferson's note]

[7] *oestrum:* Passionate impulse.

[8] *Phyllis Whately:* A condescending reference to the African American poet Phillis Wheatley (1753–1784), whose *Poems* (1773) was popular in England, going through at least four printings.

[9] *Dunciad:* Alexander Pope's satirical poem on Dullness, first published in 1728.

[10] *Ignatius Sancoh:* Charles Ignatius Sancho (1729–1780), born a slave on a slave ship, was eventually taken to England, where he emerged as an internationally prominent man of letters. His *Letters of the Late Ignatius Sancho, an African* was published in London in 1782.

[11] *Shandean:* In imitation of the eponymous antihero of Laurence Sterne's *Tristram Shandy* (1760–1767).

epistolary[12] class in which he has taken his own stand, we are compelled to enrol him at the bottom of the column. This criticism supposes the letters published under his name to be genuine, and to have received amendment from no other hand; points which would not be of easy investigation. The improvement of the blacks in body and mind, in the first instance of their mixture with the whites, has been observed by every one, and proves that their inferiority is not the effect merely of their condition of life. We know that among the Romans, about the Augustan age[13] especially, the condition of their slaves was much more deplorable than that of the blacks on the continent of America. The two sexes were confined in separate apartments, because to raise a child cost the master more than to buy one. . . . With the Romans, the regular method of taking the evidence of their slaves was under torture. Here it has been thought better never to resort to their evidence. When a master was murdered, all his slaves, in the same house, or within hearing, were condemned to death. Here punishment falls on the guilty only, and as precise proof is required against him as against a freeman. Yet notwithstanding these and other discouraging circumstances among the Romans, their slaves were often their rarest artists. They excelled too in science, insomuch as to be usually employed as tutors to their master's children. Epictetus, Terence, and Phædrus, were slaves.[14] But they were of the race of whites. It is not their condition then, but nature, which has produced the distinction. — Whether further observation will or will not verify the conjecture, that nature has been less bountiful to them in the endowments of the head, I believe that in those of the heart she will be found to have done them justice. That disposition to theft with which they have been branded, must be ascribed to their situation, and not to any depravity of the moral sense. The man in whose favour no laws of property exist, probably feels himself less bound to respect those made in favour of others. When arguing for ourselves, we lay it down as a fundamental, that laws, to be just, must give a reciprocation of right: that, without this, they are mere arbitrary rules of conduct, founded in force, and not in conscience; and it is a problem which I give to the master to solve, whether the religious precepts against the violation of property were not framed for him as well as his slave? And whether

---

[12] *epistolary:* Letter writing.

[13] *Augustan age:* The Roman Emperor Augustus ruled from 27 B.C. to A.D. 14.

[14] *Epictetus, Terence, and Phædrus, were slaves:* Epictetus (A.D. c.50–c.138) was a philosopher, Terence (c.190 B.C.–c.159 B.C.) a comic playwright, and Phædrus (first century A.D.) a writer of fables.

the slave may not as justifiably take a little from one who has taken all from him, as he may slay one who would slay him? That a change in the relations in which a man is placed should change his ideas of moral right and wrong, is neither new, nor peculiar to the colour of the blacks. Homer[15] tells us it was so 2600 years ago.

'Ημισυ, γὰρ τ' ἀρετής ἀποαίνυται εὐρύοπα Ζεὺ
'Αφνερος, ευτ' ἂν μιν κατὰ δουλιον ἦμαρ ξλησιν.
— Od. 17, 323.

Jove fix'd it certain, that whatever day
Makes man a slave, take half his worth away.

But the slaves of which Homer speaks were whites. Notwithstanding these considerations which must weaken their respect for the laws of property, we find among them numerous instances of the most rigid integrity, and as many as among their better instructed masters, of benevolence, gratitude, and unshaken fidelity. The opinion that they are inferior in the faculties of reason and imagination, must be hazarded with great diffidence. To justify a general conclusion, requires many observations, even where the subject may be submitted to the Anatomical knife, to Optical glasses, to analysis by fire or by solvents. How much more then where it is a faculty, not a substance, we are examining; where it eludes the research of all the senses; where the conditions of its existence are various and variously combined; where the effects of those which are present or absent bid defiance to calculation; let me add too, as a circumstance of great tenderness, where our conclusion would degrade a whole race of men from the rank in the scale of beings which their Creator may perhaps have given them. To our reproach it must be said, that though for a century and a half we have had under our eyes the races of black and of red men, they have never yet been viewed by us as subjects of natural history. I advance it, therefore, as a suspicion only, that the blacks, whether originally a distinct race, or made distinct by time and circumstances, are inferior to the whites in the endowments both of body and mind. It is not against experience to suppose that different species of the same genus, or varieties of the same species, may possess different qualifications. Will not a lover of natural history then, one who views the gradations in all the races of animals with the eye of philosophy, excuse an effort to keep those in the department of man as distinct as nature has formed them? This unfortunate difference of colour, and perhaps of faculty, is

[15] *Homer:* The passage that follows is from the epic poem *The Odyssey*, generally attributed to the Greek poet Homer, who lived sometime before 700 B.C.

a powerful obstacle to the emancipation of these people. Many of their advocates, while they wish to vindicate the liberty of human nature, are anxious also to preserve its dignity and beauty. Some of these, embarrassed by the question, 'What further is to be done with them?' join themselves in opposition with those who are actuated by sordid avarice only. Among the Romans emancipation required but one effort. The slave, when made free, might mix with, without staining the blood of his master. But with us a second is necessary, unknown to history. When freed, he is to be removed beyond the reach of mixture. . . .

QUERY XVIII
The particular customs and manners that may happen to be received in that State?

It is difficult to determine on the standard by which the manners of a nation may be tried, whether *catholic*[16] or *particular*. It is more difficult for a native to bring to that standard the manners of his own nation, familiarized to him by habit. There must doubtless be an unhappy influence on the manners of our people produced by the existence of slavery among us. The whole commerce between master and slave is a perpetual exercise of the most boisterous passions, the most unremitting despotism on the one part, and degrading submissions on the other. Our children see this, and learn to imitate it; for man is an imitative animal. This quality is the germ of all education in him. From his cradle to his grave he is learning to do what he sees others do. If a parent could find no motive either in his philanthropy or his self-love, for restraining the intemperance of passion towards his slave, it should always be a sufficient one that his child is present. But generally it is not sufficient. The parent storms, the child looks on, catches the lineaments of wrath, puts on the same airs in the circle of smaller slaves, gives a loose to the worst of passions, and thus nursed, educated, and daily exercised in tyranny, cannot but be stamped by it with odious peculiarities. The man must be a prodigy who can retain his manners and morals updepraved by such circumstances. And with what execrations should the statesman be loaded, who permitting one half the citizens thus to trample on the rights of the other, transforms those into despots, and these into enemies, destroys the morals of the one part,

---

[16] *catholic:* Universal; wide-ranging.

and the amor patriæ of the other. For if a slave can have a country in this world, it must be any other in preference to that in which he is born to live and labour for another: in which he must lock up the faculties of his nature, contribute as far as depends on his individual endeavours to the evanishment of the human race, or entail his own miserable condition on the endless generations proceeding from him. With the morals of the people, their industry also is destroyed. For in a warm climate, no man will labour for himself who can make another labour for him. This is so true, that of the proprietors of slaves a very small proportion indeed are ever seen to labour. And can the liberties of a nation be thought secure when we have removed their only firm basis, a conviction in the minds of the people that these liberties are of the gift of God? That they are not to be violated but with his wrath? Indeed I tremble for my country when I reflect that God is just: that his justice cannot sleep forever: that considering numbers, nature and natural means only, a revolution of the wheel of fortune, an exchange of situation, is among possible events: that it may become probable by supernatural interference! The Almighty has no attribute which can take side with us in such a contest. — But it is impossible to be temperate and to pursue this subject through the various considerations of policy, of morals, of history natural and civil. We must be contented to hope they will force their way into every one's mind. I think a change already perceptible, since the origin of the present revolution. The spirit of the master is abating, that of the slave rising from the dust, his condition mollifying, the way I hope preparing, under the auspices of heaven, for a total emancipation, and that this is disposed, in the order of events, to be with the consent of the masters, rather than by their extirpation.

BENJAMIN BANNEKER AND THOMAS JEFFERSON

Letter Exchange (1791)

The free black Benjamin Banneker (1731–1806) was an extraordinarily gifted mathematician, astronomer, inventor, and natural historian. His genealogy anticipates the tangled racial genealogies of *Clotel*. Banneker's grandmother on his mother's side, Molly Welsh, was a white Englishwoman who was convicted of a crime and deported to the colony of Maryland as an indentured servant. After serving out her time, she purchased a farm and two slaves, but eventually freed the slaves and married one of them, "Bannaka," who claimed to be an African prince. She and her husband eventually changed their name to "Banneker." Their eldest daughter, Mary, married a slave from Guinea, who took on the name Banneker; their first child was Benjamin. Taught to read and write by Molly, Benjamin also attended Baltimore's Quaker schools. When, as an adult, he gained a reputation as a gifted scientist, some of the local Quakers and other abolitionists began to publicize his achievements in order to challenge racist notions of black inferiority.

Banneker completed his first *Almanac* at age sixty, a compilation of his lifelong astronomical studies. The Quaker publishers of the volume sent a copy to then-Secretary of State Thomas Jefferson, along with Banneker's letter to Jefferson, which challenged the racialist views propounded in *Notes on the State of Virginia* and pointed to the ideological contradictions of the Declaration of Independence. Jefferson seemed genuinely impressed with both the *Almanac* and Banneker's eloquent letter. As he remarked in a subsequent letter of 30 August 1791 to the distinguished French mathematician, the Marquis de Condorcet, Banneker's achievements suggest that "the want of talents observed in them [blacks] is merely the effect of their degraded condition, and not proceeding from any difference in the structure of the parts on which intellect depends." Banneker's letter to Jefferson was regularly reprinted by abolitionists; William Wells Brown printed a version of the exchange in a chapter on Banneker in *The Black Man, His Antecedents, His Genius and His Achievements* (1863). The source of the Banneker letter below is John R. B. Latrobe, *Memoir of Benjamin Banneker* (Baltimore: John D. Toy, 1845), 14–16; Jefferson's letter is taken from *The Works of Thomas Jefferson*, vol. 6, ed. Paul Leicester Ford (New York: G. P. Putnam's Sons, 1904), 309–310.

MARYLAND, BALTIMORE COUNTY
Near Ellicotts' Lower Mills, August 19th, 1791.

THOMAS JEFFERSON, *Secretary of State.*

Sir: — I am fully sensible of the greatness of that freedom, which I take with you on the present occasion, a liberty which seemed to me scarcely allowable, when I reflected on that distinguished and dignified station in which you stand, and the almost general prejudice and prepossession which is so prevalent in the world against those of my complexion.

I suppose it is a truth too well attested to you, to need a proof here, that we are a race of beings who have long laboured under the abuse and censure of the world, that we have long been considered rather as brutish than human, and scarcely capable of mental endowments.

Sir, I hope I may safely admit, in consequence of that report which hath reached me, that you are a man far less inflexible in sentiments of this nature than many others, that you are measurably friendly and well disposed towards us, and that you are ready and willing to lend your aid and assistance to our relief, from those many distressed and numerous calamities, to which we are reduced.

Now, sir, if this is founded in truth, I apprehend you will readily embrace every opportunity to eradicate that train of absurd and false ideas and opinions, which so generally prevails with respect to us, and that your sentiments are concurrent with mine, which are that one universal father hath given being to us all, and that he hath not only made us all of one flesh, but that he hath also without partiality afforded us all the same sensations, and endued us all with the same faculties, and that however variable we may be in society or religion, however diversified in situation or colour, we are all of the same family, and stand in the same relation to him.

Sir, if these are sentiments of which you are fully persuaded, I hope you cannot but acknowledge, that it is the indispensable duty of those who maintain for themselves the rights of human nature, and who profess the obligations of christianity, to extend their power and influence to the relief of every part of the human race, from whatever burthen or oppression they may unjustly labour under, and this I apprehend a full conviction of the truth and obligation of these principles should lead all to.

Sir, I have long been convinced, that if your love for yourselves and for those inestimable laws, which preserve to you the rights of human nature, was founded on sincerity, you could not but be solicitous that every individual of whatever rank or distinction, might with you equally enjoy the blessings thereof, neither could you rest satisfied, short of the most active diffusion of your exertions, in order, to their promotion from any state of degradation, to which the unjustifiable cruelty and barbarism of men may have reduced them.

Sir, I freely and cheerfully acknowledge that I am of the African race, and in that colour which is natural to them of the deepest dye, and it is under a sense of the most profound gratitude to the supreme ruler of the Universe, that I now confess to you, that I am not under that state of tyrannical thraldom, and inhuman captivity, to which too many of my brethren are doomed, but that I have abundantly tasted of the fruition of those blessings, which proceed from that free and unequalled liberty, with which you are favored, and which, I hope you will willingly allow, you have received from the immediate hand of that being, from whom proceedeth every good and perfect gift.

Sir, suffer me to recall to your mind that time in which the arms and tyranny of the British crown were exerted with every powerful effort in order to reduce you to a state of servitude; look back, I entreat you, on the variety of dangers to which you were exposed; reflect on that time in which every human aid appeared unavailable, and in which even hope and fortitude wore the aspect of inability to the conflict, and you cannot but be led to a serious and grateful sense of your miraculous and providential preservation; you cannot but acknowledge, that the present freedom and tranquillity which you enjoy, you have mercifully received, and that it is the peculiar blessing of heaven.

This, sir, was a time in which you clearly saw into the injustice of a state of slavery, and in which you had just apprehension of the horrors of its condition; it was now, sir, that your abhorrence thereof was so excited, that you publicly held forth this true and invaluable doctrine, which is worthy to be recorded and remembered in all succeeding ages. "We hold these truths to be self-evident, that all men are created equal, and that they are endowed by their creator with certain inalienable rights, that among these are life, liberty and the pursuit of happiness."

Here, sir, was a time in which your tender feelings for yourselves had engaged you thus to declare, you were then impressed with proper ideas of the great valuation of liberty, and the free possession of those blessings to which you were entitled by nature; but, sir, how pitiable is it to reflect that although you were so fully convinced of the benevolence of the Father of mankind, and of his equal and impartial distribution of those rights and privileges which he had conferred upon them, that you should at the same time counteract his mercies, in detaining by fraud and violence so numerous a part of my brethren, under groaning captivity and cruel oppression, that you should at the same time be found guilty of that most criminal act, which you professedly detested in others with respect to yourselves.

Sir, I suppose that your knowledge of the situation of my brethren, is too extensive to need a recital here; neither shall I presume to prescribe methods by which they may be relieved, otherwise than by recommending to you and all others, to wean yourselves from those narrow prejudices which you have imbibed with respect to them, and as Job proposed to his friends, "put your souls in their souls stead";[1] thus shall your hearts be enlarged with kindness and benevolence towards them, and thus shall you need neither the direction of myself nor others, in what manner to proceed herein.

And now, sir, although my sympathy and affection for my brethren hath caused my enlargement thus far, I ardently hope that your candour and generosity, will plead with you in my behalf, when I make known to you, that it was not originally my design; but that having taken up my pen in order to direct to you as a present, a copy of an almanac, which I have calculated for the succeeding year, I was unexpectedly and unavoidably led thereto.

This calculation, sir, is the production of my arduous study in this my advanced stage of life; for having long had unbounded desires to become acquainted with the secrets of nature, I have had to gratify my curiosity herein through my own assiduous application to astronomical study, in which I need not to recount to you the many difficulties and disadvantages which I have had to encounter.

And although I had almost declined to make my calculation for the ensuing year, in consequence of that time which I had allotted therefor, being taken up at the Federal Territory, by the request of Mr. Andrew Ellicott,[2] yet finding myself under several engagements to printers of this State, to whom I had communicated my design, on my return to my place of residence, I industriously applied myself thereto, which I hope I have accomplished with correctness and accuracy, a copy of which I have taken the liberty to direct to you, and which I humbly request you will favorably receive, and although you may have the opportunity of perusing it after its publication, yet I choose to send it to you in manuscript previous thereto, that thereby you might not only have an earlier inspection, but that you might also view it in my own hand-writing.

And now, sir, I shall conclude and subscribe myself, with the most profound respect, your most obedient humble servant,

B. BANNEKER.

---

[1] *"put your souls . . . stead"*: Job 16.4.
[2] *Andrew Ellicott*: A surveyor and mathematician from Maryland, Andrew Ellicott (1754–1820) surveyed the site of the national capitol with Banneker's assistance during the early 1790s.

THOMAS JEFFERSON, *Secretary of State. Philadelphia.*

N. B.　Any communication to me, may be had by direction to Mr. Elias Ellicott, merchant, in Baltimore Town.

B. B.

TO BENJAMIN BANNEKER

PHILADELPHIA Aug. 30. 1791.

Sir, — I thank you sincerely for your letter of the 19th instant and for the Almanac it contained. No body wishes more than I do to see such proofs as you exhibit, that nature has given to our black brethren, talents equal to those of the other colors of men, and that the appearance of a want of them is owing merely to the degraded condition of their existence, both in Africa & America. I can add with truth, that no body wishes more ardently to see a good system commenced for raising the condition both of their body & mind to what it ought to be, as fast as the imbecility of their present existence, and other circumstances which cannot be neglected, will admit. I have taken the liberty of sending your Almanac to Monsieur de Condorcet,[3] Secretary of the Academy of Sciences at Paris, and member of the Philanthropic society, because I consider it as a document to which your whole colour had a right for their justification against the doubts which have been entertained of them. I am with great esteem, Sir Your most obedt humble servt.

---

[3] *Condorcet:* The Marquis de Condorcet (1743–1794), a French mathematician and philosopher, was best known for his philosophy of historical progress, particularly his belief in the eventual perfection of man.

DAVID WALKER

From *Walker's Appeal*

David Walker (c. 1790–1830), one of the most influential and controversial black abolitionists of the early national period, was born free in Wilmington, North Carolina, the son of a slave father (who died before his birth) and a free mother. As a free black, he traveled widely in the South and became a vigorous critic of slavery. In 1827 he moved to Boston, opened a clothing store, and served as the Boston sales agent of *Freedom's Journal,* the first African American newspaper. A year later he married Eliza, a fugitive slave, and during the few remaining years of his life engaged in a number of antislavery and antiracist activities, continuing his association with black newspapers, speaking before black organizations, and writing and attempting to disseminate his *Walker's Appeal, in Four Articles, Together with a Preamble, to the Colored Citizens of the World, But in Particular, and Very Expressly to those of the United States of America* (1829). Though the book became notorious for its militant assertion that blacks, when faced with the possibility of enslavement, should "kill or be killed," an assertion that led Southerners to blame Walker for Nat Turner's insurrection of 1831, the overarching intention of the volume was not to push blacks toward a race war (unless whites offered no other choice) but to argue for blacks' rights to freedom and dignity in the United States. In developing his argument, Walker challenged whites' racist assumptions about black inferiority, particularly as set forth in Jefferson's *Notes on the State of Virginia,* attacked African colonizationism, and called for blacks to take responsibility for their moral, educational, and economic uplift. Walker died under uncertain circumstances in 1830. According to legend, he was murdered by white racists, but evidence suggests he died from consumption a week after his daughter succumbed to a similar illness. The *Appeal* remained highly influential among black abolitionists. In 1848 it was republished as part of a volume titled *Walker's Appeal, With a Brief Sketch of His Life. By Henry Highland Garnet. And also Garnet's Address to the Slaves of the United States of America* (New York: J. H. Tobitt), from which the selection below is taken.

My beloved brethren: The Indians of North and of South America — the Greeks — the Irish subjected under the king of Great Britain — the Jews that ancient people of the Lord — the inhabitants of the islands of the sea — in fine, all the inhabitants of the earth, (except however, the sons of Africa) are called *men,* and of course are, and ought to be free. But *we,* (coloured people) and our children are *brutes!!* and of course are and ought to be SLAVES to the American people and their children forever! to dig their mines and work their farms; and thus go on enriching them, from one generation to another with our blood and our tears!!

I promised in a preceding page to demonstrate to the satisfaction of the most incredulous, that we, (colored people of these United States of America) are the *most wretched, degraded* and abject set of beings that ever *lived* since the world began, and that the white Americans

having reduced us to the wretched state of *slavery*, treat us in that condition *more cruel* (they being an enlightened and christian people)
than any heathen nation did any people whom it had reduced to our
condition. These affirmations are so well confirmed in the minds of all
unprejudiced men who have taken the trouble to read histories, that
they need no elucidation from me. But to put them beyond all doubt, I
refer you in the first place to the children of Jacob, or of Israel in
Egypt, under Pharaoh and his people. Some of my brethren do not
know who Pharaoh and the Egyptians were — I know it to be a fact
that some of them take the Egyptians to have been a gang of *devils*, not
knowing any better, and that they (Egyptians) having got possession of
the Lord's people, treated them *nearly* as cruel as *christian Americans*
do us, at the present day. For the information of such, I would only
mention that the Egyptians, were Africans or colored people, such as
we are — some of them yellow and others dark — a mixture of
Ethiopians and the natives of Egypt — about the same as you see the
colored people of the United States at the present day, — I say, I call
your attention then, to the children of Jacob, while I point out particularly to you his son Joseph among the rest, in Egypt.

"And Pharaoh, said unto Joseph, thou shalt be over my house, and
"according unto they word shall all my people be ruled; only in the
"throne will I be greater than thou."

"And Pharaoh said unto Joseph, see, I have set thee over all the land
"of Egypt."

"And Pharaoh said unto Joseph, I am Pharaoh, and without thee
"shall no man lift up his hand or foot in all the land of Egypt."[1]

Now I appeal to heaven and to earth, and particularly to the American people themselves who cease not to declare that our condition is
not *hard*, and that we are comparatively satisfied to rest in wretchedness and misery, under them and their children. Not, indeed, to show
me a colored President, a Governor, a Legislator, a Senator, a Mayor,
or an Attorney at the Bar. — But to show me a man of color, who
holds the low office of a constable, or one who sits in a Juror Box,
even on a case of one of his wretched brethren, throughout this great
Republic!! — But let us pass Joseph the son of Israel a little further in
review, as he existed with that heathen nation.

"And Pharaoh called Joseph's name Zaphnathpaaneah; and he
"gave him to wife Asenath the daughter of Potipherah priest of On.
"And Joseph went out over all the land of Egypt."[2]

---

[1] See Genesis, chap. xli. v. 40, v. 41, v. 44. [Walker's note.]
[2] v. 45. [Walker's note.]

Compare the above, with the American institutions. Do they not institute laws to prohibit us from marrying among whites? I would wish, candidly, however, before the Lord, to be understood, that I would not give *a pinch of snuff* to be married to any white person I ever saw in all the days of my life. And I do say it, that the black man, or man of color, who will leave his own color (provided he can get one who is good for any thing) and marry a white woman, to be a double slave to her just because she is *white*, ought to be treated by her as he surely will be, viz; as a NIGER!!! It is not indeed what I care about intermarriages with the whites, which induced me to pass this subject in review; for the Lord knows, that there is a day coming when they will be glad enough to get into the company of the blacks, notwithstanding, we are, in this generation, levelled by them almost on a level with the brute creation; and some of us they treat even worse than they do the brutes that perish. I only made this extract to show how much lower we are held, and how much more cruel we are treated by the Americans, than were the children of Jacob, by the Egyptians. . . .

But to prove farther that the condition of the Israelites was better under the Egyptians than ours is under the whites. I call upon the professing christians, I call upon the philanthropist, I call upon the very tyrant himself, to show me a page of history, either sacred or profane, on which a verse can be found, which maintains, that the Egyptians heaped the *insupportable insult* upon the children of Israel by telling them that they were not of the *human family.* Can the whites deny this charge? Have they not, after having reduced us to the deplorable condition of slaves under their feet, held us up as descending originally from the tribes of *Monkeys* or *Orang-Outangs?* O! my God! I appeal to every man of feeling — is not this insupportable? Is it not heaping the most gross insult upon our miseries, because they have got us under their feet and we cannot help ourselves? Oh! pity us we pray thee, Lord Jesus, Master. — Has Mr. Jefferson declared to the world, that we are inferior to the whites, both in the endowments of our bodies and of minds? It is indeed surprising, that a man of such great learning, combined with such excellent natural parts, should speak so of a set of men in chains. I do not know what to compare it to, unless, like putting one wild deer in an iron cage, where it will be secured, and hold another by the side of the same, then let it go, and expect the one in the cage to run as fast as the one at liberty. So far, my brethren, were the Egyptians from heaping these insults upon their slaves, that Pharaoh's daughter took Moses, a son of Israel, for her own, as will appear by the following.

"And Pharaoh's daughter said unto her, [Moses' mother] take this
"child away, and nurse it for me and I will pay thee thy wages. And the
"woman took the child [Moses] and nursed it.

"And the child grew, and she brought him unto Pharaoh's daughter
"and he became her son. And she called his name Moses: and she said
"because I drew him out of the water."[3]

In all probability, Moses would have become Prince Regent to the
throne, and no doubt, in process of time but he would have been
seated on the throne of Egypt. But he had rather suffer shame, with the
people of God, than to enjoy pleasures with that wicked people for a
season. O! that the colored people were long since of Moses' excellent
disposition, instead of courting favor with, and telling news and lies to
our *natural enemies,* against each other — aiding them to keep their
hellish chains of slavery upon us. Would we not long before this time,
have been respectable men, instead of such wretched victims of oppression as we are? Would they be able to drag our mothers, our
fathers, our wives, our children and ourselves around the world in
chains and hand-cuffs as they do, to dig up gold and silver for them
and theirs? This question, my brethren, I leave for you to digest; and
may God Almighty force it home to your hearts. Remember that
unless you are united, keeping your tongues within your teeth, you
will be afraid to trust your secrets to each other, and thus perpetuate
our miseries under the *christians!!!!!* [☞ ADDITION, — Remember,
also to lay humble at the feet of our Lord and Master Jesus Christ,
with prayers and fastings. Let our enemies go on with their butcheries,
and at once fill up their cup. Never make an attempt to gain our freedom or *natural right,* from under our cruel oppressors and murderers,
until you see your way clear; when that hour arrives and you move, be
not afraid or dismayed; for be you assured that Jesus Christ the king of
heaven and of earth who is the God of justice and of armies, will surely
go before you. And those enemies who have for hundreds of years
stolen our *rights,* and kept us ignorant of Him and His divine worship,
he will remove. Millions of whom, are this day, so ignorant and avaricious, that they cannot conceive how God can have an attribute of justice, and show mercy to us because it pleased Him to make us black —
which color, Mr. Jefferson calls unfortunate!!!!!! As though we are not
as thankful to our God for having made us as it pleased himself, as
they (the whites) are for having made them white. They think because
they hold us in their infernal chains of slavery that we wish to be

---

[3] See Exodus, chap. ii, v. 9, 10. [Walker's note.]

white, or of their color — but they are dreadfully deceived — we wish to be just as it pleased our Creator to have made us, and no avaricious and unmerciful wretches, have any business to make slaves of or hold us in slavery. How would they like for us to make slaves of, or hold them in cruel slavery, and murder them as they do us? But is Mr. Jefferson's assertion true? viz. "that it is unfortunate for us that our Creator has been pleased to make us black." We will not take his say so, for the fact. The world will have an opportunity to see whether it is unfortunate for us, that our Creator *has made us* darker than the *whites.*

Fear not the number and education of our *enemies,* against whom we shall have to contend for our lawful right; guaranteed to us by our Maker; for why should we be afraid, when God is, and will continue (if we continue humble) to be on our side?

The man who would not fight under our Lord and Master Jesus Christ, in the glorious and heavenly cause of freedom and of God — to be delivered from the most wretched, abject and servile slavery, that ever a people was afflicted with since the foundation of the world, to the present day — ought to be kept with all of his children or family, in slavery, or in chains, to be butchered by his *cruel enemies.* ▱] . . .

I have been for years troubling the pages of historians to find out what our fathers have done to the *white Christians of America,* to merit such condign punishment as they have inflicted on them, and do continue to inflict on us their children. But I must aver, that my researches have hitherto been to no effect. I have therefore come to the immovable conclusion, that they (Americans) have, and do continue to punish us for nothing else, but for enriching them and their country. For I cannot conceive of any thing else. Nor will I ever believe otherwise until the Lord shall convince me.

The world knows, that slavery as it existed among the Romans, (which was the primary cause of their destruction) was, comparatively speaking, no more than a *cypher,* when compared with ours under the Americans. Indeed, I should not have noticed the Roman slaves, had not the very learned and penetrating Mr. Jefferson said, "When a mas-"ter was murdered, all his slaves in the same house or within hearing, "were condemned to death."[4] — Here let me ask Mr. Jefferson, (but he is gone to answer at the bar of God, for the deeds done in his body while living,) I therefore ask the whole American people, had I not rather die, or be put to death than to be a slave to any tyrant, who

[4] See his notes on Virginia. [Walker's note.]

takes not only my own, but my wife and children's lives by the inches? Yea, would I meet death with avidity far! far!! in preference to such *servile submission* to the murderous hands of tyrants. Mr. Jefferson's very severe remarks on us have been so extensively argued upon by men whose attainments in literature, I shall never be able to reach, that I would not have meddled with it, were it not to solicit each of my brethren, who has the spirit of a man, to buy a copy of Mr. Jefferson's "Notes on Virginia," and put it in the hand of his son. For let no one of us suppose that the refutations which have been written by our white friends are enough — they are *whites* — we are *blacks*. We, and the world wish to see the charges of Mr. Jefferson refuted by the blacks *themselves,* according to their chance: for we must remember that what the whites have written respecting this subject, is other men's labors and did not emanate from the blacks. I know well, that there are some talents and learning among the coloured people of this country, which we have not a chance to develope, in consequence of oppression; but our oppression ought not to hinder us from acquiring all we can. — For we will have a chance to develope them by and by. God will not suffer us, always to be oppressed. Our sufferings will come to an *end,* in spite of all the Americans this side of *eternity.* Then we will want all the learning and talents among ourselves, and perhaps more, to govern ourselves. — "Every dog must have its day,"[5] the American's is coming to an end.

But let us review Mr. Jefferson's remarks respecting us some further. Comparing our miserable fathers, with the learned philosophers of Greece, he says: "Yet notwithstanding these and other discouraging "circumstances among the Romans, their slaves were often their rarest "artists. They excelled too in science, insomuch as to be usually em- "ployed as tutors to their master's children; Epictetus, Terence and "Phædrus, were slaves, — but they were of the race of whites. It is not "their *condition* then, but *nature,* which has produced the distinction."[6] See this, my brethren!! Do you believe that this assertion is swallowed by millions of the whites? Do you know that Mr. Jefferson was one of as great characters as ever lived among the whites? See his writings for the world, and public labors for the United States of America. Do you believe that the assertions of such a man, will pass away into oblivion unobserved by this people and the world? If you do you are much mis-

[5] *"Every dog must have its day":* Attributed to John Heywood (1497?–1580?), a British writer known for his proverbs and epigrams.

[6] See his notes on Virginia. [Walker's note.]

taken — See how the American people treat us — have we souls in our bodies? are we men who have any spirits at all? I know that there are many *swell-bellied* fellows among us whose greatest object is to fill their stomachs. Such I do not mean — I am after those who know and feel, that we are MEN as well as other people; to them, I say, that unless we try to refute Mr. Jefferson's arguments respecting us, we will only establish them.

But the slaves among the Romans. Every body who has read history, knows, that as soon as a slave among the Romans obtained his freedom, he could rise to the greatest eminence in the State, and there was no law instituted to hinder a slave from buying his freedom. Have not the Americans instituted laws to hinder us from obtaining our freedom. Do any deny this charge? Read the laws of Virginia, North Carolina, &c. Further: have not the Americans instituted laws to prohibit a man of colour from obtaining and holding any office whatever, under the government of the United States of America? Now, Mr. Jefferson tells us that our condition is not so hard, as the slaves were under the Romans!!!!

It is time for me to bring this article to a close. But before I close it, I must observe to my brethren that at the close of the first Revolution in this country with Great Britain, there were but thirteen States in the Union, now there are twenty-four, most of which are slave-holding States, and the whites are dragging us around in chains and hand-cuffs to their new States and Territories to work their mines and farms, to enrich them and their children, and millions of them believing firmly that we being a little darker than they, were made by our creator to be an inheritance to them and their children forever — the same as a parcel of *brutes!!*

Are we MEN!! — I ask you, O my brethren! are we MEN? Did our creator make us to be slaves to dust and ashes like ourselves? Are they not dying worms as well as we? Have they not to make their appearance before the tribunal of heaven, to answer for the deeds done in the body, as well as we? Have we any other master but Jesus Christ alone? Is he not their master as well as ours? — What right then, have we to obey and call any other master, but Himself? How we could be so *submissive* to a gang of men, whom we cannot tell whether they are as *good* as ourselves or not, I never could conceive. However, this is shut up with the Lord and we cannot precisely tell — but I declare, we judge men by their works.

The whites have always been an unjust, jealous unmerciful, avaricious and blood thirsty set of beings, always seeking after power and authority. — We view them all over the confederacy of Greece, where they were first known to be any thing, (in consequence of education) we see them there, cutting each other's throats — trying to subject each other to wretchedness and misery, to effect which they used all kinds of deceitful, unfair and unmerciful means. We view them next in Rome, where the spirit of tyranny and deceit rated still higher. — We view them in Gaul, Spain and in Britain — in fine, we view them all over Europe, together with what were scattered about in Asia and Africa, as heathens, and we see them acting more like devils than accountable men. But some may ask, did not the blacks of Africa, and the mulattoes of Asia, go on in the same way as did the whites of Europe. I answer no — they never were half so avaricious, deceitful and unmerciful as the whites, according to their knowledge.

But we will leave the whites or Europeans as heathens and take a view of them as christians, in which capacity we see them as cruel, if not more so than ever. In fact, take them as a body, they are ten times more cruel, avaricious and unmerciful than ever they were; for while they were heathens they were bad enough it is true, but it is positively a fact that they were not quite so audacious as to go and take vessel loads of men, women and children, and in cold blood and through devilishness, throw them into the sea, and murder them in all kind of ways. While they were heathens, they were too ignorant for such barbarity. But being christians, enlightened and sensible, they are completely prepared for such hellish cruelties. Now suppose God were to give them more sense, what would they do. If it were possible would they not *dethrone* Jehovah and seat themselves upon his throne? I therefore, in the name and fear of the Lord God of heaven and of earth, divested of prejudice either on the side of my colour or that of the whites, advance my suspicion, whether they are *as good by nature* as we are or not. Their actions, since they were known as a people, have been the reverse, I do indeed suspect them, but this, as I before observed, is shut up with the Lord, we cannot exactly tell, it will be proved in succeeding generations. — The whites have had the essence of the gospel as it was preached by my master and his apostles — the Ethiopians have not, who are to have it in its meridian splendor — the Lord will give it to them to their satisfaction. I hope and pray my God, that they will make good use of it, that it may be well with them. . . .

Oh! coloured people of these United States, I ask you, in the name of that God who made us, have we, in consequence of oppression, nearly lost the spirit of man, and, in no very trifling degree, adopted that of brutes? Do you answer, No? — I ask you, then, what set of men can you point me to, in all the world, who are so abjectly employed by their oppressors as we are by our *natural enemies?* How can, Oh! how can those enemies but say that we and our children are not of the HUMAN FAMILY, but were made by our creator to be an inheritance to them and theirs forever? How can the slave-holders but say that they can bribe the best coloured person in the country, to sell his brethren for a trifling sum of money, and take that atrocity to confirm them in their avaricious opinion, that we were made to be slaves to them and their children? How could Mr. Jefferson but say,[7] "I advance it there-"fore as a suspicion only, that the blacks, whether originally a distinct "race, or made distinct by time and circumstances, are *inferior* to the "whites in the endowments both of body and mind?" "It," says he, "is "not against experience to suppose, that different species of the same "genus, or varieties of the same species, may possess different qualifi-"cations." [Here, my brethren listen to him.] ☞ "Will not a lover of "natural history then, one who views the gradations in all the races of "*animals* with the eye of philosophy, excuse an effort to keep those "in the department of MAN as *distinct* as nature has formed them?" I hope you will try to find out the meaning of this verse — its widest sense and all its bearings: whether you do or not, remember the whites do. This very verse, brethren, having emanated from Mr. Jefferson, a much greater philosopher the world never afforded, has in truth injured us more, and has been as great a barrier to our emancipation as any thing that has ever been advanced against us. I hope you will not let it pass unnoticed. He goes on further and says: "This *unfortu-*"*nate* difference of colour, and *perhaps* of *faculty,* is a powerful ob-"stacle to the emancipation of these people. Many of their advocates, "while they wish to vindicate the liberty of human nature are anxious "also to preserve its *dignity* and *beauty.* Some of these, embarrassed "by the question, 'What further is to be done with them?' join them-"selves in opposition with those who are actuated by sordid avarice "only." Now I ask you candidly, my suffering brethren in time, who are candidates for the eternal worlds, how could Mr. Jefferson but have given the world these remarks respecting us, when we are so submissive to them, and so much servile deceit prevails among our-selves — when we so *meanly* submit to their murderous lashes, to which neither the Indians or any other people under heaven would submit? No, they could die to a man, before they would suffer such things from men who are no better than themselves, and *perhaps not*

---

[7] See his notes on Virginia [Walker's note.]

so good. Yes, how can our friends but be embarrassed, as Mr. Jefferson says, by the question, "What further is to be done with these people?" for while they are working for our emancipation, we are, by our treachery, wickedness and deceit, working against ourselves and our children — helping ours, and the enemies of God, to keep us and our dear little children, in their infernal chains of slavery!! Indeed, our friends cannot but relapse and join themselves 'with those who are actuated by *sordid avarice* only!!!!' For my part, I am glad Mr. Jefferson has advanced his position for your sake; for you will either have to contradict or confirm him by your own actions and not by what our friends have said or done for us; for those things are other men's labors and do not satisfy the Americans who are waiting for us to prove to them ourselves that we are MEN before they will be willing to admit the fact; for I pledge you my sacred word of honor that Mr. Jefferson's remarks respecting us have sunk deep into the hearts of millions of the whites and never will be removed this side of eternity. For how can they, when we are confirming him every day by our *groveling submissions* and *treachery?*

I aver that when I look upon these United States and see the ignorant deceptions and consequent wretchedness of my brethren, I am brought ofttimes solemnly to a stand, and in the midst of my reflections I exclaim to my God, 'Lord didst thou make us to be slaves to our brethren, the whites?' But when I reflect that God is just, and that millions of my wretched brethren would meet death with glory — yea, more, would plunge into the very mouths of cannons and be torn into particles as minute as the atoms which compose the elements of the earth, in preference to a mean submission to the lash of tyrants, I am with streaming eyes, compelled to shrink back into nothingness before my Maker, and exclaim again, thy will be done, O Lord God Almighty. . . .

In conclusion, I ask the candid and unprejudiced of the whole world, to search the pages of historians diligently, and see if the Antediluvians — the Sodomites — the Egyptians — the Babylonians — the Ninevites — the Carthagenians — the Persians — the Macedonians — the Greeks — the Romans — the Mahometans — the Jews[8] — or devils, ever treated a set of human beings, as the white Christians of America do us, the blacks, or Africans. — I also ask the attention of

---

[8] *Antediluvians . . . Jews:* For the most part, references to ancient peoples who once held great power.

the world of mankind to the declaration of these very American people, of the United States.

A Declaration made July 4, 1776.

It says,[9] "When in the course of human events, it becomes neces-
"sary for one people to dissolve the political bands which have con-
"nected them with another, and to assume among the Powers of the
"earth, the separate and equal station to which the laws of nature and
"of nature's God entitle them, a decent respect for the opinions of
"mankind requires that they should declare the causes which impel
"them to the separation. We hold these truths to be self evident, that
"all men are created equal, that they are endowed by their Creator
"with certain unalienable rights; that among these are life, liberty, and
"the pursuit of happiness; that to secure these rights, governments are
"instituted among men, deriving their just powers from the consent
"of the governed; that whenever any form of government becomes
"destructive of these ends it is the right of the people to alter or to
"abolish it, and to institute a new government laying its foundation on
"such principles, and organizing its powers in such form as to them
"shall seem most likely to effect their safety and happiness. Prudence,
"indeed, will dictate that governments long established should not be
"changed for light and transient causes; and accordingly all experience
"hath shewn, that mankind are more disposed to suffer, while evils are
"sufferable, than to right themselves by abolishing the forms to which
"they are accustomed. But when a long train of abuses and usurpa-
"tions, pursuing invariably the same object, evinces a design to reduce
"them under absolute despotism, it is their right, it is their duty to
"throw off such government, and to provide new guards for their
"future security." See your declaration, Americans!! Do you understand your own language? Hear your language, proclaimed to the
world, July 4, 1776 — ☞ "We hold these truths to be self evident —
"that *ALL* MEN ARE CREATED EQUAL! *that they are endowed by their*
"*Creator with certain unalienable rights; that among these are life, lib-*
"*erty, and the pursuit of happiness!!*" Compare your own language
above, extracted from your Declaration of Independence, with your
cruelties and murders inflicted by your cruel and unmerciful fathers on
ourselves on our fathers and on us, men who have never given your
fathers or you the least provocation!!!

Hear your language further! ☞ "But when a long train of abuses
"and usurpations, pursuing invariably the same object, evinces a design

[9] See the Declaration of Independence of the United States. [Walker's note.]

"to reduce them under absolute despotism, it is their *right,* it is their "*duty,* to throw off such government, and to provide new guards for "their future security."

Now, Americans! I ask you candidly, was your sufferings under Great Britain one hundredth part as cruel and tyrannical as you have rendered ours under you? Some of you, no doubt, believe that we will never throw off your murderous government, and "provide new "guards for our future security." If Satan has made you believe it, will he not deceive you?[10] Do the whites say, I being a black man, ought to be humble, which I readily admit? I ask them, ought they not to be as humble as I? or do they think they can measure arms with Jehovah? Will not the Lord yet humble them? or will not these very coloured people, whom they now treat worse than brutes, yet under God, humble them low down enough? Some of the whites are ignorant enough to tell us, that we ought to be submissive to them, that they may keep their feet on our throats. And if we do not submit to be beaten to death by them, we are bad creatures and of course must be damned, &c. If any man wishes to hear this doctrine openly preached to us by the American preachers, let him go into the Southern and Western sections of this country — I do not speak from hearsay — what I have written, is what I have seen and heard myself. No man may think that my book is made up of conjecture — I have travelled and observed nearly the whole of those things myself, and what little I did not get by my own observation, I received from those among the whites and blacks, in whom the greatest confidence may be placed.

The Americans may be as vigilant as they please, but they cannot be vigilant enough for the Lord, neither can they hide themselves, where he will not find and bring them out.

---

[10] The Lord has not taught the Americans that we will not some day or other throw off their chains and hand-cuffs, from our hands and feet, and their devilish lashes (which some of them shall have enough of yet) from off our backs. [Walker's note.]

HENRY CLAY

From *African Colonization*

Jefferson's belief that blacks and whites could never live together in harmony in the United States was a central tenet of the American Colonization Society (ACS), which was founded in December 1816 with the goal of transporting the free blacks to Africa. Among the prominent members of the ACS were Harriet Beecher Stowe's father, Lyman Beecher, and the congressman, nationalist, and perennial presidential candidate from Kentucky, Henry Clay (1777–1852), who would eventually become one of the principal architects of the Compromise of 1850. Clay helped to found the ACS and later served as its president from 1836 until his death in 1852.

The colonizationists conceived of themselves as moderate reformers who were helping to bring about the end of slavery in the U.S. by shipping the nation's blacks to their "natural" home in Africa. In an effort to achieve their goals, the colonizationists purchased land in Africa and founded the country of Liberia. William Lloyd Garrison, Frederick Douglass, and most other abolitionists were infuriated by what they regarded as the ACS's racist agenda of creating a white America. Douglass in particular challenged the claim that blacks were "aliens" in the United States, underscoring in numerous speeches, which were often angrily directed at Clay, that blacks had fought in the American Revolution and helped to develop the nation, and therefore had as much right to U.S. citizenship as whites. Clay, in his speech on African colonization at the 1827 annual meeting of the ACS, called on federal and state legislatures to offer financial support to the Society. In order to make his case for such support, he provided an overview of the ACS's goals and assumptions. The text of the speech is from *The Life, Correspondence, and Speeches of Henry Clay. In Six Volumes*, ed. Calvin Colton, vol. 5 (New York: A. S. Barnes, 1857), 330–33.

It is now a little upward of ten years since a religious, amiable, and benevolent resident of this city,[1] first conceived the idea of planting a colony,[2] from the United States, of free people of color, on the western shores of Africa. He is no more, and the noblest eulogy which could be pronounced on him would be, to inscribe upon his tomb, the merited epitaph, "Here lies the projector of the American Colonization Society."

Among others, to whom he communicated the project, was the person who now has the honor of addressing you. My first impressions, like those of all who have not fully investigated the subject, were

---

[1] *resident of this city:* A reference to Elias B. Caldwell (1776–1825), who was one of the founders of the American Colonization Society.
[2] *colony:* Liberia, founded in 1822 by the American Colonization Society.

against it. They yielded to his earnest persuasions and my own reflections, and I finally agreed with him that the experiment was worthy of a fair trial. A meeting of its friends was called, organized as a deliberative body, and a Constitution was formed. The Society went into operation. He lived to see the most encouraging progress in its exertions, and died in full confidence of its complete success. The Society was scarcely formed before it was exposed to the derision of the unthinking; pronounced to be visionary and chimerical by those who were capable of adopting wiser opinions; and the most confident predictions of its entire failure were put forth. It found itself equally assailed by the two extremes of public sentiment in regard to our African population. According to one (that rash class which, without a due estimate of the fatal consequence, would forthwith issue a degree of general, immediate, and indiscriminate emancipation), it was a scheme of the slaveholder to perpetuate slavery. The other (that class which believes slavery a blessing, and which trembles with aspen sensibility at the appearance of the most distant and ideal danger to the tenure by which that description of property is held), declared it a contrivance to let loose on society all the slaves of the country, ignorant, uneducated, and incapable of appreciating the value or enjoying the privileges of freedom. The Society saw itself surrounded by every sort of embarrassment. What great human enterprise was ever undertaken without difficulty? What ever failed, within the compass of human power, when pursued with perseverance and blessed by the smiles of Providence? The Society prosecuted undismayed its great work, appealing for succor to the moderate, the reasonable, the virtuous, and religious portions of the public. It protested, from the commencement, and throughout all its progress, and it now protests, that it entertains no purpose, on its own authority or by its own means, to attempt emancipation, partial or general; that it knows the general government has no constitutional power to achieve such an object; that it believes that the States, and the States only, which tolerate slavery, can accomplish the work of emancipation; and that it ought to be left to them, exclusively, absolutely, and voluntarily, to decide the question.

The object of the Society was the colonization of the free colored people, not the slaves, of the country. Voluntary in its institution, voluntary in its continuance, voluntary in all its ramifications, all its means, purposes, and instruments, are also voluntary. But it was said that no free colored persons could be prevailed upon to abandon the comforts of civilized life and expose themselves to all the perils of a settlement in a distant, inhospitable, and savage country; that, if they could be induced to go on such a quixotic expedition, no territory could be procured for their establishment as a colony; that the plan was altogether incompetent to effectuate its professed object; and that it ought to be rejected as the idle dream of visionary enthusiasts. The Society has outlived, thank God, all these disastrous predictions. It has survived to swell the list of false prophets. It is no longer a question of speculation whether a colony can or can not be planted from the United States of free persons of color on the shores of Africa. It is a matter demonstrated; such a colony, in fact, exists, prospers, has made successful war, and honorable peace, and transacts all the multiplied business of a civilized and Christian community. It now has about five hundred souls, disciplined troops, forts, and other means of defense, sovereignty over an extensive territory, and exerts a powerful and salutary influence over the neighboring clans.

Numbers of the free African race among us are willing to go to Africa. The society has never experienced any difficulty on that subject, except that its means of comfortable transportation have been inadequate to accommodate all who have been anxious to migrate. Why should they not go? Here they are in the lowest state of social gradation; aliens — political, moral, social aliens — strangers, though natives. There, they would be in the midst of their friends, and their kindred, at home, though born in a foreign land, and elevated above the natives of the country, as much as they are degraded here below the other classes of the community. . . .

The Society has experienced no difficulty in the acquisition of a territory, upon reasonable terms, abundantly sufficient for a most extensive colony. And land in ample quantities, it has ascertained, can be procured in Africa, together with all rights of sovereignty, upon conditions as favorable as those on which the United States extinguish the Indian title to territory within their own limits.

In respect to the alleged incompetency of the scheme to accomplish its professed objects, the Society asks that that object should be taken to be, not what the imaginations of its enemies represent it to be, but what it really proposes. They represent that the purpose of the Society is, to export the whole African population of the United States, bond and free; and they pronounce this design to be unattainable. They declare that the means of the whole country are insufficient to affect the transportation to Africa of a mass of population approximating to two million of souls. Agreed; but that is not what the Society contemplates. They have substituted their own notion for that of the Society. What is the true nature of the evil of the existence of a portion of the

African race in our population? It is not that there are some, but that
there are so many among us of a different caste, of a different physical,
if not moral, constitution, who never can amalgamate with the great
body of our population. In every country, persons are to be found
varying in their color, origin, and character, from the native mass. But
this anomaly creates no inquietude or apprehension, because the
exotics, from the smallness of their number, are known to be utterly
incapable of disturbing the general tranquillity. Here, on the contrary,
the African part of our population bears so large a proportion to the
residue, of European origin, as to create the most lively apprehension,
especially in some quarters of the Union. Any project, therefore, by
which in a material degree, the dangerous element in the general mass,
can be diminished or rendered stationary, deserves deliberate consideration.

The Colonization Society has never imagined it to be practicable, or
within the reach of any means which the several governments of the
Union could bring to bear on the subject, to transport the whole of the
African race within the limits of the United States. Nor is that necessary to accomplish the desirable objects of domestic tranquillity, and
render us one homogeneous people. The population of the United
States has been supposed to duplicate in periods of twenty-five years.
That may have been the case heretofore, but the terms of duplication
will be more and more protracted as we advance in national age; and I
do not believe that it will be found, in any period to come, that our
numbers will be doubled in a less term than one of about thirty-three
and a third years. I have not time to enter now into details in support
of this opinion. They would consist of those checks which experience
has shown to obstruct the progress of population, arising out of its
actual augmentation and density, the settlement of waste lands, etc.
Assuming the period of thirty-three and a third, or any other number
of years, to be that in which our population will hereafter be doubled,
if, during that whole term, the capital of the African stock could be
kept down, or stationary, while that of European origin should be left
to an unobstructed increase, the result, at the end of the term, would
be most propitious. Let us suppose, for example, that the whole population at present of the United States, is twelve millions, of which ten
may be estimated of the Anglo-Saxon, and two of the African race. If
there could be annually transported from the United States an amount
of the African portion equal to the annual increase of the whole of that
caste, while the European race should be left to multiply, we should
find at the termination of the period of duplication, whatever it may

be, that the relative proportions would be as twenty to two. And if the process were continued, during a second term of duplication, the proportion would be as forty to two — one which would eradicate every cause of alarm or solicitude from the breasts of the most timid. But the transportation of Africans, by creating, to the extent to which it might be carried, a vacuum in society, would tend to accelerate the duplication of the European race, who by all the laws of population, would fill up the void space.

This Society is well aware, I repeat, that they can not touch the subject of slavery. But it is no objection to their scheme, limited, as it is, exclusively to those free people of color who are willing to migrate, that it admits of indefinite extension and application, by those who alone, having the competent authority, may choose to adopt and apply it. Our object has been to point out the way, to show that colonization is practicable, and to leave it to those States or individuals who may be pleased to engage in the object, to prosecute it. We have demonstrated that a colony may be planted in Africa, by the fact that an American colony there exists. The problem which has so long and so deeply interested the thoughts of good and patriotic men, is solved; a country and a home has been found to which the African race may be sent, to the promotion of their happiness and our own.

THOMAS R. DEW

From *Review of the Debate in the Virginia Legislature*

In the wake of Nat Turner's bloody slave revolt in Southampton County, Virginia, in August 1831, the Virginia legislature took up the question of slavery during the winter of 1831–32. After considering possibilities for emancipation and colonization, the legislators went on record with their strong support for maintaining slavery in Virginia. This debate can be regarded as a critical turning point in proslavery thinking in the South, as formerly defensive supporters of slavery now began to adopt a more militant and aggressive posture on the centrality of slavery to Southern culture. A professor of political law at the College of William and Mary, Thomas R. Dew (1802–1846) was an interested observer of the debate in the Virginia legislature, and his 1832 tract, *Review of the Debate*, quickly became one of the most influential proslavery documents. It circulated widely during the 1830s and achieved renewed prominence during the 1850s when it was republished in Charleston, South Carolina, as part of a collection of Southern defenses of slavery, *The Pro-Slavery Argument* (1852). In *Review*, Dew challenged Jefferson's notion that slavery gave rise to ugly passions, arguing for slavery's social benefits throughout history. Like many proslavery writers to follow, he asserted that slavery offered distinct advantages to the slave class that simply were unavailable to workers in the Northern market economy, and he saw nothing in slavery that went against the moral precepts of the Bible. Nevertheless, by the late 1830s he came to believe that Virginia would be better off as an all-white state and that slavery was more appropriate to the lower South. The selection is from Thomas R. Dew, *Review of the Debate in the Virginia Legislature of 1831 and 1832* (Richmond, VA: T. W. White, 1832), 106–12.

1st. It is said slavery is wrong, in the *abstract* at least, and contrary to the spirit of Christianity. To this we answer as before, that any question must be determined by its circumstances, and if, as really is the case, we cannot get rid of slavery without producing a greater injury to both the masters and slaves, there is no rule of conscience or revealed law of God which *can* condemn us. The physician will not order the spreading cancer to be extirpated although it will eventually cause the death of his patient, because he would thereby hasten the fatal issue. So if slavery had commenced even contrary to the laws of God and man, and the sin of its introduction rested upon our hands, and it was even carrying forward the nation by slow degrees to final ruin — yet if it were *certain* that an attempt to remove it would only hasten and heighten the final catastrophe — that it was in fact a "vulnus immedicabile"[1] on the body politic, which no legislation could safely remove, then, we would not only not be found to attempt the extirpation, but we would stand guilty of a high offence in the sight of both God and man, if we should rashly make the effort. But the original sin of introduction rests not on our heads, and we shall soon see that all those dreadful calamities which the false prophets of our day are pointing to, will never in all probability occur. With regard to the assertion, that slavery is against the spirit of Christianity, we are ready to admit the general assertion, but deny most positively that there is anything in the Old or New Testament, which would go to show that slavery, when

---

[1] *"vulnus immedicabile"*: Incurable wound.

once introduced, ought at all events to be abrogated, or that the master commits any offence in holding slaves. The children of Israel themselves were slave holders, and were not condemned for it. All the patriarchs themselves were slave holders — Abraham had more than three hundred — Isaac had a "great store"[2] of them, — and even the patient and meek Job himself, had *"a very great household."*[3] When the children of Israel conquered the land of Canaan, they made one whole tribe "hewers of wood and drawers of water,"[4] and they were at that very time under the special guidance of Jehovah; they were permitted expressly to purchase slaves of the heathens, and keep them as an inheritance for their posterity — and even the Children of Israel might be enslaved for six years. When we turn to the New Testament, we find not one single passage at all calculated to disturb the conscience of an honest slave holder. No one can read it without seeing and admiring that the meek and humble Saviour of the world in no instance meddled with the established institutions of mankind — he came to save a fallen world, and not to excite the black passions of men and array them in deadly hostility against each other. From no one did he turn away; his plan was offered alike to all — to the monarch and the subject — the rich and the poor — the master and the slave. He was born in the Roman world, a world in which the most galling slavery existed, a thousand times more cruel than the slavery in our own country — and yet he no where encourages insurrection — he nowhere fosters discontent — but exhorts *always* to implicit obedience and fidelity. What a rebuke does the practice of the Redeemer of mankind imply upon the conduct of some of his nominal disciples of the day, who seek to destroy the contentment of the slaves, to rouse their most deadly passions, to break up the deep foundations of society, and to lead on to a night of darkness and confusion! "Let every man (says Paul), abide in the same calling wherein he is called. Art thou called *being* a servant? care not for it; but if thou mayest be made free use *it* rather." (1 *Corinthians*, vii. 20, 21.) Again; "Let as many servants as are under the yoke, count their own masters worthy of all honor, that the name of God and his doctrines be not blasphemed; and they that have believing masters, let them not despise *them,* because they are brethren, but rather do them service, because they are faithful and beloved partakers of the benefit. These things teach and

[2] *"great store"*: Genesis 26.14.
[3] *"a very great household"*: Job 1.3.
[4] *"hewers of wood and drawers of water"*: Joshua 9.21.

exhort." (1 *Tim.* vi. 1, 2.) Servants are even commanded in Scripture to be faithful and obedient to unkind masters. "Servants, (says Peter,) be subject to your masters with all fear; not only to the good and gentle, but to the froward. For what glory is it if when ye shall be buffeted for your faults ye take it patiently; but if when ye do well and suffer for it, ye take it patiently, this is acceptable with God." (1 *Peter,* ii. 18, 20.) These, and many other passages in the New Testament, most convincingly prove, that slavery in the Roman world was nowhere charged as a fault or crime upon the holder, and everywhere is the most implicit obedience enjoined. . . .

2dly. *But it is further said that the moral effects of slavery are of the most deleterious and hurtful kind;* and as Mr. Jefferson has given the sanction of his great name to this charge, we shall proceed to examine it with all that respectful deference to which every sentiment of so pure and philanthropic a heart is justly entitled.

"The whole commerce between master and slave," says he, "is a perpetual exercise of the most boisterous passions — the most unremitting despotism on the one part, and degrading submission on the other. Our children see this, and learn to imitate it, for man is an imitative animal — this quality is the germ of education in him. From his cradle to his grave, he is learning what he sees others do. If a parent had no other motive, either in his own philanthropy or self love, for restraining the intemperance of passion towards his slave, it should always be a sufficient one that his child is present. But generally it is not sufficient. The parent storms, the child looks on, catches the lineaments of wrath, puts on the same airs in the circle of smaller slaves, gives a loose to his worst of passions, and thus nursed, educated, and daily exercised in the worst of tyranny, cannot but be stamped by it with odious peculiarities."[5] Now we boldly assert that the fact does not bear Mr. Jefferson out in his conclusions. He has supposed the master in a continual passion — in the constant exercise of the most odious tyranny, and the child, a creature of imitation, looking on and learning. But is not this master sometimes kind and indulgent to his slaves? does he not mete out to them, for faithful service, the reward of his cordial approbation? Is it not his interest to do it? and when thus acting humanely, and speaking kindly, where is the child, the creature of imitation, that he does not look on and learn? We may rest assured, in this intercourse between a good master and his servant, more good

---

[5] "The. . . . odious peculiarities": See p. 342 in this volume.

than evil *may* be taught the child; the exalted principles of morality and religion may thereby be sometimes indelibly inculcated upon his mind, and instead of being reared a selfish contracted being, with nought but self to look to — he acquires a more exalted benevolence, a greater generosity and elevation of soul, and embraces for the sphere of his generous actions a much wider field. Look to the slave holding population of our country, and you every where find them characterized by noble and elevated sentiment, by humane and virtuous feelings. We do not find among them that cold, contracted, calculating *selfishness,* which withers and repels every thing around it, and lessens or destroys all the multiplied enjoyments of social intercourse. Go into our national councils, and ask for the most generous, the most disinterested, the most conscientious, and the least unjust and oppressive in their principles, and see whether the slave holder will be past by in the selection. Edwards[6] says that slavery in the West Indies seems to awaken the laudable propensities of our nature, such as "frankness, sociability, benevolence, and generosity. In no part of the globe is the virtue of hospitality more prevalent than in the British sugar islands. The gates of the planter are always open to the reception of his guests — to be a stranger is of itself a sufficient introduction."

Is it not a fact, known to every man in the South, that the most *cruel masters* are those who have been unaccustomed to slavery. It is well known that northern gentlemen who marry southern heiresses, are much severer masters than southern gentlemen. And yet, if Mr. Jefferson's reasoning were correct, they ought to be much milder: in fact, it follows from his reasoning, that the authority which the father is called on to exercise over his children, must be seriously detrimental; and yet we know that this is not the case; that on the contrary, there is nothing which so much humanizes and softens the heart, as this *very authority;* and there are none, even among those who have no children themselves, so disposed to pardon the follies and indiscretion of youth, as those who have seen most of them, and suffered greatest annoyance. There may be many cruel relentless masters, and there are unkind and cruel fathers too; but both the one and the other make all those around them shudder with horror. We are disposed to think that their example in society tends rather to strengthen, than weaken the principle of benevolence and humanity.

---

[6] *Edwards:* A reference to Bryan Edwards (1743–1800), author of *The History of the British Colonies in the West Indies* (1793).

Let us now look a moment to the slave, and contemplate *his* position. Mr. Jefferson has described him as hating, rather than loving his master, and as losing, too, all that *amor patriae* which characterizes the true patriot. We assert again that Mr. Jefferson is not borne out by the fact. We are well convinced that there is nothing but the mere relations of husband and wife, parent and child, brother and sister, which produce a closer tie, than the relation of master and servant. We have no hesitation in affirming, that throughout the whole slave holding country, the slaves of a good master, are his warmest, most constant, and most devoted friends; they have been accustomed to look up to him as their supporter, director and defender. Every one acquainted with southern slaves, knows that the slave rejoices in the elevation and prosperity of his master; and the heart of no one is more gladdened at the successful debut of young master or miss on the great theatre of the world, than that of either the young slave who has grown up with them, and shared in all their sports, and even partaken of all their delicacies — or the aged one who has looked on and watched them from birth to manhood, with the kindest and most affectionate solicitude, and has ever met from them, all the kind treatment and generous sympathies of feeling tender hearts. . . .

The fact is that all of us, and the great author of the Declaration of Independence is like us in this respect, are too prone to judge of the happiness of others by ourselves — we make *self* the standard, and endeavor to draw down every one to its dimensions — not recollecting that the benevolence of the omnipotent has made the mind of man pliant and susceptible of happiness in almost every situation and employment. We might rather die than be the obscure slave that waits at our back, — our education and our habits, generate an ambition that makes us aspire at something loftier — and disposes us to look upon the slave as unsusceptible of happiness in his humble sphere, when he may indeed be much happier than we are, and have his ambition too, — but his ambition is to excel all his fellow slaves in the performance of his servile duties — to please and to gratify his master — and to command the praise of all who witness his exertions. Let the *wily philanthropist,* but come and whisper into the ears of such a slave, that his situation is degrading and his lot a miserable one — let him but light up the dungeon in which he persuades the slave that he is caged — and that moment, like the serpent that entered the garden of Eden, he destroys his happiness and his usefulness. We cannot, therefore, agree with Mr. Jefferson, in the opinion that slavery makes the unfeeling tyrant and the ungrateful dependant; and in regard to

Virginia especially, we are almost disposed, judging from the official returns of crimes and convictions, to assert, with a statesman who has descended to his tomb, (Mr. Giles,)[7] "that the whole population of Virginia, consisting of three *castes* — of free white, free colored, and slave colored population, is the soundest and most moral of any other, according to numbers, in the whole world, as far as is known to me."

[7] *Mr. Giles:* The Virginian politician William Giles (1762–1830) was a strong advocate of slavery and states' rights.

JOHN C. CALHOUN

From *On the Reception of Abolition Petitions*

Between 1836 and 1844, Southern congressmen, in alliance with some Northern supporters, successfully sponsored a series of gag rules that prohibited the reception of antislavery petitions in the House of Representatives. In 1837, Senator John C. Calhoun (1782–1850), a former representative and vice president, took to the floor to defend the legality of the gag rules and to warn abolitionists against trying to meddle in Southern affairs. Having earlier in the decade spearheaded South Carolina's unsuccessful efforts to nullify the federal government's tariff on imports, Calhoun now called on the slave states to resist all efforts by federal legislators to encroach on their right to own property (i.e., slaves). Convinced that slavery was guaranteed by the Constitution, Calhoun, in the course of this famous speech, not only defended the legality of slavery and the gag rules but also propounded his belief that slavery was a "positive good." Influenced by Aristotle and other classical writers, he presented slavery as central to the development of human civilization. Among Calhoun's other influential speeches and writings were "Speech on the Importance of Domestic Slavery" (1838), "Speech on the Slavery Question" (1850), in which he opposed the Compromise of 1850 as an encroachment on states' rights, and *Disquisition on Government,* published posthumously in 1854. The text of "On the Reception of Abolition Petitions, Delivered in the Senate, February 6th, 1837" is from *Speeches of John C. Calhoun, Delivered in the House of Representatives, and in the Senate of the United States,* ed. Richard K. Crallé (New York: D. Appleton and Company, 1864), 629–32.

They who imagine that the spirit now abroad in the North, will die away of itself without a shock or convulsion, have formed a very inadequate conception of its real character; it will continue to rise and spread, unless prompt and efficient measures to stay its progress be adopted. Already it has taken possession of the pulpit, of the schools, and, to a considerable extent, of the press; those great instruments by which the mind of the rising generation will be formed.

However sound the great body of the non-slaveholding States are at present, in the course of a few years they will be succeeded by those who will have been taught to hate the people and institutions of nearly one-half of this Union, with a hatred more deadly than one hostile nation ever entertained towards another. It is easy to see the end. By the necessary course of events, if left to themselves, we must become, finally, two people. It is impossible under the deadly hatred which must spring up between the two great sections, if the present causes are permitted to operate unchecked, that we should continue under the same political system. The conflicting elements would burst the Union asunder, powerful as are the links which hold it together. Abolition and the Union cannot co-exist. As the friend of the Union I openly proclaim it, — and the sooner it is known the better. The former may now be controlled, but in a short time it will be beyond the power of man to arrest the course of events. We of the South will not, cannot surrender our institutions. To maintain the existing relations between the two races, inhabiting that section of the Union, is indispensable to the peace and happiness of both. It cannot be subverted without drenching the country in blood, and extirpating one or the other of the races. Be it good or bad, it has grown up with our society and institutions, and is so interwoven with them, that to destroy it would be to destroy us as a people. But let me not be understood as admitting, even by implication, that the existing relations between the two races in the slaveholding States is an evil: — far otherwise; I hold it to be a good, as it has thus far proved itself to be to both, and will continue to prove so if not disturbed by the fell spirit of abolition. I appeal to facts. Never before has the black race of Central Africa, from the dawn of history to the present day, attained a condition so civilized and so improved, not only physically, but morally and intellectually. It came among us in a low, degraded, and savage condition, and in the course of a few generations it has grown up under the fostering care of our institutions, reviled as they have been, to its present comparatively civilized condition. This, with the rapid increase of numbers, is conclusive proof of the general happiness of the race, in spite of all the exaggerated tales to the contrary.

In the mean time, the white or European race has not degenerated. It has kept pace with its brethren in other sections of the Union where slavery does not exist. It is odious to make comparison; but I appeal to all sides whether the South is not equal in virtue, intelligence, patriotism, courage, disinterestedness, and all the high qualities which adorn our nature. I ask whether we have not contributed our full share of talents and political wisdom in forming and sustaining this political fabric; and whether we have not constantly inclined most strongly to the side of liberty, and been the first to see and first to resist the encroachments of power. In one thing only are we inferior — the arts of gain; we acknowledge that we are less wealthy than the Northern section of this Union, but I trace this mainly to the fiscal action of this Government, which has extracted much from, and spent little among us. Had it been the reverse, — if the exaction had been from the other section, and the expenditure with us, this point of superiority would not be against us now, as it was not at the formation of this Government.

But I take higher ground. I hold that in the present state of civilization, where two races of different origin, and distinguished by color, and other physical differences, as well as intellectual, are brought together, the relation now existing in the slaveholding States between the two, is, instead of an evil, a good — a positive good. I feel myself called upon to speak freely upon the subject where the honor and interests of those I represent are involved. I hold then, that there never has yet existed a wealthy and civilized society in which one portion of the community did not, in point of fact, live on the labor of the other. Broad and general as is this assertion, it is fully borne out by history. This is not the proper occasion, but if it were, it would not be difficult to trace the various devices by which the wealth of all civilized communities has been so unequally divided, and to show by what means so small a share has been allotted to those by whose labor it was produced, and so large a share given to the nonproducing classes. The devices are almost innumerable, from the brute force and gross superstition of ancient times, to the subtle and artful fiscal contrivances of modern. I might well challenge a comparison between them and the more direct, simple, and patriarchal mode by which the labor of the African race is, among us, commanded by the European. I may say with truth, that in few countries so much is left to the share of the laborer, and so little exacted from him, or where there is more kind attention paid to him in sickness or infirmities of age. Compare his condition with the tenants of the poor houses in the more civilized portions of Europe — look at the sick, and the old and infirm slave, on one hand, in the midst of his family and friends, under the kind super-intending care of his master and mistress, and compare it with the for-lorn and wretched condition of the pauper in the poor house. But I will not dwell on this aspect of the question; I turn to the political; and here I fearlessly assert that the existing relation between the two races in the South, against which these blind fanatics are waging war, forms the most solid and durable foundation on which to rear free and stable political institutions. It is useless to disguise the fact. There is and always has been in an advanced stage of wealth and civilization, a con-flict between labor and capital. The condition of society in the South exempts us from the disorders and dangers resulting from this conflict; and which explains why it is that the political condition of the slave-holding States has been so much more stable and quiet than that of the North. The advantages of the former, in this respect, will become more and more manifest if left undisturbed by interference from without, as the country advances in wealth and numbers. We have, in fact, but just entered that condition of society where the strength and durability of our political institutions are to be tested; and I venture nothing in pre-dicting that the experience of the next generation will fully test how vastly more favorable our condition of society is to that of other sec-tions for free and stable institutions, provided we are not disturbed by the interference of others, or shall have sufficient intelligence and spirit to resist promptly and successfully such interference.

ALBERT BARNES

From *An Inquiry into the Scriptural Views of Slavery*

In response to the arguments of writers like Calhoun, who claimed that slavery was a "positive good," Albert Barnes (1798–1870), a Presbyterian clergyman from Philadelphia, published two major antislavery books: *An Inquiry into the Scriptural Views of Slavery* (1846) and *The Church and Slavery* (1857). He was particularly intent on refuting the proslavery notion that slavery was sanctioned by the Bible. Thus he challenged proslavery claims that Abraham and other great patriarchs of the Bible had slaves, that God taught the importance of hierarchy and obedience to masters and slaves alike, and that the account in Genesis of Noah's curse on Ham (despite the fact that Ham is never explicitly described as black) helps to "explain" blacks' putative inferiority. In *Inquiry*, Barnes placed particular emphasis on the New Testament's account of the teachings of Jesus and his disciples, arguing that the advent of Jesus brought a redemptive spirit of love that crossed racial boundaries and in effect redefined human history. Like William Wells Brown, who credited a Quaker with helping him to escape from slavery, Barnes made a special point of emphasizing the truly Christian nature of the Quakers' antislavery commitments. The selection is taken from Albert Barnes, *An Inquiry into the Scriptural Views of Slavery* (Philadelphia: Perkins & Purves, 1846), 344–46, 380–84.

The Christian religion teaches that "God hath made of one blood all the nations of men for to dwell on all the face of the earth," (Acts xvii. 26,) and that as the children of the common Father they are regarded as equal. All the right which one human being has ever been supposed to have over another, in virtue of any superiority in rank, complexion, or blood, is evidently contrary to this doctrine of the Bible in regard to the origin and equality of the human race. The *common nature* which man has, is not affected, in any respect, by the colour of his hair or his skin, by the difference of his stature, by national physiognomy, or by any ethnographical distinctions in the form of the skull. This common nature, as distinct from the brute creation, remains the same under every external appearance, and every form of intellectual and moral development. A man may be wiser or less wise than I am; he may have more or less property; he may have a more richly endowed, or an inferior mental capacity, but this does not affect our common nature. He is in every respect, notwithstanding our difference in these things, as completely a human being as myself; and he stands in precisely the same relations towards the Creator and Father of all. He, like myself, has an immortal soul, and is placed in a state of probation, as a candidate for everlasting happiness or everlasting wo. He has an intellect capable of an endless progression in knowledge; and God has given him the right to improve it to the utmost. He is endowed with a conscience, which, like his immortal intellect, for ever constitutes an impassable line between him and the inferior races of the animal creation. In virtue of this endowment, it is his right and privilege to seek to know the will of God, and to act always with reference to the future state on which he is soon to enter. He is a sinner, and, as such, is placed in substantially the same circumstances with all others before God, in reference to the rewards of heaven or the pains of hell. It was with reference to this *common nature* that redemption was provided. It was our common nature which the Son of God assumed when he became incarnate, and, *in* that assumption, and in all his sufferings for man, he regarded the race as having such a common nature. He was not a *Jew,* except by the accident of his birth; but he was a *man,* and in his human frame there was as distinct a relation to the African and the Malay, as there was to the Caucasian. The blood that flowed in his veins, and that was shed on the cross for human redemption, was the blood of a human being — a descendant of Adam — and had as much reference, when it warmed his heart with benevolence, and when it was shed on the cross, to a descendant of Ham as to the posterity of Japheth or Shem. Every human being has a right to feel that when the Son of God became incarnate he took *his* nature upon him, and to regard him as the representative of that common humanity. It is on the basis of that common nature that the gospel is commanded to be preached to 'every creature,' and any one human being has a right to consider that gospel as addressed to him with as specific an intention as to any other human being whatever. It is on the basis of that common nature also that the Holy Spirit is sent down from heaven to awaken, convict, and convert the soul; and any human being, no matter what his complexion, may regard the promise of the Holy Spirit to be as much addressed to him as to any other one — though that other one may have a more comely form or complexion; may be clothed in the imperial purple, or may wear a coronet, or a crown. In *all respects* pertaining to our common origin; to our nature as distinct from the brute creation; to the fall and to redemption; to the rights of conscience and to the hopes of glory, the human race is regarded in the Bible as on a level. There is an entire system of things which contemplates *man as such* as distinguished from the inferior creation; not one of which pertains to a brute, however near the brute may seem to approximate a human being, and each one of which is as applicable to one human being as to another.

If these views are correct, then all the reliance which the system of slavery has ever been thought to derive from the supposed fact that one class of human beings is essentially inferior to another, is a false reliance. At all events, such views will find no support in the Bible, and they must be left to be maintained by those who recognise the Christian Scriptures as of no authority. A man acting on the views laid down in the Bible on this subject, would never *make* a slave; a man acting on these views would not long *retain* a slave; and Christianity, by laying down this doctrine of the essential equality of the race, has stated a doctrine which *must* sooner or later emancipate every human being from bondage. . . .

The defence of slavery from the Bible is to be, and will soon be abandoned, and men will wonder that any defence of such a system could have been attempted from the word of God. If the authors of these defences could live a little longer than the ordinary term of years allotted to man, they would themselves wonder that they could ever have set up such a defence. Future generations will look upon the defences of slavery drawn from the Bible, as among the most remarkable instances of mistaken interpretation and unfounded reasoning furnished by the perversities of the human mind.

One thing further is settled. If the Bible could be shown to defend and countenance slavery as a good institution, it would make thousands of infidels — for there are multitudes of minds that will see more clearly that slavery is against all the laws which God has written on the human soul, than they would see that a book sanctioning such a system had evidence of divine origin. If slavery is to be defended, it is not to be by arguments drawn from the Bible, but by arguments drawn from its happy influences on agriculture, commerce, and the arts; on the increase of population and national prosperity; on morals and social intercourse; on the military strength which it gives a people; on the smiling villages, the neat dwellings, the school-houses and churches, which it rears and adorns; on its influence in promoting chastity and purity of life; on its elevating the black man, and making him more intelligent and happy than he would be in his own land; on its whole benevolent bearing on the welfare of the slave, in this world and the world to come. Whether these considerations in its favour are sufficient to defend the institution, may be safely left to the results of an examination by those who are disposed to engage in it.

From the whole train of reasoning which I have pursued, I trust it will not be considered as improper to regard it as a position clearly demonstrated, that the fair influence of the Christian religion would everywhere abolish slavery. Let its principles be acted out; let its maxims prevail and rule in the hearts of all men, and the system, in the language of the Princeton Repertory,[1] 'would SPEEDILY come to an end.' In

---

[1] *Princeton Repertory:* Probably a reference to the *Biblical Repertory*, edited by Charles Hodge (1797–1878), who was associated with the Princeton Theological Seminary.

what way this is to be brought about, and in what manner the influence of the church may be made to bear upon it, are points on which there may be differences of opinion. But there is one method which is obvious, and which, if everywhere practised, would certainly lead to this result. It is, *for the Christian church to cease all connection with slavery.* Happily we have, on this subject, one most beautiful and instructive example of what might be done by all Christian churches — the example of the Society of Friends. Humbly commending that example to the churches of the Lord Jesus Christ in this land, as one eminently prudent, Christian, and wise, I would submit this whole argument to the candid judgment of the Christian public, to all who love liberty and value the rights of man.

The history of emancipation among the Quakers is an exceedingly interesting and instructive portion of the history of our country; and in the calm, and prudent, and persevering measures which they have adopted, is probably to be found the true way in which our country can be, and is to be, freed from this great evil. They have aimed at two things — and two only — both of them legitimate, both of them prudent and wise: — *first* to remove slavery from their own body; and *then* to bear their solemn testimony, in regard to the evil, to the world. The first object was pursued year after year by patient and manly discussion, and by faithful and affectionate dealing with their brethren; — and the period at last arrived — a most triumphant period in the history of their body — when they could announce to the world that the evil of slavery was not attached to any portion of their denomination; when there was not a "Friend" who claimed a right of property in his fellow-man. The other object they have as steadily pursued. They have borne, without ambiguity, and without hesitancy, and with nothing of a spirit of denunciation, their 'testimony' in regard to the evil of the system before the world. They offer no forced interference. They use no harsh words. They impugn no man's motives. They interfere with no rights protected by law. But they are a plain-spoken people. They use intelligent language. They do not attempt to blink the subject, or to cover up the evil. They make no apology for slavery; they never speak of it as right; they never speak of it as sanctioned by the Bible; they never even speak of the difficulty of emancipation; they use no metaphysical distinctions on the question whether it is a moral, or a political, or a social wrong, or on the question whether it is in all cases a sin. They leave the impression that *they* regard it as a wrong in every sense of the word, and that they themselves deemed it *so great* a wrong that they were willing to make great sacrifices, that their own denomination might be freed from it totally and for ever; and they leave this solemn testimony to go forth to the world for what it is worth.

Now here, I am persuaded, is a wise model for all other denominations of Christian men, and the true idea of all successful efforts for the removal of this great evil from the land. Let all the evangelical denominations but follow the simple example of Quakers in this country, and slavery would soon come to an end. There is not vital energy enough; there is not power of numbers and influence enough out of the church, to sustain it. Let every religious denomination in the land *detach itself* from all connection with slavery, without saying a word against others; let the time come when, in all the mighty denominations of Christians, it can be announced that the evil has ceased *with them* FOR EVER; and let the voice from each denomination be lifted up in kind, but firm and solemn testimony against the system — with no 'mealy' words; with no attempt at apology; with no wish to blink it; with no effort to throw the sacred shield of religion over so great an evil — and the work is done. There is no public sentiment in this land — there could be none created, that would resist in the power of such testimony. There is no power *out* of the church that could sustain slavery an hour if it were not sustained *in* it. Not a blow need be struck. Not an unkind word need be uttered. No man's motive need be impugned; no man's proper rights invaded. All that is needful is, for each Christian man, and for every Christian church, to stand up in the sacred majesty of such a solemn testimony; to free themselves from all connection with the evil, and utter a calm and deliberate voice to the world, AND THE WORK WILL BE DONE.

MARTIN R. DELANY

Southern Customs — Madame Chevalier

Born in what is now West Virginia, Martin R. Delany (1812–1885) was the son of a free black seamstress and a plantation slave. In the early 1820s he moved to western Pennsylvania, and by the late 1830s he had emerged as an important black leader in Pittsburgh. During the 1840s he edited one of the first black newspapers, *The Mystery,* and in 1847 he became the coeditor of Frederick Douglass's *North Star.* Though he had worked closely with Douglass to support programs of black elevation in the United States, Delany broke with Douglass around the time of the

Compromise of 1850, and in one of his best-known works, *The Condition, Elevation, Emigration, and Destiny of the Colored People of the
United States* (1852), urged African Americans to emigrate to Central and
South America. In the late 1850s and early 1860s he attempted to form a
black colony in Africa but abandoned that plan soon after the outbreak of
the Civil War. During the war he recruited troops for the Union army, and
in 1865 he received a commission as major. Disillusioned with Reconstruction and its aftermath, he spent the final years of his life developing
plans to help Southern blacks emigrate to Africa.

   In their antislavery writings, African American writers, in the tradition
of David Walker, regularly challenged white racists' views of black inferiority. One of the unusual aspects of Delany's essay, which appeared in the
22 June 1849 issue of the *North Star,* the source of this selection, is that it
attacks the antiblack racism of both whites and blacks, warning African
Americans in particular against adopting the racist views of their white
oppressors.

   "Madame Chevalier" as she is called, is a dark mulatto woman of
what the Spanish creoles term as sambo color, and takes her name
from a slaveholding cotton planter in the Red river county not far distant above Compte[1] by the name of Chevalier. This woman has had a
young and interesting daughter, (whose name we forbear to mention
at present lest it may hereafter become a source of annoyance to her,
should she as she solemnly declares she will do, if an honorable opportunity ever occurs, come to the North again to reside,) for several years
at school in the city of Cincinnati, who during the period of Gilmer's
"High School"[2] was a pupil of that institution. I _____ is a comely
and interesting young girl now about fifteen years of age, a pure
Louisiana quadroon of the Japanese complexion. The mother who is a
native Virginian having been taken south when young, eventually
falling into the hands of this man Chevalier, who at once adopted her
as his paramour, for the first time came to Cincinnati in May bringing
two sons, handsome youths of twelve and fourteen with her, for the
purpose of placing them at school at Oberlin and taking her daughter

---

   [1] *Red river county . . . Compte:* Deriving its name from an eighteenth-century
French fort, Compte refers to an area in southeastern Louisiana; the Red River extends
from Texas through Oklahoma to Louisiana.
   [2] *Gilmer's "High School":* The Reverend Hiram S. Gilmore established a school for
blacks, the "Cincinnati High School," in 1844; it was discontinued in 1854.

home with her, as she alleged, to finish her education in a French Seminary at New Orleans.

The daughter, as is customary with Southerners, was sent to Cincinnati without the mother, the father coming and making arrangements in person, during which period she has been under the protection and boarded in the family of a very respectable colored lady, Mrs. T_____ who keeps a reserved private boarding house, while her husband, an enterprising industrious man, trades on the river. But an absence of nearly five years began to give the mother impressions concerning the daughter, which she at once determined to realise — hence the reason of her coming instead of the father, to make arrangements for the education of her boys. Although the paramour and mistress, being herself a slave, like the slaves generally she was uneducated, and if we mistake not unable to read; consequently so incompetent to discharge duties necessary in making arrangements for the education of her boys, that she declined to discharge that duty herself, employing Mrs. T _____ , the guardian of her daughter, to take the youths to Oberlin and make arrangements for their education.

Notwithstanding the ignorance and enslavement of this woman, added to which was the double degradation of her situation in concubinage — yet this wreck of a woman — this creature — this victim of human depravity had great fault to find with Mrs. T _____ , not for any delinquency on her part of attention to the daughter, but forsooth, because she did not prohibit her from the company and society of colored people altogether, except the necessary association with her class at school; with an effrontery only befitting that ignorance the natural offspring of self degradation, this woman, observed to Mrs. T _____ , with indignance — "Me let my daughter associate with such people indeed! why I have *slaves* at home as goodlooking as they!" the pitiable creature, forgetting that she herself at the same time was a slave — intimating, as we learned, although she did not express it in so many words, that she would prefer to see her daughter in *concubinage* to a white, than respectably married to a colored man! Who could believe that slavery was capable of thus reducing to the deepest abyss of degradation the image of God, created a little lower than the angels? — capable of so obscuring the human vision as to induce it to voluntarily close the windows of the soul and shut out the glaring light of Heaven, preferring darkness to light — preferring ignorance to intelligence — preferring disgrace to respectability — misery to happiness, because their deeds are evil and full of corruption.

But why reflect and animadvert upon the conduct of this miserable wretched woman — she is an ignorant bondee — she knew no better, and if she did, she acted precisely as she had been taught by her master and paramour, who in all probability, is but training up the daughter as a superior *rival* to her *mother*. This will not be thought improbable by those acquainted with Southern customs, but the ignorant slave mother little suspects such an event. She is but a type of hundreds of such poor miserable beings who coming to the North disseminate the prejudices instilled into them at the South by the wily slave-holder, whose only object is to effectually prevent concord and union among the colored people. Hence, the frequent silly attempts at the establishment of "Quadroon Societies," "Dead-head Societies,"[3] as one in existence we believe is now termed, and such like ridiculous feints at superiority of descent. But all this has emanated from slavery, ignorance, and arrogance; hence, the impudence and infamy of Madam Chevalier can easily be extenuated, although we may not be so charitably disposed towards those who under far more favorable auspices in the non-slaveholding states, endorse the doctrine and adopt this hideously deformed creature of our oppressors, endeavoring to rear it up in our midst. All that is necessary for us to do is to stamp our foot upon it and crush it level to the earth. We conversed with the young girl of doubtful destination, giving her some good advice, who promised us with tears in her eyes, that if possible, she would return to the embraces of virtue and respectability — protesting that it was not her desire at all to return South, laying the charge of all the consequences upon the shoulders of her mother!

[3] *"Quadroon . . . Dead-head Societies":* A scornful reference to blacks who attempted to "pass" as whites; a "quadroon" was one-fourth (or less) "black."

FREDERICK DOUGLASS

Colorphobia in New York!

Throughout his long career, Douglass regularly attacked the key assumptions informing whites' racial prejudice, particularly the concept of racial difference. In one of his best-known lectures, "The Claims of the Negro Ethnologically Considered" (1854), he contested the views of the racialist ethnologists of the 1840s and 1850s, who made "scientific" assertions about blacks' supposed inferiority to whites and argued for the exclusively white origins of Western civilization (for examples of this sort of writing, see the two selections that follow this one). In response to the ethnologists, Douglass pointedly emphasized the indebtedness of Western culture to black African sources, insisting that the mixing of races and traditions was a fact of human history. Three decades after this famous speech, following the death in 1882 of his wife, Anna, Douglass married a white woman, Helen Pitts, and presented his interracial marriage as a model that might help Americans to transcend their racial hatreds and even the concept of race itself. In an interview printed in the 26 January 1884 *Washington Post,* Douglass declared: "You may say that Frederick Douglass considers himself a member of the one race which exists." In this earlier selection from the 25 May 1849 *North Star,* "Colorphobia in New York!," Douglass boldly points to connections between racial and sexual anxieties.

The fifth of May will long be remembered as the most trying day ever experienced by the unfortunate victims of colorphobia in the city of New York. The disease was never more malignant or general than on that day. The streets were literally crowded with persons of all classes afflicted with this terrible malady. Whole omnibus loads were attacked at the same moment, and their hideous and unearthly howls were truly distressing, excruciating. It will be impossible to describe, or give the reader any correct idea either of the extent of the disease or the agony it seemed to occasion. Like most epidemics, its chief havoc was among the baser sort. The suffering here was fearful and intense. If the genteel suffered from the plague, they managed to suppress and control their feelings better than what are called the "lower orders." But, even here, there could be no successful concealment. The strange plague defied all concealment, and would show itself in spite of veils, white pocket handkerchiefs, parasols, hats, bonnets and umbrellas. In the refined the presence of the plague might be seen by a distortion of the countenance, a red and furious look about the cheek, a singular turn up of the nose, and a *"lower me!"* expression of the eyes.

Among the low and vulgar the symptoms were different; — the hand clinched, head shaking, teeth grating, hysteric yells and horrid imprecation, marked the presence of the disease and the agony of the miserable creatures who were its unfortunate victims. Persons who, at a distance of thirty or forty yards, appeared the very pictures of health, were found, on a nearer approach, most horribly cut and marred.

But the effect upon the outward man was not half so strange and

dreadful as that upon the mind. Here all was utter ruin. GOUGH's description of "delirium tremens"[1] would not be much out of place in
describing one haunted and afflicted with colorphobia. Monsters, gob-
lins, demons, snakes, lizards and scorpions — all that was foul, strange
and loathsome — seized upon their bewildered imaginations. Pointing
with outstretched arm towards us, its victims would exclaim, as if
startled by some terrible sight — "Look! look!" "Where?" "Ah, what?"
"Why?" "Why, don't you see?" "See what?" "Why, that BLACK!
BLACK! *black!*" Then, with eyes turned up in horror, they would exclaim in the most unearthly manner, and start off in a furious gallop —
running all around us, and gazing at us, as if they would read our very
hearts. The whole scene was deeply afflicting and terrible.

But to the cause of this wide-spread plague, or rather the manifestation of it. We think it can all be made plain to the dullest comprehension. There had arrived in New York, a few days previous, two
English LADIES,[2] from London — friends of FREDERICK DOUGLASS —
and had taken apartments at the Franklin House, Broadway; and were
not only called upon at that Hotel by Mr. DOUGLASS, but really
allowed themselves to take his arm, and to walk many times up and
down Broadway, in broad-day light, when that great thoroughfare
was crowded with pure American ladies and gentlemen. Such an open,
glaring outrage upon *pure American* tastes had never before been perpetrated. Two ladies, elegantly attired, educated, and of the most
approved manners, faultless in appearance and position, actually
walking, and leaning upon the arm of a person, with a skin not colored like their own! Oh! monstrous! Was it not enough to cause the
very stones to leap up with indignation from the pavement! and to
"stir them up to mutiny and rage"?[3] More and worse still, these ladies
appeared wholly indifferent to, and oblivious of, all the indignation
and fury going on about them; but walked, talked and acted as though
nothing unusual was passing. In a word, they seemed to forget that

---

[1] *"delirium tremens"*: Trembling and anxiety brought on by an excessive consumption of alchohol; John Gough and other temperance reformers of the day regularly
warned of this condition. See *Clotel*, note 7, p. 168.

[2] *two English* LADIES: The British abolitionist Julia Griffiths (?–1895) and her sister
Eliza Griffiths. In November 1853, William Lloyd Garrison insinuated that Douglass
was sexually involved with Julia Griffiths, who had been living with Douglass and his
wife, Anna, while helping Douglass with the day-to-day operations of *Frederick Douglass' Paper*. Shortly thereafter, Julia returned to England.

[3] *"stir them up to mutiny and rage"?*: Shakespeare, *Julius Caesar* III.vi.64–65.

they were in the greatest Commercial Emporium of this, the mightiest
Nation in the world, and to act as though they had been in the paltry
city of London!! instead of New York. What could they have been
thinking about? How strange that they had not made themselves
acquainted with the institutions and customs of the great Nation,
upon whose sacred soil they were *allowed* to land? How singular that
their friends had not warned them against such a monstrous outrage
upon the established customs of this, the *"freest"* country in the
world? They certainly must have been deceived. It is impossible "that
nature so could err."[4] "Charms, conjuration — mighty magic,"[5] must
have bewildered and misled them. They would have been kindly
received and hospitably entertained by some of the most respectable
and refined families in the city of New York; but, with a strange hallu-
cination, they preferred to identify themselves with the most despised
and injured portion of all the people of America — and thus to make
themselves of no reputation, and cut themselves off from all sympathy
and attention of the highly favored and accomplished sons and daughters of America. Before quitting this subject, we wish to call attention
to certain singular inconsistencies connected with the development of
the feeling, called (erroneously) prejudice against color. The first is
this. The poor creatures who seemed most disturbed by the fact that
these ladies walked through the streets of New York in company with
a colored man, felt in no wise shocked at seeing ladies seated in their
gilded carriages, with colored persons seated near them, driving their
horses and otherwise assisting such ladies. All this was perfectly right.
They were in the capacity of servants. Hence New York toadyism is
rather pleased than disgusted. It is not with colored servants that New
York loafers are displeased; but with colored *gentlemen.* It is with the
colored man as a gentleman that they feel the most intense displeasure.
They cannot bear it, and they must pour out their pent-up wrath,
whenever an opportunity is afforded for doing so.

In this same Franklin Hotel, in which we could not be allowed to dine
on account of our color, we saw a large number of colored waiters in the
nearest proximity to white gentlemen and ladies, without offence.

We, however, tire of this subject. This prejudice is so unjust, unnatural and irrational, that ridicule and indignation seem to be the only
weapons with which to assail it.

---

[4] *"that nature so could err"*: Shakespeare, *Othello* I.viii.18.
[5] *"Charms . . . magic"*: Shakespeare, *Othello* I.iii.101–102.

Our friends informed us that when they landed, they were assured that they had reached the shores of a free country, and were congratulated upon that fact. But they had scarcely reached the hotel, when they were informed that a friend of theirs, who was not deemed unfit to be associated with in London, and who would have been kindly received at the best hotels in that city, and in Paris, would not be allowed to take dinner with them at the Franklin Hotel, in the city of New York. In this free country one is not permitted to choose and enjoy the society of his friends, without being subjected to innumerable insults and annoyances.

We shall not, however, despair on this point. A marked improvement has already taken place in the manner of treating colored travelers, and the change is going on still. Nothing, however, facilitates this more than such examples of fidelity to principle, and indifference to a corrupt and brutal public opinion, as is presented in the conduct of these two English ladies, and others. This prejudice must be removed; and the way for abolitionists and colored persons to remove it, is to act as though it did not exist, and to associate with their fellow creatures irrespective of all complexional differences. We have marked out this path for ourselves, and we mean to pursue it at all hazards.

JOSIAH C. NOTT AND GEORGE R. GLIDDON

From *Types of Mankind*

The late 1830s and 1840s saw an upsurge of writing on human racial differences by highly regarded scientists of what came to be termed the "American School" of ethnology. These ethnologists gained international stature for writings that seemed to offer scientific "proof" of black inferiority and difference. Central to the arguments of many of these writers was the theory of polygenesis — the idea that blacks and whites and other racial groups had had separate moments of divinely induced creation. The scientific racialists supported their theories through the close study of the physical, social, and mental characteristics of peoples of differing racial types. Philadelphia physician and researcher Samuel Morton (1799–1851), president of the Academy of Natural Sciences at Philadelphia, pursued his investigation of racial difference through a comparative analysis of skull size and shape, and emerged as one of the most celebrated founders of the "American School"; his books *Crania Americana* (1839) and *Crania Ægyptiaca* (1844) inspired the researches and writings of the Swiss biologist Louis Agassiz (1807–1873), a professor of zoology and geology at Harvard; Josiah C. Nott (1804–1873), a physician from Mobile, Alabama, who authored *Two Lectures on the Natural History of the Caucasian and Negro Races* (1844); and George R. Gliddon (1809–1857), an Englishman who, while serving as vice-consul at Cairo, examined mummified skulls and concluded that the ancient Egyptians were white. Nott's and Gliddon's researches culminated in *Types of Mankind* (1854), a widely disseminated, massive compendium of "facts" about the races that appeared to offer scientific legitimation to those who would argue for blacks' lower place in the social hierarchy, whether as slaves in the South or as marginalized noncitizens in the North. The selection is taken from J. C. Nott and Geo. R. Gliddon, *Types of Mankind: Ethnological Researches, Based upon the Ancient Monuments, Paintings, Sculptures, and Crania of Races, and upon Their Natural, Geographical, Philological, and Biblical History: Illustrated by Selections from the Inedited Papers of Samuel George Morton, M.D.* (Philadelphia: Lippincott, Grambo & Co., 1854), 49–50, 259–60.

Mr. Luke Burke, the bold and the able Editor of the *London Ethnological Journal*, defines Ethnology to be "a science which investigates the mental and physical differences of Mankind, and the organic laws upon which they depend; and which seeks to deduce from these investigations, principles of human guidance, in all the important relations of social existence." To the same author are we indebted not only for the most extensive and lucid definition of this term, but for the first truly philosophic view of a new and important science that we have met with in the English language.

The term "Ethnology" has generally been used as synonymous with "Ethnography," understood as the Natural History of Man; but by Burke it is made to take a far more comprehensive grasp — to include the whole mental and physical history of the various Types of Mankind, as well as their social relations and adaptations; and, under this comprehensive aspect, it therefore interests equally the philanthropist, the naturalist, and the statesman. Ethnology demands to know what was the primitive organic structure of each race? — what [is] such race's moral and psychical character? — how far a race may have been, or may become, modified by the combined action of time and moral and physical causes? — and what position in the social scale Providence has assigned to each type of man?

Such is the scope of this science — born, we may say, within our own generation — and we propose to examine mankind under the above two-fold aspect, while we point out some of the more salient results towards which modern investigation is tending. The press everywhere teems with new books on the various partitions of the wide field of Ethnology; yet there does not exist, in any language, an attempt, based on the highest scientific lights of the day, at a systematic treatise on Ethnology in its extended sense. MORTON was the first to conceive the proper plan; but, unfortunately, lived not to carry it out; and although the present volume falls very far below the just requirements of science, we feel assured that it will at least aid materially in suggesting the right direction to future investigators.

The grand problem, more particularly interesting to all readers, is that which involves the *common origin* of races; for upon the latter deduction hang not only certain religious dogmas, but the more practical question of the equality and perfectibility of races — we say "more practical question," because, while Almighty Power, on the one hand, is not responsible to Man for the distinct origin of human races, these, on the other, are accountable to Him for the manner in which their delegated power is used towards each other.

Whether an original diversity of races be admitted or not, the *permanence* of existing physical types will not be questioned by any Archæologist or Naturalist of the present day. Nor, by such competent arbitrators, can the consequent permanence of moral and intellectual peculiarities of types be denied. The intellectual man is inseparable from the physical man; and the nature of the one cannot be altered without a corresponding change in the other. . . .

To one living in, or conversant with, the Slave-States of North America, it need not be told, that the Negroes, in ten generations, have not made the slightest physical approach either towards our aboriginal population, or to any other race. As a mnemonic, we here subjoin, sketched by a friend, the likenesses of two Negroes (Figs. 179, 180), who ply their avocations every day in the streets of Mobile; where anybody could in a single morning collect a hundred others quite as strongly marked. Fig. 179 (whose portrait was caught when, chuckling with delight, he was "shelling out corn" to a favorite hog) may be considered caricatured, although one need not travel far to procure, in daguerreotype, features fully as animal; but Fig. 180 is a fair average, sample of ordinary field-Negroes in the United States.

Fig. 179.   Fig. 180.

Mr. LYELL,[1] in common with tourists less eminent, but in this question not less misinformed, has somewhere stated, that the Negroes in America are undergoing a manifest improvement in their physical type. He has no doubt that they will, in time, show a development in skull and intellect quite equal to the whites. This unscientific assertion is disproved by the cranial measurements of Dr. Morton.

That Negroes imported into, or born in, the United States become more intelligent and better developed in their *physique* generally than their native compatriots of Africa, every one will admit; but such intelligence is easily explained by their ceaseless contact with the whites, from whom they derive much instruction; and such physical improvement may also be readily accounted for by the increased comforts with which they are supplied. In Africa, owing to their natural improvidence, the Negroes are, more frequently than not, a half-starved, and therefore half-developed race; but when they are regularly and adequately fed, they become healthier, better developed, and more humanized. Wild horses, cattle, asses, and other brutes, are greatly improved in like manner by domestication: but neither climate nor food can transmute an ass into a horse, or a buffalo into an ox.

One or two generations of domestic culture effect all the improvement of which Negro-organism is susceptible. We possess thousands of the second, and many more of Negro families of the eighth or tenth generation, in the United States; and (where unadulterated by white blood) they are identical in physical and in intellectual characters. No one in this country pretends to distinguish the native son of a

[1] *Mr. LYELL:* Sir Charles Lyell (1797–1875) was an influential British geologist and evolutionary theorist.

Negro from his great-grandchild (except through occasional and ever-apparent admixture of white or Indian blood); while it requires the keen and experienced eye of such a comparative anatomist as Agassiz to detect structural peculiarities in our few African-born slaves. The "improvements" among Americanized Negroes noticed by Mr. Lyell, in his progress from South to North, are solely due to those ultra-ecclesiastical amalgamations which, in their illegitimate consequences, have deteriorated the white element in direct proportion that they are said to have *improved* the black.

SAMUEL A. CARTWRIGHT

From *Diseases and Peculiarities of the Negro Race*

In 1851, *De Bow's Review* featured a four-part series on the "Diseases and Peculiarities of the Negro Race," authored by Samuel A. Cartwright (1793–1862), a respected New Orleans physician and race theorist. Devoted to the promotion of Southern commerce, *De Bow's Review*, the source of this selection, was published in New Orleans from 1846 to 1861 and emerged as one of the most widely influential journals of the period. Cartwright's extended essay on the "peculiarities" of blacks was intended to help masters better manage their slaves. Convinced by the scientific racialists that blacks were of a different "species" from whites, and convinced that slavery was a positive good for blacks and whites alike, Cartwright was unable to imagine a motive for slave flight other than physical or mental illness.

DYSÆSTHESIA ÆTHIOPICA, OR HEBETUDE OF MIND AND OBTUSE SENSIBILITY OF BODY — A DISEASE PECULIAR TO NEGROES — CALLED BY OVERSEERS, "RASCALITY."

Dysæsthesia Æthiopica is a disease peculiar to negroes, affecting both mind and body in a manner as well expressed by dysæsthesia, the name I have given it, as could be by a single term. There is both mind and sensibility, but both seem to be difficult to reach by impressions from without. There is a partial insensibility of the skin, and so great a hebetude[1] of the intellectual faculties, as to be like a person half asleep, that is with difficulty aroused and kept awake. It differs from every other species of mental disease, as it is accompanied with physical signs or lesions of the body discoverable to the medical observer, which are always present and sufficient to account for the symptoms. It is much more prevalent among free negroes living in clusters by themselves, than among slaves on our plantations, and attacks only such slaves as live like free negroes in regard to diet, drinks, exercise, etc. It is not my purpose to treat of the complaint as it prevails among free negroes, nearly all of whom are more or less afflicted with it, that have not got some white person to direct and to take care of them. To narrate its symptoms and effects among them would be to write a history of the ruins and dilapidation of Hayti, and every spot of earth they have ever had uncontrolled possession over for any length of time. I propose only to describe its symptoms among slaves.

From the careless movements of the individuals affected with the complaint, they are apt to do much mischief, which appears as if intentional, but is mostly owing to the stupidness of mind and insensibility of the nerves induced by the disease. Thus, they break, waste and destroy everything they handle, — abuse horses and cattle, — tear, burn or rend their own clothing, and, paying no attention to the rights of property, steal others, to replace what they have destroyed. They wander about at night, and keep in a half nodding sleep during the day. They slight their work, — cut up corn, cane, cotton or tobacco when hoeing it, as if for pure mischief. They raise disturbances with their overseers and fellow-servants without cause or motive, and seem to be insensible to pain when subjected to punishment. The fact of the existence of such a complaint, making man like an automaton or senseless machine, having the above or similar symptoms, can be clearly established by the most direct and positive testimony. That it should have escaped the attention of the medical profession, can only be accounted for because its attention has not been sufficiently directed to the maladies of the negro race. Otherwise a complaint of so common an occurrence on badly-governed plantations, and so universal among free negroes, or those who are not governed at all, — a disease radicated in physical lesions and having its peculiar and well marked symptoms and its curative indications, would not have escaped the notice of the profession. The northern physicians and people have noticed the symptoms, but not the disease from which

[1] *hebetude:* Dulling.

they spring. They ignorantly attribute the symptoms to the debasing influence of slavery on the mind, without considering that those who have never been in slavery, or their fathers before them, are the most afflicted, and the latest from the slave-holding South the least. The disease is the natural offspring of negro liberty — the liberty to be idle, to wallow in filth, and to indulge in improper food and drinks.

In treating of the anatomy and physiology of the negro, I showed that his respiratory system was under the same physiological laws as that of an infant child of the white race; that a warm atmosphere, loaded with carbonic acid[2] and aqueous vapor, was the most congenial to his lungs during sleep, as it is to the infant; that, to insure the respiration of such an atmosphere, he invariably, as if moved by instinct, shrouds his head and face in a blanket or some other covering when disposing himself to sleep; that in sleeping by the fire in cold weather he turns his head to it, instead of his feet, evidently to inhale warm air; that when not in active exercise, he always hovers over a fire in comparatively warm weather, as if he took a positive pleasure in inhaling hot air and smoke when his body is quiescent. The natural effect of this practice, it was shown, caused imperfect atmospherization or vitalization of the blood in the lungs, as occurs in infancy, and a hebetude or torpor of intellect — from blood not sufficiently vitalized being distributed to the brain; also a slothfulness, torpor and disinclination to exercise from the same cause — the want of blood sufficiently vitalized in the circulating system.

When left to himself, the negro indulges in his natural disposition to idleness and sloth, and does not take exercise enough to expand his lungs and to vitalize his blood, but dozes out a miserable existence in the midst of filth and uncleanliness, being too indolent, and having too little energy of mind to provide for himself proper food and comfortable lodging and clothing. The consequence is, that the blood becomes so highly carbonized and deprived of oxygen, that it not only becomes unfit to stimulate the brain to energy, but unfit to stimulate the nerves of sensation distributed to the body. A torpor and insensibility pervades the system; the sentient nerves distributed to the skin lose their feeling in so great a degree, that he often burns his skin by the fire he hovers over without knowing it, and frequently has large holes in his clothes, and the shoes on his feet burnt to a crisp, without having been conscious of when it was done. This is the disease called dysæsthesia — a Greek term expressing the dull or obtuse sensation that always attends the complaint. When aroused from his sloth by the

[2] *carbonic acid:* A weak acid formed when carbon dioxide dissolves in water.

stimulus of hunger, he takes anything he can lay his hands on, and tramples on the rights, as well as on the property of others, with perfect indifference as to consequences. When driven to labor by the compulsive power of the white man, he performs the task assigned to him in a headlong, careless manner, treading down with his feet or cutting with his hoe the plants he is put to cultivate — breaking the tools he works with, and spoiling everything he touches that can be injured by careless handling. — Hence the overseers call it "rascality," supposing that the mischief is intentionally done. But there is no premeditated mischief in the case, — the mind is too torpid to meditate mischief, or even to be aroused by angry passions to deeds of daring. Dysæsthesia, or hebetude of sensation of both mind and body, prevails to so great an extent, that when the unfortunate individual is subjected to punishment, he neither feels pain of any consequence, nor shows any unusual resentment, more than by a stupid sulkiness. In some cases, anæsthesiæ would be a more suitable name for it, as there appears to be an almost total loss of feeling. The term "rascality" given to this disease by overseers, is founded on an erroneous hypothesis, and leads to an incorrect empirical treatment, which seldom or never cures it.

The complaint is easily curable, if treated on sound physiological principles. The skin is dry, thick and harsh to the touch, and the liver inactive. The liver, skin and kidneys should be stimulated to activity and be made to assist in decarbonizing the blood. The best means to stimulate the skin is, first, to have the patient well washed with warm water and soap; then, to anoint it all over with oil, and to slap the oil in with a broad leather strap; then to put the patient to some hard kind of work in the open air and sunshine, that will compel him to expand his lungs, as chopping wood, splitting rails, or sawing with the crosscut or whip saw. Any kind of labor will do that will cause full and free respiration in its performance, as lifting or carrying heavy weights, or brisk walking; the object being to expand the lungs by full and deep inspiration and expirations, thereby to vitalize the impure circulating blood by introducing oxygen and expelling carbon. This treatment should not be continued too long at a time, because where the circulating fluids are so impure as in this complaint, patients cannot stand protracted exercise without resting frequently and drinking freely of cold water or some cooling beverage, as lemonade, or alternated pepper tea sweeted with molasses. In bad cases, the blood has always the appearance of blood in scurvy, and commonly there is a scorbutic[3]

---

[3] *scorbutic:* Showing signs of scurvy, a disease caused by a deficiency of vitamin C and marked by swollen and bleeding gums.

affection to be seen on the gums. After resting until the palpitation of the heart caused by the exercise is allayed, the patient should eat some good wholesome food, well seasoned with spices and mixed with vegetables, as turnip or mustard salad, with vinegar. After a moderate meal, he should resume his work again, resting at intervals, and taking refreshments and supporting the perspiration by partaking freely of liquids. At night he should be lodged in a warm room with a small fire in it, and should have a clean bed with sufficient blanket covering, and be washed clean before going to bed; in the morning, oiled, slapped, and put to work as before. Such treatment will, in a short time, effect a cure in all cases which are not complicated with chronic visceral derangements. The effect of this or a like course of treatment is often like enchantment. No sooner does the blood feel the vivifying influences derived from its full and perfect atmospherization by exercise in the open air and in the sun, than the negro seems to be awakened to a new existence, and to look grateful and thankful to the white man whose compulsory power, by making him inhale vital air, has restored his sensation, and dispelled the mist that clouded his intellect. His intelligence restored and his sensations awakened, he is no longer the *bipedum nequissimus,* or arrant rascal, he was supposed to be, but a good negro that can hoe or plow, and handles things with as much care as his fellow servants.

DANIEL WEBSTER

From *The Constitution and the Union*

On 7 March 1850, Daniel Webster (1782–1852) addressed the Senate on the importance of supporting the Compromise of 1850. By reputation America's greatest orator, and at the time a Whig senator from Massachusetts, Webster was known for his absolute, almost mystical commitment to the idea of Union, and had made his political reputation by attacking the nullification arguments of John C. Calhoun and other Southern politicians. Concerned that abolitionism was pushing the Southern states toward secession, Webster saw the Compromise of 1850 as the best possible hope for preserving the Union, a goal that he regarded as far more desirable than fighting for an immediate end to slavery. Webster, who previously as congressman, presidential candidate, secretary of state, and senator had voiced his opposition to slavery, remained hopeful that slavery in the United States would eventually come to an end. But given what he regarded as the exigencies of the time, he called on his colleagues and constituents to support a bill that, among other things, would make it the legal obligation of all U.S. citizens to return fugitive slaves to their supposed masters. Webster's support for the Compromise of 1850, the passage of which only further heightened sectional tensions, diminished his reputation as a champion of liberty and made him a particular object of wrath among antislavery reformers. In *Clotel*, Brown takes a jab at Webster by noting that the dark-complected senator was sometimes regarded as a black (with the implication that Webster, too, could become a victim of the Fugitive Slave Law). The text of Webster's speech on the compromise, "The Constitution and the Union: A Speech Delivered in the Senate of the United States, on the 7th of March, 1850," is taken from *The Great Speeches and Orations of Daniel Webster, With an Essay on Daniel Webster as a Master of English Style,* ed. Edwin P. Whipple (Boston: Little, 1879), 616–18.

Mr. President, in the excited times in which we live, there is found to exist a state of crimination and recrimination between the North and South. There are lists of grievances produced by each; and those grievances, real or supposed, alienate the minds of one portion of the country from the other, exasperate the feelings, and subdue the sense of fraternal affection, patriotic love, and mutual regard. I shall bestow a little attention, Sir, upon these various grievances existing on the one side and on the other. I begin with complaints of the South. I will not answer, further than I have, the general statements of the honorable Senator from South Carolina,[1] that the North has prospered at the expense of the South in consequence of the manner of administering this government, in the collecting of its revenues, and so forth. These are disputed topics, and I have no inclination to enter into them. But I will allude to other complaints of the South, and especially to one which has in my opinion just foundation; and that is, that there has been found at the North, among individuals and among legislators, a disinclination to perform fully their constitutional duties in regard to the return of persons bound to service who have escaped into the free States. In that respect, the South, in my judgment, is right, and the

---

[1] *Senator from South Carolina:* John C. Calhoun; see the headnote to the selection from Calhoun on p. 371.

North is wrong. Every member of every Northern legislature is bound
by oath, like every other officer in the country, to support the Constitution of the United States; and the article of the Constitution[2] which
says to these States that they shall deliver up fugitives from service is as
binding in honor and conscience as any other article. No man fulfils
his duty in any legislature who sets himself to find excuses, evasions,
escapes from this constitutional obligation. I have always thought that
the Constitution addressed itself to the legislatures of the States or to
the States themselves. It says that those persons escaping to other
States "shall be delivered up," and I confess I have always been of the
opinion that it was an injunction upon the State themselves. When it is
said that a person escaping into another State, and coming therefore
within the jurisdiction of that State, shall be delivered up, it seems to
me the import of the clause is, that the State itself, in obedience to the
Constitution, shall cause him to be delivered up. That is my judgment.
I have always entertained that opinion, and I entertain it now. But
when the subject, some years ago, was before the Supreme Court of
the United States, the majority of the judges held that the power to
cause fugitives from service to be delivered up was a power to be exercised under the authority of this government. I do not know, on the
whole, that it may not have been a fortunate decision.[3] My habit is to
respect the result of judicial deliberations and the solemnity of judicial
decisions. As it now stands, the business of seeing that these fugitives
are delivered up resides in the power of Congress and the national
judicature, and my friend at the head of the Judiciary Committee[4] has
a bill on the subject now before the Senate, which, with some amendments to it, I propose to support, with all its provisions, to the fullest
extent. And I desire to call the attention of all sober-minded men at the
North, of all conscientious men, of all men who are not carried away
by some fanatical idea or some false impression, to their constitutional
obligations. I put it to all the sober and sound minds at the North as a
question of morals and a question of conscience. What right have they,
in their legislative capacity or any other capacity, to endeavor to get
round this Constitution, or to embarrass the free exercise of the rights
secured by the Constitution to the persons whose slaves escape from

---

[2] *article of the Constitution:* Article IV, section 2.
[3] *fortunate decision:* In *Prigg* v. *Pennsylvania* (1842), the Supreme Court upheld
Congress's Fugitive Slave Law of 1793, denying states the right to develop their own legislation on fugitive slaves.
[4] *my friend . . . Committee:* James Murray Mason (1798–1871), U.S. senator from
Virginia. Mason drafted the Fugitive Slave Act of 1850.

them? None at all; none at all. Neither in the forum of conscience, nor before the face of the Constitution, are they, in my opinion, justified in such an attempt. Of course it is a matter for their consideration. They probably, in the excitement of the times, have not stopped to consider of this. They have followed what seemed to be the current of thought and of motives, as the occasion arose, and they have neglected to investigate fully the real question, and to consider their constitutional obligations; which, I am sure, if they did consider, they would fulfil with alacrity. I repeat, therefore, Sir, that here is a well-founded ground of complaint against the North, which ought to be removed, which it is now in the power of the different departments of this government to remove; which calls for the enactment of proper laws authorizing the judicature of this government, in the several States, to do all that is necessary for the recapture of fugitive slaves and for their restoration to those who claim them. Wherever I go, and whenever I speak on the subject, and when I speak here I desire to speak to the whole North, I say that the South has been injured in this respect, and has a right to complain; and the North has been too careless of what I think the Constitution peremptorily and emphatically enjoins upon her as a duty.

GEORGE FITZHUGH

From *Sociology for the South*

In the sectional war of words following the passage of the Compromise of 1850, George Fitzhugh (1806–1881), a lawyer and owner of a small plantation in Virginia, emerged as one of the most influential proslavery writers of the period, centering his defense of slavery on attacking Northern market culture. In his best-known works, *Sociology for the South, or the Failure of Free Society* (Richmond, VA: A. Morris, 1854), the source of this selection, and *Cannibals All!, or Slaves Without Masters* (1857), he contrasted what he presented as the gentle, organicist workings of Southern plantation society to the cutthroat competitive practices of Northern "free" market society. Again and again, in what was actually a rather cogent, class-based attack on capitalist culture, Fitzhugh argued that Northern "wage slaves" were significantly worse off than the South's plantation slaves. Though he had important things to say about the precarious situation of Northern workers, the logic of his position meant that he had to idealize the plantation and present blacks as happy in their place as slaves. Convinced that slavery was a positive good, Fitzhugh, in other of his writings of the 1850s, attempted to transcend issues of race by arguing for the possible value of white slavery as well.

The moral effect of free society is to banish Christian virtue, that virtue which bids us love our neighbor as ourself, and to substitute the very equivocal virtues proceeding from mere selfishness. The intense struggle to better each one's pecuniary condition, the rivalries, the jealousies, the hostilities which it begets, leave neither time nor inclination to cultivate the heart or the head. Every finer feeling of our nature is chilled and benumbed by its selfish atmosphere; affection is under the ban, because affection makes us less regardful of mere self; hospitality is considered criminal waste, chivalry a stumbling-block, and the code of honor foolishness; taste, sentiment, imagination, are forbidden ground, because no money is to be made by them. Gorgeous pageantry and sensual luxury are the only pleasures indulged in, because they alone are understood and appreciated, and they are appreciated just for what they cost in dollars and cents. What makes money, and what costs money, are alone desired. Temperance, frugality, thrift, attention to business, industry, and skill in making bargains are virtues in high repute, because they enable us to supplant others and increase our own wealth. The character of our Northern brethren, and of the Dutch, is proof enough of the justice of these reflections. The Puritan fathers had lived in Holland, and probably imported Norway rats and Dutch morality in the Mayflower.

Liberty and equality are not only destructive to the morals, but to the happiness of society. Foreigners have all remarked on the care-worn, thoughtful, unhappy countenances of our people, and the remark only applies to the North, for travellers see little of us at the South, who live far from highways and cities, in contentment on our farms.

The facility with which men may improve their condition would, indeed, be a consideration much in favor of free society, if it did not involve as a necessary consequence the equal facility and liability to lose grade and fortune. As many fall as rise. The wealth of society hardly keeps pace with its numbers. All cannot be rich. The rich and the poor change places oftener than where there are fixed hereditary distinctions; so often that the sense of insecurity makes every one unhappy; so often, that we see men clutching at security through means of Odd Fellows, Temperance Societies, &c., which provide for members; so often, that almost every State in the Union has of late years enacted laws or countenanced decisions giving more permanency to property. Entails and primogeniture[1] are as odious to us as kings were to the Romans; but their object — to keep property in our families — is as dear to us as to any people on earth, because we love our families as much. Hence laws to exempt small amounts of personal property from liability to debt are daily enacted, and hence Iowa or Wisconsin has a provision in her constitution, that the homestead of some forty acres shall be exempt from execution. Hence, also, the mighty impulse of late in favor of woman's rights. Legislatures and courts are vieing with each other which shall do most to secure married women's rights to them. The ruin of thousands upon thousands of families in the revulsion of 1837,[2] taught the necessity of this new species of entail, this new way of keeping property in the family. The ups and downs of life became too rapid to be agreeable to any who had property to lose or a family to provide for. . . .

But the chief and far most important enquiry is, how does slavery affect the condition of the slave? One of the wildest sects of Communists in France[3] proposes not only to hold all property in common, but to divide the profits, not according to each man's in-put and labor, but according to each man's wants. Now this is precisely the system of domestic slavery with us. We provide for each slave, in old age and in infancy, in sickness and in health, not according to his labor, but according to his wants. The master's wants are more costly and refined, and he therefore gets a larger share of the profits. A Southern farm is the beau ideal of Communism; it is a joint concern, in which the slave consumes more than the master, of the coarse products, and is far happier, because although the concern may fail, he is always sure of a support; he is only transferred to another master to participate in the profits of another concern; he marries when he pleases, because he

[1] *Entails and primogeniture:* The practice of limiting the inheritance of property to a fixed series of possessors, such as first-born sons.

[2] *the revulsion of 1837:* A reference to the U.S. banking crisis of 1837, usually termed the Panic of 1837.

[3] *sects of Communists in France:* A deliberately generalized reference to the various communistic and socialistic groups flourishing in France from the time of the French Revolution to the mid-nineteenth century. Fitzhugh may be referring to the emergence of the 1847 Central Republic Society of Louis August Blanqui (1815–1881) or to the recent upsurge in the U.S. of the utopian socialist communities inspired by Charles Fourier (1772–1837).

knows he will have to work no more with a family than without one, and whether he live or die, that family will be taken care of; he exhibits all the pride of ownership, despises a partner in a smaller concern, "a poor man's negro," boasts of "our crops, horses, fields and cattle;" and is as happy as a human being can be. And why should he not? — he enjoys as much of the fruits of the farm as he is capable of doing, and the wealthiest can do no more. Great wealth brings many additional cares, but few additional enjoyments. Our stomachs do not increase in capacity with our fortunes. We want no more clothing to keep us warm. We may create new wants, but we cannot create new pleasures. The intellectual enjoyments which wealth affords are probably balanced by the new cares it brings along with it.

There is no rivalry, no competition to get employment among slaves, as among free laborers. Nor is there a war between master and slave. The master's interest prevents his reducing the slave's allowance or wages in infancy or sickness, for he might lose the slave by so doing. His feeling for his slave never permits him to stint him in old age. The slaves are all well fed, well clad, have plenty of fuel, and are happy. They have no dread of the future — no fear of want. A state of dependence is the only condition in which reciprocal affection can exist among human beings — the only situation in which the war of competition ceases, and peace, amity and good will arise. A state of independence always begets more or less of jealous rivalry and hostility. A man loves his children because they are weak, helpless and dependent; he loves his wife for similar reasons. When his children grow up and assert their independence, he is apt to transfer his affection to his grand-children. He ceases to love his wife when she becomes masculine or rebellious; but slaves are always dependent, never the rivals of their master. Hence, though men are often found at variance with wife or children, we never saw one who did not like his slaves, and rarely a slave who was not devoted to his master. "I am thy servant!"[4] disarms me of the power of master. Every man feels the beauty, force and truth of this sentiment of Sterne. But he who acknowledges its truth, tacitly admits that dependence is a tie of affection, that the relation of master and slave is one of mutual good will. Volumes written on the subject would not prove as much as this single sentiment. It has found its way to the heart of every reader, and carried conviction along with it. The slave-holder is like other men; he will not tread on the worm nor break

---

[4] "I am thy servant!": From Laurence Sterne (1713–1768), A Sentimental Journey (1768).

the bruised reed. The ready submission of the slave, nine times out of ten, disarms his wrath even when the slave has offended. The habit of command may make him imperious and fit him for rule; but he is only imperious when thwarted or crossed by his equals; he would scorn to put on airs of command among blacks, whether slaves or free; he always speaks to them in a kind and subdued tone. We go farther, and say the slave-holder is better than others — because he has greater occasion for the exercise of the affections. His whole life is spent in providing for the minutest wants of others, in taking care of them in sickness and in health. Hence he is the least selfish of men. Is not the old bachelor who retires to seclusion, always selfish? Is not the head of a large family almost always kind and benevolent? And is not the slave-holder the head of the largest family? Nature compels master and slave to be friends; nature makes employers and free laborers enemies.

The institution of slavery gives full development and full play to the affections. Free society chills, stints and eradicates them. In a homely way the farm will support all, and we are not in a hurry to send our children into the world, to push their way and make their fortunes, with a capital of knavish maxims. We are better husbands, better fathers, better friends, and better neighbors than our Northern brethren. The tie of kindred to the fifth degree is often a tie of affection with us. First cousins are scarcely acknowledged at the North, and even children are prematurely pushed off into the world. Love for others is the organic law of our society, as self-love is of theirs.

Every social structure must have its substratum. In free society this substratum, the weak, poor and ignorant, is borne down upon and oppressed with continually increasing weight by all above. We have solved the problem of relieving this substratum from the pressure from above. The slaves are the substratum, and the master's feelings and interests alike prevent him from bearing down upon and oppressing them. With us the pressure on society is like that of air or water, so equally diffused as not any where to be felt. With them it is the pressure of the enormous screw, never yielding, continually increasing. Free laborers are little better than trespassers on this earth given by God to all mankind. The birds of the air have nests, and the foxes have holes, but they have not where to lay their heads. They are driven to cities to dwell in damp and crowded cellars, and thousands are even forced to lie in the open air. This accounts for the rapid growth of Northern cities. The feudal Barons were more generous and hospitable and less tyrannical than the petty land-holders of modern times.

Besides, each inhabitant of the barony was considered as having some right of residence, some claim to protection from the Lord of the Manor. A few of them escaped to the municipalities for purposes of trade, and to enjoy a larger liberty. Now penury and the want of a home drive thousands to towns. The slave always has a home, always an interest in the proceeds of the soil.

An intelligent New Englander, who was much opposed to negro slavery, boasting of his own country, told us that native New Englanders rarely occupied the place of domestic or body servants, or that of hired day laborers on public works. Emigrants alone served as menials, cleansed the streets, and worked on railroads and canals. New England is busy importing white free laborers for the home market, and catching negroes in Africa for the Brazilian market.[5] Some of the negroes die on the passage, but few after they arrive in Brazil. The masters can't afford to neglect them. Many of the white laborers die on the passage of cholera and other diseases occasioned by filth and crowding — a fourth of them probably in the first year after they arrive, for the want of employment or the neglect of employers. The horrors of the middle passage are nothing to the horrors of a deck passage up the Mississippi when cholera prevails, or the want, penury and exposure that emigrants are subjected to in our large cities. England, too, has a tender conscience about slavery, but she is importing captured African slaves into her colonies to serve as apprentices, and extending this new species of slave trade even to Asia.[6] "Expel nature with a fork, she will soon return."[7] Slavery is natural and necessary, and will in some form insinuate itself into all civilized society. — The domestic slave trade is complained of, and justly too, because it severs family ties. It is one of the evils of slavery, and no institution is without its evils. But how is it with New England? Are none of the free, the delicately reared and enlightened forced to quit the domestic hearth and all its endearments, to seek a living among strangers? Delicacy forbids our dwelling on this painful topic. The instances are before our eyes. What would induce a Virginian, rich or poor, to launch such members of his family unattended on the cold world.

---

[5] *catching negroes . . . Brazilian market:* During the 1850s there were known instances of Northern merchants illegally importing slaves from Africa to Central and South America, but most of these relatively rare cases involved New York merchants.

[6] *England . . . Asia:* A wild exaggeration, as England had banned slavery in its colonies during the 1830s and was actively working to combat the international slave trade.

[7] *"Expel nature with a fork, she will soon return":* From Horace (65 B.C.–8 B.C.), *Epistles,* Book I, Epistle 10.

More than half of the white citizens of the North are common laborers, either in the field, or as body or house servants. They perform the same services that our slaves do. They serve their employers for hire; they have quite as little option whether they shall so serve, or not, as our slaves, for they cannot live without their wages. Their hire or wages, except with the healthy and able-bodied, are not half what we allow our slaves, for it is wholly insufficient for their comfortable maintenance, whilst we always keep our slaves in comfort, in return for their past, present, or expected labor. The socialists say wages is slavery. It is a gross libel on slavery. Wages are given in time of vigorous health and strength, and denied when most needed, when sickness or old age has overtaken us. The slave is never without a master to maintain him. The free laborer, though willing to work, cannot always find an employer. He is then without a home and without wages! In a densely peopled country, where the supply of laborers exceeds the demand, wages is worse than slavery. Oh! Liberty and Equality, to what a sad pass do you bring your votaries!

NEHEMIAH ADAMS

From *A South-Side View of Slavery*

Not all post-Compromise of 1850 defenses of slavery came from the South. A number of Northern merchants and clergy continued to support the institution because they regarded it as central to the nation's economy and general well being. They also shared the racist assumptions of the Southern masters. One of the best-known Northern defenses of slavery came from a Boston Congregationalist minister, Nehemiah Adams (1806–1878), who, after touring the South in the winter of 1854, published *A South-Side View of Slavery; or, Three Months at the South* (Boston: T. R. Marvin, 1854), the source of this selection. Seeking to quell sectional conflict by portraying the Southern masters, and the institution itself, in a good light, Adams attempted to rebut the claims of Harriet Beecher Stowe, William Wells Brown, and other abolitionists, who argued that one of the worst aspects of slavery was the way it brought about the separation of the black family. In lectures of 1854 and 1855, Brown attacked Adams, dubbing him "South-Side Adams," and in 1856 he satirized him in an unpublished drama, "Experience, or, How to Give a Northern Man a Backbone."

The separation of families seems to be an inevitable feature of slavery, as it exists at present. If a man is rich and benevolent, he will provide for his servants, and tax himself to support them, let their number be never so great, buying one plantation after another, chiefly to employ his people. But the time will come when he must die, and his people are deprived of his protection. No one child, perhaps, can afford to keep them together; perhaps he has no children; then they must take their chance of separations to the widest borders of the slave States. But here individual kindness mitigates sorrow and distress. The owner of several plantations at the south, with no children, has made his slaves his heirs, on condition that they remove to Liberia.

It seems to be taken for granted that to be sold is inevitably to pass from a good to an inferior condition. This is as much a mistake as it would be to assert the same of changes on the part of domestic servants in the free States. There are as good masters as those whose death makes it necessary to scatter the slaves of an estate. The change itself is not necessarily an evil.

We must remember that slaves are not the only inhabitants, nor slave families the only families, in the land, that are scattered by the death of others. Sometimes the demand seems to be that slaves should be kept together at all events, and separations never be permitted. This is absurd, upon the least reflection. No one ought to demand or expect for them an experience better or worse than the common lot of men. Let the slaves share with us in the common blessings and calamities of divine providence. What would become of our families of five or ten children should their parents die? Can we keep our children about us always? Do none but black children go to the ends of the Union and become settled there? How many white people there are that do this, who — deplorable truth! — cannot read and write, and seldom if ever hear of their relatives from whom they are separated. Let us not require too much of slavery. Let us not insist that the slaves shall never be separated, nor their families broken up; but let it be done as in the course of nature every where, with no more pain, nor pain of any other kind, than must accrue to those who depend upon their own efforts for a living.

Facts connected with this part of the subject have given me deep respect and sympathy for those slaveholders who, from the number of instances which have come to my knowledge, it is evident are by no means few, that suffer hardship and loss in their efforts to keep the members of their slave families together. Our knowledge of distressing cases, and the indisputable truth that slavery gives the power of disposal to the owner at his will, no doubt leads us to exaggerate the number of cases in which suffering is unjustly inflicted. While we are sure to hear of distressing cruelties, ten thousand acts of kindness are not mentioned. These can not compensate, however, for the liability to abuse which there is in authority almost absolute; but still let us discriminate when we bring charges against a whole community, and let us consider how far the evils complained of are inseparable, not only from a system which is felt to be a burden, but also from human nature in every condition.

As was remarked with regard to sales by auction, it is in vain to expect that painful separations of families in a wanton manner, or by stress of circumstances, can wholly cease, in the present system. It is indeed a burdensome system, destroying itself by its own weight, unless relieved by some of those unnatural and violent expedients. It is deplored for this and other reasons by multitudes at the south, whose voices we shall hear as soon as our relations as north and south are such as will allow them to speak. In the mean time, public sentiment is fast correcting abuses under the system; and not only so, but through its influence and the power of Christian love, the condition of families and individuals among the slaves is becoming here and there as free from evil as human nature permits in a dependent condition.

CAROLINE LEE HENTZ

From *The Planter's Northern Bride*

The publication of Harriet Beecher Stowe's phenomenally popular *Uncle Tom's Cabin* put the South on the defensive and quickly led to the rise of anti-Uncle Tom novels. These novels typically portrayed benign slave masters and contented slaves who thrived in the familial, caring world of the plantation — the world extolled by Fitzhugh and other writers of proslavery tracts. Among the most notable novelistic responses to *Uncle Tom's Cabin* were William Gilmore Simms's *Woodcraft* (1852), Mary H. Eastman's *Aunt Phillis's Cabin* (1852), Maria J. McIntosh's *The Lofty and the Lowly* (1853), and Caroline Lee Hentz's *The Planter's Northern Bride* (1854). Hentz (1800-1856) was a somewhat unlikely person to respond to Stowe. Born and raised in New England, she made her reputation as a domestic novelist who was seemingly unconcerned with issues of slavery and race; her most popular novel, *Linda* (1850), focused on the travails of a young woman who suffers various forms of domestic persecution. Also, while living in Cincinnati in the early 1830s, Hentz belonged to the same literary society as Stowe, the Semi-Colon Club. But in 1834 she moved with her husband, Nicholas Hentz, to Alabama, and she came to adopt a Southern perspective on slavery and sectional conflict. Convinced that she knew slavery far better than Stowe, Hentz wrote a novel that celebrates slavery as an organic institution that values and protects slaves and women.

The selection below, taken from Hentz's, *The Planter's Northern Bride* (Philadelphia: A. Hart, 1854), 498–512, comes at a climactic moment in the novel. Moreland, owner of a slave plantation in Georgia and the hero of the novel, has married the daughter of a Northern abolitionist, Eulalia Hastings, who thus far has been favorably impressed by the workings of the plantation. But Moreland fears the possibility of a slave insurrection, for the apparent abolitionist Reverend Mr. Brainard (who is revealed at the novel's conclusion to be a forger and con man) has been secretly goading the slaves towards rebellion. As Eulalia and Moreland's sister, Ildegerte, look on, Moreland confronts Paul the preacher, Vulcan the blacksmith, and the other restless slaves of his plantation, invoking the heroic fidelity of the deceased slave Dilsy. Also observing the scene is the slave woman Kizzie, who cares for Moreland's children.

A long, winding blast of the bugle-horn summoned the labourers from the field, the carpenter and blacksmith from their shops, the spinsters from their wheels, the weaver from her loom, and emptied, as if by magic, the white-washed cabins. The negroes, one and all, had been told to attend their master's call, expressed by that sounding blast. It was just before the sunset hour, — one of those mild, glowing days, that so often diffuse over the aspect of a Southern winter the blandness of summer and the haziness of autumn. Eulalia and Ildegerte stood in the portico, spectatresses of a scene which made their hearts throb high in their bosoms. Ildegerte's eyes flashed with excitement. Eulalia's cheek was the bed of its coming and vanishing roses. She saw her husband standing, as she had seen him once before, the centre of a dark ring, but she gazed with far different emotions. It could not be said that she feared for him. His superiority was so manifest, that it suggested, at once, the idea of triumph — the triumph of mind over matter. He seemed to her an angel of light surrounded by the spirits of darkness, and, knowing that he was defended by the breastplate of righteousness, she was assured of his safety as well as his power.

Moreland waited till they had all gathered, and they came with halting, lingering steps, very unlike their former cheerful alacrity; then, telling them to follow him, he led the way to the grave of the old prophetess, Dilsy, at whose burial he had made with them a solemn covenant, which *he* had kept inviolate. It was long since any of them had approached the burying-ground. In all their nightly meetings they had avoided passing it, fearing that the spirits of the dead would sweep their cold wings in their faces, or seize them with their stiff and icy fingers, or shriek in their ear some unearthly denunciation. As they walked through the place of graves, the long, dry yellow grass broke and crumpled under their steps, and the brambles twisted round their ankles. They had neglected their dead. The autumn leaves lay thick, damp, and rotting on the sods that covered them, choking the vines and plants, which, in happier hours, had been cultured there.

Moreland stopped by the headstone, which his own hand had placed at Dilsy's grave, and indicated by a commanding gesture the places they were to assume. Paul, the preacher, stood nearest to him, his arms folded on his brawny chest, and his hoary locks of wool bent so low they seemed scattering their powder on the ground. Vulcan, the blacksmith, black and sullen as a thunder-cloud, stood on his left. The women, who had most of them been excluded from the secret deliberations, hung timidly in the rear, curiosity and apprehension struggling in them for mastery. And beyond the edge of the burying-ground, the two children of Moreland, — the one holding the hand, the other borne in the arms of Kizzie, shone in the innocence of infancy and beauty of childhood, on the gloom and duskiness of the scene.

"More than two years have passed," said Moreland, his eyes glancing from face to face, calmly and gravely, as he spoke, "since I stood on this spot, on which the grave-clods had just been thrown, and you all stood around me then, just as you are gathered now. At that hour, I renewed the vows of protection and kindness to you which I uttered, when a boy, in the ear of a dying mother. I told you, if I ever proved unkind, unjust, and tyrannical, if I ever forgot my duties to you as a master and a friend, to meet me here, in this solemn enclosure, and remind me of what I then said. You all promised then, to continue faithful, trustworthy, and obedient, and, judging of the future by the past, I believed you. And yet," he added, his voice deepening into sternness and his eye kindling with indignation, "you have basely deceived me; you have been listening to a traitor and a villain, and plotting against your master and your friend. Under pretence of worshipping God, you have been engaged in the service of Satan, and doing the work of devils. I know all your horrible plans. I know what holiday frolics you are preparing. Which of you has a word to say in his defence? Which of you can look me in the face and say he does not deserve the severest punishment, for treachery and ingratitude to a master as kind and forbearing as I have ever been? Paul, you have taken upon you the office of a preacher of the gospel of peace, who, on all occasions, are the voice of your brethren; look up, speak, and if you have one word to say in your justification and theirs, let us hear it, and hear it quickly."

"No, massa!" cried Paul, slowly raising his head, without lifting his eyes; "got noting to say — noting — only Massa Brainard."

"Poor, deluded creatures!" said Moreland, "poor, blind tools of an artful, selfish, false, and cold-hearted hypocrite, who cares no more for you than the grass you are trampling under your feet. I pity you; for I sent the wretch in your midst, believing him to be a man of God. He has beguiled you with promises of freedom. What is the freedom he can offer you? Nothing but poverty, degradation, and sorrow. If you could compare your condition with those of the free coloured people at the North, you would shudder to think of all that you have escaped. Listen! You are slaves, and I am free; but I neither made you slaves nor myself a free man. We are all in the condition in which we were born. You are black, and I am white; but I did not give you those sable skins, nor myself this fairer complexion. You and I are as God Almighty made us, and, as I expect to give an account of the manner in which I fulfil my duties as a master, so you will be judged according to your fidelity, honesty, and uprightness as servants. The Bible says — 'Can the Ethiopian change his skin?'[1] No, he cannot! but there is no reason why he should have a black heart, because his skin is black. Free! how willingly would I make you free this moment, if, by so doing, I could make you better and happier! Free! I would to heaven you were all free, — then I, too, should be free from a burden made intolerable by your treachery and ingratitude! I would rather, ten thousand times, cultivate these broad fields myself, than be served by faithless hands and false, hollow hearts. I have hands that can work. I would do it cheerfully, if labour was the portion God had assigned me in this world. Better, far better, the toiling limbs, than the aching heart!"

[1] *'Can the Ethiopian change his skin?'*: Jeremiah 13.23.

He paused a moment in indescribable emotion. Among those who were looking earnestly in his face, and drinking in his words with countenances expressive of shame, remorse, and returning devotion, were some who had been the playmates of his childhood, and others in whose arms he had been dandled and caressed when a little boy, and others, again, mere boys now, whom he had made the playthings of his youthful years. He remembered sitting, many and many a time, in the lap of Paul, under an old tree, teaching him to read, while the negro would twist his dark fingers in his childish locks, and pray God Almighty to bless him and make him a blessing to mankind. A sable filament was twisted in every cord that bound him to the past. The associations of bygone years rose above the painful and gloomy present, and it was far more in sorrow than in anger, that he regarded the large family whom the most consummate art had alienated from him.

"Paul," said he, turning to the preacher, whose head was drooping still lower on his breast, and whose cheeks were marked by a wet, shining streak, where silent tears were travelling, "Paul, do you remember Davy, to whom my father gave his freedom many years ago, and who afterwards bought his wife and settled in the State of New York?"

"Yes, massa!"

"Here is a letter, which I received from him a few days since. I will read it. I want you all to listen to it."[2]

Moreland took a letter from his pocket-book and read as follows: —

"DEAR YOUNG MASTER: — I hope you have not forgotten Davy, though you was a little boy when I came away. I'm very sick; the doctor says I can't live long. I'm willing to die; but there's one great care on my mind. I don't want to leave my wife and children here. I've made a considerable property, so they wouldn't be in want; but that ain't all a person wants, master. If I had life before me again, I'd come back myself, for I've never been as happy, or as respectable, as when I lived with old Master. I heard so much talk about the white people at the North being such friends to the blacks, I thought we'd be on perfect equality; but it's no such thing. They won't associate with us; and I never want my wife and children to put themselves on a level with the free negroes I see here, — they are a low, miserable set, and folks that

---

[2] This is a genuine fact, and the gentleman to whom the letter was addressed complied with the request it contained. He arrived just in time, to receive the legacy so solemnly bequeathed, and to comfort, with his presence, the dying negro. [Hentz's note]

respect themselves won't have anything to do with them. My dear young master, please come on, or, if you can't come yourself, send somebody to take back my wife and children, — I have but two daughters, if they were boys I would not care so much. I give them to you, just as if they had never been free. I bequeath you all my property too, and wish it was more. Oh! happy should I be, could I live to see the son of my dear old master before I die, — but the will of God be done. I've got somebody to write this letter for me, for I am too weak to sit up; but I'll put my name to it, that you may know it comes from

DAVY

"If you can't come or send directly, please write a line, just to ease my dying thoughts."

"This letter," said Moreland, "was dictated by one who has tasted the joys of freedom, as it exists among the black people at the North. His condition is far better than the majority, for he has acquired property, while most of them are miserably poor. Listen to me, sons and daughters of Africa! If I thought freedom would be a blessing to you, it should be yours. East, West, or North, anywhere, everywhere, you might go, and I would bid you God speed; but I would as soon send those poor sheep on the hill-side, among ravening wolves, as cast you amid such friends as this pretended minister of God represents! Which of you wants to trust him now? Which of you wants to leave your master and follow him? Tell me, for I will have no Judas in the field, ready to betray his too kind and trusting master!"

"Oh, massa!" exclaimed Paul, — completely subdued and melted, and sinking down on his knees, right on the grave of Dilsy, — "forgive us! Don't send us away! Trust us once more! We've ben 'ceived by Satan, and didn't know what we were doing!"

The moment Paul prostrated himself before his master, all but *one* followed his example, entreating for pardon, and imploring with tears and sobs not to be sent away from him. Vulcan, the blacksmith, stood firm and unmoved as the anvil in his forge. All his dark and angry passions had been whetted on the edge of the murderous weapons hidden beneath his shop, and made red hot by the flames of the midnight furnace. His stubborn knees refused to bend, and a sullen cloud added luridness to his raven-black face.

Moreland and he stood side by side; — all the rest were kneeling. The beams of the departing sun played in golden glory round the brow of Moreland; the negro seemed to absorb the rays, — he looked of more intense, inky blackness.

"Vulcan!" said his master, "if you expect my forgiveness, ask it. Dare to resist me, and you shall feel the full weight of my indignation."

"I'm my own master," cried the blacksmith, in a morose, defying tone. "I ain't a gwine to let no man set his feet on my neck. If the rest are a mind to be fools, let 'em!" and he shook his iron hand over the throng, and rolled his bloodshot eyes, like a tiger ready to spring from its lair.

The face of Moreland turned pale as marble, and lightnings kindled in his eyes. To brute force and passion he had nothing to oppose but moral courage and undaunted will; but he paused not to measure his strength with the muscles swelling out, like twisting serpents, in the negro's brandished arm. Laying his right hand commandingly on his shoulder, he exclaimed: —

"There is but one master here. Submit to his authority, or tremble for the consequences!"

Suddenly wrenching his shoulder from the hand that grasped it, the blacksmith leaped forward, and seizing his master in his gigantic arms, was about to hurl him to the ground, when a tremendous blow on the back of his head laid him prostrate and stunned at Moreland's feet. So sudden had been the attack, so instantaneous the release, that Moreland was hardly conscious how it had been effected, till the sight of Paul, standing with dilated nostrils and panting chest over the fallen giant, and brandishing with both hands a massy rail, which had been lying at the foot of the grave, made him aware who his deliverer was.

"Let me kill 'em, massa — let me kill 'em," cried Paul, swinging the rail above his head, and planting his foot on the broad breast of the rebel.

"Stop!" cried Moreland; "in the name of God, stop! He may be dead already! Let him be carried to the guard-house and there taken care of. Give him in charge to the overseer."

Four of the stoutest negroes sprang forward, eager to show their recovered zeal and loyalty, and lifted up the heavy mass of insensible flesh, which they would have beaten to jelly in their indignation, so powerful was the reaction of their feelings.

"Paul," said Moreland, holding out his hand, "true and faithful servant yet! Let the past be forgotten, or remembered only to forgive!"

"Oh! dear massa!" cried Paul, dropping the rail, and throwing his arms round Moreland's shoulders, he wept and sobbed like a child, — "you're safe and alive yet! Bless a Lord Almighty! Paul's heart always was right, but he got a mighty poor head of hisn."

When Moreland seemed under the ruffian grasp of Vulcan, the women uttered the most terrible screams; but wilder and more piercing than all the rest was the shriek that issued from the portico, that commanded a full view of the scene. Eulalia and Ildegerte, who were standing with arms interlaced, gazing on what to them was an exciting pantomime, for they could not hear one syllable of what was uttered, beheld the giant leaping on his master, and believed it the signal of death. How they reached there they knew not, for the place was at some distance from the house, — but they found themselves forcing their way through the ring just as Paul was weeping on his master's shoulder.

"All is safe!" cried Moreland, as they threw themselves into his arms, clinging to him in an agony of emotion — "all is well! Look up, my Eula! Sister, be not afraid; it is all over! Here is Paul, who is ready to die in my defence."

"Me too, master!" cried Albert, with glistening eye; "Paul struck 'fore I got a chance, or I would have killed him!"

The little golden-brown head of the infant Russell was seen peeping behind the ring, like a sunbeam playing on the cloud-edge. Kizzie, nearly distracted, had pressed as close as possible to the scene of action, after the terrible rebel was secured; and the infant, excited by the tumult, clapped its cherub hands, and glanced its beautiful hazel eyes from face to face with innocent curiosity.

"Bring that child here," said Moreland; and Albert, springing forward, bore it in triumph over the woolly heads between, to his master's extended arms.

"This child," said he, raising it aloft in its smiling beauty, "is your future master. With its first lessons of obedience to his parents and love to his God, he shall be taught his duties to you, and yours to him. Born and brought up in your midst, he will learn to regard you as a part of his own life and soul. I trust, with the blessing of God, he will live to be a better, wiser, kinder master than I have ever been, and watch over your children's interests when I am laid low in the grave."

The infant, delighted with its elevated position, laughed in its glee, while the negroes gazed upon both father and child as beings of a superior world.

The admiration, love, and devotion which the negro feels for the children of a beloved master, is one of the strongest, most unselfish passions the human heart is capable of cherishing. The partition wall of colour is broken down. The sable arms are privileged to wreathe the neck of snow, the dusky lips to press soft kisses on the cheek of living roses. And, though, in after years, the child feels the barrier of distinction drawn by the Creator's hand, in infancy it clings with instinctive affection to the dark bosom that nurses it, and sees only the loving heart through the black and sooty skin. If such are the feelings which infancy usually inspires, it is not strange that the child of such a master as Moreland should be an object of idolatry, for, notwithstanding they had been tempted from their allegiance by the irresistible arts of Brainard, the principles of strong affection and undying loyalty existed in their hearts, and now throbbed with renovated vitality — with the exception of the fierce and rebellious artisan. His was one of those animal natures which, having had a scent of blood in the breeze, snuffed it with savage delight, and, being baffled of its prey, revenged itself for its unslaked thirst in roars of defiance and deeds of violence. He was now, however, incapable of inflicting farther injury. The well-aimed blow of Paul, though not mortal, had caused a terrible concussion in his system, from which he was likely long to suffer; and he was also strongly guarded.

That night the deepest tranquillity brooded over the plantation. The stormy elements were hushed; the late troubled waters subsided into a peaceful yet tremulous expanse. Eula, exhausted by the agitation of the several preceding days, slept as quietly as the babe that rested on her bosom. But no sleep visited the wakeful eyes of Moreland. He went abroad into the stillness, the solemnity and loneliness of night, and beyond the clear and illimitable moonlight, he looked into the darkening future. The clouds of the preceding night were all swept away, and the moon glided, slowly, majestically, radiantly over the blue and boundless firmament, a solitary bark of silver navigating the unfathomable ocean of ether. Moreland walked through the long rows of cabins, whose whitewashed walls reflected, with intense brightness, the light that illumined them, and envied the repose of the occupants. The signs of the times were dark, and portentous of disunion and ruin. The lightnings might be sheathed, but they were ready, at any moment, to rend the cloud and dart their fiery bolts around. Supposing, for one moment, the full triumph of fanaticism, how fearful would be the result! The emancipation of brute force; the reign of animal passion and power; the wisdom of eighteen centuries buried under waves of barbarism, rolling back upon the world; the beautiful cotton-fields of the South left neglected and overgrown with weeds; the looms of the North idle for want of the downy fleece, and England, in all her pride and might, bleeding from the wound her own hands had inflicted. None but the native of a tropic zone, physically constructed to endure the heat of a Southern clime, can cultivate its soil and raise its staple products. That the African, *unguided by the white man's influence,* would suffer the fairest portions of God's earth to become uncultivated wildernesses, let St. Domingo, Jamaica, and the emancipated islands bear witness. Suppose the triumph of fanaticism, agriculture would inevitably languish and die; the negro, as well as the white man, would not only sink into an abyss of poverty and ruin, but the withered energies, the decaying commerce, and expiring manufactures of the North would show the interests of the two different sections of our common country to be connected by as vital a ligament as that which unites the twin-born brothers of Siam. Let the death-stroke pierce the bosom of one, the other must soon become a livid and putrifying corpse.

HARRIET JACOBS

What Slaves Are Taught to Think of the North

The author of the best-known slave narrative written by an African American woman, *Incidents in the Life of a Slave Girl,* Harriet Jacobs (1813–1897) was born a slave in Edenton, North Carolina, and, as she documents in *Incidents,* was sexually pursued by her slave master for a number of years. Eventually she chose to counter his advances by becoming sexually involved with a local white lawyer, with whom she had two children. In an amazing (and ultimately successful) effort to escape from slavery, she hid in the cramped crawl space of her grandmother's cabin for nearly seven years, and in 1842 finally made her way to New York City. By the 1850s, after she was reunited with her children, she became involved with the antislavery movement, and in 1861 published *Incidents* with the help of Lydia Maria Child, who served as her editor. During the Civil War and Reconstruction, she worked with her daughter to help the freed slaves. In this chapter from *Incidents,* Jacobs initially criticizes Southerners' attempts to deceive the slaves about life in the North. But the critique quickly enlarges to implicate all of white America in the South's racist efforts to justify blacks' enslaved and disenfranchised status in the United States. The selection is from *Incidents in the Life of a Slave Girl: Written by Herself,* ed. L. Maria Child (Boston: Published for the Author, 1861), 67–70.

Slaveholders pride themselves upon being honorable men; but if you were to hear the enormous lies they tell their slaves, you would have small respect for their veracity. I have spoken plain English. Pardon me. I cannot use a milder term. When they visit the north, and return home, they tell their slaves of the runaways they have seen, and describe them to be in the most deplorable condition. A slaveholder once told me that he had seen a runaway friend of mine in New York, and that she besought him to take her back to her master, for she was literally dying of starvation; that many days she had only one cold potato to eat, and at other times could get nothing at all. He said he refused to take her, because he knew her master would not thank him for bringing such a miserable wretch to his house. He ended by saying to me, "This is the punishment she brought on herself for running away from a kind master."

This whole story was false. I afterwards staid with that friend in New York, and found her in comfortable circumstances. She had never thought of such a thing as wishing to go back to slavery. Many of the slaves believe such stories, and think it is not worth while to exchange slavery for such a hard kind of freedom. It is difficult to persuade such that freedom could make them useful men, and enable them to protect their wives and children. If those heathen in our Christian land had as much teaching as some Hindoos, they would think otherwise. They would know that liberty is more valuable than life. They would begin to understand their own capabilities, and exert themselves to become men and women.

But while the Free States sustain a law which hurls fugitives back into slavery, how can the slaves resolve to become men? There are some who strive to protect wives and daughters from the insults of their masters; but those who have such sentiments have had advantages above the general mass of slaves. They have been partially civilized and Christianized by favorable circumstances. Some are bold enough to *utter* such sentiments to their masters. O, that there were more of them!

Some poor creatures have been so brutalized by the lash that they will sneak out of the way to give their masters free access to their wives and daughters. Do you think this proves the black man to belong to an inferior order of beings? What would *you* be, if you had been born and brought up a slave, with generations of slaves for ancestors? I admit that the black man *is* inferior. But what is it that makes him so? It is the ignorance in which white men compel him to live; it is the torturing whip that lashes manhood out of him; it is the fierce blood-hounds of the South, and the scarcely less cruel human bloodhounds of the north, who enforce the Fugitive Slave Law. *They* do the work.

Southern gentlemen indulge in the most contemptuous expressions about the Yankees, while they, on their part, consent to do the vilest work for them, such as the ferocious bloodhounds and the despised negro-hunters are employed to do at home. When southerners go to the north, they are proud to do them honor; but the northern man is not welcome south of Mason and Dixon's line,[1] unless he suppresses every thought and feeling at variance with their "peculiar institution." Nor is it enough to be silent. The masters are not pleased, unless they obtain a greater degree of subservience than that; and they are generally accommodated. Do they respect the northerner for this? I trow[2] not. Even the slaves despise "a northern man with southern principles;" and that is the class they generally see. When northerners go to the south to reside, they prove very apt scholars. They soon imbibe the sentiments and disposition of their neighbors, and generally go beyond their teachers. Of the two, they are proverbially the hardest masters.

They seem to satisfy their consciences with the doctrine that God created the Africans to be slaves. What a libel upon the heavenly Father, who "made of one blood all nations of men!" And then who *are* Africans? Who can measure the amount of Anglo-Saxon blood coursing in the veins of American slaves?

I have spoken of the pains slaveholders take to give their slaves a bad opinion of the north; but, notwithstanding this, intelligent slaves are aware that they have many friends in the Free States. Even the most ignorant have some confused notions about it. They knew that I could read; and I was often asked if I had seen any thing in the news-papers about white folks over in the big north, who were trying to get their freedom for them. Some believe that the abolitionists have already made them free, and that it is established by law, but that their masters prevent the law from going into effect. One woman begged me to get a newspaper and read it over. She said her husband told her that

---

[1] *Mason and Dixon's line:* Running between Pennsylvania and Maryland, the Mason-Dixon line was initially surveyed by Charles Mason (1730?–1787) and Jeremiah Dixon (1733–1779) between 1763 and 1767. By the early nineteenth century, the line was taken to mark the boundary between the free and slaveholding states.
[2] *trow:* Believe.

the black people had sent word to the queen of 'Merica that they were all slaves; that she didn't believe it, and went to Washington city to see the president about it. They quarrelled; she drew her sword upon him, and swore that he should help her to make them all free.

That poor, ignorant woman thought that America was governed by a Queen, to whom the President was subordinate. I wish the President was subordinate to Queen Justice.

WALT WHITMAN

Prohibition of Colored Persons

In his great epic poem "Song of Myself" (1855), Walt Whitman (1819–1892) imagines himself as a loving harborer of a fugitive slave and then as the fugitive slave himself: "I am the hounded slave, I wince at the bite of the dogs, / Hell and despair are upon me" (60). The slave's agonies become Whitman's agonies and thus to a certain extent the reader's agonies as well. Such dramatic poetic moments constitute Whitman's most sympathetic representations of African Americans. Though opposed to slavery, the New Yorker Whitman, son of a carpenter of radical political bent, was also committed to promoting the welfare of Northern white laborers. Like many white workers, Whitman not only regarded slavery as a threat to free labor but he also viewed free blacks as a threat to white men's ability to find good jobs. In "Prohibition of Colored Persons," his 1858 editorial on Oregon's proposed constitution, which simultaneously banned slavery and made it illegal for free blacks to enter the state, he sided with the white laboring classes, imagining a future in which every U.S. citizen was white. In 1859, Oregon was admitted as the thirty-third state with precisely the constitution that Whitman supported. Whitman's views on the undesirability and unnaturalness of "amalgamation" among whites and blacks of the United States are reminiscent of Jefferson's views on the subject. His rhetorical insistence on the impossibility of amalgamation between blacks and whites was of course belied by the very existence of Frederick Douglass, William Wells Brown, and the hundreds of thousands of other mixed-race individuals in the Americas, and is at odds with the more transgressive and humane energies of his poetry. Whitman's editorial appeared in the 6 May 1858 issue of the Brooklyn *Daily Times,* the source of this selection.

The new Constitution of Oregon prohibits colored persons, either slave or free, from entering the State — making an exclusively white population. This is objected to by several of the abolition Senators in the U.S. Senate — Mr. Hale[1] and others. Mr. Seward,[2] however, is going to vote in favor of the Constitution.

We shouldn't wonder if this sort of total prohibition of colored persons became quite a common thing in new Western, Northwestern, and even Southwestern States. If so, the whole matter of slavery agitation will assume another phase, different from any phase yet. It will be a conflict between the totality of White Labor, on the one side, and, on the other, the interference and competition of Black Labor, or of bringing in colored persons on any terms.

When the question assumes this shape, will not the popular feeling be in favor of the prohibition? Although at first sight it seems a cruel prohibition, we see, upon examination, much to commend it, and much that will be likely to carry the judgment of the masses of the nation in its favor. The great obstacle to Southern progress and enterprise is well known to be the fact that White Labor will not demean itself to stand, walk, sit, work, or what not, side by side with the Blacks, and on an equality with them. Zealous persons may speak of this as a prejudice, but we think every man has a right to his taste in such things — and the white workingman has in this.

Once get the whole matter presented prominently in that point of view, in new States, and to be decided on those grounds, the question of the abolition of slavery, even in the old Southern States, would arise anew, and would have to be argued in a new way. All the old objections to "abolitionism" would become powerless. Indeed, the arguments would have to be transported — either party to change sides. It would be altogether a contest with reference to the interest of the masses of the Whites, and would have to be settled on the grounds of their benefit.

And can any person of moral and benevolent feelings, then, countenance for a moment, such a plan as the total exclusion of an unfortunate race, merely on account of their color, and because there is prejudice against them? No, not if there were the shadow of a hope that battling against this prejudice will ever succeed in rooting it out in

---

[1] *Mr. Hale:* An abolitionist senator from New Hampshire, John Parker Hale (1806–1873) was nominated for president by the Free Soil Party in 1852.

[2] *Mr. Seward:* A prominent political abolitionist and senator from New York, William Henry Seward (1801–1872), helped to form the Republican party in 1855.

America. But taking a deep and wide view of the whole question, the answer might perhaps be Yes — strange as it sounds at first.

Who believes that the Whites and Blacks can ever amalgamate in America? Or who wishes it to happen? Nature has set an impassable seal against it. Besides, is not America for the Whites? And is it not better so? As long as the Blacks remain here, how can they become anything like an independent and heroic race? There is no chance for it.

Yet we believe there is enough material in the colored race, if they were in some secure and ample part of the earth, where they would have a chance to develope themselves, to gradually form a race, a nation that would take no mean rank among the peoples of the world. They would have the good will of all the civilized powers, and they would be compelled to learn to look upon themselves as freemen, capable, self-reliant — mighty. Of course all this, or anything toward it, can never be attained by the Blacks here in America.

So that prohibitions like that in the new Constitution of Oregon, are not to be dismissed at first sight as arbitrary and unjust. We think the subject will bear much further examination. We even think it not likely but it would, when thus examined, meet the approval of the best friends of the Blacks, and the farthest-sighted opponents of Slavery. For, we repeat it, once get the slavery question to be argued on, as a question of White Workingmen's Labor against the Servile Labor of Blacks, and how many years would slavery stand in two-thirds of the present Slave-States?

3

Resistance and Reform

This chapter provides a selection of key antislavery and antiracist documents from the 1830s to the time of the Civil War and beyond. The emphasis is on black resistance to slavery and, just as crucially, black resistance to the racism that pervaded Northern and Southern antebellum culture. African American resistance to slavery and racism developed during a time when social reform was high on the agenda of many political activists of the period. Inspired by social perfectionist notions that the United States could indeed become the "City upon a Hill" of Puritan imaginings, and energized by a renewal of Protestant evangelicism during the 1820s and 1830s, Northern reformers in particular championed temperance, women's rights, abolitionism, and numerous other reforms as a way of redeeming the nation. From the perspective of these reformers, slavery was both a specific social practice and a metaphor for other forms of power that thwarted individual and social regeneration. Thus slavery was invoked by feminists to talk about the patriarchal power that "enslaved" white women, and slavery was invoked by temperance reformers to talk about the corporeal appetites that "enslaved" individuals. Though this metaphorical usage of slavery allowed some individuals and groups to avoid confronting the reality of slavery on the plantation, such comparisons also worked to promote cross-racial affiliations. Temperance advocates and feminists found themselves gravitating toward antislavery even as black abolitionists gravitated toward temperance and feminism. In short, the

antislavery movement gained force in Northern culture as it participated in a larger culture of reform.

While the selections in this chapter point to a shared language of
reform, they also reveal important differences among various reformers
and groups. Whereas white abolitionists tended to emphasize the need
to abolish slavery, black abolitionists also emphasized the importance
of contesting the racist practices that marginalized and disenfranchised
the free blacks. The antislavery movement was never a monolithic
enterprise. Abolitionists who aligned themselves with William Lloyd
Garrison rejected violence, preached moral suasion, sought an immediate end to slavery, and believed it mistaken to use traditional political
means to combat slavery; by contrast, the New York-based antislavery
reformers associated with the American and Foreign Anti-Slavery Society thought it best to work pragmatically with existing political institutions to fashion policies that would bring about the eventual end of
slavery. They also rejected Garrison's support for women's public participation in antislavery activities. Among black abolitionists, there
were divisions about whether Garrisonian moral suasion or political
abolitionism made better sense. There were also divisions among black
abolitionists about whether black emigration to Africa or Haiti or some
other country might be preferable to pursuing citizenship in a nation
intent on denying blacks their political rights.

The year 1831 is generally viewed as a turning point in the antislavery movement, for 1831 saw the founding of William Lloyd Garrison's
highly influential abolitionist newspaper, *The Liberator,* the convening
in Philadelphia of the first annual black convention, and the staging of
the bloodiest slave revolt in U.S. history, Nat Turner's rebellion in Virginia. Garrison's newspaper helped to mobilize black and white abolitionists; the black convention signaled the emergence of an organized
and active black abolitionism; and the Turner rebellion inspired many
blacks, frightened many whites, and exacerbated sectional tensions.

To locate 1831 as a key year in the development of the antislavery
movement in the United States is not to deny that antislavery had crucial sources in the eighteenth and early nineteenth centuries. During
the Revolutionary struggles with England, many American patriots
proclaimed that they were resisting England's efforts to "enslave"
them, and this use of the metaphor of slavery, inspired by Enlightenment beliefs in individuals' "natural" rights, led white leaders such as
Benjamin Franklin, Anthony Benezet, and even Thomas Jefferson to
go on record against slavery. Important steps to abolish slavery in the
North were taken in the aftermath of the Revolution, as Vermont,

New Hampshire, and other New England states passed laws freeing the slaves. The poet Phillis Wheatley, the Masonic leader Prince Hall, and numerous other blacks spoke out against slavery and racism during the Revolutionary and early national period; but African American opposition to slavery and white racist practices became much more vociferous following the founding of the American Colonization Society in 1816. Philadelphia's James Forten and other African American leaders regarded the colonizationist agenda of shipping the free blacks to Africa as an insult to the blacks who had fought for the nation during the Revolutionary War and then contributed so significantly to the social and economic development of the new nation. A growing conviction among many African Americans that better-organized efforts were needed to lead the struggle for blacks' rights in the U.S. led to the founding in 1827 of the first black newspaper, *Freedom's Journal,* and to the rise of the black convention movement in the early 1830s.

The documents in this chapter date from the year 1831, beginning with the text of *The Confessions of Nat Turner.* Although post-Revolutionary America had seen three large-scale slave conspiracies — the Gabriel Prosser conspiracy of 1800, based in Virginia; the "Easter Plot" conspiracy of 1802, based in Virginia and North Carolina; and the Denmark Vesey conspiracy of 1822, based in South Carolina — this was the first such conspiracy that went forward to actual rebellion. The uprising and subsequent white backlash resulted in the deaths of well over one hundred blacks and approximately sixty whites. For Thomas R. Dew and other Southern proslavery writers, Turner's revolt raised the specter of the massive slave rebellion in San Domingo (1791–1804), which had led to the loss of over sixty thousand lives, and spoke to slave owners' needs to keep a vigilant watchfulness over their slaves. But for many abolitionists, Nat Turner, who initially planned his uprising for July 4, was a prophetic American hero, a Moses-like figure attempting to liberate his people. Dual perspectives on Turner are captured in the *Confessions.* Turner tells his story to a white legal reporter who regards him as a homicidal maniac. Yet despite the fact that his words are transcribed and framed by a white reporter, his story is still there: unlike the supposedly content Sambo slave of Southern proslavery writing, Turner developed a passionate hatred of slavery and conceived of his and his fellow slaves' violent resistance as analogous to the Israelites' resistance to their enemies in the Old Testament.

According to William Lloyd Garrison's editorial on the Nat Turner rebellion, which appeared in the 3 September 1831 issue of the *Lib-*

erator, the revolt was "the vengeance of heaven" on the "crime of oppression." Horrified by the bloody violence, Garrison called for "IMMEDIATE EMANCIPATION" (143), arguing that evangelical appeals to conscience were the most moral means for combating slavery. Garrison, like many evangelically inspired abolitionists, regarded the master-slave relationship as blasphemous, insofar as the master appeared to usurp God's place in the divine hierarchy. In the selections from Garrison, Lydia Maria Child, and Angelina E. Grimké, we see the emergence of an antislavery position that echoes Jefferson's worries about the particularly deleterious effects of slavery on the morals of the master. But these important white abolitionists also expressed genuine concerns about the plight of the slave, and in their writings they attempted to make whites identify with the enslaved. As the materials in Chapter 2 make clear, for antislavery writers to offer even basic arguments about the slaves' humanity was difficult (and controversial) in a slave culture that used the Bible and science to insist upon black inferiority and difference.

Of particular note in Grimké's *Appeal* is her dual commitment to antislavery and feminism. In his 1847 *A Lecture Delivered before the Female Anti-Slavery Society of Salem,* William Wells Brown similarly addressed the connections between these two reforms: "We are not those who would ask the men to help us and leave the women at home. We want all to help us. A million of women are in Slavery, and as long as a single woman is in Slavery, every woman in the community should raise her voice against that sin, that crying evil that is degrading her sex" (97). Arguably, some white feminist abolitionists of the antebellum period, when putting antislavery rhetoric to the service of a feminist politics, lost sight of the slave (and of the fact that, unlike the slave, white women were not literally enslaved to patriarchal authority; see Sánchez-Eppler). But the shared rhetorics and concerns of abolitionist and feminist reform helped to energize both reforms. In addition to the white reformer Grimké, a number of white and black women became involved in antislavery activity precisely because they perceived parallels between antislavery and feminism and were disturbed (as Brown was disturbed) about the vulnerability of slave women to the predatory sexual desires of masters like Thomas Jefferson. The selections from Frederick Douglass and Sojourner Truth show how antislavery and feminist reform could nourish and mutually reinforce one another.

In addition to being concerned about the plight of the nation's slaves, Douglass, Truth, and many other African American reformers were also concerned about the plight of the "free" blacks and sought to develop strategies to improve their situation. At the 1831 First Annual Convention of the People of Color, the Committee on the Condition of the Free People of Color of the United States reported to the delegates "that, in their opinion, *Education, Temperance,* and *Economy,* are best calculated to promote the elevation of mankind to a proper rank and standing among men" (*Minutes* 5). During the antebellum period, a number of black abolitionists argued that if free blacks could demonstrate their ability to "elevate" themselves in U.S. culture, their successes would refute the proslavery argument that blacks were better off under the supervisory regime of the plantation. An emphasis on black moral reform, or uplift, could at times seem to put an unfair burden on free blacks to demonstrate their ability to prosper in a racist culture that for the most part denied them education, economic opportunities, and other privileges of citizenship. Nevertheless, a number of African American reformers, even as they attacked the racism of Northern culture, urged blacks to educate themselves, become sober and temperate workers, and achieve economic self-reliance. The selections from Maria W. Stewart, Samuel E. Cornish, and Frances E. W. Harper provide three complementary perspectives on the self-help movement, which Brown, as a temperance leader, also regarded as an important component of antislavery reform.

Increasingly central to movements for black self-help was the notion that African Americans needed to create their own autonomous institutions of social reform. The antebellum period thus saw the continued growth of black churches, schools, mutual aid societies, literary societies, temperance organizations, and newspapers. As Frederick Douglass remarked in an editorial in the inaugural 3 December 1847 issue of the *North Star* (a black-edited newspaper that Garrison and others saw as unnecessarily competing with the *Liberator*): "It is neither a reflection on the fidelity, nor a disparagement of the ability of our friends and fellow-laborers, to assert . . . that the man who has *suffered the wrong* is the man to *demand redress,* — that the man STRUCK is the man to CRY OUT — and that he who has *endured the cruel pangs of Slavery* is the man to *advocate Liberty.* It is evident we must be our own representatives and advocates, not exclusively, but peculiarly — not distinct from, but in connection with our white friends" (2). Similar sentiments on the need for blacks to speak and act for themselves informed the black convention movement, which in the 1830s was fairly open to white abolitionists but by the 1840s had become more exclusively a place where blacks (mostly men) formulated policy. The five selections following Harper's black-uplift statement, ranging from Henry Highland Garnet's "Address" to the National Convention of Colored Men's "Declaration," provide examples of writings from black conventions between 1843 and 1864, and show that although African Americans were increasingly convinced of the importance of working together to redress their wrongs, there was hardly consensus on the appropriate modes of resistance and reform.

In Garnet's "Address to the Slaves of the United States of America," for example, which was delivered at the 1843 black national convention, Garnet rejected the moral-suasion tactics of Garrison and asserted that the slaves had the right to use force to overcome their oppressors. His admonitions were inspired by David Walker's similar declaration in his 1829 *Appeal* that slaves should "kill or be killed," and that "it is no more harm for you to kill a man, who is trying to kill you, than it is for you to take a drink of water when thirsty" (37). Though Garnet's call for violence was rejected both by the 1843 and 1847 black national conventions, there was an increasing militancy among abolitionists following the passage of the Compromise of 1850's Fugitive Slave Law, as former moral suasionists such as Brown came to advocate self-protective forms of violence. Brown's favorable portrayal of the Nat Turner-like Picquilo in *Clotel* is an indication of his own changing views.

Rightly fearing that the new law made Northern free blacks vulnerable to reckless fugitive-slave catchers, Philadelphia's black leaders circulated a manifesto of October 1850, "Resolutions by a Committee of Philadelphia Blacks," which boldly declared in resolution seven: "Resolved, That we endorse, to the full, the sentiment of the Revolutionary patriot of Virginia, and should the awful alternative be presented to us, will act fully up to it — 'Give me Liberty or give me Death' " (Ripley IV: 69). In his 1852 speech "What to the Slave Is the Fourth of July?," Douglass similarly asserted that the nation's Revolutionary ideology legitimated violence against arbitrary authority, though he continued to champion black uplift and nonviolent forms of antislavery activity at the 1853 black national convention, which he organized and chaired. Martin R. Delany took a different tack at an 1854 black convention, which he organized and chaired. Viewing the Fugitive Slave Law as clear evidence that blacks were "alien to the laws and political privileges of the country" (*Condition* 158), and thus could never hope to achieve citizenship in the United States, Delany in his speech to the 1854 convention, "Political Destiny," advocated black emigration to Central and South America and to Africa.

Developments of the 1850s, including the 1854 Kansas-Nebraska Act, which opened new territories for slavery, and the Supreme Court's 1857 Dred Scott ruling, in which Chief Justice Roger B. Taney asserted that blacks "had no rights which the white man was bound to respect" (qtd. Foner 292–3), encouraged a number of African Americans, including Garnet, James Holly, and Brown, to circulate calls for black emigration. In the late 1850s, Garnet and Delany championed emigration to Africa, while Holly and Brown urged African Americans to emigrate to Haiti and thereby remain in the Americas. With the advent of the Civil War, however, most blacks abandoned emigrationism and embraced the Civil War as a war against slavery. But even with the Emancipation Proclamation of January 1863 and the introduction of black troops into the conflict in the spring of that year, black leaders remained concerned that their antislavery and antiracist goals were not being taken seriously by Union leaders. They expressed their concerns at the 1864 National Convention of Colored Men in a "Declaration of Wrongs and Rights."

The documents from three decades of black conventions are followed by three documents that, in different ways, address the uses of violence to bring about social justice. In his lecture on the revolutions in San Domingo, which anticipates his support for black emigration to Haiti, Brown presents the black revolutionary leader Toussaint L'Ouverture as a black "American" patriot; in a lecture on John Brown's daring attack on Harper's Ferry, Henry David Thoreau celebrates antislavery insurrectionism as patriotic and religiously inspired; and in his historical study of blacks' participation in the Civil War, Brown extols the bravery and patriotism of the black troops who defended Milliken's Bend.

In the final selection of Chapter 3, which jumps forward to 1880, Brown in *My Southern Home* conveys his disgust and dismay at the failure of Reconstruction. At the same time, he clings to the possibility that racial harmony can emerge in the United States through interracial marriages and the development of black pride. He concludes his last published book with an image of an impending conciliatory handshake between white and black. It was Brown's hope that such a handshake would begin the process of redeeming a legacy of violation and betrayal that had its origins in Jefferson's contradictory "fathering" of slavery (and slaves) and freedom.

The Confessions of Nat Turner

In the early morning of 22 August 1831, the slave preacher Nat Turner (1800–1831) and approximately fifty fellow slaves initiated a bloody rebellion in Southampton County, Virginia, that left over two hundred dead, including at least fifty-five whites. The militia quickly captured or killed most of the rebels; Turner managed to hide out in the swamps until October 30 and was subsequently tried and executed within two weeks of his capture. While incarcerated, Turner was interviewed by a local lawyer, Thomas R. Gray, who was convinced that Turner was insane. Hoping to make money from an interview with the leader of the bloodiest slave revolt in the nation's history, Gray published the *Confessions* later that year and sold approximately fifty thousand copies. While most U.S. whites were unnerved (or horrified) by the Nat Turner rebellion, Brown and other abolitionists found Turner to be an inspiring figure. In addition to making Turner's insurrection an important part of *Clotel,* Brown devoted a chapter to Turner in *The Black Man, His Antecedents, His Genius, and His Achievements* (1863). The following is the complete text of *The Confessions of Nat Turner* (Baltimore: Thomas R. Gray, 1831), with the exception of the affidavits accompanying the Clerk's and Court's seal, the list of people killed, and the list of slaves who testified at the trial.

TO THE PUBLIC

The late insurrection in Southampton has greatly excited the public mind, and led to a thousand idle, exaggerated and mischievous reports. It is the first instance in our history of an open rebellion of the slaves, and attended with such atrocious circumstances of cruelty and destruction, as could not fail to leave a deep impression, not only upon the minds of the community where this fearful tragedy was wrought, but throughout every portion of our country, in which this population is to be found. Public curiosity has been on the stretch to understand the origin and progress of this dreadful conspiracy, and the motives which influence its diabolical actors. The insurgent slaves had all been destroyed, or apprehended, tried and executed, (with the exception of the leader,) without revealing any thing at all satisfactory, as to the motives which governed them, or the means by which they expected to accomplish their object. Every thing connected with this sad affair was wrapt in mystery, until Nat Turner, the leader of this ferocious band, whose name has resounded throughout our widely extended empire, was captured. This "great Bandit" was taken by a single individual, in a cave near the residence of his late owner, on Sunday, the thirtieth of October, without attempting to make the slightest resistance, and on the following day safely lodged in the jail of the County. His captor was Benjamin Phipps, armed with a shot gun well charged. Nat's only weapon was a small light sword which he immediately surrendered, and begged that his life might be spared. Since his confinement, by permission of the jailor, I have had ready access to him, and finding that he was willing to make a full and free confession of the origin, progress and consummation of the insurrectory movements of the slaves of which he was the contriver and head; I determined for the gratification of public curiosity to commit his statements to writing, and publish them, with little or no variation, from his own words. That this is a faithful record of his confessions, the annexed certificate of the County Court of Southampton, will attest. They certainly bear one stamp of truth and sincerity. He makes no attempt (as all the other insurgents who were examined did,) to exculpate himself, but frankly acknowledges his full participation in all the guilt of the transaction. He was not only the contriver of the conspiracy, but gave the first blow towards its execution.

It will thus appear, that whilst every thing upon the surface of society wore a calm and peaceful aspect; whilst not one note of preparation was heard to warn the devoted inhabitants of woe and death, a gloomy fanatic was revolving in the recesses of his own dark, bewildered, and overwrought mind, schemes of indiscriminate massacre to the whites. Schemes too fearfully executed as far as his fiendish band proceeded in their desolating march. No cry for mercy penetrated their flinty bosoms. No acts of remembered kindness made the least impression upon these remorseless murderers. Men, women and children, from hoary age to helpless infancy were involved in the same cruel fate. Never did a band of savages do their work of death more unsparingly. Apprehension for their own personal safety seems to have been the only principle of restraint in the whole course of their bloody proceedings. And it is not the least remarkable feature in this horrid transaction, that a band actuated by such hellish purposes, should have resisted so feebly, when met by the whites in arms. Desperation alone, one would think, might have led to greater efforts. More than twenty of them attacked Dr. Blunt's house on Tuesday morning, a little before day-break, defended by two men and three boys. They fled precipitately at the first fire; and their future plans of mischief, were entirely disconcerted and broken up. Escaping thence, each individual sought his own safety either in concealment, or by returning home, with the hope that his participation might escape detection, and all were shot down in the course of a few days, or captured and brought to trial and punishment. Nat has survived all his followers, and the gallows will speedily close his career. His own account of the conspiracy is submitted to the public, without comment. It reads an awful, and it is hoped, a useful lesson, as to the operations of a mind like his, endeavoring to grapple with things beyond its reach. How it first became bewildered and confounded, and finally corrupted and led to the conception and perpetration of the most atrocious and heart-rending deeds. It is calculated also to demonstrate the policy of our laws in restraint of this class of our population, and to induce all those entrusted with their execution, as well as our citizens generally, to see that they are strictly and rigidly enforced. Each particular community should look to its own safety, whilst the general guardians of the laws, keep a watchful eye over all. If Nat's statements can be relied on, the insurrection in this county was entirely local, and his designs confided but to a few, and these in his immediate vicinity. It was not instigated by motives of revenge or sudden anger, but the results of long deliberation, and a settled purpose of mind. The offspring of gloomy fanaticism, acting upon materials but too well prepared for such impressions. It will be long remembered in the annals of our country, and many a mother as she presses her infant darling to her bosom, will shudder at the recollection of Nat Turner, and his band of ferocious miscreants.

Believing the following narrative, by removing doubts and conjectures from the public mind which otherwise must have remained, would give general satisfaction, it is respectfully submitted to the public by their ob't serv't,

T. R. GRAY.

CONFESSION

Agreeable to his own appointment, on the evening he was committed to prison, with permission of the jailer, I visited NAT on Tuesday the 1st November, when, without being questioned at all, he commenced his narrative in the following words: —

SIR, — You have asked me to give a history of the motives which induced me to undertake the late insurrection, as you call it — To do so I must go back to the days of my infancy, and even before I was born. I was thirty-one years of age the 2d of October last, and born the property of Benj. Turner, of this county. In my childhood a circumstance occurred which made an indelible impression on my mind, and laid the ground work of that enthusiasm, which has terminated so fatally to many, both white and black, and for which I am about to atone at the gallows. It is here necessary to relate this circumstance — trifling as it may seem, it was the commencement of that belief which has grown with time, and even now, sir, in this dungeon, helpless and forsaken as I am, I cannot divest myself of. Being at play with other children, when three or four years old, I was telling them something, which my mother overhearing, said it had happened before I was born — I stuck to my story, however, and related somethings which went, in her opinion, to confirm it — others being called on were greatly astonished, knowing that these things had happened, and caused them to say in my hearing, I surely would be a prophet, as the Lord had shewn me things that had happened before my birth. And my father and mother strengthened me in this my first impression, saying in my presence, I was intended for some great purpose, which they had always thought from certain marks on my head and breast — [a parcel of excrescences[1] which I believe are not at all uncommon, particularly among negroes, as I have seen several with the same. In this case he has either cut them off or they have nearly disappeared] — My grandmother, who was very religious, and to whom I was much attached — my master, who belonged to the church, and other religious persons who visited the house, and whom I often saw at prayers, noticing the singularity of my manners, I suppose, and my uncommon intelligence for a child, remarked I had too much sense to be raised, and if I was, I would never be of any service to any one as a slave — To a mind like mine, restless, inquisitive and observant of every thing that was passing, it is easy to suppose that religion was the subject to which it would be directed, and although this subject principally occupied my thoughts — there was nothing that I saw or heard of to which my attention was not directed — The manner in which I learned to read and write, not only had great influence on my own mind, as I acquired it with the most perfect ease, so much so, that I have no recollection whatever of learning the alphabet — but to the astonishment of the family, one day, when a book was shewn me to keep me from crying, I

[1] *excrescences:* Abnormal growths. This remark on Turner's skin is supplied by Thomas Gray, who several times interrupts Turner's narrative, using brackets or parentheses, to add information or to editorialize.

began spelling the names of different objects — this was a source of wonder to all in the neighborhood, particularly the blacks — and this learning was constantly improved at all opportunities — when I got large enough to go to work, while employed, I was reflecting on many things that would present themselves to my imagination, and whenever an opportunity occurred of looking at a book, when the school children were getting their lessons, I would find many things that the fertility of my own imagination had depicted to me before; all my time, not devoted to my master's service, was spent either in prayer, or in making experiments in casting different things in moulds made of earth, in attempting to make paper, gunpowder, and many other experiments, that although I could not perfect, yet convinced me of its practicability if I had the means.[2] I was not addicted to stealing in my youth, nor have ever been — Yet such was the confidence of the negroes in the neighborhood, even at this early period of my life, in my superior judgment, that they would often carry me with them when they were going on any roguery, to plan for them. Growing up among them, with this confidence in my superior judgment, and when this, in their opinions, was perfected by Divine inspiration, from the circumstances already alluded to in my infancy, and which belief was ever afterwards zealously inculcated by the austerity of my life and manners, which became the subject of remark by white and black. — Having soon discovered to be great, I must appear so, and therefore studiously avoided mixing in society, and wrapped myself in mystery, devoting my time to fasting and prayer — By this time, having arrived to man's estate, and hearing the scriptures commented on at meetings, I was struck with that particular passage which says: "Seek ye the kingdom of Heaven and all things shall be added unto you."[3] I reflected much on this passage, and prayed daily for light on this subject — As I was praying one day at my plough, the spirit spoke to me, saying "Seek ye the kingdom of Heaven and all things shall be added unto you." *Question* — what do you mean by the Spirit. *Ans.* The Spirit that spoke to the prophets in former days — and I was greatly astonished, and for two years prayed continually, whenever my duty would permit — and then again I had the same revelation, which fully confirmed me in the impression that I was ordained for some great purpose in the hands of the Almighty. Several years rolled round, in

---

[2] When questioned as to the manner of manufacturing those different articles, he was found well informed on the subject. [Gray's note.]

[3] *"Seek . . . to you"*: Luke 12.31.

which many events occurred to strengthen me in this my belief. At this time I reverted in my mind to the remarks made of me in my childhood, and the things that had been shewn me — and as it had been said of me in my childhood by those by whom I had been taught to pray, both white and black, and in whom I had the greatest confidence, that I had too much sense to be raised, and if I was, I would never be of any use to any one as a slave. Now finding I had arrived to man's estate, and was a slave, and these revelations being made known to me, I began to direct my attention to this great object, to fulfill the purpose for which, by this time, I felt assured I was intended. Knowing the influence I had obtained over the minds of my fellow servants, (not by the means of conjuring and such like tricks — for to them I always spoke of such things with contempt) but by the communion of the Spirit whose revelations I often communicated to them, and they believed and said my wisdom came from God. I now began to prepare them for my purpose, by telling them something was about to happen that would terminate in fulfilling the great promise that had been made to me — About this time I was placed under an overseer, from whom I ran away — and after remaining in the woods thirty days, I returned, to the astonishment of the negroes on the plantation, who thought I had made my escape to some other part of the country, as my father had done before. But the reason of my return was, that the Spirit appeared to me and said I had my wishes directed to the things of this world, and not to the kingdom of Heaven, and that I should return to the service of my earthly master — "For he who knoweth his Master's will, and doeth it not, shall be beaten with many stripes, and thus have I chastened you."[4] And the negroes found fault, and murmured against me, saying that if they had my sense they would not serve any master in the world. And about this time I had a vision — and I saw white spirits and black spirits engaged in battle, and the sun was darkened — the thunder rolled in the Heavens, and blood flowed in streams — and I heard a voice saying, "Such is your luck, such you are, called to see, and let it come rough or smooth, you must surely bear it." I now withdrew myself as much as my situation would permit, from the intercourse of my fellow servants, for the avowed purpose of serving the Spirit more fully — and it appeared to me, and reminded me of the things it had already shown me, and that it would then reveal to me the knowledge of the elements, the revolution of the planets, the operation of tides, and changes of the seasons. After this

[4] *"For he . . . chastened you"*: Luke 12.47.

revelation in the year 1825, and the knowledge of the elements being made known to me, I sought more than ever to obtain true holiness before the great day of judgment should appear, and then I began to receive the true knowledge of faith. And from the first steps of righteousness until the last, was I made perfect; and the Holy Ghost was with me, and said, "Behold me as I stand in the Heavens" — and I looked and saw the forms of men in different attitudes — and there were lights in the sky to which the children of darkness gave other names than what they really were — for they were the lights of the Saviour's hands, stretched forth from east to west, even as they were extended on the cross on Calvary[5] the redemption of sinners. And I wondered greatly at these miracles, and prayed to be informed of a certainty of the meaning thereof — and shortly afterwards, while laboring in the field, I discovered drops of blood on the corn as though it were dew from heaven — and I communicated it to many, both white and black, in the neighborhood — and I then found on the leaves in the woods hieroglyphic characters, and numbers, with the forms of men in different attitudes, portrayed in blood, and representing the figures I had seen before in the heavens. And now the Holy Ghost had revealed itself to me, and made plain the miracles it had shown me — For as the blood of Christ had been shed on this earth, and had ascended to heaven for the salvation of sinners, and was now returning to earth again in the form of dew — and as the leaves on the trees bore the impression of the figures I had seen in the heavens, it was plain to me that the Saviour was about to lay down the yoke he had borne for the sins of men, and the great day of judgment was at hand. About this time I told these things to a white man, (Etheldred T. Brantley) on whom it had a wonderful effect — and he ceased from his wickedness, and was attacked immediately with a cutaneous eruption, and blood oozed from the pores of his skin, and after praying and fasting nine days, he was healed, and the Spirit appeared to me again, and said, as the Saviour had been baptised so should we be also — and when the white people would not let us be baptised by the church, we went down into the water together, in the sight of many who reviled us, and were baptised by the Spirit — After this I rejoiced greatly, and gave thanks to God. And on the 12th of May, 1828, I heard a loud noise in the heavens, and the Spirit instantly appeared to me and said the Serpent was loosened, and Christ had laid down the yoke he had borne for the sins of men, and that I should take it on and fight against

---

[5] *Calvary:* The place where Christ was crucified; see Luke 23.

the Serpent, for the time was fast approaching when the first should be last and the last should be first. *Ques.* Do you not find yourself mistaken now? *Ans.* Was not Christ crucified? And by signs in the heavens that it would make known to me when I should commence the great work — and until the first sign appeared, I should conceal it from the knowledge of men — And on the appearance of the sign, (the eclipse of the sun last February) I should arise and prepare myself, and slay my enemies with their own weapons. And immediately on the sign appearing in the heavens, the seal was removed from my lips, and I communicated the great work laid out for me to do, to four in whom I had the greatest confidence. (Henry, Hark, Nelson, and Sam) — It was intended by us to have begun the work of death on the 4th July last — Many were the plans formed and rejected by us, and it affected my mind to such a degree, that I fell sick, and the time passed without our coming to any determination how to commence — Still forming new schemes and rejecting them, when the sign appeared again, which determined me not to wait longer.

Since the commencement of 1830, I had been living with Mr. Joseph Travis, who was to me a kind master, and placed the greatest confidence in me; in fact, I had no cause to complain of his treatment to me. On Saturday evening, the 20th of August, it was agreed between Henry, Hark and myself, to prepare a dinner the next day for the men we expected, and then to concert a plan, as we had not yet determined on any. Hark, on the following morning, brought a pig, and Henry brandy, and being joined by Sam, Nelson, Will and Jack, they prepared in the woods a dinner, where, about three o clock, I joined them.

Q. Why were you so backward in joining them.

A. The same reason that had caused me not to mix with them for years before.

I saluted them on coming up, and asked Will how came he there, he answered, his life was worth no more than others, and his liberty as dear to him. I asked him if he thought to obtain it? He said he would, or lose his life. This was enough to put him in full confidence. Jack, I knew, was only a tool in the hands of Hark, it was quickly agreed we should commence at home (Mr. J. Travis') on that night, and until we had armed and equipped ourselves, and gathered sufficient force, neither age nor sex was to be spared, (which was invariably adhered to.) We remained at the feast, until about two hours in the night, when we went to the house and found Austin; they all went to the cider press and drank, except myself. On returning to the house, Hark went to the door with an axe, for the purpose of breaking it open, as we knew we were strong enough to murder the family, if they were awaked by the noise; but reflecting that it might create an alarm in the neighborhood, we determined to enter the house secretly, and murder them whilst sleeping. Hark got a ladder and set it against the chimney, on which I ascended, and hoisting a window, entered and came down stairs, unbarred the door, and removed the guns from their places. It was then observed that I must spill the first blood. On which, armed with a hatchet, and accompanied by Will, I entered my master's chamber, it being dark, I could not give a death blow, the hatchet glanced from his head, he sprang from the bed and called his wife, it was his last word, Will laid him dead, with a blow of his axe, and Mrs. Travis shared the same fate, as she lay in bed. The murder of this family, five in number, was the work of a moment, not one of them awoke; there was a little infant sleeping in a cradle, that was forgotten, until we had left the house and gone some distance, when Henry and Will returned and killed it; we got here, four guns that would shoot, and several old muskets, with a pound or two of powder. We remained some time at the barn, where we paraded; I formed them in a line as soldiers, and after carrying them through all the manœuvres I was master of, marched them off to Mr. Salathul Francis', about six hundred yards distant. Sam and Will went to the door and knocked. Mr. Francis asked who was there, Sam replied it was him, and he had a letter for him, on which he got up and came to the door; they immediately seized him, and dragging him out a little from the door, he was dispatched by repeated blows on the head; there was no other white person in the family. We started from there for Mrs. Reese's, maintaining the most perfect silence on our march, where finding the door unlocked, we entered, and murdered Mrs. Reese in her bed, while sleeping; her son awoke, but it was only to sleep the sleep of death, he had only time to say who is that, and he was no more. From Mrs. Reese's we went to Mrs. Turner's, a mile distant, which we reached about sunrise, on Monday morning. Henry, Austin, and Sam, went to the still, where, finding Mr. Peebles, Austin shot him, and the rest of us went to the house as we approached, the family discovered us, and shut the door. Vain hope! Will, with one stroke of his axe, opened it, and we entered and found Mrs. Turner and Mrs. Newsome in the middle of a room, almost frightened to death. Will immediately killed Mrs. Turner, with one blow of his axe. I took Mrs. Newsome by the hand, and with the sword I had when I was apprehended, I struck her several blows over the head, but not being able to kill her, as the sword was dull. Will turning around and discovering it, despatched her also. A general destruction of property and search for money and ammunition, always succeeded the murders. By this time my company amounted to fifteen, and nine men mounted, who started for Mrs. Whitehead's, (the other six were to go through a by way to Mr. Bryant's, and rejoin us at Mrs. Whitehead's,) as we approached the house we discovered Mr. Richard Whitehead standing in the cotton patch, near the lane fence; we called him over into the lane, and Will, the executioner, was near at hand, with his fatal axe, to send him to an untimely grave. As we pushed on to the house, I discovered some one run round the garden, and thinking it was some of the white family, I pursued them, but finding it was a servant girl belonging to the house, I returned to commence the work of death, but they whom I left, had not been idle; all the family were already murdered, but Mrs. Whitehead and her daughter Margaret. As I came round to the door I saw Will pulling Mrs. Whitehead out of the house, and at the step he nearly severed her head from her body, with his broad axe. Miss Margaret, when I discovered her, had concealed herself in the corner, formed by the projection of the cellar cap from the house; on my approach she fled, but was soon overtaken, and after repeated blows with a sword, I killed her by a blow on the head, with a fence rail. By this time, the six who had gone by Mr. Bryant's, rejoined us, and informed me they had done the work of death assigned them. We again divided, part going to Mr. Richard Porter's, and from thence to Nathaniel Francis', the others to Mr. Howell Harris', and Mr. T. Doyle's. On my reaching Mr. Porter's, he had escaped with his family. I understood there, that the alarm had already spread, and I immediately returned to bring up those sent to Mr. Doyle's, and Mr. Howell Harris'; the party I left going on to Mr. Francis', having told them I would join them in that neighborhood. I met these sent to Mr. Doyle's and Mr. Harris' returning, having met Mr. Doyle on the road and killed him; and learning from some who joined them, that Mr. Harris was from home, I immediately pursued the course taken by the party gone on before; but knowing they would complete the work of death and pillage, at Mr. Francis' before I could get there, I went to Mr. Peter Edwards', expecting to find them there, but they had been here also. I then went to Mr. John T. Barrow's, they had been here and murdered him. I pursued on their track to Capt. Newit Harris', where I found the greater part mounted, and ready to start; the men now amounting to about forty, shouted and hurraed as I rode up, some were in the yard, loading their guns, others drinking. They said Captain Harris and his family had escaped, the property in the house they destroyed, robbing him of money and other valuables. I ordered them to mount and march instantly, this was about nine or ten o'clock, Monday morning. I proceeded to Mr. Levi Waller's, two or three miles distant. I took my station in the rear, and as it 'twas my object to carry terror and devastation wherever we went, I placed fifteen or twenty of the best armed and most to be relied on, in front, who generally approached the house as fast as their horses could run; this was for two purposes, to prevent their escape and strike terror to the inhabitants — on this account I never got to the houses, after leaving Mrs. Whitehead's, until the murders were committed, except in one case. I sometimes got in sight in time to see the work of death completed, viewed the mangled bodies as they lay, in silent satisfaction, and immediately started in quest of other victims — Having murdered Mrs. Waller and ten children, we started for Mr. William Williams' — having killed him and two little boys that were there; while engaged in this, Mrs. Williams fled and got some distance from the house, but she was pursued, overtaken and compelled to get up behind one of the company, who brought her back, and after showing her the mangled body of her lifeless husband, she was told to get down and lay by his side, where she was shot dead. I then started for Mr. Jacob Williams, where the family were murdered — Here we found a young man named Drury, who had come on business with Mr. Williams — he was pursued, overtaken and shot. Mrs. Vaughan was the next place we visited — and after murdering the family here, I determined on starting for Jerusalem[6] — Our number amounted now to fifty or sixty, all mounted and armed with guns, axes, swords and clubs — On reaching Mr. James W. Parker's gate, immediately on the road leading to Jerusalem, and about three miles distant, it was proposed to me to call there, but I objected, as I knew he was gone to Jerusalem, and my object was to reach there as soon as possible; but some of the men having relations at Mr. Parker's it was agreed that they might call and get his people. I remained at the gate on the road, with seven or eight; the others going across the field to the house, about half a mile off. After waiting some time for them, I became impatient, and started to the house for them, and on our return we were met by a party of white men, who had pursued our blood-stained track, and who had fired on those at the gate, and dispersed them, which I knew nothing of, not having been at that time rejoined by any of them — Immediately on discovering the whites, I ordered my men to halt and form, as they

---

[6] *Jerusalem:* A neighboring town, seventy miles east of Richmond, Virginia.

appeared to be alarmed — The white men, eighteen in number, approached us in about one hundred yards, when one of them fired, (this was against the positive orders of Captain Alexander P. Peete, who commanded, and who had directed the men to reserve their fire until within thirty paces) — And I discovered about half of them retreating, I then ordered my men to fire and rush on them: the few remaining stood their ground until we approached within fifty yards, when they fired and retreated. We pursued and overtook some of them who we thought we left dead; (they were not killed) after pursuing them about two hundred yards, and rising a little hill, I discovered they were met by another party, and had haulted, and were re-loading their guns, (this was a small party from Jerusalem who knew the negroes were in the field, and had just tied their horses to await their return to the road, knowing that Mr. Parker and family were in Jerusalem, but knew nothing of the party that had gone in with Captain Peete; on hearing the firing they immediately rushed to the spot and arrived just in time to arrest the progress of these barbarous villains, and save the lives of their friends and fellow citizens). Thinking that those who retreated first, and the party who fired on us at fifty or sixty yards distant, had all only fallen back to meet others with ammunition. As I saw them re-loading their guns, and more coming up than I saw at first, and several of my bravest men being wounded, the others became panick struck and squandered over the field; the white men pursued and fired on us several times. Hark had his horse shot under him, and I caught another for him as it was running by me; five or six of my men were wounded, but none left on the field; finding myself defeated here I instantly determined to go through a private way, and cross the Nottoway river at the Cypress Bridge, three miles below Jerusalem, and attack that place in the rear, as I expected they would look for me on the other road, and I had a great desire to get there to procure arms and ammunition. After going a short distance in this private way, accompanied by about twenty men, I overtook two or three who told me the others were dispersed in every direction. After trying in vain to collect a sufficient force to proceed to Jerusalem, I determined to return, as I was sure they would make back to their old neighborhood, where they would rejoin me, make new recruits, and come down again. On my way back, I called at Mrs. Thomas's, Mrs. Spencer's, and several other places, the white families having fled, we found no more victims to gratify our thirst for blood, we stopped at Majr. Ridley's quarter for the night, and being joined by four of his men, with the recruits made since my defeat, we mustered now about forty strong. After placing out sentinels, I laid down to sleep, but was quickly roused by a great racket; starting up, I found some mounted, and others in great confusion; one of the sentinels having given the alarm that we were about to be attacked, I ordered some to ride round and reconnoitre, and on their return the others being more alarmed, not knowing who they were, fled in different ways, so that I was reduced to about twenty again; with this I determined to attempt to recruit, and proceed on to rally in the neighborhood, I had left. Dr. Blunt's was the nearest house, which we reached just before day; on riding up the yard, Hark fired a gun. We expected Dr. Blunt and his family were at Maj. Ridley's, as I knew there was a company of men there; the gun was fired to ascertain if any of the family were at home; we were immediately fired upon and retreated, leaving several of my men. I do not know what became of them, as I never saw them afterwards. Pursuing our course back and coming in sight of Captain Harris', where we had been the day before, we discovered a party of white men at the house, on which all deserted me but two, (Jacob and Nat,) we concealed ourselves in the woods until near night, when I sent them in search of Henry, Sam, Nelson, and Hark, and directed them to rally all they could, at the place we had had our dinner the Sunday before, where they would find me, and I accordingly returned there as soon as it was dark and remained until Wednesday evening, when discovering white men riding around the place as though they were looking for some one, and none of my men joining me, I concluded Jacob and Nat had been taken, and compelled to betray me. On this I gave up all hope for the present; and on Thursday night after having supplied myself with provisions from Mr. Travis's, I scratched a hole under a pile of fence rails in a field, where I concealed myself for six weeks, never leaving my hiding place but for a few minutes in the dead of night to get water which was very near; thinking by this time I could venture out, I began to go about in the night and eaves drop the houses in the neighborhood; pursuing this course for about a fortnight and gathering little or no intelligence, afraid of speaking to any human being, and returning every morning to my cave before the dawn of day, I know not how long I might have led this life, if accident had not betrayed me, a dog in the neighborhood passing by my hiding place one night while I was out, was attracted by some meat I had in my cave, and crawled in and stole it, and was coming out just as I returned. A few nights after, two negroes having started to go hunting with the same dog, and passed that way, the dog came again to the place, and having just gone out to walk about, discovered me and barked, on which thinking myself discovered, I spoke to them to beg concealment. On making myself known they fled from me. Knowing then they would betray me, I immediately left my hiding place, and was pursued almost incessantly until I was taken a fortnight afterwards by Mr. Benjamin Phipps, in a little hole I had dug out with my sword, for the purpose of concealment, under the top of a fallen tree. On Mr. Phipps' discovering the place of my concealment, he cocked his gun and aimed at me. I requested him not to shoot and I would give up, upon which he demanded my sword. I delivered it to him, and he brought me to prison. During the time I was pursued, I had many hair breadth escapes, which your time will not permit you to relate. I am here loaded with chains, and willing to suffer the fate that awaits me.

I here proceeded to make some inquiries of him, after assuring him of the certain death that awaited him, and that concealment would only bring destruction on the innocent as well as guilty, of his own color, if he knew of any extensive or concerted plan. His answer was, I do not. When I questioned him as to the insurrection in North Carolina[7] happening about the same time, he denied any knowledge of it; and when I looked him in the face as though I would search his inmost thoughts, he replied, "I see sir, you doubt my word; but can you not think the same ideas, and strange appearances about this time in the heaven's might prompt others, as well as myself, to this undertaking." I now had much conversation with and asked him many questions, having forborne to do so previously, except in the cases noted in parenthesis; but during his statement, I had, unnoticed by him, taken notes as to some particular circumstances, and having the advantage of his statement before me in writing, on the evening of the third day that I had been with him, I began a cross examination, and found his statement corroborated by every circumstance coming within my own knowledge or the confessions of others whom had been either killed or executed, and whom he had not seen nor had any knowledge since 22d of August last, he expressed himself fully satisfied as to the impracticability of his attempt. It has been said he was ignorant and cowardly, and that his object was to murder and rob for the purpose

---

[7] *the insurrection in North Carolina:* During September 1831 there were rumors of slave revolts in Fayetteville and several other North Carolina towns. Though there may have been a few isolated small slave uprisings, for the most part these rumors were used by some whites to justify "retributive" violence against North Carolina's free and enslaved blacks.

of obtaining money to make his escape. It is notorious, that he was never known to have a dollar in his life; to swear an oath, or drink a drop of spirits. As to his ignorance, he certainly never had the advantages of education, but he can read and write, (it was taught him by his parents,) and for natural intelligence and quickness of apprehension, is surpassed by few men I have ever seen. As to his being a coward, his reason as given for not resisting Mr. Phipps, shews the decision of his character. When he saw Mr. Phipps present his gun, he said he knew it was impossible for him to escape as the woods were full of men; he therefore thought it was better to surrender, and trust to fortune for his escape. He is a complete fanatic, or plays his part most admirably. On other subjects he possesses an uncommon share of intelligence, with a mind capable of attaining any thing; but warped and perverted by the influence of early impressions. He is below the ordinary stature, though strong and active, having the true negro face, every feature of which is strongly marked. I shall not attempt to describe the effect of his narrative, as told and commented on by himself, in the condemned hole of the prison. The calm, deliberate composure with which he spoke of his late deeds and intentions, the expression of his fiend-like face when excited by enthusiasm, still bearing the stains of the blood of helpless innocence about him; clothed with rags and covered with chains; yet daring to raise his manacled hands to heaven, with a spirit soaring above the attributes of man; I looked on him and my blood curdled in my veins.

I will not shock the feelings of humanity, nor wound afresh the bosoms of the disconsolate sufferers in this unparalleled and inhuman massacre, by detailing the deeds of their fiend-like barbarity. There were two or three who were in the power of these wretches, had they known it, and who escaped in the most providential manner. There were two whom they thought they left dead on the field at Mr. Parker's, but who were only stunned by the blows of their guns, as they did not take time to re-load when they charged on them. The escape of a little girl who went to school at Mr. Waller's, and where the children were collecting for that purpose, excited general sympathy. As their teacher had not arrived, they were at play in the yard, and seeing the negroes approach, she ran up on a dirt chimney, (such as are common to log houses,) and remained there unnoticed during the massacre of the eleven that were killed at this place. She remained on her hiding place till just before the arrival of a party, who were in pursuit of the murderers, when she came down and fled to a swamp, where, a mere child as she was, with the horrors of the late scene before her, she lay concealed until the next day, when seeing a party go up to the house, she came up, and on being asked how she escaped, replied with the utmost simplicity, "The Lord helped her." She was taken up behind a gentleman of the party, and returned to the arms of her weeping mother. Miss Whitehead concealed herself between the bed and the mat that supported it, while they murdered her sister in the same room, without discovering her. She was afterwards carried off, and concealed for protection by a slave of the family, who gave evidence against several of them on their trial. Mrs. Nathaniel Francis, while concealed in a closet heard their blows, and the shrieks of the victims of these ruthless savages; they then entered the closet where she was concealed, and went out without discovering her. While in this hiding place, she heard two of her women in a quarrel about the division of her clothes. Mr. John T. Baron, discovering them approaching his house, told his wife to make her escape, and scorning to fly, fell fighting on his own threshold. After firing his rifle, he discharged his gun at them, and then broke it over the villain who first approached him, but he was overpowered, and slain. His bravery, however, saved from the hands of these monsters, his lovely and amiable wife, who will long lament a husband so deserving of her love. As directed by him, she attempted to escape through the garden, when she was caught and held by one of her servant girls, but another coming to her rescue, she fled to the woods, and concealed herself. Few indeed, were those who escaped their work of death. But fortunate for society, the hand of retributive justice has overtaken them; and not one that was known to be concerned has escaped.

The Commonwealth, ⎫
        vs.   ⎬   Charged with making insurrection,
Nat Turner. ⎭   and plotting to take away the lives of
divers free white persons, &c. on the 22d of August, 1831.

The court composed of — , having met for the trial of Nat Turner, the prisoner was brought in and arraigned, and upon his arraignment pleaded *Not guilty;* saying to his counsel, that he did not feel so.

On the part of the Commonwealth, Levi Waller was introduced, who being sworn, deposed as follows: *(agreeably to Nat's own Confession.)* Col. Trezvant[8] was then introduced, who being sworn, nar-

---

[8] The committing Magistrate. [Gray's note.]

rated Nat's Confession to him, as follows: *(his Confession as given to Mr. Gray.)* The prisoner introduced no evidence, and the case was submitted without argument to the court, who having found him guilty, Jeremiah Cobb, Esq. Chairman, pronounced the sentence of the court, in the following words: Nat Turner! Stand up. Have you any thing to say why sentence of death should not be pronounced against you?

Ans. I have not. I have made a full confession to Mr. Gray, and I have nothing more to say.

Attend then to the sentence of the Court. You have been arraigned and tried before this court, and convicted of one of the highest crimes in our criminal code. You have been convicted of plotting in cold blood, the indiscriminate destruction of men, of helpless women, and of infant children. The evidence before us leaves not a shadow of doubt, but that your hands were often imbrued in the blood of the innocent; and your own confession tells us that they were stained with the blood of a master; in your own language, "too indulgent."[9] Could I stop here, your crime would be sufficiently aggravated. But the original contriver of a plan, deep and deadly, one that never can be effected, you managed so far to put it into execution, as to deprive us of many of our most valuable citizens; and this was done when they were asleep, and defenceless; under circumstances shocking to humanity. And while upon this part of the subject, I cannot but call your attention to the poor misguided wretches who have gone before you. They are not few in number — they were your bosom associates; and the blood of all cries aloud, and calls upon you, as the author of their misfortune. Yes! You forced them unprepared, from Time to Eternity. Borne down by this load of guilt, your only justification is, that you were led away by fanaticism. If this be true, from my soul I pity you; and while you have my sympathies, I am, nevertheless called upon to pass the sentence of the court. The time between this and your execution, will necessarily be very short; and your only hope must be in another world. The judgment of the court is, that you be taken hence to the jail from whence you came, thence to the place of execution, and on Friday next, between the hours of 10 A.M. and 2 P.M. be hung by the neck until you are dead! dead! dead! and may the Lord have mercy upon your soul.

---

[9] *"too indulgent":* These are not Turner's words; in the "Confessions" he calls the master "kind" (see p. 434 in this volume).

WILLIAM LLOYD GARRISON

To the Public

In the 3 September 1831 issue of his antislavery newspaper, *The Liberator,* William Lloyd Garrison (1805–1879) exclaimed on the Nat Turner rebellion: "What we have so long predicted, — at the peril of being stigmatized as an alarmist and declaimer, — has commenced its fulfillment. The first step of the earthquake, which is ultimately to shake down the fabric of oppression, leaving not one stone upon another, has been made." Garrison blamed Southerners for the bloodshed, but most Southerners had a different perspective, calling for the suppression of Garrison's *Liberator* and other antislavery publications, which they blamed for inciting rebellion among the otherwise "contented" slaves. These Southerners believed it was no coincidence that Turner's revolt occurred the same year that Garrison began editing his radical abolitionist paper, which was published weekly in Boston from January 1831 to December 1865.

Born in Newburyport, Massachusetts, Garrison came to antislavery reform after working for several years as a printer and temperance reformer. In 1828 he joined forces with the abolitionist Benjamin Lundy (1789–1839), who edited the antislavery newspaper *The Genius of Universal Emancipation.* Disillusioned by Lundy's support for gradual emancipation and African colonization, Garrison soon broke with Lundy and by the early 1830s had asserted the principles that would guide his politics for the next thirty years: an unconditional call for immediate emancipation, a condemnation of the Constitution as proslavery, a rejection of Union with slaveholding states, and a commitment to moral suasion over violence. In 1833 he organized the American Anti-Slavery Society, which remained one of the most effective antislavery organizations of the period. His support for women's rights and moral suasion led to a schism in his abolitionist organization in 1840 and the emergence of the more pragmatic American and Foreign Anti-Slavery Society. During the 1840s and 1850s, Brown, who shared Garrison's views on the immorality of the American Constitution and the importance of having women participate in antislavery reform, worked as a lecturing agent for Garrison's American Anti-Slavery Society. In the editorial "To the Public," which appeared in the 1 January 1831 inaugural issue of the *Liberator,* the source of the following selection, Garrison invokes Jefferson's language in the Declaration to point to the unfinished work of the American Revolution.

In the month of August, I issued proposals for publishing "THE LIB-ERATOR" in Washington city; but the enterprise, though hailed in different sections of the country, was palsied by public indifference. Since that time, the removal of the Genius of Universal Emancipation[1] to the Seat of Government has rendered less imperious the establishment of a similar periodical in that quarter.

During my recent tour for the purpose of exciting the minds of the people by a series of discourses on the subject of slavery, every place that I visited gave fresh evidence of the fact, that a greater revolution in public sentiment was to be effected in the free states — *and particularly in New-England* — than at the south. I found contempt more bitter, opposition more active, detraction more relentless, prejudice more stubborn, and apathy more frozen, than among slave owners themselves. Of course, there were individual exceptions to the contrary. This state of things afflicted, but did not dishearten me. I determined, at every hazard, to lift up the standard of emancipation in the eyes of the nation, *within sight of Bunker Hill[2] and in the birth place of liberty.* That standard is now unfurled; and long may it float unhurt by the spoliations of time or the missiles of a desperate foe — yea, till every chain be broken, and every bondman set free! Let southern oppressors tremble — let their secret abettors tremble — let their northern apologists tremble — let all the enemies of the persecuted blacks tremble.

I deem the publication of my original Prospectus unnecessary, as it has obtained a wide circulation. The principles therein inculcated will be steadily pursued in this paper, excepting that I shall not array myself as the political partisan of any man. In defending the great cause of human rights, I wish to derive the assistance of all religions and of all parties.

Assenting to the "self-evident truth" maintained in the American Declaration of Independence, "that all men are created equal, and endowed by their Creator with certain inalienable rights — among which are life, liberty and the pursuit of happiness," I shall strenuously contend for the immediate enfranchisement of our slave population. In Park-street Church, on the Fourth of July, 1829, in an address on slavery, I unreflectingly assented to the popular but pernicious doctrine of

---

[1] *the Genius of Universal Emancipation:* An antislavery paper edited by Benjamin Lundy (1789– 1839). Garrison served as an editor from 1829 to 1830.

[2] *Bunker Hill:* The site of a famous Revolutionary battle fought in Boston on 17 June 1775.

gradual abolition. I seize this opportunity to make a full and unequiv-ocal recantation, and thus publicly to ask pardon of my God, of my country, and of my brethren the poor slaves, for having uttered a senti-ment so full of timidity, injustice and absurdity. A similar recantation, from my pen, was published in the Genius of Universal Emancipation at Baltimore, in September, 1829. My conscience is now satisfied.

I am aware, that many object to the severity of my language; but is there not cause for severity? I *will be* as harsh as truth, and as uncom-promising as justice. On this subject, I do not wish to think, or speak, or write, with moderation. No! no! Tell a man whose house is on fire, to give a moderate alarm; tell him to moderately rescue his wife from the hands of the ravisher; tell the mother to gradually extricate her babe from the fire into which it has fallen; — but urge me not to use moderation in a cause like the present. I am in earnest — I will not equivocate — I will not excuse — I will not retreat a single inch — AND I WILL BE HEARD. The apathy of the people is enough to make every statue leap from its pedestal, and to hasten the resurrection of the dead.

It is pretended, that I am retarding the cause of emancipation by the coarseness of my invective, and the precipitancy of my measures. *The charge is not true.* On this question my influence, — humble as it is, — is felt at this moment to a considerable extent, and shall be felt in com-ing years — not perniciously, but beneficially — not as a curse, but as a blessing; and posterity will bear testimony that I was right. I desire to thank God, that he enables me to disregard "the fear of man which bringeth a snare," and to speak his truth in its simplicity and power. And here I close with this fresh dedication:

> Oppression! I have seen thee, face to face,
> And met thy cruel eye and cloudy brow;
> But thy soul-withering glance I fear not now —
> For dread to prouder feelings doth give place
> Of deep abhorrence! Scorning the disgrace
> Of slavish knees that at thy footstool bow
> I also kneel — but with far other vow
> Do hail thee and thy hord of hirelings base: —
> I swear, while life-blood warms my throbbing veins,
> Still to oppose and thwart, with heart and hand,
> Thy brutalising sway — till Afric's chains
> Are burst, and Freedom rules the rescued land, —
> Trampling Oppression and his iron rod:
> *Such is the vow I take* — SO HELP ME GOD!

LYDIA MARIA CHILD

From *An Appeal in Favor of That Class of Americans Called Africans*

Child's *An Appeal,* published in Boston in 1833, provided the first comprehensive discussion of race and slavery in the United States. In her book, Child presented historical backgrounds, legal analyses, and descriptive accounts of the moral and political evils of slavery, and she denounced antiblack racism in the slave South and the free North. Her antislavery convictions were energized by her interactions with William Lloyd Garrison in the early 1830s; and with the publication of *An Appeal* she emerged as one of the most important and influential white abolitionists. In publishing such a book in 1833, Child took enormous risks. She had been acclaimed in genteel circles in the Northeast for her novels *Hobomok* (1824) and *The Rebels* (1825), for her domestic treatises *The Frugal Housewife* (1829) and *The Mother's Book* (1831), and for her children's magazine, *Juvenile Miscellany,* which she founded in 1826. But when she turned to antislavery writing, she came under vitriolic attack from many of her fellow New Englanders, who thought it improper for a woman to involve herself with public affairs. The Boston Athenaeum revoked her library privileges, sales of her books diminished, and enough people canceled their subscriptions to *Juvenile Miscellany* to force her to cease its publication in 1834. A revised edition of *An Appeal in Favor of that Class of Americans Called Africans* (New York: John S. Taylor) appeared in 1836 and is the source of the selection below. In the excerpts that follow, Child, having exposed the horrors of the African slave trade, turns to the problem of slave ownership and sets her sights on Jefferson.

We now come to the influence of this diabolical system on the *slave-owner;* and here I shall be cautioned that I am treading on delicate ground, because our own countrymen are slaveholders. But I am yet to learn that wickedness is any the better for being our own. Let the truth be spoken — and let those abide its presence who can.

The following is the testimony of Jefferson, who had good opportunities for observation, and who certainly had no New-England prejudices: "There must, doubtless, be an unhappy influence on the manners of the people, produced by the existence of slavery among us. The whole commerce between master and slave is a perpetual exercise of the most boisterous passions; the most unremitting despotism on the one part, and degrading submission on the other. Our children see this and learn to imitate it; for man is an imitative animal. The parent storms; the child looks on, catches the lineaments of wrath, puts on the same airs in a circle of smaller slaves, gives loose to the worst of passions, and thus nursed, educated, and daily exercised in tyranny, cannot but be stamped by it with odious peculiarities. The man must be a prodigy, who can retain his morals and manners undepraved in such circumstances."[1]

In a community where all the labor is done by one class there must of course be another class who live in indolence; and we all know how much people that have nothing to do are tempted by what the world calls pleasures; the result is, that slaveholding states and colonies are proverbial for dissipation. Hence, too, the contempt for the industry, which prevails in such a state of society. — Where none work but slaves, usefulness becomes degradation. The wife of a respectable mechanic, who accompanied her husband from Massachusetts to the South, gave great offence to her new neighbors by performing her usual household avocations; they begged her to desist from it, (offering the services of their own blacks), because the sight of a white person engaged in any labor was extremely injurious to the slaves; they deemed it very important that the negroes should be taught, both by precept and example, that they alone were made to work!

Whether the undue importance attached to merely external gentility, and the increasing tendency to indolence and extravagance throughout this country, ought to be attributed, in any degree, to the same source, I am unable to say; if *any* influence comes to us from the example and ridicule of the slaveholding states, it certainly must be of this nature.

There is another view of this system, which I cannot unveil so completely as it ought to be. I shall be called bold for saying so much; but the facts are so important, that it is a matter of conscience not to be fastidious.

The negro woman is unprotected either by law or public opinion. She is the property of her master, and her daughters are his property. They are allowed to have no conscientious scruples, no sense of shame, no regard for the feelings of husband, or parent; they must be entirely subservient to the will of their owner, on pain of being

---

[1] *"There must . . . circumstances"*: From Jefferson's *Notes on the State of Virginia*; see p. 342 in this volume.

whipped as near unto death as will comport with his interest, or quite
to death, if it suit his pleasure.

Those who know human nature would be able to conjecture the
unavoidable result, even if it were not betrayed by the amount of
mixed population. Think for a moment, what a degrading effect must
be produced on the morals of both blacks and whites by customs like
these!

Considering we live in the nineteenth century, it is indeed a strange
state of society where the father sells his child, and the brother puts
his sister up at auction! Yet these things are often practised in our
republic. . . .

I have more than once heard people, who had just returned from
the South, speak of seeing a number of mulattoes in attendance where
they visited, whose resemblance to the head of the family was too
striking not to be immediately observed. What sort of feeling must be
excited in the minds of those slaves by being constantly exposed to the
tyranny or caprice of their own brothers and sisters, and by the knowledge that these near relations, will on a division of the estate, have
power to sell them off with cattle?

But the vices of white men eventually provide a scourge for themselves. They increase the negro race, but the negro can never increase
theirs; and this is one great reason why the proportion of colored population is always so large in slaveholding countries. As the ratio
increases more and more each year, the colored people must eventually
be the stronger party; and when this result happens, slavery must
either be abolished, or government must furnish troops, of whose
wages the free states must pay their proportion. . . .

I shall perhaps be asked why I have said so much about the slave-
trade, since it was long ago abolished[2] in this country? There are several good reasons for it. In the first place, it is a part of the system; for
if there were no slaves, there could be no slave-trade; and while there
are slaves, the slave-trade *will* continue. In the next place, the trade is
still briskly carried on in Africa, and slaves are smuggled into these
States through the Spanish colonies. In the third place, a very extensive
internal slave-trade is carried on in this country. The breeding of
negro-cattle for the foreign markets, (of Louisiana, Georgia, Alabama,
Arkansas, and Missouri), is a very lucrative branch of business. Whole

---

[2] *slave-trade . . . abolished:* By an act of 1807, the U.S. Congress prohibited the
international slave trade; the act ultimately worked to foster the slave trade within
the U.S.

coffles of them, chained and manacled, are driven through our Capital on their way to auction. Foreigners, particularly those who come here with enthusiastic ideas of American freedom, are amazed and disgusted at the sight.[3] A troop of slaves once passed through Washington on the fourth of July, while drums were beating, and standards flying. One of the captive negroes raised his hand, loaded with irons, and waving it toward the starry flag, sung with a smile of bitter irony, "Hail Columbia! *happy* land!" . . .

The disgrace of such scenes in the capital of our republic cannot be otherwise than painful to every patriotic mind; while they furnish materials for the most pungent satire to other nations. A United States senator declared that the sight of a drove of slaves was so insupportable that he always avoided it when he could; and an intelligent Scotchman said, when he first entered Chesapeake Bay, and cast his eye along our coast, the sight of the slaves brought his heart into his throat. How can we help feeling a sense of shame, when we read Moore's contemptuous couplet,

> "The fustian flag that proudly waves,
>   In splendid mockery, o'er a land of slaves?"[4]

The lines would be harmless enough, if they were false; the sting lies in their truth.

Finally, I have described some of the horrors of the slave-trade, because when our constitution was formed, the government pledged itself not to abolish this traffic until 1808. We began our career of freedom by granting a twenty years' lease of iniquity — twenty years of allowed invasion of other men's rights — twenty years of bloodshed, violence, and fraud! And this will be told in our annals — this will be heard of to the end of time!

While the slave-trade was allowed, the South could use it to advance their views in various ways. In their representation to Congress, five slaves counted the same as three freemen;[5] of course, every fresh cargo was not only an increase of property, but an increase of *political*

---

[3] See the second volume of Stuart's "Three years in North America." Instead of being angry at such truths, it would be wise to profit by them. [Child's note.]

[4] *"The fustian . . . slaves?":* From Thomas Moore, "To the Lord Viscount Forbes." See *Clotel*, p. 176, n. 1.

[5] *five slaves . . . three freemen;:* A reference to the three-fifths clause of the Constitution, which allowed Southern slave states to count each slave as three-fifths of a person when determining congressional representation.

power. Ample time was allowed to lay in a stock of slaves to supply the new slave states and territories that might grow up; and when this was effected, the prohibition of foreign commerce in human flesh, operated as a complete *tariff*, to protect the domestic supply.

Every man who buys a slave promotes this traffic, by raising the value of the article; every man who owns a slave, indirectly countenances it; every man who allows that slavery is a lamentable *necessity*, contributes his share to support it; and he who votes for admitting a slave-holding State into the Union, fearfully augments the amount of this crime.

ANGELINA E. GRIMKÉ

From *Appeal to the Christian Women of the South*

Born and raised in a slaveholding family in Charleston, South Carolina, Angelina E. Grimké (1805–1879) and her older sister Sarah M. Grimké (1792–1873) moved to Philadelphia in the 1820s, and by the 1830s had become staunch Garrisonian abolitionists and advocates of women's rights. Angelina was regarded as a particularly shocking cultural figure for having the temerity to lecture on abolitionism before mixed audiences of men and women. Chastised by the domestic theorist and educator Catharine Beecher for her unwomanly politicking, Grimké responded in *Letters to Catharine Beecher* (1838) by asserting connections between women's rights and antislavery. She declared: "The investigation of the rights of the slave has led me to a better understanding of my own" (117). That same year she married the abolitionist Theodore Dwight Weld, author of the influential *Slavery As It Is* (1839), a compilation of horrible incidents about slavery that would have a major impact on Catharine Beecher's sister, Harriet Beecher Stowe (see the Weld selection on pp. 265–70). In *Appeal to the Christian Women of the South* (New York: American Anti-Slavery Society, 1836), the source of this selection, Grimké urges Southern women to use their influence to help bring about the end of slavery. Challenging key tenets of the proslavery argument, including Jefferson's notion that emancipation would lead to bloodshed, Grimké in effect calls on Southern women to rebel against their own "enslavement" to patriarchy.

I have thus, I think, clearly proved to you seven propositions, viz.: First, that slavery is contrary to the declaration of our independence. Second, that it is contrary to the first charter of human rights given to Adam, and renewed to Noah. Third, that the fact of slavery having been the subject of prophecy, furnishes *no* excuse whatever to slavedealers. Fourth, that no such system existed under the patriarchal dispensation. Fifth, that *slavery never* existed under the Jewish dispensation; but so far otherwise, that every servant was placed under the *protection of law,* and care taken not only to prevent all *involuntary* servitude, but all *voluntary perpetual* bondage. Sixth, that slavery in America reduces a *man* to a *thing,* a "chattel personal," *robs him* of *all* his rights as a *human being,* fetters both his mind and body, and protects the *master* in the most unnatural and unreasonable power, whilst it *throws him out* of the protection of law. Seventh, that slavery is contrary to the example and precepts of our holy and merciful Redeemer, and of his apostles.

But perhaps you will be ready to query, why appeal to *women* on this subject? *We* do not make the laws which perpetuate slavery. *No* legislative power is vested in *us; we* can do nothing to overthrow the system, even if we wished to do so. To this I reply, I know you do not make the laws, but I also know that *you are the wives and mothers, the sisters and daughters of those who do;* and if you really suppose *you* can do nothing to overthrow slavery, you are greatly mistaken. You can do much in every way: four things I will name. 1st. You can read on this subject. 2d. You can pray over this subject. 3d. You can speak on this subject. 4th You can *act* on this subject. I have not placed reading before praying, because I regard it more important, but because, in order to pray aright, we must understand what we are praying for; it is only then we can "pray with the understanding and the spirit also."

1. Read then on the subject of slavery. Search the Scriptures daily, whether the things I have told you are true. Other books and papers might be a great help to you in this investigation, but they are not necessary, and it is hardly probable that your Committees of Vigilance[1] will allow you to have any other. The *Bible* then is the book I want you to read in the spirit of inquiry, and the spirit of prayer. Even the enemies of Abolitionists, acknowledge that their doctrines are drawn

---

[1] *Committees of Vigilance:* Groups of Southern whites who attempted to suppress abolitionists' writings.

from it. In the great mob in Boston,[2] last autumn, when the books and papers of the Anti-Slavery Society, were thrown out of the windows of their office, one individual laid hold of the Bible and was about tossing it out to the ground, when another reminded him that it was the Bible he had in his hand. *"O! 'tis all one,"* he replied, and out went the sacred volume, along with the rest. We thank him for the acknowledgment. Yes, *"it is all one,"* for our books and papers are mostly commentaries on the Bible, and the Declaration. Read the *Bible* then, it contains the words of Jesus, and they are spirit and life. Judge for yourselves whether *he sanctioned* such a system of oppression and crime.

2. Pray over this subject. When you have entered into your closets, and shut to the doors, then pray to your father, who seeth in secret, that he would open your eyes to see whether slavery is *sinful*, and if it is, that he would enable you to bear a faithful, open and unshrinking testimony against it, and to do whatsoever your hands find to do, leaving the consequences entirely to him, who still says to us whenever we try to reason away duty from the fear of consequences, *"What is that to thee, follow thou me."*[3] Pray also for that poor slave, that he may be kept patient and submissive under his hard lot, until God is pleased to open the door of freedom to him without violence or bloodshed. Pray too for the master that his heart may be softened, and he made willing to acknowledge, as Joseph's brethren did, "Verily we are guilty concerning our brother," before he will be compelled to add in consequence of Divine judgment, "therefore is all this evil come upon us."[4] Pray also for all your brethren and sisters who are laboring in the righteous cause of Emancipation in the Northern States, England and the world. There is great encouragement for prayer in these words of our Lord. "Whatsoever ye shall ask the Father *in my name, he will give* it to you"[5] — Pray then without ceasing, in the closet and the social circle.

3. Speak on this subject. It is through the tongue, the pen, and the press, that truth is principally propagated. Speak then to your relatives, your friends, your acquaintances on the subject of slavery; be not

---

[2] *mob in Boston:* In October 1835, a mob attacked William Lloyd Garrison and the British abolitionist George Thompson (1804–1878); Garrison was dragged through the streets on a rope.

[3] *"What . . . thou me":* John 21.22.

[4] *"Verily . . . upon us":* Genesis 42.21.

[5] *"Whatsoever . . . to you":* John 16.23.

afraid if you are conscientiously convinced it is *sinful,* to say so openly, but calmly, and to let your sentiments be known. If you are served by the slaves of others, try to ameliorate their condition as much as possible; never aggravate their faults, and thus add fuel to the fire of anger already kindled, in a master and mistress's bosom; remember their extreme ignorance, and consider them as your Heavenly Father does the *less* culpable on this account, even when they do wrong things. Discountenance *all* cruelty to them, all starvation, all corporal chastisement; these may brutalize and *break* their spirits, but will never bend them to willing, cheerful obedience. If possible, see that they are comfortably and *seasonably* fed, whether in the house or the field; it is unreasonable and cruel to expect slaves to wait for their breakfast until eleven o'clock, when they rise at five or six. Do all you can, to induce their owners to clothe them well, and to allow them many little indulgences which would contribute to their comfort. Above all, try to persuade your husband, father, brothers and sons, that *slavery is a crime against God and man,* and that it is a great sin to keep *human beings* in such abject ignorance; to deny them the privilege of learning to read and write. The Catholics are universally condemned, for denying the Bible to the common people, but, *slaveholders must not* blame them, for *they* are doing the *very same thing,* and for the very same reason, neither of these systems can bear the light which bursts from the pages of that Holy Book. And lastly, endeavour to inculcate submission on the part of the slaves, but whilst doing this be faithful in pleading the cause of the oppressed.

> "Will *you* behold unheeding,
> Life's holiest feelings crushed,
> Where *woman's* heart is bleeding,
> Shall *woman's* voice be hushed?"[6]

4. Act on this subject. Some of you *own* slaves yourselves. If you believe slavery is *sinful,* set them at liberty, "undo the heavy burdens and let the oppressed go free."[7] If they wish to remain with you, pay them wages, if not let them leave you. Should they remain teach them, and have them taught the common branches of an English education; they have minds and those minds, *ought to be improved.* So precious a talent as intellect, never was given to be wrapt in a napkin and buried in the earth. It is the *duty* of all, as far as they can, to improve their

[6] "*Will you . . . be hushed?*": From Elizabeth Margaret Chandler (1807–1834), "Think of Our Country's Glory," in *Poetical Works,* ed. Benjamin Lundy (1836).
[7] "*undo . . . free*": Isaiah 58.6.

own mental faculties, because we are commanded to love God with *all our minds,* as well as with all our hearts, and we commit a great sin, if we *forbid or prevent* that cultivation of the mind in others, which would enable them to perform this duty. Teach your servants then to read &c, and encourage them to believe it is their *duty* to learn, if it were only that they might read the Bible. . . .

What can I say more, my friends, to induce *you* to set your hands and heads, and hearts, to this great work of justice and mercy. Perhaps you have feared the consequences of immediate Emancipation, and been frightened by all those dreadful prophecies of rebellion, bloodshed and murder, which have been uttered. "Let no man deceive you;"[8] they are the predictions of that same "lying spirit" which spoke through the four thousand prophets of old, to Ahab[9] king of Israel, urging him on to destruction. *Slavery* may produce these horrible scenes if it is continued five years longer, but Emancipation *never will.*

I can prove the *safety* of immediate Emancipation by history. In St. Domingo in 1793 six hundred thousand slaves were set free in a white population of forty-two thousand. That Island "marched as by enchantment towards its ancient splendor," cultivation prospered, every day produced perceptible proofs of its progress, and the negroes all continued quietly to work on the different plantations, until in 1802, France determined to reduce these liberated slaves again to bondage. It was at *this time* that all those dreadful scenes of cruelty occurred, which we so often *unjustly* hear spoken of, as the effects of Abolition. They were occasioned *not* by Emancipation, but by the base attempt to fasten the chains of slavery on the limbs of liberated slaves.

In Guadaloupe eighty-five thousand slaves were freed in a white population of thirteen thousand. The same prosperous effects followed manumission here, that had attended it in Hayti; every thing was quiet until Buonaparte sent out a fleet to reduce these negroes again to slavery,[10] and in 1802 this institution was reestablished in that Island. In 1834, when Great Britain determined to liberate the slaves in her West India colonies, and proposed the apprenticeship system; the planters of Bermuda and Antigua, after having joined the

---

[8] *"Let no man deceive you":* Paul 5.6.

[9] *Ahab:* The idolatrous king of I Kings 16–22.

[10] *Buonaparte . . . slavery:* In 1802 Napoleon Bonaparte sent French military forces to the West Indian island of Guadeloupe in an effort to restore French authority over the rebellious black population; by 1803 he had succeeded in reintroducing slavery to this French colony.

other planters in their representations of the bloody consequences of Emancipation, in order if possible to hold back the hand which was offering the boon of freedom to the poor negro; as soon as they found such falsehoods were utterly disregarded, and Abolition must take place, came forward voluntarily, and asked for the compensation which was due to them, saying, *they preferred immediate emancipation*, and were not afraid of any insurrection. And how is it with these islands now? They are decidedly more prosperous than any of those in which the apprenticeship system was adopted, and England is now trying to abolish that system, so fully convinced is she that immediate Emancipation is the *safest* and the best plan.

And why not try it in the Southern States, if it *never* has occasioned rebellion; if *not* a *drop* of *blood* has ever been shed in consequence of it, though it has been so often tried, why should we suppose it would produce such disastrous consequences now. "Be not deceived then, God is not mocked," by such false excuses for not doing justly and loving mercy. There is nothing to fear from immediate Emancipation but *every thing* from the continuance of slavery.

FREDERICK DOUGLASS

The Rights of Women

In July 1848, three hundred delegates, including forty men, gathered in Seneca Falls, New York, for the first women's rights convention in the United States. Frederick Douglass, one of those delegates, promoted the Seneca Falls convention in the *North Star,* and at the convention he had the honor of seconding Elizabeth Cady Stanton's daring proposal that women be granted full rights to the elective franchise. That proposal became part of the convention's "Declaration of Sentiments," an assertion of women's rights that was modeled on Jefferson's Declaration of Independence. Like William Lloyd Garrison, William Wells Brown, and other abolitionists, Douglass saw resemblances between the subordinate positions of women and blacks and sought equal rights for all. Though he shared some of his culture's assumptions about men's particular suitability for leadership roles, he supported women's causes throughout his career, attending numerous women's rights conventions. Douglass's account of the Seneca Falls convention is taken from the 28 July 1848 issue of the *North Star.*

One of the most interesting events of the past week, was the holding of what is technically styled a Woman's Rights Convention, at Seneca Falls. The speaking, addresses, and resolutions of this extraordinary meeting, were almost wholly conducted by women; and although they evidently felt themselves in a novel position, it is but simple justice to say, that their whole proceedings were characterized by marked ability and dignity. No one present, we think, however much he might be disposed to differ from the views advanced by the leading speakers on that occasion, will fail to give them credit for brilliant talents and excellent dispositions. In this meeting, as in other deliberative assemblies, there were frequently differences of opinion and animated discussion; but in no case was there the slightest absence of good feeling and decorum. Several interesting documents, setting forth the rights as well as the grievances of woman, were read. Among these was a declaration of sentiments, to be regarded as the basis of a grand movement for attaining all the civil, social, political and religious rights of woman. As these documents are soon to be published in pamphlet form, under the authority of a Committee of women, appointed by that meeting, we will not mar them by attempting any synopsis of their contents. We should not, however, do justice to our own convictions, or to the excellent persons connected with this infant movement, if we did not, in this connection, offer a few remarks on the general subject which the Convention met to consider, and the objects they seek to attain.

In doing so, we are not insensible that the bare mention of this truly important subject in any other than terms of contemptuous ridicule and scornful disfavor, is likely to excite against us the fury of bigotry and the folly of prejudice. A discussion of the rights of animals would be regarded with far more complacency by many of what are called the *wise* and the *good* of our land, than would be a discussion of the rights of woman. It is, in their estimation, to be guilty of evil thoughts, to think that woman is entitled to rights equal with man. Many who have at last made the discovery that negroes have some rights as well as other members of the human family, have yet to be convinced that woman is entitled to any. Eight years ago, a number of persons of this description actually abandoned the anti-slavery cause,[1] lest by giving

---

[1] *"Eight years ago . . . cause."*: A reference to the 1840 schism in William Lloyd Garrison's American Slavery Party which led to the founding of the American and Foreign Anti-Slavery Society. Garrison had insisted on the importance of continuing to work for women's rights.

their influence in that direction, they might possibly be giving countenance to the dangerous heresy that woman, in respect to rights, stands on an equal footing with man. In the judgment of such persons, the American slave system, with all its concomitant horrors, is less to be deplored than this *wicked* idea. It is perhaps needless to say, that we cherish little sympathy for such sentiments, or respect for such prejudices. Standing as we do upon the watch-tower of human freedom, we cannot be deterred from an expression of our approbation of any movement, however humble, to improve and elevate the character and condition of any members of the human family. While it is impossible for us to go into this subject at length, and dispose of the various objections which are often urged against such a doctrine as that of female equality, we are free to say, that in respect to political rights, we hold woman to be justly entitled to all we claim for man. We go farther, and express our conviction that all political rights which it is expedient for man to exercise, it is equally so for woman. All that distinguishes man as an intelligent and accountable being, is equally true of woman; and if that government is only just which governs by the free consent of the governed, there can be no reason in the world for denying to woman the exercise of the elective franchise, or a hand in making and administering the laws of the land. Our doctrine is, that "Right is of no sex." We therefore bid the women engaged in this movement our humble God-speed.

SOJOURNER TRUTH

I Am a Woman's Rights

In the summer of 1851, Sojourner Truth (1797–1883) addressed a women's rights convention in Akron, Ohio, taking the podium in order to challenge the pronouncements of a group of ministers on the inferiority of women. A prepossessing advocate of the rights of blacks and women, Sojourner Truth, who never learned to read or write, emerged as one of the most prominent reformers of the 1850s, known in particular for her passionate, religious, and often folksy speeches. Born a slave in New York's Ulster County, she saw at least five of her children sold into slavery, though she successfully sued for the return of one of her sons two years after her emancipation in 1827. Taking the name of Van Wagener from an employer, she was known as Isabella Van Wagener until 1843, when she had a visionary conversion experience that left her convinced that God wanted her to preach the truth as an itinerant speaker. As Sojourner Truth, she lectured widely in the northeast and midwest on Americans' sins against blacks and women, and with the publication of the *Narrative of Sojourner Truth* (1850), an account of her life that she dictated to Olive Gilbert, gained even greater renown. During the Civil War she helped to recruit and raise supplies for the black troops. An account of one of her 1851 speeches on women's rights appeared in the 21 June 1851 issue of the *Anti-Slavery Bugle,* the source of this selection.

May I say a few words? Receiving an affirmative answer, she proceeded; I want to say a few words about this matter. I am a woman's rights. I have as much muscle as any man, and can do as much work as any man. I have plowed and reaped and husked and chopped and mowed, and can any man do more than that? I have heard much about the sexes being equal; I can carry as much as any man, and can cut as much too, if I can get it. I am as strong as any man that is now. As for intellect, all I can say is, if woman have a pint and man a quart — why cant she have her little pint full? You need not be afraid to give us our rights for fear we will take too much, — for we cant take more than our pint'll hold. The poor men seem to be all in confusion, and dont know what to do. Why children, if you have woman's rights give it to her and you will feel better. You will have your own rights, and they wont be so much trouble. I cant read, but I can hear. I have heard the bible and have learned that Eve caused man to sin. Well if woman upset the world, do give her a chance to set it right side up again. The Lady has spoken about Jesus, how he never spurned woman from him, and she was right. When Lazarus[1] died, Mary and Martha came to him with faith and love and besought him to raise their brother. And Jesus wept — and Lazarus came forth. And how came Jesus into the world? Through God who created him and woman who bore him. Man, where is your part? But the women are coming up blessed be God and a few of the men are coming up with them. But man is in a tight place, the poor slave is on him, woman is coming on him, and he is surely between a hawk and a buzzard.

[1] *Lazarus:* The brother of Mary and Martha of Bethany, Lazarus was restored to life by Jesus after having spent four days in a tomb; see John 11.1–44, 12.1, 2.

MARIA W. STEWART

An Address, Delivered at the African Masonic Hall

An important black activist of the 1830s, Maria W. Stewart (1803–1879) was born in Hartford, Connecticut, and eventually moved to Boston, where in 1826 she married James W. Stewart, a shipping agent, who died three years later. Galvanized by the publication of David Walker's 1829 *Appeal,* she adopted the antislavery cause and in 1832 lectured in Boston's Franklin Hall to the predominately white New England Anti-Slavery Society. In her 1833 "An Address," she lectured to a black Masonic society. In these and other lectures of the 1830s, Stewart combined a call for abolitionism with attacks on the racist practices that kept Northern free blacks marginalized and disenfranchised. A deeply religious woman, Stewart spoke prophetically of America as a modern City of Babylon and warned, in the manner of a Jeremiah, of God's impending apocalyptic judgment. Rejecting colonization and emigration as solutions to African Americans' problems, she urged blacks to take the primary role in fighting for their rights to U.S. citizenship. Though not as prominent a cultural figure after the 1830s, Stewart continued to work for antislavery and antiracist causes, attending antislavery and women's rights conventions and occasionally lecturing. Stewart's "An Address, Delivered at the African Masonic Hall, Boston, February 27, 1833," was reprinted in *Productions of Mrs. Maria W. Stewart* (1835) and in a volume she worked on just before her death, *Meditations from the Pen of Mrs. Maria W. Stewart* (Washington, DC: n. p., 1879), the source of this selection.

African rights and liberty is a subject that ought to fire the breast of every free man of color in these United States, and excite in his bosom a lively, deep, decided, and heart-felt interest. When I cast my eyes on the long list of illustrious names that are enrolled on the bright annals of fame among the whites, I turn my eyes within and ask my thoughts, "Where are the names of *our* illustrious ones?" It must certainly have been for the want of energy on the part of the free people of color that they have been long willing to bear the yoke of oppression. It must have been the want of ambition and force that has given the whites occasion to say that our natural abilities are not as good, and our capacities by nature inferior to theirs. They boldly assert that did we possess a natural independence of soul, and feel a love for liberty within our breasts, some one of our sable race, long before this, would have testified it, notwithstanding the disadvantages under which we labor. We have made ourselves appear altogether unqualified to speak in our own defense, and are therefore looked upon as objects of pity and commiseration. We have been imposed upon, insulted, and derided on every side; and now, if we complain, it is considered as the height of impertinence. We have suffered ourselves to be considered as dastards, cowards, mean, faint-hearted wretches; and on this account (not because of our complexion) many despise us, and would gladly spurn us from their presence.

These things have fired my soul with a holy indignation, and compelled me thus to come forward and endeavor to turn their attention to knowledge and improvement, for knowledge is power. I would ask, is it blindness of mind or stupidity of soul or the want of education that has caused our men who are sixty or seventy years of age never to let their voices be heard nor their hands be raised in behalf of their color? Or has it been for fear of offending the whites? If it has, O ye fearful ones, throw off your fearfulness and come forth, in the name of the Lord and in the strength of the God of Justice, and make yourselves useful and active members in society; for they admire a noble and patriotic spirit in others, and should they not admire it in us? If you are men, convince them that you possess the spirit of men; and as your day so shall your strength be. Have the sons of Africa no souls? Feel they no ambitious desires? Shall the chains of ignorance forever confine them? Shall the insipid appellation of "clever negroes" or "good creatures" any longer content them? Where can we find among ourselves the man of science, or a philosopher, or an able statesman, or a counsellor at law? Show me our fearless and brave, our noble and gallant ones. Where are our lecturers on natural history and our critics in useful knowledge? There may be a few such men among us, but they are rare. It is true, our fathers bled and died in the revolutionary war, and others fought bravely, under the command of Jackson,[1] in defense of liberty. But where is the man that has distinguished himself in these modern days by acting wholly in the defense of African rights and liberty? There was one; although he sleeps, his memory lives.[2]

---

[1] *under the command of Jackson:* A reference to the free blacks who fought with Andrew Jackson during the War of 1812; see William C. Nell's text of Jackson's Two Proclamations on pp. 262–65.

[2] *his memory lives:* In all likelihood, a reference to David Walker; see the selection from Walker on pp. 348–60.

I am sensible that there are many highly intelligent gentlemen of color in these United States in the force of whose arguments, doubtless, I should discover my inferiority; but if they are blessed with wit and talent, friends and fortune, why have they not made themselves men of eminence by striving to take all the reproach that is cast upon the people of color, and in endeavoring to alleviate the woes of their brethren in bondage? Talk, without effort, is nothing. You are abundantly capable, gentlemen, of making yourselves men of distinction; and this gross neglect on your part causes my blood to boil within me. Here is the grand cause which hinders the rise and progress of the people of color. It is the want of laudable ambition and requisite courage.

Individuals have been distinguished according to their genius and talents ever since the first formation of man, and will continue to be while the world stands. The different grades rise to honor and respectability as their merits may deserve. History informs us that we sprung from one of the most learned nations of the whole earth; from the seat, if not the parent of science; yes, poor, despised Africa was once the resort of sages and legislators of other nations, was esteemed the school of learning, and the most illustrious men of Greece flocked thither for instruction. But it was our gross sins and abominations that provoked the Almighty to frown thus heavily upon us and give our glory unto others. Sin and prodigality have caused the downfall of nations, kings, and emperors; and were it not that God in wrath remembers mercy, we might indeed despair; but a promise is left us: "Ethiopia shall again stretch forth her hands unto God."[3]

But it is no use for us to boast that we sprung from this learned and enlightened nation, for this day a thick mist of moral gloom hangs over millions of our race. Our condition as a people has been low for hundreds of years, and it will continue to be so, unless, by true piety and virtue, we strive to regain that which we have lost. White Americans, by their prudence, economy, and exertions, have sprung up and become one of the most flourishing nations in the world, distinguished for their knowledge of the arts and sciences, for their polite literature. While our minds are vacant and starving for want of knowledge, theirs are filled to overflowing. Most of our color have been taught to stand in fear of the white man from their earliest infancy, to work as soon as they could walk, and to call "master" before they scarce could lisp the name of *mother*. Continual fear and laborious servitude have in some

[3] *"Ethiopia . . . God"*: Psalms 68.31.

degree lessened in us that natural force and energy which belong to man; or else, in defiance of opposition, our men, before this, would have nobly and boldly contended for their rights. But give the man of color an equal opportunity with the white from the cradle to manhood, and from manhood to the grave, and you would discover the dignified statesman, the man of science, and the philosopher. But there is no such opportunity for the sons of Africa, and I fear that our powerful ones are fully determined that there never shall be. Forbid, ye Powers on high, that it should any longer be said that our men possess no force. O ye sons of Africa, when will your voices be heard in our legislative halls, in defiance of your enemies, contending for equal rights and liberty? How can you, when you reflect from what you have fallen, refrain from crying mightily unto God, to turn away from us the fierceness of his anger, and remember our transgressions against us no more forever. But a God of infinite purity will not regard the prayers of those who hold religion in one hand, and prejudice, sin, and pollution in the other; he will not regard the prayers of self-righteousness and hypocrisy. Is it possible, I exclaim, that for the want of knowledge we have labored for hundreds of years to support others, and been content to receive what they choose to give us in return? Cast your eyes about, look as far as you can see; all, all is owned by the lordly white, except here and there a lowly dwelling which the man of color, midst deprivations, fraud, and opposition has been scarce able to procure. Like King Solomon, who put neither nail nor hammer to the temple, yet received the praise; so also have the white Americans gained themselves a name, like the names of the great men that are in the earth, while in reality we have been their principal foundation and support. We have pursued the shadow, they have obtained the substance; we have performed the labor, they have received the profits; we have planted the vines, they have eaten the fruits of them.

I would implore our men, and especially our rising youth, to flee from the gambling board and the dance-hall; for we are poor, and have no money to throw away. I do not consider dancing as criminal in itself, but it is astonishing to me that our young men are so blind to their own interest and the future welfare of their children as to spend their hard earnings for this frivolous amusement; for it has been carried on among us to such an unbecoming extent that it has become absolutely disgusting. "Faithful are the wounds of a friend, but the kisses of an enemy are deceitful."[4] Had those men among us, who

---

[4] "*Faithful . . . deceitful*": Proverbs 27.6..

have had an opportunity, turned their attention as assiduously to mental and moral improvement as they have to gambling and dancing, I might have remained quietly at home and they stood contending in my place. These polite accomplishments will never enroll your names on the bright annals of fame who admire the belle void of intellectual knowledge, or applaud the dandy that talks largely on politics, without striving to assist his fellow in the revolution, when the nerves and muscles of every other man forced him into the field of action. You have a right to rejoice, and to let your hearts cheer you in the days of your youth; yet remember that for all these things God will bring you into judgment. Then, O ye sons of Africa, turn your mind from these perishable objects, and contend for the cause of God and the rights of man. Form yourselves into temperance societies. There are temperate men among you; then why will you any longer neglect to strive, by your example, to suppress vice in all its abhorrent forms? You have been told repeatedly of the glorious results arising from temperance, and can you bear to see the whites arising in honor and respectability without endeavoring to grasp after that honor and respectability also?

But I forbear. Let our money, instead of being thrown away as heretofore, be appropriated for schools and seminaries of learning for our children and youth. We ought to follow the example of the whites in this respect. Nothing would raise our respectability, add to our peace and happiness, and reflect so much honor upon us, as to be ourselves the promoters of temperance, and the supporters, as far as we are able, of useful and scientific knowledge. The rays of light and knowledge have been hid from our view; we have been taught to consider ourselves as scarce superior to the brute creation; and have performed the most laborious part of American drudgery. Had we as a people received one-half the early advantages the whites have received, I would defy the Government of these United States to deprive us any longer of our rights.

I am informed that the agent of the Colonization Society has recently formed an association of young men for the purpose of influencing those of us to go to Liberia who may feel disposed. The colonizationists are blind to their own interest, for should the nations of the earth make war with America, they would find their forces much weakened by our absence; or should we remain here, can our "brave soldiers" and "fellow-citizens," as they were termed in time of calamity, condescend to defend the rights of the whites and be again deprived of their own, or sent to Liberia in return? Or, if the colonizationists are the real friends to Africa, let them expend the money which they collect, in erecting a college to educate her injured sons in this land of gospel, light, and liberty; for it would be most thankfully received on our part, and convince us of the truth of their professions, and save time, expense, and anxiety. Let them place before us noble objects worthy of pursuit, and see if we prove ourselves to be those unambitious negroes they term us. But, ah, bethinks their hearts are so frozen toward us they had rather their money should be sunk in the ocean than to administer it to our relief; and I fear, if they dared, like Pharaoh, king of Egypt, they would order every male child among us to be drowned. But the most high God is still as able to subdue the lofty pride of these white Americans as He was the heart of that ancient rebel. They say, though we are looked upon as *things,* yet we sprang from a scientific people. Had our men the requisite force and energy they would soon convince them by their efforts, both in public and private, that they were men, or things in the shape of men. Well may the colonizationists laugh us to scorn for our negligence; well may they cry: "Shame to the sons of Africa." As the burden of the Israelites was too great for Moses to bear, so also is our burden too great for our noble advocate to bear. You must feel interested, my brethren, in what he undertakes, and hold up his hands by your good works, or in spite of himself his soul will become discouraged and his heart will die within him; for he has, as it were, the strong bulls of Bashan[5] to contend with.

It is of no use for us to wait any longer for a generation of well educated men to arise. We have slumbered and slept too long already; the day is far spent; the night of death approaches; and you have sound sense and good judgment sufficient to begin with, if you feel disposed to make a right use of it. Let every man of color throughout the United States, who possesses the spirit and principles of a man, sign a petition to Congress to abolish slavery in the District of Columbia, and grant you the rights and privileges of common free citizens; for if you had had faith as a grain of mustard seed, long before this the mountains of prejudice might have been removed. We are all sensible that the Anti-Slavery Society has taken hold of the arm of our whole population, in order to raise them out of the mire. Now all we have to do is, by a spirit of virtuous ambition, to strive to raise ourselves; and I am happy to have it in my power thus publicly to say that the colored inhabitants of this city, in some respects, are beginning to improve. Had the free people of color in these United States nobly and boldly contended

[5] *bulls of Bashan:* See Psalms 22.12.

for their rights, and showed a natural genius and talent, although not so brilliant as some; had they held up, encouraged and patronized each other, nothing could have hindered us from being a thriving and flourishing people. There has been a fault among us. The reason why our distinguished men have not made themselves more influential, is because they fear that the strong current of opposition through which they must pass would cause their downfall and prove their overthrow. And what gives rise to this opposition? Envy. And what has it amounted to? Nothing. And who are the cause of it? Our whited sepulchres, who want to be great, and don't know how; who love to be called of men "Rabbi, Rabbi;" who put on false sanctity, and humble themselves to their brethren for the sake of acquiring the highest place in the synagogue and the uppermost seat at the feast. You, dearly beloved, who are the genuine followers of our Lord Jesus Christ — the salt of the earth, and the light of the world — are not so culpable. As I told you in the very first of my writing, I tell you again, I am but as a drop in the bucket — as one particle of the small dust of the earth. God will surely raise up those among us who will plead the cause of virtue and the pure principles of morality more eloquently than I am able to do.

It appears to me that America has become like the great City of Babylon, for she has boasted in her heart: "I sit a queen, and am no widow, and shall see no sorrow!"[6] She is, indeed, a seller of slaves and the souls of men; she has made the Africans drunk with the wine of her fornication; she has put them completely beneath her feet, and she means to keep them there; her right hand supports the reins of government and her left hand the wheel of power, and she is determined not to let go her grasp. But many powerful sons and daughters of Africa will shortly arise, who will put down vice and immorality among us, and declare by Him that sitteth upon the throne that they will have their rights; and if refused, I am afraid they will spread horror and devastation around. I believe that the oppression of injured Africa has come up before the Majesty of Heaven; and when our cries shall have reached the ears of the Most High, it will be a tremendous day for the people of this land; for strong is the arm of the Lord God Almighty. Life has almost lost its charms for me; death has lost its sting, and the grave its terrors; and at times I have a strong desire to depart and dwell with Christ, which is far better. Let me entreat my white brethren to awake and save our sons from dissipation and our daughters from ruin. Lend the hand of assistance to feeble merit; plead the cause of

---

[6] "I . . . no sorrow!": Revelation 18.7.

virtue among our sable race; so shall our curses upon you be turned into blessings; and though you should endeavor to drive us from these shores, still we will cling to you the more firmly; nor will we attempt to rise above you; we will presume to be called your equals only.

The unfriendly whites first drove the native American from his much loved home. Then they stole our fathers from their peaceful and quiet dwellings, and brought them hither, and made bond-men and bond-women of them and their little ones. They have obliged our brethren to labor; kept them in utter ignorance; nourished them in vice, and raised them in degradation; and now that we have enriched their soil, and filled their coffers, they say that we are not capable of becoming like white men, and that we never can rise to respectability in this country. They would drive us to a strange land. But before I go, the bayonet shall pierce me through. African rights and liberty is a subject that ought to fire the breast of every free man of color in these United States, and excite in his bosom a lively, deep, decided, and heartfelt interest.

SAMUEL E. CORNISH

Responsibility of Colored People in the Free States

A free black born in Delaware, Samuel E. Cornish (1796–1858) moved to Philadelphia in 1816, where he was licensed to preach in 1819. In the early 1820s he moved to New York City, and in 1827 cofounded with John B. Russwurm (1799–1851) the first black newspaper, *Freedom's Journal*, which managed to stay in business for the next two years. Despite the newspaper's demise in 1829, Cornish remained devoted to the cause of black uplift in the United States, attacking white prejudice while at the same time urging blacks to take responsibility for their own elevation. He supported the black convention movement of the 1830s, worked with William Lloyd Garrison's American Anti-Slavery Society, and founded the influential African American newspaper *Colored American* in 1837. Convinced that one of the best arguments against slavery and racism was the existence of a thriving community of Northern free blacks, Cornish again and again preached self-help doctrines to his readers, urging them to better themselves socially by bettering themselves economically. In this editorial from *Colored American*, which appeared in the issue of 4 March 1837, the source of this selection, Cornish urges his readers to adopt temperate habits in the marketplace, and specifically calls on blacks to eschew alcoholic beverages. The cause of temperance reform was promoted by many African American leaders, including Stewart, Brown, Douglass, Harper, and Delany.

Brethren, God hath laid on us great responsibility — we have to act an important part, and fill an important place, in the great cause of humanity and religion — and in the work of emancipation. On *our* conduct and exertions much, very much depend. It is our part, by virtue, prudence and industry, to uphold the hands of our devoted and sacrificing friends — let us not be found wanting. Should we prove unworthy [of] our few privileges, we shall furnish our enemies the strongest arguments with which to oppose the emancipation of the slave, and to hinder the elevation of the free.

On the other hand, should we establish for ourselves a character — should we as a people, become more religious and moral, more industrious and prudent, than other classes of community — it will be impossible to keep us down. This we should do; we are more oppressed and proscribed than others, therefore we should be more circumspect and more diligent than others.

We live in an age of reform, and if we lay not hold of every means of reformation and improvement, we shall be left in the back ground, and the contrast between our condition and that of our white brethren will be widened — then let us as a whole people, avail ourselves of every measure, calculated to cultivate the mind and elevate the morals. No oppressed COLORED AMERICAN, who wishes to occupy that elevation in society, which God has designed he should occupy, should be intemperate or even touch, as a beverage, intoxicating drinks, none should be idle or extravagant, none profane the Sabbath nor neglect the sanctuary of God, but all, all should be up and doing, should work while it is day. We owe it to ourselves and we owe it to the poor slaves, who are our brethren.

On *our* conduct, in a great measure, *their* salvation depends. Let us show that we are worthy to be freemen; it will be the strongest appeal to the judgement and conscience of the slave-holder and his abettors, that can be furnished; and it will be a sure means of our elevation in society, and to the possession of all our rights as men and citizens. But brethren we are encouraged in these matters — we rejoice that there is a redeeming spirit abroad in the land: and merely suggest these things, to stir up your pure minds by way of remembrance.

FRANCES E. W. HARPER

The Colored People in America

Frances Ellen Watkins Harper (1825–1911) was one of the most prolific and popular African American writers of the nineteenth century,
authoring four novels, several widely praised volumes of poems, and a
number of essays and short stories. Born in Baltimore to free black parents who died when she was young, Frances Watkins was raised by her
uncle William Watkins, a prominent educator and abolitionist. She taught
at schools in Ohio and Pennsylvania, and in the early 1850s left teaching
to lecture for the Maine Anti-Slavery Society and other antislavery organizations. In 1857 she shared the podium with Brown in Boston and gave a
series of lectures on slavery, temperance, and black uplift. She married
Fenton Harper of Cincinnati, Ohio, in 1860, and after his death four years
later she resumed lecturing, supporting the cause of black suffrage and
urging blacks to work for their uplift through temperance, education, and
economic empowerment. In 1892 she published her best-known work of
fiction, *Iola Leroy,* a novel that owes a particular debt to *Clotelle; or, The
Colored Heroine.* "The Colored People of America," a classic statement
on white racism and black uplift, was the concluding essay of Frances
Ellen Watkins's *Poems on Miscellaneous Subjects* (Boston: J. B. Yerrinton
& Son, 1854), the source of the text of this selection. Prefaced by William
Lloyd Garrison, the volume, which included several poetic "responses" to
Stowe's *Uncle Tom's Cabin,* sold approximately twelve thousand copies in
its first four years in print and was reprinted at least twenty times during
Harper's lifetime.

Having been placed by a dominant race in circumstances over
which we have had no control, we have been the butt of ridicule and
the mark of oppression. Identified with a people over whom weary
ages of degradation have passed, whatever concerns them, as a race,
concerns me. I have noticed among our people a disposition to censure
and upbraid each other, a disposition which has its foundation rather,
perhaps, in a want of common sympathy and consideration, than
mutual hatred or other unholy passions. Born to an inheritance of misery, nurtured in degradation, and cradled in oppression, with the scorn
of the white man upon their souls, his fetters upon their limbs, his
scourge upon their flesh, what can be expected from their offspring,

but a mournful reäction of that cursed system which spreads its baneful influence over body and soul; which dwarfs the intellect, stunts its development, debases the spirit, and degrades the soul? Place any nation in the same condition which has been our hapless lot, fetter their limbs and degrade their souls, debase their sons and corrupt their daughters; and, when the restless yearnings for liberty shall burn through heart and brain — when, tortured by wrong and goaded by oppression, the hearts that would madden with misery, or break in despair, resolve to break their thrall, and escape from bondage, then let the bay of the bloodhound and the scent of the human tiger be upon their track; — let them feel that, from the ceaseless murmur of the Atlantic to the sullen roar of the Pacific, from the thunders of the rainbow-crowned Niagara to the swollen waters of the Mexican gulf, they have no shelter for their bleeding feet, or resting place for their defenceless heads; — let them, when nominally free, feel that they have only exchanged the iron yoke of oppression for the galling fetters of a vitiated public opinion; — let prejudice assign them the lowest places and the humblest positions, and make them "hewers of wood and drawers of water;"[1] — let their income be so small that they must from necessity bequeath to their children an inheritance of poverty and a limited education; and tell me, reviler of our race! censurer of our people! if there is a nation in whose veins runs the purest Caucasian blood, upon whom the same causes would not produce the same effects; whose social condition, intellectual and moral character, would present a more favorable aspect than ours? But there is hope; yes, "blessed be God!" for our down-trodden and despised race. Public and private schools accommodate our children; and in my own southern home, I see women whose lot is unremitted labor, saving a pittance from their scanty wages to defray the expense of learning to read. We have papers edited by colored editors, which we may consider an honor to possess, and a credit to sustain. We have a church that is extending itself from east to west, from north to south, through poverty and reproach, persecution and pain. We have our faults, our want of union and concentration of purpose; but are there not extenuating circumstances around our darkest faults — palliating excuses for our most egregious errors? and shall we not hope, that the mental and moral aspect which we present is but the first step of a mighty advancement, the faintest corruscations[2] of the day that will dawn

[1] "hewers of wood and drawers of water;": Joshua 9.21.
[2] corruscations: Coruscations — sudden gleams or flashes of light.

with unclouded splendor upon our down-trodden and benighted race, and that ere long we may present to the admiring gaze of those who wish us well, a people to whom knowledge has given power, and righteousness exaltation?

HENRY HIGHLAND GARNET

Address to the Slaves of the United States of America

Henry Highland Garnet (1815–1882) was born a slave in New Market, Maryland. In 1825 he escaped to New York City with his mother, father, and sister, and began a serious course of education. He attended the New York African Free School, the Noyes Academy in Canaan, New Hampshire, and the Oneida Institute in Whitesboro, New York, where he decided to become a Presbyterian minister. Licensed to preach in 1842, he accepted the pastorate of the predominately white Liberty Street Presbyterian Church in Troy, New York, that same year.

Garnet was regarded as a radical in the antislavery movement. He rejected the moral suasion position of the Garrisonians in favor of the political abolitionism of the Liberty Party, which was founded in 1840. On 16 August 1843, at the National Convention of Colored Citizens held at Buffalo, New York, Garnet delivered to over seventy delegates his famous speech, "An Address to the Slaves of the United States of America." Drawing on the nation's Revolutionary ideology, Garnet, in rejecting the Garrisonians' unqualified commitment to nonviolence, presented slave resistance as an act of patriotism and self-defense. With Garrisonian abolitionists in the majority at the convention, Garnet came under fire, but after much debate the "Address" failed by only one vote in winning the endorsement of the convention's delegates. Brown and Frederick Douglass, Garnet's principal adversaries at the convention, joined the majority in voting against Garnet's ideas. Five years later the white abolitionist John Brown helped to finance the publication of Garnet's speech in a volume that also included Walker's *Appeal*. That volume, *Walker's Appeal, With a Brief Sketch of His Life. By Henry Highland Garnet. And also Garnet's Address to the Slaves of the United States of America* (New York: J. H. Tobitt, 1848), is the source of the text below.

By the early 1850s, Douglass, Brown, and many other black abolitionists had come to share Garnet's view of the appropriateness of slave resistance. Later in the decade, however, Garnet was once again the focus of

Douglass's and Brown's anger, as they opposed his support for the African Civilization Society, which encouraged black emigration to Africa. In spite of his views on emigration, Garnet joined with most African American leaders in championing the Civil War as a war against slavery. After the war he continued to work for reforms that would help to improve the situation of African Americans, even as he kept his eye on Africa as a possible site for black emigration. In 1882 Garnet accepted an appointment as U.S. minister to Liberia, where he died later that year.

PREFACE.

The following Address was first read at the National Convention held at Buffalo, N.Y., in 1843. Since that time it has been slightly modified, retaining, however, all of its original doctrine. The document elicited more discussion than any other paper that was ever brought before that, or any other deliberative body of colored persons, and their friends. Gentlemen who opposed the Address, based their objections on these grounds. 1. That the document was war-like, and encouraged insurrection; and 2. That if the Convention should adopt it, that those delegates who lived near the borders of the slave states, would not dare to return to their homes. The Address was rejected by a small majority; and now in compliance with the earnest request of many who heard it, and in conformity to the wishes of numerous friends who are anxious to see it, the author now gives it to the public, praying God that this little book may be borne on the four winds of heaven, until the principles it contains shall be understood and adopted by every slave in the Union.

H.H.G.

Troy, N.Y., April 15, 1848.

ADDRESS TO THE SLAVES OF THE U.S.

BRETHREN AND FELLOW CITIZENS:

Your brethren of the north, east, and west have been accustomed to meet together in National Conventions, to sympathize with each other, and to weep over your unhappy condition. In these meetings we have addressed all classes of the free, but we have never until this time, sent a word of consolation and advice to you. We have been contented in sitting still and mourning over your sorrows, earnestly hoping that before this day, your sacred liberties would have been restored. But, we have hoped in vain. Years have rolled on, and tens of thousands have been borne on streams of blood, and tears, to the shores of eternity. While you have been oppressed, we have also been partakers with you; nor can we be free while you are enslaved. We therefore write to you as being bound with you.

Many of you are bound to us, not only by the ties of a common humanity, but we are connected by the more tender relations of parents, wives, husbands, children, brothers, and sisters, and friends. As such we most affectionately address you.

Slavery has fixed a deep gulf between you and us, and while it shuts out from you the relief and consolation which your friends would willingly render, it afflicts and persecutes you with a fierceness which we might not expect to see in the fiends of hell. But still the Almighty Father of Mercies has left to us a glimmering ray of hope, which shines out like a lone star in a cloudy sky. Mankind are becoming wiser, and better — the oppressor's power is fading — and you, every day, are becoming better informed, and more numerous. Your grievances, brethren, are many. We shall not attempt, in this short address, to present to the world, all the dark catalogue of this nation's sins, which have been committed upon an innocent people. Nor is it indeed, necessary, for you feel them from day to day, and all the civilized world look upon them with amazement.

Two hundred and twenty-seven years ago, the first of our injured race were brought to the shores of America. They came not with glad spirits to select their homes, in the New World. They came not with their own consent, to find an unmolested enjoyment of the blessings of this fruitful soil. The first dealings which they had with men calling themselves Christians, exhibited to them the worst features of corrupt and sordid hearts; and convinced them that no cruelty is too great, no villainy, and no robbery too abhorrent for even enlightened men to perform, when influenced by avarice, and lust. Neither did they come flying upon the wings of Liberty, to a land of freedom. But, they came with broken hearts, from their beloved native land, and were doomed to unrequited toil, and deep degradation. Nor did the evil of their bondage end at their emancipation by death. Succeeding generations inherited their chains, and millions have come from eternity into time, and have returned again to the world of spirits, cursed, and ruined by American Slavery.

The propagators of the system, or their immediate ancestors very soon discovered its growing evil, and its tremendous wickedness, and secret promises were made to destroy it. The gross inconsistency of a people holding slaves, who had themselves "ferried o'er the wave," for freedom's sake, was too apparent to be entirely overlooked. The voice of Freedom cried, "emancipate your Slaves." Humanity supplicated with tears, for the deliverance of the children of Africa. Wisdom urged her solemn plea. The bleeding captive plead his innocence, and pointed to Christianity who stood weeping at the cross. Jehovah frowned upon the nefarious institution, and thunderbolts, red with vengeance, struggled to leap forth to blast the guilty wretches who maintained it. But all was vain. Slavery had stretched its dark wings of death over the land, the Church stood silently by — the priests prophesied falsely, and the people loved to have it so. Its throne is established, and now it reigns triumphantly.

Nearly three millions of your fellow citizens, are prohibited by law, and public opinion, (which in this country is stronger than law), from reading the Book of Life.[1] Your intellect has been destroyed as much as possible, and every ray of light they have attempted to shut out from your minds. The oppressors themselves have become involved in the ruin. They have become weak, sensual, and rapacious. They have cursed you — they have cursed themselves — they have cursed the earth which they have trod. In the language of a Southern statesman, we can truly say, "even the wolf, driven back long since by the approach of man, now returns after the lapse of a hundred years, and howls amid the desolations of slavery."

The colonists threw the blame upon England. They said that the mother country entailed the evil upon them, and that they would rid themselves of it if they could. The world thought they were sincere, and the philanthropic pitied them. But time soon tested their sincerity. In a few years, the colonists grew strong and severed themselves from the British Government. Their Independence was declared, and they took their station among the sovereign powers of the earth. The declaration was a glorious document. Sages admired it, and the patriotic of every nation reverenced the Godlike sentiments which it contained. When the power of Government returned to their hands, did they emancipate the slaves? No; they rather added new links to our chains. Were they ignorant of the principles of Liberty? Certainly they were not. The sentiments of their revolutionary orators fell in burning elo-

---

[1] the Book of Life: The Bible.

quence upon their hearts, and with one voice they cried, LIBERTY OR DEATH.[2] O, what a sentence was that! It ran from soul to soul like electric fire, and nerved the arm of thousands to fight in the holy cause of Freedom. Among the diversity of opinions that are entertained in regard to physical resistance, there are but a few found to gainsay that stern declaration. We are among those who do not.

SLAVERY! How much misery is comprehended in that single word. What mind is there that does not shrink from its direful effects? Unless the image of God is obliterated from the soul, all men cherish the love of Liberty. The nice discerning political economist does not regard the sacred right, more than the untutored African who roams in the wilds of Congo. Nor has the one more right to the full enjoyment of his freedom than the other. In every man's mind the good seeds of liberty are planted, and he who brings his fellow down so low, as to make him contented with a condition of slavery, commits the highest crime against God and man. Brethren, your oppressors aim to do this. They endeavor to make you as much like brutes as possible. When they have blinded the eyes of your mind — when they have embittered the sweet waters of life — when they have shut out the light which shines from the word of God — then, and not till then has American slavery done its perfect work.

TO SUCH DEGRADATION IT IS SINFUL IN THE EXTREME FOR YOU TO MAKE VOLUNTARY SUBMISSION. The divine commandments, you are in duty bound to reverence, and obey. If you do not obey them you will surely meet with the displeasure of the Almighty. He requires you to love him supremely, and your neighbor as yourself — to keep the Sabbath day holy — to search the Scriptures — and to bring up your children with respect for his laws, and to worship no other God but him. But slavery sets all these at naught and hurls defiance in the face of Jehovah. The forlorn condition in which you are placed does not destroy your moral obligation to God. You are not certain of Heaven, because you suffer yourselves to remain in a state of slavery, where you cannot obey the commandments of the Sovereign of the universe. If the ignorance of slavery is a passport to heaven, then it is a blessing, and no curse, and you should rather desire its perpetuity than its abolition. God will not receive slavery, nor ignorance, nor any other state of mind, for love, and obedience to him. Your condition does not absolve you from your moral obligation. The diabolical injustice by which your liberties are

---

[2] *LIBERTY OR DEATH:* A reference to the famous credo of Virginia's Revolutionary patriot Patrick Henry (1736–1799).

cloven down, NEITHER GOD, NOR ANGELS, OR JUST MEN, COMMAND YOU
TO SUFFER FOR A SINGLE MOMENT. THEREFORE, IT IS YOUR SOLEMN AND
IMPERATIVE DUTY TO USE EVERY MEANS, BOTH MORAL, INTELLECTUAL,
AND PHYSICAL, THAT PROMISE SUCCESS. If a band of heathen men should
attempt to enslave a race of Christians, and to place their children
under the influence of some false religion, surely, heaven would frown
upon the men who would not resist such aggression, even to death. If,
on the other hand, a band of Christians should attempt to enslave a
race of heathen men and to entail slavery upon them, and to keep them
in heathenism in the midst of Christianity, the God of heaven would
smile upon every effort which the injured might make to disenthrall
themselves.

Brethren, it is as wrong for your lordly oppressors to keep you in
slavery, as it was for the man thief to steal our ancestors from the coast
of Africa. You should therefore now use the same manner of resistance,
as would have been just in our ancestors, when the bloody foot prints
of the first remorseless soul thief was placed upon the shores of our
fatherland. The humblest peasant is as free in the sight of God, as the
proudest monarch that ever swayed a sceptre. Liberty is a spirit sent out
from God, and like its great Author, is no respector of persons.

Brethren, the time has come when you must act for yourselves. It is
an old and true saying, that "if hereditary bondmen would be free,
they must themselves strike the blow."[3] You can plead your own
cause, and do the work of emancipation better than any others. The
nations of the old world are moving in the great cause of universal
freedom, and some of them at least, will ere long, do you justice. The
combined powers of Europe have placed their broad seal of disapprobation upon the African slave trade.[4] But in the slave holding parts of
the United States, the trade is as brisk as ever. They buy and sell you
as though you were brute beasts. The North has done much — her
opinion of slavery in the abstract is known. But in regard to the South,
we adopt the opinion of the New York Evangelist — "We have
advanced so far, that the cause apparently waits for a more effectual
door to be thrown open than has been yet."[5] We are about to point

[3] *"if hereditary bondmen . . . blow"*: A paraphrase of a line from canto 2, stanza 76 of Lord Byron's *Childe's Harold's Pilgrimage* (1818).
[4] *combined powers of Europe . . . slave trade*: A reference to the Quintuple Treaty (1841) signed by Britian, Austria, Prussia, France, and Russia, which permitted the seiz-ing of vessels engaged in the slave trade.
[5] *"We have advanced . . . yet"*: A paraphrase of an antislavery editorial in the 27 July 1843 issue of a Presbyterian weekly newspaper, the *New York Evangelist*.

you to that more effectual door. Look around you, and behold the bosoms of your loving wives, heaving with untold agonies! Hear the cries of your poor children! Remember the stripes your fathers bore. Think of the torture and disgrace of your noble mothers. Think of your wretched sisters, loving virtue and purity, as they are driven into concubinage, and are exposed to the unbridled lusts of incarnate devils. Think of the undying glory that hangs around the ancient name of Africa: — and forget not that you are native-born American citizens, and as such, you are justly entitled to all the rights that are granted to the freest. Think how many tears you have poured out upon the soil which you have cultivated with unrequited toil, and enriched with your blood; and then go to your lordly enslavers, and tell them plainly, that YOU ARE DETERMINED TO BE FREE. Appeal to their sense of justice, and tell them that they have no more right to oppress you, than you have to enslave them. Entreat them to remove the grievous burdens which they have imposed upon you, and to remunerate you for your labor. Promise them renewed diligence in the cultivation of the soil, if they will render to you an equivalent for your services. Point them to the increase of happiness and prosperity in the British West Indies, since the act of Emancipation.[6] Tell them in language which they cannot misunderstand, of the exceeding sinfulness of slavery, and of a future judgment, and of the righteous retributions of an indignant God. Inform them that all you desire, is FREEDOM, and that nothing else will suffice. Do this, and for ever after cease to toil for the heartless tyrants, who give you no other reward but stripes and abuse. If they then commence the work of death, they, and not you, will be responsible for the consequences. You had far better all die — *die immediately,* than live slaves, and entail your wretchedness upon your posterity. If you would be free in this generation, here is your only hope. However much you and all of us may desire it, there is not much hope of Redemption without the shedding of blood. If you must bleed, let it all come at once — rather, *die freemen, than live to be slaves.* It is impossible, like the children of Israel, to make a grand Exodus from the land of bondage. THE PHARAOHS ARE ON BOTH SIDES OF THE BLOOD-RED WATERS! You cannot remove en masse to the dominions of the British Queen — nor can you pass through Florida, and overrun Texas, and at last find peace in Mexico. The propagators of American slavery are spending their blood and treasure, that they may plant the black flag in

---

[6] *act of Emancipation:* The Emancipation Act of 1833 ended slavery in the British empire.

the heart of Mexico, and riot in the halls of the Montezumas.[7] In the language of the Rev. Robert Hall, when addressing the volunteers of Bristol, who were rushing forth to repel the invasion of Napoleon, who threatened to lay waste the fair homes of England, "Religion is too much interested in your behalf, not to shed over you her most gracious influences."[8]

You will not be compelled to spend much time in order to become inured to hardships. From the first moment that you breathed the air of heaven, you have been accustomed to nothing else but hardships. The heroes of the American Revolution were never put upon harder fare, than a peck of corn, and a few herrings per week. You have not become enervated by the luxuries of life. Your sternest energies have been beaten out upon the anvil of severe trial. Slavery has done this, to make you subservient to its own purposes; but it has done more than this, it has prepared you for any emergency. If you receive good treatment, it is what you could hardly expect; if you meet with pain, sorrow, and even death, these are the common lot of the slaves.

Fellow-men! patient sufferers! behold your dearest rights crushed to the earth! See your sons murdered, and your wives, mothers, and sisters, doomed to prostitution! In the name of the merciful God! and by all that life is worth, let it no longer be a debateable question, whether it is better to choose LIBERTY or DEATH!

In 1822, Denmark Veazie,[9] of South Carolina, formed a plan for the liberation of his fellow men. In the whole history of human efforts to overthrow slavery, a more complicated and tremendous plan was never formed. He was betrayed by the treachery of his own people, and died a martyr to freedom. Many a brave hero fell, but History, faithful to her high trust, will transcribe his name on the same monument with Moses, Hampden, Tell, Bruce, and Wallace, Toussaint L'Ouverture, Lafayette and Washington.[10] That tremendous move-

---

[7] *halls of the Montezumas:* A reference to efforts by slaveholding Texas to seize Mexican territory during the late 1830s and early 1840s; Montezuma was an Aztec emperor of the early sixteenth century.

[8] *"Religion . . . gracious influences":* From an 1804 speech by the British clergyman Robert Hall (1764–1831), which responded to Napoleon's threats to invade England.

[9] *Denmark Veazie:* A reference to Denmark Vesey's 1822 efforts to bring about a slave insurrection in Charleston, South Carolina. After the conspiracy was betrayed by nervous house servants, Vesey, a free black Charleston carpenter, was executed.

[10] *Moses . . . Washington:* A list of revolutionary heroes from antiquity to the nineteenth century. Moses led the Jewish people out of slavery in Egypt; John Hampden (1594–1643) helped to lead the Puritan opposition to Charles I during the late 1630s and early 1640s; William Tell was the legendary (perhaps apocryphal) Swiss freedom fighter of the twelfth century; the Scotts Robert Bruce (1274–1329) and William Wallace

ment shook the whole empire of slavery. The guilty soul thieves were overwhelmed with fear. It is a matter of fact, that at that time, and in consequence of the threatened revolution, the slave states talked strongly of emancipation. But they blew but one blast of the trumpet of freedom, and then laid it aside. As these men became quiet, the slaveholders ceased to talk about emancipation: and now behold your condition to-day! Angels sigh over it, and humanity has long since exhausted her tears in weeping on your account!

The patriotic Nathaniel Turner followed Denmark Veazie. He was goaded to desperation by wrong and injustice. By Despotism, his name has been recorded on the list of infamy, but future generations will number him among the noble and brave.

Next arose the immortal Joseph Cinque,[11] the hero of the Amistad. He was a native African, and by the help of God he emancipated a whole ship-load of his fellow men on the high seas. And he now sings of liberty on the sunny hills of Africa, and beneath his native palm trees, where he hears the lion roar, and feels himself as free as that king of the forest. Next arose Madison Washington,[12] that bright star of freedom, and took his station in the constellation of freedom. He was a slave on board the brig Creole, of Richmond, bound to New Orleans, that great slave mart, with a hundred and four others. Nineteen struck for liberty or death. But one life was taken, and the whole were emancipated, and the vessel was carried into Nassau, New Providence. Noble men! those who have fallen in freedom's conflict, their memories will be cherished by the true hearted, and the God-fearing, in all future generations; those who are living, their names are surrounded by a halo of glory.

We do not advise you to attempt a revolution with the sword,

(1272?–1305) championed popular resistance to England during the thirteenth century; Toussaint L'Ouverture (1743–1803) was one of the leaders of the late-eighteenth-century Haitian uprising against French colonialism; and the Marquis de Lafayette (1757–1834) and George Washington (1732–1799) were celebrated American Revolutionary military leaders. Having further demonstrated his revolutionary commitments during the French Revolution and the Revolution of 1830, Lafayette remained popular in the United States.

[11] *Joseph Cinque:* Joseph Cinqué was one of the leaders of the 1839 slave mutiny on the Spanish slave ship the *Amistad.* The U.S. Navy seized the ship and mutineers, but in 1841 the U.S. Supreme Court granted the rebels their freedom. Abolitionists helped Cinqué and others to return to Africa.

[12] *Madison Washington:* Madison Washington was one of the leaders of the 1841 slave mutiny on the slave ship *Creole,* which was in the process of transporting slaves from Virginia to Louisiana. Washington and his compatriots guided the ship to Nassau, in the Bahamas, where the former slaves were granted asylum and liberated.

because it would be INEXPEDIENT. Your numbers are too small, and
moreover the rising spirit of the age, and the spirit of the gospel, are
opposed to war and bloodshed. But from this moment cease to labor
for tyrants who will not remunerate you. Let every slave throughout
the land do this, and the days of slavery are numbered. You cannot be
more oppressed than you have been — you cannot suffer greater cruelties than you have already. RATHER DIE FREEMEN, THAN LIVE TO BE
SLAVES. Remember that you are THREE MILLIONS.

It is in your power so to torment the God-cursed slaveholders, that
they will be glad to let you go free. If the scale was turned, and black
men were the masters, and white men the slaves, every destructive
agent and element would be employed to lay the oppressor low. Danger and death would hang over their heads day and night. Yes, the
tyrants would meet with plagues more terrible than those of Pharaoh.
But you are a patient people. You act as though you were made for the
special use of these devils. You act as though your daughters were
born to pamper the lusts of your masters and overseers. And worse
than all, you tamely submit, while your lords tear your wives from
your embraces, and defile them before your eyes. In the name of God
we ask, are you men? Where is the blood of your fathers? Has it all run
out of your veins? Awake, awake; millions of voices are calling you!
Your dead fathers speak to you from their graves. Heaven, as with a
voice of thunder, calls on you to arise from the dust.

Let your motto be RESISTANCE! RESISTANCE! RESISTANCE! — No
oppressed people have ever secured their liberty without resistance.
What kind of resistance you had better make, you must decide by the
circumstances that surround you, and according to the suggestion of
expediency. Brethren, adieu. Trust in the living God. Labor for the
peace of the human race, and remember that you are three millions.

NATIONAL CONVENTION OF COLORED PEOPLE

From *Report of the Committee on Abolition* (1847)

At the 1847 National Convention of Colored People in Troy, New
York, which Brown attended shortly after the publication of his *Narrative,* Garnet again delivered his "Address to the Slaves." Angered by Garnet's militancy, a committee chaired by Frederick Douglass issued a
"Report of the Committee on Abolition," which attacked Garnet's ideas

as both immoral and impractical. The "Report" was adopted by the convention's delegates and appears in *Proceedings of the National Convention of Colored People, and Their Friends, Held in Troy, N.Y., on the 6th, 7th, 8th and 9th October, 1847* (Troy, NY: J. C. Kneeland, 1847), the source of this selection.

The Committee appointed to draft a Report respecting the best means of abolishing Slavery and destroying Caste in the United States, beg leave most respectfully to Report: That they have had the important subjects referred to them, under consideration, and have carefully endeavored to examine all their points and bearings to the best of their ability; and from every view they have been able to take they have arrived at the conclusion that the best means of abolishing slavery is proclamation of truth, and that the best means of destroying caste is the mental, moral and industrial improvement of our people.

First, as respects Slavery. Your Committee find this monstrous crime, this stupendous iniquity, closely interwoven with all the great interests, institutions and organizations of the country; pervading and influencing every class and grade of society, securing their support, obtaining their approbation, and commanding their homage. Availing itself of the advantage which age gives to crime, it has perverted the judgment, blunted the moral sense, blasted the sympathies, and created in the great mass — the overwhelming majority of the people — a moral sentiment altogether favorable to its own character, and its own continuance. Press and pulpit are alike prostituted, and made to serve the end of this infernal institution. The power of the government and the sanctity of religion, church and state, are joined with the guilty oppressor against the oppressed — and the voice of this great nation is thundering in the ear of our enslaved fellow countrymen the terrible fiat, *you shall be slaves or die!* The slave is in the minority, a small minority. The oppressors are an overwhelming majority. The oppressed are three millions, their oppressors are seventeen millions. The one is weak, the other is strong; the one is without arms, without means of concert, and without government; the other possess every advantage in these respects; and the deadly aim of their million of musketry, and loud-mouthed cannon tells the down-trodden slave in unmistakable language, *he must be a slave or die.* In these circumstances, your committee are called upon to report as to the best means of abolishing slavery. And without pretending to discuss all the ways which have been suggested from time to time by various parties and factions, though did time permit, they would gladly do so, they beg at once to state their entire disapprobation of any plan of emancipation involving a resort to bloodshed. With the facts of our condition before us, it is impossible for us to contemplate any appeal to the slave to take vengeance on his guilty master, but with the utmost reprobation. Your Committee regard any counsel of this sort as the perfection of folly, suicidal in the extreme, and abominably wicked. We should utterly frown down and wholly discountenance any attempt to lead our people to confide in brute force as a reformatory instrumentality. All argument put forth in favor of insurrection and bloodshed, however well intended, is either the result of an unpardonable impatience or an atheistic want of faith in the power of truth as a means of regenerating and reforming the world. Again we repeat, let us set our faces against all such absurd, unavailing, dangerous and mischievous ravings, emanating from what source they may. The voice of God and of common sense, equally point out a more excellent way, and that way is a faithful, earnest, and persevering enforcement of the great principles of justice and morality, religion and humanity. These are the only invincible and infallible means within our reach with which to overthrow this foul system of blood and ruin. Your Committee deem it susceptible of the clearest demonstration, that slavery exists in this country, because the people of this country WILL its existence. And they deem it equally clear, that no system or institution can exist for an hour against the earnestly-expressed WILL of the people. It were quite easy to bring to the support of the foregoing proposition powerful and conclusive illustrations from the history of reform in all ages, and especially in our own. But the palpable truths of the propositions, as well as the familiarity of the facts illustrating them, entirely obviate such a necessity.

Our age is an age of great discoveries; and one of the greatest is that which revealed that this world is to be ruled, shaped and guided by the *marvelous might of mind*. The human voice must supersede the roar of cannon. Truth alone is the legitimate antidote of falsehood. Liberty is always sufficient to grapple with tyranny. Free speech — free discussion — peaceful agitation, — the foolishness of preaching these, under God, will subvert this giant crime, and send it reeling to its grave, as if smitten by a voice from the throne of God. Slavery exists because it is popular. It will cease to exist when it is made unpopular. Whatever therefore tends to make Slavery unpopular tends to its destruction. This every Slaveholder knows full well, and hence his opposition to all discussion of the subject. It is an evidence of intense feeling of alarm, when John C. Calhoun calls upon the North to put down what he is pleased to term "this plundering agitation." Let us give the Slaveholder what he most dislikes. Let us expose his crimes and his foul abominations. He is reputable and must be made disreputable. He must be regarded as a moral leper — shunned as a loathsome wretch — outlawed from Christian communion, and from social respectability — an enemy of God and man, to be execrated by the community till he shall repent of his foul crimes, and give proof of his sincerity by breaking every chain and letting the oppressed go free. Let us invoke the Press and appeal to the pulpit to deal out the righteous denunciations of heaven against oppression, fraud and wrong, and the desire of our hearts will soon be given us in the triumph of Liberty throughout all the land. . . .

Your Committee would further recommend the adoption of the following Resolutions as embodying the sentiments of the foregoing Report:

Resolved, That our only hope for peaceful Emancipation in this land is based on a firm, devoted, and unceasing assertion of our rights, and a full, free and determined exposure of our multiplied wrongs.

Resolved. That, in the language of inspired wisdom, there shall be no peace to the wicked, and that this guilty nation shall have no peace, and that we will do all that we can to *agitate!* AGITATE!! AGITATE!!! till our rights are restored and our Brethren are redeemed from their cruel chains.

All of which is respectfully submitted,

FREDERICK DOUGLASS,   JOHN LYLE,
ALEXANDER CRUMMELL.[1]   THOS. VAN RENSSELAER.

---

[1] *ALEXANDER CRUMMELL:* The best-known of Douglass's fellow signees, Alexander Crummell (1819–1898) was born free in Brooklyn, New York, attended several New York schools, and was ordained an Episcopal priest in 1844. After a stint as pastor to the Church of the Messiah in New York City, he journeyed to England in 1849 and attended Cambridge University, graduating in 1853. He then accepted an appointment as Episcopal missionary to Liberia, and he remained in that country for twenty years. Among his publications are *The Future of Africa* (1862) and the posthumous *Africa and America* (1891).

COLORED NATIONAL CONVENTION

Resolutions Adopted (1853)

In 1853, the year of the publication of *Clotel,* Frederick Douglass presided over one of the most important African American conventions of the 1850s. Rejecting the pessimism that followed the Compromise of 1850, Douglass and his fellow delegates met in Rochester, New York, to express their renewed optimism that blacks could one day achieve political equality in the United States. Over the course of the three-day convention, the delegates formulated plans to turn this possibility into a reality. Their optimism was buoyed by their excitement at Northern whites' enthusiastic responses to Stowe's *Uncle Tom's Cabin*; most participants were relatively unconcerned that the final chapters of the novel seemed to endorse Liberian colonization. (In fact, just a few months before the convention Stowe sent a letter to a New York meeting of the American and Foreign Anti-Slavery Society to express her regrets about the novel's ending, saying that if she were to rewrite the novel she would not have sent George Harris to Liberia.) The group's proclamation of "Resolutions Adopted" is taken from *Proceedings of the Colored National Convention, Held in Rochester, July 6th, 7th and 8th, 1853* (Rochester: Office of *Frederick Douglass' Paper,* 1853).

Whereas, The social condition of the colored inhabitants of this country, in its developments, shows, beyond a question, the necessity of social reform, and a better regulation of our domestic habits; therefore,

Resolved, That this Convention urge upon the clergy, who are not only our spiritual, but our social and moral instructors, to begin the reform, by urging upon the people who attend their preaching the necessity of a social reform; to use more untiring exertion than heretofore; to induce parents to pay more attention to the domestic education of their children; to prepare them for a better condition in society; to instill in them a desire for their elevation in society; to instill in them a desire for better occupations than the mass are brought up to; to give them higher notions of what the genius and spirit of the country requires of us, than they now have; to teach them more regular habits; and this Convention would urge upon parents the fact, that while the mass of the people are generally employed in menial service, from necessity, while this may not, of itself, bring reproach upon a people, yet it must be admitted that, should we bring up our children to the same employment, it will, of necessity, engraft upon them unstable habits — a disregard for the mechanical branches, as well as unfit them for regular employments; and instead of elevating their character for the future, we shall place them beneath our own position, and give them rather the downward, than the upward tendency.

Resolved, That to secure a more permanent attention to business habits than heretofore, and the acquisition of mechanical branches, it is necessary that some decisive measure be taken to open and secure the avenues of mechanical trades to our youth; and that, as a primary measure, it is necessary that it be known to parents and youth who are willing to take colored apprentices in their workshops; and further, that it is now expedient that intelligence offices be established, which shall register the names and places of business of such mechanics as are willing to employ colored youth; and also the names, age, residence, &c., of such youth as are desirous of learning trades.

Resolved, That it is the duty of colored men, in any way connected with mechanical or business houses, enjoying the confidence of their employers, to use all fair and honorable means to secure for themselves business advantages, and especially, to secure the admission of their children, or the children of others into mechanical establishments; and in every way practicable to use their influence to secure and extend business advantages and business connection to those now excluded from it.

Resolved, That it is now expedient and necessary for those who have accumulated some means, to employ such means in some one or more of the general avenues of business and profit, and to make for themselves a better business character than we now possess, and thus open and secure the way for the development of new business, and right business talent.

Resolved, That the attempt to create a successful colony on the coast of Liberia is an attempt to accomplish an end in violation of the admitted laws of human civilization, and in violation of the physical laws of the human constitution.

Resolved, That, as for the American Colonization Society, we have no sympathy with it, having long since determined to plant our trees on American soil, and repose beneath their shade.

Resolved, That the several towns and cities represented in this Convention be, and are hereby advised to procure copies of Garrison's

Thoughts on Colonization:[1] and that they be advised to reiterate the resolves and addresses contained in the first part of that work, on the head of the Free People of Color.

Resolved, That in recognizing the power of the press, and the vast influence it exerts in making apparent the spirit and character of a people, we are happy in congratulating ourselves upon the fact that in *Frederick Douglass' Paper*[2] we possess a correct exponent of the condition of our people, as well as an able, firm, and faithful advocate of their interests, and that, consequently, we cheerfully recommend it as worthy of our hearty and untiring support.

Resolved, That we welcome the newspaper recently established in Cleveland, Ohio, edited by William H. Day,[3] as a powerful auxiliary to our cause and as an efficient lever for promoting our elevation; and that we pledge it that hearty support which its importance [deserves].

Whereas, It is not generally known to the colored citizens and others that there is, in the city of Alleghany, Pa., an institution of learning — a regularly incorporated college for the education of colored youth and others;[4] therefore,

Resolved, That this Convention will give publicity to that institution by publishing, among the proceedings of this body, a notice of its existence.

Resolved, That a committee of one from each State represented be appointed to report an especial address to the Free People of Color of the United States; and also, that we recommend the next "National Convention" to be holden within two years, at some suitable place, which may hereafter be agreed upon.

Resolved, That the Colored People of the United States gratefully appreciate the services of the distinguished pioneer of the doctrine of universal, unconditional, and immediate emancipation, William Lloyd Garrison, and his noble co-adjutors, eliciting, as they do, our undying

---

[1] *Garrison's Thoughts on Colonization:* A reference to William Lloyd Garrison's *Thoughts on African Colonization* (1832). Garrision strongly opposed the American Colonization Society's attempts at shipping U.S. free blacks to the African colony of Liberia.

[2] *Frederick Douglass' Paper:* Frederick Douglass edited his antislavery *Frederick Douglass' Paper* from 1851 to 1860.

[3] *William H. Day:* A well-known black abolitionist from Ohio, William Howard Day (1825– 1900) founded the abolitionist newspaper *The Aliened American* in 1853.

[4] *college for the education of colored youth and others:* A reference to the Allegheny Institute and Mission Church, later named Avery College, founded in the late 1840s by the white philanthropist Charles A. Avery (1784–1858).

affection; and when we forget them, may our tongues cleave to the roof of our mouths, and our right hands forget their cunning.

Resolved, That we recommend the parents and guardians of colored children to avail themselves of every opportunity for their ingress to those schools and academia wherein there is no proscription of race or color.

Resolved, That we recognize in "Uncle Tom's Cabin" a work plainly marked by the finger of God, lifting the veil of separation which has too long divided the sympathies of one class of the American people from another; and that we feel and know that such sympathies once awake, and flowing in the proper human direction, must be the first step in that happy human brotherhood which is to be the ultimate destiny and crowning glory of our race.

Resolved, That we, as American citizens, are entitled to the right of elective franchise, in common with the white men of this country; and whenever any of our people have the use of that privilege, it is their duty to vote and vote only for such men, irrespective of party, as are known to be opposed to slavery and the Fugitive Slave Law.

Resolved, That the secretaries, in conjunction with Frederick Douglass, be appointed a Committee on Publication.

[The following resolutions have direct bearing upon the plan of organization, and in the report should be placed immediately after it:]

Resolved, That the Council shall be delegated to select its various committees.

Resolved, That the Council have power to offer a premium for prize essays on different subjects agreed on by the Council.

Resolved, That the said Council shall hear and grant petitions, and be governed by the rules of legislative bodies, and their decisions shall be final.

Resolved, That any State applying for admission into this Union, shall be admitted on such terms as may hereafter be agreed upon.

Resolved, That in establishing a National Council for our own special improvement, and a Manual Labor School for the education of our children in science, literature, and mechanical arts, this Convention do this, not to build ourselves up as a distinct and separate class in this country, but as a means to a great end, viz: the equality in political rights, and in civil and social privileges with the rest of the American people.

MARTIN R. DELANY

From *Political Destiny of the Colored Race on the American Continent*

As coeditor of the *North Star,* Martin Delany worked with Frederick Douglass to encourage moral reform and black elevation in the United States. But two key events during the fall of 1850 contributed to his disillusionment and increasingly confrontational stance. First, after having been admitted to Harvard Medical School during the summer of 1850, Delany was abruptly asked to leave in the fall by the dean, Oliver Wendell Holmes, who caved in to students' demands that Harvard remain an all-white institution. At around the same time, Congress approved the Compromise of 1850, with its infamous Fugitive Slave law. Delany subsequently began to explore the possibility of black emigration, and in response to Douglass's 1853 Rochester national black convention, he convened a rival National Emigration Convention of Colored Men in Cleveland. At this 1854 convention Delany delivered the keynote address, "Political Destiny," which counseled African Americans to emigrate to Central or South America on the grounds that white racists would never allow blacks to become U.S. citizens. A few years later he called for black emigration to Africa. Delany's emigrationism influenced the Haitian emigration movement of the late 1850s and early 1860s, which Brown initially championed. However, during the Civil War both Delany and Brown supported the Union's cause and abandoned their emigration plans. By the 1870s, Delany was angered by the failure of Reconstruction and sought to help blacks emigrate to Africa. The selection from Delany's "Political Destiny," which first appeared in the *Proceedings of the National Emigration of Colored People* (1854), is taken from the Appendix to F. A. Rollin, *Life and Services of Martin R. Delany* (Boston: Lee and Shepard, 1868), 327, 329–38, 353–54.

To the Colored Inhabitants of the United States: —
Fellow-Countrymen: The duty assigned us is an important one, comprehending all that pertains to our destiny and that of our posterity, present and prospectively. And while it must be admitted that the subject is one of the greatest magnitude, requiring all that talents, prudence, and wisdom might adduce, and while it would be folly to pretend to give you the combined result of these three agencies, we shall

satisfy ourselves with doing our duty to the best of our ability, and that in the plainest, most simple, and comprehensive manner.

Our object, then, shall be to place before you our true position in this country (the United States), the improbability of realizing our desires, and the sure, practicable, and infallible remedy for the evils we now endure.

We have not addressed you as *citizens,* — a term desired and ever cherished by us, — because such you have never been. We have not addressed you as *freemen,* because such privileges have never been enjoyed by any colored man in the United States. Why, then, should we flatter your credulity, by inducing you to believe that which neither has now, nor never before had, an existence? Our oppressors are ever gratified at our manifest satisfaction, especially when that satisfaction is founded upon false premises; an assumption on our part of the enjoyment of rights and privileges which never have been conceded, and which, according to the present system of the United States policy, we never can enjoy. . . .

Let it then be understood, as a great principle of political economy, that no people can be free who themselves do not constitute an essential part of the *ruling element* of the country in which they live. Whether this element be founded upon a true or false, a just or an unjust basis, this position in community is necessary to personal safety. The liberty of no man is secure who controls not his own political destiny. What is true of an individual is true of a family, and that which is true of a family is also true concerning a whole people. To suppose otherwise, is that delusion which at once induces its victim, through a period of long suffering, patiently to submit to every species of wrong; trusting against probability, and hoping against all reasonable grounds of expectation, for the granting of privileges and enjoyment of rights which never will be attained. This delusion reveals the true secret of the power which holds in peaceable subjection all the oppressed in every part of the world.

A people, to be free, must necessarily be *their own rulers;* that is, *each individual* must, in himself, embody the *essential ingredient* — so to speak — of the *sovereign principle* which composes the *true basis* of his liberty. This principle, when not exercised by himself, may, at his pleasure, be delegated to another — his true representative. . . .

In the United States our degradation being once — as it has in a hundred instances been done — legally determined, our color is sufficient, independently of costume, education, or other distinguishing marks, to keep up that distinction.

In Europe when an inferior is elevated to the rank of equality with the superior class, the law first comes to his aid, which, in its decrees, entirely destroys his identity as an inferior, leaving no trace of his former condition visible.

In the United States, among the whites, their color is made, by law and custom, the mark of distinction and superiority; while the color of the blacks is a badge of degradation, acknowledged by statute, organic law, and the common consent of the people.

With this view of the case, — which we hold to be correct, — to elevate to equality the degraded subject of law and custom, it can only be done, as in Europe, by an entire destruction of the identity of the former condition of the applicant. Even were this desirable, which we by no means admit, with the deep-seated prejudices engendered by oppression, with which we have to contend, ages incalculable might reasonably be expected to roll around before this could honorably be accomplished; otherwise, we should encourage, and at once commence, an indiscriminate concubinage and immoral commerce of our mothers, sisters, wives, and daughters, revolting to think of, and a physical curse to humanity.

If this state of things be to succeed, then, as in Egypt, under the dread of the inscrutable approach of the destroying angel, to appease the hatred of our oppressors, as a license to the passions of every white, let the lintel of each door of every black man be stained with the blood of virgin purity and unsullied matron fidelity.[1] Let it be written along the cornice in capitals, "The *will* of the white man is the rule of my household." Remove the protection to our chambers and nurseries, that the places once sacred may henceforth become the unrestrained resort of the vagrant and rabble, always provided that the licensed commissioner of lust shall wear the indisputable impress of a *white* skin.

But we have fully discovered and comprehended the great political disease with which we are affected, the cause of its origin and continuance; and what is now left for us to do is to discover and apply a sovereign remedy, a healing balm to a sorely diseased body — a wrecked but not entirely shattered system. We propose for this disease a remedy. That remedy is emigration. This emigration should be well advised, and like remedies applied to remove the disease from the physical system of man, skillfully and carefully applied, within the

---

[1] *lintel . . . fidelity:* An allusion to Exodus 12.22–23.

proper time, directed to operate on that part of the system whose greatest tendency shall be to benefit the whole.

Several geographical localities have been named, among which rank the Canadas. These we do not object to as places of temporary relief, especially to the fleeing fugitive, — which, like a palliative, soothes, for the time being, the misery, — but cannot commend them as permanent places upon which to fix our destiny, and that of our children, who shall come after us. But in this connection we would most earnestly recommend to the colored people of the United States generally, to secure, by purchase, all of the land they possibly can while selling at low rates, under the British people and government; as that time may come, when, like the lands in the United States territories generally, if not as in Oregon and some other territories and states, they may be prevented entirely from settling or purchasing them, — the preference being given to the white applicant.

And here we would not deceive you by disguising the facts that, according to political tendency, the Canadas, as all British America, at no very distant day, are destined to come into the United States.

And were this not the case, the odds are against us, because the ruling element there, as in the United States, is, and ever must be, white; the population now standing, in all British America, two and a half millions of whites to but forty thousand of the black race, or sixty-one and a fraction whites to one black! — the difference being eleven times greater than in the United States, — so that colored people might never hope for anything more than to exist politically by mere sufferance; occupying a secondary position to the whites of the Canadas. The Yankees from this side of the lakes are fast settling in the Canadas, infusing, with industrious success, all the malignity and negro-hate inseparable from their very being, as Christian democrats and American advocates of equality.

Then, to be successful, our attention must be turned in a direction towards those places where the black and colored man comprise, by population, and constitute by necessity of numbers, the *ruling element* of the body politic, and where, when occasion shall require it, the issue can be made and maintained on this basis; where our political enclosure and national edifice can be reared, established, walled, and proudly defended on this great elementary principle of original identity. Upon this solid foundation rests the fabric of every substantial political structure in the world, which cannot exist without it; and so soon as a people or nation lose their original identity, just so soon must that nation or people become extinct. Powerful though they may have been, they must fall. Because the nucleus which heretofore held them together, becoming extinct, there being no longer a centre of attraction, or basis for a union of the parts, a dissolution must as naturally ensue as the result of neutrality of the basis of adhesion among the particles of matter. . . .

Our friends in this and other countries, anxious for our elevation, have for years been erroneously urging us to lose our identity as a distinct race, declaring that we were the same as other people; while at the very same time their own representative was traversing the world, and propagating the doctrine in favor of a *universal Anglo-Saxon predominance.* The "universal brotherhood," so ably and eloquently advocated by that Polyglot Christian Apostle[2] of this doctrine, had established as its basis a universal acknowledgment of the Anglo-Saxon rule.

The truth is, we are not identical with the Anglo-Saxon, or any other race of the Caucasian or pure white type of the human family, and the sooner we know and acknowledge this truth the better for ourselves and posterity.

The English, French, Irish, German, Italian, Turk, Persian, Greek, Jew, and all other races, have their native or inherent peculiarities, and why not our race? We are not willing, therefore, at all times and under all circumstances to be moulded into various shapes of eccentricity, to suit the caprices and conveniences of every kind of people. We are not more suitable to everybody than everybody is suitable to us; therefore, no more like other people than others are like us.

We have, then, inherent traits, attributes, so to speak, and native characteristics, peculiar to our race, whether pure or mixed blood; and all that is required of us is to cultivate these, and develop them in their purity, to make them desirable and emulated by the rest of the world.

That the colored races have the highest traits of civilization, will not be disputed. They are civil, peaceable, and religious to a fault. In mathematics, sculpture and architecture, as arts and sciences, commerce and internal improvements as enterprises, the white race may probably excel; but in languages, oratory, poetry, music, and painting, as arts and sciences, and in ethics, metaphysics, theology, and legal jurisprudence, — in plain language, in the true principles of morals,

---

[2] *that Polyglot Christian Apostle:* A reference to the peace reformer Elihu Burritt; see "Narrative of the Life and Escape of William Wells Brown," see note 31, p. 71.

correctness of thought, religion, and law or civil government, there is no doubt but the black race will yet instruct the world.

It would be duplicity longer to disguise the fact that the great issue, sooner or later, upon which must be disputed the world's destiny, will be a question of black and white, and every individual will be called upon for his identity with one or the other. The blacks and colored races are four sixths of all the population of the world; and these people are fast tending to a common cause with each other. The white races are but one third of the population of the globe, — or one of them to two of us, — and it cannot much longer continue that two thirds will passively submit to the universal domination of this one third. And it is notorious that the only progress made in territorial domain, in the last three centuries, by the whites, has been a usurpation and encroachment on the rights and native soil of some of the colored races.

The East Indies, Java, Sumatra, the Azores, Madeira, Canary, and Cape Verde Islands; Socotra,[3] Guardifui,[4] and the Isle of France; Algiers, Tunis, Tripoli, Barca,[5] and Egypt in the North, Sierra Leone in the West, and Cape Colony in the South of Africa; besides many other islands and possessions not herein named; Australia, the Ladrone Islands,[6] together with many others of Oceanica;[7] the seizure and appropriation of a great portion of the Western Continent, with all its islands, were so many encroachments of the whites upon the rights of the colored races. Nor are they yet content, but, intoxicated with the success of their career, the Sandwich Islands[8] are now marked out as the next booty to be seized in the ravages of their exterminating crusade.

We regret the necessity of stating the fact, but duty compels us to the task, that, for more than two thousand years, the determined aim of the whites has been to crush the colored races wherever found. With a determined will they have sought and pursued them in every quarter of the globe. The Anglo-Saxon has taken the lead in this work of universal subjugation. But the Anglo-American stands preeminent for

---

[3] *Socotra:* An island in the Indian Ocean.

[4] *Guardifui:* A Cape at East Africa.

[5] *Barca:* Cyrenaica — an ancient district in North Africa.

[6] *Ladrone Islands:* Now called the Mariana Islands, a group of fifteen islands east of the Philippines.

[7] *Oceanica:* Islands of the central and south Pacific.

[8] *Sandwich Islands:* Former name of the Hawaiian islands.

deeds of injustice and acts of oppression, unparalleled, perhaps in the annals of modern history.

We admit the existence of great and good people in America, England, France, and the rest of Europe, who desire a unity of interests among the whole human family, of whatever origin or race.

But it is neither the moralist, Christian, nor philanthropist whom we now have to meet and combat, but the politician, the civil engineer, and skilful economist, who direct and control the machinery which moves forward, with mighty impulse, the nations and powers of the earth. We must, therefore, if possible, meet them on vantage ground, or, at least, with adequate means for the conflict.

Should we encounter an enemy with artillery, a prayer will not stay the cannon shot, neither will the kind words nor smiles of philanthropy shield his spear from piercing us through the heart. We must meet mankind, then, as they met us — prepared for the worst, though we may hope for the best. Our submission does not gain for us an increase of friends nor respectability, as the white race will only respect those who oppose their usurpation, and acknowledge as equals those who will not submit to their oppression. This may be no new discovery in political economy, but it certainly is a subject worthy the consideration of the black race.

After a due consideration of these facts, as herein recounted, shall we stand still and continue inactive — the passive observers of the great events of the times and age in which we live; submitting indifferently to the usurpation by the white race of every right belonging to the blacks? Shall the last vestige of an opportunity, outside of the continent of Africa, for the national development of our race, be permitted, in consequence of our slothfulness, to elude our grasp, and fall into the possession of the whites? This, may Heaven forbid. May the sturdy, intelligent Africo-American sons of the Western Continent forbid.

Longer to remain inactive, it should be borne in mind, may be to give an opportunity to despoil us of every right and possession sacred to our existence, with which God has endowed us as a heritage on the earth. For let it not be forgotten that the white race — who numbers but *one* of them to *two* of us — originally located in Europe, besides possessing all of that continent, have now got hold of a large portion of Asia, Africa, all North America, a portion of South America, and all of the great islands of both hemispheres, except Paupau, or New Guinea, inhabited by negroes and Malays, in Oceanica; the Japanese Islands, peopled and ruled by the Japanese; Madagascar, peopled by

negroes, near the coast of Africa; and the Island of Hayti, in the West
Indies, peopled by as brave and noble descendants of Africa as they
who laid the foundation of Thebias,[9] or constructed the everlasting
pyramids and catacombs of Egypt, — a people who have freed themselves by the might of their own will, the force of their own power, the
unfailing strength of their own right arms, and their unflinching determination to be free.

Let us, then, not survive the disgrace and ordeal of Almighty displeasure, of two to one, witnessing the universal possession and control by the whites of every habitable portion of the earth. For such
must inevitably be the case, and that, too, at no distant day, if black
men do not take advantage of the opportunity, by grasping hold of
those places where chance is in their favor, and establishing the rights
and power of the colored race.

We must make an issue, create an event, and establish for ourselves
a position. This is essentially necessary for our effective elevation as a
people, in shaping our national development, directing our destiny,
and redeeming ourselves as a race.

If we but determine it shall be so, it *will* be so; and there is nothing
under the sun can prevent it. We shall then be but in pursuit of our
legitimate claims to inherent rights, bequeathed to us by the will of
Heaven — the endowment of God, our common Parent. A distinguished economist has truly said, "God has implanted in man an infinite progression in the career of improvement. A soul capacitated for
improvement ought not to be bound by a tyrant's landmarks."[10] This
sentiment is just and true, the application of which to our case is
adapted with singular fitness.

Having glanced hastily at our present political position in the world
generally, and the United States in particular, — the fundamental disadvantages under which we exist, and the improbability of ever attaining citizenship and equality of rights in this country, — we call your
attention next to the places of destination to which we shall direct emigration.

The West Indies, Central and South America, are the countries of
our choice, the advantages of which shall be made apparent to your

[9] *Thebias:* Thebes; an ancient city in Upper Egypt.
[10] *"God has . . . .tyrant's landmarks":* The probable source is John Locke
(1632–1704); see, for example, "Of Slavery," in *Two Treatises on Civil Government*
(1690).

entire satisfaction. Though we have designated them as countries, they are, in fact, but one country, relatively considered, a part of this, the Western Continent. . . .

From the earliest period after the discovery, various nations sent a representative here, either as adventurers and speculators, or employed laborers, seamen, or soldiers, hired to work for their employers. And among the earliest and most numerous class who found their way to the New World were those of the African race. And it has been ascertained to our minds, beyond a doubt, that when the continent was discovered, there were found in the West Indies and Central America tribes of the black race, fine looking people, having the usual characteristics of color and hair, identifying them as being originally of the African race; no doubt, being a remnant of the Africans who, with the Carthaginian expedition, were adventitiously cast upon this continent, in their memorable adventure to the "Great Island," after sailing many miles distant to the west of the "Pillars of Hercules," — the present Straits of Gibraltar.[11]

We would not be thought to be superstitious, when we say, that in all this we can "see the finger of God." Is it not worthy of a notice here, that while the ingress of foreign whites to this continent has been voluntary and constant, and that of the blacks involuntary and but occasional, yet the whites in the southern part have *decreased* in numbers, *degenerated* in character, and become mentally and physically *enervated* and imbecile; while the blacks and colored people have studiously *increased* in numbers, *regenerated* in character, and have grown mentally and physically vigorous and active, developing every function of their manhood, and are now, in their elementary character, decidedly superior to the white race? So, then, the white race could never successfully occupy the southern portion of the continent; they must, of necessity, every generation, be repeopled from another quarter of the globe. The fatal error committed by the Spaniards, under Pizarro,[12] was the attempt to exterminate the Incas and Peruvians, and fill their places by European whites. The Peruvian Indians, a hale, hardy, vigorous, intellectual race of people, were succeeded by those

---

[11] *Carthaginian expedition . . . Gibraltar:* A reference to the possible journey of ancient Africans to the New World (the "Great Island"); the Pillars of Hercules are promonotories flanking the east entrance to the Strait of Gibraltar, which is between Europe and Africa.

[12] *Pizarro:* During the 1530s, the Spanish explorer Francisco Pizarro (1476–1541) invaded and conquered Peru.

who soon became idle, vicious, degenerated, and imbecile. But Peru, like all the other South American states, is regaining her former potency, just in proportion as the European race decreases among them. All the labor of the country is performed by the aboriginal natives and the blacks, the few Europeans there being the merest excrescences on the body politic — consuming drones in the social hive.

Had we no other claims than those set forth in a foregoing part of this address, they are sufficient to induce every black and colored person to remain on this continent, unshaken and unmoved.

But the West Indians, Central and South Americans, are a noble race of people; generous, sociable, and tractable — just the people with whom we desire to unite; who are susceptible of progress, improvement, and reform of every kind. They now desire all the improvements of North America, but being justly jealous of their rights, they have no confidence in the whites of the United States, and consequently peremptorily refuse to permit an indiscriminate settlement among them of this class of people; but placing every confidence in the black and colored people of North America.

NATIONAL CONVENTION
OF COLORED MEN

Declaration of Wrongs and Rights
Made by the Colored Men of the United States of America in Convention Assembled, in Syracuse, N.Y., Oct. 4, 1864.

Despite Lincoln's 1863 Emancipation Proclamation and an effort during the spring and summer of 1864 to make black soldiers' pay equal to that of whites, African American leaders remained concerned that a brokered settlement to the Civil War would result in the perpetuation of slavery in the South and the continued marginalization of blacks in the North. In October 1864, black leaders convened a national convention in Syracuse, New York, to discuss the war situation. Frederick Douglass was elected the convention's president; Brown, one of six delegates from Massachusetts, served with Douglass on the Committee on Credentials. The culminating "Declaration of Wrongs and Rights" drew heavily on Jefferson's Declaration to argue for African Americans' rights to U.S. citizenship.

The selection is taken from *Proceedings of the National Convention of Colored Men, Held in the City of Syracuse, N.Y., October 4, 5, 6, and 7, 1864* (Boston: J. R. Rock and Geo. L. Ruffin, 1864), 41–43.

1st. As a branch of the human family, we have for long ages been deeply and cruelly wronged by people whose might constituted their right; we have been subdued, not by the power of ideas, but by brute force, and have been unjustly deprived not only of many of our natural rights, but debarred the privileges and advantages freely accorded to other men.

2d. We have been made to suffer well-nigh every cruelty and indignity possible to be heaped upon human beings; and for no fault of our own.

3d. We have been taunted with our inferiority by people whose statute-books contained laws inflicting the severest penalties on whomsoever dared teach us the art of reading God's word; we have been denounced as incurably ignorant, and, at the same time, have been, by stern enactments, debarred from taking even the first step toward self-enlightenment and personal and national elevation; we have been declared incapable of self-government by those who refused us the right of experiment in that direction, and we have been denounced as cowards by men who refused at first to trust us with a musket on the battle-field.

4th. As a people, we have been denied the ownership of our bodies, our wives, homes, children, and the products of our own labor; we have been compelled, under pain of death, to submit to wrongs deeper and darker than the earth ever witnessed in the case of any other people; we have been forced to silence and inaction in full presence of the infernal spectacle of our sons groaning under the lash, our daughters ravished, our wives violated, and our firesides desolated, while we ourselves have been led to the shambles[1] and sold like beasts of the field.

5th. When the nation in her trial hour called her sable sons to arms, we gladly went to fight her battles: but were denied the pay accorded to others, until public opinion demanded it; and then it was tardily granted. We have fought and conquered, but have been denied the laurels of victory. We have fought where victory gave us no glory, and

---

[1] *shambles:* Butcher's shop or stall; slaughterhouses.

where captivity meant cool murder on the field, by fire, sword, and halter; and yet no black man ever flinched.

6th. We are taxed, but denied the right of representation. We are practically debarred the right of trial by jury; and institutions of learning which we help to support are closed against us.

We submit to the American people and world the following Declaration of our Rights, asking a calm consideration thereof:

1st. We declare that all men are born free and equal; that no man or government has a right to annul, repeal, abrogate, contravene, or render inoperative, this fundamental principle, except it be for crime; therefore we demand the immediate and unconditional abolition of slavery.

2d. That, as natives of American soil, we claim the right to remain upon it: and that any attempt to deport, remove, expatriate, or colonize us to any other land, or to mass us here against our will, is unjust; for here were we born, for this country our fathers and our brothers have fought, and here we hope to remain in the full enjoyment of enfranchised manhood, and its dignities.

3d. That, as citizens of the Republic, we claim the rights of other citizens. We claim that we are, by right, entitled to respect; that due attention should be given to our needs; that proper rewards should be given for our services, and that the immunities and privileges of all other citizens and defenders of the nation's honor should be conceded to us. We claim the right to be heard in the halls of Congress; and we claim our fair share of the public domain, whether acquired by purchase, treaty, confiscation, or military conquest.

4th. That, emerging as we are from the long night of gloom and sorrow, we are entitled to, and claim, the sympathy and aid of the entire Christian world; and we invoke the considerate aid of mankind in this crisis of our history, and in this hour of sacrifice, suffering, and trial.

Those are our wrongs; these a portion of what we deem to be our rights as men, as patriots, as citizens, and as children of the common Father. To realize and attain these rights, and their practical recognition, is our purpose. We confide our cause to the just God, whose benign aid we solemnly invoke. To him we appeal.

WILLIAM WELLS BROWN

From *St. Domingo: Its Revolutions and Its Patriots*

For many black abolitionists, the slave rebellion in San Domingo against French colonial authority provided a more compelling model for slave insurrection than Nat Turner's comparatively limited rebellion. Sparked by the French Revolution and the refusal of Haitian planters to permit mulatto participation in the French National Assembly, the San Domingo insurrection, which resulted in the deaths of tens of thousands of blacks and whites between 1791 and 1804, ultimately led to the emergence of Haiti as an independent black nation in the Americas. Like many African Americans of the period, Brown was inspired by the heroic leadership of Toussaint L'Ouverture (c. 1744–1803), a self-educated former slave who helped to guide the rebellion, eventually becoming the governor of San Domingo in 1801. In 1802 Napoleon sent troops to the region in a last-gasp effort to regain control of the blacks. Toussaint L'Ouverture was arrested and deported to France, where he died in prison a martyr to the principles of liberty in an age of revolution. Haitian independence was achieved in 1804 with the help of Thomas Jefferson, who offered U.S. aid to the black government because he feared that a strong French presence in Haiti posed a threat to the recently purchased Louisiana territory. Brown, who would promote black emigration to Haiti during 1861 and 1862, lectured on San Domingo in London and Philadelphia in 1854. Drawing on John R. Beard's *The Life of Toussaint L'Ouverture* (1853), he presented Toussaint as an exemplary "American" revolutionary whose life testified to blacks' fierce desires for liberty. The selection is taken from Brown, *St. Domingo: Its Revolutions and Its Patriots. A Lecture* (Boston: Bela Marsh, 1855), 35–38.

We cannot close without once more reviewing the character of Toussaint. Of all the great men of St. Domingo, the first place must be given to him. He laid the foundation for the emancipation of his race and the independence of the island. He fought her battles, and at last died in a cold prison for her sake and his fidelity to the cause of freedom. As an officer in battle he had no superior in Hayti. He defeated the French in several pitched battles, drove the English from the island, and refused a crown when it was offered to him. When his friends advised him to be on his guard against the treachery of Leclerc,[1] he replied, "For one to expose one's life for one's country when in danger is a sacred duty; but to arouse one's country in order to save one's life is inglorious." From ignorance he became educated by his own exertions. From a slave he rose to be a soldier, a general, and a governor, and might have been a king. He possessed a rare genius, which showed itself in the private circle, in the council-chamber, and on the field of battle. His very name became a tower of strength to his friends and a terror to his foes.

The history of Toussaint, placed by the side of that of Napoleon,[2] presents many striking parallels. Both born in a humble position, they raised themselves to the height of power by the force of their character. Both gained renown in legislation and government, as well as in war. Both fell the moment they had attained supreme authority. Both finished their career on a barren rock.

The parallels, however, have their contrast. Toussaint fought for liberty; Napoleon fought for himself. Toussaint gained fame by leading an oppressed and injured race to the successful vindication of their rights; Napoleon made himself a name and acquired a sceptre by supplanting liberty and destroying nationalities, in order to substitute his own illegitimate despotism. Napoleon transferred Toussaint from the warm and sunny climate of the West Indies to the cold climate of the north of France; the English transferred Napoleon from the cold climate of France to the warm climate of St. Helena.[3]

This was indeed retribution; for the man of the cold regions died in the tropics, to atone for his crime in having caused the man of the tropics to end his days in the cold regions. While Toussaint's memory will be revered by all lovers of freedom, Napoleon will be detested.

And, lastly, Toussaint's career as a Christian, a statesman, and a general, will lose nothing by a comparison with that of Washington. Each was the leader of an oppressed and outraged people, each had a

---

[1] *Leclerc:* A French general under the command of Napoleon Bonaparte, Charles Victor Emmanuel Leclerc (1772–1802) led French forces against the black revolutionaries of San Domingo, seizing Touissant and deporting him to France, where he died in a dungeon.

[2] *Napoleon:* The French general Napoleon Bonaparte (1769–1821), who was emperor from 1804 to 1815, led French military forces against numerous countries during the late 1790s and early 1800s in what came to be known as the Napoleonic wars.

[3] *St. Helena:* A British island in the south Atlantic Ocean, St. Helena is best known as the place of exile of Napoleon Bonaparte, who was shipped there in 1815 after being taken as a prisoner of war.

powerful enemy to contend with, and each succeeded in founding a government in the New World. Toussaint's government made liberty its watchword, incorporated it in its constitution, abolished the slave-trade, and made freedom universal amongst the people. Washington's government incorporated slavery and the slave-trade, and enacted laws by which claims were fastened upon the limbs of millions of people. Toussaint liberated his countrymen; Washington enslaved a portion of his, and aided in giving strength and vitality to an institution that will one day rend asunder the UNION that he helped to form. Already the slave in his chains, in the rice swamps of Carolina and the cotton fields of Mississippi, burns for revenge.

In contemplating the fact that the slave would rise and vindicate his right to freedom by physical force, Jefferson said: —

> "Indeed, I tremble for my country when I reflect that God is just; that his justice cannot sleep forever; that, considering numbers, nature, and natural means only, a revolution of the wheel of fortune, an exchange of situation, is among possible events; that it may become probable by supernatural interference! The Almighty has no attribute which can take side with us in such a contest.
>
> "What an incomprehensible machine is man! who can endure toil, famine, stripes, imprisonment, and death itself, in vindication of his own liberty, and the next moment be deaf to all those motives whose power supported him through his trial, and inflict on his fellow-men a bondage, one hour of which is fraught with more misery than ages of that which he rose in rebellion to oppose."[4]

And, should such a contest take place, the God of Justice will be on the side of the oppressed blacks. The exasperated genius of Africa would rise from the depths of the ocean, and show its threatening form; and war against the tyrants would be the rallying cry. The indignation of the slaves of the south would kindle a fire so hot that it would melt their chains, drop by drop, until not a single link would remain; and the revolution that was commenced in 1776 would then be finished, and the glorious sentiments of the Declaration of Independence, "That all men are created equal, and endowed by their Creator with certain inalienable rights, among which are life, liberty, and the pursuit of happiness," would be realized, and our government would no longer be the scorn and contempt of the friends of freedom in other lands, but would really be the LAND OF THE FREE AND HOME OF THE BRAVE.

---

[4] "*Indeed . . . . oppose*": From Jefferson's *Notes on the State of Virginia* and "Observations"; see *Clotel*, note 2, p. 157.

HENRY DAVID THOREAU

From *A Plea for Captain John Brown*

In the wake of the Supreme Court's 1857 Dred Scott ruling, which upheld the constitutionality of slavery and denied blacks the right to U.S. citizenship, there was a growing sense among abolitionists that violence might well be the only way to bring about the end of slavery. The militant white abolitionist John Brown shared this belief and on 16 October 1859 led twenty-one men, including five blacks, in an effort to seize the federal arsenal at Harper's Ferry in western Virginia and inspire a massive slave uprising. Following his capture and execution in December of that year, Brown was celebrated in the North as a patriotic martyr in the American Revolutionary tradition. Henry David Thoreau (1817–62) had met Brown earlier in the decade when Brown visited Concord, Massachusetts, to raise funds to support armed attacks on proslavery settlers in Kansas. An advocate of nonviolent reform in his best known works, "Resistance to Civil Government" (1849) and *Walden* (1854), Thoreau was increasingly disturbed by the government's participation in the violence of the slave system. In "Slavery in Massachusetts" (1854) he attacked Northern complicity in the Compromise of 1850's Fugitive Slave Law, and when he heard news of Brown's attack and capture, he delivered "A Plea for Captain John Brown" on 30 October 1859 in the Concord Town Hall. William Wells Brown later celebrated the heroism of John Brown and his black allies in a chapter of *The Negro in the American Rebellion* (1867). The selection from Thoreau's lecture is taken from *Echoes of Harper's Ferry*, ed. James Redpath (Boston: Thayer and Eldridge, 1860), 17–18, 37–42.

I trust that you will pardon me for being here. I do not wish to force my thoughts upon you, but I feel forced myself. Little as I know Captain Brown, I would fain do my part to correct the tone and the statements of the newspapers, and of my countrymen generally, respecting his character and actions. It costs us nothing to be just. We can at least express our sympathy with, and admiration of, him and his companions, and that is what I now propose to do.

First, as to history. I will endeavor to omit, as much as possible, what you have already read. I need not describe his person to you, for probably most of you have seen and will not soon forget him. I am told that his grandfather, John Brown, was an officer in the Revolution; that he himself was born in Connecticut about the beginning of this century, but early went with his father to Ohio. I heard him say that his father was a contractor who furnished beef to the army there, in the war of 1812; that he accompanied him to the camp, and assisted him in that employment, seeing a good deal of military life, more, perhaps, than if he had been a soldier, for he was often present at the councils of the officers. Especially, he learned by experience how armies are supplied and maintained in the field — a work which, he observed, requires at least as much experience and skill as to lead them in battle. He said that few persons had any conception of the cost, even the pecuniary cost, of firing a single bullet in war. He saw enough, at any rate, to disgust him with a military life; indeed, to excite in him a great abhorrence of it; so much so, that though he was tempted by the officer of some petty office in the army, when he was about eighteen, he not only declined that, but he also refused to train when warned, and was fined for it. He then resolved that he would never have any thing to do with any war, unless it were a war for liberty. . . .

It was his peculiar doctrine that a man has a perfect right to interfere by force with the slaveholder, in order to rescue the slave. I agree with him. They who are continually shocked by slavery have some right to be shocked by the violent death of the slaveholder, but no others. Such will be more shocked by his life than by his death. I shall not be forward to think him mistaken in his method who quickest succeeds to liberate the slave. I speak for the slave when I say, that I prefer the philanthropy of Captain Brown to that philanthropy which neither shoots me nor liberates me. At any rate, I do not think it is quite sane for one to spend his whole life in talking or writing about this matter, unless he is continuously inspired, and I have not done so. A man may have other affairs to attend to. I do not wish to kill nor to be killed, but I can foresee circumstances in which both these things would be by me unavoidable. We preserve the so-called peace of our community by deeds of petty violence every day. Look at the policeman's billy and handcuffs! Look at the jail! Look at the gallows! Look at the chaplain of the regiment! We are hoping only to live safely on the outskirts of *this* provisional army. So we defend ourselves and our hen-roosts, and maintain slavery. I know that the mass of my countrymen think that the only righteous use that can be made of Sharpe's rifles and revolvers[1] is to

---

[1] *Sharpe's* [sic] *rifles and revolvers:* Weapons produced by Sharps Rifle Manufacturing Company of Hartford, Connecticut, which was founded in 1851 by Christian Sharps.

fight duels with them, when we are insulted by other nations, or to hunt Indians, or shoot fugitive slaves with them, or the like. I think that for once the Sharpe's rifles and the revolvers were employed in a righteous cause. The tools were in the hands of one who could use them.

The same indignation that is said to have cleared the temple once will clear it again. The question is not about the weapon, but the spirit in which you use it. No man has appeared in America, as yet, who loved his fellow-man so well, and treated him so tenderly. He lived for him. He took up his life and he laid it down for him. What sort of violence is that which is encouraged, not by soldiers but by peaceable citizens, not so much by laymen as by ministers of the gospel, not so much by the fighting sects as by the Quakers, and not so much by Quaker men as by Quaker women?

This event advertises me that there is such a fact as death — the possibility of a man's dying. It seems as if no man had ever died in America before, for in order to die you must first have lived. I don't believe in the hearses, and palls, and funerals that they have had. There was no death in the case, because there had been no life; they merely rotted or sloughed off, pretty much as they had rotted or sloughed along. No temple's vail was rent, only a hole dug somewhere. Let the dead bury their dead. The best of them fairly ran down like a clock. Franklin — Washington — they were let off without dying; they were merely missing one day. I hear a good many pretend that they are going to die; or that they have died, for aught that I know. Nonsense! I'll defy them to do it. They haven't got life enough in them. They'll deliquesce like fungi, and keep a hundred eulogists mopping the spot where they left off. Only half a dozen or so have died since the world began. Do you think that you are going to die, sir? No! there's no hope of you. You haven't got your lesson yet. You've got to stay after school. We make a needless ado about capital punishmen — taking lives, when there is no life to take. *Memento mori!*[2] We don't understand that sublime sentence which some worthy got sculptured on his gravestone once. We've interpreted it in a grovelling and snivelling sense; we've wholly forgotten how to die.

But be sure you do die, nevertheless. Do your work and finish it. If you know how to begin, you will know when to end.

These men, in teaching us how to die, have at the same time taught us how to live. If this man's acts and words do not create a revival, it

[2] *Memento mori!*: A reminder of death.

506 Resistance and Reform

will be the severest possible satire on the acts and words that do. It is the best news that America has ever heard. It has already quickened the feeble pulse of the North, and infused more and more generous blood into her veins and heart, than any number of years of what is called commercial and political prosperity could. How many a man who was lately contemplating suicide has now something to live for!

One writer says that Brown's peculiar monomania made him to be "dreaded by the Missourians as a supernatural being." Sure enough, a hero in the midst of us cowards is always so dreaded. He is just that thing. He shows himself superior to nature. He has a spark of divinity in him.

> "Unless above himself he doth erect himself,
> How poor a thing is man!"[3]

Newspaper editors argue also that it is a proof of his *insanity* that he thought he was appointed to do this work which he did — that he did not suspect himself for a moment! They talk as if it were impossible that a man could be "divinely appointed" in these days to do any work whatever; as if vows and religion were out of date as connected with any man's daily work, — as if the agent to abolish Slavery could only be somebody appointed by the President, or by some political party. They talk as if a man's death were a failure, and his continued life, be it of whatever character, were a success.

When I reflect to what a cause this man devoted himself, and how religiously, and then reflect to what cause his judges and all who condemn him so angrily and fluently devote themselves, I see that they are as far apart as the heavens and earth are asunder.

The amount of it is, our *"leading men"* are a harmless kind of folk, and they know *well enough* that *they* were not divinely appointed, but elected by the votes of their party.

Who is it whose safety requires that Captain Brown be hung? Is it indispensable to any Northern man? Is there no resource but to cast these men also to the Minotaur?[4] If you do not wish it, say so distinctly. While these things are being done, beauty stands veiled and music is a screeching lie. Think of him — of his rare qualities! such a man as it takes ages to make, and ages to understand; no mock hero,

---

[3] *"Unless . . . is man!":* From William Wordsworth, *The Excursion* (1814), book fourth: 330–31.

[4] *Minotaur:* In Greek mythology, a monster with the head of a bull on the body of a man who devoured youths.

nor the representative of any party. A man such as the sun may not rise upon again in this benighted land. To whose making went the costliest material, the finest adamant;[5] sent to be the redeemer of those in captivity; and the only use to which you can put him is to hang him at the end of a rope! You who pretend to care for Christ crucified, consider what you are about to do to him who offered himself to be the saviour of four millions of men.

Any man knows when he is justified, and all the wits in the world cannot enlighten him on that point. The murderer always knows that he is justly punished; but when a government takes the life of a man without the consent of his conscience, it is an audacious government, and is taking a step towards its own dissolution. Is it not possible that an individual may be right and a government wrong? Are laws to be enforced simply because they were made? or declared by any number of men to be good, if they are *not* good? Is there any necessity for a man's being a tool to perform a deed of which his better nature disapproves? Is it the intention of law-makers that *good* men shall be hung ever? Are judges to interpret the law according to the letter, and not the spirit? What right have *you* to enter into a compact with yourself that you *will* do thus or so, against the light within you? Is it for *you* to *make up* your mind — to form any resolution whatever — and not accept the convictions that are forced upon you, and which ever pass your understanding? I do not believe in lawyers, in that mode of attacking or defending a man, because you descend to meet the judge on his own ground, and, in cases of the highest importance, it is of no consequence whether a man breaks a human law or not. Let lawyers decide trivial cases. Business men may arrange that among themselves. If they were the interpreters of the everlasting laws which rightfully bind man, that would be another thing. A counterfeiting law-factory, standing half in a slave land and half in a free! What kind of laws for free men can you expect from that?

I am here to plead his cause with you. I plead not for his life, but for his character — his immortal life; and so it becomes your cause wholly, and is not his in the least. Some eighteen hundred years ago Christ was crucified; this morning, perchance, Captain Brown was hung. These are the two ends of a chain which is not without its links. He is not Old Brown any longer; he is an angel of light.

---

[5] *adamant:* An impenetrable or unyielding substance.

I see now that it was necessary that the bravest and humanest man in all the country should be hung. Perhaps he saw it himself. I *almost fear* that I may yet hear of his deliverance, doubting if a prolonged life, if *any* life, can do as much good as his death.

"Misguided"! "Garrulous"! "Insane"! "Vindictive"! So ye write in your easy chairs, and thus he wounded responds from the floor of the Armory, clear as a cloudless sky, true as the voice of nature is: "No man sent me here; it was my own prompting and that of my Maker. I acknowledge no master in human form."

And in what a sweet and noble strain he proceeds, addressing his captors, who stand over him: "I think my friends, you are guilty of a great wrong against God and humanity, and it would be perfectly right for any one to interfere with you so far as to free those you willfully and wickedly hold in bondage."

And referring to his movement: "It is, in my opinion, the greatest service a man can render to God."

"I pity the poor in bondage that have none to help them; that is why I am here; not to gratify any personal animosity, revenge, or vindictive spirit. It is my sympathy with the oppressed and the wronged, that are as good as you, and as precious in the sight of God."

You don't know your testament when you see it.

"I want you to understand that I respect the rights of the poorest and weakest of colored people, oppressed by the slave power, just as much as I do those of the most wealthy and powerful."

"I wish to say, furthermore, that you had better, all you people at the South, prepare yourselves for a settlement of that question, that must come up for settlement sooner than you are prepared for it. The sooner you are prepared the better. You may dispose of me very easily. I am nearly disposed of now; but this question is still to be settled — this negro question, I mean; the end of that is not yet."

I foresee the time when the painter will paint that scene, no longer going to Rome for a subject; the poet will sing it; the historian record it; and, with the Landing of the Pilgrims and the Declaration of Independence, it will be the ornament of some future national gallery, when at least the present form of Slavery shall be no more here. We shall then be at liberty to weep for Captain Brown. Then, and not till then, we will take our revenge.

WILLIAM WELLS BROWN

Battle of Milliken's Bend

In a key Civil War battle of June 1863, Confederate troops attacked a Union garrison near Vicksburg, Mississippi, at Milliken's Bend on the Mississippi River, and were repulsed by the black soldiers defending the supply line. This was one of the first battles involving black troops, and their courage and skills were widely praised in the North. Brown described the battle in a chapter of *The Negro in the American Rebellion: His Heroism and His Fidelity* (Boston: Lee & Shepard, 1867), the source of this selection. A historical overview of blacks' participation in the American Revolution, the War of 1812, and the Civil War, the book was written with the express purpose of developing black pride, confuting white racists' notions of black inferiority, and making the case for African American citizenship. It appeared several months before the 1867 publication of *Clotelle*, Brown's final revision of his novel, which in a similar spirit portrayed the heroic contributions of blacks to the war effort.

On the 7th of June, 1863, the first regular battle was fought between the blacks and whites in the valley of the Mississippi. The planters had boasted, that, should they meet their former slaves, a single look from them would cause the negroes to throw down their weapons and run. Many Northern men, especially copperheads,[1] professed to believe that such would be the case. Therefore, all eyes were turned to the far off South, the cotton, sugar, and rice-growing States, to see how the blacks would behave on the field of battle; for it is well known that the most ignorant of the slave population belonged in that section.

The following account of the fight is from an eye witness: —

"My informant states that a force of about five hundred negroes, and two hundred men of the Twenty-third Iowa, belonging to the second brigade, Carr's division (the Twenty-third Iowa had been up the river with prisoners, and was on its way back to this place), was surprised in camp by a rebel force of about two thousand men. The first intimation that the commanding officer received was from one of the black men, who went into the colonel's tent, and said, 'Massa, the

---

[1] *copperheads:* Northerners who sympathized with the South during the Civil War.

secesh are in camp.' The colonel ordered him to have the men load
their guns at once. He instantly replied, 'We have done did dat now,
massa.' Before the colonel was ready, the men were in line, ready for
action. As before stated, the rebels drove our force towards the gun-
boats, taking colored men prisoners and murdering them. This so
enraged them that they rallied, and charged the enemy more heroically
and desperately than has been recorded during the war. It was a genuine bayonet-charge, a hand-to-hand fight, that has never occurred to
any extent during this prolonged conflict. Upon both sides men were
killed with the butts of muskets. White and black men were lying side
by side, pierced by bayonets, and in some instances transfixed to the
earth. In one instance, two men — one white and the other black —
were found dead, side by side, each having the other's bayonet through
his body. If facts prove to be what they are now represented, this
engagement of Sunday morning will be recorded as the most desperate
of this war. Broken limbs, broken heads, the mangling of bodies, all
prove that it was a contest between enraged men: on the one side, from
hatred to a race; and, on the other, desire for self-preservation, revenge
for past grievances, and the inhuman murder of their comrades. One
brave man took his former master prisoner, and brought him into
camp with great gusto. A rebel prisoner made a particular request,
that *his own* negroes should not be placed over him as a guard."

Capt. M. M. Miller, of Galena, Ill., who commanded a company in
the Ninth Louisiana (colored) Regiment, in a letter, gives the following
account of the battle: —

"We were attacked here on June 7, about three o'clock in the morning, by a brigade of Texas troops, about two thousand five hundred in
number. We had about six hundred men to withstand them, five hundred of them negroes. I commanded Company I, Ninth Louisiana. We
went into the fight with thirty-three men. I had sixteen killed, eleven
badly wounded, and four slightly. I was wounded slightly on the head,
near the right eye, with a bayonet, and had a bayonet run through my
right hand, near the forefinger; that will account for this miserable
style of penmanship.

"Our regiment had about three hundred men in the fight. We had
one colonel wounded, four captains wounded, two first and two second lieutenants killed, five lieutenants wounded, and three white
orderlies killed, and one wounded in the hand, and two fingers taken
off. The list of killed and wounded officers comprised nearly all the
officers present with the regiment, a majority of the rest being absent
recruiting.

"We had about fifty men killed in the regiment and eighty wounded; so you can judge of what part of the fight my company sustained. I never felt more grieved and sick at heart, than when I saw how my brave soldiers had been slaughtered, — one with six wounds, all the rest with two or three, none less than two wounds. Two of my colored sergeants were killed; both brave, noble men, always prompt, vigilant, and ready for the fray. I never more wish to hear the expression, 'The niggers won't fight.' Come with me, a hundred yards from where I sit, and I can show you the wounds that cover the bodies of sixteen as brave, loyal, and patriotic soldiers as ever drew bead on a rebel.

"The enemy charged us so close that we fought with our bayonets, hand to hand. I have six broken bayonets to show how bravely my men fought. The Twenty-third Iowa joined my company on the right; and I declare truthfully that they had all fled before our regiment fell back, as we were all compelled to do.

"Under command of Col. Page, I led the Ninth and Eleventh Louisiana when the rifle-pits were retaken and held by our troops, our two regiments doing the work.

"I narrowly escaped death once. A rebel took deliberate aim at me with both barrels of his gun; and the bullets passed so close to me that the powder that remained on them burnt my cheek. Three of my men, who saw him aim and fire, thought that he wounded me each fire. One of them was killed by my side, and he fell on me, covering my clothes with his blood; and, before the rebel could fire again, I blew his brains out with my gun.

"It was a horrible fight, the worst I was ever engaged in, — not even excepting Shiloh.[2] The enemy cried, 'No quarter!' but some of them were very glad to take it when made prisoners.

"Col. Allen, of the Sixteenth Texas, was killed in front of our regiment, and Brig.-Gen. Walker was wounded. We killed about one hundred and eighty of the enemy. The gunboat 'Choctaw' did good service shelling them. I stood on the breastworks[3] after we took them, and gave the elevations and direction for the gunboat by pointing my sword; and they sent a shell right into their midst, which sent them in all directions. Three shells fell there, and sixty-two rebels lay there when the fight was over.

[2] *Shiloh:* One of the bloodiest battles of the Civil War, the battle of Shiloh (6–7 April 1862), which took place near the Shiloh Church in Tennessee, resulted in the deaths of over ten thousand men on each side and has usually been regarded as a Union victory.

[3] *breastworks:* Hastily constructed defensive barriers generally standing breast high.

"My wound is not serious but troublesome. What few men I have left seem to think much of me, because I stood up with them in the fight. I can say for them that I never saw a braver company of men in my life.

"Not one of them offered to leave his place until ordered to fall back. I went down to the hospital, three miles, to-day to see the wounded. Nine of them were there, two having died of their wounds. A boy I had cooking for me came and begged a gun when the rebels were advancing, and took his place with the company; and, when we retook the breastworks, I found him badly wounded, with one gun-shot and two bayonet wounds. A new recruit I had issued a gun to the day before the fight was found dead, with a firm grasp on his gun, the bayonet of which was broken in three pieces. So they fought and died, defending the cause that we revere. They met death coolly, bravely: not rashly did they expose themselves, but all were steady and obedient to orders."

This battle satisfied the slave-masters of the South that their charm was gone; and that the negro, as a slave, was lost forever. Yet there was one fact connected with the battle of Milliken's Bend which will descend to posterity, as testimony against the humanity of slave-holders; and that is, that no negro was ever found alive that was taken a prisoner by the rebels in this fight.

WILLIAM WELLS BROWN

From *My Southern Home*

After touring several Southern states in the winter of 1879-80, Brown published *My Southern Home* in May 1880. More than half the book consists of Brown's autobiographical reflections on slave life, as he retells — often with significant variations — some of the stories that make up his *Narrative*, his several memoirs, and *Clotel*. He also devotes at least a third of the book to excoriating the Southern states for abandoning the goals of Reconstruction. Angered by the persistence of antiblack racism and discrimination, he encourages blacks to consider moving North, hoping that a black exodus may encourage Southerners to realize just how crucial blacks are to the Southern economy. In addition to blaming the plight of the South's African Americans on white racists, he criticizes blacks themselves for allegedly failing to take full responsibility for their uplift by adopting temperance and industry. In the book's final chapter, which is printed in its entirety below, Brown, like Frederick Douglass during this time, encourages "amalgamation" between whites and blacks as a way of ending racial strife. In the context of *Clotel*, Brown's appeal for marriages between blacks and whites, along with the book's accompanying image of a cross-racial handshake, encourages us to reimagine the relationship between Thomas Jefferson and Sally Hemings as a kind of rehearsal for a deracialized, progressive, reformative union between blacks and whites that promises to redeem the United States. But even as Brown encourages amalgamation, he strongly asserts the importance of developing black pride. The selection is from Brown, *My Southern Home: Or, The South and Its People* (Boston: A. G. Brown & Co., 1880).

In America, the negro stands alone as a race. He is without mate or fellow in the great family of man. Whatever progress he makes, it must be mainly by his own efforts. This is an unfortunate fact, and for which there seems to be no remedy.

All history demonstrates the truth that amalgamation is the great civilizer of the races of men. Wherever a race, clan, or community have kept themselves together, prohibiting by law, usage, or common consent, inter-marriage with others, they have made little or no progress. The Jews, a distinct and isolated people, are good only at driving a bargain and getting rich. The Gipsies commence and stop with trading horses. The Irish, in their own country, are dull. The Coptic race[1] form but a handful of what they were — those builders, unequalled in ancient or modern times. What has become of them? Where are the Romans? What races have they destroyed? What races have they supplanted? For fourteen centuries they lorded it over the semi-civilized world; and now they are of no more note than the ancient Scythians, or Mongols, Copts, or Tartars.[2] An un-amalgamated, inactive people will decline. Thus it was with the Mexicans, when Cortes[3] marched on Mexico, and the Peruvians, when Pizarro[4] marched on Peru.

---

[1] *Coptic race:* Ancient Egyptians.

[2] *Scythians, or Mongols, Copts, or Tartars:* References to ancient peoples who possessed what Brown regards as distinct racial or ethnic identities: the Scythians resided in southeast Europe and Asia; the Mongols in Asia; and the Tartars in Asia and eastern Europe.

[3] *Cortes:* The Spanish explorer Hernán Cortés (1485–1547) conquered Mexico in 1520.

[4] *Pizarro:* See Martin Delany, "Political Destiny," p. 496, n. 12.

The Britons were a dull, lethargic people before their country was invaded, and the hot, romantic blood of Julius Caesar and William of Normandy coursed through their veins.

Caractacus,[5] king of the Britons, was captured and sent to Rome in chains. Still later, Hengist and Horsa,[6] the Saxon generals, imposed the most humiliating conditions upon the Britons, to which they were compelled to submit. Then came William of Normandy, defeated Harold at Hastings,[7] and the blood of the most renowned land-pirates and sea-robbers that ever disgraced humanity, mixed with the Briton and Saxon, and gave to the world the Anglo-Saxon race, with its physical ability, strong mind, brave and enterprising spirit. And, yet, all that this race is, it owes to its mixed blood. Civilization, or the social condition of man, is the result and test of the qualities of every race. The benefit of this blood mixture, the negro is never to enjoy on this continent. In the South where he is raised, in the North, East, or West, it is all the same, no new blood is to be infused into his sluggish veins.

His only hope is education, professions, trades, and copying the best examples, no matter from what source they come.

This antipathy to amalgamation with the negro, has shown itself in all of the States. Most of the Northern and Eastern State Legislatures have passed upon this question years ago. Since the coming in of the present year, Rhode Island's Senate refused to repeal the old law forbidding the intermarriage of whites and blacks. Thus the colored man is left to "paddle his own canoe" alone. Where there is no law against the mixture of the two races, there is a public sentiment which is often stronger than law itself. Even the wild blood of the red Indian refuses to mingle with the sluggish blood of the negro. This is no light matter, for race hate, prejudice and common malice all die away before the melting power of amalgamation. The beauty of the half-breeds of the South, the result of the crime of slavery, have long claimed the attention of writers, and why not a lawful mixture? And then this might help in

> "Making a race far more lovely and fair,
> Darker a little than white people are:

---

[5] *Caractacus:* British chieftan who opposed the Romans, circa A.D. 50.

[6] *Hengist and Horsa:* Brothers who led the Teutonic (Germanic) invasion of Britain circa A.D. 440.

[7] *William of Normandy, defeated Harold at Hastings:* A reference to the Norman Conquest of 1066, in which England's King Harold (c.1022–1066) was defeated by William, Duke of Normandy (c.1027–1087), who became William I, King of England.

Stronger, and nobler, and better in form,
Hearts more voluptuous, kinder, and warm;
Bosoms of beauty, that heave with a pride
Nature had ever to white folks denied."

Emigration to other States, where the blacks will come in contact with educated and enterprising whites, will do them much good. This benefit by commercial intercourse is seen in the four thousand colored people who have come to Boston, where most of them are employed as servants. They are sought after as the best domestics in the city. Some of these people, who were in slavery before the war, are now engaged in mercantile pursuits, doing good business, and showing what contact will do. Many of them rank with the ablest whites in the same trades. Indeed, the various callings are well represented by Southern men, showing plainly the need of emigration. Although the colored man has been sadly at fault in not vindicating his right to liberty, he has, it is true, shown ability in other fields. Benjamin Banneker,[8] a negro of Maryland, who lived a hundred years ago, exhibited splendid natural qualities. He had a quickness of apprehension, and a vivacity of understanding, which easily took in and surmounted the most subtile and knotty parts of mathematics and metaphysics. He possessed in a large degree that genius which constitutes a man of letters; that quality without which judgment is cold, and knowledge is inert; that energy which collects, combines, amplifies, and animates.

The rapid progress made in acquiring education and homesteads by the colored people of the South, in the face of adverse circumstances, commends the highest admiration from all classes.

The product of their native genius and industry, as exhibited at county and State Agricultural Fairs, speak well for the race.

At the National Fair, held at Raleigh, N.C., in the autumn of 1879, the exhibition did great credit to the colored citizens of the South, who had the matter in charge. Such manifestations of intellectual and mechanical enterprise will do much to stimulate the people to further development of their powers, and higher facilities.

The colored people of the United States are sadly in need of a National Scientific Association, to which may be brought yearly reports of such investigations as may be achieved in science, philosophy, art, philology, ethnology, jurisprudence, metaphysics, and what-

---

[8] *Benjamin Banneker:* See Banneker's letter exchange with Thomas Jefferson on pp. 343–48 in this volume.

ever may tend to unite *the race in their moral, social, intellectual and physical improvement.*

We have negro artists of a high order, both in painting and sculpture; also, discoverers who hold patents, and yet the world knows little or nothing about them. The time for the negro to work out his destiny has arrived. Now let him show himself equal to the hour.

In this work I frequently used the word "Negro," and shall, no doubt, hear from it when the negro critics get a sight of the book. And why should I not use it? Is it not honorable? What is there in the word that does not sound as well as "English," "Irish," "German," "Italian," "French?"

"Don't call me a negro; I'm an American," said a black to me a few days since.

"Why not?" I asked.

"Well, sir, I was born in this country, and I don't want to be called out of my name."

Just then, an Irish-American came up, and shook hands with me. He had been a neighbor of mine in Cambridge. When the young man was gone, I inquired of the black man what countryman he thought the man was.

"Oh!" replied he, "he's an Irishman."

"What makes you think so?" I inquired.

"Why, his brogue is enough to tell it."

"Then," I said, "why is not your color enough to tell that you're a negro?"

"Arh!" said he, "that's a horse of another color," and left me with a "Ha, ha, ha!"

Black men, don't be ashamed to show your colors, and to own them.

Selected Bibliography

This bibliography is divided into two sections, "Works Cited" and "Suggestions for Further Reading." All books and articles quoted in the general introduction, chapter introductions, and headnotes are listed in "Works Cited." The "Suggestions for Further Reading" provides a primary bibliography of Brown's works and a secondary bibliography in Brown studies. "Critical Studies on Brown" lists works devoted exclusively to Brown, but many of the works listed in "Literary and Historical Studies" also have chapters or sections on Brown. "Suggestions for Further Reading" also includes selected bibliographies keyed to the three areas covered by the historical documents in Part Two. Some of the books and articles that appear in "Works Cited" are not listed again in "Suggestions for Further Reading." A recommended starting point for further reading on Brown is William Edward Farrison's excellent biography, *William Wells Brown: Author and Reformer.*

WORKS CITED

Andrews, William L. "The 1850s: The First Afro-American Literary Renaissance." *Literary Romanticism in America.* Ed. Andrews. Baton Rouge: Louisiana State UP, 1981. 38–60.

Berlin, Ira. *Many Thousands Gone: The First Two Centuries of Slavery in North America.* Cambridge: Harvard UP, 1998.

Brown, Josephine. *Biography of an American Bondman, by His Daughter.* Boston: R. F. Wallcut, 1856.

Brown, William Wells. *The Black Man, His Antecedents, His Genius, and His Achievements.* 1863. Miami: Mnemosyne Publishing Inc., 1969.

———. *A Lecture Delivered before the Female Anti-Slavery Society of Salem, at Lyceum Hall. Nov. 14, 1847.* Boston: Massachusetts Anti-Slavery Society, 1847.

———. "Letter to Frederick Douglass." *North Star* 16 Jan. 1851: 3.

———. *Three Years in Europe; or, Places I Have Seen and People I Have Met.* London: Charles Gilpin, 1852.

Callender, James. [Untitled.] *Richmond Recorder* 1 Sept. 1802: 2.

———. [untitled] *Richmond Recorder* 22 Sept. 1802:2.

Castronovo, Russ. *Fathering the Nation: American Genealogies of Slavery and Freedom.* Berkeley: U of California P, 1995.

Davis, David Brion. "American Slavery and the Revolution." *Slavery and Freedom in the Age of the American Revolution.* 1983. Ed. Ira Berlin and Ronald Hoffman. Urbana: U of Illinois P, 1986. 262–80.

Delany, Martin R. *The Condition, Elevation, Emigration and Destiny of the Colored People of the United States.* 1852. New York: Arno, 1969.

Douglass, Frederick. *My Bondage and My Freedom.* 1855. Ed. William L. Andrews. Urbana: U of Illinois P, 1987.

———. "Our Paper and Its Prospects." *North Star* 3 Dec. 1847: 2.

duCille, Ann. *The Coupling Convention: Sex, Text, and Tradition in Black Women's Fiction.* New York: Oxford UP, 1993.

Ellis, Joseph J. *American Sphinx: The Character of Thomas Jefferson.* New York: Knopf, 1997.

Ellis, Joseph J., and Eric S. Lander. "Founding Father." *Nature* 5 Nov. 1998: 68–9.

Ernest, John. *Resistance and Reformation in Nineteenth-Century African-American Literature.* Jackson: UP of Mississippi, 1995.

Finkelman, Paul. "Jefferson and Slavery: 'Treason Against the Hopes of the World.'" *Jeffersonian Legacies.* Ed. Peter S. Onuf. Charlottesville: U of Virginia P, 1993. 181–221.

Foner, Eric. *Free Soil, Free Labor, Free Man: The Ideology of the Republican Party before the Civil War.* New York: Oxford UP, 1970.

Foster, Eugene A., et al. "Jefferson Fathers Slave's Last Child." *Nature* 5 Nov. 1998: 27–28.

Fredrickson, George M. *The Black Image in the White Mind: The Debate on African-American Character and Destiny, 1817–1914.* New York: Harper Torchbooks, 1972.

Garrison, William Lloyd. "The Insurrection." *Liberator* 3 Sept. 1831: 143.

Gilmore, Paul. " 'De Genewine Artekil': William Wells Brown, Blackface Minstrelsy, and Abolitionism." *American Literature* 69 (1997): 743–80.

Gordon-Reed, Annette. *Thomas Jefferson and Sally Hemings: An American Controversy.* Charlottesville: UP of Virginia, 1997.

Grimké, Angelina E. *Letters to Catharine Beecher.* Boston: Knapp, 1838.

Hawthorne, Nathaniel. *The House of the Seven Gables.* 1851. New York: Penguin, 1981.

Jacobs, Harriet A. *Incidents in the Life of a Slave Girl. Written by Herself.* 1861. Ed. Jean Fagan Yellin. Cambridge: Harvard UP, 1987.

Jefferson, Thomas. *The Works of Thomas Jefferson.* Vol. 6. Ed. Paul Leicester Ford. New York: G. P. Putnam's Sons, 1904.

———. *Writings.* Ed. Merrill Peterson. New York: Library of America, 1984.

Jordan, Winthrop D. *White over Black: American Attitudes toward the Negro, 1550–1812.* Chapel Hill: U of North Carolina P, 1968.

Levine, Robert S. "Pierre's Blackened Hand." *Leviathan: A Journal of Melville Studies* 1 (1999): 23–44.

Marryat, Frederick. *A Diary in America: With Remarks on Its Institutions.* 1839. Ed. Sydney Jackman. New York: Knopf, 1962.

Melville, Herman. *Moby-Dick; or, The Whale.* 1851. Ed. Harrison Hayford, Hershel Parker, and G. Thomas Tanselle. Evanston and Chicago: Northwestern UP and The Newberry Library, 1988.

Minutes and Proceedings of the First Annual Convention of the People of Colour, Held by Adjournments in the City of Philadelphia. Philadelphia: n.p., 1831.

"New Work by William W. Brown." *The Liberator* 3 Feb. 1854: 19.

Quinby, Lee, ed. *Genealogy and Literature.* Minneapolis: U of Minnesota P, 1995.

Rachman, Stephen. " 'Es lässt sich nicht schreiben': Plagiarism and 'The Man of the Crowd.' " *The American Face of Edgar Allan Poe.* Ed. Shawn Rosenheim and Stephen Rachman. Baltimore: Johns Hopkins UP, 1995. 49–87.

Ripley, C. Peter, et al., eds. *The Black Abolitionist Papers.* 5 vols. Chapel Hill: U of North Carolina P, 1985–92.

Sánchez-Eppler, Karen. "Bodily Bonds: The Intersecting Rhetorics of
    Feminism and Abolition." *Representations* 24 (1988): 28–59.
Stowe, Harriet Beecher. *Uncle Tom's Cabin*. 1852. Ed. Elizabeth
    Ammons. New York: Norton, 1994.
Walker, David. *Appeal, in Four Articles; Together with a Preamble,
    To the Coloured Citizens of the World, but in Particular, and
    Very Expressly, to Those of the United States of America*. 1830.
    New York: Hill, 1995.
Weinauer, Ellen. "Plagiarism and the Proprietary Self: Policing the
    Boundaries of Authorship in Herman Melville's 'Hawthorne and
    His Mosses.'" *American Literature* 69 (1997): 697–717.
Whitman, Walt. *Leaves of Grass*. Ed. Jerome Loving. New York:
    Oxford UP, 1990.

SUGGESTIONS FOR FURTHER READING

Works by Brown

*Narrative of William W. Brown, A Fugitive Slave. Written by Him-
    self*. Boston: American Anti-Slavery Society, 1847.
*A Lecture Delivered before the Female Anti-Slavery Society of Salem,
    at Lyceum Hall, Nov. 14, 1847*. Boston: Massachusetts Anti-
    Slavery Society, 1847.
Ed. *The Anti-Slavery Harp: A Collection of Songs for Anti-Slavery
    Meetings Compiled by William W. Brown, A Fugitive Slave*.
    Boston: Bela Marsh, 1848.
*A Description of William Wells Brown's Original Panoramic Views
    of the Scenes in the Life of an American Slave, from His Birth in
    Slavery to His Death or His Escape to His First Home of Free-
    dom on British Soil*. London: Charles Gilpin, 1850.
Three Years in Europe; or, Places I Have Seen and People I Have Met.
    London: Charles Gilpin, 1852.
*Clotel; or, The President's Daughter: A Narrative of Slave Life in the
    United States*. London: Partridge & Oakey, 1853.
*The American Fugitive in Europe: Sketches of Places and People
    Abroad*. Boston: John P. Jewett, 1855.
St. Domingo: Its Revolutions and Its Patriots. A Lecture. Boston:
    Bela Marsh, 1855.
The Escape; or, A Leap for Freedom. A Drama in Five Acts. Boston:
    R. F. Walcutt, 1858.
*Memoir of William Wells Brown, an American Bondman, Written by
    Himself*. Boston: Boston Anti-Slavery Office, 1859.

Miralda; or, The Beautiful Quadroon. A Romance of American Slavery, Founded on Fact. In *Weekly Anglo-African,* 1 December 1860–16 March 1861.

The Black Man, His Antecedents, His Genius, and His Achievements. New York: Thomas Hamilton, 1863.

Clotelle: A Tale of the Southern States. Boston: James Redpath Publishers, 1864.

Clotelle; or, The Colored Heroine. A Tale of the Southern States. Boston: Lee & Shephard, 1867.

The Negro in the American Rebellion: His Heroism and His Fidelity. Boston: Lee & Shephard, 1867.

The Rising Son; or, The Antecedents and Advancement of the Colored Race. Boston: A. G. Brown, 1874.

My Southern Home: or, The South and Its People. Boston: A. G. Brown, 1880.

For a generous sampling of speeches and letters by Brown, see *The Black Abolitionist Papers.* Ed. C. Peter Ripley et al. 5 vols. Chapel Hill: U of North Carolina P, 1985–92.

Bibliography

Ellison, Curtis W. *William Wells Brown and Martin R. Delany: A Reference Guide.* Boston: G. K. Hall, 1976.

Biographies

Brown, Josephine. *Biography of an American Bondman, by His Daughter.* Boston: R. F. Wallcut, 1856

Farrison, William Edward. *William Wells Brown: Author and Reformer.* Chicago: U of Chicago P, 1969.

Critical Studies on Brown

Andrews, William L. "Mark Twain, William Wells Brown, and the Problem of Authority in New South Writing." *Southern Literature and Literary Theory.* Ed. Jefferson Humphries. Athens: U of Georgia P, 1990. 1–21.

Dorsey, Peter A. "De-authorizing Slavery: Realism in Stowe's *Uncle Tom's Cabin* and Brown's *Clotel.*" *ESQ* 41 (1995): 257–88.

Ernest, John. "The Reconstruction of Whiteness: William Wells Brown's *The Escape; or, A Leap for Freedom.*" *PMLA* 113 (1998): 1108–21.

2

2

Fabi, M. Giulia. "The 'Unguarded Expressions of the Feelings of the Negroes': Gender, Slave Resistance, and William Wells Brown's Revisions of *Clotel*." *African American Review* 27 (1993): 639–54.

Farrison, William Edward. "Clotel, Thomas Jefferson, and Sally Hemings." *CLA Journal* 17 (1973): 147–74.

Gilmore, Paul. " 'De Genewine Artekil': William Wells Brown, Blackface Minstrelsy, and Abolitionism." *American Literature* 69 (1997): 743–80.

Heermance, J. Noel. *William Wells Brown and Clotelle: A Portrait of the Artist in the First Negro Novel*. Hamden, CT: Archon, 1969.

Levine, Robert S. " 'Whiskey, Blacking, and All': Temperance and Race in William Wells Brown's *Clotel*." *The Serpent in the Cup: Temperance in American Literature*. Ed. David S. Reynolds and Debra J. Rosenthal. Amherst: U of Massachusetts P, 1997. 93–114.

Lewis, Richard O. "Literary Conventions in the Novels of William Wells Brown." *CLA Journal* 29 (1985): 129–56.

Mulvey, Christopher. "The Fugitive Self and the New World of the North: William Wells Brown's Discovery of America." *The Black Columbiad: Defining Moments in African American Literature and Culture*. Ed. Werner Sollors and Maria Diedrich. Cambridge: Harvard UP, 1994. 99–111.

Literary and Historical Studies

Andrews, William L. "The Novelization of Voice in Early African American Narrative." *PMLA* 105 (1990): 23–34.

———. *To Tell a Free Story: The First Century of Afro-American Autobiography, 1760–1865*. Urbana: U of Illinois P, 1986.

Baker, Houston A., Jr. *The Journey Back: Issues in Black Literature and Criticism*. Chicago: U of Chicago P, 1980.

Bell, Bernard W. *The Afro-American Novel and Its Tradition*. Amherst: U of Massachusetts P, 1987.

Bentley, Nancy. "White Slaves: The Mulatto Hero in Antebellum Fiction." *American Literature* 65 (1993): 501–22.

Berzon, Judith R. *Neither White Nor Black: The Mulatto Character in American Fiction*. New York: New York UP, 1978.

Blassingame, John W. *The Slave Community: Plantation Life in the Antebellum South*. New York: Oxford UP, 1972.

Bryant, Jerry H. *Victims and Heroes: Racial Violence in the African American Novel*. Amherst: U of Massachusetts P, 1997.

Carby, Hazel. *Reconstructing Womanhood: The Emergence of the Afro-American Woman Novelist*. New York: Oxford UP, 1987.

Cassuto, Leonard. *The Inhuman Race: The Racial Grotesque in American Literature and Culture.* New York: Columbia UP, 1997.

Castronovo, Russ. *Fathering the Nation: American Genealogies of Slavery and Freedom.* Berkeley: U of California P, 1995.

duCille, Ann. *The Coupling Convention: Sex, Text, and Tradition in Black Women's Fiction.* New York: Oxford UP, 1993.

Ernest, John. *Resistance and Reformation in Nineteenth-Century African-American Literature.* Jackson: UP of Mississippi, 1995.

Fahey, David H. *Temperance and Racism: John Bull, Johnny Reb, and the Good Templars.* Lexington: U of Kentucky P, 1996.

Fleischner, Jennifer. *Mastering Slavery: Memory, Family, and Identity in Women's Slave Narratives.* New York: New York UP, 1996.

Foster, Frances Smith. *Witnessing Slavery: The Development of Ante-bellum Slave Narratives.* Westport, CT: Greenwood, 1979.

Fox-Genovese, Elizabeth. *Within the Plantation Household: Black and White Women of the Old South.* Chapel Hill: U of North Carolina P, 1988.

Gates, Henry Louis, Jr. *Figures in Black: Words, Signs, and the "Racial" Self.* New York: Oxford UP, 1987.

Genovese, Eugene D. *Roll, Jordan, Roll: The World the Slaves Made.* New York: Vintage, 1976.

Ginsberg, Elaine K., ed. *Passing and the Fictions of Identity.* Durham: Duke UP, 1996.

Gutman, Herbert G. *The Black Family in Slavery and Freedom, 1750–1925.* New York: Vintage, 1977.

Herzog, Kristin. *Women, Ethnics, and Exotics: Images of Power in Mid-Nineteenth-Century American Fiction.* Knoxville: U of Tennessee P, 1983.

Horton, James Oliver. *Free People of Color: Inside the African American Community.* Washington, DC: Smithsonian Institution P, 1993.

Jackson, Blyden. *A History of Afro-American Literature.* Vol I. Baton Rouge: Louisiana State UP, 1989.

Levine, Lawrence W. *Black Culture and Black Consciousness: Afro-American Folk Thought from Slavery to Freedom.* New York: Oxford UP, 1977.

Loggins, Vernon. *The Negro Author: His Development in America to 1900.* 1931. Port Washington, NY: Kennikat P, 1959.

Moses, Wilson Jeremiah. *Black Messiahs and Uncle Toms: Social and Literary Manipulations of a Religious Myth.* University Park: Pennsylvania State UP, 1993.

Nelson, Dana D. *The Word in Black and White: Reading "Race" in American Literature, 1638–1867*. New York: Oxford UP, 1992.

Paterson, Orlando. *Slavery and Social Death: A Comparative Study*. Cambridge: Harvard UP, 1982.

Raboteau, Albert J. *Slave Religion: The "Invisible Institution" in the Antebellum South*. New York: Oxford UP, 1978.

Redding, J. Saunders. *To Make a Poet Black*. 1939. Ithaca: Cornell UP, 1988.

Smith, Valerie. *Self-Discovery and Authority in Afro-American Narrative*. Cambridge: Harvard UP, 1987.

Sollors, Werner. "National Identity and Ethnic Diversity: 'Of Plymouth Rock and Jamestown and Ellis Island'; or, Ethnic Literature and Some Redefinitions of America." *History and Memory in African-American Culture*. Ed. Geneviève Fabre and Robert O'Meally. New York: Oxford UP, 1994. 92–121.

——— . *Neither Black Nor White Yet Both: Thematic Explorations of Interracial Literature*. New York: Oxford UP, 1997.

Stepto, Robert B. *From Behind the Veil: A Study of Afro-American Narrative*. Urbana: U of Illinois P, 1979.

Stuckey, Sterling. *Going Through the Storm: The Influence of African American Art in History*. New York: Oxford UP, 1994.

Sundquist, Eric J. *To Wake the Nations: Race in the Making of American Literature*. Cambridge: Harvard UP, 1993.

Takaki, Ronald T., ed. *Violence in the Black Imagination: Essays and Documents*. New York: Oxford UP, 1993.

Wiegman, Robyn. *American Anatomies: Theorizing Race and Gender*. Durham: Duke UP, 1995.

Wonham, Henry B., ed. *Criticism and the Color Line: Desegregating American Literary Studies*. New Brunswick: Rutgers UP, 1996.

Yarborough, Richard. "The First-Person in Afro-American Fiction." *Afro-American Literary Study in the 1990s*. Ed. Houston A. Baker, Jr., and Patricia Remond. Chicago: U of Chicago P, 1989. 105–20.

——— . "Race, Violence, and Manhood: The Masculine Ideal in Frederick Douglass's 'The Heroic Slave.' " *Frederick Douglass: New Literary and Historical Essays*. Ed. Eric J. Sundquist. New York: Cambridge UP, 1990. 166–88.

Yellin, Jean Fagan. *The Intricate Knot: Black Figures in American Literature, 1776–1863*. New York: New York UP, 1972.

Zafar, Rafia. *We Wear the Mask: African Americans Write American Literature, 1760–1870*. New York: Columbia UP, 1997.

Zanger, Jules. "The 'Tragic Octoroon' in Pre-Civil War Fiction." *American Quarterly* 18 (1966): 63–70.

Sources and Revisions

Davis, David Brion. *The Problem of Slavery in the Age of Revolution, 1770–1823.* Ithaca: Cornell UP, 1975.

Finkelman, Paul. *Slavery and the Founders: Race and Liberty in the Age of Jefferson.* New York: M. E. Sharpe, 1996.

French, Scott, and Edward L. Ayers. "The Strange Career of Thomas Jefferson: Race and Slavery in American Memory, 1943–1993." *Jeffersonian Legacies.* Ed. Peter S. Onuf. Charlottesville: U of Virginia P, 1993. 418–56.

Gordon-Reed, Annette. *Thomas Jefferson and Sally Hemings: An American Controversy.* Charlottesville: UP of Virginia, 1997.

Gossett, Thomas, F. *Uncle Tom's Cabin and American Culture.* Dallas: Southern Methodist UP, 1985.

Hedrick, Joan D. *Harriet Beecher Stowe: A Life.* New York: Oxford UP, 1994.

Hirschfeld, Fritz. *George Washington and Slavery: A Documentary Portrayal.* Columbia: U of Missouri P, 1997.

Karcher, Carolyn L. *The First Woman in the Republic: A Cultural Biography of Lydia Maria Child.* Durham: Duke UP, 1994.

Morgan, Edmund. *American Slavery, American Freedom: The Ordeal of Colonial Virginia.* New York: Norton, 1975.

Quarles, Benjamin. *The Negro in the American Revolution.* 1961. Chapel Hill: U of North Carolina P, 1996.

Weinauer, Ellen M. " 'A Most Respectable Looking Gentleman': Passing, Possession, and Transgression in *Running a Thousand Miles for Freedom.*" *Passing and the Fictions of Identity.* Ed. Elaine K. Ginsberg. Durham: Duke UP, 1996. 37–56.

Race, Slavery, Prejudice

Boulton, Alexander O. "The American Paradox: Jeffersonian Equality and Racial Science." *American Quarterly* 47 (1995): 467–93.

Faust, Drew Gilpen, ed. *The Ideology of Slavery: Proslavery Thought in the Old South.* Baton Rouge: Louisiana State UP, 1981.

Fredrickson, George M. *The Black Image in the White Mind: The Debate on African-American Character and Destiny, 1817–1914.* New York: Harper Torchbooks, 1972.

Freehling, William H. *The Road to Disunion: Secessionists at Bay. 1776–1854.* New York: Oxford UP, 1990.

Freimark, Vincent, and Bernard Rosenthal, eds. *Race and the American Romantics.* New York: Schocken, 1971.

Gates, Henry Louis, Jr., ed. *"Race," Writing, and Difference.* Chicago: U of Chicago P, 1986.

Gossett, Thomas F. *Race: The History of an Idea in America.* 1963. New York: Oxford UP, 1997.

Hinks, Peter P. *To Awaken My Afflicted Brethren: David Walker and the Problem of Antebellum Slave Resistance*. University Park: Pennsylvania State UP, 1997.

Horsman, Reginald. *Race and Manifest Destiny: The Origins of American Racial Anglo-Saxonism*. Cambridge: Harvard UP, 1981.

Jordan, Winthrop D. *White over Black: American Attitudes toward the Negro, 1550–1812*. Chapel Hill: U of North Carolina P, 1968.

Litwack, Leon F. *North of Slavery: The Negro in the Free States, 1790–1860*. Chicago: U of Chicago P, 1961.

Lott, Eric. *Love and Theft: Blackface Minstrelsy and the American Working Class*. New York: Oxford UP, 1993.

Miller, William Lee. *Arguing About Slavery: The Great Battle in the United States Congress*. New York: Knopf, 1996.

Nelson, Dana. *National Manhood: Capitalist Citizenship and the Imagined Fraternity of White Men*. Durham: Duke UP, 1998.

Peterson, Merrill D. *The Great Triumvirate: Webster, Clay, and Calhoun*. New York: Oxford UP, 1987.

Roediger, David. *The Wages of Whiteness: Race and the Making of the American Working Class*. New York: Verso, 1991.

Stanton, William. *The Leopard's Spots: Scientific Attitudes toward Race in America, 1815–1859*. Chicago: U of Chicago P, 1972.

Tise, Larry E. *Proslavery: A History of the Defense of Slavery in America, 1700–1840*. Athens: U of Georgia P, 1987.

Williamson, Joel. *New People: Miscegenation and Mulattoes in the United States*. New York: Free, 1980.

Resistance and Reform

Bell, Howard Holman. *A Survey of the Black Convention Movement, 1830–1861*. 1953. New York: Arno, 1969.

Blackett, R. J. M. *Building an Antislavery Wall: Black Americans in the Atlantic Abolitionist Movement, 1830–1860*. Baton Rouge: Louisiana State UP, 1983.

Cooper, Frederick. "Elevating the Race: The Social Thought of Black Leaders, 1827–1850." *American Quarterly* 24 (1972): 604–25.

Genovese, Eugene D. *From Rebellion to Revolution: Afro-American Slave Revolts in the Making of the New World*. New York: Vintage, 1981.

Kraditor, Aileen S. *Means and Ends in American Abolitionism: Garrison and His Critics in Strategy and Tactics, 1834–1850*. New York: Vintage, 1970.

Levine, Robert S. *Martin Delany, Frederick Douglass, and the Politics of Representative Identity.* Chapel Hill: U of North Carolina P, 1997.

Mayer, Henry. *All on Fire: William Lloyd Garrison and the Abolition of Slavery.* New York: St. Martin's, 1998.

McFeely, William S. *Frederick Douglass.* New York: Norton, 1991.

Miller, Floyd J. *The Search for a Black Nationality: Black Emigration and Colonization, 1787–1863.* Urbana: U of Illinois P, 1975.

Mills, Bruce. *Lydia Maria Child and the Literature of Reform.* Athens: U of Georgia P, 1994.

Moses, Wilson Jeremiah. *The Golden Age of Black Nationalism, 1850–1925.* New York: Oxford UP, 1978.

Pease, Jane H., and William H. Pease. *They Who Would Be Free: Blacks' Search for Freedom, 1830–1861.* 1974. Urbana: U of Illinois P, 1990.

Peterson, Carla L. *"Doers of the Word": African-American Women Speakers and Writers in the North (1830–1880).* New York: Oxford UP, 1995.

Quarles, Benjamin. *Black Abolitionists.* New York: Oxford UP, 1969.

Sánchez-Eppler, Karen. "Bodily Bonds: The Intersecting Rhetorics of Feminism and Abolition." *Representations* 24 (1988): 28–59.

Stuckey, Sterling. *Slave Culture: Nationalist Theory and the Foundations of Black America.* New York: Oxford UP, 1987.

Ullman, Victor. *Martin R. Delany: The Beginnings of Black Nationalism.* Boston: Beacon, 1971.

Walters, Ronald G. *American Reformers, 1815–1860.* New York: Hill, 1978.

Yacovone, Donald. "The Transformation of the Black Temperance Movement." *Journal of the Early Republic* 8 (1988): 281–97.

Yellin, Jean Fagan. *Women and Sisters: The Antislavery Feminists in American Culture.* New Haven: Yale UP, 1989.